# Ruth Rendell

# HARM DONE

# GOING WRONG

ARROW

This edition published in 2004 by Arrow Books,
an imprint of Random House UK Ltd,
20 Vauxhall Bridge Road, London SW1V 2SA

*Harm Done* first published in 1999 by Hutchinson
*Going Wrong* first published in 1990 by Hutchinson

Printed and bound in Great Britain by
Bookmarque Ltd, Croydon, Surrey

# HARM DONE

The Children's Crusade, he called it after it was all over, because children played such a big part in it. Yet it wasn't really about children at all. Not one of them was physically injured, not one of them suffered bodily pain or was even made to cry beyond the common lot of people of their age. The mental pain they endured, the emotional traumas and psychological damage – well, those were another thing. Who knows what impression certain sights leave on children? And who can tell what actions those impressions will precipitate? If any. Perhaps, as people once believed, they are character-forming. They make us strong. After all, the world is a hard place and we may as well learn it young. All childhoods are unhappy, said Freud. But then, thought Wexford, some childhoods are unhappier than others.

These children, the crusaders, were witnesses. There are many who believe children should never be permitted to be witnesses. As it is, laws are in place to protect them from exploitation by the law. But who will stop them seeing what they witnessed in the first place? His daughter Sylvia, the social worker, said that she sometimes thought, after what she had seen, that all children should be taken from their parents at birth. On the other hand, if any busybody of a social worker tried to take her children away from her she'd fight him tooth and nail.

The children in question, in Wexford's questions and questioning, came from all over Kingsmarkham and the other small towns and villages, from an estate the newspapers, in their current favourite word, called 'infamous', from the millionaires' row they called 'leafy' and from the middle-class in between. They were given, or occasionally baptised with, the names that became popular in the eighties and nineties: Kaylee and Scott, Gary and Lee, Sasha and Sanchia.

In one class in Kingsmarkham St Peter's Primary School it was tactless to ask after someone's father because most of the children were unsure about who their fathers were. Raised on crisps and chips and chocolate and take-away, they were nevertheless the healthiest generation of children the country has ever known. If one of them had been smacked he or she would have taken the perpetrator to the European Court of Human Rights. Mental torture was another story and no one knew what that story was, though many tried to write it every day.

The eldest of the children Wexford was interested in was on the upper limits of childhood. She was sixteen, old enough to marry, though not to vote, old enough to leave school if she so chose and leave home too if she wanted to.

Her name was Lizzie Cromwell.

# Chapter 1

On the day Lizzie came back from the dead the police and her family and neighbours had already begun the search for her body. They worked on the open countryside between Kingsmarkham and Myringham, combing the hillsides and beating through the woods. It was April but cold and wet, and a sharp north-east wind was blowing. Their task was not a pleasant one; no one laughed or joked and there was little talking.

Lizzie's stepfather was among the searchers but her mother was too upset to leave the house. The evening before the two of them had appeared on television to appeal for Lizzie to come home, for her abductor or attacker, whatever he might be, to release her. Her mother said she was only sixteen, which was known already, and that she had learning difficulties, which was not. Her stepfather was a lot younger than her mother, perhaps ten years, and looked very young. He had long hair and a beard, and wore several earrings, all in the same ear. After the television appearance several people phoned Kingsmarkham Police Station and gave it as their opinion that Colin Crowne had murdered his stepdaughter. One said he had buried her on the building site down York Street, a quarter of a mile down the road from where the Crownes and Lizzie lived on the Muriel Campden Estate. Another told Detective Sergeant Vine that she had heard Colin

Crowne threaten to kill Lizzie 'because she was as thick as two planks'.

'Those folks as go on telly to talk about their missing kids,' said a caller who refused to give her name, 'they're always the guilty ones. It's always the dad. I've seen it time and time again. If you don't know that you've no business being in the police.'

Chief Inspector Wexford thought she was dead. Not because of what the anonymous caller said, but because all the evidence pointed that way. Lizzie had no boyfriend, she was not at all precocious, she had a low IQ and was rather slow and timid. Three evenings before, she had gone with some friends on the bus to the cinema in Myringham but at the end of the film the other two girls had left her to come home alone. They had asked her to come clubbing with them but Lizzie had said her mother would be worried – the friends thought Lizzie herself was worried at the idea – and they left her at the bus-stop. It was just before eight thirty and getting dark. She should have been home in Kingsmarkham by nine fifteen but she didn't come home at all. At midnight her mother had phoned the police.

If she had been – well, a different sort of girl, Wexford wouldn't have paid so much attention. If she had been more like her friends. He hesitated about the phrase he used even in his own mind, for he liked to keep to his personal brand of political correctness in his thoughts as well as his speech. Not to be absurd about it, not to use ridiculous expressions like 'intellectually challenged', but not to be insensitive either and call a girl such as Lizzie Cromwell mentally handicapped or retarded. Besides, she wasn't either of those things, she could read and write, more or less, she had a certain measure of independence and went about on her own. In daylight, at any rate. But she wasn't fit just

4

the same to be left alone after dark on a lonely road. Come to that, what girl was?

So he thought she was dead. Murdered by someone. What he had seen of Colin Crowne he hadn't much liked but he had no reason to suspect him of killing his stepdaughter. True, some years before he married Debbie Cromwell, Crowne had been convicted of assault on a man outside a pub and he had another conviction for taking and driving away – in other words, stealing – a car. But what did all that amount to? Not much. It was more likely that someone had stopped and offered Lizzie a lift.

'Would she accept a lift from a stranger?' Vine had asked Debbie Crowne.

'Sometimes it's hard to make her like understand things,' Lizzie's mother had said. 'She'll sort of say yes and no and smile – she smiles a lot, she's a happy kid – but you don't know if it's like sunk in. Do you, Col?'

'I've told her never talk to strangers,' said Colin Crowne. 'I've told her till I'm blue in the face, but what do I get? A smile and a nod and another smile, then she'll just say something else, something loony, like the sun's shining or what's for tea.'

'Not loony, Col,' said the mother, obviously hurt. 'You know what I mean.'

So when she had been gone three nights and it was the morning of the third day Colin Crowne and the neighbours on either side of the Crownes on the Muriel Campden Estate started searching for Lizzie. Wexford had already talked to her friends and the driver of the bus she should have been on but hadn't been on, and Inspector Burden and Sergeant Vine had talked to dozens of motorists who used that road daily around about that time. When the rain became torrential, which happened at about four in the afternoon, they called off the search for that day but

5

they were set to begin again at first light. Taking DC Lynn Fancourt with him, Wexford went over to Puck Road for another talk with Colin and Debbie Crowne.

When it was built in the sixties, on an open space which would now be called a 'green field area', between the top of York Street and the western side of Glebe Road, the three streets and block of flats on a green in the midst of them, it had been called the York Estate. The then chairman of the housing committee, who had done *A Midsummer Night's Dream* for his School Certificate and was proud of the knowledge thus gained, named the streets after characters in that comedy, Oberon, Titania and Puck. This last had always been a problem to tenants, the police and the local authority because of the opportunity it gave the local youth of transforming, with a can of spray paint and the minimum effort, an innocent name into an obscenity.

Muriel Campden had been the Chair (as she must now be designated) of Kingsmarkham Borough Council longer than anyone else and when she died the York Estate was renamed after her. A move was afoot to erect a statue of her on the green opposite the council offices, a building newly named the Municipal Centre. Half the population was in favour and half was vehemently opposed.

'I'd have thought this place was memorial enough,' said Wexford, eyeing the triangle of squat sixties houses in the midst of which reared up a truncated tower, six storeys high. Ariel, Oberon and Puck Roads looked as if built out of absorbent breeze blocks that had soaked up the rain of two dozen wet winters and had rendered them the darkest shade of charcoal. 'Very appropriate for Muriel Campden. She was a dark, grey, gloomy sort of woman.' He pointed to the street sign at the beginning of Puck Road, once more defaced. 'Look at that. You'd think they'd get bored with doing it.'

'Little things please little minds, sir,' said Lynn just as the door was opened and they were admitted to number 45 by the occupier of number 47. This was a neighbour called Sue Ridley who conducted them into the presence of Debbie and Colin Crowne, sitting side by side on a sofa. They were both smoking cigarettes and both watching, or at any rate looking at, a television quiz show.

Debbie jumped up and screamed when they came in, 'They've found her! She's dead!'

'No, no, Mrs Crowne, we've no news for you. Nothing has happened. May I sit down?'

'Do what you want,' said Colin Crowne in customary surly tones.

He lit a cigarette and gave his wife one without asking her. The atmosphere in the small room was already thick with smoke. Rain beat relentlessly on the windows. On the screen a quiz contender, asked if Oasis was a town in Saudi, a pop group or a West End cinema, was unable to answer. Debbie Crowne called fretfully to her neighbour to make another cup of tea, would you, Sue, love?

Wexford and his team had already asked all the relevant questions and he was there more to convince Mrs Crowne that everything was being done that could be done to elicit more information. But he did press once more for the names of any relatives or even friends living in distant parts of the country to whom Lizzie might conceivably have gone. Such a man or woman would have to have been marooned on a newspaper-less, radio-less and TV-less island in perhaps the Outer Hebrides not to have known that Lizzie Cromwell had vanished and that the police

7

were hunting for her, but he still asked. For something to say, for the sake of something to distract Debbie Crowne's mind from the horror of her fears.

The doorbell rang at the very moment Sue Ridley brought in their tea, four mugs of it with the teabags still in as well as the milk and no spoons. She deposited the mugs in a bunch on the table and went to answer the door, saying it would be her partner, come back from going out with the search party.

Her loud shout made Wexford jump. 'You naughty girl, wherever have you been!'

Everybody stood up, the door opened and a girl came in, water running from her hair and clothes as if she had just stepped out of a bathful of it. Debbie Crowne screamed and, screaming, threw her arms round her daughter, oblivious of her soaking clothes.

'I'm cold, Mum,' said Lizzie, smiling waterily through chattering teeth. 'I'm ever so cold.'

She was back and safe, and apparently unharmed, and that, at first, was all that mattered. Wexford left, deputing Mike Burden and Lynn Fancourt to talk to Lizzie after she had had a hot bath. He was to question her himself on the following day and several times on subsequent days because her response was far from satisfactory. In other words, she refused – or was unable – to say where she had been.

He said nothing, he knew nothing, of this when he walked into his own house at six, early for him, but he did tell his wife Lizzie Cromwell was found. 'Rather, she seems to have come back of her own accord. It'll be on the news at nine.'

'Where had she been?' said Dora.

'I don't know. Off with some boy, I dare say. That's usually what it is. The fact that their parents don't know there *is* a boy means nothing.'

'I suppose it was the same with us. I suppose Sylvia and Sheila had boyfriends we never knew about, as well as the ones we did. Which reminds me, Sylvia is bringing Robin and Ben to us for the night. Neil's away somewhere and she's got this new job.'

'Ah, The Hide helpline. I didn't know she had to work nights.'

'I wish she didn't have to. It's far too much for her, with her day job as well. I don't suppose The Hide pays much.'

'If I know anything about it,' said Wexford, 'The Hide pays nothing at all.'

He was on the phone to Burden when his elder daughter arrived with his grandsons. Burden had made the call, incensed at Lizzie Cromwell's refusal to talk.

'You mean she won't say where she's been?'

'I thought she *couldn't* talk. I honestly thought she was dumb. Well, she's not entirely normal, is she?'

'She can talk,' said Wexford repressively. 'I've heard her.'

'Oh, so have I – now.'

'And she's as normal as you are or as normal as half the people in this place. It's just that she's not a genius.' Wexford cleared his throat. 'Like you and your ilk,' he added nastily, for Burden had just gained membership of Mensa on an IQ rumoured to be 152. 'Why won't she say where she's been?'

'I don't know. Scared. Obstinate. Doesn't want her mum and Earrings to know, I'd guess.'

'OK, we'll have another go tomorrow.'

Wexford's daughter Sylvia was a social worker. She had been a mature student when she studied for her sociology degree, for she had married at eighteen. The two boys who came running out of the kitchen when their grandfather put down the phone

9

were the offspring of that marriage. Wexford said hallo to them, admired a new Nintendo and a Gameboy, and asked if their mother was still in the house.

'She's talking to Gran,' said Ben in the tone of disgust someone might use when castigating deeply antisocial behaviour.

All parents have a favourite among their children, though they may, like Wexford, strive always to conceal that preference. He had failed to hide his bias in favour of his younger daughter and he knew it, so he kept on trying. With Sylvia he was more effusive, he never missed giving her a kiss each time they met, listened attentively when she spoke to him and pretended not to be ruffled when she rubbed him up the wrong way. For Sylvia lacked her sister's charm and, although pleasant enough to look at, was without Sheila's beauty. She was an opinionated, didactic, often aggressive feminist, with a talent for saying the wrong thing, a fault-finder, bad at marriage but expert at rearing children. She was also – and Wexford knew it – good as gold, with an oversized social conscience.

He found her sitting at the kitchen table with a mug of tea in front of her, lecturing her mother on domestic violence. Dora had apparently asked the classic question, the one that, according to Sylvia, betrays ignorance of the whole subject: 'But if their husbands beat them why don't they leave?'

'That question is just so typical', Sylvia was saying, 'of the sort of woman who is completely out of touch with the world around her. Leave, you say. Where is she – we'll say she, not they – where is she to go? She's dependent on him, she has nothing of her own. She has children – is she to take her children? Sure, he beats her, he breaks her nose and knocks out her teeth, but afterwards, every time, he says he's sorry,

10

he won't do it again. She wants to keep things normal, she wants to keep the family together – oh, hi, Dad, how are things?'

Wexford kissed her, said things were fine and how was work on the crisis line.

'The helpline, we call it. I was telling Mother about it. Mind you, it breaks your heart, all of it. And some of the worst is the attitude of the public. It's extraordinary, but a lot of people still think there's something *funny* about a man beating up a woman. It's a joke, it's a seaside postcard kind of thing. They ought to see some of the injuries we see, some of the *scars*. And as for the police . . .'

'Now, Sylvia, wait a minute.' Wexford's resolutions flew out of the window. 'We have a programme here in Mid-Sussex for dealing with domestic violence, we emphatically do not treat assaults on women in the home as a routine part of married life.' His voice rose. 'We're even putting in place a scheme to encourage friends and neighbours to report evidence of domestic violence. It's called Hurt-Watch and if you haven't heard about it you should have.'

'All right, all right. But you have to admit all that's very new. It's very recent.'

'It sounds like the Stasi or the KGB to me,' said Dora. 'The nanny state gone mad.'

'Mother, suppose it is a nanny state, what's wrong with having a nanny to look after you? I've often wished I could afford one. Some of these women are utterly helpless, no one *cared* about them until the refuges started. And if that isn't evidence enough of the need, there aren't refuge places enough, there aren't *half* enough to meet the need . . .'

Wexford left the room quietly and went to find his grandsons.

The boys' school was on the outskirts of Myfleet and

11

next morning Wexford drove them there before going on to work. His route took him through the Brede Valley, under Savesbury Hill and along the edge of Framhurst Great Wood, and he never went that way without thankfulness that the bypass, started the previous year, had been shelved on a change of government. Newbury was completed but Salisbury would never be built and nor would Kingsmarkham (insofar as you could ever say 'never' in connection with such things). It was unusual to feel glad about frugality, relieved that something couldn't be afforded, but this was a rare instance of that happening. The Yellow Caddis would be saved and the Map butterfly. You could even say that some kinds of wildlife benefited from the bypass plans, since the badgers retained their old setts and gained man-made new ones, while the butterfly had two nettle plantations to feed on instead of just one.

At the point where the bypass was due to start and where work on it had begun, earth had been shifted by diggers and excavators. No one, it appeared, had any intention of restoring the terrain to its former level, and grass and wild plants had grown over the new landscape of mounds and declivities, so that in the years to come these hills and valleys would seem a natural phenomenon. Or so Wexford said, commenting on the strange scenery.

'And in hundreds of years, Grandad,' said Robin, 'archaeologists may think those hills were the burial ground of an ancient tribe.'

'Very likely,' said Wexford, 'good point.'

'Tumuli,' Robin said, savouring the word, 'that's what they'll call them.'

'Are you pleased?' Ben asked.

'What, that they didn't build the bypass? Yes, I am, very pleased. I didn't like them cutting down the trees and tearing up the hedges. I didn't like the road building.'

'I did,' said Ben. 'I liked the diggers. I'm going to drive a JCB when I'm grown up and then I'll dig up the whole world.'

It was the loveliest time of the year, unless early May, still a month off, might be more lush and floral, but now in April the trees were misted over with green and pale amber and the Great Wood, which in May would be carpeted with bluebells, showed celandines and aconites, both bright gold, studding the forest floor. After he had dropped the boys at the school gate and waited a moment or two to see them shepherded into the building, he drove back, musing on children's taste, and on the beauties of nature and when children first were affected by them. Girls sooner than boys, he thought, girls as young as seven, while boys seemed not to notice scenery, rivers and hills, woodland, the distant landscape of downs and the high skyscape of clouds, until well into their teens. And yet all the great nature poets had been men. Of course, Sylvia might be right and there had been great women poets too, born to be unrecognised and waste their sweetness on the desert air.

Meanwhile, he had a girl to talk to, one who might or might not care about pastoral beauty and badgers and butterflies, but who seemed amiable enough and who smiled timorously when her stepfather scolded her and when she was soaked to the skin. Not a wild teenager, not a rebel.

She was sitting on the sofa in the front room of 45 Puck Road, watching a dinosaur cartoon video, designed for children half her age, called *Jurassic Larks*. Or staring unseeing at it, Wexford thought.

Anything rather than have to look at him and Lynn Fancourt.

At a nod from Wexford, Lynn picked up the remote off the table. 'I think we'll have this off, Lizzie. It's time to talk.'

As the pink brontosaurus faded and the pterodactyl with baby ichthyosaur in its mouth vanished in a flicker, Lizzie made a deprecating sound, a kind of snort of protest. She went on staring at the blank screen.

'You won't get anything out of her,' Debbie Crowne said. 'She's that obstinate, you might as well talk to a brick wall.'

'How old are you, Lizzie?' Wexford asked.

'She's sixteen.' Debbie didn't give her daughter a chance to answer. 'She was sixteen in January.'

'In that case, Mrs Crowne, perhaps it would be best for us to talk to Lizzie on her own.'

'What, not have me here?'

'The law requires a parent or responsible adult to be present only when a child is under sixteen.'

Lizzie spoke, though she didn't turn her head. 'I'm not a child.'

'If you would, please, Mrs Crowne.'

'Oh, all right, if you say so. But she won't say anything.' Debbie Crowne put her hand up to her mouth as if she had just recollected something. 'If she *does* say something you'll tell me, won't you? I mean, she could have been anywhere, with anyone. There's no knowing, is there? I mean, she could be *pregnant*.'

Lizzie made the same sound she had when her video was turned off. Saying, 'It's all very well grunting like that, but I reckon she ought to be examined,' Debbie Crowne left the room, shutting the door rather too smartly behind her. The girl didn't move.

'You were away from your home for three days,

Lizzie,' Wexford said. 'You'd never done anything like that before, had you?'

Silence. Lizzie bent her head still further so that her face was entirely concealed by hanging hair. It was pretty hair, red-gold, long and wavy. The hands in her lap had bitten nails. 'You didn't go alone, did you? Did someone take you away, Lizzie?'

When it was clear she wasn't going to answer that either, Lynn said, 'Whatever you did or wherever you went, no one is going to punish you. Are you afraid of getting into trouble? You won't.'

'No one is going to harm you, Lizzie,' said Wexford. 'We only want to know where you went. If you went away because you wanted to be with someone you like you've a right to do that. No one can stop you doing that. But, you see, everyone was looking for you, the police and your parents and your friends were all looking for you. So now we have a right too. We've a right to know where you were.'

The grunt came again, a straining sound like that made by someone in pain. 'I can understand you might not want to tell me,' Wexford said. 'I can go away. You could be alone with Lynn. You could talk to Lynn. Would you like that?'

She looked up then. Her face, a rather pretty pudgy face, freckled about the nose and forehead, was blank, her pale-blue eyes vacant. She moistened her thin pink lips. Frown lines appeared as if she was concentrating hard but as if the intellectual effort of whatever it was was too much for her. Then she nodded. Not as people usually nod, repeating several times the up-and-down motion of the head, but just once and jerkily, almost curtly.

'That's good.' Wexford went out of the room into the hall, a narrow passage that contained a bicycle and a crate full of empty bottles. He tapped on a door at the end and was admitted into a kitchen-diner. Colin Crowne was nowhere to be seen. His wife was sitting in the dining area on a high stool up at a counter, drinking coffee and smoking a cigarette. 'There's a chance your daughter may feel more able to talk to DC Fancourt on her own.'

'If you say so, but if she won't talk to her own mother . . .'

'What would your attitude be if it turns out she's been with a boyfriend?'

'She hasn't,' said Debbie Crowne, stubbing out her cigarette in a saucer, 'so I couldn't have an *attitude*.'

'Let me put it another way. Could she be afraid of what would happen if you found out she had been with a boyfriend?'

'Look, she hasn't got a boyfriend. I'd know. I know where she is every minute of the day, I have to, she's not – well, you know what she is. She's a bit – she's got to be looked after.'

'Nevertheless, she was out on her own with friends on Saturday evening and though she went to Myringham with them, they left her to come home on her own.'

'Well, they shouldn't have. I've told them over and over not to leave Lizzie to do things on her own. I've *told* them and her.'

'They're sixteen, Mrs Crowne, and they don't always do as they're told.'

She shifted off the subject to one obviously nearer to her heart. 'But what about like I said if she's pregnant, she ought to have a medical, she ought to be looked at. Suppose he did something to her, we don't know what he did.'

'Are you suggesting she was raped?'

'No, I'm not, of course I'm not, I'd know that all right.'

Then if she hasn't a boyfriend and she wasn't

raped, how could she possibly be pregnant? He didn't say it aloud but went back to the living-room, first knocking on the door. Lynn was there but the girl was gone.

'I couldn't exactly stop her, sir. She wanted to go upstairs to her bedroom and I couldn't stop her.'

'No. We'll leave it for now.' In the car he asked her what had been the result of the interview, if there had in fact been an interview. 'Did she say anything?'

'She told me a lot of lies, sir. I know they were lies. It was as if – well, she'd realised she had to say something to get us to leave her alone. Unfortunately for her, she has rather a limited imagination, but she tried.'

'So what tall stories did this limited imagination come up with?'

'She was waiting at the bus-stop and it was raining. A lady – that's how she put it – a lady came along in a car and offered her a lift but she refused because Colin had told her never to accept lifts from strangers. The bus didn't come and it was pouring with rain so she went into an empty house with boarded-up windows – the house with the apple tree, she calls it – and sat on the floor waiting for the rain to stop . . .'

'I don't believe it!'

'I said you wouldn't. I didn't.'

'How did she get in?'

'The door wasn't locked. She pushed it open. Then when the rain had stopped and she thought she'd go back to the bus-stop she couldn't get out because someone had come along and locked her in. She stayed in there for three nights and three days with nothing to eat, though she could get water from a tap, and she found blankets to wrap herself in and keep herself warm. Then the door was unlocked, she escaped and caught the bus home.'

No one believed Lizzie's story but it was worth going to Myringham and taking a look.

'No need for you to do that, sir,' Lynn said. She meant it was beneath someone of his rank. 'I can do it.'

'It's either that or back to the paperwork,' said Wexford.

Vine had talked to the two friends, Hayley Lawrie and Kate Burton, and both said they had walked with Lizzie to the bus-stop. They had promised not to leave her alone but they hadn't, not really, only for five minutes, the bus was due in five minutes. Hayley said she wished now she had stayed with Lizzie till the bus came but Kate said it didn't matter anyway because no harm had come to Lizzie.

The bus-stop was the nearest one to the cinema where they had been but still it was on the outskirts of Myringham, on the old Kingsmarkham Road. The first thing Wexford noticed was the derelict house. The bus-stop was directly in front of it. All its windows boarded up, half the slates off its roof, its front gate hanging from a single hinge, the house stood in an overgrown patch of garden in which the one beautiful thing about the whole place was the cherry tree in rose-pink blossom. Not an apple, as Lizzie had said, but a Japanese kanzan. The front door of the house had been painted an aggressive dark green some twenty years before and now the paint was peeling. Wexford turned the blackened brass knob and pushed it, wondering how he would feel about Lizzie if the door yielded. But it was locked.

They went round the back. Here the boards were hanging off one of the windows, or someone had been at work attempting to remove them. Wexford made a quick decision. 'We'll get in that way. And afterwards we'll have the window properly boarded up. Do the owner a service, whoever he or she may be.'

Perhaps Lizzie had got in that way or out that way or both. The aperture was big enough for small or slight people to squeeze through but Donaldson had to enlarge it for Wexford with the aid of tools from the car boot. Wexford stepped in over the ledge and Lynn and Donaldson followed. Inside it was cold, damp and smelt of fungus. Floorboards had been taken up to disclose black pits, in some of which oily water lay. Most of the furniture had been taken out long ago, though a black horsehair settee remained in the room where they were and the iron basket in the fireplace was full of empty crisp packets and cigarette ends. Paper hung from the walls in long curling swathes.

In the only other downstairs room, apart from the kitchen, two oil paintings still hung on mildewed walls, one of a stag drinking from a pool, the other of a girl of vaguely Pre-Raphaelite appearance picking up shells on a beach. No blankets anywhere. Upstairs still remained to explore. Wexford was inspired to investigate the filthy hole of a kitchen. He tried both taps. One was dry while the other emitted a trickle of rusty water, red as blood. Lizzie hadn't drunk from that. The back door had no key in its lock and no bolts. Wooden battens had been nailed across its architrave. Lizzie hadn't come in through the front door either. It was bolted on the inside. The bolts were rusty and couldn't have been drawn back without the use of tools.

'Can we get up the stairs, Lynn?' Wexford asked. 'They look as if someone's been at them with a pickaxe.'

'Just about, sir.' Lynn eyed him, not the staircase, as if she doubted his athleticism rather than the stability of treads and risers.

An attempt had apparently been made to replace the treads or remove them or widen the whole structure and had been abandoned, but not until the staircase was partially demolished. Wexford let Lynn go first, not so much out of politeness as from knowing that this way, if he fell over backwards, he wouldn't fall on top of a small, slim woman who probably weighed less than eight stone. He trod gingerly, holding on, perhaps unwisely, to the rickety banister, and got safely to the top. His efforts were rewarded by the sight of a large grey blanket covering some sort of tank or at any rate large cuboid object. There was nothing else at all in the two small attic bedrooms.

'I suppose she could have wrapped herself in this,' said Lynn, extending to Wexford the hand she had brought away damp from contact with the blanket. 'Though it smells a bit musty.' Above them, through a hole in the stained plaster, the edge of a tile could be seen and beyond, a segment of blue and white sky.

'She might have drunk from a bathroom tap,' said Wexford, 'if there were a bathroom.' He shook his head. 'She may have been here but not for three days.'

'Does it matter, sir?' Lynn asked as they made their way back down the perilous staircase. 'I mean, she's back and she's not hurt. Is it any of our concern where she was?'

'Maybe not. Maybe you're right. I suppose it's just because I'd like to *know*.'

He said much the same thing to Burden next day when the inspector protested about his interest in something so trivial. They were not at the police station but in the Olive and Dove, for a beer at the end of the day's work.

'Only I don't seem to have done any work,' said Wexford, 'just filled in those damned forms.'

'Perhaps we're beating crime at last.'

'You jest. I don't suppose a crime was committed against Lizzie Cromwell or that she committed one but I'd like to know. *Three days* she was away, Mike, three days and three nights. She wasn't in that house – oh, we could only establish that for sure by taking her fingerprints and going over the place – but I know she wasn't. She couldn't have got in or if she had she couldn't have got out again and restored that window to the way it was when we found it. She lied about drinking water from a tap, she lied about wrapping herself in a blanket and she lied about being locked in and then let out. So she wasn't there at all. I'm wondering if it would be worth putting out a call for that woman, the one who offered her a lift.'

'That may be a lie too.'

'True. It may be.' Wexford downed the last of his best bitter. 'So where was she?'

'With a man. They're always with a man, you know that. The fact that her mother says there's no boyfriend means nothing and saying she never had the chance to meet a boyfriend means nothing either. It doesn't matter what a girl looks like or how simple she is – all right, don't look like that, you know what I mean – or how shy or whatever, the instinct in young human beings to reproduce is so powerful that the most unlikely ones get together like – like magnets.'

'I hope there'll be no reproduction in this case, though I agree the most likely thing is that she was with a man, a boy. It still doesn't tell us where.'

'At his place, of course.'

'Ah, but there's the difficulty. If he's her age the

21

most likely thing is that he lives with parents or one parent and maybe siblings. If he's older he's likely to be married or, as they put it these days, "in a relationship". The other people involved would know of her disappearance. Somebody would have come to us.'

'He could have taken her to a hotel.'

'For *three days and three nights*, Mike? Is he that well off? No, the only possibility that I can see is that he lives alone in a room or flat of his own and that he took her there. He kept her indoors for the whole of the three days and three nights and no one in the house or block of flats saw her. I don't like it, I don't really believe it, but we know what Sherlock Holmes said.'

Burden had heard it too often from Wexford's lips to be in any doubt about it. 'If all else is impossible that which remains must be so, or something like that.' He went to renew their drinks. Although he wasn't going to say so, or not yet, he was sick of Lizzie Cromwell and bored with the whole thing. Wexford, in his opinion, was beginning to get obsessive again, only in the past when he had a bee in his bonnet it was over events rather more earth-shaking than this. But if, when he returned to their table with the two halves of Adnams, he hoped that Wexford would choose a new subject of conversation he was disappointed.

'So when her friends left her at the bus-stop she was waiting for this guy to come along in a car, was she? Why a bus-stop then? Why not somewhere warm and dry like a café?'

'Because she had to make her friends believe she was waiting for a bus.' Burden said it repressively. He hoped he might have had the last word.

'You're fed up with this, aren't you? I know you are, I can tell. I won't bore you much longer. I think you're right about her reason for waiting at the bus-stop, but I'd like to dig a little deeper into that. Why did she want to make her friends believe she was waiting for a bus?'

'So they wouldn't know about the boyfriend.'

'But why wouldn't she want them to know? Wouldn't she be proud of having a boyfriend? Especially one with a car and a place to take her? She could have trusted them. They'd be the last to tell her mother.'

'Maybe he's married.'

'Then he wouldn't have a place to take her,' said Wexford and, though Burden waited for the next phase of this reasoning, he said no more about it. 'Hurt-Watch meeting in the morning,' he said instead. 'Remember? Ten sharp. Southby will be there, in case I haven't told you.'

At the prospect of an encounter with the new Assistant Chief Constable Designate, Burden groaned softly. Operation Safeguard, which the programme had originally been called, held very little interest for him. His personal belief was that what happened in the home belonged in the home and should come as little as possible within the province of the law. But he knew where Wexford's sympathies lay, so he held his tongue.

Next morning, half an hour before the meeting was due to begin, a woman came into the police station on her way to work to say that she had seen Lizzie Cromwell at the bus-stop the previous Saturday evening. It was a matter of chance that Wexford spoke to her at all. He and Barry Vine happened to be passing the desk in the foyer of the building where she was talking to the duty sergeant. Even so, Barry came out with the usual formula, that he

23

would see to it, that it was hardly necessary for Wexford to . . .

Bother my pretty little head about it, Wexford thought but he didn't say aloud. 'We'll go up to my office,' he said.

# Chapter 2

It was Friday now and Lizzie had come home on
Tuesday afternoon. Wexford imparted this information to Mrs Pauline Ward, surprised that she seemed
not to know it already. 'May I ask why you didn't
come before?' he asked her.

'I never saw her picture till last night. It was in a
paper wrapping up a crab.'

'It was what?'

'Look, I don't take a paper. I mean, a daily paper.
And I don't watch television news. I watch television
but not the news. It upsets me. I mean, if it's not
atrocities in Albania or kids burnt to death in a fire
it's baby seals getting clubbed to death. So I don't
look at it any more.'

'The crab, please, Mrs Ward.'

She was in her mid-fifties, smartly dressed, her
skirt too short and her eyelids too blue, but a
handsome, well-kept woman who had arrived – and
parked it on the parking place reserved for the
Assistant Chief Constable Designate – in a dark-blue
Audi, polished to a gleam. When she smiled, as she
now did, she showed a fine set of bright white teeth.

'Oh, the crab,' she said. 'Yes, I stopped off at that
good fishmonger in York Street on my way home
from work last evening. I had a friend coming to
supper and I'd nothing for a starter, so I thought a
crab would be nice and the fishmonger wrapped it
up in this newspaper. *The Times*, I think it was.

Anyway, when I unwrapped my crab I saw her picture and I remembered seeing her on Saturday night.'

'I see. And when your friend came, did you say anything to her about it?'

'Him,' said Mrs Ward. 'It's a him, my friend.' Her tone was that of a woman who would hardly bother to buy a crab for a female guest. 'Well, no, I didn't. Should I have?'

'He might have told you Lizzie Cromwell was found. That is, unless he too shies away from the news.'

Pauline Ward gave him a suspicious sideways look. 'I don't know whether he does or not. We don't talk about that sort of thing.' She very nearly but not quite tossed her head. 'Don't you want to know about Saturday night?'

Wexford nodded.

'All right then. I work in Myringham. I'm the manager of the Crescent Minimarket on the Heaven Spent mall and we stay open till eight thirty on Saturdays. It was twenty to nine when I left. I had to lock up and go to my car so, what with one thing and another, it was ten to when I drove past that bus-stop.'

Wexford interrupted her. 'How can you be so sure of the time?'

'I always do, to the minute. I'm a clock-watcher. Well, I suppose I'm a watch-watcher. I noted the time when I left, and I saw that digital clock on the Midland Bank just when I started driving off and it said eight fifty-four. I thought, that can't be right, not as late as that, and I checked it with my watch and the clock on the car – I knew they were both right to the nearest second – and they both said eight forty-nine. Well, I thought, I'll go into the Midland and tell them (and I did, I went in on the Tuesday). And by the time I'd thought that, about the bank I mean, I was passing that bus-stop and the girl was there, and I thought, poor thing, having to wait for a bus in the rain. Shall I offer her a lift, I thought, and then I thought, no, better not, because you never know, do you?'

So this wasn't the woman who had offered Lizzie a lift and had her offer rejected. But ten to nine . . . Had the girl really waited at the bus-stop for twenty minutes?

'Are you quite sure it was ten to nine?'

'I've told you, haven't I? I always know the time. What d'you want to know all this for, anyway, if she's come back?'

'I can't tell you that, Mrs Ward.'

She got up. 'Aren't you going to thank me? I didn't have to come in here, you know. I wouldn't have if I hadn't happened to buy that crab.'

He took her downstairs and at the exit doors she looked back over her shoulder and said, 'You have an attitude problem, you know. You want to get it sorted.'

Wexford restrained his laughter until she had gone. He certainly had a problem but it wasn't one of attitude. Rather, he was allowing himself to be ridiculously involved in this Lizzie Cromwell business. She was back, as everyone kept telling him, she had been away with a boyfriend, but she was back and no harm was done. Had the boyfriend kept her waiting at that bus-stop for twenty minutes? In the rain? Perhaps. It was possible. It struck him – and the idea was very unwelcome – that Lizzie, sweet, childishly pretty, not very bright and probably highly gullible, was the kind of person of whom the unscrupulous would take advantage.

Did she go to a special school? And if not, why not? Even if she did, would that school be the kind of place to nurture her self-confidence and her street wisdom? He doubted it. But he resolved to turn his back on Lizzie and her problems and her family. It wasn't a police matter. Police time and the taxpayers' money had been wasted on it but that happened all the time. You had to be thankful there was no crime, there was no fatality or even injury, and some would say the money and time had been well spent when the outcome was such a happy one. So goodbye, Lizzie Cromwell, and let's hope you're not pregnant.

The Hurt-Watch meeting passed off uneventfully, even satisfactorily. For once, Wexford and Malcolm Southby were in agreement. Both wanted to prioritise (Southby's word, Wexford wasn't in agreement with that) domestic violence as serious crime, and both thought providing women who were its victims with mobile phones and pagers a good move. Simply knowing the police were on their side was to take a step in the right direction.

'What about the ones who are victims but who have never called us?' Karen Malahyde asked. 'There's a lot of secrecy goes on in this area, you know. A good many of these women will do almost anything not to admit to being victims.'

'I hardly see what we can do about that, DS Malahyde,' said Southby, who was parsimonious with the taxpayers' money, 'short of supplying every lady in Greater Kingsmarkham with expensive electronic equipment.' Even when he approved a cause, the Assistant Chief Constable Designate could scarcely resist sarcasm. He elaborated. 'Oh, excuse me, only those in a meaningful relationship, of course' and he cackled with laughter at his own wit.

Karen, who didn't think it amusing, kept a straight and glowering face while deploring the sycophantic smiles of certain of her fellow officers. 'That's all very well, sir.' She didn't quite dare say that was all very

funny and she knew the 'sir' didn't justify everything. 'But don't we have to do more to find out
where the victims are? I mean, the ones who'll
conceal what happens to them at any price?'

'We have Hurt-Watch, Karen,' said Wexford and
got a look from Southby for using her Christian
name. 'We're alerting everyone through advertising
in the *Courier* and leafleting every household. A
police representative – and that'll be one of us – will
go on *Newsroom South-East* and talk about it. I don't
see at the moment what more we can do.'

'OK. Thank you, sir. It's just that the whole
business is on the increase – but, thanks.'

He had concentrated on the meeting for the hour
that it lasted and he also had resisted smiling,
without much difficulty, at the ACC's wit. The
moment it was over, the thought came winging back
into his head: talking of secrecy, what was there
about this boyfriend that he had to be concealed
from Lizzie's friends as well as her parents and why
wouldn't she admit to him now?

The Hide was probably not the dullest and least
interesting looking structure in the whole of Kingsmarkham. The Muriel Campden tower was uglier
and some office blocks starker, but among sizeable
houses standing in their own grounds The Hide had
no rivals in the category of boring buildings not
worth a second glance. That few people would have
given it that second glance or even noticed it at all
had been a factor in its purchase by Griselda Cooper
and Lucy Angeletti as a centre and temporary home
for the victims of domestic violence.

It was necessary for the house to be inconspicuous
yet appear to have nothing to hide, dreary without
being sinister, and dull with a dullness that excited

no comment. Once it had been numbered 12 Kingsbrook Valley Drive, but the number-plate had been removed and no name-plate lettered *The Hide* replaced it. Its telephone number was ex-directory. Only its helpline number was known. Every call-box in Kingsmarkham, Stowerton, Pomfret and the villages had posted up in its interior on a card The Hide's helpline number. But there was nothing on the cards about where the house was or its purpose, or who sought and found sanctuary there.

Almost the first question Sylvia Fairfax had asked when she first went to work for the helpline was, 'Why the secrecy?'

'In nine cases out of ten,' Griselda Cooper said, 'husbands or partners or boyfriends, whoever's responsible for the abuse, come looking for them. This way it makes it harder to find them. Not impossible but harder.'

'But they do get here?'

'Some do. We had one got over the wall. It's ten feet high with barbed wire on the top but he got over. After that we changed the barbed wire for razor wire.'

The garden was large. Trellis raised the height of the walls between The Hide and numbers 10 and 14 Kingsbrook Valley Drive. The lawn was mown and the shrubs occasionally pruned but otherwise the garden was untended. There was a swing and a climbing frame for the children and Lucy Angeletti, who was The Hide's fund-raiser, was trying to get enough money together to create a proper play area.

The neighbours at numbers 10 and 14, and at numbers 8 and 16 too, had got wind of this intention and were mounting a rival campaign to put a stop to it. The Hide and its occupants were not popular in Kingsbrook Valley Drive. People thought it constituted a danger to the peace of the area and an encouragement to crime. The house itself was a big square box without wings or gables or porch, built in 1886 by a man with a large family who wanted to save expense. Even the roof, though not entirely flat, was scarcely discernible from the street, being concealed by a bald brick wall that ran round the top of the house above the third-floor windows. Dull reddish-brown brick was the building material used and the only decorations on the house were the buff-coloured stone facings around the flat sash windows. All this was half hidden by the laurel bushes which dominated the front garden and by the two ilexes, cemetery trees whose leaves never fell but merely grew darker and dustier with time.

Inside, it was quite different, pale colours and pretty curtains, and pictures on the walls. Well, posters rather than pictures. Lucy had had the bright idea of buying sheets of wrapping paper, the kind that has flower paintings on it or maps of the world or *La Dame à la Licorne*, and getting them framed. The furniture was from second-hand shops or contributed by supporters and the floor covering came from the carpet warehouse on the Stowerton Road where all the stock was cheap because it had been damaged by fire. There was never sufficient money. Lucy's hair had gone grey through worrying about getting enough funds to keep The Hide going, though perhaps it would have changed colour anyway as premature greyness ran in her family.

Lack of money was the reason Sylvia and Jill Lewis and Davina Crewe got no pay for answering the phone to the women who appealed for help and sometimes for refuge. Ideally, the helpline should have operated from elsewhere. But there was no elsewhere. Griselda Cooper lived on the premises and Lucy Angeletti in a one-bedroom flat in Stowerton. The Hide had no offices apart from two poky rooms in the basement at number 12 Kingsbrook Valley Drive. The two phone lines manned by Jill and Davina, sometimes by Griselda and Lucy, and now by Sylvia, were in a room on the top floor alongside Griselda's tiny flat. Space was so precious that the other two rooms on that floor had been converted into bedsits for fugitive women, two single beds in one and three plus a cot in the other. It wasn't ideal but it was the best they could do.

There was no lift. Sylvia had to toil up three flights of stairs, from the ground floor where the living-rooms were, the lounge and the television room and the children's playroom and the kitchen and the laundry room, through the first and second storeys, given over entirely to bedsits and bathrooms – more bathrooms were another priority when Lucy could get the funds – and up to the top where the phones were. Children were usually playing on the stairs. They weren't supposed to, or slide down the banisters but, when the playroom was crowded and it was raining, they hadn't much choice.

Sylvia worked at The Hide two evenings a week, not always the same evenings, up till midnight. Her husband was usually at home to look after the boys and if he couldn't be there she knew they could go to her parents. She had taken on the job partly from the pressures of her social conscience and her commitment to women's causes, and partly to get herself out of the house. When she was at home she and Neil either sat in silence or addressed each other through the medium of their children, or quarrelled. Although she never talked about the state of her marriage to her mother or her father, she did to friends and she was fast making a friend of Griselda Cooper.

Griselda's shift ended when she took over but sometimes she stayed on for half an hour or even longer to talk. She was a dozen years or more older than Sylvia, a single woman who had a lover who took her out and about, and away when she had a weekend off, an enviable lot. Sylvia couldn't help being envious, though Griselda had no children and now never would have. One evening she told Griselda about her marriage, that she and Neil had married very young and discovered too late they were less than well-suited.

'Too late?' said Griselda, who had been divorced.

'I couldn't break up the family. If we split up it would devastate my kids.'

'That sounds like the sort of thing some of our callers say. He's half killed her and he will again, and she knows he will but she can't break up the family.'

The phone rang and Griselda picked up the receiver. 'The Hide helpline. How can I help you?' She spoke in the calmest, warmest and most comforting tone she could achieve, and that was very calm and warm and comforting.

Sylvia could tell there was silence at the other end. There often was. Women lost their nerve or didn't know what to say or, worst of all, the man of the house had come into the room where the phone was.

Griselda waited, repeating her words, 'How can I help you,' then, 'We're here to help you,' and 'Won't you tell me what your problem is? Anything you say will be in confidence.'

After ten minutes' perseverance she put the phone down regretfully. 'I could hear her breathing,' Griselda said. 'I heard her sigh. God knows, I hope she'll call back. Maybe she will and you'll take it.'

'What you were saying just now,' Sylvia said, 'before the call came, about a man half killing a woman but still she won't break up the family, Neil has never laid a finger on me. And, d'you know, working here and listening to all this, hearing from

33

these women and what they go through, has done me good. I mean, it's actually done my *marriage* good.'

'You're joking.'

'The other night I went home from here and it was the middle of the night, of course, and I went home and got into bed – oh, yes, we share a bed – crazy, eh? – and I got into bed beside him – he was asleep, sleeping so peacefully, like a child, and I – I thought, you've always been kind to me and gentle and patient, and I've never appreciated that. And I – I put my arm round him, and lay beside him and hugged him. That's something I haven't done for years ...'

'Come on,' said Griselda, 'don't cry. Well, *do* cry if it makes you feel better.'

She put her arm round Sylvia but only for a moment because the phone was ringing again.

A designer in textiles who lived and worked in Pomfret had had her entire stock stolen. The collection, quilted coats and waistcoats, bedcovers and throws, as well as batik wall hangings, dresses, table-cloths and napkins, had been housed in the basement, which had been converted two years before into a workshop. The basement window was barred and the door into the area double-locked and bolted, but the window of the cloakroom, a cupboard-sized place containing lavatory and diminutive wash-basin, was open. Whoever had got through that window must have been thin and lithe, and he or she had evidently removed the entire haul through the same aperture.

'Or unbolted and unlocked that door from the inside,' said Inspector Burden, 'taken the stuff out, gone back, bolted and locked the door again and escaped through that broken window.'

'I couldn't do it,' said Wexford sadly. 'If it were

twice the size I couldn't.' He looked critically at Burden, whose new taupe-coloured suit enhanced his slimness. 'And I'm bound to say you couldn't either, Mike. Did they put a kid in there? A kind of Oliver Twist?'

'God knows. We've found no prints apart from her own and the guy she lives with. She values the stuff that's gone at fifty thousand pounds.'

'Does she now? I thought these crafts people were supposed to be on the breadline. You know what they say, that they'd make more dosh going out cleaning than they do from their exquisite needlework, pots, batik et cetera.'

'That's what she *values* it at. It's got nothing to do with whether she can sell it or not. By the way, before I forget, we've had another mum phoned up to say her daughter's missing.'

Wexford banged the desk top with both fists. 'Why didn't you say so before?'

Burden didn't answer. Always particular about his appearance, he fingered his tie, also a shade of taupe but patterned discreetly in dark red and pale blue, and looked about him for a mirror. A very small one had always hung on Wexford's yellow wall between the door and the filing cabinet.

'It's gone,' Wexford said impatiently. 'I don't like mirrors or "looking glasses", as my old dad used to call them. I look in one to shave in the morning, I have to, and that's enough for the day. I'm not a male model.'

'Evidently,' said Burden, by now studying the best image of his face and neck he could get, their reflection in the glass that covered Wexford's Chagall print. 'I don't know what's wrong with this tie, it goes crooked whatever I do.'

'For God's sake, take it off then. Or do as I do and have two ties to wear on alternate days, the blue one on Mondays, Wednesdays and Fridays and the red one on Tuesdays and Thursdays, and vice versa the next week. Now perhaps you'll tell me about this missing girl.'

Burden sat down on the other side of Wexford's desk. 'It's almost certainly nothing, Reg. Do you know that there are more than forty thousand teenagers missing in this country? Of course you do. Anyway, this one won't be missing, she's not a child, she's eighteen and she's probably done a Lizzie Cromwell.'

'And what might that be?'

'I mean she's gone off with a boy or gone to visit friends, or dropped out or something.'

'What do you mean, "dropped out"?'

'She's at university somewhere. She came home here for the weekend, went out on Saturday night and hasn't been seen since.'

'Time was,' said Wexford, 'when universities used to stop undergraduates leaving the place to go home or anywhere else at weekends. Pity the custom's changed. I suppose the mother knows she hasn't just gone back to her college – had they had a family row, for instance?'

'She says not. And the girl hasn't gone back. Barry's checked with her hall of residence and her supervisor.'

'What's she called and where's her home?'

'She's called Rachel Holmes, Oval Road, Stowerton. The mother's Mrs Rosemary Holmes, divorced, lives alone when the girl's not there. She's a medical secretary in Dr Akande's practice.'

Turning away from his reflection, a ghostly face dimly mirrored behind Chagall's flying lovers, Burden began to explain. Rachel had gone out at eight or thereabouts on Saturday night with the intention of meeting a group of friends in a pub. Her mother didn't know which pub nor yet where Rachel was going afterwards, but it would have been some club or a friend's house. It was unlikely that she would be home before two or three next morning.

'When she was younger,' Mrs Holmes had said to Detective Sergeant Barry Vine, 'I made her carry a mobile with her and she'd ring me to tell me where she was. But you can't do that when they're over eighteen, can you? She's at university, after all. I don't know what she's doing when she's there, do I? I don't know what time she comes in at night when she's there. So what's the point of worrying if she's late when she's at home. I do worry, though, of course I do. I didn't sleep a wink on Saturday night.'

'So she phoned us today, did she?' Wexford asked.

'Phoned and came in to report a missing person.'

'Why did she wait so long?'

'Don't know. Vine got the impression the girl's one of these bolshie teenagers, the kind who might give her mother a hard time if she reported her missing when she's just off somewhere up to her own devices.'

Wexford sat silent for a moment. He was anxious not to become obsessive, not to let a single not very important case take over and dominate his mind. But he was also aware that it is very hard to alter one's nature, especially at his age. This was the way he was and to attempt a change would be a violation of his character and not necessarily otherwise advantageous.

'You surely aren't thinking of going to see Mrs Holmes?' said Burden almost derisively. 'Barry's got it in hand.'

'I'm thinking of going back to see the Crownes and Lizzie Cromwell.' Wexford got up. 'If they know the Holmeses or the two girls know each other it would be very interesting indeed.'

# Chapter 3

'No, we don't know her,' Debbie Crowne said, spitting out the words. 'She's not our class, is she? The likes of her wouldn't want to know the likes of us.'

Since Rachel Holmes and her mother lived in a back-street terrace, in a poor little house rather smaller than the one he was now in, Wexford wondered at the fine distinction Mrs Crowne made. But at the same time he knew he was being disingenuous. There *was* a difference. Rosemary Holmes owned her house, she had a white-collar job – if that description could be applied to a woman – and Rachel was at university. Somehow, if she had begun in the working class, Mrs Holmes had elevated herself a grade or two, while the Crownes had remained where they started. In some ways he didn't like these gradations but he knew they were a fact of life, not a culture specific or, as some said, confined to this country.

'Were she and Rachel at the same school?'

As soon as he said it he knew he had made things worse. Lizzie herself gave him one of her lowering looks, head drooping but nervous rabbit's eyes peering upwards. It was an expression more usually seen in children half her age.

Her mother said, 'There's two years between them, you said. That's like centuries when you're her age.'

'But Lizzie does go to Kingsmarkham Comprehensive,' he persisted, 'where Rachel went?'

'Along with a couple of thousand others. Anyway, she's in the Learning Difficulties stream.' Debbie Crowne eyed him with the same expression as her daughter's. 'That's like the bottom of the pile.'

Nevertheless, they must have been at the same school at the same time over a period of years, perhaps as many as four. Was that the link? Was there a link? Colin Crowne came into the room before any more was said. Wexford studied him while Mrs Crowne talked about Lizzie, repeating her fears as to what might have happened to her during her absence from home and averting in querulous tones to the possibility of her being pregnant. She kept glancing at her husband while she talked.

Most people would have called Colin Crowne handsome. He was tall and slim, dark-haired and dark-eyed with firm, clear-cut features. But the length of his hair and the beard that might have been just a week-long failure to shave, as well as the triple earring arrangement, gave him a sinister look. His wife's faded appearance, her pinched face and dry, shaggy hair, contrasted almost ludicrously with the impression he gave of youth and sensuality. Wexford remembered them on television when Crowne had made an eloquent appeal for Lizzie's return, staring into the camera and enunciating his words clearly and with what seemed like real emotion, while his wife had sat by, biting her lip and only just restraining her tears. If it wasn't true, what that caller had said, that those who appeared on television to appeal for the return of a missing child were often themselves responsible for that child's death, there was a grain of truth in it.

There had been cases of a parent, later found guilty of child murder, whose outpourings of grief over that child's disappearance moved viewers to tears. And such behaviour wasn't necessarily hypo-critical; these people felt genuine grief, real emotion and sometimes bitter regret. What, after all, is likely to pain you more and stimulate more remorse than committing murder? But Lizzie wasn't dead, Lizzie had come back. He had no reason at all to suppose Crowne responsible for her three-day absence or guilty of anything in connection with her.

After a moment's soul-searching, he decided to mention the derelict house in Myringham to Lizzie. Even supposing she had spoken to Lynn Fancourt in confidence, no discretion had been asked for. Besides, the truth must be that she had never been in the place. Perhaps a girl such as she couldn't be blamed for lying, but she had lied.

He spoke to her gently. 'Lizzie, you were never in that house by the bus-stop, were you? You told' – he sought for words she would understand – 'the woman police officer, you told her you had been three days in that house and wrapped yourself in blankets? You told her you took water from a tap, but that wasn't really true, was it?'

He saw at once from their reaction, or because there was no reaction, that Colin and Debbie Crowne had been told the same story. The likelihood was that Lizzie, rather than being afraid to tell this fantasy to her mother and stepfather, had only thought it up in the moments before she revealed it to Lynn. Prob-ably she had gone through the whole tale again to Debbie Crowne once he and Lynn had left.

Now she said, with the liar's too vehement indig-nation, 'Yes, it was! I did go there!'

'There was no water in the taps, Lizzie. It was very cold. There was a blanket but it was damp.'

'I did go there!'

Crowne said roughly, 'There you are, you've got your answer. What more d'you want?'

A great deal. But it would be useless, and perhaps pointless, to persist. And yet Wexford was suddenly sure that she *had* been in that house, not for three days and nights certainly, but she had been inside it, she knew it. She had seen that blanket and had at least attempted to get water from the taps. Had Rachel been there too?

Burden had implied that it would be quite unnecessary for Wexford to go to Oval Road, Stowerton; that this was an altogether different missing person case from that of Lizzie Cromwell, for Rachel was older, for the most part living away from home and an intelligent young woman very much in charge of her own life. But since then all inquiries had had negative results. None of her relatives had heard from her and it seemed that none of her friends was harbouring her.

A second call to the University of Essex revealed only that she had not turned up to the lecture she was due to attend at ten that morning. But a different picture was emerging. Rachel, apparently, had never intended to go straight to the pub but first to her friend's home in Framhurst. Because the Framhurst-to-Stowerton bus route had been discontinued when work on the bypass began, an arrangement had been made for Caroline Strang's mother, who would be passing that way on her way home from work, to pick her up at eight on the Kingsmarkham Road, five minutes from Oval Road, take her to Framhurst to pick up Caroline, then drive the two girls to the Rat and Carrot. Vine had talked to Mrs Strang and been told that she had reached the pick-up point some minutes after eight owing to a traffic hold-up, and had parked and waited.

'They're always late for everything, these girls. I know, I've got two and I thought I'd got there long before Rachel even though I was late.' She had waited for ten minutes, then driven off. 'I'd have gone to her house only I don't know where she lives. I'd got the phone number but not the address.'

Caroline Strang thought Rachel must have been confused about the arrangement and gone straight to the Rat and Carrot. Nevertheless, she had phoned her home before she herself left but got no reply. She naturally supposed no one had answered the phone because Rachel was on her way to the pub and her mother was out.

Vine talked to the remaining three young people Caroline and Rachel were to meet that night. All said she hadn't come. None was worried. They supposed she had changed her mind. Vine concluded they were very casual indeed about such matters as forgetfulness, indecisiveness, phoning to explain or apologising when a better prospect for the evening turned up.

There was a chance Rachel had gone to Kingsmarkham by bus and Vine had talked to bus drivers. The buses on the Stowerton–Kingsmarkham––Pomfret run had no conductors and it was the driver who took the money and issued tickets. Vine showed Rachel's photograph to the drivers of the eight-ten bus and the eight-thirty-two bus. Neither remembered her but one said he was sure he wouldn't remember her and the other said that he had no memory for faces.

That convinced Wexford Rachel hadn't been on the bus, for to any man she would be unforgettable, an exceptionally good-looking girl with luxuriant dark hair, large dark eyes and voluptuous features: full mouth, rounded chin and high, smooth forehead. These seemed an inheritance from her handsome mother. If Rosemary Holmes was forty, she was not much more. Wexford could imagine her being frequently flattered by people taking her and her daughter for sisters. Her own dark hair was plaited and coiled at the nape of her neck, an old-fashioned style that suited her oval face. She was very slim, with long, shapely legs. Dr Akande must keep his medical secretary well hidden, Wexford thought, for he would have remembered this woman if he had ever seen her in the medical centre.

In his own mind he had compared the Crownes' home with this one, but theirs, though clean enough, betrayed the fact that none of them took much interest in their surroundings, while Rosemary Holmes's house was furnished with taste if not much expense. Well-tended houseplants grew green and lush in troughs on both window-sills in the living-room, a big bowl of orange tulips was on the table and one wall was fitted from floor to ceiling with bookshelves. British country people might be class-conscious still, but there was a warped reasoning behind their élitism and their sense of inferiority.

Though he knew he was wrong to do it, Wexford couldn't help linking the two cases in his mind, and now he had somehow convinced himself that because Lizzie had come back after three days and three nights, Rachel would come back too and after the same period of time. That would be tomorrow afternoon, Tuesday afternoon. So he was unable entirely to share Mrs Holmes's fear. When she said, as she now did, 'I keep thinking I'll never see her again,' he felt strangely as if he were in possession of some superior knowledge, some secret information, that it would be cruel not to reveal to her. And yet, of course, he wasn't, he knew nothing; he had no reason to align one girl's disappearance with another's. To tell her that everything would be all right, that she

43

had no need to worry, would be the unkindest thing, for which of us can say that we guess right more often than we guess wrong?

'Are you', she asked him, 'going to – well, search for her? I mean, the way you see people on television searching – in a line – with sticks? Beating the – well, you know, the ground?' She began to wring her hands. Wexford understood very well what she meant: that they would only do that if they had good reason to believe her daughter was dead.

'It's early days for that, Mrs Holmes.' Karen Malahyde saved him the trouble of answering. 'Let's wait a while. Rachel has only been missing since Saturday evening, that's less than forty-eight hours.'

They had already inquired about boyfriends. Vine had asked her and now Karen did so again. 'You say there's no boyfriend now, but what about in the past, when she was living here with you and going to school?'

Rosemary Holmes gave two names. She had done so before, to other police officers, but if she felt impatient with these repetitions she gave no sign of it. She was anxious to help, she would have done anything to assist in finding her daughter and done it without complaint.

'And yourself, Mrs Holmes?' Karen asked it delicately. 'Are you perhaps in a relationship?'

'I've got someone, yes. But you're not thinking –?'

'We're really not thinking anything at the moment,' Wexford said, reflecting that nothing could have been further from the truth. 'We're asking questions and sizing up the information we get, that's all. It's useful for us at this stage to have the names and addresses of all your friends and your daughter's, Mrs Holmes.'

She named a doctor with a practice in Flagford.

They had been going out for about a year and sometimes they spent weekends together. Rachel, she said in a burst of frankness, didn't like him but she hadn't liked any friend of her mother's. So high is the profile of a doctor of medicine in society that Wexford immediately placed Dr Michael Devonshire beyond suspicion, then, with quick self-admonition, put him back inside it again. A medical man was also a man and you never could tell.

'You went out yourself on Saturday evening, Mrs Holmes?'

She flushed faintly. 'Well, yes. May I ask how you know that?'

'Caroline Strang phoned here at about twenty-five past eight. You weren't here.'

'Michael took me out to dinner. It's ridiculous, I know, but I feel guilty about being out when – when whatever was happening to Rachel was happening.'

'Did you know about this arrangement with Mrs Strang?'

Rosemary Holmes said uneasily, 'I knew someone was picking her up on the Kingsmarkham Road. She said. I thought it was a – well, one of the boys she was meeting.' Suddenly she burst out, 'You can't stop them doing things, you know. You can't keep tabs on them all the time.' Again she dropped her guard. 'I don't suppose it's important, I just want to say that we have our problems, Rachel and I. I mean, she's a lovely girl, a really marvellous person and I get on with her fine, but she doesn't exactly get on with me. I expect that's quite usual with people her age, isn't it?'

'Quite usual, Mrs Holmes,' said Karen.

Back in the car Wexford suggested she speak to Michael Devonshire, perhaps catch him before his evening surgery. 'Though he obviously has an alibi with Rachel's mother. Do you think it worth taking a second look at that house in Myringham?'

'But Rachel never went near Myringham, sir.' Karen sounded surprised.

'So far as we know.'

'Surely it's just coincidence that Lizzie Cromwell went missing the Saturday before last and Rachel Holmes disappeared last Saturday.'

'But we don't like coincidence, do we? We know that when events happen in sequence or according to a pattern those events are most likely linked.'

Karen looked dubious. As well she might, Wexford thought, as well she might. He must rid his mind of tying in one girl's disappearance with the other's. There was no point in returning to the derelict house just as there was no real link between the girls – except for their having attended the same school. Except for their both being young and pretty and unattached and female. Except for their disappearing on successive Saturday nights . . . Stop it, he said to himself, but when he encountered Burden at the end of the day's work, it was to the Rat and Carrot instead of the Olive and Dove that he suggested they go for their evening drink, a twice-weekly event when they could make it.

Burden gave him a sidelong look. 'She never got there, you know. Rachel Holmes, I mean. Whatever happened to her happened in Stowerton. Waiting for a bus.'

'Like Lizzie Cromwell,' said Wexford.

'You've no reason to connect the two, none at all. Rachel shouldn't have been waiting for a bus, we know that, she should have been waiting for a lift. But they're so dozy, these young girls, they're as forgetful as old people. Now if Lizzie Cromwell had been found dead and *then* Rachel Holmes had disappeared, I'd have said, now you're talking. No,

46

it's just that you've got another one of your obsessions. I thought you'd given all that stuff up but you haven't, you're as bad as ever.'

'Can the leopard change his spots?' asked Wexford rhetorically, 'or the Ethiopian his skin?'

'If I'd said that you'd have called me a racist.'

The nearest bus-stop to Kingsbrook Valley Drive was at the eastern end of the High Street. From there it was ten minutes' walk to the Rat and Carrot, an ornate Victorian building on the corner of Kingsbrook Valley Drive and Savesbury Road. The area was mainly residential but there were two shops next to the pub, one of them a small supermarket and the other a jeweller, and opposite it a pharmacist. All were closed by now and the jeweller had taken the valuable stock out of his window and pulled down a metal grille to cover it.

It was a district of hotchpotch housing, thirties bungalows neighbouring on near-mansions and seventies blocks of flats alternating with gloomy houses dating from the late nineteenth century. The Rat and Carrot was the residents' local. Not long ago the pub had been called the Duke of Albany but that was considered by whoever rules in these matters to be outdated and meaningless to most people, so it had been given this new, and to those who rechristened it amusing, name. Unfortunately, within six months local people were dubbing it the Rotten Carrot and this sobriquet stuck.

It evidently put itself out to supply everything patrons could want from a pub, as well as a good many things that probably wouldn't have occurred to them. 'Good' meals were served in the restaurant as well as the bar; snacks and sandwiches were available all day long, the pub ran its own lottery and gave away scratch cards as prizes in contests to guess the number of pints consumed there each day or how much money had been raised in the bar for charity since Christmas, and the Rats' Hard Rock Club met every Tuesday and Thursday evening. Children were welcome in the King Rat Kids' Room where orange juice and Coke were on sale, or on fine days outside in the play area, furnished as it was by a large purple dinosaur, a giant Yogi Bear, two climbing frames and a huge Loony Tune character with a table and chairs in a cavity where its stomach should have been. As Wexford remarked, you could have been forgiven for entirely missing the point that the primary purpose of a public house was to sell alcoholic drinks to customers.

He and Burden went in through the main entrance, under a sign informing patrons that the licensee was one Andy Honeyman, edging their way between boards advertising bumper breakfasts, line dancing and a talent contest (Be The Next Posh Spice).

'I wouldn't much care to live down here,' said Burden gloomily. 'Summer evenings must be a nightmare.'

'Ah, well,' said Wexford, carrying their drinks to a table, 'in the midst of life we are in Karaoke. It could happen to you, you know. That pub down your road, it's a free house. Get a change of licensee and you too could have a view of cartoon characters from your living-room windows and aspiring Spice Girls warbling away half the night.'

Pretending not to hear, Burden surveyed the place, glass in hand. The bar was very brightly decorated. Red and gold flock wallpaper shared the walls with mock linenfold panelling, there were a number of pictures of doe-eyed girls, gambolling kittens, wistful dogs and mountainous panoramas, and all the chairs were black and gold with pale primrose upholstery. The girl who walked about wiping the already spotless tables wore skin-tight scarlet leggings and earrings that hung to her collar-bones.

Apart from her and them, the only other person in the bar was a bearded man of about forty, whom she addressed as Andy and who was sitting on a high stool behind the counter reading *Sporting Life*.

Burden shook his head ponderously in the manner of one asking what the world was coming to. 'Rachel Holmes,' he said, 'you can't understand what a girl like her would be doing in a place like this.'

'I dare say a good many men ask her that question,' said Wexford gravely.

'You what? Oh, yes, I see. Right. But seriously, a good-looking girl from a nice background who's got into a university – what would she find here?'

'Her friends, presumably. Anyway, she didn't find anything, she didn't come. Ah, more custom. I can't say I'm sorry. I don't much care for being the only people in a pub, do you?'

Two men had come in, closely followed by a man and a woman. 'As a matter of fact, I prefer it,' said Burden. 'I like a bit of hush.'

Wexford grinned because that was the response he had expected. 'I've just thought of something. Mrs Strang was late, she didn't get to the pick-up point – outside the Flag, was it? – until some minutes after eight, let's say at least five past eight. Just suppose, though, that Rachel *wasn't* late, that Rachel got there on the dot of eight or even a couple of minutes to. And someone else came along and offered her a lift and she took it.'

'Why would she? She was waiting for Mrs Strang.'

'True. But I've got an idea about that . . .'

He broke off and edged his chair back to allow for the passage of a group of women who had just come into the Rat and Carrot by the swing doors. There were four of them, two young and two in early middle age, and Wexford was immediately struck by the air of wariness and timidity most of them had. But the one who led the way up to the bar, a thin and rather beautiful young woman in jeans and shabby sweater whose long black hair was tied back with a chiffon scarf, had a resolute manner as if before coming in here she had gritted her teeth and sworn to stick to her purpose. Screwed her courage to the sticking place, he thought.

The others followed her and stood in a line along the counter. The black-haired woman cleared her throat but this had no effect on Honeyman who kept his eyes on his *Sporting Life*.

There was a brief silence, then – and Wexford heard her draw in her breath – she said in a voice probably higher pitched than her normal tone, 'We'd like a drink, please. Two glasses of white wine and two of lager and lime.'

The licensee slammed the paper shut and looked up. 'You come from that place up the road, don't you?'

She took a step nearer the bar. '*What*?'

'That house that's full of women who've walked out on their menfolk. You come from there.'

An older woman, taking courage, said, 'That's a funny way of putting it but what if we do?'

'I'll tell you what. I'm not serving you, that's what.'

The black-haired woman had gone very pale. Wexford thought he saw the hand that rested on the counter begin to tremble. 'You can't do that,' she said. 'What reason have you got for doing that?'

'Don't have to have a reason. You ask anyone if I'm not within my rights to refuse to serve anyone I don't want to serve.'

'He is, too,' Burden said softly.

Wexford nodded. He doubted if the women

50

would put up a fight and they didn't. They said no more but turned away and made for the door.

The licensee called after them, 'You'd best go down the High Street where they don't know where you're from. They'll serve you there till they find out who you are.'

The black-haired woman turned round and said in ringing tones, 'You bastard!'

'Charming,' said Honeyman when the door swung to behind them. 'I wonder if you gentlemen heard that? Ladylike, wouldn't you say?'

Wexford got up, went to the counter and, having ordered two more halves of Adnams, said that he was a police officer and showed his warrant card.

Honeyman said rather too hastily, 'I was right, wasn't I? I don't need a reason for not serving people.'

'You were within your rights but you must have had a reason and I've been wondering what it is.'

The licensee filled the two tankards. 'It's on the house.'

'No, it's not, thanks all the same.' Wexford produced a fiver and put it down with precision. 'We came in here to ask you about the missing girl, Rachel Holmes, but just tell me about those women first, will you?'

'They live in a house in Kingsbrook Valley Drive, up the road here, actually.' Honeyman's whole manner had changed, becoming obsequious and conciliatory. Even his voice was different, the South of England burr shed and replaced by a refined drawl. 'They're what they call battered women, if you know what I mean. Or they say they are. Husbands gave them a little tap when they cut up rough, if the truth were known.'

'All right, I get the picture. But what have they done to get up your nose?'

51

'Let me tell you. There was two of them in here a couple of weeks back and some poor devil comes in and gets hold of one of them, asks her to come home, she's left him with the kids, if you please. Well, of course, she's not going to do as he asks, is she? Don't suppose she ever has. So she struggles and gives him a push and he starts slapping her around, which he was driven to, and then the other one joins in, banging on his back with her fists, and then I had to intervene. Naturally, as I'm sure you'll agree, out you go, I said, the lot of you and don't come back. Actually, I regret having to put him out, he seemed a decent fellow. You know something? Well, of course you do. When folks got married in the old days the woman used to have to say she'd obey him. Pity that was ever changed, if you ask me.'

'I don't know that I do ask you, Mr Honeyman,' Wexford said blandly. 'I'm rather inclined to think I wouldn't want your advice on anything much.' He watched Honeyman blink his eyes and slightly recoil. 'But you could take some. You'd be well advised to call us next time a decent fellow slaps a woman around on your premises. And now perhaps you'd like to tell me if to your knowledge this girl has ever been in here.'

A deep red flush had suffused Honeyman's face. It was probably a relief to him to have something to look at and be distracted by. He stared at the photograph Wexford showed him, then muttered, 'I don't know, I don't recall.'

Burden, who had come up to the counter, said, 'Does that mean you never saw her meet her friends in here on a Saturday night? She's very good-looking, isn't she? Not the sort of face you'd forget.'

'I may have seen her.' The burr was back and the sulkiness. 'I reckon I did, maybe two or three months back. She was in here with some other kids – well, I don't mean kids,' he said quickly, remembering what the law said about selling alcohol to those under-age, 'they was all over eighteen – and they had a bar meal.'

'But you didn't see her on Saturday night?'

'Absolutely not,' said Honeyman, shaking his head to give a kind of earnest vehemence to his denial.

'Sylvia's working there,' Wexford said when he and Burden were outside and approaching The Hide. 'I can't remember if I told you. Answering calls on the helpline among other things. Have you ever hit a woman?'

'Of course I haven't,' Burden said, shocked. 'What a question.'

'Oh, I don't know. I haven't either. D'you know what Barry said to me the other day? "All men hit their wives some time or other", that's what he said. I was a bit taken aback.'

'My God.' Burden sounded horrified. 'I hope and trust we haven't got a wife-beater on the team. That would be a fine thing, just when Hurt-Watch has got going. And by the way, just how are we to go about distributing those pagers and mobiles? We may know that domestic violence is very prevalent in all societies but how many prosecutions for assaults on wives and girlfriends have there been in our area? Precious few. Presumably that doesn't mean male-female relationships are more idyllic here or men more easygoing. It's just because in the past women haven't called us and haven't wanted our intervention.'

'So how are we going to find the ones that are in danger? Is that what you mean? Maybe by consulting the people who run this place.'

Wexford stopped outside The Hide and looked up at the windows. Those on the ground floor were almost entirely hidden by the tall evergreens which

53

filled the front garden. From a top-floor window a white face framed in black hair looked back at him and he recognised its owner as the woman who had shouted at Andy Honeyman.

'There'll have to be some such method. We can't very well put an ad in the *Courier* offering free communication systems to anyone who applies. As Southby says, the entire female population would want one.'

Burden obviously wasn't much interested. 'Talking of the female population,' he said, 'what was this idea of yours?'

'Idea?'

'You said you'd an idea about Rachel waiting for Mrs Strang. Presumably you meant you'd found some sort of answer.'

'Oh, right. Yes. But I wouldn't go as far as that. I only wondered if Rachel and Mrs Strang had ever met. I mean, would they recognise each other?'

Burden seemed mystified. He gave Wexford a dark look and said he had better be getting home, his mother and father-in-law were visiting and he was inexcusably late already. And Wexford went home too, with Burden's remarks to nag at him while he ate his dinner and afterwards, when a television documentary on a European single currency failed to hold his attention. Operation Safeguard, and its subsidiary scheme Hurt-Watch, would only work if he and his team probed the whole domestic-violence situation.

A ludicrous picture presented itself to him of 500 mobile phones and pagers landing in his office, perhaps even on his desk, and he without a clue as to which women were eligible to receive them and which would be affronted to be offered what amounted to a defence against and protection from the men who shared their lives. Once that hurdle had been got over, how were they to react when a call on one of these mobiles was received? Go to the caller's home and arrest the perpetrator. Simple. Only most of the time it wouldn't be as clear-cut as that. She'd say she didn't want him charged, she didn't want him taken from the house, he was the bread-winner, he'd promised not to do it again, he was sorry, he was ashamed, she shouldn't have called the police, only she was frightened and hurt and at her wits' end, but she didn't want the family broken up . . . He must talk to Sylvia. Meanwhile, there was this missing girl, Rachel Holmes.

Dora seemed quite keen on the boring television programme, which meant he couldn't turn it off. The evening would stay light till past eight so he went out into the garden and walked about, finally sitting down in the little paved area, which was the centrepiece of Dora's rose garden. His seat was one of a pair of French café chairs which Sheila had given them for Christmas, a very elegant affair of pale-grey metal scrolls and twists and curlicues, but not the most comfortable to sit on. Above him the sky was a deepening blue and heading this way, probably by now passing over Pomfret, was a red and yellow balloon whose passengers he could see waving to him. Or waving to someone. Wexford waved back and in doing so nearly fell off his delicate and perilous seat.

Tomorrow would be Tuesday and in the afternoon Rachel Holmes would come back. Both girls had been to the same school, both were still in their teens, both were attractive, if in very different ways, each was the child of a divorced mother, both had been waiting for a bus, one returning from an evening out with friends, the other anticipating such an evening. Both had gone missing on a Saturday, and on successive Saturdays. In spite of all that, Burden would say it was a ridiculous assumption to make. He was making it every time the girl entered his thoughts. It kept him from worrying about Rachel as he should be worrying. Did it also prevent him taking all possible steps and measures to find her?

Should he, for instance, have put Rosemary Holmes on television? Should he have instituted a search of the countryside between Stowerton and Kingsmarkham? Perhaps the question he should be asking himself was, would he have done so if Lizzie Cromwell hadn't gone missing exactly a week before and come home three nights and three days later?

The balloon sailed overhead and a little breeze sprang up to ruffle the new leaves and send a shower of petals scattering off the pear tree. The pretty chair was so uncomfortable it might have been designed as an instrument of torture. Sit on it for twelve hours under bright lights and answer the interrogator's questions ... My God, he thought. He got up and went into the house, resolving to talk to Caroline Strang's mother first thing in the morning.

# Chapter 4

The search began at two on Tuesday afternoon.
There were ten uniformed officers, some of them
reinforcements from the Regional Crime Squad, and
sixteen members of the public, all volunteers from
among neighbours and friends of the Holmeses.
Rosemary Holmes wanted to join them but Wexford
advised against it. He still believed, against the odds,
that Rachel would turn up later in the afternoon and
what he had discovered in Framhurst that morning
only reinforced his belief. Olga Strang had never met
Rachel, had never even seen a photograph of her.
The two girls had met at university, not through
living only five miles apart or having been to the
same school. Rachel was a stranger to her and she to
Rachel.

'How were you to know her?' Wexford had asked.
'You were to give her a lift but how were you to
recognise her?'

'You mean, she wore a yellow ribbon and I wore a
big red rose? There was nothing like that. I never
thought about it, I was just *there* and she was
supposed to be *there* but she wasn't.'

A scatty woman who seemed unable to collect her
thoughts for two minutes at a time, Mrs Strang gave
the impression of being harassed by everything in
her surroundings and perhaps by life itself. The
cottage she lived in with her husband and three
children was in a state of frightening disorder,

papers mixed with clothes, chairs laden with newspapers and magazines, used cups and glasses set or left beside vases of dead flowers, an iron switched on, its red light glistening, standing up-ended between a naked loaf of bread and an open packet of kettle descaler.

She herself, perhaps about to use the iron, wore a diaphanous dressing-gown over blouse and slip, and clutched in her left hand something made of crumpled red material that might have been a skirt or a pair of trousers. Without relinquishing her hold on it, she sat on the edge of the table, crumpling the red stuff to a worse state of creasedness while running her right hand through her wispy reddish-gold hair.

'I won't keep you long,' Wexford said. 'I can see you're getting ready to go to work.' He couldn't keep his eyes off that iron that seemed to come closer and closer to her muslin frills as she swayed nervously back and forth. 'But did Rachel know the make of your car, for instance? Its colour?'

'Oh, I don't know, I can't answer.'

'Had Caroline described you to her?'

'You'll have to ask her. I can't remember.' She brightened and suddenly smiled. 'I knew she had dark hair. I was looking for a dark-haired girl. And Caroline said she was very good-looking.'

'Mrs Strang, you're about to singe your – er, dressing-gown on that iron.'

'Am I? Oh God. Thank you. Caroline's not here, she's back at college, you could phone her and ask her. Or I could. I must get this skirt ironed, you must excuse me, I'm late . . .'

He knew enough. Rachel had no more idea as to the woman due to give her a lift than that she was middle-aged and driving a car. Someone else had come along at eight and picked her up, and when

Rachel said, 'Mrs Strang?' or some such thing, this woman had agreed, had fallen in with the misapprehension and used it to her advantage.

Was she the same woman who had offered a lift to Lizzie Cromwell? And had Lizzie, in spite of what she said, accepted it? To risk acting on this wild intuition would be criminal. There must be a search and next day, if she hadn't come home, he would have Rosemary Holmes up before the television cameras. But she'd come home. She'd walk into the house in Oval Road. She wouldn't be distraught or soaked to the skin, she would simply stroll in and after her mother had had hysterics, ask what all the fuss was about. Or else, instead, she'd turn up at her university, with a considerable amount of explaining to do. He turned his attention to his post, first to the document which lay uppermost on his desk.

If someone addresses you, in a letter, by your given name and signs himself 'yours always', you may confidently expect your correspondent to be a close friend. This printout of an e-mail began 'Dear Reg' and ended 'Yours always, Brian', but Wexford would not have placed Brian St George, editor of the *Kingsmarkham Courier*, in that intimate category. The very sight of it filled him with apprehension. No communication he had ever received from St George had been supportive or even co-operative with police strategy. He had looked at this one without putting on his reading glasses and it was a glazed muzziness of dancing print that he stared at for a moment. But he knew that was no good and, after what was only a brief hesitation, he put on his glasses and read St George's letter.

Dear Reg,
    It has come to my attention that the infamous paedophile, Henry Thomas Smith, is due to be

released from detention at the end of this week. His home was and still is on the Muriel Campden Estate in Kingsmarkham and I have been reliably informed that he intends to return to the house, currently occupied by his daughter and her partner, when he leaves prison, where he has been for the past nine years, on 17 April.

Now, a large number of parents with young children, to whom Smith must pose a threat, live on the Muriel Campden Estate and my intention is to run a lead story in this week's edition of the *Courier*, informing interested parties of Smith's return. I am sure you will agree that Smith is a dangerous man and that no child can be safe while he remains at large.

I will be interested to receive your comments. If the Mid-Sussex Constabulary would care to supply me with a statement of Smith's current situation and perhaps their general opinion on the arrangements made for released paedophiles, I will be delighted to print it.

With my very good wishes,

Yours always,

Brian.

Wexford sighed. It wasn't only a wonder what induced St George to call him by his first name and end in that affectionate way, but a mystery why the man should want to. At their last meeting, which had been in connection with the hostage-taking over the proposed Kingsmarkham bypass he, Wexford, had been atrociously (but justifiably) rude to the editor of the *Courier* and had received a good deal of abuse in return. The answer, no doubt, was that St George wanted something. Wexford's approval?

He decided – quite quickly – not to reply. After all, much as he would have liked to, he couldn't stop St

George and the *Courier* in their mission. Barring an injunction to restrain them, they would go ahead whatever happened. He tried to remember Smith but could recall only a newspaper photograph from long ago of a fat-faced man with bloated chin and forehead. That didn't mean much. Anyone would look dreadful in one of those blown-up snaps. Smith, the man, had entirely faded from his memory. Of course the crime, whatever it was, hadn't happened in the Kingsmarkham area and it wasn't he who had arrested him.

He was wondering whether he was capable of summoning up Smith's CV or dossier on his computer, of filling with useful information the pretty blue screen over which clouds swam and birds flew, when Barry Vine came in.

'How's the Rachel Holmes search going?' Wexford asked.

'Nothing new, sir. But I came to tell you something else. You know we had a second clothes robbery?'

'Oh, yes. The First Gear boutique.'

'Well, we've got someone for both, the First Gear and the craftswoman, the designer. You were right when you said they used a child to get in. A sort of Oliver Twist, were your words if I remember rightly. I don't know how old Oliver Twist was – I can't say I've ever read the book or seen the film – but this kid's four.'

For a moment Wexford said nothing. Smith's face, the remembered face, reappeared in some picture frame of his mind and he asked himself which was worse, to use a small child sexually or to teach that child to break and enter and steal. The former, of course, no question about it, but still . . .

'You mean this villain – what's his name, by the way?'

'Flay. Patrick Flay. He lives in Glebe Road.'

'This Patrick Flay put a child of four through that fanlight and instructed him how to open the door?'

'Not quite, sir,' said Vine. 'It was a girl, his own daughter, and while it was a fanlight the first time, my belief is that this second time she went in through the cat flap.'

'The *cat flap*?'

'Yes, sir. It's a sort of trapdoor that hangs on hinges that the cat pushes open with its head and . . .'

'I know what it *is*.' Wexford shook his head, more in sorrow than in anger. 'Before the things were invented they used to cut a hole in the door and the story is that Isaac Newton cut a hole for his cat and when she had kittens he cut six more holes.'

Vine stared at him. 'He must have been bonkers.'

'Well, no. They didn't have Mensa in those days but he was just as bright as Mr Burden. He was a great physicist, he discovered gravity, among other things. But that's the point, that very clever people can be daft in some ways. Anyway, I don't believe it. I told you just to make it plain that I know what a cat flap is. Where's this Flay? Downstairs?'

'He's called his solicitor and the guy's on his way.'

'I hope and trust you haven't brought the little girl along as well?'

Vine looked a little affronted. 'I left her with her mum, sir. I've talked to her . . .'

'In the presence of her mother, I hope?'

'Of course. Mother claims to know nothing about it, but the child – she's called Kaylee, K-A-Y-L-double-E – told me her dad got her to wear gloves. He said it was cold and she must keep them on, and they went out together and round the back of this house where her dad showed her the little door that belonged to "the pussy cat", I quote, and he said never to tell what she did, so she wasn't going to tell me. But afterwards her dad gave her a Dracula.'

'Gave her a *what*?'

'It's a kind of ice-cream,' said Vine.

They went downstairs together. On the way Wexford asked if the missing textiles had been discovered and Vine had to admit that they had not. Flay, a man of twenty-five who wore his reddish hair in dreadlocks, though he was white and that hair was sparse, sat at the table in the interview room, smoking while he awaited his solicitor. PC Martin Dempsey sat on a chair inside the door, his back to the wall, his eyes fixed impassively on the table legs.

Vine switched on the recorder and said, 'Detective Chief Inspector Wexford and Detective Sergeant Vine have entered the room at four fifty-two. Present also are Police Constable Dempsey and Patrick John Flay.'

'I'm not saying a word till my lawyer gets here,' said Flay.

Wexford didn't answer. He had been sitting down for no more than a minute when Lynn Fancourt brought the solicitor in. This was a young man Wexford had never seen before but whom he knew to be James Beamish of Proctor, Beamish, Green in Kingsmarkham High Street. Vine noted his arrival and began questioning Flay, whose sullen expression had changed to one of pleasurable anticipation once his solicitor was beside him. His smiles turned to laughter when Vine asked him about his daughter. 'You've got that wrong for a start. She's not my kid, she's the wife's. I'm like her stepdad. The wife had her before we like moved in together.'

'You seem to have a good relationship with her,' said Wexford.

'What with Kaylee? Of course I do. I love kids.'

'You love her so much that you teach her to go into someone else's house and steal someone else's property.'

'I don't know what you're talking about,' said Flay, grinning widely. 'If you believe what a four-year-old kid, practically a toddler, tells you you're barking. She's got an imagination, has Kaylee. She tells stories, right? Well, some would call them lies. I mean, I wouldn't, not me, I'm a tolerant sort of guy, but there's some as'd give a kid a clip round the ear for telling the sort of porkies Kaylee tells.'

'So you didn't make her wear gloves and put her through a fanlight into the householder's cloakroom and then through a cat flap into the householder's basement?'

Wexford was aware of how ridiculous it all sounded. Any outsider would almost have thought Flay's mirth justified. He was looking at Beamish now, grinning and shaking his head.

'You didn't teach her how to open the window and put the property out from the inside.'

'Zilch. Are you kidding?'

'Kaylee wasn't taught to enter that house and steal the owner's property?'

Beamish raised his eyes languidly. 'My client has already told you no, Mr Wexford.'

Wexford was thinking how to rephrase his questions when a note was brought to him by Lynn Fancourt. He didn't even glance at it he was so sure it was to tell him Rachel Holmes had come back, but he spoke into the recorder to announce he was leaving the room and that Lynn had taken his place. Outside, he unfolded the paper. Not a word about Rachel but a message from the Assistant Chief Constable Designate asking him to call him as a matter of urgency. Of course, it was a bit early for Rachel's return. If she came back at the same time as Lizzie Cromwell had returned, she wouldn't be in Stowerton before six. The moment he was back in his office he phoned Southby.

'Smith,' said the voice that always barked out its clipped sentences. 'Henry Thomas Smith. Mean anything to you?'

Would he have known if he hadn't had St George's letter? Wexford would never have thought he had reason to be grateful to the editor of the *Kingsmarkham Courier*. 'Paedophile, sir,' he said promptly. 'He's been inside for nine years, coming out and home here next Friday.'

'Right.' Southby sounded faintly disappointed. 'I just thought you should know that the local rag's going to run one of their in-the-public-interest stories about it. On Friday. I dare say it will pass off without incident.'

So Southby too had had a letter from St George. I wonder if that one began *Dear Malcolm*, thought Wexford. He started up the computer and after several false moves resulting in rather frightening admonitions on the screen, managed to access – hateful computer language but nevertheless a source of pride when you got it right – Henry Thomas Smith.

'Born South Woodford, London E18,' he read, '20 February 1928, the third son of George and Annie Smith, of Churchfields, South Woodford. Educated Buckhurst Hill County High School until age sixteen. Convicted of gross indecency 1949 and again in 1952, sent to prison on the first offence for two months and on the second for eighteen months. Convicted of gross indecency with a minor in 1958 and sent to prison for eight years.'

Sickened by the dreary repetition almost as much as by the squalid nature of the offences, Wexford pressed the page-down key and was gratified to find that it worked. It actually did the job it claimed to do, which was far from being the case, in his opinion, with most computer moves. But this time it did what he wanted and up on to the screen came the last page of Smith's sorry catalogue. Wexford drew in his breath. It was for manslaughter that the man had gone to prison nine years before, having been sentenced originally to fifteen years for his part in the rape and subsequent death of a twelve-year-old boy.

Two other men had been involved, of whom one had received the same sentence as Smith and the other eight years. There was no mention in the dossier of Smith's marriage or marriages and nothing about a daughter. Wexford noted that he must be an old man now, more than seventy. Would he still be a danger to children? You would have to know the man and know a lot more about paedophilia than he did to answer that. But of one thing he was sure: that there was something wrong with a society that set free such a monster, even a worn-out, aged, broken monster, into a community with a bigger population of small children than anywhere else in the neighbourhood.

By nine he knew he had been wrong and the Rachel Holmes disappearance wasn't going to follow Lizzie Cromwell's pattern. A kind of guilt overwhelmed him, as if it was his fault she hadn't come back. He was thankful he had said nothing of that hope and certainty of his except to Burden. What he said to Burden would remain between them. He tried to compensate by suggesting that the search went on after dark but even he had to admit this was impossible, for it was a black, moonless night of heavy rain.

Vine, whom he phoned before he went to bed, told him he had had to let Patrick Flay go. Without enough evidence to charge him he was obliged to release the man, still laughing, in the company of his solicitor. For a while Wexford stood at the landing window, looking out at the night. It was a habit of his, to stare out, when all was still and silent, and it amused him to see that Sylvia did it too. Maybe you could inherit a gene of meditative sky-watching. Rain fell steadily, insistently, long silver needles of it puncturing the dark. He thought then of Lear's words when he reproaches himself for having paid too little attention to the plight of the homeless and dispossessed – *poor, houseless wretches, who bide the beating of this pitiless storm*, the women who cried to Sylvia for help, such victimised children as Kaylee Flay and the missing girl. But she, probably, was dead by now, lying in a waterlogged ditch.

In Detective Sergeant Vine's opinion people like the Flays – and he made no such reservations as Sylvia Fairfax did – shouldn't be allowed to have children and if by some contravention of the law they did have them, should not be allowed to bring them up. What was the care system for if not to protect children against the likes of Patrick Flay? Why was there fostering and adoption if these processes weren't put to better use?

He arrived at the ground-floor flat in Glebe Road, the half of a shabby, run-down house, to find both Patrick Flay and Kaylee's mother at home, and the little girl, when he began to talk to her, firmly set on the stained and battered sofa between them, squeezed between them, with no possibility of escape. She was a child of mixed race, born of a white mother, a woman as fair, freckled and ginger-haired as Patrick. But Kaylee had dark-brown hair in tight ringlets all over her head, dark-brown eyes and a light-olive skin. Under the left one of those eyes was a darker mark, a bruise which hadn't been there before, and Vine knew, as surely as if he had seen the blow struck, that one of those two had hit her in the face. Jackie Flay, perhaps, but more probably Patrick, and Vine also knew why that blow had been inflicted.

A choking feeling of impotence and frustration almost inhibited him from speaking and, as he afterwards told Wexford, the worst part was knowing there was little he could do about it.

'You can notify the Social Services,' said Wexford. 'There's a good case here for threatening the Flays with putting the child into care. So what happened?'

'Kaylee told me it *hadn't* happened. She's an intelligent kid, you know. I mean, she's really very bright. She just said none of it was true, she had made it up. In other words, just what Flay said. And he had the nerve to say to her, "You know what happens to you when you tell lies, don't you, Kaylee?" And he was grinning in that revolting way of his.'

'And the mother?'

'She just sat there, silly-scared, if you know what I mean, looking as if she'd say anything and do anything to stay on the right side of Flay. She probably held the kid while Flay hit her. I can just hear him saying it, "You say you never did it, you never went there – right? You want my fist in your face again?"'

Wexford shook his head. 'Jackie Flay may be just as much a victim. And the worst thing is that Flay'll get the child to do it again, he'll get her into the habit of it and soon she won't even consider telling the truth – poor little Olivia Twist.'

Vine, who had been frowning gloomily, brightened a little and said, 'What happened to him, sir? This Oliver Twist?'

'He got saved by an old gentleman who turned out, by an amazing coincidence, to be his own grandfather.'

'That won't happen to Kaylee.'

'Probably not, though I dare say she has no more idea who her grandfathers are than Oliver had.'

Vine considered this, pursing his lips and nodding. 'Why would a woman want to marry Flay? If they're married. Why would any woman shack up with him? Does she want to be a victim and make her kid a victim?'

'You're getting into deep waters, Barry, when you start asking why anyone would marry anyone else. It's a mystery. But I doubt if many people choose to be victims unless they're masochists and masochists are few. The thing is people want to be part of a couple, what they call these days "being in a relationship". And most of them would rather have a bad one than none at all. It's nature. By the way, you didn't really mean you hit your wife, did you?'

'Me? Oh, right. It was just the once. She hit me and I hit her back. That's all I mean.'

Wexford had spent the best part of the morning in Oval Road, where Rosemary Holmes, who knew Lizzie Cromwell's story, had perhaps also believed her daughter would return on the previous evening. But Rachel hadn't come home and Rosemary was distraught, pacing the room and at one point throwing herself into an armchair where she collapsed in a storm of tears. Wexford asked himself why on earth he had thought this disappearance would have a happy outcome just because Lizzie's had. Thank God he hadn't let his ridiculous hunch impede the search or prevent any serious investigation.

The searchers had begun again soon after first light, combing the rain-drenched fields, glad of shelter inside the quiet dimness of woodlands, but while the rain remained no more than a drizzle, pressing on. Karen Malahyde and Lynn Fancourt had widened the inquiry beyond Rachel's immediate circle of friends, had talked to people she had been at school with. They were now in Brighton with the girl's father, Rosemary's divorced husband, hearing how he hadn't seen his daughter for the past seven years. Michael Devonshire, the Flagford GP, had not only taken Rosemary out to dinner but admitted frankly that he had spent most of the night with her, leaving the house in Oval Road at five the next morning.

Rachel had now been missing for four nights and almost four days. Uneasily, Wexford set up a press conference for five that afternoon – his reluctance stemming from the certainty that Brian St George would be there – and at that conference, as part of it, Rosemary Holmes would make her appeal for Rachel's return. She shrank from it, at first flatly refusing. She was too little in command of herself, she told Wexford, she would make a mess of it.

'That doesn't much matter,' he said to her gently. 'I don't want to sound cynical but the more emotion you show and the more . . . well, frankly, upset, you appear to be, the more likely the appeal is to succeed.'

'But they don't care, those viewers. They're just going to gloat.'

'I wouldn't be so sure of that, Mrs Holmes. There are a lot of people out there who have real sympathy for you.'

And your attractions may have some effect, he thought, not saying it aloud, your pretty, youthful face and nice voice, not to mention that figure and those legs. We live in a world where good looks get you everything, where the preservation of youth is at a premium. Those journalists would write better stories and longer ones because this woman was beautiful and had a voice like a Shakespearean actress. The photographers would take more trouble and the television cameramen be more enthusiastic.

And would all that bring Rachel back? No one could tell him.

A car was sent for Rosemary Holmes at four thirty. Wexford saw with approval that in spite of her terrible anxiety, she had dressed herself with care for this confrontation in a black suit and pink-and-white blouse. She had made up her face for the cameras. Her hair was newly washed and her nails painted pink pearl. St George's reporter stared as if he had never seen a presentable woman before. The cameras closed in before she had taken her seat at the table between Wexford and Burden.

'Look this way, Rosemary!'

'Just turn your head a fraction, Rosemary!'

'Thank you, that's great. Just one more, Rosemary, and I'm done.'

Wexford clenched his teeth. Why couldn't they call her Mrs Holmes? Did they think that using her first name would allay her anxiety, put her at her ease, make her *happier*? It was such crass impertinence.

He listened while she made her appeal in that rich, modulated voice, her eyes downcast. 'If you are holding my – my beloved daughter, please let her go, let her come back to me. Please have mercy on us, she's all I've got and I – I'm all she's got. *Please*. She's a lovely, good, clever girl, she's never done harm to anyone in the whole of her short life. Please send her back to me . . .'

And here Rosemary Holmes could sustain the steadiness of her voice no longer. She broke into sobs, her throat heaving, her pretty hands flying to her face, her weeping eyes. Wexford helped her to her feet and took her out. He sent for tea and left her in his office with Lynn Fancourt. Burden would conduct the rest of the press conference, they didn't really need him, but he made his way back downstairs all the same and was just in time to hear someone, not the *Courier* reporter, ask in strident tones if it was true that Thomas Smith would be coming out next day and returning to his home in Oberon Road.

'No questions will be answered not relevant to the Rachel Holmes disappearance,' Burden snapped.

The reporter took no notice. 'Will he be coming out tomorrow?'

'No,' said Burden with perfect truth. Smith's release date was not Thursday but Friday. 'That ends the conference. Thank you very much, ladies and gentlemen.'

Wexford went back upstairs. What must it be like to be a paedophile? To want to have sex with small children? Something told him that if you could imagine it, just as if you could imagine being a sadist or a necrophile, really live it yourself in imagination, then you would understand. *To understand all is to forgive all* ought to be changed to, *to imagine is to understand* and leave off the forgiving bit. In the Lord's Prayer, which he hadn't said in church or anywhere else for forty years, there was a bit about forgiving us our trespasses as we forgive those that trespass against us.

Against *us*, not against other people. He couldn't forgive those offences against others, and God, if there was a God, ought not to either. Maybe religious people would call that blasphemy.

In his office he thought about going home, put some of these papers in his expensive hide briefcase – another gift from Sheila. Did she ever let him and Dora buy things like that? – paperwork to do at home, worse luck. The phone rang but he didn't dare think of not answering it.

A voice he didn't recognise, they were always

changing, said, 'I have a Mrs Holmes on the line for you, sir.'

And then the beautiful tones he had heard no more than half an hour ago, appealing for her daughter's return: 'Rachel's home. She was here at home when I got back. I'm so happy, I still can't believe it, but it's true, she's home.'

# Chapter 5

She was twenty-four hours late but she had come back. He felt curiously gratified because he had been right, especially as she was so obviously unharmed, a beautiful girl, tall and slim, with a flawless skin and dark, shining hair. It was plain, though, that she was far from pleased to see him and Karen Malahyde. She didn't want them there. If it had been left to her, Wexford thought, the police would never have been notified of her return.

He could almost see inside her head, imagine her thinking, I'll just quietly go back to Essex and then Mum can tell them after I've gone. It's nothing to do with them, it's my business. She had greeted them by saying in a loud and surly tone that she had a bad headache.

'You should see a doctor,' Wexford said. 'You must do that anyway.'

Rachel had flushed brilliantly. 'I don't need a doctor. I've just got a headache. No one's done anything to me.'

What she meant was clear. But she explained, her eyes on Karen Malahyde. 'It's because I'm a woman. People just assume a woman must have been raped. Well, I haven't been. I'd know.'

A very strange remark, Wexford thought it. How could she not know? How could anyone not know? 'Have you been assaulted in any way?'

'No. Not in *any* way.'

He wasn't imagining the scorn in her voice. She was one of those clever girls, brought up to have a high opinion of themselves, who when as young as this show their self-confidence in contempt for others they estimate as lower down the intelligence scale. Police officers would come into that category, he thought with concealed amusement.

'Have you been given any substances? I was thinking of a blood test.'

'I don't know,' she said sharply. 'I don't know what I've been given, I can't remember. But I'm not having any blood test. If you've got AIDS in mind I've told you I've not been raped.'

He hadn't had it in mind. 'I would like a doctor to see you.'

'I wouldn't and I won't.' She said savagely, 'I won't see a doctor and I won't have a doctor see me. I hate doctors. I never go near them. If I need anything like that I go to an alternative practitioner. Chinese medicine or a herbalist.'

'I hardly think a herbalist would be much use in the present situation,' Wexford said drily. He thought of Rosemary Holmes's friendship with her doctor. Was that the cause of Rachel's dislike of orthodox medicine? Perhaps. 'If you're so set against a doctor I can't compel you. Now perhaps you'll tell us where you've been.'

They were wonderful banisters to slide down, dark-red mahogany polished over a century by a hundred hands, many of them gloved, and in the staircase's early life, by half a dozen housemaids. The banisters flowed, an unbroken river of wood, from the top floor to the basement, unbroken but not consistent in their gradient, for while on the main areas of the flights they declined at an angle of forty-five degrees, above the bends they became briefly almost vertical and at the landings they relaxed into the horizontal. It was at the second landing that Sylvia, toiling up, stepped back to avoid contact with a protruding foot as a child of about six came flying down, hanging on with both hands and shrieking at the top of his lungs. Shrieking, Sylvia had often thought, seemed a natural concomitant of pleasure in the under-sevens. His momentum was just insufficient to carry him on across the landing horizontal to the next downward slope and, waving to Sylvia, he cried, 'Give us a push, Miss!'

This was the way the children at The Hide tended to address her and Lucy and Griselda, as if they were teachers at school. Deciding not to admonish him, but dreading an accident, she put out her hand and gave him a feeble shove in the middle of his back.

'Harder,' he said. 'Go *on*.'

Sylvia pushed a very little harder, the little boy slid along the straight and tipped over on to the next slope with another shriek. She watched him reach the bend and, more riskily, negotiate the vertical banister at the bend in safety, before climbing up the last flight. Lucy was in the helpline room and the two phones were quiet.

'I'm not on my own, am I?'

'Afraid so,' Lucy said. 'Jill's got flu and Davina's giving up. She says she can't afford an unpaid job and that I understand.'

'What do I do', Sylvia asked, 'if both phones ring at the same time?'

'It seldom happens, thank God, it's not as if we're in the centre of a big city. But if it does you'll just have to put one on hold. Use your own judgement which one.'

'When they get their mobiles we'll have a lot more, won't we? Though I suppose that's not something we should complain about.'

Lucy laughed. 'No, we shouldn't but I know what you mean. I'm going to leave you to hold the fort now.'

After she had gone Sylvia stood by the window, looking down into this garden and the next one, and those behind, all the big, shrubby, well-treed gardens, divided from each other by walls of stone or brick, or creeper-hung fences or cypress or yew hedges. Apart from this one, all the leafy gardens were empty of people but for one man mowing a distant lawn, the hum of the mower faintly audible as its owner took advantage of a rainless day. In The Hide's garden two toddlers supervised by their mothers clambered up the climbing frame while bigger children occupied the swing. The banister slider came out into the garden while she watched, holding a red, white and blue football, which he dropped on to the grass and kicked hard at the trunk of a flowering cherry, dislodging from its blossoms a cascade of petals. The pink shower he achieved evidently pleased him, for he aimed another harder kick at the tree and when it had the effect he wanted, gave one of his famous shrieks.

She turned back into the room. Two of its walls were papered with press cuttings of domestic-violence cases. Big black letters, big stark photographs, a haggard woman with a black eye, another with a split lip, a well-known black boxer whose smile showed his dazzling teeth, an equally famous white footballer wearing his notorious scowl. The former had put his girlfriend into a wheelchair for life, the latter had killed his wife by accident while punching her head. On the wall above the table where the phones were hung a calendar and a large sheet of card that showed details of the four refuges in the area and what space, if any, was available in each of them. The current situation was that there was no room at the Kingsmarkham Hide and none in Myringham, but the smaller house in Sewingbury had one room free and the most distant of all, a one-time B & B outside Lewes, had two. Sylvia had read all the cases on the walls several times over and now, for the intervals of quiet, she brought a book with her.

The phone ringing, after a quarter of an hour of silence, made her jump. She picked up the receiver. 'The Hide. How can I help you?'

A woman's voice, cultured, gentle, diffident, said, 'I'm not one of those battered women, you know.'

'Right,' said Sylvia cheerfully. 'Would you like to tell me what your problem is? Take your time. I've plenty. Everything you say will be in absolute confidence.'

She heard the rough intake of breath and its expulsion before the woman spoke again. 'I would like to know if you could recommend a psychiatrist.'

Sylvia was a little taken aback. 'This is The Hide helpline line. Are you sure you have the right number?'

'Oh, yes,' the woman said. 'I know who you are and I'd like you to recommend a psychiatrist. My husband says he'll stop hitting me if I put myself in the hands of a good psychiatrist.'

'There are lots of bits I can't remember,' Rachel Holmes said. 'You just have to accept that. I've got a sort of amnesia. It's the shock, I expect.'

'Let's have the bits you do remember,' said Karen Malahyde drily. If this girl was going to be uppity, was going to try to put her down, she too could be crushing. 'Begin at the beginning, will you? At eight on Saturday evening. You were to be picked up by Mrs Strang at eight?'

'You know all that,' the girl said. 'You don't want

me to repeat it, I suppose? I was early. My mother's boyfriend was calling for her and I thought I'd get out of their way.' This last remark was accompanied by a resentful glance in her mother's direction. 'I don't come home all that often and I'd have thought the least she could do was give up a night out with *him* just for once ...'

'But, Rachel,' Rosemary protested faintly, 'you were going out yourself, you'd told me you were going out.'

'Oh, what's the use?'

Rachel seemed about to expand on her resentment but Karen Malahyde cut in with a swift and rather curt, 'Let's get back to your movements on Saturday night, can we?'

'I left here at a few minutes to eight.' Rachel was sullen now. 'I got to the bus-stop opposite the Flag when it was just on eight. There's a seat there and I sat down to wait. I'd have thought all that was pretty obvious.'

Wexford couldn't help recalling how Mrs Holmes had said, no more than an hour or so before, that her daughter was a 'good, lovely, clever girl'. Clever she might well be. 'Did you know Mrs Strang's car, its colour and make?' he asked.

The girl gave an impatient sigh, but at last she spoke more reasonably. 'I know I ought to have found that out. I ought to have found out what the woman looked like but I didn't and I've been punished for that, haven't I?'

'You tell us,' said Wexford equably.

'I am telling you. A car came along and stopped. A woman was driving it – oh, she was about fifty, I suppose. Maybe more, I don't know,' said Rachel with the indifference of an eighteen-year-old for the age of anyone over thirty-five. 'She wound down the passenger window and I went over and said hi or

79

something and I'm Rachel, and she said, Get in, Rachel, and I did. I just thought she was Mrs Strang, I took it for granted. When I was sitting down she said, I'm Vicky, but I didn't know what Mrs Strang was called, did I?'

'Mrs Strang's name is Olga.'

'Pity no one told me that earlier. Still,' said Rachel with unusual graciousness, 'they weren't to know, were they? Anyway, I did call her Vicky and we talked, and I suppose I didn't take much notice of where we were going. If I had it wouldn't have helped. I don't know those villages, I've never been to Framhurst, so I wouldn't know where we went. It was country, I know that, fields and woods and whatever. I was talking to her, she wanted to know all about me . . .'

'What, she asked you to talk about yourself?'

'Yes and you could say I fell for it. I told her my parents were divorced and I lived with my mother, and that I'd be nineteen in June and I was at university – oh, and all sorts of things about my friends and what I liked doing, and my interests and everything.' She laughed suddenly, an angry, self-mocking sound. 'Vicky was a good listener,' she said bitterly.

'Where did she take you?'

'I don't know. I didn't take any of it in. You see, I simply trusted her to take me to her house and pick up Caroline. She talked about Caroline. Of course I see now that she could talk about Caroline because I'd talked about her first, said we'd met in our first term at Essex and then found out we lived near each other, and how Caroline was doing Latin American studies and I was doing anthropology. She talked about Caroline's Spanish being so good because they'd lived in Spain for a year when she was a child and I said I'd never known that, and of course it

80

wasn't true, it was all made up – but you can see why I trusted her, can't you?'

'What happened when you got to where you were going?'

Rachel sighed. 'I wish I could tell you where it was and describe the house but I can't. I have a vague impression of shingles on the front of the house and a fir tree – well, a sort of Christmas tree – but that's all. I didn't look, I didn't know then that I'd have to remember. Vicky unlocked the front door and we went inside, and she called out "Caroline!" as if Caroline was somewhere getting ready or something. My God, she was such a good actress I'd have sworn I heard Caroline answer.' She looked at her mother. 'Can I have a drink of water?'

Rosemary Holmes shot out of her chair, happy to obey any commands now she had her daughter back. Karen watched with carefully disguised disapproval as she came running back with a tall glass that had ice in it and a bottle of Perrier.

Taking it without a word of thanks, Rachel tipped the ice into an ashtray and filled the glass with water. 'I'll go on now, shall I?'

'If you please,' said Wexford.

'Vicky asked me to sit down and I did, and she offered me a drink and I said yes, which was a big mistake, but I didn't know that.'

'How a big mistake?' Karen asked.

'She put something in it. She must have . . .'

'Oh, Rachel . . .!' It was a wail from Rosemary Holmes, a cry of anguish.

'I've told you they didn't do anything to me!' Rachel was almost shouting. 'Not what you mean, anyway. There's no need to make a fuss.' She seemed to notice the effect her rage was having on the two police officers, their quiet awareness that might cover disapproval, and she lowered her voice. 'I asked for vodka with tonic or lemonade or whatever and she brought it,' she said. 'She wouldn't have anything herself because she'd be driving Caroline and me to the Rotten Carrot. Oh, yes, I'd told her where we were going, she wasn't a thought reader. My drink tasted like a normal vodka and tonic, and it didn't have any weird effects, not at first.

'I did start wondering why Caroline was taking so long as I must have been there ten minutes. We were supposed to be at the Rotten Carrot by eight thirty and it was past that. Vicky offered me another drink – "Freshen your glass" was what she said – but I wouldn't, I was starting to feel a bit woozy. And then this man came into the room. At first I thought he must be Caroline's brother, though he'd have been old for that. He was maybe thirty, a small, thin guy with weird eyes.'

'What does weird mean?'

For a moment Karen thought Rachel was going to shout at her to consult a dictionary, so contemptuous was her glance, but she only gave one of her impatient sighs. 'Strange,' she said, 'piercing but sort of dull. Like stones. He had rather a high voice and he didn't look at you while he was talking.' She drank some of her mineral water and set the glass down. 'And after that I don't remember, I don't remember what happened till the middle of the next day, the middle of Sunday.'

'Oh, Rachel!' exclaimed Rosemary Holmes once more.

'Oh, Rachel,' her daughter mocked. 'I've told you, I know I wasn't – touched. What Granny would call "interfered with".' She looked at Wexford as if she would include him in the Granny category. 'I was lying on a bed and Vicky – I'm sure it was Vicky and not him – had taken off my jeans and my sweater. I was in my top and bra and pants, *and nobody'd done anything else to me.* Right? Is that clear? Vicky brought me a cup of tea and said to get up and have a bath and dress.' She hesitated. 'So I did,' she said. 'I mean, I argued, I said, where was I and to take me home, but when I saw there was no way of getting out – she'd locked me in and wouldn't let me out till I'd had a bath – I just did it. I suppose I thought I'd be better able to get away from there if I was clean and dressed and everything.

'Vicky had taken away my jeans and given me a skirt, a longish sort of A-line skirt it was, awful, but I wasn't going to go out there in just my knickers, so I put it on and went out and *he* was there – she called him Jerry – and she told me to cook the lunch.'

'She told you to cook the lunch?' Wexford said in a neutral tone. The incredulity was in his face.

'I was to cook the lunch and clear it away and wash up. I said, "Don't be ridiculous" and that I was going home, she was to take me home *now*. I knew it was a crime to take someone away and shut them up against their will, and I said that to them and Vicky said "Too bad" or something like that. I tried to run to the front door – well, I did run to the front door but it was locked on three locks, so I tried a window but all the windows were locked and I think they were double glazed too. I didn't tell you I felt awfully ill, like an outsize hangover it was, a tremendous headache and sort of trembling and shivering. So in the end I just did what she said. I said could I have some paracetamol first and she gave me two capsules. I saw her take them out of the paracetamol pack so I knew they were OK.'

She laughed that same bitter laugh. 'Then I peeled some potatoes and washed a cauliflower – I'm not much of a cook, I've never had to cook.' Rachel eyed her mother reproachfully just as she must have looked at her when, in the past, any tentative suggestions had been made that she might care to learn how to boil an egg or grill a chop. 'They watched me all the time, Vicky and Jerry. Anyway, we ate the lunch and then I washed up and Vicky said to get the vacuum cleaner and clean the bedrooms, but not *her* bedroom, the door to that was locked. I said, "Can I go home if I do?" and Vicky said, "We'll see," so I cleaned the bedrooms and when I came back she gave me a great pile of Jerry's socks and said to mend them. "Darn" them was what she said and I didn't know what that meant . . .'

'Rachel,' said Wexford, interrupting her, for he could stand it no longer, 'have you ever read a novel called *The Franchise Affair* by Josephine Tey?'

She looked at him with raised eyebrows. 'What?'

'It's about a young girl who accuses two women of kidnapping her and forcing her to do their housework. The accusation is false. She has, in fact, been away with a man she picked up in an hotel. The novel is sometimes set as a GCSE text.'

The flush that spread across Rachel's face was one of the most intense and glowing he had ever seen. But he knew that it is not only guilt and shame that make us blush. Being suspected of lying may be just as effective in causing a rush of blood to the face.

'Have you read it?' he asked, gently this time.

'Yes, I have,' she said.

'Well?'

Rachel spoke in a high voice, near to hysteria. 'You came here and – and wanted me to talk to you and I said yes – I said I'd tell you everything – and now I – I have – you – you don't believe me! You accuse me of getting it out of a book!'

'Did you darn his socks?' asked Karen, barely concealing her amusement.

'No, because I can't! I don't know how! I got supper instead and put my jeans and shirt in the

84

washing machine and washed up, and all the time this Jerry never said a word, he just watched me. Why won't you believe me?'

'Go on,' said Wexford.

'Not if that woman's going to laugh at me.'

'I'm not laughing,' said Karen. 'Even you must have felt it was pretty ludicrous trying to get you to mend his socks. Did you try to escape?'

'They hadn't a phone or if they had I couldn't find it. I tried all the windows. I tried to attract someone's attention but there wasn't anyone, it was just a country lane. Cars went past but the drivers couldn't see me. I got up in the night but Vicky'd locked my bedroom door. I could have broken the window if I'd really tried but there were bars outside.'

'This was a bungalow?'

'No – yes, just one floor, yes. But big, a lot of rooms. On the Monday I felt better, the headache had worn off. Vicky got me up early and told me to defrost the fridge and clean the oven. Then I was to take Jerry his breakfast in bed. That was the only time Vicky touched me. She shook me to wake me up and slapped my face. I'd – no one had ever slapped me before. I didn't know what to do, I don't know how to fight people. It was a shock, being hit like that. I took Jerry's breakfast in on a tray, it was cereal and toast and honey and an orange. He was sitting up in bed in striped pyjamas, and he took the tray and said, "Thanks." That was the only time he spoke to me, though he spoke to Vicky.'

Rachel seemed to have forgotten her restraint. Now she was voluble, pouring it all out. 'I did housework all day and cooked. I suppose I thought that if I did it they'd let me go. I had plenty to eat and Vicky offered me drinks but I wouldn't have them in case she'd doctored them with whatever that was. But I did a silly thing. On Tuesday I started feeling ill, it was my period coming, and I asked Vicky for a paracetamol and again the pack came out. But she'd done something to it, put capsules with this drug in through the plastic so the foil seal wasn't broken. And that deceived me, so I took two and they had the same effect as the first one, only worse, and I don't know what I did for the rest of the day, I can't remember anything, I may have done housework, had some food, I don't know, but when I woke up it was midday today and I was lying there' – she looked dubiously in Wexford's direction – 'well, in a bit of a mess, and there was a packet of Tampax beside me and my jeans and sweater.

'I felt dreadful but Vicky made me wash my sheets. She hung them on the line herself, she wouldn't let me outside. And then, at about six, she said I could go home. I had such a hangover I could hardly see. Jerry wasn't around. Vicky unlocked the front door and took me out to the car, the same one we'd come in. I could have run away then but I felt so ill and besides I didn't see the point. I let her bring me back here and she dropped me off where she'd picked me up.'

It was not Wexford or Karen Malahyde who eventually persuaded Rachel to be seen by a doctor, but Lynn Fancourt, who seemed to strike some chord with her or ignite some spark of affinity. Perhaps it was only that Lynn was nearer her own age. Not that Devonshire, though, she said, pulling a face as if she could smell something nasty. So it was Dr Akande whom she saw and, after more grumbling and truculence, allowed him to take a blood sample and peer into her eyes and down her throat.

'I think she was given Rohypnol,' Wexford said. 'Akande found no trace of it but it's virtually undetectable anyway and by now it would have passed out of her system.'

Burden raised his eyebrows. 'Is that the stuff they call the rape drug? No smell, no taste, put in drink it sedates and next day the subject has a massive hangover but can't remember what's happened to her.'

'More or less.'

'Then we find out who in the area's been prescribed Rohypnol and Bob's your uncle.'

'Not quite,' said Wexford. 'Rohypnol's only obtainable on prescription now and only, in fact, on private prescription, but until recently you could buy it over the counter, anyone could buy it.'

Burden, who had been walking up and down, not so much pacing as strolling while he considered, sat down on the edge of Wexford's desk. 'How much of this tale of hers do we believe? I mean, is it any less of a farrago of lies than Lizzie Cromwell's story?'

Wexford was silent, thinking. He had begun by not believing it. The parallels with *The Franchise Affair*, a favourite book of his, had been responsible in part for his incredulity, but gradually, as Rachel went on, he had doubted his own disbelief. Now he was in a state of half-belief. That a middle-aged woman had taken Rachel to a house somewhere in the countryside he could give credence to. And that she had been drugged and locked up, all that was possible. But the silent stony-eyed Jerry and the demands that Rachel cook and do housework, most of all that she darn the man's socks, these must be figments or fantasies. 'What's a farrago, anyway?' he said irrelevantly.

'God knows. It's just a phrase, a figure of speech, a "farrago of lies" is. You're such a pedant, you are. You ought to have been a professor among the dreaming spires.'

'Maybe I should at that,' said Wexford wistfully.

'You talk about a tissue of lies – well, you don't but I might – so I suppose a farrago is something like that, like sort of embroidered material or something.'

Wexford watched him resume his walking, take up a station at the window, against which a sudden shower was dashing hailstones. 'She's described those two people quite circumspectly,' he said. 'The woman in her fifties, grey-haired, blue-eyed, wearing a wedding ring, overweight – but any normal person's overweight to these girls.' Wexford tightened his belly, as people always do when talking of fatness or thinness in others. 'The man about thirty, small, she says around five foot four, dark receding hair and the stony eyes. She sticks to these descriptions, she's repeated them twice to me and given the same details to Lynn. I believe in them.'

Apparently fascinated by the hailstones that stung the glass, Burden didn't turn his head. 'Does it matter? No harm's been done. She wasn't hurt. It probably did her good, cooking and cleaning and all that, spoilt little madam.'

'You know better than that, Mike. I don't have to tell you that taking someone away and detaining her against her will is a very serious offence. Not to mention drugging her. And now it's happened to two young women. It's false imprisonment. Of course it matters.'

'All right. Point taken. You mean you think this Vicky woman took Lizzie away too?'

'You remember she mentioned a woman offering her a lift, which she didn't accept? Well, I think she did accept it and she too was taken to this house for the same purpose, whatever that was.'

'The woman and the man were mother and son, were they?'

'Don't know. It's possible.' Wexford thought of the

strange relationships he came across in the course of his work, the bizarre combinations of disparate types and the unlikely conjunctions of ages. He wasn't going to draw any facile conclusions about this one. 'What on earth are you gawping at?' he asked. 'You've seen hailstones before, haven't you?'

'Come and look at this.'

Wexford got up. Through the streaming window he could see two people sheltering from the hail in a shop doorway. Both wore sandwich boards, the woman's cut out in the shape of a girl child, the man's in the shape of a boy, faces and hair and clothes painted in quite realistically, one bearing the words: *Save Our Children* and the other: *Paedophile Out*. The storm ceased as abruptly as it had started, both of them stepped out on to the pavement and crossed the road, holding up hands to halt the traffic. Taking no notice of the honking of horns and yells of motorists, they reached the police station side and stood looking up at the windows.

Wexford rubbed at the steam on the glass left by his breath. 'The man's Colin Crowne,' he said. 'I don't know the woman's name but she's from the Muriel Campden Estate too, Oberon Road, I think.'

'Where Smith returns tomorrow,' said Burden in fatalistic tones. 'Shall we get on over there and kill two birds with one stone?'

'And have a word with those two first.'

But by the time they reached the forecourt the two people and their child-shaped sandwich boards had gone.

For no apparent reason, the Muriel Campden Estate was designed so that no house faced another, but all, looking inwards from the three sides of the triangle, fronted on the squat tower in its centre. Around this building, from all the windows on the second floor, at bedroom-window height in the houses, a banner had been hung, bearing the same legends in red and black paint as those on the sandwich boards. It girdled the tower like a belt, running almost all the way round and announcing to anyone looking out of windows or passing by: *Paedophile Out. Keep Away From Our Children*. Of the sandwich-board bearers there was no sign.

In the raised flowerbeds at the foot of the tower, hail had beaten the tulips to death. Orange-and-green-striped, feather-edged, they lay broken and crushed against the pale chalky soil. And the pink-blossoming street trees, cherries and prunus, had dropped all their petals in one mighty shedding under the hail's onslaught. The pavements were slippery with them, bright mother-of-pearl under the blazing sun, which had suddenly come out. In the distance, beyond these charcoal-coloured houses, these anthracite walls and roofs, the green meadows shone brilliantly enough to hurt the eyes.

Wexford rang the bell of number 16 Oberon Road. Standing on the doorstep, he had only to turn his head to receive the full force of that banner, some twenty yards away. But it would be the same wherever you lived on the triangle. The protestors had seen to that. Here, though, at this point, by careful design and strategic positioning, the single word Paedophile stood out most assertively.

The woman who opened the door looked sixty but was probably forty. She had the appearance of someone who has never taken the least care of herself, who has never heard that it is possible to file and clean one's nails, keep one's hair clean, go to a dentist, iron one's clothes and smell sweet. Her face was greasy and her hair the same dull charcoal as the fabric of the house she lived in, fastened back with an elastic band. She wore a dress that should have had a belt but was unbelted and was probably, by the shape and style of it, a hand-down from her grandmother, wrinkled brown stockings and bedroom slippers. The smell of her, as Burden remarked later, was very like that emanating from the hamburger stall set up in Queen Street on market day. Her teeth – but he said he didn't want to remember her teeth, he wanted to put them right out of his mind.

'Ms Smith?' said Wexford. 'Ms Suzanne Smith?'

'That's me. What d'you want?'

'Chief Inspector Wexford and Inspector Burden, Kingsmarkham CID. May we come in a minute?'

She stepped back and when they were inside, slammed the door hard. 'Haven't I got enough to put up with,' she asked of no one in particular, 'with that scum out there?' In the living-room a man sat staring at the television screen. He took no notice whatever of the newcomers; Suzanne Smith might have come into the room alone, or, as far as he was concerned, no one at all had come in.

'You expect your father to come home here on Friday – tomorrow, that is?' Wexford asked.

'I reckon,' she said. 'He's nowhere else to go, the old bugger.'

This remark stirred the man at the other end of the room. He took his eyes from the screen, turned his head and stared in their direction. Suzanne Smith made a kind of introduction: 'That's my fiancé.'

Neither policeman acknowledged him. 'We're not anticipating trouble,' Burden said with a confidence he didn't feel, 'but I'll leave you this number.' He wrote it down and handed it to her. 'And if need be you can speak to me, Inspector Burden. B-U-R-D-E-N – have you got that?'

She nodded. Loyalty to her father forgotten – or perhaps Wexford had misinterpreted her tone – she made a sound of exasperation, a 'huh' noise, and cast up her eyes.

The man at the other end of the room spoke. 'That's right, girl,' he said, and he added in a voice so deeply vindictive and vicious that Wexford found himself flinching, 'Put the likes of him in the gas chamber'd be best. Or the chair.'

Outside, in the relatively wholesome air, Burden remarked that Suzanne Smith's 'fiancé' probably had no idea capital punishment had ceased in this country over thirty years before. His whole notion of life came from television; so much transatlantic culture had he absorbed from that source that he believed death by gas chamber or electrocution were United Kingdom options.

'So long as he and she don't give the wretched Smith up to the mob,' said Wexford.

'You're joking, I hope,' Burden said severely.

'So do I hope. There is no mob, there's only a banner. We must look on the bright side.'

Wexford looked about him. The sun had gone in but the day was still bright and the sky blue, with scurrying clouds rushing across its face. The belt-banner flapped in the breeze. In two of the gardens men who looked civilised and law-abiding mowed their lawns. 'This isn't a very pretty place,' he said, 'but it's quite nice, isn't it? It's comfortable, rustic, the air's pure and if it's not like wine it's like the best mineral water. There's no vandalism or very little. If the local authority plant trees they don't get pulled up. Hail spoils the tulips, not human hands. A far cry from those inner-city estates one reads about, wouldn't you say? Those places where the old go in terror of their lives or daren't go out at all, where gangs roam the walkways and the residents deal in controlled substances.'

'Sure. So what are you getting at?'

'Just that – let's hope it stays that way. And now we'll pay a call on the Crowne family, shall we?'

Inevitably, the banner was visible from this front room too. Lizzie Cromwell was sitting in the window, gazing at it, as if she expected it to change shape, fall off or be joined at any moment by even more inflammatory material. Wexford, deterred neither by the smoky atmosphere nor Debbie Crowne's grim expression and headful of heated rollers, pulled up a chair beside Lizzie and proceeded to tell her what in fact had happened to her on Saturday two weeks before.

'After you'd waited twenty minutes for the bus you accepted a lift from a lady in a white car and she drove you to a house in the country. There was a man there. Her name was Vicky and his was Jerry. They gave you something to drink which made you sleepy and made you forget a lot of what happened to you. I'm right, aren't I, Lizzie?'

She turned to face him. He thought how healthy she looked and blooming, her face flushed and her eyes bright and knowing. 'I'm not supposed to say.'

'Who told you not to say? The woman who took you away? The man, Jerry?' Lizzie didn't get a chance to answer. Debbie Crowne interposed herself between Wexford and her daughter. There was a strong smell, suddenly, of overheated hair. He saw that she was trembling.

'What is it, Mrs Crowne?'

'I'll tell you what it is. She's pregnant, that's what it is. He's made my daughter pregnant.'

# Chapter 6

Wexford's first reaction was to say, 'It's not possible to tell so soon. It's less than a fortnight.'

'Where have you been living?' Debbie Crowne asked rudely. 'On the moon? I done a test, haven't I? A home pregnancy kit's what they call them in case you didn't know. And I done it and she's fallen pregnant. If I'd done it last week it'd have shown the same. And what I'd like to know is, what are you going to do about it?'

'It would help us to do something', said Burden, 'if Lizzie would tell us the truth about what happened to her.'

'She's scared, isn't she? He raped her and she's scared what he might do.'

At the word 'raped', Lizzie's eyelids flickered. It was as if something hot or a very bright light had suddenly been brought close up to her face. Her head jerked back.

'Did you sleep a lot while you were there, Lizzie?' Wexford asked. 'Did they give you drinks to make you sleep?'

'I don't know,' she said. 'I'm not to say. I'll be punished if I say.'

Burden looked at Colin Crowne who had just come into the room. 'You won't be punished, Lizzie. No one will punish you. If you tell us about them and about the house you went to and where it was, they will be caught and punished. I'm sure you understand that, don't you?'

Debbie Crowne shouted suddenly, 'You leave her alone! It's not right, bullying her in her condition. She could have a miscarriage!'

Surely the best thing imaginable, Wexford thought, then castigated himself for callousness. 'No one is bullying Lizzie,' he began but the rest of his sentence dwindled away as Lizzie broke in, and he forgot that he had once thought her meek and not inclined to rebellion.

'No, I won't, I won't have a miscarriage. I'm going to have my baby, I want my baby. Then I can go away from here and get a flat and live with my baby. I can get away from you and *him*, and have my own place and be – be *happy*!' Her face crumpled and she burst into a storm of tears.

'Now see what you've done,' said Debbie Crowne. 'That's rubbish, that is. Wants her baby! She ought to have had the morning-after pill. If she'd had the morning-after pill the day she come back ...'

'She wouldn't be in the shit now,' said Colin Crowne.

'Farrago,' said Wexford next morning. 'I looked it up in the dictionary. It doesn't mean anything like tissue, it means "mixed fodder for cattle" and it comes from the Latin. Interesting, don't you think?'

Burden threw the *Kingsmarkham Courier* down on Wexford's desk. 'It only confirms what I said about you being a pedant. Have you seen the paper?'

With a hint of that feeling that is usually described as a sinking of the heart, Wexford said, 'Why? Should I have?' He knew what he was likely to see but not how bad it would be. 'Oh, God,' he said, 'what's the point of doing this, I wonder. What does St George get out of it?'

'A boost to his circulation, I suppose. God knows it needs it.'

The headline was: SMITH FREED, and under that, KINGSMARKHAM PAEDOPHILE COMES HOME.

All parents with small children, [Wexford read] will live in terror from this weekend onwards, knowing that Thomas Smith, convicted paedophile and child-killer is back in their midst. Released after serving eight years of a fifteen-year prison sentence, Smith, seventy-one, is expected to return today to the home he left nearly a decade ago in Oberon Road on Kingsmarkham's Muriel Campden Estate.

'He could only have spelt it out more thoroughly if he'd given the house number,' he said gloomily. 'I wonder why he didn't.'

An elderly man by now, Smith is nevertheless understood to have admitted he may still be a danger to children. His home in Oberon Road, currently occupied by his daughter Ms Suzanne Smith and her partner Mr Garry Wills, backs on to Kingsmarkham's only public park with its children's play area. Until an order is in place restraining Smith from places frequented by children, such as York Park, this popular venue for youngsters will most likely stand empty, and that at the most favourable season of the year for outdoor play . . .

'I can't stand his English or his reporter's English, never mind the content,' said Wexford. 'That word "paedophile", no one knew what it meant five years ago – well, no one but psychiatrists and Greek scholars. Now it's on everyone's lips. Even a moron like that Colin Crowne knows what it means.'

'There's a leading article as well,' said Burden. 'Would you like me to give you a synopsis? It won't do you any good to read it yourself. Your blood pressure's showing all over your face as it is.'

Wexford sighed. 'OK. What does it say?'

'That paedophiles should be kept under restraint for the whole of their natural lives, given the option of castration, never allowed within any area where even one child may live, given more severe sentences in the first place – all that, if not necessarily in that order. Oh, and he – it's St George himself this time, by the way – he says the Government aren't acting fast enough and how about these steps they are supposed to be taking to monitor released paedophiles? It couldn't be worse.'

'I don't know about that. He could have advocated compulsory castration.' Wexford dropped the paper on the floor where he couldn't see it. 'I've been thinking about that banner thing, Mike. We don't have any powers to make them take it down, do we?'

'I doubt it. We could if it led to trouble. Then it'd be an offence against public order. But it hasn't led to trouble.'

'Not yet. Smith's not home yet, but he will be today. I dreamt about the Muriel Campden Estate last night and I woke up yelling there was a bomb planted under the tower. Dora thought I'd gone mad. What are we going to do about Lizzie Cromwell?'

'It's a job for Lynn now, don't you reckon? Get Lynn round there and see if she can ferret out what really happened. Rachel Holmes got on fine with her, so why not Lizzie?'

'They're a very different type of girl, Mike. But it's a good idea. Lynn should persuade Mrs Crowne to take Lizzie to her GP, that's a priority. When he or she confirms it I'll believe she's two weeks pregnant.'

The hunt for the house with the shingles on its front and the big Christmas tree hadn't yet begun but Wexford, whose knowledge of the surrounding area was considerable, had given it thought. He had pictured villages in his mind's eye, seeing their churches and clustering cottages, bigger houses, village greens with war memorials, and had been presented with several possible bungalows, but none of these stood alone in open countryside. Seeing stretches of roads and lanes, dipping valleys and swelling hills, was harder. So, on the previous evening he had driven back and forth across the area where the bypass was to have been built.

To himself he confessed that he enjoyed going there to gloat. There was a sweet almost physical pleasure in seeing, bursting into fresh leaf, trees scheduled last year to be felled, in hearing the song of birds going to roost and driving along the one narrow road through Framhurst Great Wood, eyeing through the long still glades the tiny blossoms of celandine and wood anemones on the forest floor. He had even lingered on the edge of it, parking the car for a moment or two, while he reflected that here, on this very spot, he and everyone else in Kingsmarkham had expected to see by this time a huge trunk road ripping through the wasted valley. It did him good, he sometimes thought, to sit and look and rejoice, it brought him a calm satisfaction. And he felt revived and keen again when he started the car, and set off for Framhurst and Savesbury and Myfleet.

All the way along the roads, some of them narrow lanes with high banks studded with primroses and cowslips, he looked for a house that would conform to Rachel Holmes's description. But although a shingled front is a feature of many Sussex dwellings, there were few of these in the area and even fewer that were bungalows. After driving around for an hour, going as far as Myringham in one direction and Stringfield in the other, he had come across only two, and of these one was in the centre of a hamlet and in any case was a house on two floors. The other, on the edge of downland, had no trees near it apart from its own Leyland cypress hedge.

That had been last evening. This morning he resolved to take Rachel reconnoitring with him and Karen Malahyde, and to go south of the town, always supposing she had kept her promise and not yet returned to the University of Essex.

Sylvia had been at The Hide for no more than ten minutes when the doorbell rang. It wasn't one of her days for being there and it wasn't one of her times. In fact, it was the day she was owed to take off from her regular job and she had been at home, planning a morning in the garden and an afternoon at the cinema, when Lucy Angeletti phoned and said that Jill Lewis still had flu and she had a morning meeting set up with Myringham Housing Department, and could she possibly be an angel and come in? Just for a few hours till Griselda took over at three. So of course she had said yes and had phoned her mother to ask her to pick up the boys from school, just in case she was late, and had come down here by eleven.

When she was herself a child, when she was ten, no one would have thought twice about letting her come home from school alone. No one would have considered it unsafe for her to bring her little sister home with her. But these days everyone was terrified of letting their kids out of their sight for five minutes. And they would be even more frightened after reading the *Courier*, as she had done that morning, taking it and her cup of tea back to bed with her. Presumably, there had been paedophiles when she was a child, there must have been, and just as many – human nature didn't change – but you seldom heard about them, while today there seemed to be one behind every bush and round every corner.

She was hanging up her raincoat in the hall and there was no one else about apart from two three-year-olds sitting on the stairs, so it seemed obvious that she should answer the door. But even as she put up her hand to the latch she remembered instructions she had received during her brief training for this job. Be careful when you answer the door, look through the spyhole first, put the chain on. It could be a violent spouse or partner looking for the woman he had assaulted and who had escaped from him. So Sylvia drew back her hand, put on the chain, lifted up the little circular flap over the spyhole and squinted through it.

A very old, anxious-looking woman was what she saw. She slipped off the chain and opened the door. The woman held out a sheaf of papers fastened to a clipboard. She spoke as if she had learnt her words by heart and painstakingly. 'I wonder if you would care to put your name to the Kingsbrook Residents' Association's petition? It is a protest against the residential home where they plan to make a children's playground.'

'Do you mean The Hide?' said Sylvia.

'That is what they call it, yes. You may care to read some literature I have here first. It fully explains the situation and why the Kingsbrook Residents are so strongly opposed to it.'

Sylvia had difficulty suppressing her laughter. She put one hand up to her mouth, took a deep breath and said in a polite tone, 'This *is* The Hide.'

'This is? This house?' The woman couldn't have sounded more aghast. She rallied, as people do, by taking refuge in unreasoning attack. This hadn't been learnt in advance. 'How on earth is one supposed to know? There's no name up, there's no number. It ought to be against the law for a house not to have a number.'

'Right. I'll tell the police,' said Sylvia and, closing the door, burst into laughter. She would tell the police, she'd tell her father if she saw him that evening. It would amuse him. She climbed the stairs. A black woman with two small children in tow came out of one of the bedrooms as she crossed the first landing. Black people were thin on the ground in Kingsmarkham and its environs, though there were more now than a year ago, and Sylvia wondered where she had come from and what her particular story was. She was tall and majestic, her braided hair wound and woven into a crown on top of her head. Sylvia said hallo and that it was raining again, and passed on to the top floor.

Lucy Angeletti was there and she was on the phone. It didn't sound as if she was answering a distress call. She heard Lucy say, 'Yes, well, thanks. If someone will call this morning I'll show him or her the letter I've had. Goodbye.'

Sylvia raised an eyebrow.

'A death threat,' Lucy said. 'Anonymous, of course. *You have got my wife. If she don't come back I will kill you, bitch.*'

'Was that the police you were phoning? Are they sending someone round?'

'It won't be your dad,' said Lucy, laughing. 'He's too high-ranking. But just so that they know. I'll leave you to it then, shall I? We've got a new woman coming in any minute. She's been at the Pomfret police house all night with a baby and a two-year-old. She'll have our last available room and after that I don't know what we'll do. And now I must get over to Myringham.'

From the window, Sylvia watched the woman arrive. She came in a taxi, for the payment of which Sylvia knew the Social Services Department would have provided her with a voucher. The baby was tiny, snuggled up like a nestling bird in the harness the woman wore across her thin chest. The toddler was crying, pushing fists into his eyes. Lucy came out of the front door and down the steps, and took the case the woman had brought out of the back of the cab. The driver did nothing to assist her. The voucher, Sylvia thought, probably didn't allow for a tip. She watched the taxi reverse down the drive between the green banks of shrubs and was back to her desk when the phone started ringing.

'The Hide. How can I help you?'

Silence. There usually was silence or else a hurried rush of speech. Most women were embarrassed about phoning. Guiltless, they were ashamed. After all, they were complaining to outsiders about the man they had chosen for their life partner. They often began with excuses for themselves or for the man who had beaten them. While the silence endured, she thought of the woman she had spoken to the other night, the one whose husband abused her because he said she was mad and would only stop when she found a cure for her madness. From her, once she had unburdened herself, they had heard no more and Sylvia had no way of knowing if her advice to go to the police had been taken.

She said again, 'This is The Hide. How may I help you?'

A voice said abruptly, 'Is that the Women's Aid Federation of England?'

'No, this is The Hide helpline. We offer you the same kind of service as the Women's Aid Federation. Can I help you?'

'What will you – what will you do for me?'

Sylvia spoke very gently. 'Won't you tell me what the problem is? Has someone hurt you? Have you been hurt?'

'It was last night. Before he left for work. He's at work now, he'll be back around eleven, maybe sooner. I thought he'd broken my arm but he hasn't. It's not broken if I can move it, is it? I'm all over bruises and my face is a real sight.'

Sylvia looked at the clock. It was nearly ten thirty. She didn't ask why the woman hadn't phoned before, why she had waited so long. She guessed what it must have cost her to have phoned at all, the sacrifice of pride and privacy, the revealing to a stranger what her marriage had come to.

'The best thing for you to do is go straight to your nearest police station. Are you in Kingsmarkham?' The woman wouldn't want to give her address, Sylvia sensed, but she got a grudging murmur of assent. 'Would you tell me your name?'

'I'd rather not.'

'That's fine. That's quite all right. It doesn't matter. Go to Kingsmarkham Police Station. Do you know where it is? It's in the High Street at the beginning of the Pomfret Road, opposite Tabard Road. I'll phone them and alert them to expect you. Will you do that?'

'Oh, I don't know . . .'

'I'll phone them as soon as I've said goodbye to you. I'll tell them to expect you in half an hour.'

'Goodbye,' the voice said abruptly. 'Thank you. Goodbye.'

The phone went down and dialling tone began. No means of knowing if her caller would take her advice was available to Sylvia, but she phoned Kingsmarkham Police, spoke to Sergeant Camb whom she had known since she was in her teens and told him to expect the arrival of a woman with a badly bruised face, name unknown. The phone rang immediately she put the receiver down. A man this time.

'Fucking bitch,' said the voice. 'Frigid lesbian cow. Do you know what I'm going to do to you? I'm going to ...'

Sylvia held the receiver at arm's length. She noted that the hand holding it was shaking, her whole arm was trembling. Lucy had laughed when she told her the last time it had occurred and said she knew all about that shaking and trembling, it had happened to her, but it wouldn't always. She would get used to these calls and eventually take them in her stride.

Obscenities gobbled and chattered out of the receiver. Sylvia put it down and drew a deep breath. Was it the husband of the woman who wouldn't give her name? Had he come home while she was still talking? She desperately hoped not. That was the worst of this job. Half the time, more than half, you didn't know what the outcome had been, you couldn't guess the next phase in a caller's perilous life.

No more calls came for half an hour, three-quarters of an hour. Then the phone rang. Perhaps because there had been silence for so long, the bell seemed more than usually loud and insistent. A shrill phone bell, a soft cultured voice.

'My name is Anne. I don't want to give you my surname.'

'That's fine,' said Sylvia. 'Will you tell me what your problem is?'

A hesitation, then in a slightly bewildered tone, 'But surely it's always the same problem, isn't it?'

'Basically, perhaps it is. The details vary. Usually it's a woman who's been hurt but not always. It may not be physical, it may be psychological abuse.'

The laugh she gave was unearthly, cold and echoing, the least humorous laughter Sylvia had ever heard. 'Oh, there's nothing psychological about my hurt, I can tell you.'

'I'd like to help you,' Sylvia said. She hazarded the Christian name she didn't entirely believe in, 'I'd really like to help you, Anne. Won't you tell me what's wrong?'

'I'd have to see you, I'd have to be face to face with someone, it's a long story, it would take days, weeks.'

She stopped and a silence followed. Sylvia listened to the silence, discerning faint breathing sounds.

Then, piteously, desperately, a cry for help if Sylvia had ever heard one, came on a thin, keening note out of the receiver, 'What shall I do?'

'Are you in Kingsmarkham?'

'Yes.'

'Is there anyone else in the house with you?'

'He's in the garden. The baby's with him. I can see them from the window. Oh God, he's coming in, I can't talk, I shouldn't have rung you, he'll want to know who I was speaking to – what shall I say?'

'Phone again when you're alone,' Sylvia said in the calmest tone she could muster. 'I'll say goodbye now.'

There was no answer. The phone went down. Sylvia sat hunched over the desk, her head in her hands. It had shaken her, that call. So far it was the worst she had had. There was something particularly horrible in the fact that this was a middle-class woman – yes, Sylvia had to admit this – a woman perhaps gently brought up and living in this country, in this town, who could speak in the tones of a victim of imprisonment and torture. She imagined the man coming into the room, taking the phone from her, hitting her with his free hand, and she shuddered.

On this job you needed a drink, she sometimes thought, but that was impossible, she knew where that would lead, drinking at midday. She told herself there were others to think about besides 'Anne' and made herself phone Kingsmarkham Police Station again, but no woman with a bruised face had come in.

'Describe the house to me again,' Wexford said. They were in Karen Malahyde's car. Karen was driving, with Rachel Holmes in the passenger seat and Wexford in the back.

'I've *told* you.' One thing you could say for Rachel, she wasn't scared of the police. 'It stood all on its own with fields and woods around, there weren't any other houses, it had shingle tiles all over its front – well, not all over, just over the top part, the rest was red brick – and a big tree in the front garden. I think it was a pine tree, maybe a Scots pine.'

'You said a Christmas tree before.'

'That's a pine, isn't it? I don't know but I know what I saw. I've been thinking about it, shutting my eyes and trying to make a picture form, and what I see is a Christmas tree sort of tree.'

What she meant was that the tree was coniferous but Wexford didn't correct her. He knew how easy it would be to put her off and drive her into a sullen silence. If only he knew equally how to put her into a cheerful and responsive mood! 'Now, Rachel,' he said, 'while you were being kept a prisoner you must have known that on your release the police would be involved. Did you think of that?'

'Sometimes I thought I'd never be released.'

'All right, but you've made it plain you weren't particularly frightened by your ordeal. While you were with Vicky and ... er, Jerry, you no doubt thought that when the time came the police would want you to recall as much as you could of your

106

surroundings. Did you, for instance, take note of what you could see from the windows?'

Rachel sniffed. She had an unattractive habit of sniffing where others might have shrugged. 'They gave me that stuff, you know they did. You said what it was. It messed up my memory. Anyway, all you could see was fields. That's all there was, just fields for miles and miles.'

They drove south from Stowerton towards Flagford. There were few stretches of this road bare of houses but all were widely separated, each from its nearest neighbours, which might be a quarter of a mile away. And the architecture was varied, ranging from farmhouses and what had perhaps been dower houses to cottages, converted barns, modern villas and even, on the outskirts of Flagford, a couple of blocks of flats, thinly disguised as mansions, but few bungalows. Rachel made a sullen face and Wexford guessed this was because they were passing either Dr Devonshire's home or the medical centre where he practised.

The village itself was not worth lingering in, for Rachel was adamant that the place to which she had been taken was surrounded by open meadows. Karen took byways and narrow lanes, through woodland and on to the downs. The great sweep of gentle hills and higher peaks was inhabited only by sheep. Not a house was in sight. Rachel, moreover, insisted that she had been nowhere near here, nowhere like this terrain at all. 'I said *fields*,' she said, 'fields and woods; it wasn't hilly.'

'You'll be hard put', Karen said crisply, 'to find anywhere round here that isn't hilly.'

She didn't like Rachel, Wexford had noticed, and she let her dislike show. A not altogether helpful attitude in this situation. 'Drive on,' he said. 'Keep north of the downs.'

South-west of Pomfret they came upon a house that perfectly answered Rachel's description, or so Wexford thought. It was what is known as a chalet bungalow, its upper floor consisting of only one room and that up in the roof, and it stood alone in an isolated place at a crossroads, though the roads in question were no more than narrow lanes. On its upper storey were scallop-shaped shingles while its lower floor was of pale reddish brick. The windows were latticed panes and its front door a lead-and-glass anachronism. In the front garden, which was otherwise lawn and gravel drive, stood a tall and beautiful tree, its shape roughly that of a Lombardy poplar, and evidently deciduous, for it was just coming into leaf, its elegant skeleton misted over with a delicate tracery of pale bright green. Wexford thought it might be a swamp cypress, native to the bayous of Louisiana, and said so.

'I said a pine tree,' said Rachel.

'A pine or a fir. Let's settle for a coniferous tree, shall we?'

'Then why hasn't that one got – what d'you call it? Needles, right – why hasn't it got needles?'

Wexford wasn't going to get into that one. 'Could this be the house?'

'No,' said Rachel, 'it's not a bit like it.'

'It answers your description,' said Karen.

'The front door's wrong. I know I haven't said anything about the front door but I remember now and that one's wrong. The tree's wrong and the door and the tiles are the wrong colour. And', said Rachel triumphantly, 'it wasn't on a crossroads.'

They took her home. She was evidently relieved. On Sunday she would return to Colchester and the University of Essex, and put her experience with Vicky and Jerry in the house with the pine tree behind her. If the house she described ever existed, as Karen said on the way back to Kingsmarkham. If there was a house. She was cleverer at invention than Lizzie Cromwell but not much cleverer.

'Then what happened to those two girls that they're so anxious to hide from us?' Wexford asked.

'Rape, apparently, in Lizzie's case.'

'I don't believe that.'

Karen's look had something of disappointment in it, as if she had hitherto categorised him as a man who took rape seriously but now had cause to change her mind. 'She *is* pregnant, sir.'

'So far as we know. And if she is there are other ways of getting there.' Wexford looked hard at her. 'Another time, Sergeant Malahyde, make your dislike of the girl a bit less obvious, will you? What you'd no doubt call emotional involvement has no place in police practice.'

No general practitioner in the area had prescribed Rohypnol to a patient in the past two years. If any had it would have been next to impossible to get a name out of him or her. Pharmacists in Kingsmarkham, Stowerton and Pomfret all said they had stocked it but did so no longer. None had any records of purchases but four of them kept no records of this kind of sale.

While Rachel Holmes was being driven about the countryside, helping (or obstructing) the police in their inquiries, the GP who attended the Crowne family confirmed Lizzie's pregnancy. That is, Debbie Crowne and her daughter said she had confirmed it. To Wexford the doctor declined to give any information about her patient.

Lizzie had had several long conversations with Lynn Fancourt, on whom she was developing a 'crush'. 'I'd like to be a policeman when I grow up,' she said; a statement which Lynn saw as so pathetic

109

it nearly brought tears to that tough young woman's eyes.

'A police *officer*, Lizzie,' she said gently.

'A police *officer*, that's what I meant.'

'And I think you're grown-up now, aren't you? People can't have babies till they're grown-up.' If only that were true!

'If I get a flat to live in, Mum could come and look after my baby while I did my training to be a policeman – I mean, a police *officer*. I wouldn't want *him* near my baby but Mum'd be OK.'

Lynn told Wexford Lizzie appeared to dislike Colin Crowne intensely. She suspected sexual abuse. Lizzie's pregnancy was beginning to show, which was absurd if conception had only taken place two weeks previously. But when she asked about Colin Crowne and, emboldened by the girl's evident desire to list all Colin's faults, all the 'nasty things' he said and did, hinted that sexual relations might have taken place between her and him, Lizzie laughed so incredulously and was so obviously amazed at the idea that she almost gave up. But perhaps her hints had been too oblique. She spelt things out more freely.

'I'd give him a punch he wouldn't forget if he ever come near me,' Lizzie said, more aggressive than Lynn had ever known her.

It was her renewed laughter that did more to convince Lynn than her stalwart denials. She wasn't in the least upset. On the other hand, relaying Rachel's story to her seemed to cause distress. She didn't want to hear. She had abandoned her tale of spending three days and nights in the derelict house, saying instead that she had never been there, that it was a 'dream'.

No one had taken her to any other sort of house either, no one had taken her anywhere, she had roamed the countryside, sleeping in barns and under hedges. It had been to get away from *him*. It had been to get away from Colin who said she was mental. He was always getting at her because she wasn't brainy.

'Did you like Jerry, Lizzie?' Lynn asked.

She gave a small sigh of relief when Lizzie, distracted by her dislike of Colin, said, 'Don't know any Jerry. I liked Vicky all right.'

It was the only breakthrough but it wasn't much of one.

# Chapter 7

It was dark when Thomas Smith, always called Tommy, came home to Oberon Road. He came on foot from the station and because those who interested themselves in his return were certain it would be by cab or in a police car or even a prison van, his arrival went unnoticed. The last train brought him to Kingsmarkham and it was just after eleven thirty when he rang the bell of the house of which he was the tenant. No doubt he had possessed a key, but during the eight years he had been in prison that key had been mislaid. The house was in darkness, as if no one lived there.

His daughter Suzanne opened the door. He entered without a word and she closed the door after him.

'You've aged,' he said when she switched on the light.

'I suppose you think you haven't.'

Six years had passed since she had last visited him. She didn't like the looks she got in there. Everyone knew what he was in for and took it out on him. But why take it out on her? It wasn't her fault. She watched him walk into the living-room and look out of the window. He knew there was something hanging out of the windows in the tower but he hadn't lingered to look at it by the light of the solitary street lamp and the few lights on in the flats. The street lamp was still on, though it would go out

112

in twenty minutes. He read the legend on the banner impassively. He had very little feeling left and reacted to nothing, cared about nothing except staying alive, though why he desired life he couldn't have said. A chaplain in the prison had once told him he was in danger of losing his soul and Tommy had shrugged his shoulders.

Now he said to his daughter, 'What's that thing?'

She didn't answer. He made out the word 'paedophile' and if he flinched it didn't show. He turned away from the window, said, 'That chap of yours, is he still here?'

'He's my fiancé,' she said.

Tommy Smith laughed. His was the kind of laughter that sounded as if it came from an instrument and by a mechanism long disused. It was as if he were speaking a language learnt at his mother's knee but for years superseded by a different and harsher idiom. In the quiet, mostly dark house it echoed a little.

'I got your bed ready,' she said and added, 'in the back.'

'Taken my room, have you? You and your fiancé?' Into that last word he put infinite scorn. 'I don't want anything to eat or drink,' he said, as if she had asked.

He picked up the suitcase he had left in the hall and went upstairs without turning on more lights to guide him. His daughter waited at the foot until he had disappeared. She opened the front door and looked out into the silent, empty street, the rows of houses, the tower and the banner, which swayed a little in the wind. When, on the stroke of midnight, the street lamps went out, she closed the front door, bolted it and put on the chain. Then she too went to bed.

In the large, inconvenient, rather beautiful and

113

incompletely modernised former rectory where she lived with her husband and her sons, Sylvia lay awake, worrying about The Hide. The woman who had come in that morning (yesterday morning by now) had taken the last available room for herself and her children. What would they do when the next caller appealed for sanctuary? Only a couple of hours after that woman's arrival another had rung and asked, with such hope and innocence, 'Can I come and stay with you? Can I bring my baby?' And then, when Sylvia had asked for details of her problem, 'Would I get a flat for myself and my baby?'

Some had such optimistic expectations, others almost none. Some wanted no more than a listening ear, another human being to confide in, while there was always one who thought that once she had taken that initial small step – that vast, enormous, almost impossible step – all else would follow: substantial accommodation be found for her, the law invoked on her behalf, the man who was the author of her troubles chastised, warned and brought to behave as she believed he would when first she threw in her lot with his.

What became of the ones who phoned in but never went to the police or the Social Services? The one with the battered face, for instance? And what about the woman called Anne who had laughed that dreadful bitter laugh when Sylvia mentioned psychological abuse and who had sounded so terrified when she saw her husband coming in from the garden?

What had been her fate when he confronted her and perhaps understood whom she had been phoning? Had he hit her again? Injured her again? And what of the baby she had mentioned? Where did that baby come into all this? It worried Sylvia, it kept her awake at night, lying beside the nice, kind, dull man she had ceased to love long ago. He was as likely to raise his hand to her, she thought, as he was to change into the interesting, exciting and charming lover she had expected him to be when she married him. A lot of those abusive spouses and partners, 'fiancés' and boyfriends were charming men – courteous, considerate and altogether delightful to all but the women they lived with. Sylvia wondered why this was. She had asked her father what he thought when she called round last evening to collect Robin and Ben.

'To throw a blanket of deceit over their true activities maybe,' he had replied. 'Only you'll think that so psychologically unsound I hesitate to say it.'

'Yes, it can't be that,' she had said in her dismissive way. 'That's ridiculous,' then wished she'd been nicer to him as she often did wish.

He made considerable efforts to behave as if he loved her as much as he loved her sister. She noticed the efforts but her awareness didn't make her feel tenderly towards him. She thought he ought not to prefer Sheila. Why did he? She loved her two sons equally, she made no difference between them, for she genuinely had no favourite.

He'd gone on talking to her as if she hadn't snapped at him. 'We've got a meeting set up for next Wednesday. The ACCD and I, and a couple of people from the Regional Crime Squad and a woman called Griselda Cooper from The Hide. It's to discuss methods of supplying those mobiles to women in need.'

Confiding in her, she thought, making a conscious effort to talk about things he calculated she'd be interested in.

'Do you know Ms Cooper?'

She observed the 'Ms', uncharacteristically used. A placating tactic, no doubt. 'Well, of course I do,' she said sharply. 'We haven't got a staff of hundreds, more's the pity.'

Now, lying wakeful beside Neil, she remembered her sharpness. She was too old for this behaviour. What was wrong with her, anyway, that she couldn't get on with her own husband and her own father? Her own mother, come to that. She was great with children. She was marvellous with the disadvantaged, the poor, the socially excluded. Everyone said so. Why not with her kind, forbearing father? And then a thought so daring and bold came to her that she sat bolt upright in bed. Hadn't she always maintained, hadn't she been taught this in therapy, that the proper thing to do in such circumstances, was to 'talk it through'? Why, then, not talk it through with her father?

She said it aloud, half waking Neil, so that he muttered at her, 'What's the matter? What's wrong?'

Talking to him of their differences had only ever resulted in his retorting that there was nothing to talk about, they were incompatible, that was all, but must remain together for their sons' sake. She looked at him in the dim half-light of dawn, at his closed eyes, the frown lines on his forehead that never relaxed, then she bent over and gently kissed his cheek. He smiled in his sleep. That smile brought tears to her eyes and she thought, when he's asleep I still love him. She lay down again, close up beside him.

A beautiful day, the first really fine day for a month. The sky was blue, the sun shining and every blade of grass, every new leaf, every spring flower bright and fresh, fed by weeks of rain. Wexford and Dora were going to London by train to shop, to visit the Bonnard exhibition at the Tate and in the evening see Sheila in the revival of Somerset Maugham's *Home and Beauty* at the Theatre Royal, Haymarket. Because it was such nice weather they walked to the station, discussing on the way whether they would have to leave immediately after the curtain fell in order to catch the last train home or if the play would end early enough for them to have a glass of champagne with Sheila in her dressing-room.

Burden was in his garden. His wife had planted box all around a formal flowerbed and now he had to decide how to trim it. To cut it square or up to a point? To turn each small bush into a ball? He doubted if he was capable of this last. Wasn't it, anyway, too early in the year to cut it at all? Perhaps he should just trim off the bits that stuck out. He decided to leave it for now and mow the lawn instead.

On the Muriel Campden Estate the street sign had been repainted and the loop in the P of Puck restored entire. It wouldn't last, as Hayley Lawrie remarked to Kate Burton on their way to the Crownes' house to ask Lizzie Cromwell to accompany them to the new shopping arcade in Myringham. Kate had just had her sixteenth birthday and wanted to spend the fifty pounds her father and stepmother and two half-brothers had sent her for a birthday present.

Lizzie, who hadn't been to school since her abduction and didn't intend to go back, said she couldn't come out because she was pregnant and had to rest. The two girls were astounded at her news, astounded, delighted and somewhat overawed. Details were demanded. Who, why and when? Lizzie had scarcely begun to answer when Colin Crowne came in, lighting a cigarette from the stub of the last one. He had overheard Lizzie say she couldn't come out and, anxious to get rid of her, said what was she, simple or something? Of course she must go, it would do her good, they weren't living in

117

'olden times'. Kate, who fancied Colin, cast him languishing looks, of which he took no notice, having other fish to fry.

When the girls had gone, he and his wife went down the road to call on Brenda Bosworth, the mother of three small children. The young Bosworths were out playing, unsupervised, in York Park with a number of other children from the estate. Colin and Debbie and Brenda Bosworth walked to the end of Puck Road and into Oberon Road where they rang the doorbell of Tommy Smith's house. Suzanne withdrew the bolts and opened the door but kept the chain on. This allowed it to stand about six inches ajar.

'Where is he?' asked Colin Crowne.

'What's that to you?' said Suzanne.

'Is he inside?'

'Maybe he is and maybe he isn't.'

'We want a straight answer to a straight question.' Brenda Bosworth elbowed Colin aside and tried to get sight of the hallway behind Suzanne. 'And that question is,' she cried theatrically, 'where is the infamous paedophile, Thomas Smith?'

'Fuck off the lot of you,' said Suzanne and slammed the door in her face.

Undaunted, they went round the back, Colin first, with the two women following. The house was semi-detached, with a gate of wire netting on a wooden frame between the side wall and the fence dividing this garden from next door's. Colin kicked the gate open and they walked through into the back garden. It presented a startling contrast to those on either side of it, both of which were trim, with neat lawns and flowerbeds. The Smiths' grew nettles, thistles and docks as luxuriantly as the next-door gardens grew tulips and wallflowers. In among the weeds, where the neighbours on one side had a bird-bath, lay a rusty iron bedstead.

Colin, Debbie and Brenda took no notice of any of this. Having peered at the front window as they passed and seen that the curtains were drawn, they now made for the french windows. Through these they saw Garry Wills, the man they knew as Suzanne's fiancé, watching television and a yard from him, in an armchair, a much older man who was doing nothing at all, just staring at the opposite wall. He was short and stocky, with a bloated, puffy face and iron-grey hair, surprisingly long and luxuriant. The hands that lay slack in his lap were large and thickly veined, his nails as thick and yellow as hooves. He was dressed in grey flannel trousers far too big for him and a blue and white striped T-shirt far too young for him.

Debbie Crowne banged on the window. Garry Wills turned his head and scowled at her. The other man moved not at all but continued to stare straight ahead of him, even his hands remaining perfectly still on his bony knees.

'We've seen you, Tommy Smith,' Debbie shrieked. 'We know it's you.'

'We know you're in there,' said Colin, as if Smith were hiding in a cupboard. 'Don't think you can get away with this.'

Suzanne Smith's fiancé turned his eyes back to the screen. Smith stayed immobile. He might have been a waxwork of himself. At a loss how to act, Colin and Debbie Crowne and Brenda Bosworth walked away back to the front of the house where, in the street, they encountered two women carrying sheets of cardboard mounted on broom handles. One said, *Paedophile Go Away* and the other, *Protect Our Children*. The banner still rested, like a belt, round the waist of the tower. Colin persuaded the women to

119

join forces with him, Debbie and Brenda, whereupon the lot of them made their way into York Park where they collected all the children playing on the swings, see-saws and climbing frames, and brought them back, protesting, to Oberon Road.

With the exception of Brenda Bosworth they assembled outside the Smith house, chanting, 'Ban the paedo' and 'Save our children', to the tune of 'Men of Harlech'. Very soon heads appeared out of the windows of the tower and the neighbours came out of their houses to swell their numbers. Brenda Bosworth went back to her own house where she phoned the *Kingsmarkham Courier*. No one was in the offices except the woman who took the small ads but she gave Brenda Brian St George's home number. Brenda phoned him and, showing some contempt for a newspaper that only appeared once a week, asked how she could get hold of *Independent Television News*. He would do that, St George said, gladly abandoning his earlier plans to spend the day at a point-to-point.

A train crash, owing to a signal failure on the line between Bath and Bristol, occupied the media that Saturday to the exclusion of almost all other news. Almost all, because at approximately the same time as the engine of the local train ploughed into the last carriage of the Paddington-to-Bristol *INTERCITY*, a bomb exploded in a Belfast pub, killing no one but injuring four people. Therefore television and radio showed little interest in the Kingsmarkham fracas and although both the *Sunday Mirror* and the *Mail on Sunday* responded favourably to Brian St George's frenzied efforts to get his story recognised as major, nothing of what he had written appeared in their pages on the following day.

There having been a football match of international

significance on the Saturday afternoon, occupying a television channel from three till five, most of the residents of Puck, Ariel and Oberon Roads, occupied in watching it, had no inclination to follow Colin and Debbie Crowne and Brenda Bosworth into battle.

'A bit of a damp squib' was the comment of a peace-loving neighbour of the Smiths, who had watched the Crowne–Bosworth activities and listened for as long as he could bear it to the chanting. But at five to three, just before the soccer was due to start, he walked round to York Street where he encountered two police officers on the beat, PC Martin Dempsey and WPC Lydia Wingate.

They went back with him to Oberon Road and advised the chanters and banner carriers to go home. Colin Crowne argued with them but not for long. The children who had been removed from York Park were whinging about missing their lunch and noisily demanding food, so by three fifteen everyone had departed or 'dispersed to their homes', as PC Dempsey put it.

He and Lydia Wingate went into the tower and up in the lift to the second floor where they banged on the door of a flat tenanted by John and Rochelle Keenan. Martin Dempsey asked them to take the banner down. Expecting a refusal, he got meek acquiescence – John Keenan would have agreed to anything so long as he could watch the soccer – and by the time Dempsey and Wingate were on their way back to York Street, Keenan had sent Rochelle round to the neighbours and together they had removed the strip of cloth with its inflammatory lettering. On the corner, Dempsey looked back and saw to his surprise and gratification that it had gone.

Not in all this time had Tommy Smith shown his face at any window or door of number 16 Oberon Road. Suzanne Smith ventured out at four and came back three-quarters of an hour later with two carrier bags of shopping. The place was dead, not a soul about, for everyone was watching the match, including her father and her fiancé. Garry Wills left the house alone at seven to go to the pub, as was his habit, but instead of the Crown and Anchor in York Street, his usual venue, he thought it wiser to go further afield to the Rat and Carrot, where no one knew him.

The Sunday papers were full of the bomb and the rail crash. With her morning tea Wexford took them upstairs to his wife who was having a lie-in after her late night, but first he checked that there was nothing in them about Smith. A mile away, in the triangle of streets with the central tower, all was as yet calm. The banner had disappeared. The curtains in the front window of 16 Oberon Road remained drawn. At ten Colin Crowne was still in bed, sleeping off a hangover, the result of drinking round at Brenda Bosworth's until the small hours with Brenda and her live-in lover Miroslav Zlatic. Brenda and Miroslav were also still asleep, so the two small boys and the small girl had got up on their own, got their breakfast unaided and taken themselves off to York Park with two little Keenans and three children called Hebden from Ariel Road.

Saturday had been one of the most enjoyable days of Lizzie Cromwell's life. For once she had been fêted and admired. Hayley had bought her ice-cream and Kate, having treated them all to lunch out of her birthday money, persuaded her to have a vodka and blackcurrant to 'build her up'. She had to look after herself now she was pregnant, they said. After several illegal drinks in a pub that boasted it never closed, they went back to Kate's mother's flat on the Stowerton Road, had fish and chips and mushy peas fetched in by Kate's brother Darryl, and watched a video of *LA Confidential*.

Lizzie hadn't got home till nearly midnight. She expected trouble but none came, for, as Debbie said, 'It's too late for that, isn't it?'

And Colin said, 'No point in shutting the stable door after the bloody horse has bolted.'

Next day looked like being nearly as good, for soon after ten Kate and Hayley called for her with another girl whose name was Charlotte. This Charlotte, as well as being over six feet tall and stunningly beautiful, with red hair that reached to her waist, knew hundreds of boys, including four who all had motor bikes and were coming over from Pomfret to meet up by the bandstand at eleven. The four girls all went down to the High Street, and bought Twix bars and crisps from the only shop in the town centre open on a Sunday, then they made their way into the park.

The day's promise was destined not to be fulfilled, for the boys failed to turn up. Lizzie and Kate and Hayley and Charlotte hung about the bandstand for a long time, eating their crisps and chocolate, and eventually lying down on the grass to listen to Lizzie's account of the origin of her pregnancy. Each time she told this story she gave a different account of events and by this time she had invented three possible fathers for the child. Hayley noticed this and pointed it out, but Lizzie said not to argue with her, she mustn't be upset in her condition.

When it was obvious the boys weren't coming, they all got up and trailed back. Not the way they had come, for that would have brought them out into the High Street, but via the children's playground, which was in that part of the park closest to the Muriel Campden Estate. A young Keenan and a young Bosworth were on the swings, another Bosworth and two Hebdens were on the climbing frame and the rest of them were kicking a ball about. The four girls lingered and Hayley said she was going down the slide, she'd never dared to when she was little.

Most of the houses in Oberon Road backed on to the park but only those numbered between 14 and 19 actually overlooked the playground. Hayley, descending the slide for the second time, looked up and saw a man standing at an upstairs window, apparently staring at the children in the playground. It wasn't number 16 and it wasn't Tommy Smith, but the man next door but one at number 18, the one who had fetched the police on the previous afternoon. Tony Mitchell was six inches taller than Smith and twenty years younger but Hayley didn't let these minor matters bother her. Descending with a whoosh, arms and legs in the air, she screamed out, 'The paedo! The paedo's up there, watching us!' The other girls took up the cry and so did the children, bored by now with what the playground had on offer. With Hayley in the lead, they started back for the Muriel Campden Estate, running now, and all yelling, 'The paedo, the paedo!'

They pounded down the passage that led into Oberon Road, Lizzie running with the best of them, her condition forgotten. Nine children and four teenagers all shouting at the tops of their voices make a considerable noise. Heads appeared at windows in Oberon Road and Puck Road, doors flew open and people came out into their front gardens to see what was going on.

'That old paedo's up at his window watching the kids,' Charlotte gasped and Lizzie cried equally breathlessly, 'He's watching them and he's going to come down and get them!'

Brenda Bosworth, who had come out in her night-dress with a coat over it, let out a loud scream and seized hold of her Sean, her Dean and her Kelly, clutching all three of them to her in a protective embrace, but let them go again when Colin Crowne began ushering all the children into his own house, declaring that they would be safe there until 'something had been done about it'. He slammed the front door on them, and he and Debbie marched up the road to number 16.

By this time John and Rochelle Keenan had appeared on the lawn that surrounded the tower, where they were joined by a dozen other people, two of whom, young men, had armed themselves, one with a length of lead piping and the other with a brick. The banners with *Paedophile Go Away* and *Protect Our Children* now reappeared, carried by Joe Hebden and a pal of his who had dropped in to talk about a twenty-five-year-old Triumph Herald he was trying to sell for two hundred pounds. The Triumph Herald man was only the first of many strangers to the estate who came to join in the fray. How they knew about it, how news of it had reached and fired them, remained a mystery. But by the time the majority of Muriel Campden parents had gathered on the lawn where Brenda Bosworth was haranguing them on 'this menace in our midst', people were streaming into Ariel Road from all parts of King-smarkham, most on foot but some in cars or on motor bikes, as well as a party in a minibus.

The peacemaker, Tony Mitchell, whom Hayley had mistaken for Tommy Smith, saw it all but this time did nothing. Last evening, while he was out watering his front garden, an old woman had gone by, spat at him and called him a Quisling, an epithet he was far too young to understand. He hadn't liked it, though, and he hadn't liked his neighbour at 19 turning her back when he said good-evening, so he resolved to stick his neck out no further. He told his wife not to get involved and she said she wouldn't. She just quietly popped across the road to the tower, borrowed her sister Rochelle Keenan's Camcorder and, from an upstairs window, began recording the whole thing on videotape.

The three streets were now packed with cars. Drivers, trying to get in through the approach road from York Street, left their hands on horns and shouted out of their windows. One of them was Brian St George, who abandoned his car to block the roadway and went off into Oberon Road on foot. The crowd on the lawn cheered and clapped Brenda Bosworth, and two men had the idea of carrying her on their shoulders to take up a position outside number 16.

There they stood, flanked by the banner carriers, while something like a hundred people assembled behind them. Things were still quite orderly, with the crowd merely chanting once more, this time to 'Abide With Me', the tune a suggestion of a Manchester United supporter and not because it was Sunday. Who threw the first brick was never established. The stack of bricks stood in the front garden of 21 Oberon Road, whose occupants were out for the day, ready for use in the building of a wall to separate their lawn from the pavement and replace the wire fence. The bricklayer had left them there on Friday, covered up with a plastic sheet.

John Keenan pulled off this sheet but whether he actually picked up a brick no one knew. But somebody did and hurled it at number 16. This first brick, flying past Brenda Bosworth's ear, caused her bearers to duck and the banner carriers to retreat, but it missed its mark and crashed against the front wall of the Smiths' house instead of through the window.

The noise it made slightly daunted everyone and the crowd hesitated.

It was at this point that a man called Carl Meeks realised that there were fewer children about than there should have been. Notably, his own son. He shouted out, 'Where's my Scott?' and John Keenan took up the cry with, 'What's happened to my Gary?'

Brenda Bosworth jumped down from her bearers' shoulders, assured herself with a glance round that her children were missing and screamed out, 'He's got them! The paedo's got them in there!'

All the little Bosworths, Keenans, Hebdens and Scott Meeks were inside the Crowne house where, although any of them could have opened the front door and escaped, they preferred to remain and enjoy themselves eating the crisps they found in the kitchen and watching one of Colin Crowne's porn videos. Colin had shut them in there, but no one knew that and somehow Colin had forgotten all about it. So he too began shouting that Smith had got the children and he too threw a brick. This time it didn't miss but went through the front window of number 16. A hail of bricks followed it and when the bricks ran out the crowd threw stones they picked out of the tower flowerbeds. Someone could be heard shrieking inside the Smith house. It was Suzanne herself but Linda Meeks claimed to recognise the voice of her son Scott, whereupon the crowd surged forward up to the gate of number 16, to kick that gate down, to trample down the flimsy wire fence and form a human battering ram against the front door.

The police arrived just as the door went down. Suzanne had rung them when the first brick was thrown. She would have phoned before but for her fiancé saying that if anyone had told him someone belonging to him would call the police he'd never have believed them. What Smith thought no one knew. He sat silently in his upright chair, doing nothing except for getting up sometimes to make himself another cup of tea. Between nine in the morning and three in the afternoon he had drunk fifteen cups.

The police dispersed the crowd and arrested John Keenan, Brenda Bosworth and Miroslav Zlatic, all of whom would be charged with making an affray and causing criminal damage. They sent a carpenter round to rehang the front door of number 16 Oberon Road and board up the broken windows. Sergeant Joel Fitch had a long talk with its occupants about the situation and their future, or rather he talked in Smith's presence, but whether Smith listened or cared was another matter. Should he remain where he was or be moved? And if moved, taken where? Possibly a police station would be the best, though temporary, sanctuary for him. But not Kingsmarkham, where the only accommodation was two cells, both currently occupied by John Keenan and Miroslav Zlatic, Brenda having been released because there was no one to look after her children.

Those children, along with the small Keenans and Hebdens, were not discovered for some hours. By the time Debbie and Colin and Lizzie got home, they had left, having consumed everything edible in the house, helped themselves to the 500 duty-free cigarettes Colin had brought back from a day trip to France and gone down to Kingsbrook weir for a swim.

When things had quietened down, Shirley Mitchell came out of her house and on to the green where she picked up all the litter dropped during the course of the afternoon and put it into a plastic bin liner: crisp packets and chocolate wrappers and a couple of Coke cans. There was no one about to hear her angry mutterings on the theme of those too ignorant to value their environment.

Later in the evening a man came out of number 16 Oberon Road, carrying a suitcase. It was Suzanne Smith's fiancé and he was heading for the station to catch the last train for London. He had a pal in Balham he could stay with. When it had 'all blown over' he might come back, he told Suzanne, but the way things were the stress was too much for him.

Wexford watched it all on television, on the Sunday night news at ten to nine. Most of the footage came from an amateur video and this was acknowledged, though no names were mentioned. He thought it unhelpful that included in the news item was a still of Thomas Smith, one of those rogues' gallery photographs that make the subject look like a hideous and debased thug. Of course, it was quite likely that Smith was just that, he thought with a sigh, and he hoped he wouldn't have to meet him but feared he soon would.

The sight of the Smiths' house, even after the boarding-up had taken place, shocked Dora deeply. Such a thing would have been unthinkable when she first came to live in Kingsmarkham and the place was a quiet, law-abiding, peaceful country town.

'Not all that law-abiding,' said Wexford.

'Nothing like it is now, Reg, you know that.'

'Yes, of course I do. What are we going to do with this chap, this Smith? Lock him up for ever?'

'Wouldn't that be best? It makes me shudder to think of him.'

'It makes us all shudder,' said Wexford.

Rumour ran wild around the Muriel Campden Estate. Shirley Mitchell had received £5000 for her video, she had received £10,000, she had received no more than £500, she had got nothing. It wasn't even her video that had been used but another made by a professional cameraman secreted into the Keenans' flat. Tony Mitchell had personally smashed his sister-in-law's movie camera and as a result he and Shirley were splitting up.

The children had been snatched by Smith but Colin Crowne had rescued them. Or only the Bosworth children had been snatched and it was Miroslav Zlatic who had done the rescuing. Smith had committed suicide, or had told Suzanne he intended to commit suicide. Far from being charged with anything, Brenda Bosworth was to be recommended for a bravery medal.

All these stories proliferated. More important and more dangerous was one that began to do the rounds on Monday morning. The man who had been seen leaving 16 Oberon Road at nine thirty the previous night wasn't Suzanne's fiancé but Smith himself. One of the Keenans' neighbours knew that for a fact because he had seen Gary Wills at his bedroom window at ten. Another older man, one of the original residents on the Muriel Campden Estate, recognised Smith; he would have known his walk anywhere and the way he carried his suitcase in his left hand.

Where had he gone? No one knew but that didn't stop them guessing.

# Chapter 8

'There's no house within twenty minutes' drive of Kingsmarkham that answers Rachel's description,' Wexford said. 'She made it up. For some reason, she doesn't want us to find Vicky and Jerry.'

'If Vicky and Jerry exist,' said Burden.

'Vicky does. Both girls admit to Vicky. So what is true and what is false? Certainly it's false that Lizzie is only two weeks pregnant, she's more like three months. And certainly it's true that Rachel wanted to keep her engagement at the Rotten Carrot but was prevented by someone or something. Both of them were taken somewhere but perhaps not to the same place. Whoever took Lizzie away managed to frighten her. If she told they would find her and punish her, something like that. But that wouldn't succeed with Rachel, so I'm wondering if while she was with this person or these people she did something she regards as shameful and she doesn't want it to come out.'

'We stand a chance of finding out if they take another girl.'

'God forbid.'

'You're always telling me where things come from,' said Burden. 'I mean expressions, quotes, that sort of thing. I bet you don't know where what you've just said comes from.'

'Where what comes from?'

'God forbid.'

131

'*What*? Oh, I see. Well, where does it come from?'

'Paul. The apostle Paul. He says it all the time in his letters.'

'How do *you* know.'

'I don't know. I just know.'

Wexford had expected another girl to be abducted on Saturday evening. While he was in London and next day during the Muriel Campden crisis his thoughts had reverted from time to time to Rachel and Lizzie, to Vicky and Jerry, and the mystery house, and he wouldn't have been at all surprised this morning to hear of another missing girl. But there had been nothing. And what was to be done about Smith overrode all other considerations.

On the Muriel Campden Estate things were quiet. Miroslav Zlatic and John Keenan with Brenda Bosworth were currently appearing in Kingsmarkham Magistrates Court but Wexford knew they would all be put on probation or bound over to keep the peace and released by lunch-time. What would be the result of Smith's showing his face outside 16 Oberon Road? He couldn't remain shut up in there for ever. And there was no knowing when some other Muriel Campden firebrand would decide that his children were in danger and make a renewed assault on the house. Wexford was beginning to revise his opinion of the estate as being different from its inner-city counterparts and its occupants law-abiding. On the other hand, wouldn't most parents of small and sub-teenage children rise in wrath and fear when a Smith came among them?

Superintendent Rogers of the uniformed branch had told him that Smith, on leaving prison, had made a private appeal for protection. He wouldn't guarantee, he said, that he was no longer a danger. He couldn't say what would happen if he had access to children. At any rate, if nothing worse than that,

132

he liked looking at them. It gave him great pleasure to watch them and he couldn't rightly see why he should relinquish that pleasure. It did no harm. Apart from the boy who died – and that, he averred, was a tragic accident – Thomas Smith maintained that he had never done any harm. He was one of those paedophiles – ' "Paedos," ' said Wexford scathingly. 'A new word enters the English language' – who insisted that children, even very small ones, desire, enjoy and need sexual relations. 'He asked for it, pestered me for it,' was his principal defence.

And if Wexford had been inclined to pity Smith, it was this attitude more than anything that made him harden his heart. 'Evil' was a word very freely bandied about these days and he looked on it with suspicion, but Smith and what he did were evil, that he knew. And when he heard how Smith justified his actions, even at this late stage, when he heard that the old man still made excuses for himself on such grounds, he felt much the same kind of fury as that displayed by the Muriel Campden residents. If his own grandsons lived anywhere near Smith's home, wouldn't he at any rate want to react as they reacted?

Still, if in no more than the interests of public order and civilised behaviour, the paedophile must be protected from his neighbours, just as little boys must be protected from him. Superintendent Rogers was in favour of removing him to Myringham, either to the police station or to the Mid-Sussex Constabulary Headquarters. Both had accommodation that could be temporarily adapted to house him. For, as Rogers said, obnoxious as the whole idea of the man and his activities might be, he had (in the Superintendent's own words) 'paid his debt to society' and was technically an innocent person, who could not legitimately be lodged in a police cell without some adaptations being made to it.

The Assistant Chief Constable Designate wanted him left where he was, at home, in his own house. For the present. His theory was that once the ringleaders, in this case John Keenan, Miroslav Zlatic and Brenda Bosworth, had appeared in court, been dealt with and severely warned, there would be no more problems. This was a community of country folk whose recent forebears had lived in cottages in villages and hamlets, who had kept their sheep and looked after the landowner's game. Such people were naturally law-abiding, peace-loving and tolerant. 'Besides,' he said, 'they'll get used to it. They will accept. They'll see no harm comes to their children and everything will simmer down.'

Detective Constable Lynn Fancourt had established a pleasant relationship with Lizzie Cromwell, albeit one that was sympathetic on her part and sycophantic on Lizzie's. Lizzie called her by her first name and felt herself privileged, even daring, to do so. On Monday afternoon Lynn had managed, in the course of a friendly talk, to extract from Lizzie an admission that she had in fact accepted a lift from the woman called Vicky and been told that Vicky drove a white car, registration number and make unknown. It was a triumph for Lynn and she decided to leave it there and revert to the subject of Lizzie's pregnancy, of which she deeply disapproved. A termination was what she advocated and as soon as possible.

Debbie said it was a funny thing but she had just missed the social worker who had been round to see Lizzie and asked her to take part in their new project. Lizzie was proud to have been one of the girls selected. No, Debbie said, she hadn't said anything about Lizzie's pregnancy and Lizzie hadn't, it didn't seem necessary and, anyway, it wasn't the social worker's business.

By now Lynn had guessed that the project was Kingsmarkham Social Services' initiative to discourage teenage pregnancies, a campaign called Project Infant Simulator, and when she went into the living-room where Lizzie was she found her with a life-size baby doll on her lap. The doll wore a Babygro over a disposable napkin and little white socks.

'I'm to keep him for the week,' said Lizzie. 'His name's Jodi.'

She seemed bemused. As well she might be, thought Lynn. She asked, 'Is he a sort of robot?' And then she realised Lizzie wouldn't know what that was, so she said, 'Does he cry and pee, and need feeding and all that?'

'He's done some crying. I changed him. I'm learning how to look after him.'

Lynn saw that Lizzie, and perhaps Debbie too, had missed the point. The provision of Jodi to selected candidates or volunteers was to demonstrate to adolescent girls the hard work, lack of sleep and overall responsibility caring for a baby entailed. Thus, they might think twice before engaging in unprotected sexual activity. Lizzie, on the other hand, saw it as training for her future.

'Well, I'm afraid you're in for some sleepless nights,' said Lynn. 'How many weeks pregnant do you think you are?' She asked it conversationally, in a friendly instead of hectoring tone and Lizzie, preoccupied with staring into Jodi's fathomless blue eyes, answered her just as casually, 'I reckon fourteen weeks, that's what Mum says. I haven't seen since February.'

Interpreting this last statement with some difficulty but pretty sure she had got it right, Lynn said, 'Jerry had nothing to do with it, did he?'

Lizzie's muttered answer was lost in a sudden sob from Jodi, who began to cry without prior warning, as indeed real babies do. Saying she had to get his bottle, she handed the robot to Lynn and went outside. DC Fancourt was left in the ridiculous situation of being landed with a weeping baby doll, down whose plastic cheeks water trickled and who mouthed piteous whimpers.

She got up and walked it up and down, the way she remembered her mother doing with her infant brother. Jodi continued to sob and weep, and thrash his arms about. His crying had reached a crescendo by the time Lizzie came back. She took him tenderly into her arms, murmured to him and slid the teat into his mouth. A sweet smile came to her lips as the robot sucked and she turned to Lynn with such a naked look of love and pride that DC Fancourt almost flinched. To question her now seemed like interrupting with practicalities the celebration of some holy rite. Lizzie, with a lump of plastic on her lap, was earth mother, priestess and the essence of sacred maternity all at once.

So Lynn waited, rather uneasily, until the bottle had been emptied, deciding to speak when Lizzie began removing Jodi's napkin and fastening on another. After all, no one, however moved by the girl's devotion – curiously it brought to Lynn's mind those orphaned ducklings who, imprinted early, attach themselves to a mother dog as surrogate – could become sentimental over these hygienic measures. 'You were going to tell me about Jerry, Lizzie,' she said.

'He never touched me,' Lizzie said. 'Never touched me and never said a word.' She realised she had betrayed herself and put one hand over her mouth.

Lynn said casually, 'Was it a nice house?'

Jodi replaced in his carrying cot, Lizzie turned on her a resentful look. 'I'm not to say, you know that.

They'll get to me and punish me. They'll drill holes in my knees, they said, they'll break my fingers. If they hurt me I could lose my baby, Mum says.'

'So you've told your mum?'

'No, I haven't,' Lizzie shouted. 'I just said, I'd like a nice bungalow like that, modern like and out in the real country, and not joined on to next door.'

'And Jerry never spoke to you, is that right?'

Lizzie said with bitterness, 'Never spoke a word, but they never do. *He* never did. Just "Leezee, Leezee".'

About to ask her to explain, Lynn was interrupted by the entry of Debbie, fetched in by the sound of Lizzie's raised voice. 'What's the matter? What have you been saying to her now?'

'I'm just leaving, Mrs Crowne. Lizzie has been very helpful.'

'Oh, has she? Well, wonders will never cease. To change the subject, I thought you lot might like to know that old paedo's gone. There you are, you didn't know, did you?' Debbie smiled complacently. 'It's funny how the police never know what the rest of the world does. He's gone, left last night. There's dozens of people saw him. He had a suitcase, one of them on wheels, and he was running like all the devils in hell was after him and pulling that case behind him. It's not likely any folks here'd stop him going, is it? Good riddance to bad rubbish is what I say. It's no good asking me', she went on, as if Lynn had asked, 'where he went, because I haven't a clue. Chucked himself under a train, hopefully, only if he'd done that there'd be a body. What amazes me is he's the criminal, he's the one ought to be hung, but it's poor John and Brenda and that Miro-what's-he-called that's up in court.'

When this conversation was relayed to him, 'If they believe he's gone, so much the better,' said

137

Wexford. 'That way we'll have a bit of hush. Sooner or later they're going to find out he's still there but unless he goes out, and I doubt if he will, there'll be no trouble.'

'I thought you subscribed to Southby's view,' Burden said.

'I do in a way. But I know that crowds are the same the world over, in city centres and rustic paradises alike, and all subject to mob psychology. Shall we go out and have another look for a bungalow?'

They knew it was a bungalow now. Both girls wouldn't be lying, not in that particular way. Lizzie had called this one 'modern', which meant forgetting about the shingles. To Smith, as Lynn said, 'modern' might mean anything put up in his lifetime, but to Lizzie it would be no more than ten years old. And this one stood alone, without neighbours. They had asked her to come with them and try to point it out but Lizzie refused. She felt ill, she said, and she was frightened, she might have that much-dreaded miscarriage. Her mum had once 'brought it on' by going for a ride in a truck on a bumpy road.

They drove to the villages along the abandoned bypass route, as far north as Myfleet, then south to Flagford, Pickvale and Sayle. Three bungalows were possibilities and one of these was soon dismissed. No one, not even Lizzie Cromwell, would call a converted train carriage, even though the conversion was recent and the house stood alone at the end of a lane, 'modern' or 'lovely'. But the bungalow on the outskirts of Pickvale was another matter. Planning restrictions forbade new building there except on a site where a previous house had been. This one probably had the vestiges of the original cottage incorporated somewhere inside it, but its outside was pristine ivory rendering, white paint and black weatherboard. No other house was in sight. Its garden was young, bleak and labour-saving, more paving than lawn, and the trees and bushes of a kind that would never grow big.

Burden rang the doorbell and they waited. A young woman answered it, a young man standing behind her. Somehow, as soon as he saw them, Wexford knew this wasn't the place. They showed their warrant cards and the young couple studied them earnestly. Unless they were consummate actors, they weren't lying when they said they knew no one called Vicky, had never heard of Jerry and the car they owned was a black BMW, presently in their garage, but which Wexford and Burden were welcome to look at.

On the way through Pickvale, taking the lane for Sayle, Burden said he thought the whole thing was a waste of time. No one had been harmed, both Rachel and Lizzie were home safely and the girls themselves were obviously anxious that no further steps should be taken.

'And that makes it all right, does it?' Wexford had been looking out of the window across the meadows to the start of the downs, but now he turned round. 'The law has been broken, and broken twice, in a very serious way. Two young women have been forcibly taken from their homes and families, and falsely imprisoned for three days. Two police investigations have been mounted at enormous cost to the taxpayer and you say no harm has been done.'

Burden would have liked to tell him not to go on so and would have done but for the presence of Donaldson the driver, whose tongue might be discreet but whose ears were not. Instead he said, 'Prolonging that investigation is just costing the taxpayer more. And for what? What kind of ...'

Wexford interrupted him. 'Look at that! That's it!'

Donaldson pulled in to the verge. They had stopped outside a house previously seen but dismissed because it had no shingles on its front. The bungalow, called Sunnybank, stood indeed upon a bank, planted with alpines and small junipers, which would have been sunny if the sky were not heavily overcast. In the middle of its front lawn grew, not a conifer as Rachel had said, but a deciduous tree with foliage the like of which Wexford had never seen before, pale yellow-green leaves shaped like a square joined to a triangle. Those leaves would, of course, have been only in bud when she was there. If she had been there, if this was the house.

'We've seen it before,' said Burden. 'We didn't give it a second glance.'

'Because the tree was wrong and there were no shingles. But we know Rachel has lied and Lizzie didn't mention shingles or a tree. This place is just what would appeal to a girl like Lizzie.'

It was dazzling white with a pink front door, unsuitable Georgian pillared portico and roof of jade-green pantiles. The separate garage was a little house in itself, also with pantiled roof and two small diamond-paned windows. In describing the house where she had been as two-storeyed, shingled and with a gravel drive, Rachel could hardly have diverged more from the truth. Had that been her purpose? To outline its opposite?

But again they were disappointed, though this time they went in, sat down and talked to Mrs Pauline Chorley for half an hour. She was in her fifties, a tall, thin woman with dyed ash-blonde hair, married to a businessman who commuted daily to London. He was there now and wouldn't be home till seven thirty. Mrs Chorley was a keen gardener, gardening occupied most of her time, that and the maintenance of her home in exquisite condition. She had painted the exterior herself last year and really thought it already needed doing again. White wasn't suitable for this country, the rain discoloured it so, but she did love white, she was crazy about it, couldn't have enough of it. And this preference showed in her furnishings of the large open-plan living–dining-room, the bright white net curtains, white carpets and cushions and fluffy rugs, and in her own clothes, the frosty white lace-trimmed blouse and glossy white pumps.

Her taste for white had its full scope in the kitchen, visible through double glass doors and as sparkling white as icebergs in an icy sea. Not in the garden, though. There she must have colour. And the view from the french windows confirmed this, the blaze of pink and orange azaleas, with the strident yellow of doronicum and Crown Imperials. It was Mrs Chorley who supplied the names, unasked.

'What's that tree in the front?'

'Lyriodendron tulipifera,' she said with perfect articulation.

Wexford said he hoped he would remember but rather doubted it. Didn't it have a common name?

'The tulip-flowering lyre tree, I suppose.' Mrs Chorley said it distastefully, as if she wondered at anyone wanting to sink so low as to call vegetation by English names. She had already told them she had never heard of Vicky or Jerry and had had no visitors to the house for months. 'I don't have time to entertain. The garden and the house take all my time. Drive? A car, d'you mean? My husband does that. I never learnt.'

And yet there was something, Wexford said when they were returning to Kingsmarkham, something he had missed or should have asked.

'That woman wouldn't have those two girls in her

house,' said Burden. 'Not in any circumstances, she wouldn't. They might make the carpets dirty. I'm sorry for that poor devil, Chorley.'

'Really? I've always thought you a bit of a fusspot about the house yourself.'

'I'm not a crazy fanatic,' said Burden huffily, 'thank you very much.'

'What is it we've failed to ask?' Wexford speculated, but Burden couldn't tell him.

Three years in the police force, ambitious and hoping for promotion, Lynn Fancourt still looked much younger than her twenty-five years. Her face was round and rosy, her eyes willow pattern china blue and her thick brown hair, short and with a fringe, cut like an old-fashioned child's under a pudding basin. People took her for eighteen and a drunk she'd arrested, for an offence against public order, asked her if her parents knew where she was at that time of night. Her home – some two hundred miles away from those parents – was the top half of a house in Framhurst with a carport at the end of the garden where she kept her Ford overnight.

Lynn usually went to work by car but lately, ever since the return of Rachel Holmes, the Fiesta had stayed in the carport. Lynn had caught the bus half-way and walked the rest. Going home was more carefully planned. One evening she walked half a mile or so to a lonely stretch of the Pomfret Road and waited at the bus-stop, not exactly thumbing for a lift but looking hopeful. On another she chose the Flagford Road where the traffic was light and the roadway darkened by overhanging trees.

The driver of the van which was the only vehicle that stopped for her, gave her such a lecherous look and was so repulsive that even if she had genuinely wanted a ride she would have turned him down.

Generally, she ended up catching the bus, but on the day she had visited Lizzie and seen her with Jodi the virtual baby, she accepted her first lift. It seemed entirely natural only to allow herself to get into a car driven by a woman. This one was middle-aged, grey-haired and friendly, her car a cream-coloured Honda. Not wanting to lead the woman to her own door, Lynn had said to drop her off in Savesbury.

Her excitement mounted when the driver took the first wrong turning and seemed to be heading in the direction of the old bypass. But she had only lost her way – 'I've no sense of direction whatsoever, my dear!' – and within ten minutes Lynn found herself set down in the middle of Savesbury village street, waving cheerfully to the departing Honda.

Then she had to walk the two miles home.

Some two hours later, Wexford was thinking about going to bed. The phone rang but it was a wrong number and he was replacing the receiver when the question he had forgotten to ask Mrs Chorley came back to him. Not so much a question, perhaps, as an *omission* in that house, which he had noticed subconsciously but had not commented on. There had been no telephone.

Or he hadn't seen one. He was trained to observe absences of things as well as their presence and he had seen no phone. These days that was so rare as to be an eccentricity. Rachel Holmes had said that the house to which she had been taken had no phone or she had been unable to find one ...

His own phone rang while he was standing there pondering. At this hour! And undoubtedly the wrong-number woman again.

He picked up the receiver and heard a voice he hadn't heard for years, the frightened child's voice of his mature, competent, controlled daughter Sylvia:

143

'Oh, Dad, something so horrible's happened. I know I'm a fool but – would you come, Dad? Would you?'

# Chapter 9

He pulled on a sweater instead of his tweed jacket
and got to The Hide a quarter of an hour later. There
he had difficulty in getting inside, due to the woman
who opened the door mistaking him for another
angry husband in search of his wife. After profuse
apologies and some relieved laughter, he found
Sergeant Fitch and PC Dempsey in the act of
arresting the man Sylvia had seen cutting the wire on
top of the wall. Quincy Miller had led them a dance
from one end of the house to the other, yelling,
'Tracy, where are you? I'm going to get you,' kicking
down two doors and punching a woman he had
never seen before and could not possibly have taken
for his wife. Tracy slept peacefully through it all and
so did her two daughters in the beds beside her.

Sylvia he found in the helpline room at the top of
the house, drinking tea and recovering from her two
confrontations with Miller, the first when he looked
up and met her eyes as he crossed the garden, the
second when he burst into this room, shook her till
her teeth chattered and bawled obscenities at her.
Wexford took her in his arms and held her in a long
comforting embrace.

After a minute or two, during which she clung to
him, she said, on a sob, 'Oh, Dad, and I thought I was
tough. All those years with the Social Services ...'

'No one', he said, 'is that tough. Believe me.'

She thought of her resolution to 'talk it through'

with him and how that no longer seemed necessary. Misery and terror were succeeded by a great calm, a warmth that spread through her like drinking something hot and strong. She caught his hand and held it.

'Show me the place,' he said. 'What's that list up there? Where are all these cuttings from?' And when she had taken him on a little tour of the room, 'What do you say when you answer the phone? What do you do?'

She told him about 'Anne' who had phoned some days before in great fear, the man who had apparently entered the room and how the phone had crashed down, and about the woman whose husband offered to stop hitting her if she went to a psychiatrist. Among her failures, those had been, so she told him about her successes too and her victories. When it got to midnight and Jill came to relieve her, Wexford said to leave her car and let him drive her home, he'd much rather she didn't drive, she could get Neil to bring her next time she was on duty. So he had driven her home, all the way out into the country, ten miles from Kingsmarkham, and seen her into the house and driven home himself, getting into bed beside Dora a few minutes before two.

It was because he was weary and a bit light-headed that he had decided to walk to work in the morning. For the fresh air and the exercise, healthy options Dr Akande was always telling him he needed. It was a beautiful day too, warm and still, the sun pleasantly hazy. He thought how pleasant it was when the litter on the pavements was fallen blossom and green pollen-dusted flowers instead of packaging and cigarette ends. In spite of sleeplessness – for he hadn't slept much after getting home – it had been a most satisfactory night, rewarding him with the affection of that difficult elder daughter whom, with luck, he might soon find he loved as much as her younger sister. At the police station he went so far as to walk upstairs, all four flights, instead of using the lift.

A brief on his desk attracted his eye and it was the first thing he read.

Action on Sex Offenders [it said].

An enhanced system for identifying and dealing with high-profile sex offenders released into the community was announced this week by the Home Secretary.

A new national steering group will be established, including representatives of the Home Office, the Association of Chief Police Officers and the Association of Chief Officers of Probation and sex offender treatment specialists.

The new group will:

Identify high-profile, difficult-to-place sex offenders while they are still in prison and assess the plans for their release;

Oversee their handling after they have been released; and

Consider any funding necessary to meet the likely additional accommodation costs. There has been obvious public concern about the way some high-profile sex offenders are released back into the community ...

You can say that again, Wexford said to himself, also reflecting that all this would be too late for Smith. But perhaps there had been a settling down on the Muriel Campden Estate. He was a great believer in people's ability to accept a situation through getting used to it. If Smith did nothing, and of course he would do nothing, if he became a high-profile offender keeping a low profile, his neighbours would do no more than ostracise him and his, and hold themselves aloof.

His reverie was interrupted by the entry into the room of Karen Malahyde. 'Another girl's gone missing, sir.'

Afterwards he regretted his facetiousness. 'Spirited away to a lovely bungalow with a tree in the front, I suppose?'

Karen didn't smile. 'I don't think so, sir. This is serious, it's a child and she's not quite three years old.'

Ploughman's Lane is Kingsmarkham's millionaires' row. Yet to the visitor it might appear not to be a street at all but rather a country road passing through woodland. And the woods of Sussex are the most beautiful in England, for the trees are taller, of more diverse kinds, their foliage more luxuriant, and among them grow the viburnum and the Wayfarer's Tree. Loveliest of all are the beeches with their branches like feathers, like spread green wings, and their trunks the smooth silvery grey of sealskin, neatest the round-crowned hornbeam whose natural shape looks as if the topiarist has been at work on it.

The great hills of the South Country
They stand along the sea;
And it's there walking in the high woods
That I could wish to be,
And the men that were boys when I was a boy
Walking along with me.

That was how Wexford felt when he came up here, though there was no sea, of course, the sea was twenty miles away. And the woods were full of houses now and had been since he was a boy. More had been added, that was all. But you still failed to see most of them until you looked, until you peered through a grove or copse, supposing some dwelling must be hiding itself behind the trees because there was a gate which told you so and a letter-box and perhaps even a name such as Woodland Lodge or The Beeches. Sylvia had once lived up here, when Neil's business was at its most prosperous, but even then her house had been among the more modest examples. The one he had come to call at now was among the more grandiose, with the tallest trees in its grounds, the longest drive, and the highest degree of invisibility from the road.

No greater contrast within a mile's radius could be found than that between this place and Glebe Road or the Muriel Campden Estate. Even those without radical leanings could hardly fail to notice it and be made, in spite of themselves, uneasy. Wexford thought of that contrast each time he came up here and as they drove along the approach to Woodland Lodge, a route to the house which was more like a country lane than a garage drive, he looked from side to side, with that same sense of the inequity of life.

The house that they reached was almost a mansion, an Arts and Crafts house dating from the first decade of the century, red brick with solid white facings, casement windows, a studded oak front door. The big double garage was evidently a conversion from the original coachhouse. Before he got out of the car he realised that from here it was quite impossible to see any neighbouring houses or for any neighbours to overlook it. This feature of Woodland Lodge, Ploughman's Lane, so advantageous to estate agents and desirable to house buyers, would be a hindrance to the police in their investigation.

He had known even before he was admitted and stood in the presence of the distraught mother and father, that this was a very different matter from the abductions of Lizzie Cromwell and Rachel Holmes.

149

The Devenishes' daughter had not been offered a lift or lured away but snatched by night from her own bed in her own bedroom in her parents' house. But that was not to say that the Cromwell and Holmes episodes were not forerunners of or rehearsals for this one.

Stephen Devenish had opened the door to Wexford and Karen Malahyde. He was very protective of his wife, intent at first on keeping her out of the investigation. She could tell them nothing, he said, she was far too upset, he didn't want her troubled, made to suffer more than she need. There was nothing she could tell them that he couldn't.

'I'm afraid I must talk to Mrs Devenish, sir,' Wexford said. 'We shan't upset her. I think she would want to help us.'

Devenish had a gracious manner, not apparently aggressive or assertive, and he gave a rueful smile as he nodded acceptance of what Wexford said. He took them into a lavishly furnished drawing-room, at one end of which french windows were open on to a terrace and a lawn. Beyond, the trees began, mature, even ancient trees, that had been here since long before the house was built, but even they were not tall enough to hide the distant blue sweep of the downs.

In the middle of a three-seater sofa upholstered in cream satin sat a small, thin woman with the pinched face and huge eyes of a flying fox. This marriage was an instance, Wexford could see at once, of that not uncommon phenomenon in which a tall, strikingly handsome man has married, and established a successful marriage with, a plain and insignificant woman. Stephen and Fay Devenish, he already knew, were both thirty-six, but while he looked in his early thirties she could have been taken for forty-five.

She got up when they entered the room and held

out her hand, gestures of a well-brought-up woman who needs more than the horror of that morning's discovery to make her forget her manners. She said in a low, sweet voice, 'Thank you for coming, it's good of you to come.'

'Sit down, darling,' Devenish said. 'You must take it easy, you have to conserve your strength.'

For what, Wexford wondered, but aloud he said, 'Your daughter, she's three years old, I believe?'

'Thirty-three months, to be precise,' said Devenish.

'And her name is – let me see – Sanchia?'

'That's right.'

'Have you any other children, Mr Devenish?'

'We have two sons. They're at school. I sent them off to school this morning, I thought it the best thing. They're called Edward and Robert, and they're twelve and ten.'

Karen said, 'Would you like to tell us what happened here last evening and this morning, Mrs Devenish?'

Although it was his wife who had been asked, Devenish said quickly, 'Last evening was just normal, an absolutely normal weekday evening. It was what happened in the night that was so – so horrendous, so terrible.' He sat down beside his wife and took her hand, drawing it on to his own knees. Next to her, he looked twice her size, a burly, though not fat, man, dark almost to swarthiness, with a Byronic head and the poet's striking features. 'Sanchia went to bed at seven as she always does and my wife read her a story, as she always does, everything was entirely normal.'

'I left the bedroom window open,' Fay Devenish said in a despairing voice, as one confessing to a dreadful solecism. 'It was a beautiful night and I left the window open. It didn't seem a dangerous thing to do, not in this place, not in England, in the summer.'

'Well, darling,' Devenish said, 'you know you do silly things sometimes.'

He spoke in a loving, almost bantering tone, but Wexford was surprised. Not 'we all do silly things sometimes' but 'you do silly things', you're the fool and to blame. 'We'll go up and see Sanchia's room in a minute,' he said. 'Did you hear anything untoward during the night?'

'I never do hear a thing, I take a sleeping pill before I go to bed.' It was a surprising admission from such a strong, healthy-looking man. 'It makes me sleep like a log. I need my rest, I've a demanding job.'

'Doing what, Mr Devenish?'

'I'm the Chief Executive of Seaward Air,' said Devenish, naming one of the principal trans-European airlines using Gatwick Airport. 'I should be there now, but obviously . . .' He lifted up his hands in a gesture of inevitability.

'And you heard nothing in the night, Mrs Devenish? Do you also take sleeping pills?'

She shook her head, then looked at Wexford with such naked pleading that he had to turn away his eyes. But he had to go on asking. 'What time would you expect Sanchia to wake up in the morning?'

Again it was Sanchia's father who spoke. 'Six. Very occasionally six thirty.' He smiled, as one paterfamilias to another. 'They all wake early at that age.'

'So you thought she was sleeping late, as she had done before?' Karen said. 'What time did you go into her room?' Devenish was evidently about to supply the answer to that but Karen said firmly, 'Mrs Devenish?'

'I – we – we overslept a bit.' She looked at her

husband as if seeking permission to continue. He nodded reassuringly. 'It was seven when I woke up. I got up and rushed in to Sanchia. I thought she must have been awake for an hour and I hadn't heard her. Of course, if she'd been there, she'd have got up and come in to us, she could have done that, but I didn't think of it, not then. I rushed into her room and the bed was empty and – Oh God – I thought – I thought . . .'

'Don't upset yourself, darling,' said Devenish. 'Try to keep calm. You know it's not wise for you to get excited. I'll tell the rest.' Once more he took his wife's hand and pulled it close against his own body. 'We thought Sanchia must have got up and gone downstairs. She'd never done that but they change so much at that age, there's always something new . . . Anyway, she hadn't. We searched for her, we even searched the garden, though all the doors had been locked and still were locked. That door' – he pointed to the french windows – 'that was locked and the key was taken out as it always is.' He nodded. 'By me,' he said as if no one else in the household would be capable of taking a key out of a lock.

Wexford got up. 'We'll see Sanchia's room now, if you please.'

The house was beautiful, immaculately kept, its woodwork typical of its period, dark, carved and highly polished, the spacious hallway and wide staircase carpeted in an ivory close-pile. Strange choice, Wexford thought. It was one thing for the childless middle-aged Mrs Chorley to enjoy and maintain pristine whiteness everywhere, but for a couple with three children, the eldest of whom was not yet in his teens? Yet it was spotless. Presumably Mrs Devenish had daily help or even a live-in maid. As they climbed the stairs, he asked.

'My wife sees to all that,' said Devenish with

pride. 'She's a splendid housewife. Not that I would stand for anything else,' and he smiled to show he was joking.

Upstairs was all ivory too and there were those articles of furniture standing about on the landing which only the wealthy have: a couple of small white-and-gilt chairs, a jardinière with a huge flower arrangement, a pink *chaise longue*. A door on the right had an enamelled medallion inset and on it the words: *Sanchia's Room*. Devenish opened the door and they went inside, the missing child's mother covering her face with her hands. She gave a low sob.

'Now sit down, darling,' said Devenish. 'It would have been better if you hadn't come up. All this is too much for you.' He lifted his eyes to give Wexford a significant look, though significant of what it was impossible to say. 'My wife isn't very strong.'

By this, Devenish seemed to mean much more than the common, though old-fashioned, usage implied. Was she recovering from some illness? Had she heart disease? Wexford couldn't guess. He surveyed the room. It was at the back of the house and its windows overlooked the garden. The carpet here was pink, the bed canopied with pink curtains. It was evidently as it had been when the child left it, was taken from it, its pink-and-white floral duvet folded back and the menagerie of furry animals – several bears, a dog, two cats and giraffe – piled at the foot. One of the windows was still open, wide enough for an adult to pass through. The other was more in the nature of a glass door and when Wexford unlocked and opened it he found that it gave on to a balcony with a wrought-iron railing. He went outside. The drop to the ground was only about fifteen feet, still too high for anyone to jump with a child in his arms.

'The bed would normally be made by this time, of

course,' Devenish said, apparently apologising. 'But, in the circumstances, I thought . . .'

Wexford made no answer to that, if answer was required. 'Have you a ladder on the premises?' he asked Devenish who had come out on to the balcony with him.

'I'm afraid we have. An extending one. It's in the garage and – again, I'm afraid, I blame myself – the garage wasn't locked. In a place like this, I mean, a country town, a very select neighbourhood, you don't expect to have to lock up the garage every night.'

'And I'm afraid the select neighbourhood is the reason you may have to,' said Wexford drily.

Devenish shrugged. 'May we shut the window now? Your people have been over everything, finger-printing and whatever, and I showed an officer the garage and the ladder.'

Wexford sat down next to Fay Devenish. Her head was still in her hands but now she took them away and looked at him, presenting a ravaged face, marked with tears. 'Mrs Devenish,' he said, 'what kind of a child is Sanchia? She's thirty-three months old, so presumably she is talking quite well and has a strong, clear voice?' He was thinking of children accompanying their mothers to supermarkets. The voice of the three-year-old is the most ear-splitting of all. 'And she has been walking for a year and a half?'

Fay Devenish hesitated, then said, 'She was a late walker, she was eighteen months before she walked.' Her voice was monotonous, all on one level, as if she had been drugged. 'And she doesn't talk much, not as much as she should.'

'Darling, please don't make my child out to be retarded.' Devenish's genial and indulgent manner softened the harshness of the reproof. 'Chief Inspector, Sanchia is simply one of those children who

155

come rather late to talking. My sons both walked at a year and were fluent by two. Sanchia's a girl and maybe it's that which makes the difference.'

Karen's intake of breath was only what Wexford would have expected from her but he gave her a quelling look just the same. 'Would she let a stranger lift her from her bed and take her out of her bedroom down a ladder? Would she protest? Surely she'd cry out?'

The father said he didn't know, he couldn't answer that, and Wexford wondered how much time he had actually spent with his children. Had Seaward Air kept him so busy that, though he might have seen them briefly in the mornings, he usually failed to get home until after they had all gone to bed?

On a choking sob Fay Devenish said, 'She's a nice little girl, a friendly little girl, she might – she might go with someone who was – who was nice to her.' And with that she broke into a storm of tears, sobbing and swaying from side to side. Her husband took Wexford's place and put his arms round her.

It wasn't necessary to spell it out. Montague Ryder, the Chief Constable, hadn't been explicit on the phone, but he had said all that needed to be said, and Wexford hadn't named names or given details to Karen and Burden and Vine, but they understood what he meant just as he had understood Ryder. It would be wiser at this stage to keep the snatching of Sanchia Devenish out of the press, off the media, to keep it for the time being a secret.

This meant no television appearance for Stephen and Fay Devenish to appeal for the return of their child, something of a relief to Wexford who was beginning to feel that after the Crownes' appeal and Rosemary Holmes's, another would be an embarrassment. Besides, he pinned his faith on Vicky and

Jerry. Whatever lies Lizzie and Rachel had told, Vicky and Jerry came into both accounts; they existed.

'Someone'll have to go to the University of Essex, I suppose,' said Burden, 'see Rachel and get the truth out of her. I imagine she may stop lying when she's told it's a three-year-old that's been taken.'

Wexford shook his head. 'No, Mike, that won't do. I want her back here. Karen is going to Colchester to bring her back here. She can get permission from her tutor or supervisor or director of studies, whatever he or she is called. One day here will be enough. I'll drive her round myself till she finds that house and identifies these people.'

'She may refuse to come.'

'In that case,' said Wexford, 'I'll have her charged with perverting the course of justice. She's over eighteen, she's a grown woman.'

Vicky was evidently very persuasive, a woman of charm perhaps. If she hadn't been, would she have been able to entice Lizzie into her car and convince the far more intelligent Rachel that she was a friend's mother? Was she also what is called 'good' with children? Was she the kind of woman a little child will immediately take to, go with, feel at ease with? Such say, 'Suffer the little children to come unto me' and they come willingly, happily, with trust. Because if it wasn't such a Pied Piper, Wexford decided, it must be someone Sanchia knew, a relative or family friend, a frequent visitor to the house in Ploughman's Lane. How unlikely that seemed, how difficult to imagine such a person taking a ladder out of a garage at dead of night, climbing it, getting in through the window and waking that sleeping infant, taking that infant away without her uttering a single cry.

Later that day he went back to Woodland Lodge

157

and extracted from Stephen Devenish a list – a very short list – of relatives and friends Sanchia knew and saw often. 'Extracted' was the word, for Devenish was most unwilling to give it. None of these people was remotely capable, he insisted, of kidnapping a child, let alone *his* child. He gave a strange impression, as of one of whom his few friends were in awe, or deeply respected or even feared. But then he smiled and it struck Wexford, not for the first time, that he didn't seem as upset as he should be. He imagined how it would have been for him if Sylvia or Sheila had been taken from their beds when they were less than three years old. Rage and incredulity would have beset him, and panic and grief. But this man smiled, albeit ruefully. Well, people were different, you had to face it. And some were very good at concealing their feelings.

Devenish gave him a list and Fay Devenish another. The husband looked at what the wife had offered and shook his head. 'Look here, darling, you've put down Gerard Morgan and Sarah Pilgrim and – let's see – Carmel Finn, whoever she may be. None of these people has been in this house for *years* – well, certainly not since Sanchia was born.' He smiled to soften his words as he had in a similar situation that morning. 'I wouldn't have allowed it.' His wife's hand received a comforting squeeze. 'Sanchia didn't know any of them, she certainly wouldn't have gone with them. Their ugly faces would have frightened her to death.'

At that final word Fay Devenish burst once more into tears.

Wexford took the lists, doubting whether they would help him much. 'I expect you have a recent photograph of Sanchia,' he said.

They hadn't. Perhaps in a family group, Devenish said doubtfully, a snapshot that would be not anything like a portrait. Wexford looked from one to the other of them, recalling his own young parenthood when photography was not the almost weekly routine it was today, but still he and Dora had pictures faithfully and regularly taken of their daughters. And they had scarcely been well-off . . .

Alone with Devenish, who took him into a room he called the study, he asked if the man had any enemies.

'Enemies?' Stephen Devenish made it sound a ludicrous suggestion.

'Have you ever received any threats?'

'Yes, of course. Any man in my position receives threats.'

Wexford found this an astonishing response. 'Really?'

'I mean, threatening letters, I've had a few of those, the kind that are full of obscenities and the writer says he wants to kill me.'

'You take it very casually, Mr Devenish. Did you inform us? Have you kept these letters?'

'No to both. Look, I know there are people at work with me, subordinates, you know, or people who *have* been at work who don't like me, but that's a far cry from stealing my child, isn't it?'

Wexford didn't answer. When it came to people's behaviour, he knew, nothing was a far cry. He looked round the room. It was an abode of maleness but almost a parody of a study, an office where men's things were done, men's work and men's business, but where a man could luxuriate too among things alien to women. A stage designer might create something like it as set for a play about a tycoon or a politician. The furniture was all big and heavy, the woodwork mahogany with brass fittings and the upholstery tan-coloured hide. No photographs, no flowers, no calendar. Crossed swords in

159

leather scabbards hung on one wall with an unsheathed dagger beneath them. An ancient flint-lock gun reposed in a glass case and next to it, in another, a large, dead, possibly stuffed fish. The window had a blind, not curtains, and on the hearth of the black marble fireplace stood an array of polished brass fire-irons.

'What did you mean by people who "have" been at work with you, Mr Devenish?'

'Oh, only that I had to sack a chap for incompetence and drinking. The general manager he was. He resented it. Naturally, I dare say. And there've been others. But all this is reaching too far out.'

'I'll have the general manager's name just the same, sir.'

Once more out in Ploughman's Lane, Wexford peered down the drives of the houses on each side of Woodland Lodge, both of them separated from the Devenishes by a good forty feet. Vine had already called on their occupants, none of whom had heard or seen anything in the night. He and Lynn were still carrying out house-to-house inquiries.

The Chief Constable came on the phone again as soon as he got back. 'When does that local paper of yours come out, Reg?'

'Kingsmarkham's, sir, not mine. The *Courier*'s on the streets on Friday morning.'

'I see. That girl, the second one to be taken, Lizzie Crowne is she called?'

'Lizzie Cromwell,' said Wexford.

'Lizzie Cromwell. I dare say you weren't thinking of questioning her about the little girl?'

What a lot you could say, Wexford thought, and make your meaning very clear, without calling a spade a spade. 'No, sir.'

'Right. Good man.'

Lizzie Cromwell wasn't exactly backward, certainly not retarded, far from being the kind who were candidates for an institution. But she was slow, innocent, with rather a low IQ. Devenish had denied that his daughter was behind others of her age, but that was something he would deny. Everyone associated with him, his wife, his children, his home, had to be perfect, you could quickly see that. Still, eighteen months old was extraordinarily late to walk, especially these days when babies seemed to do things earlier and earlier, and if one of his daughters had been unable to talk at nearly three, Wexford thought, he would have been seriously worried.

Was there a link? Did whoever had abducted Lizzie also abduct Sanchia because there was something they liked or needed or were attracted by in the unintelligent? It was an unpleasant thought. And in that case why had the same people, if they were the same people, chosen to abduct the highly intelligent Rachel Holmes? He wished he knew what the child looked like, but in the absence of a photograph – he had refused the family group – he had no idea.

Karen brought Rachel home that evening. She hadn't wanted to come, she had refused to come, so Karen had stopped trying to persuade her, told her what she could be charged with and spoke first to her supervisor, next to the head of her department and finally to the vice-chancellor himself. Sulkily, Rachel gave in. The journey took a long time because although it was possible to drive from Colchester to Kingsmarkham without going into London, there was a traffic jam on the M25 all the way from Brentwood to the Queen Elizabeth II Bridge over the Thames and another one on the M2. It was nearly nine before they reached Stowerton, where Karen left her to spend the night in her mother's house.

161

Wexford said he would see her first thing in the morning. He had personally phoned all the people on the Devenishes' lists, even those three Devenish said Sanchia had never known. All sounded innocent, shocked, sympathetic. He asked them to tell no one of their conversations with him and they undertook not to do this, but you couldn't really trust men and women to be discreet in a situation like this one.

Most people on the Muriel Campden Estate believed that Smith no longer lived there. The man seen departing from number 16 Oberon Road was certainly Smith himself – who else could it be? The question was, where had he gone? Various answers, all speculative, were supplied. Colin Crowne said he had been moved to the Mid-Sussex Constabulary Headquarters outside Myringham. It was big enough, for one thing, and it had suites in it, he knew that for a fact. Smith ought to be locked up in a cell but they wouldn't do that, they were too soft. They would put him in a suite with luxury bathroom and fitted kitchen. Brenda Bosworth said he had been sent to a former health farm, one of those which, as everyone knew, had been converted into detention units for high-profile sex offenders who had served their time.

In the opinion of Tony Mitchell, the peacemaker, Smith had been given a flat in some distant place, probably in the North, as part of a Government Witness Protection Scheme, but John Keenan said witness of what and that was only in America anyway. His wife Rochelle adhered to the suicide theory. That was where he had been going on Saturday night, to kill himself. They would probably find his body in the river or hanging from a tree in Cheriton Forest and good riddance to bad rubbish. Miroslav Zlatic said nothing, being incapable, even after twelve months in this country, of speaking a word of English, but he waved his arms about and shouted imprecations in Serbo-Croat. Live and let live, said Sue Ridley, he won't do any harm, he's too old and worn out.

All, however, were unanimous in the belief that Smith was no longer among them. Of Suzanne and her fiancé they had seen nothing. Too ashamed to show their faces, said Debbie Crowne. Then, passing along Oberon Road on his way home from work, Joe Hebden spotted a man coming out of number 16 and putting two milk bottles out on the step. A little old man, it was, with the face of an ancient baby and a mop of grey hair, wearing a T-shirt and trousers far too big for him. He scurried back and slammed the door as if menaced by a gunman, but not before Hebden had seen who it was. Tommy Smith, beyond a doubt.

In his own words, Hebden went back to his and got straight on the blower.

# Chapter 10

Her mother had stayed at home, taking the morning off work, to be with her. As if she were a child, Wexford thought with some disgust, as if she couldn't look after herself. And it wasn't even as if the girl were moderately nice to her. Their home life must be hell. Rachel's going off to university would have been a relief.

'It's time you told us the truth, Rachel,' he said. 'You know that, don't you? You know that the latest girl to go missing is a child of not yet three years old?'

'They wouldn't have taken her.'

'Rachel, darling, how can you be sure of that?' Rosemary said it in the kindest possible way.

Perhaps it sounded like someone humouring the simple-minded, for Rachel snapped at her, 'Because she wouldn't serve their purpose. Because I was there and I know these people. You weren't and you don't.'

Karen Malahyde looked as if about to say the girl could know nothing about it, but with a glance at Wexford she restrained herself. 'Still, I think you do know where this house is that they took you to.'

'You are aware of what it looks like,' said Wexford, 'and, frankly, the description you gave us matches nothing in the neighbourhood. There is no such house. There is no house or bungalow with shingles on its front and a coniferous tree in the front garden.' Then he said, watching her mutinous, petulant face, 'However, there is a house in Sayle that has a big *deciduous* tree in its front garden, a white house called Sunnybank of just one storey, with a green pantiled roof.'

Rachel Holmes was much given to blushing, no doubt to her own mortification. She put her hands up to her face but couldn't hide the deep flush, as pink as Mrs Chorley's door, making her denial, 'I don't know what you're talking about,' particularly ineffective.

She sniffed, eyed her mother, then turned away. Not knowing where to look, she stared at the door as if longing for carpet and floorboards to part and welcome her into a concealing world below.

'Mrs Pauline Chorley,' Wexford went on, determined to be relentless. 'What can you tell us about her?'

'I've never heard of her!'

People would lie less – or learn to deceive more skilfully – if they understood how easy it is for a trained investigator to detect lying. For a while after she first told her story, when she came voluntarily into the police station, he had believed her but largely because she was a victim, because there seemed no motive for not telling the truth. Now, as she expostulated, he knew she had never heard of Pauline Chorley just as she clearly knew Pauline Chorley's house.

'I think Detective Sergeant Malahyde told you that we'd like to take you on another drive, this time to Sayle, and see if you recognise the house.'

'OK. I don't mind,' Rachel mumbled. She sat up straight and some of her old assertiveness came back. 'But I've got to get back to the university tonight. So long as you know that.'

'Would you like me to come with you to Sayle, darling?' Rosemary Holmes asked.

Wexford wondered if he had ever talked so humbly and ingratiatingly to Sylvia. He hoped not, he thought not, it obviously didn't work anyway, as Rachel showed, rounding on her mother.

'No, I would not. I'm not a child!'

It was difficult to say who was the more embarrassed by the confrontation, Pauline Chorley or Rachel Holmes. Unless this was some bizarre conspiracy, some deep-laid plot – and Wexford knew it wasn't – they had never seen each other before. Like all people in this situation who have led sheltered lives, Mrs Chorley was fearful that she was going to be accused of something she hadn't done, wouldn't have dreamt of doing, but still might find herself for years ahead suspected of a crime. Rachel stood there with hanging head. She barely reacted except to stare, quite suddenly and compulsively, at an area of the white carpet approximately in the middle of the living-room. It was as if she was looking for something that should have been there but wasn't. Wexford concluded that this was simply a technique for holding herself aloof from the situation and he insisted they go over the rest of the house.

But back in the car, she admitted that if Mrs Chorley wasn't Vicky her house was *the* house. There she had been taken by Vicky on that Saturday evening two weeks before. In those rooms she had been drugged, told to cook and mend socks, into one of those bedrooms she had been put to bed and there given 'suitable' clothes to wear. Apart from their both being women and much the same sort of age, she said, Vicky and Pauline Chorley had nothing in common. They were completely different physical types. Vicky could drive and Mrs Chorley couldn't.

Mrs Chorley was plainly nervous while Vicky wouldn't have been afraid of anything.

'You cleaned that house?' Wexford asked, remembering how he had doubted that explanation when it was first given. 'Those white carpets?'

'Yes, those carpets. And I dusted all that junk and all that naff furniture. And I cooked and everything. I *told* you. And I tried to mend the guy's socks.'

Wexford went back to the house. Pauline Chorley opened the door very tentatively and was aghast to see him again. She went white, he thought she was going to faint and he stepped quickly into the hall.

'Sit down, Mrs Chorley. That's right. Believe me, I don't suspect you of anything. I believe you too are a victim of some very unscrupulous people, but you are guilty of nothing.'

The colour returning to her thin pinched face, she gave a little nervous laugh. 'The way I go on,' she said, 'flapping around and nearly passing out, I'm amazed you don't think me guilty.'

'That's only on TV,' he said. 'Now, will you help me? Will you answer a few more questions?'

She nodded.

'Have you and your husband been away on holiday lately?'

'How could you possibly know?'

'Say I guessed.'

'We went to Cyprus for a fortnight and came back at the end of last week.'

'And you had a house-sitter, didn't you? You didn't want to leave your beautiful house' – God forgive me, he thought – 'empty and perhaps a prey to burglars, so you answered an advertisement from someone offering to house-sit. Her name was Vicky Something and she had impeccable references.'

Mrs Chorley stared at him in wonderment. 'Her name was Victoria Smith and she did have good references but I'm afraid I didn't follow them up. She was so – well, so practical and down-to-earth and nice, and obviously a really good housewife that I – well, I suppose I've been a fool.'

Not to check out references, you have, he thought, but he didn't say so.

'How about Jerry? Was he her husband, her son?'

'I never saw or heard of any Jerry. She came on her own, she was here a day and a night before we left, so that I could show her everything, if you know what I mean, and she never mentioned any Jerry.' She asked her question very tentatively and as if expecting no answer. 'What – what has she done?'

'I'm afraid I'm not at liberty to tell you that.'

'I see.'

He could tell she was relieved, she didn't really want to know, it might be too unpleasant. But she had to ask, her husband would expect her to ask. He could almost hear her thoughts.

'Will you let me have her address, please, Mrs Chorley?'

'Yes, of course, I'll be glad to.'

He was positive it was false. Not that it didn't look all right, just a normal Myringham address, a poor street of terraced houses between the bus station and, ironically, the police station. But it would be a place this Victoria Smith – Smith indeed, was it likely? – would have lighted on by consulting a street plan or a driver's road map. He thanked Mrs Chorley, promised to let her know what came of it and on the doorstep asked her a final question.

'A phone? Yes, of course we have one. It's in my bedroom. But I mostly use a mobile and have it with me when I'm out in the garden.'

If anything more was needed to confirm Rachel's account, this was it. The phone was in the principal bedroom and Vicky had kept that bedroom door locked. He went back to the car. Mrs Chorley would have something to tell her husband when he returned home from his long commuting that evening. Was he the kind of man who would be interested and laugh and long to know the outcome? Or the other kind, one only too happy to have an excuse for admonishing and berating his wife for her carelessness?

Rachel was sitting in the back, mouth set, brows drawn together. 'Can I go back to Essex now?'

'Sorry, Rachel,' said Karen, 'we've got a few more questions we'd like answers to.' She was driving. 'Back to the police station, sir?'

Wexford nodded. He said nothing.

They went back through Pomfret. After about ten minutes Rachel said, 'I haven't done anything wrong, you know. You haven't any right to keep on at me like this.' When neither Wexford nor Karen replied, she repeated what she had said, but more querulously.

'You've done your best to obstruct police business,' Wexford said quietly, 'and you're lucky not to be charged with that.'

Tasneem Fowler was a woman of Pakistani parentage, born in west London, who had been married at seventeen to an Englishman and had two children before she was twenty. At the group therapy sessions sometimes conducted by Griselda Cooper she had told the others that for years she had endured her husband's brutality and when he beat her, as he did most frequently on a Saturday night, she had never called the police. She was afraid that if she did so Terry Fowler, the bread-winner, would be taken away and the family broken up. But when he broke her jaw and knocked out three of her teeth – previously he had never knocked out more than one at a time – after a week-long stay in hospital, she had been afraid to go home and had come to The Hide.

Things should have been better for her after that and in many respects they were. Some satisfactory dental work had been done on her damaged mouth, she had the promise of a flat from Kingsmarkham Borough Council and had signed up with Myringham University as a mature student to take a BA degree. But when she came to The Hide she had had to leave her sons behind. They were only six and four, and got on well with their father who had never raised his hand to them. Tasneem had a legal separation from her husband and awaited a divorce but she had no chance of getting custody of Kim and Lee while she had no home.

What she hadn't aired at the group therapy was that every day she spoke to her friend and former next-door neighbour in Ariel Road, Maria Michaels, to ask about the boys, how they were and sometimes if they had forgotten her. She phoned from the pay phone in the hall at The Hide or Maria phoned her. Tasneem was afraid to go home to see them and their father wouldn't allow them to come and see her.

'I'll go and see them if you like,' Sylvia said to her. 'I'll say I'm a social worker. Well, I *am* a social worker.'

'You're very kind.'

'I know how I'd feel if I were separated from my boys.'

Sylvia felt like crying but she controlled herself and next day she went round to the Muriel Campden Estate and gained admittance to 27 Ariel Road by saying she was from the Council's Family Department. Terry Fowler was a weedy little man and as fragile-looking as his wife. Sylvia, who was a big woman, tall and well-built, thought that if he tried anything with her she'd give him as good as she got, she wouldn't stand for it. But she knew how fallacious was this argument. Men *are* stronger than women and abused women are often too demoralised even to try to fight back.

He might be little, but he was as aggressive as a small game bird. A frustrated sergeant major, Sylvia thought, one who wouldn't have had a hope in hell of finding himself in that position but who nourished secret dreams of power and bullying. Realised through domination of his little boys? She didn't think so. Although he spoke curtly to her, barking out 'yes' and 'no' and 'right', with them he was gentle and patient. People were very odd.

Out in the hall, as she was leaving, the older boy Kim said, 'Our mummy's gone away and she's never coming back.'

A heart-strings wrencher if ever there was one, Sylvia thought as she walked back along Oberon Road. That was something she wouldn't be telling. She had hoped to have a moment alone with those boys, tell them their mother sent her love, but there had been no opportunity. When she got home she phoned The Hide and spoke to Tasneem, telling her that she had been to Ariel Road and that all was well, the children were happy and healthy. Tempted to tell a lie, to say they missed their mother and sent her messages, she restrained herself. It wouldn't do.

After Sylvia had rung off, Tasneem remained where she was, in the big hallway of The Hide, holding the receiver. She had felt a real physical pain in the area where her heart was when Sylvia said the boys were happy. Healthy was one thing, was good, but that they were happy, which meant happy without her, was one of the greatest hurts she had ever known, worse than when Terry smashed up her face. Perhaps Sylvia had made it up, perhaps she thought hearing Kim and Lee were happy would *please* her. Maria Michaels never said anything like that. She only said the children were OK. Just that, just OK. But Tasneem had understood. She knew OK meant they weren't ill or in danger and that was all she really wanted. Once more unhooking the phone from the wall, she put twenty pee in and dialled Maria's number. Best to do it now before there was a queue for the phone as there often was in the evening.

Maria answered. She was Tasneem's friend and a nice woman but she had this funny habit of calling you 'my darling' almost every sentence she spoke.

'Happy, my darling? Who told you that? A social worker? You want to steer clear of the social, my darling. Need I say more?'

'You mean they're not happy?' Now thinking of them being miserable was just as bad.

'Now I didn't say that, my darling. But you know what kids are. They miss their mummy, naturally they do, so you couldn't call them exactly over the moon. Now I've got some news for you. That old paedo's come home, that Smith. You never knew him, did you? Before he went to prison, I mean. You weren't here then, my darling, you're too young, but he's come back as large as life.'

'What's a paedo?' said Tasneem.

'A paed-o-phile, one of them that messes about with children, only this one murdered them as well.'

Tasneem began to cry. She wailed and sobbed, and banged her head against the wall until Lucy Angeletti came down to see what was going on.

When she had given a precise description of Vicky and Jerry, filling in all sorts of details like eye colour and the clothes he and Vicky wore, and coming as near to estimating their ages as she could, Rachel returned to her insistence that while at Sunnybank she had been made to do housework, cook and mend clothes. 'And it's got nothing to do with *The Franchise Affair*,' she said sulkily. 'It really happened.' She shrugged her shoulders as if exasperated by the whole exercise. 'Jerry never said a word, he just sat there and stared at me. I'll tell you something, though, something I've just remembered, as a matter of fact. Vicky wasn't very well. I mean she'd something wrong with her. She coughed a lot and she got tired. It was that which made me –'

'Made you what, Rachel?'

'Nothing. It doesn't matter.'

Wexford looked hard at her, thinking that it probably meant a lot. But she had been helpful, she had told them more than anyone else had. He asked her to describe the car. Of course she didn't know the registration number, but she was able to tell him it was 'average size' and what she rather surprisingly called 'middle of the market'; a white, or rather cream, car and an automatic.

'Now I'd like to know why they let you go and how they did.'

'They just did,' she said in her sullen mode. 'I'd vacuumed the place and dusted, and I said I was going. "I'm going now," I said, and she just said I could and she'd drive me back.'

'Just like that?' said Wexford. 'They'd abducted you, and virtually imprisoned you and drugged you, they'd forced you to work and do menial tasks, yet when you said you were going they didn't argue, they just agreed.'

'Not Jerry,' she said, 'Jerry never spoke.'

'Right. Vicky, then. Vicky just agreed?'

'I've *told* you.'

'I'm wondering what else happened in that house, Rachel. Did you do any damage to something or

173

someone? Did you do something you think might get you into trouble? Is that it?'

'I didn't do anything!' she shouted. 'You've called me a criminal but it's what was done to me you should be thinking about. What was done to *me*.'

'All right, Rachel. So Vicky drove you home, did she?'

'No, she didn't drive me back, she just took me to the bus-stop and left me there, and I waited for hours before the Kingsmarkham bus came. Can I go back to Essex now or is that too much to ask?'

'You can go.'

After she had gone Wexford looked at all the collated information gathered that day. It seemed that the Devenish extended family and friends could all be cleared of suspicion. Apart from that, the most useful piece of evidence had come from the people living opposite Woodland Lodge. They were a couple called Wingrave. During the night Sanchia had been taken, Moira Wingrave had seen a car driven out of the Devenishes' drive. It had been at about two in the morning.

Wexford blessed insomniacs, not those like Stephen Devenish but the ones who never took sleeping pills. Wakeful, Moira Wingrave had seen car lights through her bedroom curtains, had got up to look, not because she was suspicious but for something to do, something to look at, to distract her mind from those awful hours of sleeplessness. And of course she had looked at the clock, something she did at least once an hour throughout the night.

By the time she got to the window, walking slowly and carefully so as not to wake her husband, the car had come out of the Woodland Lodge drive and its headlights blazed in her face, dazzling her, almost blinding her, so that she had been unable to tell what colour it was, still less its make and registration number. She couldn't tell who was driving it, man or woman.

No other neighbour had seen anything. No one had heard any sounds from Woodland Lodge. And yet a small child had been carried out of that house by a stranger, awakened from sleep, lifted from her bed, taken down a ladder, put into a strange car, all without uttering a cry. Her abductor could have covered her mouth; she would have struggled and kicked. He or she could have gagged her, carried her away inside a sack. Wexford contemplated such horrors grimly. But he didn't believe in them. 'The case of the child who didn't cry in the night,' he said.

'I suppose she could have been drugged,' said Burden in his gloomy way. 'We know Vicky uses drugs. Could she have been given Rohypnol?'

'She still had to be wakened from sleep by someone she didn't know. She still had to see a strange face looking down at her. Did this stranger clap a gag over her mouth while he injected her with something in a hypodermic? By the way, a young couple live at the Myringham address. William Street is a tarted-up former slum between the nick and the bus station. Yuppies live there in jerry-built cottages that were put up to last ten years and have lasted, more or less, for a hundred.'

'Jerry-built,' said Burden. 'How appropriate.'

'Only unfortunately it isn't. The occupiers have never heard of him or his mother, or whatever she is.'

Burden, who usually left this sort of intuitive speculation to Wexford, said surprisingly, 'I wonder why she picked William Street? Can there be a William Street in the entire country that isn't a squalid dump? Why choose that particular place?'

'There's a William Street in London, in Knightsbridge, that's very grand, but I know what you mean. Are you saying that she had some connection with the place? Used to live there once or her parents did or someone she knew well? And that's why she picked it.'

'A person of limited imagination would do that. It might be worth doing a house-to-house. Pity we haven't got a photo. Or the number of that car.'

'If we had a photo and a car number we'd have found her by now, Mike. But let's do your house-to-house. Or Myringham will. They've only got to cross the road.' Wexford got up. 'It's late and we've got that Hurt-Watch meeting in the morning.'

Detective Sergeant Vine had talked to Moira Wingrave at two when she had told him what she had heard the previous night. Although not an excitable man, rather a discreet man with a deadpan face, Vine must have shown her something of what he had felt at receiving from her the single piece of real evidence he had retrieved from his afternoon's slog. For, after he had gone, from originally being angry with herself for not having seen or heard more, exasperated for failing to notice that car number, she began to feel herself an important contributor to this inquiry. With luck she might even get on to television or at least into the *Kingsmarkham Courier*.

That would take some manoeuvring, she thought, as she remembered the policeman telling her that everything she said was in confidence and he would be grateful if what she had told him she kept to herself. But the disappearance of the little Devenish girl would certainly be on the radio and television news, and once it was 'in the public domain' – Moira liked this phrase and repeated it to herself – she would be free to talk to whom she chose and particularly tell of the significant part she had played in the investigation of a kidnapping.

On their four television sets the Wingraves had every channel it was possible to obtain. Moira managed to find a news programme at three and another at three forty-five, while one of the many radio stations produced a news summary for her at five to four. The remarkable thing was that there was nothing on any of them about the child's disappearance. This made Moira feel a mixture of excitement at being the only one to know about it – apart from the parents, of course – and indignation at the ineffectiveness of the media. When her husband came home he'd bring the *Evening Standard* from London but she'd bet anything you liked there would be nothing in it about whatever she was called, Sasha or Sandra Devenish.

The woman who cleaned the house twice weekly came in at four. Now her daughters were both at school, Tracy Miller did cleaning jobs all day, starting at nine in the morning, and was so much in demand that she was unable to come to Moira till mid-afternoon. This was a nuisance because Bryan Wingrave always came in at six sharp and disliked Tracy being around the place, but what could Moira do about it? She had to have a cleaner, even one who had a face like Cindy Crawford, a figure like a sixteen-year-old and wore her long black hair in a plait down her back.

Tracy was a bit of a mystery, anyway. She had been working here for six months now and still Moira had no idea where she lived, whether she had a husband or lived with a boyfriend or had children or what. This seemed to make her anonymous and belonging nowhere, an isolated woman who, for all Moira knew, might shut herself up in a cupboard after her day's usefulness was over, like the vacuum cleaner she so vigorously applied. At any rate, she seemed to be a kind of recluse, friendless, discreet and quiet. She never spoke unless she was first spoken to and Moira wasn't in the business of speaking to what she would have called, if she hadn't been afraid of losing Tracy, the charwoman.

But today she did speak to Tracy beyond, that is, telling her there were fingermarks on the mirrors and the coffee table hadn't come up very well. The point was that she had to tell someone and telling Tracy was really like confiding one's secrets to a brick wall.

She merely listened while dusting, made no response until Moira was finished and said only, 'That poor mother.'

'Well, yes, exactly what I said to the policeman, that poor mother, I said. But if it's not in the public domain how can they possibly hope to catch whoever it is?'

'Search me,' said Tracy.

Bryan came home soon after that, bringing the evening paper with him. No missing child story – Moira had known there wouldn't be – and there was nothing on the BBC's six o'clock news either. She paid Tracy her twenty-five pounds at seven and saw her off the premises, forgetting to tell her not to say a word. But whom could she tell, anyway? No one who counted. She was a charwoman, for God's sake.

Quiet, secretive Tracy went home to Kingsbrook Valley Drive, an address that would very much have surprised Moira Wingrave, and to a house whose purpose she didn't know existed. Domestic violence was what Mrs Wingrave would have called 'in the matrimonial domain' and therefore between husband and wife, a private matter to be hushed up.

Tracy let herself in with her key and went through the house to the play area in the garden where she had the best chance of finding her children at this hour. But there she found only Tasneem Fowler, tidying up toys after the little girls' departure.

Tracy's daughters, she told their mother, were indoors watching a video and already in their nightdresses ready for bed.

'Thanks, you're a star,' said Tracy, who could talk volubly to people she liked. 'Hey, what d'you reckon, there's a kid gone missing up in millionaires' row. The old bat I work for told me. Little girl, under three and from one of the biggest houses up there. Just goes to show money doesn't bring happiness.'

'Missing?' said Tasneem. 'A child?'

'Like I said, a little girl. She's called Sandra Something. I like that name, don't you? If I ever have another one, which I'll never have with *him*, so help me God, I wouldn't mind calling her Sandra.'

But Tasneem wasn't listening. She gave a loud cry, half-way to a scream. 'It's that paedo! Up where my kids are. It's that paedo's taken her!'

# Chapter 11

The morning was beautiful, the sky blue and the sun shining through a thin veil of mist. On the Muriel Campden Estate all was still and silent but for birdsong from the park. Those few people who went to work early were just getting up. Soon after seven the milk float came round and the milkman left a bottle or two – no longer pint glass bottles but litre-sized plastic cartons – on most doorsteps. Half an hour later the sixteen-year-old Darren Meeks arrived, pushing his stolen supermarket trolley, to deliver the papers.

Maria Michaels, who was due to leave for work at eight thirty, picked up her copy of the *Sun* from the doormat and took it to the kitchen where she was breakfasting off a cup of tea and a croissant. The phone conversation she had had with Tasneem Fowler the evening before was much on her mind, though she had said nothing about it to anyone but Monty Smith who lived with her. There had been no opportunity, anyway, as it was ten thirty before Tasneem had got through to her, having queued up for a long time to get to The Hide pay phone.

The missing little girl would be the *Sun*'s lead story, Maria was sure of that. But it wasn't. And it wasn't just absent from the front page, she couldn't find it anywhere. What was going on? She took a cup of tea up to Monty who was unemployed and therefore still in bed, and asked him what he thought.

'It's not right,' said Monty, taking the tea and the paper from her. 'They're hushing it up. Nothing on the telly and now nothing in the paper. How would you and me feel if we'd got kids?'

'Bloody frantic, my darling. I don't blame the paper, though, I blame the police.'

'They're always on the side of the criminal,' said Monty. 'Paedos, rapers, robbers, manslaughterers, you name it, they can't do no wrong.'

'People ought to be warned. I'll just give Rochelle a phone before I go to work, my darling. My God, look at the time, better get cracking.'

So Maria phoned Rochelle Keenan and because she couldn't remember the name Tasneem had given her, told her a child called Shawna or Shana or something was missing and the police weren't doing a thing about it. After she had rung off Rochelle phoned Brenda Bosworth, embellishing her story to make it more acceptable to that sensation-loving woman's ears, and telling her Tommy Smith had snatched a baby from its own cot in its own bedroom and taken it away in a stolen car. Brenda wanted to know why it hadn't been on the telly or in the *Mirror* and Rochelle said the police didn't want it to come out that they'd left Smith at large.

It was Brenda who, at that moment, was the first to call herself and Miroslav, Colin Crowne, Joe Hebden and the Keenans by a name later taken up by the newspapers. 'It's time the Kingsmarkham Six acted,' she said.

She went round in person to tell the news to Shirley Mitchell (who had already heard it from her sister), said the Kingsmarkham Six were mustering, shook her fist at the Smiths' house and passed on to notify Hebdens, Meekses and Crownes. Shirley went upstairs and looked out of the back-bedroom window from where she had a good view of the Smiths' back garden, but it looked much the same as usual, the rusty bedstead still there, though half hidden now by the weeds, which had grown taller by a foot.

Her husband was about to leave for work. She told him Smith and Suzanne had stolen a baby girl called Sarah and had her inside the house with them.

'Smith's not interested in girls,' said Tony Mitchell. 'It's always been boys with him.'

'Then he's changed. Being in prison's changed him.'

'Load of rubbish,' said Tony. 'You might as well say you've started fancying women. Don't you get involved. You want to keep yourself to yourself. If I've told you that once I've told you five hundred times.'

By the time he was out of sight, heading for the bus-stop in York Street, a crowd was gathering in Oberon Road, with Brenda Bosworth in the vanguard. By now the sun was hot, the mist had melted away and the silence was broken by twenty voices chanting: 'We want Smith! We want Smith!'

Organising the continued search for Sanchia Devenish, Wexford was too busy to attend the Hurt-Watch meeting. Burden went in his place. Wexford had been in his office since half past eight, reviewing the progress made in tracking down Victoria Smith, or rather, the progress not made. In accordance with Burden's suggestion, Barry Vine and two officers from Myringham had carried out a house-to-house inquiry in William Street and come up with nothing. No one recognised the middle-aged woman and the young man described, no one had heard of a Vicky or a Jerry. Electoral registers going back twenty years had been consulted but the only Victoria in William

Street had been checked out and found to have died two years before.

Wexford had stopped reading and begun thinking, just sitting there with his eyes half closed and his hands folded, reflecting on what might make someone choose a particular false address. If not because she once lived in that street, because she regularly walked along it on her way to work or had been to school there or had a parent living there or a child living there, or went to a dentist or a doctor or a chiropodist there. Once he had found out that no doctor or dentist or chiropodist operated from William Street, and that there was no school there and never had been, he had to think again.

Of course it was more than possible, it was even likely, that Vicky had simply picked that address out of a street plan of Myringham. It was what he would do in the unlikely event of his needing a false address. But if not by this means, how else could he find her? His train of thought was interrupted by the phone ringing. It was Sylvia. She never phoned him at work, it was almost unheard of.

He restrained himself from asking what was wrong, was her mother all right, and simply said a cheerful, 'Hallo, darling.'

'Dad, is there a child missing in Kingsmarkham, a little girl?'

Something tightened in his chest. 'Why do you ask?'

'I'll tell you. One of the women at The Hide heard it at the place where she works and she told me when I came on last night. Well, not when I came on actually. Not till I'd been on quite a while. I was in the helpline room and she put her head round the door on her way to bed. It was all of eleven, otherwise I'd have phoned you.'

It went against the grain with him to admit this

carefully guarded secret, even, perhaps especially, to a member of his family. He said cautiously, 'A little girl is missing, yes. There are reasons for not making it public just yet. We hope to find her and then it need never be made public.'

'Would the reasons have something to do with Thomas Smith?'

'I can't answer that, Sylvia.'

'Only his neighbours, all that mob that went mad the other day, they know about it. One of our women told a friend of hers on the Muriel Campden and it'll be all round the place by now.'

'Oh God,' said Wexford. 'Thanks for telling me, Sylvia' and he added, 'You may have averted a nasty situation.'

He didn't say what he wanted to, that she certainly would have averted it if she had called him at eleven the previous night. Their relationship had never been so good; let it stay that way. The only thing to do now was put a call through to Superintendent Rogers and suggest some of his people get over to Oberon Road immediately. The uniformed branch was responsible for crowd control, but he might as well go up there himself – why not?

Where did that woman work, the one who had found out about Sanchia Devenish and passed on her information? He should have asked Sylvia. But no doubt it was in Ploughman's Lane or Winchester Drive, somewhere near the Devenishes. Too late to worry about that now, he thought, as Donaldson drove him along the High Street and turned up York Street.

He expected to hear chanting or singing or even just roaring long before the Muriel Campden Estate was reached, but there was silence, or rather, a hush, as if up here even the normal busy sounds of a country town on a weekday had been subdued. The entrance to the triangle of streets was blocked by a police car in the familiar Mid-Sussex Constabulary scarlet, blue and canary yellow, stationary across the road and at right angles to it. The uniformed officer at the wheel Wexford didn't recognise. He said to Donaldson, 'I'll walk the rest of the way.'

It was hot for early May, the sun blazing down by now, white on the pavements, black in the shade. He could see a crowd ahead of him, an ambulance parked half-way along Oberon Road. It pulled away and its siren sounded just as he passed the gate of number 20. The sight of the Smiths' house almost stopped him short. The window panes which the council had replaced only the day before were once more smashed, the front door was gone and some-one, somehow, had succeeded in dislodging several tiles from the roof. Outside the gate stood Sergeant Joel Fitch and in front of the gaping hole where the front door had been a WPC called, he thought, Wendy Brodrick. The crowd, huddled together, had retreated to the green to stare.

'Who was in the ambulance?' he asked Fitch.

'Suzanne Smith, sir. She got hit on the head with a brick. They threw the same bricks they threw on Sunday. Someone had piled them all up again and they just used them.'

'Everything gets recycled these days,' said Wexford.

'It's a blessing the little girl *wasn't* in there, sir. They'd very likely have murdered her.'

'Where's Mr Rogers?'

'Inside with Smith. He's going to bring him out. Here's the van now.'

The crowd, which had been silent, began a mutter-ing. The sound of it rose and fell, rose again and a woman shouted out, 'Nobody's taking me away in no Black Maria!' It was Brenda Bosworth, arm in arm with Miroslav Zlatic, who was also arm in arm with Lizzie Cromwell.

If 16 Oberon Road had had a garage drive things would have been much easier but the only garages on the Muriel Campden Estate were the lock-up kind, a row of them at the York Street end of Ariel Road. The van driver was obliged to park against the kerb outside number 16 and almost before he had put the handbrake on the crowd surged up to surround it.

'Get back there,' said Fitch in his resonant voice that still wasn't quite a shout. 'Go home the lot of you. There's nothing for you here.'

But the crowd wasn't going home, though it retreated a little, so that no one was any longer actually touching the van. The driver was a slender man of medium height with short-cropped golden curls. He got down and with two more uniformed men ushered the Kingsmarkham Six and their supporters back on to the grass.

'Poove,' said Colin Crowne to the driver. 'Look at his hair. Goes in for Carmen rollers, he does, the poove.'

'And perve,' said Monty Smith. 'Poove and perve' and he started laughing at his own wit.

'That's why they side with that paedo,' said Brenda. 'They're all pooves and perves, the lot of them. Birds of a feather flock together, that's what I say.'

Lizzie Cromwell shrieked with laughter, squeezing Miroslav's arm. Across the green, at her window on the second floor of the tower, Rochelle Keenan, once more in possession of her Camcorder, reached further out to make sure she missed nothing on her videotape.

Wexford went past Fitch, said 'Excuse me' to WPC Wendy Brodrick and stepped inside the half-wrecked house. He pushed the door almost closed behind him. Most of the bricks had ended up in here. Broken glass was everywhere. He trod gingerly and the glass crunched underfoot. It was such a small house that to speak to those in the living-room he hardly needed to raise his voice. 'D'you need any help, George?'

Rogers called to come in. Wexford pushed open the door. Tommy Smith was inside with Rogers, a tallish PC and a shorter one. If Wexford had been asked whether he considered Smith emotional, he would have said the man had no feeling left, either for himself or anyone else. But he would have been wrong. Smith was crying. For his own plight or for his injured daughter? Not, surely, for his past life and his crimes. The tears rolled down his puffy brown cheeks and he made no attempt to wipe them away.

'You'd better pull yourself together,' said Rogers briskly but not unkindly. 'We have to get you out of here. Or get someone out.'

Wexford knew what he meant. 'You could put a coat over – I'm sorry, I don't know your name . . .?'

'Dixon, sir.'

'You could put a coat over Dixon's head – my raincoat, if you like. It was pretty daft wearing a raincoat on a day like this, anyway – and you and I could get him out of here between us.'

'Right,' said Rogers.

Impossible not to feel pity for a weeping man, Wexford would have said a week ago, but for Smith he felt none. He looked at him and had to tense his muscles to stop himself shuddering with revulsion. Impossible to be in his presence and, if you had any imagination, not picture the things he had done, the pleasure attached to those things that swamped all concern for others.

'He's a bit taller than you,' he said to Smith in as

detached a voice as he could achieve, 'but not so's you'd notice with his head covered up. Shall we give it a go?'

'What about me?' said Smith, wiping his eyes on his sleeve.

'This is for your benefit.' Rogers wasn't pleased. 'With luck they'll take their departure once Dixon is out and you can slip away quietly in one of the cars.'

'Slip away where?' Smith looked uneasily from one to the other.

Rogers said they would come up with something. He had managed to cut his hand on a piece of broken glass and it was bleeding. Wexford, who sometimes thought he was the only man left in the world who still used handkerchiefs, handed him his clean white one. He took off his raincoat and they draped it over Dixon, covering his head and face and shoulders so that he was unrecognisable. Starting to cry again, Smith stared hopelessly at the man disguised as himself.

Wexford and Rogers were both big men so that Dixon, sandwiched between them, looked less than his five feet eight inches. As soon as the front door was pushed open howls went up from the crowd, a bit like the baying of hounds on the scent, Wexford thought. He and Rogers and Dixon stepped down on to the path and WPC Brodrick stood back to let them pass.

Policemen with linked hands, eight of them, held the crowd back but couldn't stop the baying. The banner had reappeared while Wexford was inside number 16, as well as the two boy and girl sandwich boards, one worn by fat Carl Meeks, whose belly held it out almost at right angles, and the other by Joe Hebden. The crowd started chanting, 'Paedo out, paedo out, paedo out . . .'

Wexford and Rogers with Dixon between them

made their way down the path and through the gate while the crowd strained and pushed against the linked hands and the broad backs, finally breaking through just as Dixon was shoved into the van. Rogers jumped in beside him and as Wexford stepped back the driver was already pulling away from the pavement.

He had wondered for a moment if they intended to attack him and if he would be obliged to struggle with them, but it was soon clear that no one was interested in him. He might as well have been a gatepost or a lamp standard. Brenda Bosworth, Monty Smith and John Keenan, and others whose names he didn't know, had all attached themselves to the van, grabbing hold of the door handles, hammering on the windows and shrieking at the occupants. The driver had to stop while Fitch and two PCs pulled them off, Fitch getting Monty Smith's fist in his face, for which assault on a police officer Monty was promptly arrested by PC Dempsey, shouting a triumphant, 'You're nicked!'

The van moved again, gathered speed and headed for York Street. Wexford sent Wendy Brodrick into the house, told her he would have a car come round and to bring Smith out once the coast was clear. For his part, he didn't want to see Smith again. Being in his company was a depressing experience, for this was a man and he was a man too. Probably, being a woman in his company would be easier. On the other hand, women were mothers . . .

He walked across on to the green, glad to have found a useful way of dispensing with his raincoat on what promised to be the warmest day of the year so far. Only Brenda Bosworth, Miroslav Zlatic and Lizzie Cromwell remained standing on the grass, and when they saw him approach they too moved off, still arm in arm, Lizzie giggling and thrusting forward her swelling stomach. He decided to follow them and see them safely to their homes in Puck Road. It was unlikely there would be more arrests. Prosecuting these people would be a hopeless business since it was highly unlikely anyone would give evidence against anyone else.

The remaining police officers were departing in cars, taking Monty Smith with them. Wendy Brodrick had disappeared into number 16 and when Wexford next looked over his shoulder he saw the red, yellow and blue car which had blocked the entrance road pull up outside. Not the wisest move, he thought, not the best way to avoid attracting attention, and he stopped, exasperated. Fortunately, no one remained on the green and the woman with the Camcorder had gone in and closed her window. For a moment he had been distracted from watching the three people ahead of him. A shriek made him turn round and start to run in their direction. Brenda Bosworth and Lizzie were rolling on the ground, locked together, half on the pavement, half in the council's newly planted flowerbed, Lizzie whimpering and Brenda growling, clutching a handful of the girl's blonde hair in her fist. Miroslav stood back, his arms folded, shaking his head.

A lot of things became clear to Wexford in that moment; several mysteries were solved. He grabbed hold of Brenda by the arms and tried to pull her off as Lizzie hugged herself, doubled up to protect her swollen belly. Brenda kicked Wexford, but ineffectually, and he put a stop to that by holding her in a fireman's lock. Set free and not much hurt, Lizzie got first to her knees, then up to a squatting position. Her knees were grazed and she had earth on her face. Perhaps she expected aid from Miroslav for she held out her hand for him to help her to her feet but he was looking the other way, pretending an interest in a new motor bike parked in the front garden of number 42.

'Go on home, Lizzie,' said Wexford, still holding Brenda. 'I'll come and talk to you in five minutes.'

He relaxed his hold on Brenda and propelled her to her gate, Miroslav following sheepishly behind. Brenda, turning to face Wexford once she was inside her own garden, gathered spittle in her mouth.

'Don't do it,' said Wexford.

Instead of spitting, she spoke. 'That was indecent assault, the way you were holding me. I'll have the law on you.'

'I am the law,' said Wexford, 'so shut up and get inside.'

The way she slammed the door after her made the house shake. Left outside and apparently without a key of his own, Miroslav looked to Wexford for help much as Lizzie had looked to him. Wexford shrugged and walked off, leaving him hammering on the front-room window. The flowerbed was wrecked, a mess of crushed pansies and snapped-off primulas. Wexford picked up a purple-and-orange pansy and stuck it in his buttonhole.

The Crownes' door was open and on the latch, so he rang the bell, walked straight in and found Lizzie with her mother who was washing the blood off her knees with a face-cloth and a bowl of soapy water. 'You'd better have her see the doctor,' he said. 'I doubt if there's harm done but it's best to be on the safe side.'

'That bitch,' said Debbie Crowne. 'That slag. Fighting like a bloody animal. I'll kill her, I'll poke her bloody eyes out.'

'When you've finished washing Lizzie's wounds, Mrs Crowne, I'd like a word alone with her, if you please.'

Surprisingly, Debbie went off without another

word. Wexford shut the door after her, though he couldn't stop her listening at the keyhole. Lizzie was giving him one of her truculent lowering looks, her underlip stuck out and her brows drawn together in a heavy frown.

'You're getting on for four months pregnant, aren't you, Lizzie?' he began. She nodded, still frowning.

'Miroslav Zlatic is the father, isn't he? You used to meet him in that old house outside Myringham, it was the only place you could be alone together. That's how you knew about the blanket. No doubt it was useful. Brenda found out when you and she and Miroslav were walking back, did she?'

'I don't know how,' Lizzie said innocently. 'He sort of touched me when he didn't think she was looking but she must have been looking. It must have been that. She went bonkers. Am I going to lose my baby?'

'I shouldn't think so for a moment. Babies aren't lost so easily. Is he going to leave Brenda and set up house with you when it's born?'

Lizzie shook her head. 'He can't talk, can he? All he ever said was "Leezee, Leezee". How would I know what he's going to do?'

Wexford reflected that Miroslav had got it made. Who knew how many other young women he had taken to the derelict house and made love to in silence? No doubt he had no intention of ever learning English. 'And now we know all about you and Miroslav and your baby perhaps you'll tell me what really happened in the pretty white bungalow you liked so much at Sayle. Did you do those people's housework? Sew for them and cook for them?'

She nodded, looking down again, apparently contemplating the scratches on her knees.

'Vicky and Jerry. They said to you that if you told

what had happened to you they'd seek you out and punish you. Is that right?'

Again that slow nodding. But he could tell that his guesswork and the conclusions he had drawn had deeply impressed her. How had Brenda intuited what had happened between her and Miroslav? How, equally, had he, Wexford, got it all so effortlessly right? As if he had been there, as if he, alone of all men, could speak Miroslav's own language. The look she gave him now was wondering, even respectful. Innocent, naïve and slow, she was unlike most of her kind in that she admired, and admired reverently, intelligence in others.

'They won't punish you, Lizzie, they can't. I won't let them. The best way you can help me to stop them is by telling me everything you can remember.'

She said nothing but the admiring look didn't change.

'There's a little girl missing, Lizzie. You know that, that's why you were out on the green with all the others, but perhaps you don't know that she's not yet three years old. Tommy Smith hasn't got her, that was all nonsense that someone made up. They made it up because they were afraid of him. He's gone away now and the little girl is still missing. Do you think Vicky and Jerry have got her?'

'She couldn't do housework,' said Lizzie.

'True. But that wasn't all you did, was it?'

'He never did any of that to me, not like Miroslav did.'

'No, all right. I understand that. Why did they let you go?'

'I wasn't right. I didn't do any of it right. I can do hoovering but I can't cook or mend things. Vicky said, "You're stupid, you won't do." And she brought me back in her car.'

'What did she mean, "won't do"? Won't do for what?'

'I don't know. Nobody said.'

'Tell me what she looked like.'

He expected her to say 'Just ordinary', or 'Just an old woman', the normal reaction of an unobservant person. Instead he was discovering that Lizzie was in some ways more perceptive than Rachel Holmes. 'She hadn't got any hair,' Lizzie said. 'She was bald. She had a wig, a big grey wig, but I saw her without it. I saw it hanging on a stand in her bedroom and I saw her head without any hair.'

'What happened at the meeting?'

'Not much,' said Burden. 'When does anything ever happen when Southby's in charge? That woman Griselda Cooper made some helpful suggestions about how to distribute the mobiles but our ACCD wasn't having any of it. He's set up a committee' – Burden made a disgusted face – 'to, and I quote, *consider and review the domestic-violence victim communication project.* And guess what, I'm on it.'

Wexford laughed. 'How about this unit they're setting up at Myringham? Twenty officers to have special training is what I heard.'

'I'm not on that,' said Burden, 'too senior, thank God, but Karen is, so we're going to be without her for the next three months. Any more leads to Vicky and Jerry?'

'Lizzie Cromwell gave me an interesting piece of info.' Wexford described his morning briefly, then told Burden about the wig. 'Rachel said Vicky seemed ill, she had a cough. Now what sort of illness results in a woman going bald?'

'Alopecia,' said Burden promptly.

'Yes, but where does the cough come in? Isn't it much more likely she'd had chemotherapy? She's got cancer and been treated for it with chemotherapy, which resulted, as it often does, in complete hair loss.'

'Maybe, but I don't see how it helps. You can't go along to Akande or the Royal Infirmary and ask them how many of their patients have had chemotherapy in the past few weeks. Or rather, you can but no one will tell you.'

'Let's go and have lunch, Mike. It had better be the canteen for quickness. Then I want to go back to those Devenishes and maybe you'll come with me.'

The canteen, on the top floor, had much improved in the years since Wexford had first been there. In those early days, to avoid it, he had mostly eaten out or when particularly busy, sent out for sandwiches and later the various kinds and nationalities of take-away available. On the canteen menu today were pasta, curry and risotto.

'You never see an old-fashioned steak-and-kidney pie these days,' said Burden wistfully. 'Have you noticed?'

'Of course I've noticed. I'm not supposed to eat it, anyway.'

Mention of the diet he seldom followed reminded Wexford of his doctor and thus of the other GPs in the practice. Carrying his tray of tagliatelle and salad, and a very small crème caramel, he went up to DS Vine who was sharing a table with WPC Wendy Brodrick.

'May we join you?' Wexford sat down and told the sergeant his theory. 'I don't think you'll get any joy out of those GPs, Barry, but there's just a chance when it's a matter of a young child at risk.'

'I'll give it a go, sir. I don't know if you've seen what the lab has to say yet, but they've been over that ladder in the Devenishes' garage and they're as certain as can be no one's shifted it, let alone climbed it.'

'How can they be?' asked Wendy Brodrick.

'It's a brand-new metal ladder, which was bought in plastic wrapping. Devenish removed the wrapping and simply laid the ladder on the garage floor. You can see the outline of it in the dust and there's no doubt it's never been moved. Devenish's prints alone are on it and only on the top rung.'

'Exactly. That ladder wasn't used, though another may have been.'

'What, brought there in an ordinary saloon car? Impossible, surely. We're going to have to see what more we can get out of Moira Wingrave.' Wexford turned to Wendy Brodrick who was eating a glutinous grey mass he supposed must be the risotto. 'What did you do with Smith?'

'I packed a case for him, sir, and made him a cup of tea and when the coast was clear we left. Mr Southby told me to take him to Headquarters at Myringham.'

'Have they accommodation for him?'

'They've a room with bath. Putting him in a police cell doesn't seem fair, does it, sir? After all, he's paid his debt to society.'

Wexford ignored Vine's snort and Burden's humourless 'Huh!'.

'He'll join the other 110,000 convicted paedophiles living in this country. After all, only four per cent of them are in jail. It doesn't bear thinking about, does it? So most of the time we don't think about it. What did you do? Bring him back here and await instructions?'

'I drove round the back and he didn't even have to get out of the car. Mr Southby was just coming out of his meeting and he said, take him to Myringham.

196

Well, actually, sir, he said to get shot of him as fast as I could.'

Wexford nodded. That was just like Southby, an expert at passing the buck. Send the domestic-violence issue into a committee and the child-killer ten miles up the road. 'Were you seen bringing him here?' he asked.

'I'm sure not. I was careful and there weren't many people about. He was sitting in the back. Apart from that lot up at the Muriel Campden, there aren't that many who would recognise him, sir.'

Telling Tracy Miller about the missing baby had seemed an innocent enough thing to do at the time. It was only afterwards, in the night when she couldn't sleep, that Moira Wingrave's guilt began. And those pangs of conscience continued to bring her twinges throughout the morning, pinpricks made sharper by the sight of Stephen Devenish opening the gates to his driveway, so that when she saw the two police-men coming up her drive towards her front door she was sure they knew all about it. They had come to reproach her, or worse. Yet there had been nothing on the news about it and nothing in the paper this morning . . .

She had to open the door, there was no help for it. The big policeman she recognised, the other one she had never seen before but she supposed that he too was a detective, in spite of his elegant suit in a tiny dogtooth check and his dark-green silk tie. It was all she could do to stop herself saying, 'It was me, I did it, I told.'

But they seemed uninterested in that. All they wanted was for her to tell them about the car she had seen come out of the Devenishes' drive at two in the morning and she'd already told them everything, or she thought she had. The big one, whose suit wasn't nearly so nice, but baggy and probably in need of cleaning and in a shade she always called 'men's suit grey', told her to close her eyes and try to recapture in her mind that car and what it looked like, and what colour it was and what sort of a person was driving it.

Shutting her eyes in their presence made her feel uncomfortable. Vulnerable, really. It was as if they could see so much more of her when she couldn't see them. A bit like taking off one's clothes. And with her eyes tight shut, Moira blushed. She couldn't see anything but redness and little black floaters, but suddenly, though the car wouldn't appear on the screen she was trying to create, she *remembered* two things.

'I thought it was going to hit the gatepost,' she said. 'I nearly opened the window and shouted out to be careful. I nearly did, only my husband was asleep.'

'So you didn't think this was a stranger, an intruder, say?' said the green silk tie one. 'You didn't suppose it was someone who had no right to be there?'

'Well, I didn't know. I knew it was a strange car. I mean, I thought it was some friend visiting them. Not that they've got many friends.'

The big one nodded. 'So what was the other thing?'

'The other thing?'

'That you remembered. You said there were two things.'

'Well, that was it. That I thought it was a friend of theirs.'

Green tie said, 'Who was inside the car?'

'Only the driver. Well, I think so. I couldn't see into the back.'

'And the driver was a man or a woman?'

Moira tried the eye-shutting method again. It felt easier and less embarrassing this time. A picture actually appeared. She wouldn't have believed it possible. Perhaps it was because she was relaxed. But was it a man or a woman? Just an outline, a silhouette, a faceless head. 'I don't know,' she said. 'I just don't know. I think it was a man but it might have been a woman.'

'Was there a ladder in the car, Mrs Wingrave? To accommodate a ladder either the boot or one or both rear windows would have had to be open. Did you see anything like that?'

Moira shook her head. 'The baby was on the back seat, wasn't she? There wasn't room for a ladder.'

'You mean you saw the baby on the back seat?'

'I don't know.' She felt rather huffy now. 'You *told* me the baby was on the back seat, so she must have been.'

They crossed the road and walked up the drive under the overhanging tree branches. Stephen Devenish opened the door and, standing aside to let them come in, asked if there was any news of his lost child.

'We are following up a number of leads,' said Burden.

He knew how inadequate this must sound to the bereaved father, but what else could he say? It had the merit of being true. Devenish, he thought and Wexford thought, looked a lot less distraught than Rosemary Holmes had when her daughter disappeared. Even the Crownes, in his situation, had been nearer the panic edge than this calm, courteous man who took them into the study where his wife lay on the hide-covered sofa, covered by a car rug. The room was such an abode of maleness and somehow so stern that Wexford fancied a woman might feel uncomfortable in it, but Fay Devenish had apparently chosen to relax and rest here.

'Darling,' her husband said gently, 'we expected to see Chief Inspector Wexford this afternoon, didn't we?' He turned to Burden. 'And you are?'

'Inspector Burden.'

'How do you do? We don't want to pester you but naturally we are anxious.'

The woman on the sofa looked ill. Her face was not so much white as grey and she was shivering in spite of the blanket which covered her. She struggled to sit, while pulling the blanket up to her chin. The hands which clutched its border were the pathetic little hands of a monkey clinging to the bars of its cage.

'Don't try to sit up, Mrs Devenish,' Wexford said. 'It's best for you to rest. Has your GP seen you?' These days he seemed to be always recommending people to seek medical attention.

She shook her head, then nodded.

'Of course the doctor has seen you, darling,' said Devenish and gently prised open the thin grey fingers, laying them on the blanket. 'Try and relax, that's better.' He stroked her cheek, smoothed the hair back from her forehead. 'You've nothing to tell the Chief Inspector that I can't tell him.'

Wexford nodded. 'Mr Devenish, it is impossible that whoever took Sanchia away could have used your ladder to climb up to the window of her room. And highly improbable that he or she brought a ladder along. Our investigations have shown it to be equally improbable that entry was effected to Sanchia's room from the outside. Whoever took her did so from the inside. Now, there were no signs of a break-in or a forced entry. Who, besides yourselves, has a key to this house?'

'No one at all,' said Devenish.

Burden, who had difficulty in taking his eyes off Fay Devenish, he was so shocked by the sight of her, said, 'No cleaning woman, sir, no gardener?'

'The gardener never comes into the house. My wife does the housework herself.' The surprise that showed in their faces communicated itself to him, for he said hastily, as if in defence, 'She'd be the first to tell you that since she has no profession, running our home is her job. It suits her and she has never wanted help.'

Protesting too much, thought Wexford. And what, for God's sake, was Devenish's own *profession*? He was the managing director, or something like that, of an airline.

'Your sons?'

As if on cue, after the sound of a door somewhere opening and closing, the two boys came into the room. Came tentatively and stood in the doorway, as if they expected to see something inside that no one would wish to see. The younger, Robert, looked at his mother and quickly away. The elder, Edward, who was as tall as a man but with a child's soft, vulnerable face, turned his eyes on Stephen Devenish and, curiously, unexpectedly, closed his hands into fists. As if he were going to hit him, Wexford thought. No, as if he would give it a year or two and then hit him.

But Devenish was smiling benignly at the boys. He went up to them and put an arm round each. 'They don't have a key,' he said. 'Big they may be but they're not quite old enough for a key to the door, are you, boys?'

Fay Devenish spoke for the first time. Her fall must have injured her mouth to account for her lisp and Wexford saw that she talked with difficulty. 'One of our neighbours fetched them from school and they came in by the back door. We don't lock the back door in the daytime.'

'But you do by night?'

'Of course. Always.' She sounded more than normally emphatic, almost as if she was afraid to open a chink of doubt.

The children had wriggled out from under their father's arms and retreated from the room. Devenish smiled ruefully. 'They grow up too soon as it is.'

'If no one has a key now,' said Burden, 'has anyone ever had one? Keys can be copied, you know.'

Fay Devenish turned her face into the cushion on which her head rested. Her husband drew the blanket up over her shoulders and said to the policemen, 'I'd like my wife to be left to rest now. Let us talk in the living-room.'

Unwell she might be, but she had maintained her high standards. The beautiful room had been dusted and the furniture polished, and fresh flowers were in the vases. The air was scented with the white and purple lilac that filled a huge Chinese urn. Her little daughter had vanished but still she made flower arrangements and cleaned the silver ornaments and plumped up the cushions.

'Do sit down,' said Devenish. 'I'd offer you tea, but as you've seen, my wife is hardly in any condition to make it.'

And you can't? Wexford didn't say it aloud. 'I had the impression, Mr Devenish, that you brought us in here to tell us of someone who once did have a key. Am I right?'

'Yes. But I'm feeling rather – well, I should have told you before.'

'Are you saying that this person wasn't on your list of relatives and friends?'

Trying to make light of it, Devenish gave a light,

deprecating laugh. 'I'd better come clean, hadn't I? She's a friend of my wife's, this woman, and frankly, to be absolutely honest, I can't stand her. Well, used to be her friend, only after several very unfortunate incidents – I don't think I need say more – I . . .'

'Put your foot down, Mr Devenish?'

'Oh, come.' For the first time Devenish showed irritation. 'I was going to say I persuaded my wife that she wasn't a very suitable person for a friend, especially round the children. We only had the boys then, but even so . . .'

'What's her name?' Burden asked.

Having gone so far, Devenish had to tell them. 'She's a Miss Andrews, Jane Andrews. She lives in Brighton. I don't have the address but she'll be in the phone book. She had the key because quite a long time ago, when Robert was only three, she came to stay here and look after the place while we went away on holiday. It was my wife's idea, of course. We had a cat then and she took care of the cat as well. It was soon after that that my wife agreed with me the best thing to do would be to break with her. I asked for my key back and naturally she gave it to me but that's not to say she didn't have another one cut, is it?'

Wexford nodded. He would see this Jane Andrews, follow it up, but he interpreted Devenish's remarks as paranoia. And they made him see the man in a new light. Does a normal person with a good adjustment to life suspect a friend of deviously having keys cut to his house?

He changed the subject abruptly. 'I don't suppose you've had any more of those threatening letters, have you, Mr Devenish?'

'Oh, those. No, I'd have told you.'

'Well, you didn't tell us before, sir.'

'I couldn't see why they'd be important,' Devenish said.

'I think you know why now,' Burden put in. 'They mean you've an enemy, don't they? Now do you think the writer of those letters would be capable of abducting Sanchia? Did any of them threaten to get revenge on you through a member of your family?'

'Several of them threatened to make my wife a widow and my children orphans, if you call that getting revenge through my family. They said nothing about harming *them*.'

Extraordinary terminology, Wexford was thinking as they were shown out of the room. The phrases had a biblical ring, as if they came from a psalm. One of those nasty, savage psalms that were full of fire and brimstone, and whole tribes put to the sword. Distantly, from some nether regions, he heard the sound of a cuckoo clock, cuckoo-ing five times.

# Chapter 12

The streets in the cluster were all called after geometric shapes, Rhombus, Oval, Pyramid and Rectangle. It seemed odder than flower names or girls' names or battlefields. No one knew why and since the streets had been built and named more than a hundred years ago it was unlikely anyone would ever know now. Pyramid Road had nothing to do with Egypt or mountain peaks or the tombs of kings. Like its fellows, it was a mean little street of mean little houses without front gardens or trees, originally constructed to accommodate workers in the chalk quarries.

Such back streets may be found in all English country towns but photographs of them never appear in guidebooks or on postcards. This one was now on the route of the Stowerton one-way traffic system, linking a roundabout to the beginning of the shopping area. Heavy goods vehicles rumbled along it from dawn till midnight. During the hours of darkness it was brightly lit for the benefit of the traffic and against the wishes of residents, but no lights were on now in the early afternoon of a sunny day in May.

The house Trevor Ferry lived in was almost identical in shape and size to that owned by Rosemary Holmes and only two streets away, but still there was all the difference in the world between them. Hers looked as if she had begun improving it when she moved in, perhaps ten years before, and those enhancements continued; it was comfortable, very nearly luxurious, there were books and flowers and the means of making music, and the best possible use had been made of restricted space. When he entered Trevor Ferry's house Burden, who had watched the film with his wife on Sunday evening, quoted to himself the opening line of *Who's Afraid of Virginia Woolf*, 'What a dump!'

Although, as he was to tell Burden, Ferry had been living there for nearly a year now, the living-room was still piled with the crates and boxes moved from his former home. The few pieces of furniture, fireside chairs and a wooden-armed settee, a gatelegged table and cane stools, seemed set out solely for the purpose of the maximum viewing of television. At two in the afternoon, Ferry had been watching it. Not some sports fixture of international interest, not politics, not even a quiz game, but a cheerful young woman demonstrating the mixing and baking of croissants. He had the look of the long-term unemployed, dull-faced, perpetually tired, always at a loose end.

'I haven't worked since Seaward Air said they "had to let me go",' he said. 'Nice expression that, don't you think? "We'll have to let you go", as if I'd been begging to be released. That was getting on for two years ago and d'you know how many jobs I've applied for in that time? Three hundred. Well, three hundred and twenty-one, to be precise.'

'So you've no reason to be very fond of Stephen Devenish?'

Ferry switched off the television just as Burden was about to ask him to do so. He was a small man and overweight, with the unhealthy fat of the drinker of stout and eater of junk food. But his face was pale and puffy, and he had adopted the balding man's unwise trick of combing strands of longer hair over the naked pate in an attempt to disguise it. The eyes which fixed Burden in a disconcerting stare were a pale toffee-brown, the white blood-spotted. Burden thought he knew what the man's reply would be and was astonished when Ferry said, 'Why? What's he done now?'

Burden hesitated. 'What would you expect him to have done, Mr Ferry?'

'I only meant, who else has he given the boot to. Or, come to that, been bloody to or lost his temper with.'

'You wouldn't describe him as a charming man, then?'

'He can be.'

'To women?'

'He's not one of those, what these days they call sex addicts. I'll give him that, he's devoted to his wife. I suppose he's got some good in him. I asked you what he'd done.'

'I know you did, Mr Ferry,' said Burden, who wasn't going to be spoken to like that. 'I heard you. It isn't what he's done but what's been done to him.' It was still too soon to mention the missing child to Ferry or anyone else. 'Someone's been sending him threatening letters. Anonymous letters.'

'No kidding,' said Ferry and he looked happier than he had since Burden arrived. 'Threatening what?'

Burden didn't answer. 'He's got a little daughter. She's nearly three. Have you ever seen her?' He knew at once from Ferry's expression, his obvious lack of interest, that this man had nothing to do with the kidnapping of Devenish's child.

Ferry said, 'His wife brought her into the Kingsmarkham office once – you know they've an office there, and one at Gatwick and another in Brighton. I happened to be there. I can't say I'm much of a child-lover and as for babies . . .'

'I suppose you draw unemployment benefit, Mr Ferry?'

'Yes, I do, if it's any business of the police. And I'm likely to draw it as far as I can see till it's replaced by the old age pension. Fortunately, my wife has a job.' Ferry's voice had taken on a scathing edge of sarcasm. 'Fortunately, we have no children, no *little daughters*. She went back to teaching when Devenish "let me go". Didn't want to, of course. Who would when they've been a lady of leisure living in Kingsbrook Valley Drive? And she has to work in the private sector, which means less pay.'

'You mentioned just now people Mr Devenish had been unpleasant to or with whom he'd lost his temper. Can you give me the names of any of those people.'

Ferry gave a harsh laugh. 'There'd be too many of them. The answer's practically everyone he came in contact with.'

Jane Andrews was out shopping but her mother was at home, a garrulous and highly articulate old woman who, in the space of ten minutes, had told Wexford she was seventy-two years old, a widow who had lived in this Victorian villa for forty years (and intended to die in it), that she had two daughters, Jane and Louise, that Louise too was a widow and that Jane had been married twice and divorced twice, circumstances which Mrs Probyn spoke of as if they were symptoms of a life-threatening disease.

'My daughters haven't had very happy lives, Chief Inspector. Poor Jane is one of these career women, so-called, who's sacrificed married happiness to the demands of the job. She's something in PR, which my late husband always said meant proportional representation but nowadays seems to mean public relations, whatever that may be.'

'She has always lived with you?'

'My goodness, no. One flat after another she's had, and what you might call one husband after another, I suppose. But when my husband died – I firmly believe the balance of his mind was disturbed, poor man – he left a very curious will.' Mrs Probyn said this in the manner of an old-fashioned story-teller about to relate, before an audience, a tale of mystery and suspense. She paused dramatically, then went on, 'My daughter Louise is a rich woman. Her husband left her extremely well off. She, at least, doesn't have to work. You might say that her only misfortune – apart from losing him, of course – is her failure to have children. Well, that's my view of it. But I digress. Quite reasonably, my husband felt he need leave her nothing, as he might also have felt with regard to poor Jane, whose troubles I must say have been largely of her own making. But alas, no. Under the terms of his will, this house, my home for forty years, was left to Jane, giving me only a life interest. In other words, I was to live here for the term of my natural life but in point of fact it belongs to Jane. There! What do you think of that?'

Wexford had no intention of saying what he thought of it, his principal reflection being that if he had been Jane Andrews he would have gone on occupying one of those flats rather than move in here with this loquacious harpy. But he was saved from some anodyne reply by a newcomer's arrival.

At first he thought this was a man and the illusion lasted a few seconds. A rather feminine-looking man, certainly, with tip-tilted nose and full lips, but quite tall enough, not far short of six feet, and flat-chested. Then he saw her hands and noticed the absence of an

Adam's apple. She spoke to her mother, held out her hand to him and said hallo. The voice was deep and rather harsh. She was no more dressed like a man than the average woman, her jeans and white shirt and trainers were almost a uniform, and her hair was simply fashionably short. The illusion faded.

She seemed to be in her late thirties, very slim and quite good-looking. Make-up would have improved her, for her skin was poor, pitted on the cheeks with pinprick acne scars. Her face shone with the exertion of carrying two heavy bags up the hill. She dropped them on the floor and sat down, sprawled in an armchair. He told her who he was and asked her about her friendship with Fay Devenish. He believed she was still in possession of a key to Woodland Lodge. Before answering, she suggested that her mother leave them alone.

'She does have her own sitting-room,' she said, as the old woman left the room with an offended air. 'And it's not this one. This is a big house, plenty of room for two women to live in without actually meeting all that often.' She smiled to soften the harshness of her remarks. 'I expect you think I'm being very mean. Sorry. I've only myself to blame for moving in here. I should have stayed where I was or taken my sister's offer to share with her. She doesn't live far away.'

Having no comment to make, Wexford said nothing.

'What was it you asked me about Fay?'

'I said I believed you were a friend of hers.'

'I was once,' she said, 'but no longer.'

'There was a quarrel?'

'Not between her and me, if that's what you mean.'

'Then between you and her husband?'

'Let me put it this way. He doesn't like her to have

210

friends. He told her to stop seeing me and stop – well, communicating with me. He's jealous. He's even jealous of his own children. And that's absolutely all I'm going to say.'

No policeman worth his salt takes much notice of that frequently uttered statement. 'Jealous how? Are you saying he dislikes his children? How about the little girl?' Wexford purposely used the present tense. 'Does he dislike *her*?'

'I never said anything about dislike. I said he was jealous. And I've never seen Sanchia. I just about know she exists, that's all. I haven't seen the boys for years.'

Wexford could tell she was unaware of the slip she had made. He looked at her thoughtfully. 'What became of the key, Miss Andrews?'

'What key?'

'The key the Devenishes gave you when you stayed in the house to look after their cat.'

'That was years and years ago.'

'About seven years.' Wexford was watching her carefully and he saw that a muscle in the corner of her left eye had begun twitching. It was very slight, a mere flicker, but she put up her hand and touched it with one finger to hold it still. 'Was there some reason for you to have the key copied?'

She said too quickly and too indignantly, 'That would be dishonest and I'm not dishonest. I really don't want to say any more about the Devenishes, so if you don't mind ...'

'Do you own a car, Miss Andrews?'

'Of course I do,' she said.

She sounded exasperated, but more than that. Nervous too? Most people were nervous when questioned by the police. Innocent or guilty, they were apprehensive. He tried to imagine her driving to Ploughman's Lane in the middle of the night, parking her car on the Woodland Lodge drive, entering the house and going upstairs, picking up out of her bed a child she had never seen before, preventing that child from crying out – he tried to imagine it and failed. But there was still one odd thing . . .

'Miss Andrews,' he said, 'something puzzles me, I'm bound to say.' He looked at his watch. 'I've been questioning you for the past fifteen minutes yet you've never asked why, you've never asked the reason for our coming here. I find that very strange, don't you?'

She answered quickly, with no hesitation. 'I didn't need to ask. It's because the Devenishes' baby's missing, because Sanchia's missing.'

'But how did you know that?'

'It's been in the papers, it's been on television.'

'No, it hasn't. Come to that, how did you know her name was Sanchia if you have had no contact with Mrs Devenish for seven years.'

The muscle beside her eye jumped again. She closed her eyes for a moment and, opening them, looked straight into Wexford's face. It was the way, he thought, that no one in ordinary social intercourse ever looks at anyone else.

'Well, Miss Andrews?'

'Fay told me, of course. She phoned and told me.'

'So, in spite of what you've said, you do keep in touch?'

Jane Andrews's hands clenched in her lap. 'Stephen doesn't know it but we do phone each other. Once upon a time she used to tell me *everything*. Stephen hated that. He told her I was a lesbian and – and had designs on her. It would be funny if it weren't so stupid and false. I've been *married*, actually I've been married twice. I'm likely to have done that if I were a lesbian, aren't I?'

She was more animated than during the whole of their talk. Colour had come into her pale face and her eyes were so bright they seemed full of tears.

On his way home he stopped off in Ploughman's Lane. The house Sylvia had once lived in, before she and Neil and the boys moved out into the real country, was next door but three to Woodland Lodge, if you could use such an expression about a neighbourhood in which properties were fifty yards apart. He had always liked the house, one of the smallest in this neighbourhood, its unpretentious comfortable Arts and Crafts ashlar and gables, its simple garden with strategically placed trees. The people who had bought it had added a double garage and a glazed porch. The planning department must have allowed it, he supposed, regretting past simplicity and spaciousness. Short of cutting them down, no one could do much to spoil the beauty of the trees up here, the copper beeches at their loveliest golden red in May, the horse chestnuts in flower, the oaks just coming into amber-green leaf. That place had been called, was still called, Laburnum House. The trees after which it was named were still in bud, their yellow blossoms due to appear within days. He had never liked laburnums since Sylvia, aged three, had been rushed to hospital after eating a fallen seed pod in her grandmother's garden.

The curious thought came to him that in a case like that the parents knew almost from the start their child's fate and future. Within minutes he and Dora had been told that Sylvia's stomach had been pumped, she was fine, she would *be* fine. The Devenishes knew nothing of their daughter's where-abouts, her well-being, the state of her mind, not even if she were still alive.

At Woodland Lodge the older boy Edward

answered the door. He said, without waiting to be asked, 'My mother's asleep and my father's in the garden.'

'I'll walk round and find your dad,' Wexford said, wondering, as he took the path that led round the back of the house, why a boy of twelve referred to his parents so formally instead of using his own gentler diminutive.

How did people get their lawns like that? This one was like green felt, closely shaven. Stephen Devenish was standing in the middle of it, clipping the edge of the turf round a large rosebed with a pair of long-handled shears. Strange thoughts seemed to be dodging in and out of his mind today, Wexford reflected as he walked towards him, speculations and unprecedented fancies. Why on earth, for instance, did he feel that he would have much preferred to encounter Devenish when he wasn't armed with a dangerous implement? The man was charming, gracious, courteous, patient and civilised, wasn't he? Not always. Not when he talked about Jane Andrews.

And as if he read Wexford's mind, it was to her that he immediately reverted as he laid the offensive weapon on the grass. 'I'm afraid I spoke a mite roughly about Miss Andrews when I talked to you earlier.' He smiled, that ever-present smile apparent even in the worst adversity. 'She meant well. No man likes to see an outsider come between him and his wife though, does he? An intervener, wouldn't she be called?'

'That was in divorce cases, Mr Devenish,' said Wexford. 'She was the female equivalent of a co-respondent.'

'Really?'

'As to outsiders, as you put it, most women have

women friends apart from the couples they and their husbands or partners call their friends.'

'We don't,' said Devenish. 'We have each other. We don't need anyone else. Come into the house.'

Wexford followed him. They went in through the back door into a kind of boot room and thence into a large, well-appointed, immaculate kitchen. In a dining or breakfast area, the table was laid for an evening meal for four, a white cloth instead of place mats, silver instead of bone-handled cutlery, flowers in a vase. Again he thought how peculiar it was that Fay Devenish did all this on her own without help, and apparently still did it while her baby daughter was missing, while she was distraught and while her doctor had evidently sedated her and told her to rest.

He wanted to say something like this, that frankly he was troubled, that he was like someone in a dark wood, confused and disorientated. No one could have got into this house without breaking in but on the other hand, no one could have brought in a ladder. Most significantly, no stranger could have taken Sanchia without the child's crying and disturbing her parents. He wanted to say it, he had begun to say it, when, unexpectedly and dreadfully, Stephen Devenish burst into tears. He flung his arms across the neatly laid table, lowered his head and sobbed. He shook with sobs, his shoulders heaving, his hands clenched.

Very taken aback, Wexford sat opposite him patiently. There was nothing he could do, he hardly knew why he had come. Perhaps just to see this man again, this house again. He looked about him, studying his surroundings. The counters were laden with equipment of the steamer, rice cooker, pasta maker variety. A knife block of some dark hardwood held seven or eight horn-handled knives. The walls were hung with blue and white porcelain plates,

Royal Copenhagen and Delft. There was a calendar of the Highlands and a cuckoo clock. Last time he was in the house he had heard it tell the hour, but distantly. Now, suddenly, a jaunty painted cuckoo popped out and flapping its beak, cuckoo-ed six times.

At the fourth 'cuckoo' Stephen Devenish raised his face. He had been drumming on the table with his fists, and had knocked over the pepper pot and the flower vase. One of the glasses fell over and rolled on to the floor. Wexford got up and filled another with water from the tap. He said quietly, 'Here, drink this, come on' and wondered why he couldn't lay a hand on the man's shoulder, why his reluctance to touch Devenish amounted to revulsion.

'I'm a fool,' Devenish said, sitting up, taking the water. 'I couldn't help it. I keep thinking I'll never see her again, she's dead.' His face was dry. He had cried without shedding tears. 'I'll never see her again in this world, those are the words that go round in my head.'

'While there's life there's hope,' Wexford said, in a cliché he didn't normally use.

'Yes, but is there life? Isn't it much more likely there's death?' Devenish drew in a long, shuddering breath. 'I'm sorry I broke down like that. I love my little girl, you see. I want to see her grow up.'

Wexford didn't stay long after that. Incongruously, his last thought as he left that kitchen was that when Fay Devenish woke up the first thing she would do – or would be expected to do? – was straighten, refresh and re-lay that crumpled finger-marked cloth.

So often late home that Dora no longer reproached him or even commented, Wexford nevertheless expected some kind of reproof from his elder daughter. Sylvia had called in on her mother on her

216

way home from work at Kingsmarkham Social Services and was sitting next to her on the sofa, the two of them drinking white wine. But instead of admonishing him she seemed anxious only to defend herself. 'I'm driving, Dad, so I'm positively only having one glass.'

He said, smiling, 'You know, my dear, I can't imagine you ever wilfully breaking the law.'

She flushed with pleasure. 'Can't you? That's nice.'

'If you've a moment I'd like to ask you something you might call in the field of child psychology.'

Dora sprang up. 'I'll get your dinner, Reg, I'll just put it in the microwave.'

'No, don't. I will. In a minute.' He felt a sudden distaste for the idea of expecting any such service from her. 'Sit down,' he said. 'Stay.'

Sylvia finished her wine and set down the glass. 'I'm not a psychologist, Dad, child or otherwise, though I must say people are always taking me for one. I just did a course in it for my degree.'

'You'll do,' her father said. 'Darwin said, I hope I can get it right, "Man has an instinctive tendency to speak, as we see in the babble of our young children; while no child has an instinctive tendency to bake, brew or write." Tell me at what age you'd expect a child to start talking.'

She shrugged. 'I don't know – eighteen months, two? If you mean real words and phrases. Robin was over two but Ben was talking a lot well before two. I suppose it was because his brother was always talking to him.'

'You were a very early talker, Sylvia,' Dora said. 'By eighteen months you could say anything. Sheila was later.'

'Funny how a mother remembers that. I don't, it's completely gone out of my head. So what would you

217

say are the reasons behind it when a child is talking hardly at all at thirty-three months?'

'Thirty-three *months*? That's nearly three years old.' Sylvia looked dubious. 'We're discounting brain damage, I take it?'

'Oh, I think so.'

'He or she could be deaf. That's a real possibility, but these days I'd think that would have been checked out by thirty-three months. Or, of course, it could be some sort of emotional disturbance. Tasneem Fowler at The Hide told me her older boy stopped talking for two months after the younger one was born.'

'But he'd been talking before?' said Wexford. 'He was jealous of the newcomer and that inhibited his powers of speech?'

'Probably. You must have some particular case in mind, Dad. What sort of a home does this child of yours come from?'

'Middle-class, maybe upper-middle-class, plenty of money, nice home, and that's an understatement, natural parents living together and apparently devoted, two older brothers. I would say a much-loved, much-wanted child.'

'Then I haven't a clue,' said Sylvia.

'I remember reading somewhere that Einstein didn't talk till he was three,' Dora said.

'And what on earth is that supposed to prove, Mother?'

After Sylvia had gone he watched the nine o'clock news, then a programme about a new kind of activist, the eco-warrior. A group of these people, fighting their war against genetic engineering, had uprooted a field of wheat in Shropshire and poisoned an orchard in Somerset. The wheat had been genetically altered to create a springier kind of bread and the apples were redder than normal and had no cores. He was looking at a section through a coreless apple when Dora came in and said she was taking winter clothes to the dry-cleaner's in the morning and she couldn't find his raincoat.

'Oh God,' he said, 'I lent it to a chap called Dixon to put over his head and pretend he was a paedophile.'

Dora gave him a strange look. 'Get it back. You don't want to lose it. It's a Burberry.'

She switched off the television and they went to bed. He often had interesting dreams but seldom nightmares. This dream, into which he seemed to fall at once, took him and Dora years back to when they were young and their children very young. He was sitting with Dora, admiring her appearance as she brushed her long dark hair – an ordinary enough romantic cliché – when she turned round and told him quite calmly that Sheila, their baby, had disappeared, had been stolen out of her cot. She had been into the room and found the cot empty.

His grief and terror had known no bounds. He had run through the house, calling to Sheila, begging her to come back, rushed into the street, wakened the town, the world. And then the dream shifted, as such dreams do, and he was in a television studio, being interviewed by a demonic character played by Peter Cushing. He was begging for a message to be sent to the kidnappers, offering a ransom for Sheila, and the ransom – this was the worst part, the positively most dreadful shame-making part – was his elder daughter Sylvia. Take her, he heard himself saying, and give me back Sheila. Then he woke up, sweating and trembling.

At midnight Lynn Fancourt, who had spent the evening at the cinema and afterwards had a drink in the Rat and Carrot with her boyfriend, got into a car that stopped for her at the north end of York Street. In fact, it had stopped for a red light. Lynn tapped on the passenger window and asked for a lift. The driver was a woman someone very young might describe as middle-aged and the passenger was a man of about thirty. They were going, the man said, to Myringham, but could drop her off in Framhurst if that was what she wanted.

From the conversation Lynn soon knew something funny was going on and it wasn't the something funny she was on the lookout for. When the man suggested they stop for ten minutes in a lay-by on the old bypass, she thought it was drugs and was in two minds what to do if controlled substances made their appearance. Nick them for possession? Call the station on her mobile? But she was wrong. The car stopped and both of them got in the back with her, amorously inclined. Lynn's discouraging tactics led the woman to say she quite understood and it would be best to go straight home where they could have their threesome in comfort.

It occurred to Lynn then that they had taken her for a prostitute, a new phenomenon in Kingsmarkham but not unknown. She had only herself to blame for that, tapping on car windows – and at a red light, that was an irony. They were quite nice people, pleasant and gentle, and when she said she had changed her mind they took her to Framhurst just the same and gave her their phone number in case she had second thoughts.

For more than a year now Wexford had stopped taking his local paper. The *Kingsmarkham Courier* had caused him more irritation with Brian St George's coverage of the bypass hostage-taking than he thought within the bounds of anything a man should suffer over the breakfast table. Go through that again he would not, so the paper had been given up. Neither *The Times* nor the *Independent* could ever bring him so much rage, so he would stick with them.

But since his happy relinquishment of the *Courier* his newsagent had taken on a series of new paper boys, most of them inefficient. When it rained they let the papers get wet and if they couldn't find the right one on top of their load they delivered anything that came to hand: a tabloid, maybe, or the *Financial Times*. Any of these would have been infinitely preferable to Wexford than what he saw lying face-up on his doormat. Under the masthead of an eagle with a scroll in its beak, on which the *Courier*'s name was lettered in Gothic script, the lead story leapt out at him.

He closed his eyes, but of course he had to open them again. We always do have to. 'WHERE IS SANCHIA?' the headline read in the largest Roman type available to the *Courier*'s printers, and underneath, only slightly less bold and huge, 'SMITH IN REFUGE WITH COPS'. What the story beneath would say he guessed before he read it. The gist had come into his head the moment he saw those headlines: a baby girl had disappeared, the news had been suppressed while Smith was spirited away, a huge cover-up was in progress. He hadn't, though, anticipated St George's statement – his was the byline – that Thomas Henry Smith was currently accommodated in a refurbished cell 'with all mod cons' at Kingsmarkham Police Station.

Two photographs were inserted in the text, the classic one of Smith taken on his release from prison and featured everywhere, and a portrait of Sanchia Devenish he had never seen before. It had evidently been taken when she was about six months old, for this was a baby, her round almost hairless head resting on a lacy pillow. A fuzzy picture, probably much enlarged. An adult's hand could be seen in one corner – Fay Devenish's? – and what might be the side of a pram or pushchair.

Growling to himself like a cross bear, Wexford took the paper with him into the kitchen and put the kettle on for tea. His instinct, like most people's these days when astounded, delighted, shocked or appalled, was to phone someone. But whom? Southby, of course. He had as little contact with the ACCD as he could achieve. Superintendent Rogers? The desk sergeant at the station? In the end, when he had taken up Dora's tea, when he had observed that it was raining again but had not reverted to the subject of his missing raincoat, he fell back on the old faithful and phoned Burden.

'I've seen it,' Burden said.

'I thought you'd given up that rag.'

'I have. They delivered the wrong papers.'

'You and me both. St George must have seen Wendy Brodrick bring Smith in, he was doubtless prowling about outside or loitering in a parked car. They were only there five minutes.'

'Long enough. Where did he get that picture of Sanchia?'

'God knows. Those Devenishes hadn't a photo to give us but St George gets one. Not that we'd have been interested in this, a child of six months looks nothing like how it will two years later. That photograph of St George's would no more help find Sanchia Devenish than a shot of you or me.'

Burden said thoughtfully, 'Maybe the Devenishes didn't give it to him. You know how the *Courier* organises all those contests, allegedly for charity – the guy with the biggest feet, some ghastly ferret competition, Miss Kingsmarkham till the feminists stopped it – well, I've been wondering if Sanchia was ever in a baby show, if maybe she *won* a baby show and they took the picture. She was a pretty baby, wasn't she?'

These words, uncharacteristic of Burden, moved Wexford so profoundly, driving away all his anger in a moment, bringing him instead an ache of sadness at that past tense, that he was silent. The poor little girl, he thought, please God or Fates or Furies, let whoever's got her be kind to her.

Burden said, 'Are you still there?'

'I'm here.' Wexford cleared his throat. 'The Devenishes aren't the sort of people to let their daughter compete in a baby show, are they?'

'God knows what sort of people they are. Don't ask me, you'd better ask St George.'

'I mean to,' said Wexford; then he added, with atypical relish, 'I mean to think of a way of punishing him.'

# Chapter 13

This time the trouble began in Stowerton, in Rectangle Road, not far from the homes of Trevor Ferry and Rosemary Holmes, where Joe Hebden's brother lived with his girlfriend, two children of hers and two children of his. David Hebden drove the van that delivered new copies of the *Courier* fresh off the press to every newsagent in Kingsmarkham, Stowerton and Pomfret, and his round began at six a.m. Reading was not among his skills, though he was able to decipher the headlines on the sports pages. What drew his attention to the *Courier* this wet morning was a name, one of the few he could read and which happened to be that with which his girlfriend's younger daughter had been christened.

David Hebden was very fond of little Sanchia. She was not his child but he liked her better than his own children whom he saw as coming between him and his ex-wife. For a fearful half-hour he thought something dreadful had happened to her. Why otherwise would her name be in the paper?

Asking other people to read things to him was something he avoided whenever he could, so he said nothing to any of the newsagents, simply growing more and more anxious and frustrated each time his eye lighted on that beloved name in that horrible huge print. When he got home everyone was still asleep. He rushed upstairs to look for Sanchia, found her in bed with her mother, where she must have come after he left, and woke up the whole household with his whoops of joy.

Sanchia's mother Katrina took the paper from him and read the story. After a while the other children came in and sat on the bed, seeing in this break from routine a prospect of excitement.

'The police are a disgrace,' said Katrina. 'This little kid's been missing since Monday and what do they do? Not look for her, or her body more like, oh, no, they turn the police station into a hotel with all mod cons to keep that paedophile in luxury.'

'What's a paedophile, Mum?' said Georgina, aged six.

'Ask no questions and you'll get no lies. I'm going to give Joe and Charlene a phone, Dave. Or you can, it's your duty, they've a right to know.'

Since the departure of Smith from the Muriel Campden Estate, all the excitement and most of the heat had simmered down. Another event had convulsed the residents of Puck, Ariel and Oberon Roads: Colin Crowne's assault on and destruction of Jodi the virtual baby. It had happened on the day before Lizzie Cromwell was due to return Jodi to the Social Services. After her fight with Brenda Bosworth and acknowledgement by everyone except Miroslav himself that he was the father of her child, Lizzie had seemed to lose interest in Jodi. From nursing him and feeding and changing him, putting him in his cot, lifting him up again and constantly cuddling him, she had passed rapidly to total indifference and Jodi, unattended for the first time in his short life, for he had been new-born when he came to her, began to cry. He cried and sobbed and wailed, and when the crying mechanism ran out his tape rewound and he began again.

'You can't just put him on the back burner, you know,' Debbie scolded.

Colin said nothing. Nor did he make any attempt to immobilise Jodi by removing his batteries or even smothering him. At nine at night when the robot had been crying for six hours, he picked him up by the legs and smashed him against the bathroom wall. Bits of Jodi, his limbs and his mechanism and his fine handsome head, fell into the bath where Colin stamped on them.

Lizzie didn't care, she was bored with the whole thing, but she had to explain to the social worker. Colin wasn't there, it was his day at the Job Centre for signing on. The social worker said such a thing had never happened before and what sort of a mother would Lizzie make when she had a real baby? Of course she or her mother or her stepfather would have to pay for a replacement for Jodi and did she realise how much a virtual baby cost?

Colin came home and said over his dead body would they make him pay for breaking a fucking stupid doll, and Debbie said she wouldn't either, on principle. It probably would be his dead body, anyway, Colin said, he'd already started coming out in a rash all round his waist and down his bum. No one appreciated the stress he'd suffered through having that thing in the house and God knew what it would be like with a real baby.

News of this unjust claim on the part of Kingsmarkham's Social Services Department spread round Muriel Campden like a bush fire. Almost everyone took the Crowne–Cromwell side with the exception of the Mitchells, Monty Smith and Maria Michaels. Monty Smith had been put on probation and required to pay an unimaginably large sum (which he borrowed off Maria) for hitting Sergeant Fitch, and his view was that if he had been unfairly fined why should others get off scot-free?

'How d'you make a petrol bomb?' Colin Crowne had said to Joe Hebden in the Rat and Carrot the night before.

'You what? You're barking.'

'No, I saw it on the telly. It was somewhere like Algeria or Iraq, some place like that, and this lot was throwing petrol bombs at the government. I thought to myself, they ought to do that to the council, make them sit up.'

A man neither of them had ever seen before said, 'You fill up a bottle with petrol, like a milk bottle.'

'We don't get milk bottles no more,' said Colin.

'Right. You don't. Any bottle so long as it's not plastic. Fill it up and stuff the top with a bit of rag. You put paraffin on the rag, pink or blue paraffin, don't matter, and you light it with a match and throw it. You throw it right away, mind, no hanging about or you'll go up in flames. But you don't need the hassle. You want one, I can supply it. There's a market for them things.'

'It was a joke,' said Joe.

The man only laughed and said he'd buy them a drink, then he'd like to show them something.

Joe's wife Charlene took the call from her brother-in-law at seven thirty next morning. That the child was still missing didn't much concern her. She knew that, everyone on Muriel Campden knew it, if the media didn't. But Smith in hiding at Kingsmarkham Police Station! In luxurious accommodation! Charlene was fond of saying that the world was divided into those who don't and those who do, and she was a doer. She got dressed, grabbed an umbrella and went out into the triangle, knocking on every door.

There are fat men who are solid like Carl Meeks, men

with big shoulders and bellies like convex drums, taut as if corseted but corseted in vain, and there are fat men whose obesity seems liquid, seems to slosh around inside a thin membrane, so that a pinprick would reduce them to a collapsed balloon. Brian St George, editor of the *Kingsmarkham Courier* was of the latter sort, and his liquidity was currently flowing over the arms of Wexford's chair and seeping like a tide against the edge of the desk. His shirt was meant to be white but looked, as usual, as if it had been put through the wash in company with a pair of black jeans and a red T-shirt. If he had a tie with him it must have been in his pocket. Since becoming bald, he had grown his remaining hair very long so that if you eyed him from above, as Wexford was now doing, his head looked like a big white daisy with a pinkish-yellow centre.

He had come to the police station when summoned, perhaps not much fancying the Chief Inspector's presence in the *Courier*'s offices, sat down in this chair and suffered a grilling. St George put up a spirited defence, half whining, half aggressive, and insisted he was obliged to 'improvise' because Kingsmarkham police never told him anything.

' "The Kingsmarkham Six",' said Wexford disgustedly.

'I didn't think it up,' Brian St George said as if in mitigation. 'It's vindictive, it's revenge. You know you don't treat me fairly, Reg.'

'Don't call me that,' said Wexford.

'Sorry, I'm sure. I'd been under the impression we were all old friends here. You Reg, me Brian. It's formality gone mad the way you call me "Mr St George".'

'Call it what you like but we'll keep to formality under this roof. If you believed Smith was hidden here, what stopped you phoning your old friend and checking? No, don't bother to answer. You'd have got a denial and a denial was the last thing you wanted. You'd have had no story.'

St George shifted his floppy bulk an inch or two. A gap opened between two of his shirt buttons to reveal a circle of hairy pink skin. Wexford tried not to look at it. The editor of the *Kingsmarkham Courier* took a packet of Marlboros from his pocket, looked round for an ashtray but in spite of not seeing one, lit his cigarette.

'This is a smoke-free zone,' said Wexford.

'It never used to be,' St George protested. 'Since when?'

'Since nine this morning.' Wexford looked at his watch, which showed three minutes past. 'Put that fag out, come on now.'

Slowly and with an expression of bitter regret, St George stubbed out his cigarette. 'The story's in all the nationals,' he pleaded. 'It's the *Mail*'s front-page lead.'

'Only because you told them. Apparently there have been calls coming in from them all night. Everything has to be denied. Smith is not here. Smith was here for precisely five minutes, sitting in a car in the car-park. I suppose you saw him brought in.'

'Guilty, my lord,' said St George, managing a boyish grin.

'And passed on your think-piece to the media but too late for them to upstage the *Courier*.'

'Well, what would you have done in my place, Reg? Sorry, I mean Mr Wexford.'

'Behaved like a responsible citizen, but that's an alien concept to you, I know. It's too late now to do anything about it. We must hope there's no harm done. Where did you get the photograph of Sanchia?'

'I can't reveal my sources, you know that.'

'I'm not talking about your sources, I'm talking

about a photograph you must either have got from the child's parents or have taken yourself at some earlier time.'

'It was when her dad got a big salary increase, a hundred K or whatever, and we ran a "fat cats" story. You know, "Can Airline Tycoon Justify Massive Pay Rise?"'

'What had that to do with Sanchia?'

'Human interest, you know that. Family values. Our photographer happened to see Mrs D. out with the baby. As a matter of fact, that's how we knew her first name, going through the picture archives. They were calling her Sasha and Sarah and all sorts.'

Wexford looked at him in disgust. 'We shall be not offering any information to your newspaper in future on any subject whatsoever, so you will please instruct your staff that reporters who normally come in for the twice-weekly press release will no longer be welcome.'

St George got to his feet, his whole body on the wobble. 'Now look here, you can't do this. This is outrageous, I'll go to the Chief Constable.' Echoing Dora's own words, he said, 'That's like the Stasi, it's like the KGB.'

'It may be like the Taliban for all I care,' said Wexford.

Any further comments he might have made were cut off by the noise of breaking glass from below. It sounded as if something had struck one of the windows on a lower floor. Wexford went to his window and looked out. He stood there quite still for a moment, then he turned round and beckoned to Brian St George. 'Come and see the result of your handiwork,' he said.

By eight-thirty most of the population of Kingsmarkham and the villages knew that a child was missing and a notorious paedophile under police protection. The rumour that Smith had killed Sanchia Devenish, confessed to her murder and been given refuge in Kingsmarkham Police Station to save him from being torn to pieces by all right-thinking local parents was started by a woman in Glebe Road. She was herself the mother of two, the elder of whom had been the victim of an indecent assault by a man from Stowerton. With her half-sister Jacky Flay, Jacky's daughter Kaylee and half a dozen of her neighbours she set forth on foot – it wasn't more than a quarter of a mile – and half-way there encountered a contingent from the Stowerton end of the town. This band of protesters all carried paper banners, rapidly improvised, bearing the legends: *We Want Smith* and *Save Our Babies*. If it had only continued to rain, as Wexford said later, the whole demonstration might have been avoided, as many of these people would have been reluctant to get wet. But the rain had stopped at a quarter to eight, giving place to an angrily blue sky, bright sunshine and a strong northwest wind.

The two groups met, by chance, outside the Job Centre where they paused to muster their forces. Truants from Kingsmarkham Comprehensive, the usual dispirited teenagers, were already sitting on the wall outside. They were half asleep on account of being got up early by their parents and sent to school. Nothing ever happened in this dump, according to them, so they were delighted to be asked to join the protest. Just as they were all on the march again, turning into the High Street, the bus from Stowerton stopped outside the Olive and Dove and David Hebden got off it with Katrina, her daughters Georgina and Sanchia, and his sons Grant and Jason, the children having been kept from school for a more important activity.

Recognising their purpose from the sandwich board worn by Grant (a cut-out of two children holding hands with Save the Little Children on the front and All Paedos for the Chop on the back), the Glebe Road group welcomed them with open arms and the whole party, now thirty strong, marched up the High Street past St Peter's Church. They were such an orderly group that WPC Lydia Wingate and PC Leslie Wilson, out on the beat, held up the traffic at the Kingsbrook bridge to let them cross the road.

Meanwhile, a bigger crowd was streaming out of the Muriel Campden into York Street. Missing for various reasons such as pregnancy, simple cautiousness, genuine illness and fear of paying more fines or even imprisonment, were Lizzie Cromwell, Suzanne Smith, Sue Ridley and Pete McGregor, and Monty Smith. But Brenda Bosworth was there with Miroslav Zlatic in the lead followed by Hebdens, Keenans, Carl and Linda Meeks, Maria Michaels and Shirley Mitchell, and Tasneem Fowler's Terry with Kim and Lee. Many of them were carrying what looked like full shopping bags but there was nothing particularly suspicious about this and when Lydia Wingate saw them she even failed to notice that they were the Muriel Campden residents she had encountered the previous weekend.

They joined up with the Stowerton and Glebe Road protest outside the Heaven Spent shopping mall. Joe and David Hebden were each overcome with emotion at the sight of his brother and fell into one another's arms, embracing and patting backs, both having reached their mid-thirties without doing such a thing in their lives before. This show of fraternal love put heart into the fifty or so people who had assembled and they cheered before marching on towards the police station.

But orderliness had ended with the arrival of the

Muriel Campden cohort. Here was the contrast between the effete and weary old town and the vital and energetic new, and it was as if the old had received a stimulating injection that put fire into their veins, for they began to sing as they walked, their voices low at first but rising in a steady crescendo. To the tune of 'Stand by Your Man' they chanted, 'Stand by your kids, and tell them that you love them ...' Who had been responsible for this inspired translation of Tammy Wynette's song no one seemed to know but later the consensus of opinion was that it had been Brenda Bosworth.

So they proceeded along the east end of the High Street, a troop of people all between the ages of two and forty, a company of the young, the youngest in pushchairs and the oldest with a balding head and incipient belly, all singing that perhaps best-known of country songs, if an old-fashioned one to most of them. They carried their bags and their banners, and the bright sun shone on them and the wind blew the women's hair all over the place, and just after nine o'clock they came up to the railings outside Kingsmarkham Police Station. The gates were open, the car-park, which could just be glimpsed round the side, was full of cars and there was no one about.

The protest hesitated. Carl Meeks, questioned later by the police, said that they had been taken aback to see no one. The emptiness of the place was uncanny. And even the big double doors were shut. If someone had come out, some 'responsible officer', they could have put their case to him or her. They would have told the officer, said Carl Meeks, to take Smith elsewhere, anywhere so that he was finally removed from Kingsmarkham. As it was, no one came out. But for the cars, there might have been no one inside.

Who led them on to the outer courtyard where

stood just one police car and one unmarked car? Again it was suggested it must have been Brenda Bosworth, though nobody could remember. One thing was certain. Once they began to pass through the gateway they stopped singing and a silence fell. It seemed to Shirley Mitchell that the whole town was hushed, traffic became soundless and even the blackbird in the maple tree on the forecourt ceased his song. In silence they walked to within a few yards of the steps and the double doors, and there they stopped to allow the woman they called their spokesperson to pass through. This was Brenda Bosworth who had somehow uncharacteristically found herself at the back of the crowd and had to make her way to the front of it.

While she was doing so a window in the police station opened and Sergeant Joel Fitch put his head out. What he would have said, how he would have admonished them, advised them to go home or take themselves off elsewhere, was never known, for the sight of him to Maria Michaels was like the lighting of a fuse. At once she recognised him not so much as the author of Monty Smith's troubles as the cause of his borrowing everything she had in her Co-operative Bank account to pay his fine. She plunged her hand into the Marks & Spencer bag she was carrying, pulled out a brick and hurled it at Sergeant Fitch.

Maria had been in her early youth the County of Sussex Women's Putting the Shot champion of 1984 and she could still throw further and better than most men. Luckily for him and for her, she failed to hit Fitch but only because he ducked. The brick went through the casement to the left of where his head had been. A short shocked silence was succeeded by loud cheers and the chant was taken up with renewed vigour.

'We want, we want Smith, Smith, Smith!'

The tune this time was that of 'Colonel Bogey' and it brought every passer-by to a halt outside the gates. Perhaps it was this audience that stimulated them, for a hail of cans and stones followed that first brick but only one missile struck a window and broke the glass. The rest hit brickwork and fell harmlessly into the bed of overblown wallflowers at the foot of the wall. But they had the effect of bringing half a dozen police officers running out of the double doors towards the crowd. At the same time Superintendent Rogers opened the french windows in the middle of the front of the building and stepped out on to the balcony, holding a loudhailer. He was accompanied by two other officers, one on either side of him.

'We want Smith, we want Smith, Smith, Smith!'

When the police station was designed in the early sixties the balcony was tacked on for just this purpose: for a senior policeman to stand on and admonish, harangue or reassure a deputation. Jokes had been made about it, references to palaces of justice in small South American states, places where revolution might be expected. It had never been used until today and George Rogers had to seek assistance from the nearest help available, in this case DC Archbold, to get the window open. When he finally stepped out he saw a much larger crowd than he expected, as many as fifty people, all held back by his own officers straining against them with linked hands. No more missiles had been thrown and at the sight of Rogers, with Fitch on one side of him and Archbold on the other, the chanting fell to a low mutter, an angry buzz like that of swarming bees.

On the floor above, at the window, Wexford stood with Brian St George. He had opened the window, having heard what had happened below and being anxious not to be hit by flying glass. The last person he wanted with him in this situation was St George but he could hardly send the man out of the building into, so to speak, the jaws of the protest and certainly not leave him to roam the police station, picking up whatever he might devour.

Once, Rogers, or his equivalent, would have read the Riot Act. Instead, he said into his loudhailer, 'Those persons who have thrown missiles will be dealt with accordingly. Arrests will be made. The rest of you must go home. Smith is not here and has never been here. No child has been killed. You have been misled by false rumours in newspapers. Smith presents no threat whatsoever to your children. Your children are perfectly safe.'

'Where is he then?' called someone from the crowd.

'I'm not at liberty to tell you that,' said Rogers.

'He's in there with you! You're protecting him!'

'We want, we want Smith, Smith, Smith!'

'How would you like it if a child murderer and rapist came and lived next door to your kids? Is that right? Is that fair?' This was Brenda Bosworth. 'How would you like it if the police protected him and made the mums and dads criminals?'

Much as he disliked her, Wexford had to concede that she had a point. How would he have liked it when his daughters were small? Come to that, how would Rogers feel himself, he who had married late and had two children under ten? Rogers had handled it badly. He wouldn't have said that aloud to anyone but Burden and then in the strictest privacy, but Burden wasn't there; for some reason he was late in this morning. Imagine the results of criticising Rogers to St George! Rogers should go inside now, he thought, leave it now. Make his arrests, if he could find the guilty parties. He thought what a ridiculous word 'missile' was, that it had lost its original meaning of something sent by throwing and was now irretrievably associated with a kind of rocket, a projectile bomb, nuclear or otherwise, wielded in war situations. It was strange, he reflected afterwards, that he had been thinking this at that very moment and stranger still that he and he alone witnessed what happened next.

He heard from below Rogers's parting shot, a somewhat feeble, 'I repeat, Smith is not here. He is no longer living among you and he is not in this police station.'

The men on the forecourt coaxed the crowd back, easing them through the gates and out on to the pavement. The chanting had stopped, had died away to a low muttering. Rogers went inside, followed by Fitch and Archbold, and the door to the balcony closed. Wexford was about to shut the window. Instead he opened it wider and looked down.

DS Ted Hennessy had come out of the double doors and was crossing the forecourt towards the gates. To make the threatened arrests? Or simply because until that moment, previously out of sight and earshot in the back of the building, he had come out in all innocence for some quite other purpose? Afterwards Wexford bitterly regretted having taken his eyes from the protesters to look at Hennessy, and thus having missed seeing what he later was told had happened. He saw the thing loop out of the crowd, though, saw it leave an unidentifiable hand, and he cried out, too late, 'Watch out! Get down on the ground!'

The bottle was alight, he saw the thin sheet of flame as it flew and, although it was well below him, ducked, dragging St George with him to the floor. If he hadn't, the explosion would have knocked him off his feet. It was thunderous, deafening, a roar rather than a crash, a great hissing sound like a tornado sucking up air. But not loud enough to drown the scream from the forecourt. A horrible cry it was, scarcely human, the noise you imagined an animal dying by violence might make. Wexford rolled over on to his back. He reached for St George but the man was up, craning out of the window, crying at the top of his voice, 'I saw it! I saw it all!'

Wexford got to his feet. Broken glass was everywhere, crunching under his shoes. The window was gone. Below him a car on the forecourt was burning, a column of flame hissing up into the blue air. The crowd had shrunk, people squatting or even lying on the pavement. Wexford saw Burden come in from the street, come in on his way to work and, his hands up to his face, walk slowly across the now empty forecourt. Behind him, their presence perhaps unknown to him, streamed the press pack with their cameras and their microphones.

It was too late to do anything for the man who had been close to that car. He had disappeared. He was in that inferno, burning along with the metal and the chrome and the leather, somewhere inside that hissing blaze, that eddying spiral of white smoke and black smoke, and the breath-snatching stench of burning petrol.

A groan rose from the crowd. The chain of officers continued to hold them back. Wexford found himself speechless, incapable even of making the mourning regretful moan that came from the people on the pavement. He watched the press approach, cameras flashing, heard in the distance the sound of the fire engines' sirens and then, turning to St George, did something he had never done to a man before; grabbed him by the collar of his jacket as one might take a disobedient dog by the scruff of its neck, and propelled him towards the door.

'I saw it all!' gasped St George, half strangled. 'What a piece of luck!'

# Chapter 14

The death of Ted Hennessy had done nothing to inhibit the media. Their cars filled Ploughman's Lane and Savesbury Road and Winchester Drive, and they set up camp in the front garden of Woodland Lodge. Wexford held an impromptu press conference and did his best to answer questions on the lines of, Why have you been keeping this disappearance dark? And, Can you be certain Thomas Smith has nothing to do with the missing child?

It was in vain that he repeated the simple truth: that Smith had never, in the course of his miserable career, been known to show interest in girls. He had convictions for abusing boys and had been imprisoned for the manslaughter of a boy. In the original meaning of the word he was truly a paedophile.

'He got married, didn't he?' one young woman from a national tabloid asked. 'He's got a daughter.'

'His victims have always been male,' said Barry Vine, who was on the platform with Wexford. 'Smith has nothing to do with the disappearance of Sanchia Devenish.'

Those of them who weren't laying siege to the Devenishes or on Hennessy's widow's doorstep, directed their onslaught to Suzanne Smith, convalescent at 16 Oberon Road. An unfounded rumour had got about that Suzanne was one of her father's early victims, Suzanne must have been an abused child, wretched co-partner in incest. Her head still swathed in bandages, she came out from the boarded-up house through the makeshift door and screamed at them, 'He never laid a finger on me, you filthy buggers! Poor old sod'd have never touched those dirty kids if my mum hadn't gone off and left him. That was what done it, that was what turned him bonkers for dirty kids. You fuck off the lot of you and leave us alone!'

Up in Ploughman's Lane Fay Devenish had picked up the local paper off the doormat at seven thirty. Even before Stephen Devenish had seen it, reporters were ringing his doorbell, pounding on his door, and his phone had started ringing and went on ringing non-stop. He knew better than to answer the door. One of the media people climbed up on to the garage roof and tried to get in through a fanlight. He should have had Kaylee Flay with him, as Wexford remarked when told about it.

Devenish called a taxi to take him to the police station. If he got his own car out the pack would descend on him and maybe gain entrance to the house. The cab company was called All the Sixes and its vehicles regularly plied between Kingsmarkham town, Kingsmarkham Station and the villages. The driver couldn't get through the media people and the parked cars. He left his cab and went on foot. Reporters surrounded him and some clung to him, begging to know who his fare was to be, where was he taking him and to give them a moment to talk to Sanchia's father.

The cab driver felt as if he was in a film. He thought of asking the reporters for a considerable sum to hold Mr Devenish captive, then he thought of losing his job as a result and, besides, the hero – sheriff or principal witness or driver of the stage-coach – must behave heroically, keep silent, be strong and stride boldly to the rescue. So he did his best to ignore them, marched up to the front door and rang the bell. First Devenish put his head out of a window, then he came out. The cab driver said soothingly, 'Now you keep close to me, sir, and don't say a word and you'll be OK. I'm going to take your arm and get you through this bunch of paparazzi – you won't mind that, will you?'

Devenish said he wouldn't mind that, or rather shouted that he wouldn't, for everything he said was drowned by the press pack's questions, their running feet and the clicks and flashes of their cameras. The cab driver took charge, not neglecting to get his own scowling face into the pictures as he masterfully steered Devenish to where the cab waited.

Shivering, Devenish sank into the back, said, 'Thank you. Thank you very much. Frankly, I don't know what I'd have done without you.'

The pack followed but the driver managed to lose them. When they got to the police station Devenish gave him an enormous tip. After he had gone in through the damaged double doors the driver drove twice in a double circle round the forecourt to get a good look at the broken windows and blackened front of the police station. If he got the chance later in the day, he'd come back with a camera.

Stephen Devenish asked for Wexford. No, the Chief Inspector wasn't expecting him but he thought he'd see him and there was no way he was going out there again like a fox running into the jaws of a pack of hounds. The desk sergeant sent him up in the lift and said Wexford would come out to meet him. The first press cars arrived on the forecourt by the time he reached the second floor.

In Wexford's room he didn't complain about media intrusion, but he shouted just the same and Wexford saw for the first time signs of that famous temper. Devenish crashed his fists on the desk. 'Has that paedophile got my child?'

'Please try to keep calm, Mr Devenish.'

'Just answer me!'

'Sit down, please. That's right. I understand your anger. I would feel the same myself in the circumstances. But no, Smith has not got your child.'

'How can you know that? How can you possibly know?'

'We kept her disappearance a secret', Wexford said, 'because we feared the very thing that has happened. It's an unfortunate coincidence that Smith was present in the neighbourhood at the time she went missing, but that's all it is. There is no connection – I hope you understand that.'

'Where is he now, then?'

'I can't tell you that. I'm sorry. But he is not in this building, or indeed in this town.' Wexford was tired of telling people that boys had been Smith's quarry but he repeated to Sanchia's father what he had said so many times before. 'Thomas Smith isn't interested in girls. He's a homosexual paedophile.'

'How disgusting! It makes you sick to your stomach.'

Too bad, Wexford thought, you can't have it both ways. 'We're doing everything we can to find Sanchia,' he said, 'and I can tell you, which I hope may be a comfort to you, that she is not in the hands of any known paedophile on our lists. I'm talking nationwide. No paedophile has her. In these cases, the culprit is very often a disturbed person, usually a woman, who has recently lost her own child or who cannot herself have children. That is why I was so anxious to get from you and your wife the names of all your friends and acquaintances, on the chance that such a woman might be among them.'

Wexford thought he detected a faint difference in

the man's expression, no more than a flicker, a tiny change in the iris of his eyes, a barely perceptible tightening of the mouth. Rather than pursue it, he changed the subject from the possible kidnapper of Sanchia back to the situation in Woodland Lodge on the night she was taken. 'It's not quite a question, Mr Devenish,' he said, 'of who might have a key or who might otherwise gain entrance to your home but rather of how anyone could do so without disturbing you or your wife or your sons and without Sanchia making a noise. Can you really tell me that any stranger could take your little girl out of her bed in the night, wake her and lift her up, and she not cry out or call to you?'

'I don't know.'

Wexford didn't want to ask it but he had to. He had to establish once and for all just how impaired Sanchia's intelligence and faculties were. 'She can cry out, I suppose? You have said she talks very little, but she *can* speak?'

'Of course she can,' Devenish said, quite hotly for him. 'She's not dumb. What are you saying? That she's some sort of idiot?'

'No, Mr Devenish, I'm not saying that. But you must admit yourself that the whole picture is a very strange one. Has any doctor or psychologist given an opinion on why Sanchia isn't talking at the age of two and three-quarters? Has anyone offered an explanation?'

'We haven't asked,' Devenish said. He was calm now, the colour had receded from his face and the charm was back. He spoke lightly, with his habitual half-smile. 'We never thought it necessary. She's a late developer, that's all. Forgive me, but is this to the point? Finding out why she doesn't speak isn't going to find *her*.'

'I like mysteries to be solved,' Wexford said

simply. 'I should like to solve the mystery of these threatening letters you've received. Envy makes enemies and there are plenty who must envy you. For instance, when you secured your present job and later when you received a very large salary increase, there must have been people who were passed over to make way for you. Perhaps there are those who feel they have a grievance against the airline for some real or imagined shortcoming. They might transfer this grievance on to you as the airline's representative. I'm sure you understand what I'm saying.'

'Oh, yes, of course I do. But there's nothing.'

Devenish's transparent face was one of those in which lying or truth-telling immediately shows. Now he was lying. Wexford was sure of it. And there was a stubbornness, too, revealed in those dark eyes. It wasn't just a matter of lying but of a decision not to expand on what he had said. There was nothing, he had no enemies and that was it. There could be no room for argument or persuasion.

'You hardly seem to realise', Devenish said but perfectly politely, 'that the people who send this sort of letter are mad. They don't have to have a reason. They read something in the paper and that's enough to trigger them off. They're mad.'

'I realise it, sir, I realise that this is often, though not invariably, the case. And now I'd like you to tell me something you may find similarly irrelevant but I assure you it isn't.' Wexford paused, looking steadily at the other man. 'Do you have a second home?'

'What, a cottage in the country, d'you mean? We live in the country. And we don't have a flat in London either.'

'And it would be even less necessary to ask you if an obviously devoted husband such as yourself has, or has ever had since his marriage, a relationship with another woman?'

If Devenish noticed the edge of irony to Wexford's voice and his uncharacteristic use of the third person he didn't show it. 'Chief Inspector, you must be joking.' Devenish smiled, at the same time shaking his head as at an incredibly tall story. 'You can't be serious.'

'I'm perfectly serious, sir,' Wexford said in a hard voice. 'I don't find any of this amusing. A man has died a horrible death here this morning. You'll excuse me if I concentrate on that for the time being.'

The remains of Ted Hennessy lay in the mortuary. He had been thirty-four years old, for four of those years attached to the Regional Crime Squad at Myringham. Married, with two children, as the media put it. The notice of his death in a national newspaper, not the front-page story but the announcement in the Births, Marriages and Deaths columns, said that he had been the adored husband of Laura and father of Jonathan and Kate.

Someone in that crowd had thrown the petrol bomb which killed him. He wouldn't have been in Kingsmarkham at all in the ordinary course of events. He was a reinforcement for Wexford's beleaguered team. You could say Smith and the Devenishes were responsible for his being there, which was an irony if you like.

'I don't see any irony,' said Burden.

'No, maybe not,' Wexford said. 'I really meant he wasn't here for anything real. He was here through people making a nuisance of themselves.'

He didn't explain what he meant. He had a date with Brian St George at midday. The editor of the *Kingsmarkham Courier* had failed to turn up for the press conference and Wexford thought he knew why. At any rate, he guessed or hoped he knew why. St George had 'seen it all' for himself. He had had a piece of luck and seen the petrol bomb thrown.

'I'm not saying I actually saw it, Reg,' St George began. He looked nervous. 'Not to say *saw* it. That's not exactly what I meant.'

'What did you mean, then?'

'Well, I saw it hit its target.'

'By its "target" I suppose you mean Detective Sergeant Hennessy,' Wexford said, barely suppressing rage. 'For a journalist you've a singularly unfortunate way of expressing yourself. Is that what you're going to write in that rag of yours?'

If it was possible to hurt St George's feelings, this could only be done by impugning his writing skills. He winced a little. He put his hands on his head, on the daisy-centre bald spot, and looked at Wexford loweringly. 'I never saw who threw it,' he said. 'I never meant that. If I had,' he added recklessly, 'I wouldn't tell. I don't want to be a marked man, not in my position I don't, Reg.'

'Don't call me Reg,' said Wexford.

Hennessy's widow Laura, when told of his death, said, 'I always knew the job would kill him, but not like this, not like this.'

By next morning the police station forecourt had been cleaned up, the burnt-out car – once the property of DC Archbold – removed and the broken windows boarded up. Several arrests were made and half a dozen people, including Brenda Bosworth, Maria Michaels and David Hebden, appeared in court on charges of causing criminal damage. Barry Vine and Lynn Fancourt were obliged to give up the hunt for Sanchia Devenish and, with two members of the Regional Crime Squad, track down whoever among the crowd on the pavement had thrown the petrol bomb that killed Hennessy.

It was one thing for no witnesses to come forward when throwing a brick and breaking a window was in question, quite another when a man had died as a result. Not everyone was as chicken, as Wexford put it, as Brian St George. People were anxious to talk and volunteers with information came from all over Stowerton, Kingsmarkham and the Muriel Campden Estate. The difficulty was that no one could be exactly sure who had the petrol bomb, still less who had thrown it. Hennessy's killer had been in the midst of them, was one of them, had marched with them up the High Street, talked to them and chanted 'Stand by Your Kids' with them, that everyone knew. It must have been so, but there they stopped and looked helplessly at Barry and Lynn. They couldn't absolutely say it was so-and-so, they wouldn't swear to it if it came to swearing, it was just that they *thought* ... After all, you don't want to say something's absolutely certain when it could end with the person getting life imprisonment.

Andy Honeyman, landlord of the Rat and Carrot, was profuse with his information. As Barry remarked later to Michael Burden, you'd have thought he'd been there, seen it all and taken notes and photographs. In the end it came down to a conversation he had overheard in his saloon bar. 'So this guy says, "How d'you make a petrol bomb?" I ask you, you wouldn't take it seriously, would you? And this other guy, he didn't take it seriously. "You what?" he says, "You're bonkers" or "You're barking" or something. And too right, I thought, never imagining what would come of it. And then another guy comes up ...'

'Wait a minute,' said Vine, 'I can't sort out all these guys. You don't know their names, I suppose?'

'Of course I know their names,' said Andy Honey-man. 'The first guy, he was Colin whatever, Crom-well – no, Crowne. Her ex was called Cromwell, this one's Crowne. And the other guy was Joe Hebden. Both of them come from that blot on the landscape, the Muriel Campden Estate. Well, as I say, another guy comes up ...'

'What was *his* name?'

'Don't ask me. I never saw him before. I don't know who he was but I know what he said. He told them how to make a petrol bomb, get a bottle, fill it with petrol, I leave it to your imagination. He said there was a market for the things, meaning folks would buy them, I reckon. Then he said making them was a hassle when he could supply them. There was dozens listening. I mean, there was that chap Fowler, the one with a blackie wife who's left him and gone to that bunch of slags down the road here, The Hide they call it. I know what I'd call it.'

Barry interviewed Colin Crowne and Joe Hebden and Terry Fowler. Colin said where would he get petrol, he hadn't got a car, as if possession of a motor vehicle was the only criterion for access to a fuel pump. He didn't remember the conversation in the Rat and Carrot and it was his belief it was an invention of Andy Honeyman. Anyway, he hadn't been with the protest, he'd been in bed with shingles, from which he was still suffering as anyone could see with half an eye. Joe couldn't remember the conver-sation and Terry said he had heard the word 'bomb' but he couldn't recall any guy coming up and giving advice how to make one. But Colin's rhetorical question gave Barry an idea and next day he began making inquiries at every petrol station in the town and its environs.

Lynn drove home, left her car and, out on the Savesbury Road, waited, looking forlorn, until she accepted a lift from the fourth driver and first woman driver who offered. She hadn't grey hair, or rather she had but it was dyed red, she was thin rather than thickset and certainly no more than forty-five, and she drove Lynn back into Kingsmarkham, leaving her where she asked to be let down, outside St Peter's. Lynn had to get a taxi home and wondered if she could get the fare off expenses.

The inquest on Ted Hennessy was opened and adjourned. Wexford and Burden came away from it together and Wexford put on the thin plastic mac he had bought many years before for a holiday in Ireland. 'I don't seem to be able to think of anything but that poor chap,' he said. 'It's what his wife said, not so much his death, though that's bad enough, but the manner of it. To be burned to death – you can't imagine much worse.'

'We'll get him,' said Burden, looking askance at the mac. 'No doubt about it. Him or her, we'll get them.'

'I'm afraid I don't find revenge much consolation, Mike.'

They walked down the High Street, where the sun shone brightly on wet pavements, on puddles, on lakes of water half across the roadway. A car, passing too fast, sent up a sheet of spray that just missed Burden's trouser legs. The driver, for no known reason, leant across the passenger seat at the red light and shook his fist at them.

'Let's go in the Europlate and have a coffee,' said Wexford.

The Europlate had opened six months before. Its name had nothing to do with European Monetary Union but referred solely to its menu, a suitably eclectic offering of the so-called principal dishes from the cuisine of every country in the EU. You could have Swedish meatballs, Spanish omelette, Greek salad, Irish stew, German sausage, *croque monsieur* and the Roast Beef of Old England. The trouble was that everything tasted of stir fry. The cook was reputed to be Chinese, though no one claimed to have seen him and verified this. Last time he was in there, preferring the place over the police station canteen, Wexford had asked if they did Turkish Delight and got a rather surly negative response.

The place was done up in yellow and blue. Table-cloths were dark blue and every table napkin had in its centre the ring of stars which is the emblem of the Union. They ordered coffee and were each offered a complimentary Danish pastry. Burden refused with an incredulous smile but Wexford had difficulty in resisting this sugary nut-sprinkled apricot-jam-filled confection and eventually succumbed. 'I'm going to have it,' he said. 'I know I shouldn't, but I need the comfort. It's been such a bloody week, hasn't it? There'll be an inquiry into what happened last Thursday morning and the outcome will be a resigning matter for poor old Rogers.'

'No one could have foreseen that petrol bomb. Who'd imagine petrol bombs in this place? It's not Seoul, it's not –' Burden hesitated, trying to think where else it might not be – 'Jakarta.'

Wexford started on his Danish pastry. It was the first of its kind he had eaten for more than a year and would probably be the last for another year. 'I went to Seaward Air yesterday, as you know. The head-quarters at Gatwick, not the Brighton one or the office here. I talked to Devenish's PA and his secretary – two different women, by the way, he's very grand – and to the present general manager. They all like him, they all say he's a good employer, very fair, pleasant without being too matey.'

'And?'

'Well, yes, there's an "and". The secretary talked about his bad temper, of which I saw some signs myself the other day. She's seen it directed at others, though not at her. Apparently, there was an incident when he threw some chap out of his office. Fellow forced his way in, making complaints about some relative of his being badly treated by Seaward. It was two or three years ago and before her time but she'd heard he physically threw the man out – neck and crop, as they say. The rumour was that the chap broke a rib. But it's all very vague. She doesn't know his name and I couldn't find anyone there who did.'

'You make him sound popular,' said Burden. 'You paint a very different picture from Trevor Ferry's.'

'As you said yourself, it's understandable Ferry hasn't got a good word for him.' Wexford finished his Danish pastry and picked up in his fingers the last crumbs off his plate. He said very quietly, first glancing over his shoulder, 'I believe Devenish abducted his own daughter.'

Burden looked at him. He didn't say anything.

'I don't know why he did or where he took her or where she is now but I believe she's safe and that he's hidden her.'

'I suppose I've been thinking the same thing,' Burden said.

'He blusters too much, he *cried*. Maybe it was pretend crying, as the children say. I didn't see any tears. Sometimes he seems upset about his daughter's disappearance and at others he doesn't seem to care.'

Burden nodded. 'Hidden her with someone? You must mean that.'

'First of all,' Wexford said, 'I considered a girl-friend. He's good-looking, he's young, he's well-off. His wife looks older than her age and she looks tired. And he goes on too much about his happy marriage.

The existence of a girlfriend wouldn't have surprised me.'

'You mean he was planning to leave his wife for this girlfriend but wanted to keep the child? The child is hidden with her in some secret hideaway he can afford because he's rich?'

'Something like that. But there is no girlfriend, Mike. Someone among the dozens we've talked to would know of it if he was having an affair. I know everything there is to know about him, I even know he met his wife at a staff Christmas party when he was Chief Executive at Southern Cross Rail Link and she was the Chairman's PA. There's not a breath of scandal about him. He's never even been known to have lunch with a woman. One of the ticket desk managers at Seaward was sure that if he spent a night a year away from his family that was the maximum and then only because he was absolutely obliged to attend a meeting in Brussels or Frankfurt.

'He goes to Sung Eucharist at St Peter's on Sunday mornings, the whole family goes. He never misses parents' evenings at the boys' school and he frequently takes them to sports events. He gave his wife a sapphire-and-diamond eternity ring on her thirty-fifth birthday and a new car on her thirty-sixth a week or so ago. She may look old and tired – sorry to sound so callous – but he loves her.' Wexford wiped his mouth on the EU logo. 'He seems to be one of those rare men who are totally monogamous, not from necessity or prudence but by inclination.'

'I assure you I'm monogamous by inclination,' said Burden hotly.

'You know what I mean. He wouldn't even fancy a woman he saw in the street. In other words, he doesn't commit adultery in his heart. He's a devoted husband. Do you want another coffee?'

'May as well. But this saint you're describing

kidnapped his daughter, who is incidentally also his beloved wife's daughter?'

'He's not a saint. Saints aren't arrogant and superior and insensitive to the feelings of others, and he's all those things,' Wexford said. 'The kidnapper, as you call him, was well enough known to the child for her not to cry out when she saw him. He knew exactly where she was. He had no need to break into the house because he was already in it.' Wexford signalled to the waitress, holding up the empty blue-and-yellow coffee pot. 'He drove her away in a car Mrs Wingrave opposite didn't recognise and therefore assumed it to be a stranger's. She didn't recognise it *because it was the car Devenish had given to his wife only two days before.*'

Burden looked unimpressed. 'Right, and where did he take the child in his wife's new car?'

'Not to a relative or a friend. Not to a girlfriend. That car's being gone over now. Peach and Cox went up there first thing and brought it back here. According to Mrs Devenish, it hasn't been driven since it was given to her. She hasn't been out of the house since Sanchia disappeared. So we shall soon see.' Wexford filled their two cups with fresh coffee. He picked up a Danish pastry crumb with a nut on it off the plate and put it in his mouth. 'Sanchia would have sat up in that car, she wouldn't have been lying in a cot, she's nearly three.'

'In which case she should have been strapped into a child seat.'

'I dare say he didn't bother about that. God, how irrelevant can you get? It doesn't matter whether she was in a child seat or not, she was *there* and must have left traces of herself behind, hairs, fluff from her clothes, fingerprints. Now he wouldn't dare be away from the house for long in case his wife woke up. He's the one who takes sleeping tablets, not she, though I don't suppose he took one that night. So I think he only drove Sanchia a short way and was met by someone else in a car, an accomplice, who took her from him and drove her to wherever she now is.'

'Not in the river or a grave, we hope,' said Burden.

'Who knows? He came down here in a taxi and he came in rage and despair. He put his head down on the kitchen table and wept. People weep from rage and despair and remorse though, don't they? Not simply from grief.'

Entering the police station, they met PC Dixon, whose golden curls had been even more rigorously trimmed since the smuggling out of Smith. He had been much embarrassed by the taunts of Colin Crowne and Monty Smith, even more than he was by the inquiry frequently put to him as to how were things in Dock Green. He said to Wexford, who was in the act of taking off the plastic mac, 'I've been looking for you, sir. I think you wanted to know the whereabouts of your raincoat. It never left the estate. I gave it to Jim Donaldson while he was parked in Ariel Road waiting for you.'

Just before midday Barry Vine called at the last petrol station on his list. It was a tiny place in the middle of the village of Bredeway and designed to blend in, insofar as this was possible, with its rural surroundings. Its two pumps were painted green, there were tubs of azaleas and pansies on its forecourt, and the building itself had a thatched roof. The proprietor, who was inside at the till, presiding over a counter filled with Snickers bars and Polo mints at one end and CDs and Disney videos at the other, asked Vine if he liked the set-up and described it as environmentally friendly. Vine hadn't much hope of the place but he said he was looking for someone who might have come in on the previous Thursday, quite early in the morning, before eight at any rate, and brought a vessel to be filled with petrol, some sort of can, perhaps, or bucket.

'You mean their car had run out of juice on the road somewhere?'

'Maybe. That would be the reason they gave.'

The proprietor asked a lot of questions, called to his wife who was round the back, asked her questions, offered Vine a selection of theories and finally said that it couldn't have been the Bredeway Garage because they didn't open before eight thirty in the mornings.

Vine went back to Kingsmarkham and picked up DC Archbold. The two of them started on the second phase of the project, calling on hardware stores that sold paraffin.

The doors of the big double garage stood open. Both cars were gone, Devenish's and his wife's. The front lawn was covered in red petals, the blossoms fallen from the chestnut tree. Wexford rang the bell and, when no one came, rang it again. A casement opened upstairs and Fay Devenish put her head out.

'May we have a word, Mrs Devenish?'

She didn't want to let them in, you could tell that, but she didn't know how to refuse. The inability of most ordinary middle-class people to say no was an enormous advantage to the police, Wexford often thought. One of the claims of psychotherapy was that it taught patients that it wasn't necessary or desirable for their egos and their peace of mind always to accept. Saying yes was propitiatory, a weak desire to placate and ingratiate. He sometimes wondered what would be the effect on police work if a generation grew up briefed to turn down requests and invitations.

Fay Devenish manifestly wasn't one of them. She didn't quite say how nice it was to see them but she hovered on the brink. Her husband had gone in to work just for the morning. Would they care for coffee or tea? Would they mind sitting in the study because she hadn't yet 'done' the living-room? She was in housewife's garb to the extent that Wexford hadn't seen for forty years. An old-fashioned wrap-around overall covered her blouse and skirt, and her head was tied up in a turban made from a red checked duster.

Her face was pale and shiny, untouched by make-up. Presumably, the lipstick and powder and mascara would go on after the housework was done and her husband due home. Yes, she would dress and paint, and set her hair like a wife in a fifties magazine advertisement. ('Always be fresh and neat for him, and put on something pretty when he comes home after a hard day's work.') Then he reminded himself that her little child, her only daughter, her three-year-old, was missing, and it gave him a shock; all this was so *inappropriate*.

They went into the study where, at his last visit, she had been lying on the leather sofa. Now she sat down on the edge of it and looked at them expectantly. She so nearly fitted the description he had given of her to Burden, tired and looking older than her age, that for a moment he had asked himself what on earth a clever, handsome, wealthy and successful man like Devenish saw in her. Her face was prematurely lined and her eyelids drooping. What would she look like at fifty?

'Mrs Devenish,' he began, 'I believe you know we're examining your new car, subjecting it to certain laboratory tests. You haven't driven it yourself but could anyone else have done so?'

'I wouldn't lend my car to anyone,' she said in her soft almost childish voice.

'Not even to your husband?'

He thought she winced – but why would she? 'My husband has his own car. He wouldn't need to drive mine.'

'I think you have a friend called Jane Andrews,' said Burden.

She hesitated. 'I used to have.'

'But not any longer?' Wexford watched her face for signs of dismay or concealment but there was none. 'What broke up the friendship? Do you mind telling us?'

'We grew apart,' she said. 'Friends do.'

'How did you meet in the first place?'

Her sudden distress was unexpected. 'Why do I have to tell you all this? What's it got to do with my little girl?'

'When did you last see Miss Andrews, Mrs Devenish?'

'Years ago. Six or seven years.' Suddenly she grew voluble. 'You ask how we met. We did a business studies diploma at the same time. Seventeen years ago now. The fact is that my husband dislikes her. He disapproves of her; she's been married twice and divorced twice, you know.' She must have become aware of their puzzled looks. Was a friend's complex marital history a reason for breaking a friendship? 'I don't think it's possible in a marriage to keep a friend if the other one doesn't like them,' she said, sounding confused, 'not whether it's the husband or the wife, do you?'

'I'd like to go back to the night Sanchia disappeared, Mrs Devenish.'

Wexford looked at her in silence for a moment. With her old-fashioned ways and her antiquated ideas of marriage, her housewife's uniform and her nervousness, a fear of an unspecified something that seemed to pervade her, she was a mystery and, as he had said to her husband, he liked mysteries to be solved. Fear, when it is lived with daily, abates only to a certain extent and then not for long, eats up its victim, ages her and wears her out, may drive her mad, kills her before her time. He had seen it happen before.

'You don't strike me', he said, 'as a person likely to be a heavy sleeper. Of course I don't know, I'm not a doctor, but I would say you were rather tense, very often on edge, while your husband presents on the whole a picture of a calm, steady man under his own control. Yet you and he tell me that he is the one who takes sedatives at night, not you.'

She tried a laugh. It was a pitiful, strained sound. 'I may not look a sound sleeper but I am.'

'He was drugged and you're a sound sleeper, so neither of you heard your little girl taken from her room and brought down the stairs, necessarily past your door. Remember that we know now there was no question of her being carried out through the window. She was brought along past your door and down the stairs.'

'Most mothers,' put in Burden, 'well, most parents, become light sleepers through being habituated to waking in the night when babies cry or children call out. It takes years to change that and maybe only changes after the children are grown-up if at all.'

'But you're not one of those parents, though you've had three children?'

'I heard nothing. I slept,' she said.

Leaving, Wexford turned back and said almost casually, 'What age is your older son, Mrs Devenish?'

'He's twelve.'

'Ah, yes. He looks older. So many of them do these days. Long way off driving a car yet, then?'

She hesitated. 'He's tried driving a car – well, round the front here and in the drive. That's not illegal, is it? On private land?'

'No, that's not illegal, Mrs Devenish.'

'They all want to drive, you know, and Edward's so big.'

As they were leaving she said suddenly, surprising them, 'It was dreadful about that poor man, that policeman, it was such an awful way to die.'

The report on the white VW Golf, Devenish's birthday present to his wife, confirmed most of what Wexford had expected. No fingerprints were on the steering wheel, which still held shreds of the polythene wrap that had protected it when new. The prints of five people, Devenish's, his sons', Fay Devenish's and those no doubt of the man who had delivered it to the showroom, were all over the interior. There was nothing remarkable about that.

Explicable only if Sanchia had been in the car was the presence of baby fingerprints and three fair hairs from the head of a small child. But did this mean she had been taken away in it on the night of her disappearance? Sanchia too had doubtless been among the admirers of the new car, had clambered all over the back seat while her brothers sat in the front and played with the gadgets, her mother uttered her pleasure and gratitude, and her father stood benignly by.

'Can you think of a single reason why Devenish would abduct his own child?' Burden asked over a quick drink in the Olive and Dove. 'What's his motive? What could he possibly get out of it? I mean, if there was another woman involved and he saw himself as having a future with this other woman, I could just about imagine him putting the child into her keeping so that when he and his wife divorced and Fay got custody of the kids, he'd have Sanchia. I can just about imagine it but even so it's full of holes.'

'Besides, if he did all that, what chance would he actually have of getting away with it?' said Wexford. 'Precious little. If Sanchia wasn't found beforehand, once he moved in with this woman, she would be. And there is no woman, or if there is he and she have been to such elaborate pains to conceal her existence as is only compatible with their having been planning this abduction since the affair began.'

Burden stared into the sparkling creamy head on his bitter like a clairvoyant looking into a crystal ball. 'You know something?' he said. 'I don't believe in those threatening letters. I think Devenish invented them in a clumsy effort to put us off investigating him. If he'd had them, why not keep them? Why not, at any rate, keep one? All that stuff about the letters being particularly literate, the biblical-sounding bit, that was just put in to make us think him a discerning person who'd know good prose when he saw it.'

'You may be right. If we only knew why Sanchia was taken we'd be a long way towards finding her. There's no motive for taking her nor for hiding her. No reason for taking the child from her home and torturing his wife in the process. I can see how, the mechanics of it I mean, but no matter how hard I try to imagine it I can't come up with why.'

'And can you come up with why some villain would want to kill Ted Hennessy? For nothing. For simply refusing to understand facts that had been explained a hundred times. Can you? I can't.'

# Chapter 15

When her car broke down on the old bypass Lynn had given up thinking about her entrapment of Vicky. After all, she had made several more attempts after the strange experience with the threesome couple and all had come to nothing. Vicky, she now believed, had gone to ground, had abandoned this curious plan of hers to recruit young women to do her housework – if that had been her motive – and settled down to life with or without Jerry in her own home wherever that might be. Besides, Lynn was starting to feel guilty. She shouldn't have embarked on this enterprise without permission.

On her way back to Framhurst home from work she had called in on Laura Hennessy. Laura wasn't a friend of hers and Ted hadn't been a friend, but they had worked together and Lynn had liked him and, besides, it was such an awful tragedy and, as she put it to Laura, such a *waste.* Two small children were left fatherless, there was a big mortgage outstanding on the house and if that would be covered by the compensation, it was still a worry. Lynn left the semi-detached house in Orchard Road in a dismal frame of mind, thinking what a hazardous occupation was hers, what risks she and her fellows daily ran and how little thanks, or indeed respect, they got for it.

There is no moment convenient for one's car to break down but some moments are less maddening than others. It shouldn't happen on a dark, wet night when one's boyfriend is away on business, one's contemporary and fellow officer has been burnt to death and there seems no one in the whole world worth talking to. A consolation was that when the engine simply died the Fiesta wasn't in the fast lane but far over on the left and no other traffic was on the road in either direction. It died, the car slowed down and seemed to collapse hopelessly, though of course it was all in one piece and all that had happened was that it refused to go. Lynn tried everything to make it start but it wouldn't. She wasn't very mechanically minded. She blessed the absence of traffic on the road – a lorry passed her and then a motor bike – because she didn't want help from others. The only thing to do, the obvious thing, was call the special number she had for the RAC. They would come as soon as they could and that might be very soon, in no more than ten minutes.

The rain had stopped and a misty orange moon appeared. Afterwards Lynn blessed the fact that she hadn't dropped her mobile on to the seat before she got out of the car. It was the merest chance that she didn't do this because she couldn't imagine needing the phone while simply standing outside the car to breathe the fresh night air and waiting for the RAC man. Probably it was something to do with that area of her training in which it had been impressed on her never to be separated from her phone.

The hazard lights on the Fiesta still worked though the motor didn't. They flashed on and off, on and off, in the darkness. It was the trees, the dense woods along both sides of the dual carriageway in this section of it, that made it dark and mysterious and, strangely on a wet road at night, beautiful. For the endless rain, the torrential or drizzling or misty or steady rain, the relentless daily rain, had fed these beeches with their feather fronds, these long-leaved chestnuts, these limes and hornbeams and oaks, so that they were greener than Lynn had ever seen them, greener and lusher and fresher and more luxuriant. It took her car breaking down to make her appreciate trees, she thought, and she moved to the woodland edge to look down the aisles between the trees where the rain dripped from glossy leaves, brilliant emerald in the pale moonlight.

A car drawing up made her turn round. She thought it was the RAC man but it wasn't. A white car and a woman at the wheel, leaning across and out of the passenger window to ask her if she needed help. Lynn nearly said she had already called the RAC, thank you very much, and he would be along any minute, but then she noticed that the woman was middle-aged and thickset, with unusually luxuriant grey hair. Tension gripped her, tautening her stomach muscles, and she forgot about not doing things on her own initiative.

'I don't really want to wait here for them by myself, though. If you would just take me to a garage. I'm a stranger round here but I've been told there's an all-night one at the Myfleet exit. That would be very kind.'

Lynn had never before heard herself sound so naïve and sweetly girlish. The woman pushed open the door and she got in, praying that the RAC man wouldn't come until they were on their way. Then, sitting next to the woman who could be Vicky, who surely was Vicky, feeling really bad about the poor RAC man on his way to going off duty, maybe, and home to his family and his dinner, and who would come and find her gone, the car abandoned and wonder what on earth had happened to her.

This he wouldn't guess, though. She burbled a little more to the woman about how kind she was and how awful it would have been if she hadn't come along because she, Lynn, was terribly nervous about being out alone on a lonely road in the dark, one read such awful things. It was getting more likely to be Vicky by the minute, for she hadn't even turned round to face in the direction of the Myfleet exit but was speeding up the bypass towards the Myringham turn. Lynn didn't want to show anxiety yet, it wasn't in keeping with her trusting and girlish pose. She had studied Vicky's head, quite sure now that that thickly waved dense coiffure was a wig, had had a good look round the car, had actually said what a lovely car it was, and now she was watching where they were going and telling Vicky the scenery was quite beautiful round here, she'd had no idea.

Then Vicky said it, what she had been waiting for: 'By the way, my name's Vicky.'

'Lynn,' said Lynn.

'Soon be at this garage of yours. Turn left up here.'

Vicky turned left, squeezing the car down a lane about as wide as Lynn's double bed. The fronds on the high bank, hart's-tongue ferns and dog's mercury and Lords and Ladies, brushed wetly along the side of the car. Now was the time, Lynn thought, to say this didn't look much like the way to the garage, that would be the authentic remark to make and utter in an increasingly nervous tone, but she didn't make it and Vicky didn't seem to notice.

Where were they? On the way to Myringham by a tortuous back route? Certainly they were nowhere near Sayle and the Chorley bungalow but by now a good fifteen miles away. But Vicky made her living house-sitting for people, didn't she? There had been other Sunnybanks since Rachel Holmes, at least one other Vicky had cared for and in which she had entertained Jerry. She was going to one of them now,

Lynn thought, with that little inner gasp and catching of breath that denotes excitement. She looked at her watch. Ten to ten. God, she didn't want to have to stay the night, but if there was no help for it . . .

The car crawled through this narrow wet green tunnel of a lane, came out into a slightly wider road with a little spurt like a sigh of relief. It turned left and Lynn saw in its headlights a signpost pointing to Myringham as five miles away and Upper Brede as three. Now was the time, she thought, to express anxiety. 'This isn't where I saw the garage,' she said.

'It was closed,' Vicky said. 'There's an all-night one at Upper Brede.'

Lynn didn't want to sound too intelligent. On the other hand, excessive stupidity might arouse suspicion. 'Will they have a mechanic, do you think, or just petrol pumps?'

'They've a mechanic,' Vicky said. 'Don't worry. I've used them many times.' She smiled as if she were looking at Lynn and not at the road ahead. 'Now amuse me. Tell me about yourself. After all, I've put myself out to give you a helping hand, haven't I? The least you can do is talk.'

She sounded suddenly quite cross and indignant. It must be a cue, Lynn thought, for her to start being frightened. But she did as she was told, or an approximation to what she was told, and gave Vicky an account of an entirely fictitious young woman who lived with her parents in Stowerton, had been driving their car home from an evening spent with an old school friend – a girl of course – in Kingsmarkham. She was nineteen years old and maybe Vicky would find it funny but she hadn't got a boyfriend. She worked as a veterinary assistant in Kingsmarkham but that wasn't nearly as grand as it sounded. It mostly involved clearing up messes and scrubbing floors! Lynn was proud of herself for managing to put a quite audible exclamation mark at the end of that sentence.

'Exciting life,' said Vicky.

She had changed entirely in the short space of ten minutes. From friendly geniality she had passed through brusqueness to barely concealed sneers. And now, as they entered another lane and turned almost at once into the front drive of a large well-lit, newish house, she said, rather in the tone an ill-disposed prison officer might use to a recalcitrant inmate, 'All right then, get out. Don't get any silly ideas, I'm right behind you.'

Lynn wasn't much of an actress and she didn't know how the girl she was pretending to be might react in these particular circumstances. So she did nothing at all but obey. Like a bemused sheep she scuttled out of the car and up to the front door, which at the moment of their arrival was opened from the inside. Vicky gave her an unexpected push, she stumbled over the doormat and nearly fell. Nearly but not quite. It was a funny thing to recall at that moment, but she remembered Wexford saying a miss was as good as a mile and adding that he was quoting the Duke of Wellington when someone took a pot-shot at him in Hyde Park.

She only stumbled. She looked up and found her eyes meeting a pair of stony flat grey eyes in a curiously blank face. At first she thought the face was lopsided, heavier about one cheek than the other, but it wasn't, it was an illusion. The man was a little taller than herself, thin, with receding dark hair and wearing a rather shabby pin-striped suit. He looked sad and as if he never smiled, never could, didn't know how to make the requisite muscles work. Lynn looked over her shoulder at Vicky, who was just standing there, then back at the man who must be

Jerry, and said what the nice little veterinary assistant would surely have said, 'What am I doing here? What is this place?'

'It's useless asking,' said Vicky, 'because I'm not saying. Why should I? You don't have a choice. You're here and here you stay until I decide if you'll do.'

'Do?' said Lynn.

'Do for my purposes. Say hallo to Jerry. Haven't those parents of yours taught you any manners?'

Lynn said hallo to Jerry who gave her a blank, silent stare in return.

Among the hardware stores that sold paraffin none opened before nine thirty in the morning. Vine had to revise his ideas about one of the trouble-makers buying his paraffin on the morning the bomb was thrown. He began to think he was on the wrong track altogether, for petrol and paraffin were such common and generally used commodities that certainly fifty per cent of households would have either or both accessible. But he had spent the day calling at ironmongers and hardware shops just the same in the hope, which turned out to be vain, that an assistant might tell him of a regular customer and frequent purchaser of paraffin.

By the evening he was back in the Rat and Carrot, talking once more with Andy Honeyman. Vine found it hard to understand how someone could remember what another man said and recollect the circumstances in which he had said it without being able to describe that man. Honeyman must either be lying or totally unobservant, or forgetful to the point of amnesia, for he steadily denied any knowledge of the customer in the Rat and Carrot who had told Colin Crowne how to make a petrol bomb. Nor could he remember who else had been present, apart from Colin and Terry Fowler. Heavily pressed by Vine, he finally said that there had been a woman there he knew by sight. She lived in Glebe Road and he thought her first name was Jacky. None of this was of much help to Vine who went back to the Muriel Campden Estate and began questioning Colin Crowne and Terry Fowler once more.

Colin had taken to his bed before the bomb throwing and the death of Ted Hennessy. What with the pain from his shingles and Miroslav Zlatic's refusal to listen to him or even give any sign that he understood when he asked what the Serb intended to do in the matter of providing for Lizzie's child, the stress had been too much for him, contributing to his malaise. On the following day he had been told by Kingsmarkham Social Services that their virtual babies were valued at £1254.80 apiece, that Jodi must be replaced and they intended to recover that sum from him by whatever means were in their power. Colin knew that meant the County Court and maybe the bailiffs in. He didn't want to get up when Vine arrived but Debbie said he had better, so he came down in tracksuit pants and a T-shirt.

Vine made him go through it all again, how he had only asked about making a petrol bomb out of natural curiosity. He was personally too law-abiding to have any inkling of these things but he'd seen this bit on telly, throwing bottles that blew up and set fire to cars, and naturally he'd wanted to know how it was done. Putting in a good word for his neighbour, he said that Joe Hebden was of the same way of thinking.

'But your natural curiosity didn't take you so far as to find out the name of your instructor?'

'My what?'

'The guy who told you how to do it?'

'I never asked him, did I? He put his spoke in. I

never said to him, how d'you do it. I said it to my mate. He come along and put his spoke in.'

'What did he look like?' said Vine, who had asked this question before.

Colin Crowne gave the same answer. 'Just a bloke. Twenty-something, maybe a bit more, I don't know. I wasn't to know I'd have to remember, was I?'

One of Terry Fowler's sons opened the front door. The other was sitting with his father on a sofa, watching *Crimewatch* and eating taco chips. The Crowne home was far from immaculate but this place was among the dirtiest and least cared-for Vine had ever seen. No one had cleaned it since Terry's wife left him. There was something on the floor behind the television set which Vine, quickly looking away, hoped was dog turds but feared might be from a human source.

But Terry was able, this time, to offer a scrap of help. He knew this Jacky woman through her sister whose son went to school with his two. The sisters lived next door to each other in Glebe Road but more than that he couldn't say. The little Fowler boys then began talking without a trace of diffidence or shyness about another school friend, cousin of someone or other, a boy of six who had his own computer and who had been to Florida on holiday and visited Disneyworld. Vine thought this a long way from the point – they seemed to be travelling through the ramifications of a whole cluster of Kingsmarkham families – and tried to get back to the subject of Jacky. Terry said that he had once seen her in the company of Charlene Hebden but beyond that he couldn't help.

The six-year-old Kim Fowler accompanied Vine to the door. He was what Vine's grandmother called an old-fashioned child and he apologised for the dirty floor and the dust which covered everything. 'Mum used to do it,' he said, 'but she's gone away and left us so there's no one done it. Dad says cleaning is for ladies, not guys.'

'Well,' said Vine, 'there are some guys called New Men and they do cleaning.'

'We haven't got none of them round here.' Kim stretched upwards to open the door and just made it. 'That Jacky's got a girl called Kaylee,' he said, 'and do you know what her dad did? He put her through a cat flap so she could steal things. Only he didn't go to jail because they couldn't prove it.'

Tasneem came into the helpline room just as Sylvia was putting the phone down after her fifth call of the evening. It was half past ten, a pitch-dark night and raining hard. Sylvia hadn't pulled down the blind and the rain hung on the window like a shifting, glittering veil of silver. By this time, and after all those disquieting or upsetting calls – one had been from a man with a fanatical manner and an Irish accent who had threatened to come and get her and do to her 'what they did to the blessed martyred Saint Agatha' – she was always glad of a visitor, Tasneem or Tracy or the black woman with a name she hadn't learnt to pronounce correctly, or the newcomer, Vivienne.

Tasneem stood at the window and gazed out through the water-drop veil at the wet black night. Tonight, especially, there was nothing to be seen but Tasneem often stared out there, looking, Sylvia knew, in the vague direction of York Street and the Muriel Campden Estate where Kim and Lee were.

'You don't happen to know anything about Saint Agatha, I suppose?' Sylvia said.

'Moslems don't have saints, Sylvia.'

'No, I suppose you don't. It's prophets you have.'

The phone rang. Sylvia said, 'The Hide helpline. How may I help you?'

'It's my boyfriend,' a voice said breathlessly, 'we moved in together last week – well, I moved in with him. He's always been so lovely, he's a really nice guy, everyone says so, and he's always been so gentle. Well, last night I was half an hour late home from work, the bus never came, and I didn't phone him – are you there? Can you hear me?'

'I'm here,' Sylvia said. 'I'm listening. Go on.'

'Like I said, I was half an hour late and when I came in he acted like I'd done something terrible, committed a crime or something, and he grabbed hold of me and said where had I been and who had I been with – it was only six thirty in the evening for God's sake – and then he slapped me hard on both cheeks, wham, wham. I was so shocked, I could hardly believe what had happened except that I've got a really bad bruise on the left side. He said he was sorry but then he said I ought to understand he did it because he'd been so worried.'

'Where are you now?'

'At home, at my own place. I'd kept it on, thank God I did. He's gone out for the evening, so I found this number on a card in a call-box and came in here and phoned you. Look, I can understand he was worried about me – well, up to a point I can – but you don't hit people because you're worried about them, do you?'

'Some do,' said Sylvia, 'as I'm afraid you now know. You said it all when you told me thank God you'd kept your own place on.'

'You mean I ought to stay here and not go back to him?'

'You know it without my telling you.'

'If that's what happens after I've lived with him for

271

one week what's it going to be like after six months, is that what you mean?'

Sylvia said that was what she meant and repeated that the caller knew the answers already, she just very naturally wanted reassurance and support. Putting down the phone, she told Tasneem what she had just heard.

'Terry was like that, a really nice guy and gentle and all that. From a distance, that is. It's when you get together it starts, when you're all shut up inside alone with them. I'd like to do your job, Sylvia, it'd be doing something I really know about. Terry used to call me stupid, he said I was ignorant about everything but cooking and cleaning, but if there's one thing I'm an expert in it's domestic violence.'

Sylvia took her hand and squeezed it. 'You could train to go on the helpline, Tas, but it's not paid and you've got your degree to do. Besides, once you've got your flat you won't want to come near The Hide again.'

'And I'll get my boys back, won't I?'

'I'm sure you will,' Sylvia said, though she wasn't all that sure, but she couldn't say any more because the phone was ringing again.

The threatening Irishman once more. She cut him off before he had got more than three words out, but they were three very offensive words and her hand on the phone was shaking. 'Silly, I ought to be used to it.'

'There are some things you never get used to,' said Tasneem with feeling.

'No. I think I'll tell my dad about this one, see if we can track him down.'

Griselda Cooper put her head round the door and said the roof was leaking in the north-west corner of the house with rain coming in through the ceiling. She'd had to move Vivienne into Tasneem's room, it

272

was only temporary and she hoped that was OK with Tasneem. Tasneem said she'd like the company and Sylvia asked Griselda what it was they did to Saint Agatha.

'Don't ask me. Put her on a grill or tied her to a wheel, I expect, something disgusting, anyway. Why? Does one of our charming callers want to do it to you?'

It was because she made a bargain with her captor, Lynn thought, that she was spared the Rohypnol-doctored drink that had been given to Lizzie Cromwell and Rachel Holmes on their arrival. Lynn didn't struggle or even protest much, she said her parents would be anxious and she became a little tearful, but if Vicky would promise to let her go in the morning she would agree to spend one night there. Could she phone her parents?

That made Vicky laugh. She didn't even bother to answer but, looking Lynn up and down, said, 'Those trousers you're wearing won't do. We'll have to get you into something else tomorrow.'

But Vicky didn't search her or even look in her bag where the mobile was. She seemed to accept her meekness and acquiescence as behaviour only to be expected from an independent girl of nineteen, for Vicky, as Lynn soon saw, was an egomaniac of gigantic proportions. She didn't observe or question or even have suspicions because she saw only herself, and saw herself as a figure of strength and power and rectitude. And, of course, she saw Jerry.

Set down in a chair opposite him – literally set down by Vicky, a hand on each shoulder pushing her into a sitting position – Lynn felt she owed herself congratulations on not being afraid of him. She just made it, just managed to resist and turn back the finger of fear that crept up her spine. It was his eyes as much as anything, his eyes which seemed to have more white round the irises than most people's, and his silence, so that he made her doubt if he was able to speak. If he made a sound, what kind would it be?

Ever since she had come into the house she had been thinking of the missing little girl, listening for child noises and looking round the room for child signs. But there had been no sounds. Whoever had furnished this room had no interest in their surroundings beyond requiring them to be comfortable and insulated. Beige was the predominant colour and those people had no interest in toys, either for children or grown-ups. Sanchia wasn't here, unless Vicky was cleverer than Lynn thought.

After staring at her, those eyes apparently unblinking, for ten minutes, Jerry got up and began walking about the room, picking things up and putting them down again, a book, an ashtray, a brass ornament in the shape of a tortoise. From an arrangement of flowers in a basket he took a blue iris, brought it to his nose, sniffed it, dropped it on the floor and trod on it. Not a simple treading underfoot but a concentrated manic stamping and crushing. Then he passed on to the window and stood there with his back to the room, although the curtains were drawn.

Vicky bent down and scraped the remains of the iris off the carpet, where it left a dark-blue stain. 'You can clean that off in the morning,' she said to Lynn. 'When you've had a good night's rest.'

All the time Jerry was staring at Lynn and later roving the room, she had been talking, giving some sort of explanation, or as much of an explanation as she thought fit for Lynn to know. This wasn't her house, she was house-sitting for the owners who were away on holiday. She and Jerry had only been there for three days so far. The owners liked their place to be immaculate, as Lynn could see. Keeping it that way would be her job but first, early in the morning, she, Vicky, would show her how to get Jerry's breakfast.

'Time for bed now,' she said. 'My goodness, look at the time, it's after eleven.'

At that, as if time had a particular fascination for him, Jerry spun round. He was wearing a shirt of khaki-coloured cotton buttoned up to the neck and at his sharp turn the top button came undone to reveal two strips of plaster covering a lint pad on his upper chest. Vicky went up to him and buttoned his shirt. She did it quickly as if she didn't want Lynn to see the plasters. He allowed her attentions but when she was finished sat down cross-legged on the floor with his back against the curtains. His eyes closed, his head nodding, he looked as if he was about to fall asleep in that position.

Lynn was glad to get away from him. She went upstairs, taking careful note of the geography of the house. From outside, in the dark, that it had a second floor wasn't apparent, but now she was being urged to mount another flight. Vicky was behind her, telling her to hurry up, she hadn't got all night, which seemed a strange thing to say in the circumstances. At the top Vicky showed her into a bathroom, doubtless mounting guard outside, for when Lynn came out she almost bumped into her. The door to the room that was to be hers Vicky opened from behind her. Everything happened very quickly after that and when it was too late Lynn realised how much she had underestimated the woman, for as she stepped into the room she heard a click and a snip, and felt her bag slide from her shoulder. Vicky had cut the strap with scissors. Lynn twisted round and made a grab for her but what she clutched was Vicky's hair and the grey wig came away in her hand. The door was slammed in her face and the key turned in the lock, Vicky on the outside and Lynn on the inside, without her mobile.

The scenario she had created had been quite different. Vicky would bring her to a bedroom and stand over her while she undressed and put on the night-clothes provided. With her back turned, of course, like the puritanical wardress she resembled. Her own clothes would be taken away, the door locked on her and she left to make her phone call. Things had not happened like that.

Wexford would be cross. He became a different person when he was cross – cold and stern and rather contemptuous, if never unfair. He would say she was too inexperienced to mount an operation of this kind with herself as decoy. She should have told him or Barry Vine first, she should have *asked*.

Police officers in TV sitcoms knew how to pick locks, or if they were the brute-force type, break them down with a running kick. Lynn knew that if she tried to break the door down she would make so much noise that Vicky and Jerry would come and between them they could overpower her. Besides, she very much disliked the idea of a hands-on struggle with Jerry. Though stoutly determined not to be afraid of him, she thought she might scream if he so much as laid the tip of one finger on her skin.

She went to the window and pulled back the curtains, having first switched off the light. At first she could see almost nothing beyond the fact that the rain had stopped. She opened the window, which was a casement. The lamps were still on in the room below, quite a long way below, about twenty feet, as she appeared to be in some second-floor extension built on up here perhaps only a few years back. The light down there showed in the parting between the curtains and as a thin yellow line across the wet black paving. A long way down, too far to jump, much too far when she'd be jumping on to concrete. Sheets, curtains, blankets, Lynn disliked the idea of any of those. She looked inside the cupboard. It was full of women's clothes, old clothes or the clothes of an old person, smelling musty and of camphor spray. Two of the dresses had self belts but she could see they were too flimsy for her purpose.

She sat down on the bed. She listened. The house was silent. Her watch told her the time was twenty-five past eleven. Up here it was doubtful if she would hear them go to bed but she would see the light go out. Did they share a bed? She didn't care for that idea either. It wasn't much use to her knowing if they were in bed unless she could find a way out. Somehow she must use the room, she must use what was in the room. It hadn't been designed as a prison, it was the owner's guest room. Visitors slept here, used the bathroom next door, probably enjoyed their semi-isolation at the top of the house. And if the owners weren't keen on colour and adornment they evidently were on comfort. There had been soft fluffy towels in that bathroom, new unused cakes of soap and a jar of expensive bath essence.

Vicky and Jerry hadn't taken Sanchia, that was certain. Unless they had taken her but she was no longer here now because . . . No, she wouldn't even think of that, it wasn't her job or her place to think of it. She went to the window once more. The light was still on down there. She hated to think of Jerry near a child or a child in his presence. Vicky's wig still lay on the floor, inside the door where it had fallen. Well, Vicky could come and get it after she was gone.

If you want a thing badly enough, said Lynn to herself, you can do it. Pity there wasn't a phone. People never do have phones in guest rooms, no matter how hospitable they may be, but they do have television sets and there was one in here with an aerial of zigzag metal plates standing on the top of it. There were two bed lamps, one on either side of the bed, and another standing on the dressing-table. Lynn got on to her hands and knees, and crawled under the bed. Two double sockets each held two plugs. What appliances did the others serve? She followed the lead of one of them up into the bedding and found it led to an electric blanket. The other belonged to a radio.

Each lead was about two metres long, say six and a half feet. Lynn looked about her. She opened drawers in the dressing-table but all were empty, neatly lined with white-spotted beige paper. Back to the window to check if the light was still on. It was. There was a drawer in each bedside cabinet. The one on the left-hand side contained the television remote, the one on the right an unopened box of tissues, a packet of throat pastilles, a container of nasal spray and a tiny pair of nail scissors.

Better than nothing, much better. It was no good longing for a sharp knife. The leads on the bed lamps and the aerial were thin – though, Lynn hoped, strong – and they responded well to the snip of the small fairly sharp scissors. The heavier electric cable on the blanket, radio and television set were a different matter. She worked on them until her right forefinger was sore and bleeding, and she realised she would never get through the television cable.

From somewhere far below her she heard a stair creak. She went back to the window and saw that the light was out. Lynn began to feel rather excited. Then she had a thought she at once condemned as silly. Kingsmarkham police were going to have to replace all these cables, mend everything she'd destroyed in here, not the owners, still less Vicky and Jerry. What did all that matter when she'd found them?

She set about tying the cables together. Reef knots, that was the way. The knots took up a great deal of lead. At first she had thought she had an enormous length to play with, something like eighteen metres for a drop of something like six, but the knots took it up and, when it was done and firm and looked safe to use, it wasn't more than maybe five metres long. And she still needed a length of it to tie on to something.

Tie on to what? The further away from the window the more of those five metres would be used up. Underneath the window was a radiator. Lynn examined it and saw that it was fastened to the wall by two metal brackets and to the floor by the pipes through which the water or oil or whatever passed. It felt firm enough. It would have to do. She passed the cable through the flanges on the top of the radiator and made it fast with another reef knot, a double one this time.

Again she listened to the silence of the house. Then she switched off the light. It would be harder in the dark but safer. If only she had gloves! She put one leg over the window-sill, blessing the trousers Vicky so disliked, then the other. Sitting on the ledge, her legs dangling, she realised that this was going to take some resolution, the very letting go and depending on that thin cable. Even the thick blanket and radio leads looked weak now. She turned herself over, still holding on to the sill, and lay on the window-ledge on her pelvis, her legs outstretched.

The darkness was deep, inside the room and outside. She took hold of the cable in her right hand, eased herself away from the window, still holding the ledge with her left hand, and brought both feet on to the wall. It had a rough surface, as if the rendering had been worked on with a pargeting tool. The pattern was formed in a kind of bas-relief in which none of the raised portions protruded more than half an inch, but it was enough to get a better foothold than on an absolutely flat surface. Lynn tried to grip with her toes but her shoes were stiff and had leather soles.

She climbed back into the room, took them off and hung them round her neck by their laces. Her socks came off too and she tucked them into her shoes. Back on the window-sill, she went through the same process and found it much easier this time. Perhaps going back and starting again had been a good idea. Now she could grip the protrusions in the bas-relief much more satisfactorily.

The worst part, as she had known it would be, was letting go, taking her left hand from the sill on to the cable and depending entirely on it. She hadn't foreseen how the cable would stretch and swing, and the radiator give a long groaning creak. But it held. Gripping it as firmly as she could, she moved her right foot down a few inches, then her left, then her right. Her hands slipped on the cable then and she began to slide, desperately trying to walk down the wall, running instead, until her feet slipped off it, she swung in the air about ten feet up, and from above came a crunch, a clatter and a grinding, wrenching sound.

Lynn dropped then, the cable running through and burning her fingers, to land on her feet, her legs wide apart. But she was upright and she was sound. Up above her she couldn't see much except a whitish thing on the window-sill with the cable still attached to it. She weighed only eight and a half stone but her weight had pulled the radiator away from the wall. Would the pipes have gone too? Was there any water or oil in there when the heating was off? She wasn't going to stay to find out and, with pictures of pipes spouting water and the house flooding passing through her mind, she put on her socks and shoes and fled.

Through the side entrance, round to the front. Not a light on in the house, not a light anywhere. Only those who have lived in the country, better still in a house outside a village, know how dark the countryside can be at midnight. Without a torch it is virtually impossible to go for a walk. But after a while you get used to the dark, as Lynn did. Absolute blackness becomes black and grey, then grey and black, then the varied shades of monochrome, like a very old, very dark film.

She was walking along the lane which was the way they had arrived. At the crossroads she went close up to the signpost but still she was unable to read the directions on it. But she had noted where she was on the way here and she would find it again. Left here for Bredeway and the bridge over the river. Suddenly, ahead of her, on the right-hand side, she saw a light, and she made her way towards it, keeping close up against the hedge. She hadn't got her bag with her, nor her mobile, but her warrant card she had. Carry it *on* you, Barry Vine had once told her. Not in your bag or your overcoat pocket but on you, in an inside pocket. So she had and it was there, against her heart, really, though that was a dramatic way of putting it.

The light was upstairs in a thatched cottage by the bridge. It must have been generally brighter here, for she could read the name Bridge Cottage and she noted it as another pointer to where she was. She rang the doorbell. No one answered. She rang again and again, banged on the door, using the knocker and her fist. She even thought of throwing stones at the window but she might break it and she didn't want to be responsible for causing more damage.

There was no one at home. They left that light on to make people like her, or more dangerous people, think someone was there. She turned away, closed the gate behind her and walked on over the bridge. If Vicky had heard the noise wrenching the radiator off the wall had made, would she come after her? It was likely enough. But Lynn knew she would be more than a match for Vicky on her own. A sign on the left side ahead said something, that this was the beginnings of a village, Bredeway probably. Close up, she could just read it: Bredeway. Drive Carefully Through Our Village. Chance'd be a fine thing, thought Lynn. Her car was still up there on the bypass, unless someone had nicked it or driven into it.

The village was mostly in darkness, though there were lights in two of the cottages and one biggish house was ablaze with light. That was the one, thought Lynn. She could hear the noise from the place before she was inside the gate, music, shouting, laughter, and as she entered the garden she could see people dancing in the brightly lit front room. Her warrant card in her hand, she rang the doorbell, then knocked. They might not hear the bell.

A girl of about eighteen opened the door. She didn't wait for Lynn to explain. 'Oh God, I'm sorry,' she said. 'The people next door rang and said they were phoning the police and we promised not to make so much noise but, I don't know how it is, you get carried away, don't you? It's my boyfriend's eighteenth birthday party. I didn't think the police would actually come. Oh God, I feel so terrible . . .'

'All I want', said Lynn, 'is to use your phone, if I may.'

'Of course you may, of course. Come in. Have a

drink. There's only Football Red and Football White, we've drunk the champers. Look, we'll be as quiet as mice while you're phoning, I promise.'

# Chapter 16

At some time during the night she had gone up into that room and retrieved her wig. A complicated structure of blue-grey puffs and whorls and curled wisps, it sat on top of a grim face, in which the crags and cracks had appeared early, if the age she had given was a true one. She looked a lot more than fifty-five. Her neck was thick but her face drawn and pinched. The ringless hands looked swollen and her ankles bulged above the tops of her lace-up shoes.

In a gruff, mannish voice, she kept saying she hadn't done anything wrong. She had been trying to help Jerry, that was all, caring for him as she always did. Wexford said nothing. He was waiting for James Beamish to arrive. The solicitor representing Jerry had turned up ten minutes before and was in the next interview room with his client and Burden and DC Cox. Jerry Dover, his name was, according to her. *She* was Victoria Cadbury, and his late mother's sister.

Both of them had been up when the two squad cars arrived at one thirty a.m., Jerry sitting cross-legged on the hall floor, swaying from side to side and keening softly. Vicky had been on the top floor, trying to pull a heavy metal radiator off the window-sill but lacking the strength for it. Neither of them had gone in pursuit of Lynn Fancourt. Jerry Dover looked incapable of being left on his own, though Vicky must have left him when she went for her interviews, for the night she had spent at Mrs Chorley's house and later to seek her prey. Wexford had only caught a glimpse of him when he arrived at the station himself this morning, but that was enough to define him as mad, or to put it more correctly, severely schizophrenic, the kind of person they used to describe as 'unfit to plead'.

The house in Upper Brede had been searched and the garden inspected. Of course there was no sign of Sanchia Devenish and no evidence that she had ever been there. It seemed that no child had lived there or been there for many years. The house belonged to a couple called Jackson. Vicky Cadbury had been house-sitting for them while they were on a Greek island. They were due home tomorrow to find their spare bedroom's electrics dismantled and its radiator torn off the wall. Wexford had to give grudging approval to Lynn Fancourt. After all, she had caught this pair on her own initiative, but to the cost of a good deal of the taxpayers' money – unless the householders' insurance would pay up – and in some ways it served her right that her car, which she had left on the old bypass, had been vandalised during the night and its radio stolen.

At first he had thought he would have liked to have been there and see her snatch off Vicky's wig but already he was beginning to feel pity for these two. A tragic, if ludicrous, story would emerge and, coincidentally with that thought, came James Beamish, brisk and cocky as ever.

Karen, none too pleased to have to postpone her domestic-violence training owing to pressure here, spoke into the recording device: 'Present are Victoria Mary Cadbury, Chief Inspector Wexford and Sergeant Malahyde. Mr James Beamish has just entered the room. The time is nine thirty-two.'

'Ms Cadbury,' Wexford began, 'or is it Mrs?'

'Miss, Ms, or Vicky, I don't care, call me what you like. But not "Mrs". I've never been married.'

'At some time in April, did you abduct a young woman called Elizabeth Cromwell and take her to your home and keep her prisoner against her will? And did you a week later abduct Rachel Holmes and keep her a prisoner against her will?'

Vicky shrugged her shoulders. They were heavy shoulders, such as people develop who have been on anabolic steroids. 'So what? It wasn't my home, I've done nothing wrong, I didn't hurt them, I fed them, I saved them off the street. God knows what would have happened to them, out there on the street. I made them dress decently, in a skirt instead of those trousers.' She shook her head. 'It's them that's done wrong to us. That Rachel girl stuck a penknife in Jerry. She found a knife in a drawer, you never know what's about when it's not your house, and went up to Jerry, who's harmless, who wouldn't hurt a fly, and stuck it in his chest. I thought she'd got the lung, I thought he'd bleed to death. I drove her back after that, of course I did, once I'd dressed Jerry's wound. I'd been a nurse and it's just as well, isn't it? Jerry might have died.'

So that was what had made Rachel Holmes lie, Wexford thought. She was afraid of the trouble that might ensue if it was known she stabbed Jerry Dover, so she invented a house with shingled walls and a big conifer in the front garden.

'So you did abduct these two young women?'

'My client has just said she did, Mr Wexford,' said Beamish.

'Very well. For what purpose?'

'You need not answer that,' said Beamish.

'I want to answer it. I want you all to know I wasn't doing anything wrong, I was doing a kindness. I did it for my nephew.' Vicky looked defiantly from Wexford to Karen and from Karen to James Beamish. She seemed not to understand that Beamish was on her side, although his function had been explained to her. 'I love that boy,' she said. 'D'you understand that, any of you? D'you understand you can just love someone without sex and stuff being involved, and when they're not your own kid? His mum and dad are dead. I've looked after him since all that started. You've seen him, you know what I mean.'

Beamish, who hadn't seen Jerry Dover, looked puzzled. No one enlightened him.

'He's been in and out of those places, psychiatric wards, they're worse than the old Bedlam was, so for the past ten years he's been with me. He lives with me. I give him his drugs and his meals, he doesn't eat much. I'm not saying he's not a bit destructive, he is, but he's harmless.' Vicky said in a different, shriller tone, 'I've got cancer.'

No one said anything. Wexford nodded.

'I don't say I've *had* cancer, I say I've got it. Because I have, once a cancer patient, always a cancer patient. I know, like I said, I've been a nurse. But it's worse than that, I'm going to die. It's breast cancer I've got, you always say you've got the cancer where it started, but it's in my lungs now. They say they don't know, but I know. I've got a year at best.'

'What has this got to do with the abductions, Ms Cadbury?' Karen asked.

'You were looking for someone to look after Jerry, weren't you?' said Wexford. 'A kind of wife for him, am I right? A young woman to cook and clean and mend his clothes? Someone to care for him?'

'Not for sex,' said Vicky sharply. 'Jerry doesn't know what sex is and he doesn't want to know. But they'd have got married, to be on the safe side.' She didn't explain what she meant by the 'safe side'.

'And there was plenty in it for the lucky girl. Her and Jerry, they'd come in for my house when I'm gone, nice modern house with a washer and a spin drier, and all the linen and cutlery and whatever.'

'Did you explain that to these young women?' Wexford asked drily.

'I would've if I'd found a suitable one. I'd have taken her to my place in Guildford and shown her what she'd be getting. I couldn't do that with the wrong sort, or the first one to complain; you'd have found us and then there'd be no more getting Jerry a wife. Like you have now,' she added, 'like you've knocked all that on the head.'

Her delusive state grew more and more apparent as she talked. Schizophrenia can be genetic, Wexford knew, perhaps always is. Back in the sixties and seventies those Victorian theories of inherited madness, of whole families afflicted, had been derided. Today it was seen that the nineteenth-century writers were not so far wrong.

'But the girls didn't suit,' he said gently. 'They weren't quite what you were looking for, and you were afraid you'd die and leave your nephew alone without anyone to care for him?'

'Really, Mr Wexford,' said Beamish, 'I can't have this.'

But Vicky said, looking calmly into his eyes, 'Yes. Yes, that's exactly right.'

Burden came out, then Wexford. 'Barking mad, that Jerry,' Burden said, casting up his eyes. 'He shouldn't be allowed out alone.'

'He's not.'

'False imprisonment', said Burden in a severe tone, 'is a very serious offence.'

'I know. I've been telling you that for the past three weeks. And it's no good saying no harm was done. They'll appear in court tomorrow and both will be remanded for psychiatric reports.' He sighed. 'Rachel Holmes stuck a knife in Dover's chest.'

'Ah, so that's the answer. I asked him what the plaster was doing there. He didn't answer so I asked him a second time and then the poor devil did speak. He put his hands over it and said, "Hurt, hurt."'

It was all pathetic, Wexford thought, a sad, ridiculous story. When Vicky Cadbury was dead, who would look after Jerry Dover? The state? More likely was his release 'into the community', only there was no community, just neighbours who would be afraid of him or regard him much as people in times past had regarded the village idiot, and he would end up, at the beginning of the twenty-first century, a crazy beggar on the street. 'There's nothing more I can do in there,' he said, 'so I'm going to pay another visit to Miss Jane Andrews and, since there's nothing more you can do in there, you may as well come with me.'

'My daddy said I wasn't to tell.'

Sitting on her mother's knee, playing with her mother's long hair, Kaylee Flay smiled virtuously. She took hold of a lock of Jacky Flay's hair and twisted it round and round her forefinger, while giving Vine a coy sideways glance.

'You told Kim Fowler,' said Vine.

'That's different. He's a *boy*, he's not a grown-up.'

He thought how intelligent she was, this four-year-old who had come out of the lowest stratum of society, almost the socially excluded. Somewhere he had read that, for all the claims that every child of today had an equal opportunity for education and betterment, those from her group were the least likely to avail themselves of it. It made him angry when he looked at her bright face and keen eyes, and knew that she was using that intelligence, which should have been channelled into the right paths, to deceive authority. That was the real crime, to pervert a child like this one, to corrupt her into becoming a criminal's aide and to make stealing a game, in which success was rewarded.

Jacky Flay hadn't said a word once she had told him she didn't mind him questioning Kaylee. She sat there apathetically, her arms round the child's waist, turning her head slowly round and round to make her hair more accessible to Kaylee. She seemed to enjoy this rough caressing and pulling. Vine asked her about the evening she had been in the Rat and Carrot. Had she been alone or with Patrick?

'I don't like you and my dad going out in the evening,' said Kaylee.

'Now you know Auntie Josie was only next door.'

'I don't like Auntie Josie.'

'Yes, you do, Kaylee. You do like Auntie Josie. You're a naughty girl to say that.'

'And you're naughty', said Kaylee, 'to go out and leave me on my own. I could get burnt up in a fire or that paedo could come and take me.'

'Mrs Flay, I asked you if you and your partner were together in the Rat and Carrot that evening?'

'What if we was? Leave off pulling, Kaylee, you're hurting me.'

'Did you hear someone in that bar describe how to make a petrol bomb?'

'I don't know what you're talking about,' said Jacky.

Kaylee got off her mother's lap. She slid to the ground, climbed up on to another chair and sat there with her legs dangling. 'My daddy', she said conversationally, 'got two bottles and he put this stuff in them and it smelt awful, pooh, and he stuffed up the tops with socks, they was my socks what I've grown out of, and he took some more stuff out of the heater that's in my bedroom and put that on the socks and he said they was petrol bombs and they was for killing the paedo, so there!'

Jacky Flay let out a loud scream. She made a dash for Kaylee, one arm upraised, but the child dodged her hand and Vine, wondering what he was letting himself in for, snatched her up in his arms and held her high in the air.

Mrs Probyn was in the act of seeing someone out when they arrived. The woman who was leaving was so like Jane Andrews, was a more feminine version of her, that there was no doubt this was her sister. Although it was a surprise visit, Mrs Probyn seemed delighted to see them and introduced her daughter on the doorstep. 'This is my daughter, Mrs Sharpe. These are the policemen I was telling you about, Louise, the ones that had some important business with Jane which I, of course, was not permitted to hear.'

She smiled brightly to show the good child that this treatment was only to be expected from the troublesome child. Louise Sharpe was plumper than her sister and less stylish, only her very expensive jewellery, a huge diamond in the engagement ring above her wedding band, diamond earrings and a Cartier watch on her left wrist, giving any indication of her affluence. Apart from these, she wore a longish floral skirt and a cotton sweatshirt bearing the logo of a well-known sportswear manufacturer. Her dark hair was untidy and in need of a good cut, and her pale face was bare of make-up but for some smudged black stuff circling her eyes.

She gave her mother a kiss that was just a peck in the air two inches from her cheek and remarked that she must get back as she didn't care to leave 'new staff' on their own for too long in the circumstances. Saying to Wexford and Burden, in the ludicrous expression often uttered when no words have been exchanged, that it was nice to have met them, she went down the path to her car, a new red Mercedes.

'Your daughter has a big house?' Wexford asked as Mrs Probyn ushered them into the living-room she was discouraged from occupying.

'Louise? Oh, yes, huge house, six bedrooms, three bathrooms – well, she's very well-off, as I believe I told you.' Mrs Probyn laughed merrily. '*Noblesse oblige*, you know.' Like most people, she seemed to have only a muddled idea of what the phrase meant, Wexford thought. 'I think it's important to keep up appearances, don't you? I will say for poor Jane, she does make the best of herself. She used to have lovely long hair, you know, but she would have it cut off. Said it was too much trouble, if you please. Louise looks a rag-bag most of the time but her carelessness in that regard doesn't extend to her home, I'm glad to say. She has a truly beautiful home, a real abode of bliss for a child – what a pity, as I always say, she had no children of her own.'

'She never thought of adoption?' Burden hazarded.

'Well, yes, she did try to adopt a baby from one of those countries, Romania or Albania, one of those places in the *Eastern Bloc*, as the powers-that-be call it. She had all the papers, but something went wrong, don't ask me what, and then of course poor James died, her husband that is.' Mrs Probyn giggled and put her hand over her mouth like a schoolgirl. 'But I'm not supposed to talk about it. Jane says I gossip too much and not to talk about family things. But what I say in response to that is, what else can I talk about? What else do I know? I'm not exactly out in the great world, am I? I'm not in the corridors of power or the – the Weather Centre, am I?'

They were saved from replying by the entry into the room of Jane Andrews, alerted no doubt by the sound of her mother's giggle and raised voice. She was well-dressed today in a short black dress and yellow jacket, the male image discarded, but she looked aghast. She turned white under the heavy make-up. Wexford had thought cosmetics would improve her looks but now he changed his mind. Her face was a painted mask. This time she made no attempt to expel Mrs Probyn from the room. 'I was upstairs working,' she said. 'I didn't hear the bell.'

'They didn't ring the bell, Jane. They arrived just as Louise was going and the door was open.'

'Oh, was Louise here?' Jane Andrews looked as if she wanted to say more but bit back the words. 'I didn't hear her come,' she said instead.

'She came to see me.' Mrs Probyn's unconcealed gratification made her seem senile. 'Not everyone who comes to this house wants your company you know, my dear, hard though that may be for you to grasp.'

Jane Andrews turned towards Wexford. 'What did you want to see me about?'

Burden answered her. He said quietly, 'Miss Andrews, we know your relationship with Stephen Devenish isn't a sexual one. But there is some kind of relationship with him, isn't there?'

The effect on her was startling. She burst out laughing. The laughter was the kind that has no amusement in it, only incredulity and wonder at the folly of human assumptions. It held relief too. 'I never would have expected that,' she said. 'Even from the police I wouldn't. What can I do to make it plain to you how much I loathe and despise Stephen

293

Devenish? How can I explain to you what a bastard he is?'

'Language, Jane,' said Mrs Probyn.

Wexford ignored her. 'You've already done so, Miss Andrews,' he said. 'Or, rather, you've given a strong impression of doing so. Perhaps you'll fill in the details.'

She hesitated. Her own vehemence seemed to put a check on her. 'He is an absolute bastard,' she said more quietly.

'So you said. But is there a reason for your saying so? Or is it a case of Dr Fell?'

'Of what?'

Unexpectedly, Mrs Probyn intervened and recited,

'I do not love thee, Dr Fell,
The reason why I cannot tell,
But this one thing I know full well,
I do not love thee, Dr Fell.'

He thought it would anger her daughter. To his astonishment, it made her laugh, it made her human. 'I've never heard that before, Mother,' she said, and to Wexford, 'I certainly don't love Stephen, I dislike him awfully, but of course I can tell you why. He's a sexist tyrant, he makes Fay his slave, he rules that house like the despot he is and I loathe him.'

'And perhaps you've said as much, Miss Andrews, which is why your friendship with his wife was broken off? Perhaps his wife is a loyal wife who doesn't care for these criticisms of a husband she is obviously very attached to?'

She shrugged. 'Perhaps. I don't suppose she did like it. They have no friends now, either of them. Well, he may have at work, cronies, business acquaintances, if you can call those people friends.'

'Or perhaps none of this is true. Perhaps his

declared dislike of you and your unquestionable dislike of him are a blind to conceal a friendship and an alliance.' She leant forward, tried to speak. Wexford held up his hand. 'No, one moment, let me finish, please. I am not suggesting, as I've already said, that there is or has ever been any sexual relationship. You might be useful to him and he to you. That's all I'm saying. And that, if we had recorded this conversation and were able to play it back, even you might say that you protested your dislike of him too violently to be credible.'

'If you're suggesting, and I think you are,' said Jane Andrews, once more aggressive, 'that I, or I and Stephen Devenish together, have abducted his daughter and are keeping her here, then you are mad.'

'Oh, Jane,' said her mother.

'Oh, Mother, yes. That's what they mean.'

'But you don't like Mr Devenish. That's why we never see that nice Fay any more, isn't it? Because you and Mr Devenish don't get on.'

The wake of Ted Hennessy took place on the following day. The Chief Constable and the Assistant Chief Constable were there, as well as Wexford and his entire team, and the members of the Regional Crime Squad, a junior Minister in the Home Office and Hennessy's cousin who happened to be a famous television comedian. Not on account of the Minister but owing to the presence of the comedian, film of the whole thing was shown on the BBC's early evening news.

As he was leaving Mitchell came up to him to say how sorry he was about Hennessy. 'We're having a whip-round at Muriel Campden, collecting for the poor guy's widow.' He gave Carl Meeks a baleful look. 'Well, some of us are.'

Returning to his car, Wexford remarked to Donaldson that it was the thought that counted and did he know what had become of his raincoat.

'A Mrs Hebden came up to me in the car, sir, and said you were in her house and you wanted to walk back, it being such a nice day for a change, and to give her your raincoat to take in to you.'

'And you did?'

'Yes, I did, sir. I hope I did right.'

Wexford didn't answer. He went upstairs where he had been due to see Lynn Fancourt five minutes before. She was waiting for him in his office, tense, her shoulders hunched, picking at her nails. Allowing none of the amusement he felt and none of the underlying approbation to show in his face, he gave her a five-minutes-long lecture on the inadvisability of showing this kind of initiative, of taking matters into her own hands and pursuing secret personal goals as if she were some kind of private eye instead of part of a team. That was not the way to look to promotion. This was amateurish, not enterprising. Lynn squirmed at 'private eye' and again at 'amateurish' but she said nothing, though frequently nodding her head in an earnest fashion.

Petrol bombs and nail bombs. Patrick Flay admitted that he made both in his kitchen in Glebe Road. In an interview room at Kingsmarkham Police Station, when asked why by Barry Vine, he first said that it was just a matter of interest, to see if he could, but later confessed he made the bombs for sale.

'Who were you going to sell them to?'

'You'd be surprised,' said Flay. He was becoming increasingly confident that he had done nothing wrong, or rather, that he had committed no indictable offence. 'There's a market for weapons. It's an industry. Don't you watch no TV? Supplying arms is big business worldwide.'

'That's tanks and guns and missiles and whatever,' said DC Archbold, 'not your piddling petrol in a Ribena bottle.'

'Not so piddling,' said Flay, 'when you think what it can do. It's a funny thing, you know, how it's getting harder all the time just to get hold of a glass bottle. All cans it is these days and plastic.'

'You were going to tell me who you sold your petrol bombs to,' said Vine.

'Was I? Pardon me but I don't think you asked. As a matter of fact, I never *sold* none of them. I *give* one of them away, for a sample like, and one of my nail bombs. Then' – Flay assumed a pious caring expression – 'on account of the tragedy what happened here, I destroyed all my stock. Search the place if you want, be my guest.'

'We will, you can be sure of that. So you didn't make a profit on them. Who did you give the sample to?'

'Colin Crowne,' said Flay.

'So you've said before. Crowne was ill in bed with shingles.'

'I can't help that. I don't know what he done with it. I give it to him in the Rotten Carrot, that's all I know. And it's no use asking me if I saw who threw it – *if* it was one of mine – because I wasn't there. You got all this out of my Kaylee, didn't you? Don't trouble to deny it. You got it out of Kaylee when her mum was out of the room, you wormed it out of her, she's only four years old and that's illegal what you done.'

'Mrs Flay was present throughout the interview,' Vine said stiffly.

'You can tell that to the judge,' said Flay, 'when I've writ about you to the Chief Constable.'

A warrant was obtained and the house of which Jacky Flay was the tenant was searched. Nothing was found, neither petrol nor nail bombs, nor stolen goods.

# Chapter 17

Both boys resembled their father, but in different ways, each favouring a different aspect of him, so that Edward had his height, his dark wavy hair, high forehead and straight nose, while Robert shared his eye colour, sensitive, rather full mouth, his high cheek-bones and his grace of movement. Their mother seemed to have contributed nothing to their genetic make-up; not a trace of her could be seen in either young face. Did the little girl look like her? Wexford had no means of knowing. The people on the Muriel Campden Estate and in the Glebe Road area had records of their children not only filling albums but on film. The Devenishes of Ploughman's Lane had one picture, and that taken by a newspaper when Sanchia was a baby, out in her pram.

'We don't take photographs of people,' Edward explained, if it was an explanation. 'We take them of places.'

Wexford was questioning each of them individually, in the presence, of course, of their mother. He asked Edward first to cast his mind back to when Sanchia disappeared, to close his eyes and attempt to recreate that night, beginning with the exact time he had gone to bed, if he had read in bed, when he had put the light out and how soon he had fallen asleep. The boy followed this procedure, or Wexford thought he did, and said he didn't read much and never in bed. He had been playing a computer game and left it on by mistake, so that it was still on when he woke in the night and he had to get up and turn it off.

'What woke you?' Wexford asked him.

The boy said he didn't know and added, with the first sign of perception he had shown, 'You don't ever know what wakes you because by the time you're awake it's stopped.' He hadn't known what time it was either. It might have been the sound of someone coming up or going downstairs.

'That wouldn't wake you, Edward,' Fay Devenish said. 'Dad or I often go up or downstairs after you're in bed and you don't wake up.'

'Then I don't know,' the boy said and he gave his mother a look Wexford couldn't interpret. It seemed resentful yet puzzled. 'I said I didn't know and I don't.'

'Are you fond of your sister?'

'Of course I am. She's my *sister*.'

Fay Devenish began to cry. Most boys of twelve, brought up as these had been, in this environment, would have gone up to their mother and put an arm round her shoulders, at least told her not to cry, in some way comforted her. Edward sat stony-faced. He looked away. She dabbed at her eyes, seemed to be making a stoical effort at controlling herself.

Wexford went on, 'Did you ever think you would have been happier *without* your sister? If, for instance, your sister had never been born?'

Fay made a little murmur of protest, the sound a woman might make if she cut herself or was stung by an insect.

'I'm sorry, Mrs Devenish, but I'd like him to answer.'

She nodded, rather hopelessly.

'Edward?'

The boy, whose expression hadn't changed, said, 'I

300

don't know. I got used to having her around.' He hesitated. 'I suppose I thought it was funny, I mean it was strange, having her when me and Robert were so old.'

'But you never thought of harming her in any way?'

'Chief Inspector, I'm sorry, but I can't have this.' To his knowledge, Fay had never been so assertive. Colour had come into her face and her eyes were bright. 'I can't sit by and hear you ask him things like that.'

'Very well, Mrs Devenish. That's all, Edward.'

'Can I go now?'

'You can go. Tell your brother I'll see him next.'

He was smaller than Edward but would probably attain his height in two years' time. Many children, especially boys, have inquiring or mystified expressions, not surprising, Wexford thought, when you considered the state of the world they lived in. But in the eyes of these two was something more than that, something they shared but he had seen in few others, a look of bitter bewilderment. It was particularly evident when they looked at their mother.

He asked Robert about that night but the boy could remember even less than his brother. To the question as to whether he had been fond of Sanchia he replied that he supposed so: 'I liked her all right.'

Wexford noticed this past tense if Fay Devenish did not. But she gasped when Robert said, 'She's dead, isn't she? The kids at school say she's dead.'

'Do you know a friend of your mother's called Jane, Robert? Miss Jane Andrews?'

Before the boy could answer, Fay said quickly, too quickly, 'She's not a friend of mine.'

'Robert?'

'I think so. A long time ago. We never see her any more.'

301

Wexford said he had nothing more to ask him. The child went away and his mother began crying again. 'She's not a friend of mine, she's not. You shouldn't have said that in front of my children.'

'It's understandable that you're upset, Mrs Devenish, but there are one or two more things I must settle while I'm here.'

'That's all right, but you shouldn't have ... Oh, what's the use?' She pulled tissues out of the box on a side table, dried her eyes and blew her nose. 'I won't cry any more. What is it you want to know?'

'It's not so much what I want to know as what I want to have. When I asked you for a photograph of Sanchia you offered me only a family group. I refused it then but I'd like it now. It's better than nothing.'

'My husband will be home in a minute.'

'That's fine. It's best for you not to be alone too much. But it's not a reason for your not finding a photograph for me. All we have at present is a poor smudgy shot taken by the *Courier* and we don't even have the original.'

'I saw that picture in the paper,' she said, as if answering him, as if explaining. 'The person who took it, I didn't even know they were taking it.'

'Perhaps you'll have a look now.' A conviction that Devenish's homecoming would put an end to everything useful he could accomplish here, made him urgent. 'Please, Mrs Devenish.'

She went reluctantly. They had been in the living-room and he heard her go into the study, then upstairs. Once more he asked himself why the missing little girl wouldn't or couldn't speak, why those boys' eyes were so troubled, and a fresh question, also to be unanswered, was why their mother had cried when he had simply asked her elder son if he was fond of his sister. And did she now dislike Jane Andrews so much that she wept at the imputation the woman might be her friend?

She came back and he noticed changes in her. She had powdered her face and made up her eyes and mouth, put on perfume and changed her shoes for a more elegant pair. Something had been done to make her hair look thicker and the resulting arrangement had been sprayed with lacquer.

'Here,' she said, 'I'm afraid that's the best I can do.'

Two snapshots. He could see at a glance that they were pairs or groups of people, not a single one of the child alone, but now was no time to take a closer look. Fay Devenish jumped at the sound of her husband's key in the lock.

Wexford said quickly, 'May I take these? They'll be returned to you, of course.'

'Yes, take them.'

She might have been a spy passing the plans to an enemy agent, so low and urgent was her voice, more a hiss than a whisper. She stood up, running her hands down her dress as if she could smooth away weariness and pain and anxiety.

'I was just leaving,' Wexford said as Devenish came into the room.

The man kissed his wife. It was a far from casual kiss but passionate, the kind of kiss, Wexford thought, a little embarrassed, that should never be bestowed and received in the presence of others. Devenish's lips lingered on Fay's passive half-open mouth, then he drew slowly away. To Wexford he extended his hand, smiling, warm, said, amazingly, that he was afraid they were giving the police a great deal of trouble. Wexford resisted saying, as he always did resist, that he was only doing his job. Walking back to his car, he asked himself if it was his imagination that Mrs Devenish had wanted him to stay longer, would have been content for him to sit

303

down and talk it all over once again. Yet she had dressed up for her husband's homecoming and responded gratefully to his kiss.

'I've been wondering about the older boy, Edward,' Wexford said to Burden later in the Europlate. 'They don't give much away, those children. They're cagey and secretive, their eyes are puzzled. I have even wondered if they were abused children.'

'The father?' said Burden.

'One would suppose so. There's no evidence. It may be that this whole affair of Tommy Smith put the idea into my head and it's hardly an idea, it's more a thought without foundation.'

'The fact is', said Burden, 'that child abuse is the fashion. You can't open a newspaper without reading of some fresh terrible case somewhere. It's ghastly but it's not that common and I can't see Stephen Devenish in that role.'

'I'm not so sure. He looks capable of violence and we know he has a bad temper. What are you going to eat? Three kinds of herring with new potatoes – that's Swedish – or maybe Hungarian goulash. Is Hungary in the European Union?'

'God knows,' said Burden. 'I'm reading the blackboard. Sparkling water to drink, inevitably?'

'When we find that child we'll have a bottle of the Widow.'

Wexford ordered the herring and potatoes and Burden Bacalhao from Portugal. 'Dried salted cod with something done to it. We had it when we were in the Algarve last year.'

'It sounds disgusting. I got some photographs from Mrs Devenish. D'you want to see them? They're not up to much, just out-of-focus family groups really.'

Burden gave the pictures Wexford laid on the

table-cloth a fleeting glance. 'Worse than useless, I'd say. I don't know why you're bothering with them. Either Devenish took her or one of his sons.'

'If it was one of those boys Sanchia is dead.'

Burden looked at him. 'You mean Devenish could have hidden her somewhere, he may even have engaged a nanny and set her and the nanny up in a rented flat somewhere, that's a possibility. But if one of her brothers took her he must have killed her. He'd have nowhere to hide her and no wish to hide her, as far as I can see. He'd have taken her because he was jealous of her position in the family, killed her to get her out of the way – and then what?'

'Hidden the body.' Wexford poured mineral water for both of them. 'And hidden it somewhere nearby. His mother says he can drive. Perhaps he can. He may be able to drive a car in theory but I doubt very much if he could manoeuvre it out of that drive by night. They're both big boys, either of them could have carried her and probably she wouldn't have cried if either had lifted her out of her cot. So if Edward did it – or, come to that, if Robert did it – he killed his sister somewhere in the garden, possibly by strangling her, and back we come to your point.'

'What then? Either is strong enough to carry a three-year-old some distance, but dig a grave and bury her? How long would it have taken? Would they even know how to set about it?'

Their food was brought by the Europlate's proprietor, a fat man who for some reason always wore a starched and spotlessly white apron, though he was not the cook. In the opinion of some of his patrons it was done to give him a French appearance. He combined in his looks supposedly typical features of many of the Union's members, being black-haired and moustached like a Spanish bullfighter, with the regular thin-lipped profile of the Scandinavian, the olive skin of the Greek and the high cheekbones of the Slav. Some said his name was Henri, others Henrik or Heinrich, and he was called by all these. But his English was spoken in the pure accent of the Lowland Scot and now, as he set each plate down, he expressed the opinion that a wee bi'o'fish would set them up for the day, as it fed the brain.

'I can do with some of that,' Burden said when Henri had returned to the back regions. 'We know it wasn't one of the boys, though, don't we? It has to be Devenish, or according to my as yet unfed brain it has to be. Why he took her and where he put her we don't know but we can be pretty sure if he took her she's alive.'

'Fathers do kill their children, you know that.'

'Sure, and it's a monstrous crime but it's usually accidental, the result of violent abuse. Devenish had no reason to do it.'

'No reason in your estimation, maybe. How about jealousy? How about seeing her as the one person with the power of coming between him and his wife? Of separating him from his wife? He looks as if he's in love with his wife. He greets her as passionately as if they've known each other a year and been parted for the past six months. We know a lot about these people by now, Mike, but we know very little of their feelings. What do we ever actually know of anyone's feelings, come to that, even when they're our nearest and dearest? Devenish may have disliked and resented Sanchia. Sanchia may have been her mother's favourite, preferred over her sons – preferred over *him*?'

'I sometimes wish', said Burden, 'that we had ordinary normal people to deal with.'

'Are there any? Do you realize, Mike, that you've contrived a possible scenario for Devenish? I don't think you meant to but you have. He's sexually abused all his children and now turned to the little girl. This happens in her bed during the night. He doesn't in fact take a sleeping pill, he only tells his wife he does. That night he paid his usual visit to her, accidentally killed her, carried her body downstairs and buried her in the garden.'

'How about the car, then?'

. 'Not in the garden. No, you're right. He took the body away somewhere and buried it.'

Burden put down his knife and fork. He wiped his mouth on a dark-blue napkin with the EU logo in its centre and picked up the menu. Suddenly he said, 'I don't feel like eating any more. I was going to have the Olde English Summer Pudding or the zabaglione but all this talk of what Devenish may or may not have done has rather put me off. Silly, isn't it? I'm not usually like that.'

'I shall have a pudding,' said Wexford stoutly. 'I shall have something called *rød grød*, which I am certain I'm not pronouncing correctly. As Henri said, I have to feed my brain.'

'Are you going to arrest him?'

'Henri?'

'No, Devenish, of course.'

'Not yet,' said Wexford. 'He won't run away, you know. He's absolutely confident he's safe. I'd say he always is, in everything he does. He knows best, he is right, Devenish rules OK. Doubtless it's the secret of his success, total confidence in himself.' .

'I'd like to see what happens to this famous confidence', said Burden viciously, 'when we get him in court.'

'I'm dining with a client – remember?'

Once upon a time, when her husband made that remark, and made it ten minutes before he was going

307

out to his engagement, Sylvia would, in his words, have laid into him. She had been known to lean against the front door, holding it shut, while she lectured him on her rights as a woman and told him that the children were his as well as hers. But she had spent half the day at a seminar entitled 'Psychological Abuse in Relationships' and it was either this or, more likely, her experiences at The Hide, which affected her, so that she asked herself if today's lecturer would have on many occasions accused her of verbal abuse. It chastened her, she liked to think of herself as virtuous, upright and politically correct, and she forced out pleasant words: 'That's all right. I'm on a short shift, the eight to midnight, so I'll ask Mother to have Robin and Ben, shall I?'

'It might be best.' He said it abstractedly, then, 'Do as you like. I'd better go, I'll be late.'

What had she expected? That he'd go down on his knees? A goodbye kiss, even a goodbye? The front door closed after him. She phoned her mother, packed the boys' pyjamas and clothes for the morning. It was still half-term, so her father wouldn't have to take them to school.

Could she keep it up, being nice to Neil, if most of the time he behaved as if she wasn't there? Would they ever have sex again? Would *she* ever have sex again, since she couldn't imagine it with any other man?

She got her sons into the car and drove to her mother's. It was a strange thing but often she worked so hard she didn't notice the weather and at six in the evening she saw for the first time that it wasn't raining and was going to be a fine night. The sky looked different, hazy rather than clear, and the massed clouds had split into a delicate feathering. A full moon, such as was due to rise tonight, always made working on the helpline less stressful. After a particularly disturbing encounter with a woman on the helpline, she liked to stand at that window, watch the sailing moon and look at the gardens bathed in its pale, cold light.

Therapy, really. Her father did it too. Perhaps she had picked it up from him. Modelling herself on the parent of the opposite sex, a bad thing, said the psychologist inside Sylvia. She could have sworn that night that the moon moved – well, it did of course, but not fast, not so that one could see it move. Counsellers sometimes suggested their clients alleviate pressure by watching the tranquil movements of goldfish swimming in circles. Well, the moon was her goldfish.

It would be a long time before night fell. The sun came out palely just as she arrived. Her father came out to meet her and welcome the boys. She knew he was trying hard to be nicer to her, just as she was trying to be nicer to Neil, and if she felt a certain resentment that her own father had to *try* she didn't show it. She kissed him back and asked herself, but only herself, what was wrong with her that comparative strangers like those people at The Hide all liked her, while her own family . . .

'Stay a little while?' he asked her. 'We were outside in the garden. It's almost the first chance we've had this year. I'll wait till after you've gone, then I'll take the boys down to the river.'

She used to get angry because her mother did the garden as well as the housework and cooking. That kind of feminism seemed very old hat now. That her mother enjoyed the things she did and was very well-suited to housewifery had never seemed to enter into her calculations. She sat down in a cane chair and her mother brought a tray of homemade lemonade, ice-cold with lemon slices and sugared rims to the glasses.

'You've got some new photos.' She hadn't really looked at them beyond seeing that they were photographs, but as soon as she picked them up she did.

'They're your father's, something to do with work. He emptied his pockets on to the table.' Dora laughed. 'You know how he does.'

Keys, change, a perfectly ironed white handkerchief – another cause with her in the past for pontificating against male supremacy – and these photographs. She picked up the top one. It showed a family group, man, woman, two boys a bit older than her own children, a baby in the woman's arms. They were standing in a garden in front of a house and Sylvia recognised the place at once. It was Ploughman's Lane. She had once lived just down the road, though in a rather more modest house. This one was called Woodland Lodge. In her mind's eye she could see the name-plate by the gates at the entrance to the drive. One of the finest houses up there, this was. She had been inside once, collecting for something, and she remembered the elegant broad staircase and the carved woodwork.

These people weren't there then, or if they were, she didn't recognise them. The woman who had left her in the hall and went away to find a five-pound note had been elderly. But that had been several years ago when her own boys were very small and she was very young, and she and Neil were still getting along . . .

She turned to the next photograph and the next. The baby was older here, maybe a year older. Impossible to tell if it was a boy or a girl, the hair was very short, the child's expression a blank, and his or her clothes the uniform of the modern infant: tracksuit pants and sweatshirt. Mother and child were alone, and Sylvia looked closely at this one, laying it down with a sigh.

Wexford came out of the house and sat down opposite her. He picked up the picture she had already looked at and watched her while she studied the remaining two. In neither of them could the child be clearly seen, for he or she had turned away from the camera. The father of this family was by far the most striking member of the group, dwarfing the woman and her sons, his grin broad compared with their tentative smiles.

'Tell me something, Dad. How did St Agatha die?'

'Don't ask me. There's a dictionary of martyrs in the living-room.' He thought about it. 'It's on the third shelf from the bottom with all the other dictionaries.'

Sylvia went indoors and came back with the *Oxford Book of Martyrs*. She didn't open it but once again picked up one of the photographs.

'I don't suppose you're going to tell me who these people are?'

'Is there any reason why you want me to?'

'Only that the woman is a victim of domestic violence. Oh, you can't see any bruises, you can't see healed fractures, but that's what she is and no doubt that grinning idiot is what you'd call the perpetrator.'

Very taken aback, he asked her how she could tell. He had been with Fay Devenish half a dozen times, and in her company and that of her husband together, and had seen nothing. Of course he had noted that she was a thoroughgoing old-fashioned housewife and that Stephen Devenish expected a high standard of cleanliness in his home; he had noticed they kept themselves to themselves and had few friends, but that surely was a far cry . . .

'How can I tell? Hard to say. I just can. You get to know when you're always meeting women in her situation. There's a vulnerable look, a cowed look

311

and something worn that comes into these women's faces, especially when the abuse is sustained over a long period. Look at her now, Dad, in the light of what I've said.'

He looked. He looked particularly at the picture in which she was alone with her little daughter, standing in the garden, smiling diffidently, a cautious, shy, self-deprecating woman who seemed here to wish to efface herself entirely if only she were allowed to. Her body language expressed a reluctance to be photographed at all and as if she were submitting only under pressure. The child had her back to the camera, her face pressed into her mother's long skirt.

'There's no bruise you can see,' Sylvia said. 'He's careful to hit her where the bruises won't show. If he's careless and he happens to leave marks on her arms or her legs she'll cover them up with long sleeves and long skirts.'

'I should have known,' Wexford said. 'I should have seen for myself.'

'Maybe you have to be trained to recognise it. You know, Dad, I can't only see it in her, I can see it in him. The arrogance, the grace, the charm, the smile. He's the type. Oh, there are many types but he's one of them.'

Wexford sat silent for a moment, thinking of the implications. What did this mean for Stephen Devenish? Suddenly he had become a different person, a monster, as much a criminal as the thug who punches a bystander in a pub brawl. If it was true, if Sylvia was right. He thought of how hard it would be to ask Fay Devenish and how much harder for her to answer.

'Do you remember a couple of weeks back I asked you why a child of nearly three was apparently mute? And you gave me several possible reasons?'

'Dad, are you saying that this child is the missing little girl Sanchia?'

He nodded. 'This is the Devenish family.'

'Then the reason's plain. She doesn't speak because she's witnessed her father beating up her mother. I'm not saying it's direct, I mean like, "my mother talks and you hit her, so I won't run that risk, I won't talk," though it's something like that. But it's more complex, it's protective behaviour all right – look at the way she's hiding herself in her mother's skirt. How about the boys? How has it affected them?'

'God knows, Sylvia. Now you've told me I can say what in fact I did think at the time, that the older one looks as if he's biding his time until *he's* old enough to hit his father.'

'Maybe, or maybe the father's encouraging them to hit her too. Oh, you needn't look like that, Dad. It happens. And don't ask why she puts up with it, will you? Where can she go? Where can she take her children? She can't keep herself – at least, I suppose not – so who will keep her? And she doesn't tell people because, believe it or not, she's ashamed. *She's* ashamed. She dreads the neighbours knowing, friends knowing. She's ashamed because *real* women, women who are beautiful enough and clever enough, and really good about the house, they don't get abused. They get admired and cherished. If she were like that, if she could only come up to her husband's standard, she wouldn't get beaten either.

'Probably no one knows about it, or maybe she's told her parents, if she has parents, and they say she's exaggerating, he's a good provider, he's faithful, she's making a fuss about nothing. Or she tells just one girlfriend and the friend tells her to leave him but won't take her and her children in, so what's the use?'

Jane Andrews, Wexford thought. She would be that friend and confidante. But there had been a quarrel and she had been sent away – because she knew and Devenish couldn't bear anyone to know? Or Fay, like many a person who entrusts to another the deep and painful secrets of the heart, could no longer tolerate the company of the woman she had confided in?

Sylvia was leafing through the *Martyrs* book, stopping, making a face and flinching. 'God, she had a kind of double mastectomy, they cut her breasts off. I wish I hadn't read it!'

'It was a long time ago,' said Wexford gently, 'and maybe it never happened.'

'It was in people's minds, though, wasn't it? They must have done things like that or it wouldn't – it wouldn't be in here.'

'Violence and cruelty are always with us, Sylvia. By telling me what you've just told me about the Devenishes, you may have put a stop to some of it. Think of that instead of St Agatha.'

After she had gone he understood that she had also shown him the way Sanchia's abduction had been planned, the way it had happened, the despair and last-ditch remedy, the complicity of others, the final painful but necessary sacrifice. It was as if a whole panorama of revelations, causes, consequences and seemingly endless cruelty unrolled before his eyes. He saw the paradox of the innocent victim declared guilty and the ruthless perpetrator emerging guiltless. And what on earth was he going to do about it?

# Chapter 18

A glassy lake of flowers had covered the police station forecourt since the previous week. People who had never known Ted Hennessy, even those whose only knowledge of CID work came from television serials or who hated the police, all these had brought flowers and left them lying in their slippery sheaths of cellophane under the falling rain and now the blaze of the sun. Many names on cards were those of Muriel Campden residents.

Wexford, returning to the place from Hennessy's funeral, wondered not for the first time at the current passion for mourning with flowers still in their wrapping. When had it begun? Probably when the custom began of placing bouquets on the site where someone had died by violence or tragic accident. Ten years ago? Not much more. It was almost always when the person who had died was someone you didn't know or hardly knew. Perhaps it was a sign of a more caring society and he was all for that, and he asked himself why no one ever thought of taking the flowers out of their wrapping and throwing away the plastic, so that all these roses and carnations might not bloom unseen.

He had been to the funeral but played no active part. Forbidden to be a bearer by his doctor, on account of his weight and his age, he had watched Burden, with Vine, Donaldson and Cox, carry Hennessy's coffin on their shoulders from the grim black undertaker's car up the aisle of St Peter's Church. The wreath from the Mid-Sussex Constabulary crowned it, a huge gaudy thing of delphiniums, gazanias and stephanotis, chosen by the Assistant Chief Constable, while Laura Hennessy's knot of white mock orange and her children's pathetic twin pink roses lay at its head.

The giving of the address had been left to Southby, who had said all the usual things about gallant officers and exceptional devotion to duty, and laying down one's life for one's friends, than which man has no greater love. But poor Ted Hennessy hadn't really laid down his life for anyone. He had only been in the wrong place at the wrong time.

Funerals depressed Wexford, not only for the obvious reasons, but because they brought out in men and women so much hypocrisy and false piety. Just looking at Southby, half sitting, half on his knees, with his hands over his eyes, mouthing prayers he hadn't uttered since primary school, sent up his blood pressure. The rest of them could go back to Laura's house for sherry and Dundee cake if they liked. He wouldn't and he was pretty sure Burden wouldn't either.

Pressmen and cameras were everywhere. A flash went off in his face as he came down St Peter's steps and for a moment the world went black. He squeezed his eyes shut and stood still in the sudden panic we all feel when threatened with blindness, real or imagined.

Burden touched his arm. 'Are you OK?'

'I think so. Do you ever dream there's something badly wrong with your eyes? You're going blind or will if you don't do something about it fast?'

'Everyone dreams that,' Burden said surprisingly. 'Everyone I've ever talked to at any rate.'

'Do they? I find that curiously comforting.'

A crowd had gathered in the High Street. As Wexford put it, God knew what they hoped to see. But perhaps it was in the same category as bringing the plastic-wrapped flowers and it made them feel they belonged, that they weren't left out, but part of this drama, this human tragedy.

'Any man's death diminishes me, is that why they're here?'

'Bit high-flown, isn't it?' Burden said. 'They just want to see themselves on television.'

They walked back, stared at by passers-by as if they were policemen from Mars and not the familiar faces any of them could have seen any day. Wexford was silent, thinking about Fay Devenish. He must see her but not yet. A strange reluctance to meet her again had taken hold of him and he asked himself if all abused women had this effect on others. They weren't wanted, they must be ostracised; in becoming victims of this kind, they put themselves outside ordinary human intercourse. These passive creatures were the ultimate objects of demonisation. It was a terrible attitude and he confronted it only for a few seconds before thrusting it out of his mind. He was avoiding seeing her because he had to see someone else first.

'Come upstairs.' He and Burden picked their way through the lake of flowers. 'I want to tell you a story, see what you think.' Under the plastic glaze, roses and fuchsias and zinnias were dying now, petals curling up, brown at the edges, their scent undergoing strange chemical changes. 'Lilies that fester smell far worse than weeds.'

'I don't see any lilies,' said prosaic Burden. 'But I know what you mean.'

'An amazing number of people want to adopt children, don't they?' Wexford said when they were

317

in his office. 'They get obsessed about it. Even normally law-abiding people, women particularly, though I hardly dare say it, they forget their principles and the rules by which they've lived, and break the law in all kinds of ways.'

'What, you mean like going to Romania and bringing back orphan babies, forging passports and birth certificates, that kind of thing?'

'That kind of thing. Do you remember Mrs Louise Sharpe?'

'No. Should I?'

'For God's sake, Mike, it's only a couple of days ago. Jane Andrews's sister.'

'Oh, her. What of it? And what about this story you're going to tell me?'

'Wait a little. Would you be surprised to learn that Mrs Sharpe has a record?'

'The life we lead,' said Burden, 'I wouldn't be surprised to hear anyone had a record. I wouldn't be surprised to hear *you* had.'

'Thanks very much. Louise Sharpe is a widow . . .'

'Not a criminal offence unless she murdered her old man.'

'I've no reason to think she did that. He had a heart attack two years ago. He was a few months under forty but he had a heart attack and it killed him. His name was James Michael Sharpe, and he was an accountant who had gone into computers in a big way and made a fortune. She was thirty-eight when he died and pregnant. The child, a girl, had to be kept on a life support machine and finally only lived two months. She and her husband, believing themselves infertile, had been trying to adopt a child for five years before she finally conceived. A home study was done, two babies were candidates or whatever the term is. In both cases the mothers changed their minds at the last moment. Then Louise Sharpe became pregnant ...'

'How do you know all this?'

'Thanks to our wonderful computer system, a lot of info is available on anyone with a criminal record.'

'You haven't said what the criminal record was for yet,' Burden grumbled.

'I'm coming to it. Her husband died and she lost her baby, a double tragedy. I don't know what happened next because I only got facts, not emotions. That part I have to imagine. Anyway, at some time in the following year she renewed her application to adopt but the situation was very different now. She was three years older, she was no longer in a long-lasting and stable marriage. Her chances of being acceptable as a potential adoptive parent were practically nil.'

The heavy throb of a diesel engine brought Wexford to the window. He looked down on the white-and-green truck owned by the local authority's contractors and the green-and-white-uniformed men with dayglo armbands as they began gathering up the flowers. 'Which today are,' he said, 'and tomorrow are cast into the oven. Only they're cast into that monstrous chewing machine.'

'What are you talking about?'

'Nothing,' said Wexford. 'Ignore me. Back to Mrs Sharpe. The first child was called Nicola and she was dead. Sharpe, as I've said, had made a lot of money and he left his widow very well-off, as the loquacious Mrs Probyn has told us. Not being short of cash, she went off and bought a baby. To Albania, in fact, where apparently you can buy gypsy babies. She was fortunate not to be caught there as God knows what would have become of her. I don't imagine an Albanian prison is a very pleasant place to spend a couple of years in. Instead, she was caught here, having tried to use the passport she had for the dead child, Nicola.'

'She had a passport for a sick baby that only lived two months?'

'Rich people are always taking their children out of the country. Maybe she planned to go abroad with the baby when she was better, only she didn't get better, she died. Louise Sharpe was lucky not to go to prison for buying the Albanian child. They had a psychiatrist in court who said she was badly mentally disturbed, so she got off with a heavy fine and Nicola the Second went back to Albania.'

'I'm beginning to see your drift,' said Burden. 'Here was a ready-made adoptive mother, a woman who longed for a child, even had a name all ready for her and a birth certificate and passport.'

'I think so.'

'Are you saying this woman, this Louise Sharpe, got into Woodland Lodge by night and abducted Sanchia Devenish? Where does Devenish himself come into all this? And what about Jane Andrews?'

'I can tell you all that too, I think.'

Once more Jane Andrews was in her 'unisex' attire, scrubbed face, trainers on her feet. She had come willingly to Kingsmarkham because, Wexford suspected, she was very anxious, now the whole scheme was over, to tell the rest of it. Her boats were burnt, she could recant nothing, and now she had to do the best she could for the friend she felt she had betrayed and the sister she had perhaps irrevocably injured, albeit with the kindest intentions. The solicitor she had at first demanded she no longer wanted. In fact, as she said to Wexford, she hoped that not more outsiders than absolutely necessary would be involved in this. Instead of an interview room, he took her upstairs into his office. Barry Vine and

Karen Malahyde had gone to Brighton to confront Louise Sharpe.

'And take Sanchia–Nicola away with us?' Karen had said.

'You must. The Social Services have been notified and a woman from Kingsmarkham Adoption Department will go with you. Sanchia must be restored to her parents as soon as possible.'

Wexford repeated this to Jane Andrews when he was seated at his desk and she was opposite him. She looked down.

She said quietly, 'He will kill her.'

'Stephen Devenish will kill his own daughter?'

'He will kill Fay. You said you knew why Fay gave Sanchia away. Maybe you've an idea but you don't know the extent of it. You're like all men, you think it's OK for a man to give his wife a little tap. That's the expression, isn't it? A little tap? Well, that wasn't the way it was with them. If he'd done to a man what he's done to her, systematically, over the years, on and on and more and more violent and brutal, he'd have been put in prison for life.'

Choosing to ignore her placing him in much the same category, Wexford said, 'Go on, please.'

'All right, I'll go on. It'll be a pleasure to go on. He hit her for the first time on their honeymoon. He caught her talking to a man who was staying in the same hotel. Just talking and maybe daring to laugh. Stephen asked her to come up to their room with him, she thought he wanted to make love and when they were inside he slapped her face so hard she fell over. In other words, he knocked her down. She wasn't to be alone with another man, he said, and now she knew what would happen to her if she was. She cried so much, she couldn't believe he'd do it, you see. It was, she thought, so unlike him that she cried and cried until he said he was sorry, it wouldn't happen again but he loved her so much he was insanely jealous, he couldn't help it. Well, of course it happened again. Too many times to go into. Even I haven't been told how many times or all the details. Her mother and father haven't, though it wouldn't be much good. Her mother never wants to hear about anything she calls "unpleasant" and her father asks her what she does to provoke her husband.

'He's broken both her arms. He hit her so hard in the eye once they thought she'd lose her sight. He cuts her. He'll take a knife from the kitchen and see to it she sees him take it, then he'll call her into that ghastly study – it's always for some imagined or invented misdemeanour – and he'll tell her to hold out her hand, and he doesn't smack it like teachers used to smack schoolchildren's hands, he cuts it across the palm with the knife.

'He's all contrite and sorry afterwards, of course, and he always says it won't happen again, but at the same time it's always her fault, she makes him do it. She's got a lover he overhears her talking to on the phone, or her skirt is too short, or she's flirtatious. That's why they haven't any friends. He beats her if she talks to a man and he's even jealous of women she likes. At the same time he says she's mad. I don't know how many times he's accused her of being a lesbian. She's never had a job because she might meet other people, men and women, at work. Besides, she has to keep the house spotless and do all the cooking, that's her function and if she's not perfect at it, or he *decides* she's not perfect, he's giving her what he calls "a little smack", which in fact means knocking her down and kicking her.'

Jane Andrews paused to draw breath. Her colour had become very high and her eyes glittered. Wexford saw that she was holding her fists clenched as if ready to strike someone and he had no doubt who that someone would be.

'All right, Miss Andrews, take it easy. I'm beginning to understand. Where do the children come into all this?'

She didn't reply. 'It was quite funny, really, you thinking he might have a girlfriend. Stephen Devenish is the most faithful husband on earth. He *loves* his victim, she's the one woman he can beat to death.' Her bitter laugh was unpleasant to hear. 'She phoned that Women's Aid helpline, you know, not long ago actually – well, it wasn't Women's Aid but one of those. He was in the garden with Sanchia, but he came in and accused her of talking to a lover. He hit her so hard she lost consciousness and she was out for five minutes.' She relaxed the fists and let her hands go limp, looked at him tiredly. 'Don't ask why she stayed, will you? Don't ask why she didn't leave him, call the police, whatever. I used to ask her that. Once.'

'Where do the children come in?'

'They're *there*, aren't they? He doesn't stop because his sons are there. I don't know what he tells them. That that's what you have to do to women to keep them in line, I suppose. Or Mummy's been naughty again. Something like that. Of course you can tell it's affected them, they're both disturbed in different ways.'

'And Sanchia?'

'Sanchia was the result of rape. We're permitted to use that word now, aren't we, about men forcing themselves on their wives? It's not their right any more, is it? Well, Stephen raped Fay when she was ill in bed because he'd beaten her so badly. She was in pain and she begged him to leave her alone but he didn't, he was a man, he said, and he needed sex or his health would suffer. So she got pregnant. When she was four months pregnant he kicked her in the stomach. He didn't want another child, he said. Fay would love the child more than him. Well, his kicking her didn't have the desired effect and Sanchia was born. Undamaged too, which was a piece of luck. Fay begged him not to hit her any more, she went down on her knees to him. If you behaved yourself like a responsible grown-up woman I wouldn't have to punish you, he said. Kneeling to your own husband, what kind of behaviour is that? And he kicked her over.'

Wexford interrupted her. 'He beat her like this in front of the child? In front of Sanchia?'

'Of course he did. She and I were no longer allowed to be friends but, as I told you, we spoke on the phone. I was all she had and that wasn't much.' Jane Andrews cleared her throat, as if she feared the sudden hoarseness of her voice betrayed an overwhelming emotion. 'I couldn't confront him with this. All that would have happened was that he'd have taken it out on Fay. I knew that. I'd spoken to him before, when she first told me, which was about seven years ago. I'd told him I'd call the police, and d'you know what he said? He denied it, he said it was all in Fay's imagination, that she was neurotic or worse and was lucky in that she had a husband who understood her. He wasn't rude to me or angry or anything, he was quite calm and charming as ever, soothing really, almost paternal. He just took it out on her afterwards.'

'But finally you were banned from the house?'

'That was when I found out he was beating her in front of Robert. Robert was only three then, the same age as Sanchia is now. It was almost as if he did it on purpose, so that the child could *see*. Well, no, not almost, he did do it on purpose. He'd take the child out of Fay's arms and lay him down, then he'd start on Fay with Robert watching. Now he'll learn what happens to women who are stupid and disobedient, he said.

'Well, I went for him, I told him it couldn't go on, I'd take Fay and the children away and have them live with me, God knows how, but I did mean it and he knew it. So he told me I wasn't wanted around his family any more. That wouldn't have stopped me seeing Fay but he took his revenge on her, he took it out on her and I couldn't stand that. We kept up our friendship on the phone, that was all we could manage, and even so Fay was afraid all the time that somehow he'd find out about the calls. I usually made the calls and when that one-four-seven-one system came in, you know, the number you dial and get the number of who made the last call, she was terrified he'd try that and find out if I'd made a call when she was out. She got me to promise only to phone at set times when he couldn't be in and she wouldn't be out.'

Wexford, who for the most part had sat silent, listening to this catalogue of suffering, now said, 'Whose idea was it to remove Sanchia?'

Jane Andrews said quickly, 'Fay's. Not mine. I never even thought of it. She told me it was either that or she'd kill herself.'

'And by "that" you mean the giving away of Sanchia for adoption so that she might not see her mother constantly abused by her father? So that she might grow up in a happy home even though this meant Mrs Devenish would never see her daughter again?'

'That's what I mean, yes. When she first suggested it I thought it was madness and I didn't see how it could work out. Then I thought of my sister Louise. You have to understand this was months ago, it took a lot of planning. Louise had had a bad experience

325

trying to adopt a baby from Eastern Europe and I thought she'd given up all ideas of adoption, but far from it. She told me she was as keen as ever, keener, desperate in fact. And the problems I'd foreseen but Fay hadn't, like getting Sanchia a birth certificate and a passport and whatever, that would all be taken care of because Louise had kept all the documents she'd had for her baby that died.'

'Was your mother in on this – this plot?'

'My mother knows nothing about it. She doesn't even yet know that Louise has got a child – Louise has a nanny and a live-in maid – and now she won't have to know, will she?' Jane Andrews paused, looking suddenly horror-stricken. 'Oh, poor, poor Louise,' she cried, 'this will kill her, to lose this one after all she's been through . . .'

'Miss Andrews, the fact is you should have known this whole operation was bound to fail. It was wrong of you to raise Mrs Sharpe's hopes and encourage her in this way. You must know that.'

'I don't see that. It could have worked, it *nearly* did.'

'And the effect on Sanchia has to be damaging.'

'Not half as damaging as living with a violent criminal.' An upsetting thought struck her. 'She won't have to go back, will she?'

'Of course she will have to go back,' Wexford said with a sigh. 'I understand, I appreciate the circumstances. But whatever Mr Devenish may have done, he is her natural father who is living in an apparently stable relationship with her natural mother.' He held up his hand as Jane Andrews started forward in her chair. 'Just a minute, Miss Andrews. I hear what you say and I believe you. But if Mrs Devenish makes no complaint to us about her husband there is nothing we can do. And if she was going to make a complaint she would have done so already, wouldn't she? According to you, this has been going on for about thirteen years.'

'He has to know what Fay did? I mean, that she took Sanchia away herself?'

There was something in the way she said it that sent a chill down Wexford's spine. He wanted to be unaffected by her, to maintain detachment, but he was unable to control his body's response, the shiver than ran through him.

All he could do was conceal it and tell her as coolly as he could that of course Devenish would have to know, adding to himself that the man should already have been told, just as Sanchia should by now have been reclaimed and returned to her parents. These things must be done at once. He didn't want to look into Jane Andrews's white, frightened face but he had to.

She repeated the words she had spoken before: 'He will kill her.'

Restoring a missing child to her parents should be one of the pleasantest of a police officer's tasks. Wexford had found missing children before; taking them home, seeing the bereft mother's face, the father's joy, had been enough to warm his heart. This time would be different and a happy occasion transformed into – he hardly knew what. Horror? Dismay? Perhaps fearful danger. But it had to be done and he had to do it.

It was useless Jane Andrews telling him she wanted as few people as possible to know of this. They had to know. Charges would have to be brought against Jane Andrews and Louise Sharpe but it was a puzzle to know what charges. At any rate, there was no great hurry. Neither of them would run away. As for Fay Devenish, he couldn't bring himself to think of punishing her further, and of her husband he couldn't bear to think at all. Giving himself an unusual injunction, to play it by ear, he had Donaldson drive him to Ploughman's Lane and Woodland Lodge.

It was the first time he had been there since Sylvia's, and then Jane Andrews's, revelations. In the light of them, the idyllic place looked different, not a peaceful sylvan corner of Kingsmarkham lying snugly between the old market town and the downs, but sinister, covert, the beautiful trees there for the purpose of hiding what went on beneath their shelter. Yet no one would imagine, looking at the house which seemed on this fine sunny afternoon to nestle comfortably in a leafy dell, that inside it a continuous crime was perpetrated, an ongoing perpetual assault on a defenceless creature. So delightful was the picture and so peaceful the atmosphere that for a moment he doubted. Jane Andrews had invented it, imagined it, contrived this story to cover the truth. There had been some other motive for Fay Devenish giving away her own child. But as soon as he saw her, for it was she who opened the door to him, he knew it was all true, and he was almost at a loss for words.

At least Stephen Devenish was away from home. He was at Seaward Air in the Brighton office. She told him so, as if he couldn't possibly have wanted to see her – it must be her husband he was in search of.

'I'm glad to have the chance of seeing you alone, Mrs Devenish.'

'My sons will soon be home.'

Did she think she needed protection from *him*? 'I want to talk to you', he said, 'without your sons. On your own. I have something to tell you.'

She knew. She read it in his face and she went as

white as the ivory linen blouse she wore. For a moment he thought she was going to faint and he wished he had brought Lynn with him or Wendy Brodrick. But she recovered, even managed a dreadful strained smile, and he thought how recovering from pain and shock was her life, she was used to it.

He was going towards the study where, once before, he had talked to her as she lay on the hide sofa, her face marked and swollen, her speech impeded, but she laid a thin light hand on his arm, said, 'No, not in there. Please don't let's go in there.'

He remembered what Jane Andrews had said about that room, that male place, darkly panelled, leather-furnished, with the swords and the dagger on the wall, as the scene of many of her injuries. Instead, he followed her into a room designated her province, the kitchen.

On the refectory table where Devenish had wept stood a large wooden bowl brimming with fruit, pale-yellow apples, dark-green pears, gleaming oranges, golden bananas and grapes like jade beads. Everywhere was spotless, as if newly spring-cleaned. Two of the casement windows were open and the fresh white curtains fluttered in a breeze which ruffled the leaves of the herbs, basil and sage and savory and marjoram, in glazed earthenware pots on the sill. The little painted doors on the cuckoo clock were shut.

He motioned to her to sit down at the table and he took a chair opposite her. It was an immense relief to him, a comfort almost, that she had no bruises on her face, no marks or scars, so that he could tell himself that perhaps it wasn't so bad after all, perhaps there had been exaggerations. Her eyes met his and she looked away. And then he told her. He told her that Sanchia was found, that she was safe and content in the home of a Mrs Louise Sharpe, but that Mrs Sharpe had not abducted her.

'You did that yourself, Mrs Devenish.' It was a statement, not a question. 'You need not tell me why. I know why.'

The whitening, the threatened fainting, was past. She only sighed. 'Someone is bringing her back?'

'In about half an hour's time.'

She hesitated. She dreaded saying it but she was obliged to. The words were forced out painfully, like something stiff squeezed from a tube. 'What am I to tell my husband?'

The hard rejoinder would have been that she should have thought of that before. He wouldn't have dreamt of saying it. 'We'll come to that in a minute. Your friend Miss Andrews has told me a lot of things about you and Mr Devenish. I expect you can guess what they are. If they are true and you have been the – let's say the victim of repeated assaults . . .'

She stopped him and now the words poured out. 'You're going to say I could call you, the police that is, and bring charges against him, and have him in court, and I could leave – but where could I go? And it wouldn't stop, it wouldn't, he would just be angrier, and wherever I went he'd find me, I know he would. He says so, he says he'd find me wherever I went. There isn't any escape, not while he's alive and I'm alive, no escape at all.'

She put her fingers up to her eyes, touched her temples as if stimulating thought, then said, looking at him with pathetic bravery, with a forlorn hope, 'The only thing is that he may change. I thought he was changing a year ago when he hadn't – well, done anything to me for a whole four weeks. I mean, it didn't last, but it wasn't quite so bad for a while and then it started again, but I know he was stressed-out, there was trouble at work, and I'm – I'm not always – well, the wife he expected, the wife a man like him deserves, if you like. I know all that. He may change, do you think?'

Not believing it for a moment, Wexford said, 'The temporary loss of his daughter may make a difference; it may have shocked him into changing his ways.' Can the leopard change his spots? 'But Mrs Devenish,' he tried again, 'there is no need at all for you to put up with this treatment. What your husband does to you is just as much assault as when a man knocks down another man in a street fight.'

'I know. But *he* doesn't. He says he loves me, I'm the only woman he's ever loved. It's his duty to – well, chastise me. He says I need it or I'd go completely to pieces. He really believes that.' Her voice, low as it normally was, rose suddenly to a shriek as her control vanished. 'What will he do when he knows it was me took Sanchia? What will he do?'

'Please try to keep calm. I do understand. I understand your predicament. I will be here, I will tell him. And the other officers will come with Sanchia and stay here.' It all sounded so feeble, such a wretched compromise. He put strength and firmness into his voice. 'Please remember what I've said. You aren't obliged to put up with this. Next time he strikes you, get into your car and come straight to the police station. Will you do that?'

She was crying now, shaking with sobs, as she had never cried when her child was missing. Wexford fetched her a glass of water. She sipped it, then took the glass back to the sink, rinsed it, dried it on a tea-cloth and put it away. The back door opened and the two boys came in from school. Their entry made a physical change in her. She sat up straighter, seemed to brace herself, managed a smile. But they didn't speak to her and she didn't speak to them. She got up and put cans of Coke from the refrigerator on to the table for them with a plate of biscuits and two packets of crisps. Would Wexford like tea? He shook his head. Both he and she jumped when the doorbell rang and she gave a little scream of fear.

Edward said, 'Come on, Mum, get yourself together.'

Robert went to the door and came back with Barry Vine, Karen Malahyde, a young child care officer and Sanchia. Both boys were shocked and silent. Fay Devenish said 'Sanchia', as if she were uttering an exclamation of despair. The child stared, put her fists in her eyes, turned her back on her mother and buried her head in Karen's skirt.

'Someone make a cup of tea, will you?' Wexford said to the company, not daring to single out the young women.

But the child care officer complied.

'Where has she been?' Edward said to his mother.

'Don't ask.'

'You and Dad, you're crazy,' said Robert.

He took one of the crisp packets and walked out of the room. Barry handed round the teacups. Sanchia turned her head very slowly, looked at her mother, stuck her thumb in her mouth and squeezed her eyes tight shut. No one seemed able to think of anything to say. There was no conversation apart from Karen's remarking that it hadn't rained for a couple of days and the child care officer saying in her bright social-worker's voice how much she liked the cuckoo clock and had it come from Switzerland. At that moment the doors opened, the cuckoo came out, flapped its beak and said 'cuckoo' five times.

Another half-hour went by before Stephen Devenish came home and they had all had two more cups of tea. Fay was the first to be aware of his car, she seemed to hear it before it possibly could be heard, as if some extra sense abuse and fear had developed in her picked up inaudible sound across long distances. She stiffened, sat rigid, then began to shiver visibly.

'All right,' Wexford said. 'Stay there. Leave it to me.'

He reminded himself that the man didn't know, no one had forewarned him. No doubt, strange as the whole concept was, monster that he was, he loved his child. Human beings were beyond belief strange creatures. He didn't wait for Devenish's key to enter the lock but went outside on to the forecourt. Sanchia's father was standing beside the black Jaguar he had just stepped out of, and when he was aware of Wexford he turned and gave him his charming smile.

'I have good news for you, Mr Devenish,' Wexford said in a low, steady voice. 'Your daughter is found. Sanchia is home again with her mother.'

There was no mistaking his joy, his unfeigned delight. He crowed with triumph, punched both fists in the air like some sportsman who has scored a goal or won a set. He took Wexford's hand and pumped it up and down. He laughed with pleasure.

'Where was she? What happened to her?' A less pleasant thought seemed to strike him. 'Is she all right?'

'She seems fine. Shall we go inside?'

'But what happened to her?'

'I'm going to tell you that. In a moment. And I am going to ask you to be very understanding and patient and tolerant, Mr Devenish. Shall we go into your study? I want to speak to you alone. I'm sure you can postpone seeing Sanchia for ten minutes.'

Devenish listened with his back turned. He stood at

the window, apparently looking out, while Wexford talked. Then, when he could stand it no longer, Wexford said, 'Please sit down, Mr Devenish.'

The man turned to him a face suffused with blood. Dark veins stood out on his forehead. He sat down on the edge of the leather sofa. 'She's not sane,' he said. 'She's quite mad. I didn't know she was mad when we got married but I soon found out. It's a blessing for her she's got me or she'd just go to pieces. She's a nymphomaniac, for one thing. Not with me, I may add, with everyone else but me. Still, what can you expect. She's mad.'

Wexford was in a dilemma. He had no proof of Devenish's violence, though he believed in it absolutely. But he couldn't tell the man to leave his wife alone when Devenish would only deny he had ever assaulted her. 'It's not a matter of insanity,' he said at last, 'but she certainly needs to see a psychiatrist . . .'

'What are you going to charge her with? Kidnapping? Abduction? She ought to go to prison for life. I couldn't bear that, I love her, she needs me.'

Instead of answering, Wexford said, 'As much as anything, your wife is going to need your sympathy and your support, sir. Now you had better come and see her and your daughter.'

By this time Karen had told Fay Devenish that a woman officer trained in the area of domestic violence would be visiting her and a child care officer would be making regular calls. Fay said that after they had gone her husband would kill her. Offered a mobile for getting rapidly in touch with the police or the social services, she said they already had three mobiles in the house and there was no point in having another. Sanchia crawled under the table and sat there sucking her thumb but after about ten minutes she came out and climbed on to her mother's lap.

'What have I done to her?' Fay said. 'Have I traumatised her?'

'I shouldn't think so for a moment,' the child care officer said. 'She'll be fine.' But when Devenish appeared with Wexford Sanchia started to cry. It wasn't ordinary crying but sustained screams, pumped out hysterically. Fay sat with her head bowed, holding Sanchia round the waist but making no attempt to quieten her. Her husband walked over to her, stood beside her chair, laid a hand on her shoulder. Fay didn't move. The child continued crying, sobbing now.

'All right, darling, I know all about it,' Devenish said. 'It's not so terrible. We've got her back and that's all that matters.'

She looked at Wexford and asked if he was going to arrest her.

'We'll have a talk about that tomorrow,' he said.

There was nothing more to be done but he had never before left a situation with such reluctance. He told himself not to be melodramatic, above all, not to imagine he was leaving her to her death. Devenish would be chastened, he would know he was being watched. It was absurd to feel that the moment he, Vine and the two women were out of the house Devenish would turn upon his wife and strike her, knock her to the ground.

On the other hand, it wasn't over, the man would never change. Fay would again have her face punched and her eyes blacked, perhaps her bones broken, maybe not tonight or tomorrow, but next week or the week after. It would never cease until she left him or he killed her. And if she left him he would pursue her. Wexford had never felt so powerless.

Next day he went back as he had promised and he

did see her without Devenish. The woman officer from the Regional Crime Squad had called earlier, she told him. Fortunately, her husband had left at eight thirty for the Brighton office. DS Margaret Stamford had offered her a pager as well as a mobile, which she refused, presented her with all sorts of options for accommodation and support if she left her husband, and told her about The Hide helpline. Nothing more had been heard from Kingsmarkham Children's Department and that she felt was a relief.

'They won't take Sanchia into care, will they? I don't know why I say that, really, it might be the best thing for her if they *did* take her into care.'

'Mrs Devenish,' Wexford said, 'you are not to be charged with any offence. Indeed, the only offence you could be charged with is wasting police time and preparing such a case' – he smiled reassuringly – 'with all the paperwork would waste more police time. I would just like to reinforce what DS Stamford said to you. We can't prosecute your husband unless you are prepared to give evidence against him and you've said you aren't. I would urge you to think again and if there are any more assaults to be in touch with us as soon as possible. You can phone at any hour of the day or night. Do you understand that?'

She nodded. 'Of course,' she said, 'of course I will' and he knew she didn't mean a word of it.

So he went away and left her, but his thoughts refused to abandon her. She was with him all the rest of that day and the next, and the next. He kept thinking of ways he might act to stop it, post a man to watch the place by day and another by night, lurk outside the windows to catch Devenish when next he attacked her. It wasn't practical, it wasn't possible, he hadn't the manpower. He waited for a phone call, not from her – that he was sure would never come –

but from someone, even one of her own sons, who had found her mutilated or dying or dead.

It was beyond his imagination to picture what scenes ensued after he had gone and she was alone with Devenish. Or perhaps it was only that his mind flinched from it. She was so small and frail, and Devenish such a big, burly man who must be twice her weight. And the terrible thing was that Devenish had a *right* to be angry with his wife for what she had done, taking away his child, deceiving him, lying to him and her sons. But no one had a right to vent his anger against someone else with savage treatment and blows.

'When we found Sanchia,' he said to Burden, 'we were going to have champagne – remember? I don't feel much like it now, do you?'

'Not much,' said Burden.

Had he beaten her again? Wexford had no means of knowing. As time went on he asked Margaret Stamford to call at Woodland Lodge again and she did call. This time Fay Devenish didn't even let her get past the front door. She came out on to the step, almost closing the door behind her and whispered that she was sorry but nothing profitable could come out of another interview. Her husband was indoors, she said, and she would have to explain who her visitor was and what she had come for. Only she wouldn't explain, she would invent something, God knew what.

It sounded as if Devenish's violence towards her was continuing. And of course it was; Wexford had never really doubted that it would. Everything he might do, every action taken to support or help her, would only exacerbate his violence. Brian St George carried a story in the *Courier* of the proceedings in court where Jane Andrews and Louise Sharpe appeared on a charge of wasting police time and obstructing the police in the course of their inquiries. He wondered then what would happen to Fay when Stephen Devenish read it. A much more serious charge against Victoria Cadbury, that of abduction of two women and falsely imprisoning them, made bigger headlines. Would that also incense Devenish and thus endanger his wife? Perhaps, but he heard nothing.

He even asked Sylvia if, while operating The Hide helpline, she had ever had a call from Fay Devenish or from someone who might be Fay Devenish, but there had been nothing. If there was violence at Woodland Lodge among the high trees and in the deep peace, Fay suffered in silence.

And then, after two months, the silence and the peace came to an end.

# Chapter 19

Down in Brighton, Louise Sharpe twice attempted suicide. The first time she left her six-bedroomed, three-bathroomed house with its swimming pool and its staff of resident Filipino couple but no longer resident nanny, went down to the beach and walked into the sea until it covered her head. She was seen by a swimmer and rescued. A month later her housekeeper found her unconscious, having swallowed a packet of sleeping pills and half a bottle of gin. The psychiatrist who saw her when she came out of hospital called her actions a cry for help but Louise said she didn't want help, she wanted to die.

Number 16 Oberon Road, now no longer the Smiths' home, had been seriously damaged by the Kingsmarkham Six and their supporters, all the front windows broken, the door panels kicked in and tiles knocked off the roof. Weeks passed before the local authority's contractors moved in and during those weeks the windows and front door were boarded up and the roof covered in a big sheet of blue plastic. One night, while the Muriel Campden Estate slept, a graffitist had moved in and decorated the entire façade with pictures of bleeding corpses, decapitated torsos and their separate heads, open-mawed animal faces and such words as 'paedo', 'filth' and 'killer' in the bright colours of spray paint, pink, yellow, emerald, prussian-blue and scarlet.

The *Kingsmarkham Courier* ran a story on the appalling situation of the homeless sleeping on the streets of Myringham while accommodation stood empty in that town and particularly in Kingsmarkham. Not to mention the shameful situation of Kingsmarkham Police Station being restored to pristine condition within three weeks while 16 Oberon Road still stood derelict. On their front page they used a photograph in full colour of the graffiti.

Speculation was rife on the Muriel Campden Estate as to whom it would be allocated when the repairs were finally carried out. Debbie Crowne hankered after it for her daughter Lizzie, and Miroslav Zlatic and their child. As to marriage, she cared very little about that, whatever Lizzie might feel. She just wanted, as she said to Maria Michaels, to see them in a stable relationship with family values. Unfortunately for her ambitions, Miroslav was still with Brenda in a partnership that seemed happier than formerly and it was reported that her sons called him Dad.

Lizzie was nearly six months pregnant and what her mother termed 'as big as a house'. The social worker called occasionally, urging her to attend parenting as well as antenatal classes, but Lizzie said she was still thinking it through. It was an awkward situation, seeing that Kingsmarkham Social Services were bringing an action against Colin Crowne in the County Court for the cost of replacing Jodi the virtual baby.

Tommy Smith and Suzanne his daughter had been rehoused in a flat on the outskirts of Peterborough. The accommodation was in a bungalow block designed for pensioners and the disabled, and a long way away from any families with children. But the pensioners' families soon discovered Smith's identity. They stopped bringing their children to visit their grandparents, with the result that the other occupants of the bungalow block ostracised Smith and Suzanne, and sent them obscene letters. Suzanne's fiancé never returned and after a time she became engaged to one of the men who came to collect the tenants' recycling.

The police are particularly assiduous with their investigations when it is a matter of one of their own being killed or injured. Burden and Vine, with Cox and Lynn Fanhurst, had spent uncounted man- and woman-hours pursuing inquiries to find Hennessy's killer. All they had succeeded in doing was eliminating Colin Crowne from the inquiry. Patrick Flay recalled that he had seen Miroslav Zlatic 'holding a missile'. Vine found a Serbo-Croat speaker who taught Balkan Studies at the University of the South to interpret for him but Miroslav still said nothing, being apparently as disinclined to his own language as to English. And there the matter stood, though Burden and Vine pressed on, determined to find Hennessy's killer, not to think of giving up until they had.

Frustrated by Fay Devenish's disinclination to have her husband indicted for assault or to give evidence against him, Wexford nevertheless refused to let the Devenish affair disappear into that great recycling bin of unfinished business into which unresolved family troubles were cast and came out the other end as 'in the domestic, not police, domain'. Instead, he kept an eye. DS Karen Malahyde, while undergoing a three-day-a-week training in the handling of domestic violence, had visited Fay, taking care to do so in her husband's absence. With things back to normal, Stephen Devenish had returned to his former commitment to Seaward Air, and spent between eight and ten hours a day at the Gatwick, Brighton or Kingsmarkham offices. With the boys at their preparatory school in Sewingbury until the end of July, it was easy enough to see Fay alone.

Karen soon became at home in Woodland Lodge and managed, while with Fay, to subdue her own feminist inclinations, her loathing of housework and contempt for those who did it. After all, as she remarked to Lynn, whether the poor woman polishes the floor right is the least of her worries. She set up a meeting for Fay with Griselda Cooper and the three women had lunch together at the Europlate, Fay having ascertained that it was her husband's day at Gatwick for a trial flight to Brussels and back in one of the new Flyfast 355 Stratoslicer aircraft Seaward had bought.

The lunch was profitable only in that it brought colour into Fay's face and a light into her eyes. She hadn't had a meal out with friends since Stephen stopped her seeing Jane Andrews. Griselda tried to get her to wear an alarm device round her neck but Fay said Stephen would spot it in five minutes, smash it and probably smash her as well. One good thing had come out of all this, Karen said, and that was that at last Fay felt able to talk quite freely about what went on at home. It was no longer a dark and terrible secret, to be whispered only to one intimate friend.

The neighbours knew. Operation Hurt-Watch's policy was to alert residents in the vicinity as to what went on. Karen had herself told Moira Wingrave and met with a nervous not-in-my-backyard response. Moira said she couldn't possibly think of interfering between husband and wife, especially in a select area like this one, but other dwellers in Ploughman's Lane were more accommodating and less shocked.

'Not that any of them will know,' Karen said to

Wexford. 'It's not exactly a housing estate with paper-thin walls. He could beat her to death and they wouldn't hear her screaming. Not through two hundred yards of dense rain forest.'

Wexford himself, when not busy tracking down and prosecuting eco-warriors, speculated as to what currently went on at Woodland Lodge. He talked to his wife about it and to Sylvia. When he mentioned it to his younger daughter Sheila, all she said was that if any man she'd ever been with hit her he'd wonder what had hit *him*. Wexford knew it wasn't as simple and straightforward as that. The Devenish affair was Karen's responsibility but he sometimes called on Fay himself, talking quietly to her, trying to discover what the situation now was and looking for signs of the abuse Sylvia had taught him to recognise.

He looked for other signs too. No bruises had shown on Fay's face since the return of Sanchia but many an abusive man is crafty and inflicts physical damage where the results of it won't show. That too he had learnt. And he observed what Karen had not, that although it was high summer, Fay wore dresses with long skirts and long sleeves. She was only just thirty-six but she never showed off her arms or her shoulders and all her clothes were high-necked. This might mean not only that the covered parts of her body exhibited bruises and contusions but also that Stephen Devenish demanded the excessively modest dress of a Shaker woman or an Irvingite. Wexford sometimes asked her if she was all right and she understood perfectly what he meant, simply replying yes and he was not to worry about her.

So he ran to earth (in more ways than one) the well-intentioned, earnest people who broke the law by uprooting fields of genetically altered oilseed rape and linseed, arrested them and had them charged with causing malicious damage, and he thought about the Devenish family. Was Stephen Devenish still receiving those threatening letters? Or had there ever been any threatening letters? Wexford hadn't much belief in the one-time existence of obscene or anonymous letters the recipient declares he has thrown away. Probably they existed only in Devenish's paranoid imagination.

Nor had he ever discovered exactly what happened when Stephen and Fay were alone together after Sanchia's return. She wouldn't tell him and she wouldn't tell Karen beyond saying that Stephen more often accused her of being a 'mental case' than he formerly had. He had also frequently told her she was unfit to look after his children but whether this accusation was accompanied by blows she never said.

Sanchia had begun to talk. At the beginning of July she became three years old and by then she was forming sentences and developing a large vocabulary. Children who are late talkers speak fluently once they begin. Knowing his reasoning was unsound, Wexford nevertheless saw her speech development as a sign that she had witnessed no further violence by her father against her mother.

'It doesn't work that way, Dad,' said Sylvia. 'She was bound to start talking some time. What will happen is there'll be other traumas, she'll be hyperactive or absolutely not, or spectacularly badly behaved or too quiet, but there'll be something.'

'If he's still doing it.'

'Dream on. He's still doing it. Why would he stop?'

'What amazes me', said Dora Wexford, 'is that these are middle-class people – well, upper-middle-class if you go in for all these gradations. They're very well off, he must be earning a couple of hundred thousand a year.'

'Three hundred and seventy-five thousand, to be precise,' said Wexford.

'Well, there you are then. If they got divorced she'd still get a huge allowance. She could keep that house and he could buy himself something just as nice to live in. I don't understand it.'

'No, you don't, Mother, so you might as well not air your opinions. Domestic violence occurs in all classes, it's absolutely not just a working-class thing, which is what you're saying. You don't know what you're talking about.'

'That's me crushed,' said Dora.

Wexford laughed. 'I really ought to say, don't talk to your mother like that, only as someone or other said, Lord Melbourne, I think, "Those whose behaviour requires admonishing are seldom wise enough to profit by admonition."'

A view he had no reason to change when he went to Woodland Lodge to see her a week later. Unusually for her, her face was heavily made up, some kind of pancake foundation coating the fine pale skin but not entirely concealing the black bruise that covered her forehead, her left cheek and her left temple. Her left eye was ringed in purple and the upper lid thickly swollen. Wexford found himself in the rare situation of feeling deep embarrassment. She answered the door to him, giving a little gasp when she saw who it was.

Sanchia was with her, clinging with both hands to her skirt. Once he had observed that the sons weren't in the least like their mother but this little girl resembled Fay, even to the wide-eyed, fearful look. He glanced once more at her damaged face and hardly knew what to say, but he had to say something and that pertinent to what he was seeing. She walked ahead of him into the living-room, her hand up to the bruises, an inadequate mask for that awful evidence.

'I know you haven't walked into a door or fallen against the mantelpiece,' he said. She shook her head. It might have meant a denial or simply a dismissing of the subject. The little girl was holding a long strip of cloth, a piece of cotton material, one end of which she stuffed into her mouth, while staring at him with her mother's flying-fox eyes.

'I can't talk about it in front of her,' Fay Devenish said. 'And she's here with us and I can't send her away.'

'You can at least tell me if she witnessed it.'

Another nod. All the time that hand remained pressed against the damaged flesh, the half-closed eye.

'Mrs Devenish, I've said it before, DS Malahyde has said it, everyone would say it, you must no longer tolerate this treatment. You surely have tolerated it once too often. Next time you must come to us. You must.'

Her heavy sigh seemed to raise and sink her whole body in a wave of suffering. 'I wish I spoke another language so that we could talk in that. I wish I spoke French – well, proper French. Do you speak French?'

He shook his head.

She made an effort, an effort that was both ridiculous and moving. '*Il me cherchera et il me tuera.*'

He understood that. Or he understood enough. Her husband would hunt for her and when he had found her, kill her.

Never had he felt so impotent and helpless. He imagined arresting Devenish, talking to him with his solicitor present and the man denying everything, Fay refusing to give evidence, coming up instead with one of her ready stories, the walking-into-a-wall one, the accident-prone one. At the same time he wished he understood the man's *raison d'être*, that he could begin to understand a philosophy of life that decreed a large, heavy man beat with his fists and his feet a small, vulnerable woman, for an unreal and manufactured cause. Because she couldn't always maintain the standard of perfection he desired in her household, because she lost control over the behaviour of her children. It made no sense. It denied all human decency, kindness and civilisation. Of course Devenish was a sadist and not one content with a masochist partner or one who merely pretended pain.

But how would he, Wexford, feel if the man killed her? Wouldn't he then look back with bitter regret that he had failed to do more?

But do what?

Make sure Karen kept up her visits to Woodland Lodge. Alert Hurt-Watch and its newly trained operatives to this classic situation in their midst. Make certain the Social Services were aware and attentive. Visit there himself whenever possible and whenever safe. Never forget her.

Never let her disappear from his thoughts.

He and Dora went away on a fortnight's holiday to Portugal in July. When he found that the travel agent Dora used had booked them on a Seaward Air flight to Lisbon he felt a momentary dismay. But why on earth shouldn't they fly with Seaward Air? Even if it meant putting money in Devenish's pocket – which it did not – Fay and her children would benefit as much as the Chief Executive of the airline himself. Burden often said he allowed himself to become obsessive. Now he was over-emotional as well.

At Gatwick, waiting for their flight to be called, he was nervous of seeing Devenish. It was very unlikely, he knew. A man in Devenish's position was hardly to be found wandering among the economy-class passengers or chatting to them about how they liked the service. The trouble was that if Devenish did appear and did see them he would almost certainly invite them into some private room or sanctum of his own and produce drinks. He might even offer to upgrade their seats. Wexford would of course refuse but the refusing would in itself be unpleasant. However, there was no sign of Devenish and they boarded the plane uneventfully.

Estoril and Sintra were enjoyable, the sun shone but not too blisteringly, the food was good, the hotel comfortable and they returned in the last weekend of July, rejuvenated and tanned. Wexford immediately phoned Burden to find out what had happened, what new developments had there been and how, in general, were things.

'We've got no one for Hennessy's murder, if that's what you mean,' said Burden.

'That's only partly what I mean. Anyway, if you had it'd have been in the English papers, which I read every day like a good citizen.'

'Vicky Cadbury will never come to trial. She's dying. They say any more treatment would be useless and now it's only a matter of administering morphine to kill the pain. Jerry Dover's gone barking mad and been sectioned.'

'I don't suppose my raincoat has turned up?'

'Not that I know of. Charlene Hebden denies knowing anything about it and says she's never seen Donaldson in her life.'

Wexford faced up to something much more important. He drew breath. 'And Fay Devenish?'

'Nothing new,' said Burden. 'Karen's called on her while you were away. I gather she's found out exactly how Devenish took revenge on Fay for attempting to get his child adopted. Karen will tell you herself. It's not pleasant. Otherwise it's snafu.'

'You're picking up bad language from the Muriel Campdenites,' said Wexford, making an attempt to lighten the atmosphere and failing.

He went back to work. The newly refurbished police station had a white and glaring look in the strong morning sunshine. The whole façade had been repainted and the windows renewed in new frames. He thought of Ted Hennessy who would never see it but might have admired it. Wexford remembered, from a conversation they had once had while on a case, the man's fondness for modern innovative architecture.

Karen Malahyde had started her holiday, so whatever horrors she had to tell him would have to wait. Instead, he was obliged to face a mountain of papers relating to the arrests, offences committed and damage caused by fourteen eco-warriors in the arable country between Flagford and Sayle. Burden came in and said he had just heard that Vicky Cadbury had lapsed into a coma from which she was not expected to emerge. He sat on the edge of Wexford's desk and Wexford remarked on his suit, obviously new, very lightweight and in a fetching shade of dark caramel. His tie was caramel and black stripes. Wexford said it would be fifty pee to speak to him now and he was sorry he still hadn't done anything about getting a mirror put up in here.

The paperwork took till the next morning, till halfway through it. Vine was questioning Flay yet again, WPC Brodrick sent off to Muriel Campden where all the council's recycling bins had taken to disappearing during the night and their contents of paper and card, bottles and cans scattered on the triangular lawn, and Wexford was starting to think about lunch, when his phone rang for only the second time that morning.

'There's been a murder, sir,' said Vine's voice. 'It's just come through. Up in Ploughman's Lane. Woodland Lodge.'

Afterwards Wexford could have sworn that his heart had stopped. His heart stopped, his breath was suspended and his voice lost. Time ceased.

Vine said, 'Are you still there, sir? Can you hear me?'

Voices come back and time goes on. Healthy hearts miss no beats. It only seems as if they do. Wexford found a voice from somewhere in the depths of him, said, 'I was afraid of this. Oh God, I was afraid of it. Where's her body? At the house?'

'In the study,' said Vine, 'and it's not Mrs Devenish who's dead, it's her husband, it's Stephen Devenish.'

# Chapter 20

The great trees were darker in colour and their foliage heavier. They were like middle-aged people, handsome enough, vigorous and voluptuous, until set beside the flawless freshness of the young. The trees had no such comparison to bear, for they were all growing old, all beginning to get tired, their leaves dry and browning at the edges. Again like ageing humankind, they were fine when seen from a distance, less delectable in close-up.

Wexford looked at the trees as he got out of his car and thought how the first time he came up here to interview the Devenishes they had been in green bud. Stephen Devenish would never see them turn brown and fall. He would see nothing ever again. Wexford happened to believe it was wrong to feel satisfaction at anyone's death, but except for the circumstances, he would have felt positive pleasure and gratitude at Devenish's. Except for the circumstances . . .

He would have given a lot to find out that she was somewhere else when her husband met his death, far far away out of reach and travelling distance. But Fay never went away. She was always here and she was here now. In the kitchen, according to Lynn Fancourt who opened the front door to him and Burden. She was in her domain, the kitchen, sitting at the table, drinking tea.

'Where is he?' Wexford asked, saying 'he' because it seemed too soon after the death to say 'it'.

'In the study, sir. The Scene-of-Crimes team is there and the pathologist.'

Photographs were in the process of being taken. Perry the Scene-of-Crimes Officer was busy taking measurements and the pathologist Sir Hilary Tremlett (elevated to the House of Lords in the resignation honours as Lord Tremlett of Savesbury) was squatting on the dark-brown rug, studying the dead man's wounds. He turned his head when Wexford came in but he didn't get to his feet.

'He's been stabbed in the chest. There are three wounds, one of which was made when the knife passed clean through the heart. Another may have punctured a lung. You can take him away when you like and I'll have a better look at him in the morgue. I don't want to get blood on my shoes. They're new.'

The body lay half on the rug, half on the hardwood floor. It appeared as if Devenish, when attacked, had sunk to his knees, then tumbled over backwards. His handsome features were so white in death that they looked like the face on a marble bust. He was dressed as became a professional man leaving for the day's work, in a dark-grey suit of perfect cut, a pearl-grey shirt and a pink silk tie with a grey horizontal stripe. Or, rather, this was the appearance he must have presented when first dressed that morning. Now suit jacket and shirt were dark with blood and the pink tie spattered with it in a pattern like a bunch of roses.

'I can't be sure yet,' said Lord Tremlett, 'but I'd say whoever did this was a lot shorter than he. Wouldn't be difficult, though, he was a big chap.' Staring up at Wexford, he said as if height were a disadvantage, 'Like you.'

'When did he die?' Wexford asked.

'I knew it! I was waiting for that. You want me to say, "At precisely twelve minutes past eight, give or take a second or two." That's what you want, isn't it? Well, I can't. No one could. I can *guess*.'

'Go on then, guess,' said Wexford, bored with the man's posturing. 'Break the rule of a lifetime.'

Tremlett didn't like that. 'I didn't get into their Lordships' House on guesswork but on my reputation for accuracy and thoroughness.'

Some say with a hundred thousand pounds, said Wexford silently. 'All right, when was it? Approximately.'

'Approximately between seven thirty and eight thirty this morning. I hope you won't twist my arm, I'd take a very dim view of anything like that, but *if* you did, I might say between seven thirty and eight fifteen.'

Wexford left the room, went into the hall and asked Barry Vine who had found the body.

'She did, sir. She phoned us.'

'When?'

'Just after nine. She thought he'd gone to work and she went in there to clean the place.'

'Where were the children?'

'The boys had gone to school. It's their last day of term. I suppose the little girl was with her.' Vine hesitated. 'She says someone called on Devenish at eight this morning. Devenish let him in himself and took him into the study. She didn't see him but she heard a man's voice.'

'Mrs Devenish did?'

'That's right.'

'She told you that?'

'It was almost the first thing she said.'

'I see. No sign of the weapon, I suppose?'

'There was no knife in the study, sir. Plainly, a knife was used. There are knives in a block in the kitchen and no one's touched them. That is, no one's touched them since I got here. Lynn's in the kitchen with Mrs Devenish.'

Wexford remembered the knife block. It and the cuckoo clock were to him symbols of that kitchen, and in a curious way symbols of Stephen Devenish too.

'Right. I'll go and see her now.'

He found her where Vine said he would, said good-morning to her and that this was a dreadful business, and motioned to Lynn to come out into the hall. There, with the living-room door shut, he asked her if the clothes Fay was wearing, a long button-through dress of white-spotted blue cotton and blue straw-soled espadrilles, were what she had on when she found her husband's body.

'I asked her, sir. She said they were.'

'We'll start a search of the house immediately.'

He walked back to the kitchen. It was as immaculate and neat as before. Fay Devenish looked stunned – literally so, as if someone had given her a blow to the head and felled her. Perhaps Devenish had. She sat on one of the Windsor wheel-back chairs, pulled somewhat away from the table, bending forwards, her head bowed, her knees and feet pressed close together. Her lank, pale-brown hair hung across her cheeks. She looked up when he came in and he saw that her face was as white as if the blood had drained out of her rather than her husband.

In similar circumstances, when a woman has lost a husband by murder, Wexford would have begun with condolences as a preamble to the questions he had to ask. Here, sympathy seemed inappropriate. 'You found your husband's body.'

She lifted her head again and looked at him, straight in the eye. 'Yes.' It was plainly all she wanted to say. She had nothing else to say but she perhaps recognised that he would want more, much more, and she burst out in a hoarse, half-strangled voice, 'I can't believe it, you know. I find it quite unbelievable, it *can't* be true. I was the one who'd die, I'd be killed, that's what I thought ...'

Wexford's own sentiments too, his own fears.

'But Stephen's dead. He's been killed. I can't believe it. I couldn't when I – when I saw him. He was so big and strong and – and full of life. I still can't believe it.'

'It's true.'

'There was so much blood. How could anyone have so much blood in him?'

His own blood ran cold. It was Lady Macbeth's phrase, the grotesque and inappropriate comment that stems from the shock of looking on horrors.

'What time did you find your husband's body, Mrs Devenish?'

'It was nine this morning. Just before nine. I went in there – to – to do the room. I only thank God, I thank God, Sanchia wasn't with me. I'd left her in the playroom. She had a video on. *The Lion King* it was. She was watching a video, thank God, thank God!'

'Tell me about this man you say called on your husband at eight this morning.'

She didn't like that 'you say' and she frowned. 'You mean you don't believe me?'

'I don't mean that.' But perhaps he did. 'Tell me about him.'

'I heard his voice, I didn't see him. I thought – I thought it was one of our neighbours. I suppose my husband let him in. My husband was – well, he was going to the Brighton office and sometimes this man gets a lift with him. That's who I thought it was.'

'What is his name, this neighbour?'

She didn't know or said she didn't know. 'He lives at Laburnum House.'

Sylvia's old home. He tried to remember the name of the people who had bought it from Sylvia and Neil. Paulton? Poulson?

'I see you've cut your hand,' he said.

'*I* haven't cut it.' She looked at her hand with a kind of wonder as if she had never seen it before. Across the palm, diagonally, where the lifeline ran, was a long, deep cut. 'It bled a lot at the time,' she said.

'How did that happen?'

'Stephen did it.' She began to laugh hysterically, madwoman laughter, almost operatic, running up and down scales. Backwards and forwards she flung herself on the chair, against the table, laughing and shrieking, beating on the table top with her hands. 'He did it, he did it,' she shrieked, 'but he'll never do it again, never, never, never!'

Lynn came in, alerted by the noise. 'Get her a glass of water, will you?' Wexford said to her.

By the time it came Fay Devenish was sobbing. Lynn held the water to her lips and to the surprise of both of them, she drank greedily. She drew a long breath and expelled it on a deep sigh. Then she did something that was all the more shocking because it was performed under absolute control and quite calmly. She got up and, showing surprising strength, put up her hands, seized hold of the cuckoo clock and struggled to pull it off the wall. She tugged at it for a moment or two before succeeding, then flung the clock on the floor with all the force she could muster. It smashed in pieces. The pert little cuckoo, defeated at last, its flapping beak silenced, rolled out from the wreckage and lay on its back under the table.

Violent activity had set her hand bleeding again. She seemed not to notice the blood that poured from her palm and dripped on to the floor.

Wexford said, 'That needs treatment. It should probably be stitched.'

She shrugged. 'He bought that clock when we were on holiday in Lucerne. I always hated it. I used to feel it mocked my – my sufferings.'

Lynn got down on her knees and started picking up the pieces.

Fay said, 'You must be the only person apart from me who's ever done anything like that in this house.'

'You shouldn't be alone,' Wexford said. 'Is there anyone we can call on to be with you?'

'Jane,' she said. 'I can see Jane now.'

The body had been taken away. Peach, Cox and Archbold had searched the house in a quest for blood-stained clothing and found nothing of interest. Wexford went into the utility room where a pile of clean washing, folded but not ironed, lay on a counter. Among the items, as well as half a dozen snow-white shirts belonging to the dead man, he could see what looked like a cotton skirt, several T-shirts and another button-through cotton dress. The portholes on washing machine and drier both stood open. The utility room communicated with the kitchen where Fay Devenish still sat and Lynn Fancourt with her. He looked around him, saw the knife block and noticed that each of its slots but one was occupied by a knife. Seven knives. On the day Stephen Devenish had cried in this room, his arms flung across the table, had there been seven knives or eight?

'Bag that knife block,' he said to Cox, 'and we'll send it to forensics.' Then he inquired of Fay Devenish if there was a knife missing from the block.

'I don't think so,' she said. 'Let me see. No, they're all there.' She looked fearfully up into his face. 'You think that one of these knives . . . ?'

'I'm not thinking anything much yet, Mrs Devenish. I wondered because while there are eight slots in the block there are only seven knives.'

'There never have been any more.' She spoke flatly, her hysteria over. 'There's a reason for that. It's made to take eight knives but if you put eight in they're crowded together and when you try to pull one out it brings the next one to it with it. Do you see what I mean?'

'I think so.'

He waited for her to say that one of her kitchen knives couldn't have been used to kill her husband. She had been in the kitchen all the time and the man who killed Stephen Devenish had never entered it. He expected her to say it but instead she said, 'The knife my husband cut me with, I don't know where that came from. It wasn't one of these.'

He said no more. They would soon know, Forensics would tell them.

In the hallway he encountered Burden. 'Where's the little girl, Mike?'

'I had her taken to a neighbour. The Wingrave woman. It's not ideal but better there than here. And I've phoned the boys' school; it's the Francis Roscommon School in Sewingbury. I said I'd go over there and talk to the head teacher, but he sounds a sensible man. He said he'd tell them when he found a suitable moment. And he'll bring them home.'

'I don't want them brought home, Mike.'

Burden looked at him.

'Or, rather, I want them brought here but not left alone with their mother. I don't want her to have a chance to talk to them or they to her. Some other arrangement will have to be made.'

'You're thinking of the mysterious stranger she says called here this morning? She thought that up on the spur of the moment, didn't she?'

Wexford shrugged. He went into the study and stood at the window. From here, because the room was in a block or wing of the house that jutted forward, you could look to your left and see the front door. Had Devenish been in here to watch this man arrive? Was there a man? Or .was he a desperate woman's invention? He looked ahead of him again and saw Jane Andrews's car approaching along the long green tunnel of the driveway. Her arrival obscurely cheered him. It was better that she was here.

This, Stephen Devenish's death chamber, was also the room where so much of the regular meting out of violence to Fay Devenish mainly took place. It had been searched but he set about searching it himself. In a desk drawer he found a whip. It was the kind of whip he supposed a jockey might use, though not being familiar with this means of coercing horses he couldn't be sure. One thing was certain, Devenish hadn't used it on a horse. Another drawer held nothing but a pair of nutcrackers and an instrument that might have been pincers but whose purpose he couldn't define. It was a relief to find that the top drawer contained only paper, much of it letters in envelopes.

All this would have to be gone through. Later, though, not now. He was closing the drawer when the writing, or rather the printing, on the top envelope caught his eye. It had been torn open, the contents no doubt read and then replaced inside. Addressed to *Stephen Devenish Esq., Woodland Lodge, Ploughman's Lane, Kingsmarkham KM2 4ZC*, the lettering had been produced by a computer and printer. Hardly believing himself so competent in this area, he recognised Word for Windows, the program they used at the police station – and in millions of other locations, of course. The postmark was Brighton, the date 24 July. He took out the letter. Same computer and printer-created text.

> Dear Mr Devenish [it read]
>   I often wonder if you know what a monster you are. A psychopath, not a human being at all. Evil like yours is, in fact, quite rare. Thank God. But God won't have His revenge on you till after you have died a natural death in your comfortable luxurious bed, so He has appointed me to carry out retribution. I shall kill you. In the next few days, perhaps, or weeks or even months. But it will happen. And it will be painful, as painful as the cruelty you have inflicted on your poor wife. I will make her a widow and your children orphans and laugh for joy, as they will.

There was no signature. It often amused him to note how, without a thought, we address people we dislike, despise or distrust with the endearment 'dear'. It was even done by writers of anonymous letters. In his time he had seen many of them but never one like this. It seemed, for one thing, the work of an educated person. There was something evangelical about that last sentence, almost like a line from a psalm, and a suggestion in the mention of God and the capital letters for the Deity pronoun that the writer might be religious.

He changed his mind about not going through the drawer now. Two more letters in much the same vein came to light. Both began *Dear Mr Devenish* and both mentioned Devenish's 'cruelty' to his wife, while the second referred to his habit of cutting her with a knife. One was dated early July and the other mid-June. So perhaps Devenish hadn't lied when he said in April that he had had such letters but had destroyed them. Perhaps there had been many and they had come regularly.

When Wexford returned to Woodland Lodge in the afternoon, not two but three women were in the living-room. Jane Andrews, neat and smart in a long-skirted cream linen suit, was sitting with her friend on one of the sofas, holding her uninjured hand, while in an armchair was a woman Fay surprisingly introduced as her mother, Mrs Dodds. Thin, worn Fay in the blue cotton frock that hung on her, bore no resemblance to this tall, well-built lady in bright-green dress and matching high-heeled shoes, her 'big hair' a carefully teased golden helmet, her face skilfully painted. Cakes were on a table, with biscuits in a silver dish, and someone had made a pot of coffee. They offered Wexford a cup but he shook his head.

'Mrs Devenish, I'd like to speak to you alone, so perhaps you can spare your mother and your friend for ten minutes.'

Shepherding them outside, he called to Lynn to sit with Fay Devenish. He was thinking quickly, seeing a way to seize his chance. The study was obviously out of bounds. However much Jane Andrews had loathed Stephen Devenish she would probably balk at going into the room so soon after he met a violent death there. But it was a very big house of many rooms. Opening a door, he looked into a playroom where the television set was still on, though *The Lion King* was long over, and where toys lay scattered everywhere as Sanchia had abandoned them. With his next attempt he was luckier. Here was the dining-room. A table big enough to seat twenty – had the poor woman been obliged to hold dinner parties for Devenish's business associates? – still left room for a sideboard, drinks cabinet and occasional chairs.

He asked the two women to sit down, then said, 'Mrs Dodds, your grandsons will soon be brought home from school. I don't think it a very good idea for them to be here, do you? Your daughter needs to rest. I'm wondering if you'd have them for a few days, just to ...'

She cut him short. Her eager smile and rapturous voice changed the image he had of her as far from grandmotherly. 'I'd *love* to have them. What a splendid idea. My husband and I are always saying we never see enough of them. I wouldn't mind keeping them for a month. And they love being with us.'

'That's fine then. If you could –' His glance took in Jane Andrews as well as Mrs Dodds '– just make it appear the invitation came from you in the first place? It would – well, come better that way.'

'Of course I will.'

'You and Miss Andrews could perhaps pack some clothes for them while I'm talking to Mrs Devenish. I'm sure you know what they'll need.'

She was sitting quietly, contemplating her left hand, now bandaged. Perhaps she was thinking this was the last wound she would ever receive at Devenish's hands. Or of what she had done? Or what her rescuer, this stranger, had done?

'What time was it when you heard this man's voice, Mrs Devenish?'

'I told you. About eight. I was in the kitchen, clearing away the breakfast things. The boys were with me, waiting for their lift to school.'

'I should like to get the sequence of events right, if you please. I won't keep you longer than I can, I appreciate what a strain this must be on you.'

Fay cleared her throat. She glanced across the room and for a moment Wexford thought she was going to ask if it was necessary for Lynn to be present, but she didn't.

She sighed. 'Sanchia was awake by six thirty. She always is. I got up when I heard her, and got her dressed and downstairs. By that time my husband was up and having a shower. I went into the boys' rooms at seven and got them up. I had to go back and tell them again, but I always do have to. I was helping Sanchia with her breakfast when my husband came down. I gave him his breakfast. He always has – had – a cooked breakfast. Then the boys came down for their cornflakes and toast. I'd – I'd run out of oranges to make juice from, it's a bad time of the year for oranges, so I used some frozen juice but it wouldn't thaw out – you don't want to hear all this.'

'I want to hear everything,' said Wexford. 'Go on.'

'My husband finished his breakfast and went into the study. That was about a quarter to eight. He called to me to come in there – I – oh, I don't . . .'

Her face crumpled in distress. There were no tears, rather a twisting of her features into a grimace of dismay and pain. It was as if – and Wexford thought he read it plainly – she was asking herself, as she had always asked herself, why this man of hers had felt it needful to hurt her over and over and on and on. Why? Had she really been so bad that she deserved this?

Wexford said gently, 'Your husband called you into the study to punish you, didn't he, for failing to supply fresh orange juice?'

She sucked in her lips, bent her head, said an almost silent, 'Yes.'

'He had a knife but it wasn't a knife from the kitchen? It was a knife he happened to have with him in the study?'

No more than a nod this time.

'He told you to hold out your hand – your left hand because he had no wish to interfere with your ability to do housework – and cut you across the palm.'

'Yes.'

Very unsuitably and uncharacteristically, Wexford found himself exulting in his heart that the man was dead, had died by violence, had been *punished*. He said nothing.

Fay said in a voice that trembled, 'He was much, much worse to me after that – that business with Sanchia. Every day there was – there was – something, beatings or cutting me or kicking. Edward and Robert saw it, Sanchia saw it.'

'It's over now,' said Wexford, adding silently to himself, whatever the truth of this, whatever the outcome, there will be no more of that. 'Tell me what happened after your husband cut you.'

'I went back to the kitchen. No, I went into the downstairs cloakroom first and tied my hand up in the towel that was in there. The boys didn't see the cut but they saw my hand was tied up. They were just leaving for school. On the days I don't take them they walk about a hundred yards down the road and get a lift with a woman who's also got children at their school. I sent them off . . .'

'Excuse me – do you mean you went to the front door with them?'

She looked at him, puzzled at first. 'Did I . . . oh, I see what you mean. No, I just told them it was time to go and said goodbye to them, and they went out of the kitchen into the hall and out of the front door. I didn't actually see them leave the house but I know they did. And then, almost immediately – well, a couple of minutes later, the doorbell rang. It was this man. I heard his voice and my husband's voice, talking to him.'

He noticed that she never referred to Devenish as Stephen, but always as 'my husband', as a slave might say 'my master'. 'That would have been at eight o'clock. Did you hear him leave?'

'I don't know. I thought I heard the front door close but that could have been my husband going, only it wasn't.'

'Weren't you surprised, Mrs Devenish, that your husband said nothing to you before he left? That he didn't say goodbye to you?'

Her shaky laugh rang shockingly in that quiet place. 'Would you be surprised if someone didn't say goodbye to you when he'd just slashed you with a knife?'

'Perhaps not,' said Wexford. 'Perhaps not.'

Suddenly she sprang from her chair, looked round her wildly. 'Where's my little girl? Where's Sanchia?'

'With Mrs Wingrave.'

'I want her, I want her back! Oh God, d'you realise, I never need fear for her again!'

'Of course you can have her back.'

'I'll go and fetch her,' said Lynn.

Across the road and down another driveway, Moira Wingrave was alone in the cushiony, flock-wallpapered room she called the 'lounge', reclining on a sofa with her feet up, a long glass of something beside her that might have been virgin tomato juice or a Bloody Mary, and the television on. Sanchia was somewhere about, she said, probably upstairs with Tracy. 'Oh, yes, she's taken a great fancy to Tracy. Those simple people are always a hit with children.'

Lynn asked her if she had seen a man enter the driveway to Woodland Lodge at about eight that morning.

'What man? You don't mean poor Stephen Devenish?'

365

'Not Mr Devenish. Maybe a neighbour who lives at Laburnum House?'

'Oh, Gerry Paulton. No, why would I see him? He doesn't even know the Devenishes, does he?'

'I'd like to take Sanchia back to her mother now.'

'Please do. Be my guest. I'm not used to children and frankly I never know what to say to them.'

Tracy Miller knew. She was playing a game with Sanchia called 'round and round the room', of which Moira Wingrave would certainly have disapproved, since it consisted in the child's clambering round the master bedroom on the furniture without putting her feet to the ground, jumping from little gilt chair to Louis XVIth reproduction commode, ending up on the ivory-silk-festooned dressing-table and leaping off it into Tracy's arms. Articulate now, Sanchia said she didn't want to go home, she wanted to stay with Tracy, and began to cry. Eventually Lynn persuaded her with a bribe of Smarties which she found by a lucky chance in the bottom of her bag.

Back at home, her mother gave her a smothering hug, and covered her face and head with kisses, treatment which Sanchia struggled under. She had been back home for ten minutes when Edward and Robert arrived at the back door, driven by their head teacher in his car. They looked as children of their ages always do when caught up in tragic events, awkward, embarrassed, lost and helpless.

Edward muttered something in response to Jane Andrews's greeting. Robert said nothing. He shuffled his feet, then asked his mother if there was anything to eat. From force of habit Fay got up and fetched cans of Coke out of the fridge, bread and butter and Marmite from a larder, Mars bars from somewhere else. But when their grandmother came in both showed more enthusiasm than Wexford had ever seen from either of them. He felt content with his plan and said he must go.

Outside he met Vine, who had been paying a routine call at Sylvia's old home where Gerald Paulton, just home from work, told him that he always drove himself to Brighton. It was true that he had once had a lift from Stephen Devenish when his car was having its electrics overhauled but that had been more than a year ago.

'What a dreadful thing. I was devastated when my wife told me, just devastated. He was the nicest chap, one of the best.'

'So you didn't call at Woodland Lodge at about eight this morning, sir?'

In fiction people questioned by the police take interrogation in their stride or are merely annoyed by it. Reality is different. Gerald Paulton was shocked and frightened by Vine's question. What on earth did he mean? What was he insinuating?

'I'm not insinuating anything, sir. I'm making a routine inquiry.'

'You've got me on your list of suspects!'

'We don't have a list of suspects, Mr Paulton. This investigation has only just begun.'

'Well, I didn't go there this morning. I left for work at half past seven. Ask my wife, ask my kids, the au pair, anyone.'

At home, Wexford read and reread the copies that had been made of the anonymous letters he had found in Devenish's desk. The originals had gone to the lab for testing. He thought how much harder the universal use of computers had made the identification of anonymous letter writers, but probably policemen had said much the same thing when typewriters were invented. These letters were plainly the work of someone with more than a grudge

367

against Devenish. He must find out more about this man Devenish had allegedly turned out of his office and thrown downstairs. One thing particularly struck him: why had Devenish kept these letters, that is those which came in June and July, but not the earlier ones?

Could it be because only these specifically mentioned his abuse of his wife? Of course he didn't even know if this was so, it was just guesswork. The others might have mentioned it too.

And what need, anyway, to look further afield for Devenish's killer than his own home?

# Chapter 21

Conciliatory tactics appealed to Wexford not at all and he hoped to get through this interview with Brian St George without using any. On the other hand, he wanted information from the editor of the *Kingsmarkham Courier*, which could only be obtained from St George. If necessary, he would have to make a concession and restore to the *Courier* its old press rights with Kingsmarkham Police.

But as it happened, when he met St George in his High Street office, the editor was anxious to be helpful, even obsequious, and prepared to say and do anything in order that the *status quo* might be restored. 'The "fat cats" story, Mr Wexford? When we took that photo of Sanchia? I can't tell you precisely when it was, not off the cuff. But my PA will do so in the twinkling of an eye. Our computer system here is quite excellent.'

St George's PAs were constantly changing and none seemed more than sixteen years old. The last one had been a plump blonde who wore a micro-skirt that barely covered her buttocks. Her successor was black, six feet tall, with long, gold-beaded extensions to her dyed red hair.

'See if you can find the Devenish "fat cats" story, will you, Carly-Jo? Try two years back. And bring me a printout.'

Wexford said, 'Did you interview him?'

'Sure we did. It's all in the story. We'll be using

extracts, I expect, in this week's account of his murder.'

Rather taken aback, Wexford said, 'You will? Why is that?'

'He had quite a bit to say about enemies. He made enemies in his job, he said. For instance, the airline manager was sacked soon after he got this salary increase. It was for incompetence and he *was* incompetent, according to Devenish. He'd been hopeless from the start, lost the company untold business.'

Trevor Ferry. 'You won't be running a story about that, I trust,' said Wexford rather severely.

'Certainly not.' St George assumed an expression of extreme rectitude. 'I hope we're more responsible than that.'

'So do I.'

'We didn't use it in the "fat cats" story. I'm simply telling you what he told me. Very nice chap he was, very easy to get on with, open and honest and all that. In his position he met with a lot of envy, he said. You know, great job, megabucks, lovely wife, smashing kids, beautiful home ...'

'Yes, all right,' said Wexford. 'I do know.'

'I was only going to say, Reg, that people don't like it. They resent it. I mean, why should he have it and me not have it, that sort of thing. They don't think it's fair. Oh, here's our story.'

Carly-Jo came back with the printout, put it in front of Wexford in a sweet, heavy wave of perfume. Afraid from the tingling in his nostrils that he was going to sneeze, he pressed his forefinger against his upper lip, a sure preventative. The story, he saw at once, offered little help. It was the usual thing, beginning with a word picture of Devenish's lifestyle, then leading into a long quote from him, justifying a salary of nearly £400,000 per annum. Not a line about enemies, still less threats. Nothing about the sacked manager.

'Since you were aiming to bring the chap into hatred, ridicule and contempt, I suppose you were scared of libel.' Wexford laid down the printout.

'I don't think that's altogether fair, Reg. It's not as if we were a national daily. Most of us have to live among the people of this town. *We* don't want to make enemies either. Besides, there's something to be said for goodwill, keeping up a happy relationship with one's contributors.'

'Why did he mention enemies at all? Don't tell me, I can guess. You or your reporter asked him if he had them, if he got threats, if this so-called envy took positive form.'

'As I recall it,' said St George uncomfortably, 'he did mention threatening letters·he'd had. And of course I said there was no question but that he should take the matter to the police at once.'

'Naturally,' said Wexford drily. 'You would.'

'He laughed it off, said he'd thrown them away. They were garbage and the best place for garbage was the dustbin.'

'How original. I'm not surprised you couldn't make a story out of it. Apart from Trevor Ferry, I don't suppose he named any of these enemies, did he? He hadn't any idea who sent the letters, for instance?'

'There was some guy made a nuisance of himself that he had to put out of his office once, he said that, but he didn't name any names.'

To Burden the Devenish death was merely a nuisance that distracted him and took officers away from the hunt for Hennessy's killer. Finding the wielder of the petrol bomb and bringing him or her to court was enormously more important in his eyes than running to earth whoever had stabbed Stephen Devenish. In his customary fashion he had long since dismissed Devenish as a villain and a brute, unfit to exist. He wouldn't go so far as saying good luck to his killer, for justice mattered to him, but he resented having to surrender good men and women to the inquiry when there was still so much to be done to track down the petrol bomber.

'I suppose she did it, anyway, didn't she?' he said to Wexford over a snatched lunch at the Europlate. 'These wife-beaters who get their comeuppance, it's always the wretched abused woman who's done it. The worm has turned, that's all.'

'The fact is that only two per cent of all homicides involve abused women killing their partners.'

'Oh, come on, Reg. She's stuck it for years, he's bashed and kicked her to kingdom come, and one day it's the last straw. She breaks, she picks up the knife or whatever he cut her with and gives it to him. Tit for tat and then some.'

Wexford, who was eating Italian pasta with German asparagus, shook his head, then, seeming to think better of it, nodded. 'There's a lot more I want her to tell me. But I want to talk to the boys first. Then there's this business with the weapon.'

'You haven't found the weapon, have you?'

'The funny thing is that I don't know. I say I don't know because there were seven knives in that kitchen. Of course, one could say that there should have been eight.'

'I can't say I follow you.'

'No, well, is it true what Fay Devenish says and there never were eight knives? Or were there eight and one is missing? Or was one of the seven others used? Or is it true what Fay says that none of the kitchen knives was used? If it was one of the kitchen knives, three can be discounted because they're too small to inflict those sort of injuries and one is a saw. That leaves three.'

'We'll know more', said Burden, 'when the noble Lord, Lord Tremlett, gives you his post-mortem results. No doubt it'll be quite a simple matter to match the knife to the wounds.'

Wexford said, and to Burden his remark sounded irrelevant, 'She's got a dishwasher.'

'She's what? So have I. So have you. What's that got to do with it? The way I see it is, they have that absurd contretemps with the orange juice, he summons her to be punished, cuts her and somehow she gets hold of the knife and stabs him. Blood everywhere, lashings of it. She puts her clothes in the washing machine and has them in the drier before she phones us. Her only witness is a child of three who wasn't even there, thank God, when the killing took place. Clear as crystal, no problem.'

He pushed away his plate and drank some water. All this talk of stabbing and blood had started putting him off his food. It never seemed to have much effect on Wexford and yet, if he absolutely had to say, he'd call himself more callous than the Chief Inspector.

'When he called her into the study,' Wexford said slowly, 'the boys were still in the house.'

'So she says.'

'They very likely were if he summoned her, as you put it, at seven forty-five. But they can't have been in the house when Devenish was killed. You're not saying he submitted to having a knife stuck in him three times without a murmur? He probably shouted and screamed the place down.'

'So she didn't kill him straight after he cut her,' said Burden, taking the pudding menu from Henri. 'She went back into the study after the boys had left to walk down the road for their lift and did it then.

That need have been no later than five past eight, which left her ample time to get those clothes washed. She was probably wearing the pink dress we found among the clean wash. When you come to think of it, she was in an ideal situation to stab someone and get away with it, having the means of getting rid of blood-stains right there. As for the knife, she could have buried that anywhere in all those acres they've got. Are you going to have a pudding?' Wexford shook his head. 'Nor am I,' Burden said.

Catherine Daley, the mother of a son of eleven and a daughter of ten, told Karen Malahyde that three days a week she drove her children and the Devenish boys to school in Sewingbury and fetched them back two days a week. Fay Devenish drove all four children to school two days a week and fetched them on three. On the morning of Stephen Devenish's death it had been her turn to take all the children to school and, as was their habit, Edward and Robert Devenish had come to her house, Braemar, Ploughman's Lane, at about five past eight. It might have been nearer ten past, but they were never late, Fay saw to that, knowing that Catherine Daley would leave in her car at eight fifteen. The drive took twenty minutes and both mothers liked to have the children there in plenty of time for an eight forty-five start.

'How did the boys seem?' Karen asked her.

'What exactly do you mean?'

'Were they normally behaved? Excited? Frightened? Subdued?'

'I really don't know. Perhaps Edward was rather quiet. But then he is the quieter of the two. Robert can be rather boisterous.'

'Was he boisterous yesterday?'

'Not really. No, he wasn't. They were both quite normal.'

Wexford spoke on the phone to the sacked manager, Trevor Ferry. At eight on the previous morning, the day of Stephen Devenish's death, he had still been in bed, he said. Could anyone substantiate that? His wife could, Ferry said. Anyone else? There had been no one else in the house, Ferry said rather sullenly. What did Wexford think? That they had an au pair?

'Mr Ferry, this is a far more serious matter than that which we had to deal with when I last spoke to you. If you remember the names of any of these people you seemed then to think had reason to quarrel with Mr Devenish, will you get in touch with me, please?'

Wendy Brodrick had stayed at Woodland Lodge overnight and Lynn Fancourt was in the house now. If Fay thought this surveillance strange she said nothing about it. She was in the playroom with Sanchia, another Disney video running but the child ignoring it and playing instead with a convoy of camouflage-painted toy army vehicles that surely must once have belonged to her brothers.

Not the original but a photocopy of the threatening letter was what he showed Fay. No, she had never seen it before but she knew about these letters. Stephen had had plenty of them. He had never shown her any but he had described them to her.

'I thought he'd accuse me of sending them,' she said. 'But he never did. They were done on a computer and he knew I couldn't use a computer. He thought them well-written and I expect he thought I was too ignorant to write them. He was always saying I was ignorant.' She changed the subject. 'My sons went to stay with my mother. Did you know that?'

'She said she was going to invite them.'

Fay switched off the television by means of the remote. Although Sanchia wasn't watching the video, hadn't watched it since Wexford came into the room, she immediately set up a howl of protest: 'Put it on, put it on, put it on!'

If she had been wordless and silent before, she had made up for lost time. She came up to her mother and began hitting her with a toy army jeep.

'Oh, all right,' Fay said, 'but you're to *watch* it. I don't feel I could cope with the boys at the moment. She's bad enough but I don't want to be separated from her just the same.'

'You won't have to cope with them,' Wexford said. 'Where does your mother live?'

'My mother and my dad. He's not dead. Did you think he was? They live in Myringham.' She gave him an address. 'Are you going to ask them to keep the boys a bit longer?'

'Possibly. If you like. I want to talk to Edward and Robert, Mrs Devenish. Do you have any objection?'

She looked surprised at being asked. Then she looked defeated. As if she had been found out? Or was about to be found out? 'No, I don't think so,' she said in a weary voice. 'No, I don't mind. Would it make any difference if I did?'

He wasn't going to answer that, not when she had consented. 'I will, of course, speak to them in the presence of your mother or your father.'

As if she hadn't heard him or didn't care, she said almost dreamily, 'I never told them anything about what was going on till – well, last year, I suppose, then I told my mother what Stephen did to me, and do you know what she said? She said, "You must have done something to provoke him." And my father said, "There's not much in that. They used to say it was all right to beat your wife with a stick as long as it wasn't thicker than your thumb." And he laughed and said it was a lot of fuss about nothing. That's why I've been – well, a bit distant from them lately. The children love them.'

He nodded. Sometimes there is absolutely nothing to say. Lynn came out from the kitchen and met him in the hall. 'She's made no phone calls, sir, and the phone's been put on to the answering machine for incoming calls. Not that there've been any. I checked.'

'You've done well,' said Wexford, pleasing Lynn more than she would have thought possible.

He went into the study and sat there, trying to imagine the scene of the morning if what Fay Devenish said was true, if a man had come to the front door at eight o'clock and been admitted by Stephen Devenish, a man who brought a knife with him. In a briefcase? In a carrier bag? Or had he found a knife there, ready to hand? And did Devenish know him? Devenish had been in the study, scene of the recent latest wounding of his wife, and had seen a man he knew come to the front door. Presumably, he had no fear of this man or believed he had no reason to fear him.

They went into the study where, fifteen minutes before, perhaps only ten minutes before, Devenish had punished his wife for the heinous offence of failing to buy oranges by slashing her across the palm of her hand with a knife. What knife? The *same* knife? And where was it now? One thing was for sure, it wasn't the sheathed dagger hanging up on the wall. The blade of that was corroded with rust, he saw when he took it down.

What had happened in this room, the male room that Fay so hated, the leather-padded sword-hung room, between this man and Devenish? Threats? Demands? Refusals to comply or pay or what? Then out comes the knife and the man gives Devenish three stabs to the chest. Covered with Devenish's blood – he would be covered with blood – he had left the house, taking the bloody knife with him, and run off down the street, seen by no one.

Who could believe such a story? Still, he had heard of odder things. He must delay no longer but take himself to the Doddses' home and talk to Edward and Robert Devenish.

The call came through to him on the car phone as Donaldson was driving him northwards through the villages and along the Sewingbury-to-Myringham road. At first the line was fuzzy and the tone blurred, and he couldn't make out who was speaking to him. Then suddenly the voice of Trevor Ferry came on clear and almost too loud. 'I've remembered something. You know you asked if I could think of anyone who might have a grudge against Devenish? Well, there is someone.'

'Really?'

'Oh, and before I forget, my wife has gone along to Kingsmarkham Police Station to tell them I was definitely at home and still in bed at eight this morning. Providing an alibi is what you call it, right?'

'That's what we call it, Mr Ferry,' Wexford said, wondering why these people were quite so quick off the mark and if they had something to hide. 'Who is this someone with a grudge?'

Wexford's heart dipped a little when he said, 'I don't remember the name', leapt when he went on, 'But I can tell you the story. This guy said Devenish caused his brother's death.'

'I'll call on you, if I may, early tomorrow morning.'

'How early?' said Ferry.

'Don't worry, you'll be up. It won't be before nine thirty.'

Trevor Ferry, saying goodbye and ringing off, sounded disappointed that Wexford wasn't coming at once, rushing to him at top speed, to hear earth-shaking revelations. But a hundred sensational tales of Devenish's misdemeanours or provocations of injured fellow workers and dissatisfied customers couldn't alter the fact that Fay's version of events remained incredible. Only corroboration of her story could make it believable and what corroboration could there be?

The three-storey townhouse was almost in the centre of Myringham. Fay Devenish could hardly have grown up here, it was too recently built. Everything about it looked new, from its fresh white façade, bright paint and gleaming glass to the young struggling plants in its window-box of a front garden. Even the car on the garage drive was new, an S-registered two-door saloon in the latest shade of rose-pink.

There seemed nothing in particular here to interest boys of twelve and ten. Perhaps their grandparents took them out a lot. But not long after Wexford was inside, admitted by Fay Devenish's father, a skinny little old man whom she strongly resembled, he found himself revising his opinion. For the whole house seemed a boys' paradise and, since this could hardly have been spontaneously contrived, merely on the chance of his asking Mrs Dodds to invite her grandsons to stay, he supposed it must be like this all the time. One room they passed before ascending the stairs contained, indeed was entirely given over to, a train set. Most adults with a passion for trains have their railway hidden away on the top floor but Mr Dodds had his downstairs. He had armies on mantelpieces, toy menageries on window-sills, a video library of monsters, horrors and outer space on

379

the landing and, as far as Wexford could see through open doors, a television set in every room.

'And a video,' said Mr Dodds. 'Not much point without a video, is there? We've not long moved here, used to have a bigger place, but I've managed to squeeze all my stuff in. We've four bedrooms and the fourth's entirely for my model aircraft. I used to have dogs and cats too. Can't be done here but we've fifteen guinea-pigs in the back garden and the gerbils live in *our* bedroom.'

The two Devenish boys were in the room Mr Dodds called the lounge, each with a computer – 'I've got six,' their grandfather put in – Edward playing patience on his, Robert concentrating on a soccer game in which, from the colours the players wore, France seemed to be competing against Brazil. Mrs Dodds, dressed in scarlet today with a very short skirt, sat placidly by, reading *Vogue*. Wexford greeted her and said hallo to the boys, who took absolutely no notice of him.

How had Fay reacted to this set-up? The dogs and cats, guinea-pigs and gerbils were all right, but how about the toy soldiers and the trains? Perhaps it had been different when she was young and the Dodds family lived elsewhere. Dodds might have turned to these juvenile artefacts only as he entered his second childhood. Whatever it was, Edward and Robert obviously relished it all and he had some difficulty not only in persuading the boys but in prevailing upon Mr and Mrs Dodds to 'exit from' or 'shut down' the computers or whatever the jargon was. Mrs Dodds even said it was a shame when they were enjoying themselves so much. Wexford couldn't help thinking of Fay who had told him her parents had dismissed her complaints of Devenish's behaviour as fussing about nothing.

One thing to be thankful for about this room was

that, apart from the computers and the huge television with video recorder, there was no sign of Mr Dodds's preoccupations. Neither boy could be distracted by Lego, Godzilla or a miniature motorway. Both grandparents elected to stay while Wexford talked to them and he was thankful for it. Afterwards, no one should say that he had acted improperly. The tall older boy sat in an armchair beside his grandmother, the younger on a sofa next to his grandfather. There was something uncanny about their resemblance to the dead man. Edward already had the face of a young Lord Byron, handsome, shapely, dark-eyed, with strong, full mouth and firm jawline. And then, as Robert turned to look at his grandfather for reassurance, he caught in the angle of his head and the tilt of his nose a glimpse of Fay, and somehow this tiny flash of likeness, soon probably to fade, was the most saddening of all things ...

'I want you to tell me what happened yesterday morning,' he began, 'when you first got up and when you left for school to have your lift from Mrs Daley.' He waited until Edward nodded and Robert followed with a vigorous nodding. 'Now, you got up and came downstairs for your breakfast. That would have been about half past seven. What did you have for breakfast?'

'We always have the same,' Edward said. 'Orange juice and cornflakes – well, he has Shreddies – and toast.' He looked from one to the other of them, as if for approval. 'Am I doing it right?' was unspoken but it was there. 'My dad has – I mean, he used to have – a cooked breakfast. Eggs and bacon, and maybe a sausage and fried bread, and sometimes mushrooms.' A shadow seemed to pass across him. Wexford saw, perhaps for the first time, what is really meant by the phrase 'his face fell'. 'Mum hadn't got any oranges for the juice and Dad got furious, though she'd got frozen. He ate his breakfast and went into the study, he said he was going into the study and he did go in there.' Edward looked at his grandfather and, getting an encouraging smile, went on in a way that elderly child had not perhaps expected, 'Dad called Mum into the study and I – I shut the kitchen door, I . . .'

Wexford said, 'Go on, please, Edward. I understand what you're saying. It's all right for you to go on.'

The child was desperate and Wexford felt for him to an extent he had never empathised with his own grandchildren; he had never needed to do so.

But it was Robert who butted in and saved his brother. He said almost harshly, 'He was going to start bashing her around. I mean, Dad was. Beating or kicking her, he's always doing it.'

His grandmother gave a little scream. 'Robert, you naughty boy, how dare you tell such wicked untruths!'

Robert shrugged. Suddenly he looked decades older than his age, a little old man like his grandfather. 'I'm glad he's dead,' he said flatly.

More shrieks followed this statement. Mr Dodds shook his head sorrowfully. 'They've got powerful imaginations at that age,' he said.

Wexford intervened. 'Perhaps we'll let Edward continue now. Just one thing, Edward. Did your father take a knife with him from the block in the kitchen?'

'I don't think so. No, he didn't.'

'While your mother and father were together in the study, did you hear either of them cry out?'

Had he imagined that faint flash of alarm in Robert's eyes? Edward said, 'No. Nothing.'

Then Robert said, 'I didn't hear anything.'

'Then please go on, Edward.'

'Mum came back,' the boy said, more confident now, 'with her hand wrapped up in a towel. It was the towel from our downstairs toilet and it was quite big but the blood was coming through. He'd cut her. It's no good making that face, Gran. I'm not telling lies and you know it. You don't like hearing the truth, that's all. D'you think we liked it?'

He didn't wait for Mrs Dodds's reply. 'She got a cloth and tied it up, then she told me and Robert it was time to go down to Mrs Daley's. Mrs Daley does the school run when Mum doesn't,' he explained for the benefit of those who might not know it. 'We went out into the hall just as someone rang the doorbell. I opened the door and it was someone to see Dad, a man. I told him to go into the study and he did, and Robert and I went off to Mrs Daley's house.'

'Right,' said Robert.

# Chapter 22

The two boys were both staring at him, then Robert
looked away. If you witness your father repeatedly
beat your mother will you, in your turn, beat your
wife when the time comes? They say such cruelties
form a chain from generation to generation. Did
Stephen Devenish's father beat his mother? Wexford
dismissed these ugly thoughts – there was no point
in dwelling on them – and asked Edward if he could
describe the man he had admitted to the house.

The boy frowned. He looked as if he were
concentrating. 'He was just a man,' he said. 'Not as
tall as Dad. He was wearing jeans and a jacket, and a
shirt. And he was wearing a tie.'

'He had a briefcase,' said Robert. 'The dagger was
in the briefcase.'

His brother rounded on him. 'How do *you* know?
You can't see through leather. You don't know what
he had in the briefcase.'

'Can you make a guess at how old he was?'
Wexford knew this was unlikely, almost hopeless. To
a child of twelve everyone over twenty-five is old.

But Edward said promptly, 'About the same age as
Dad.'

'I don't suppose you saw what colour his eyes
were? Or his hair?'

Robert started laughing, throwing himself about in
his chair and kicking his legs. 'His hair was blue and
his eyes were red!'

'You're stupid,' said Edward. 'No one would think you were ten years old.' He said to Wexford, suddenly very grown-up, 'I don't remember about his hair and his eyes I didn't notice. I mean, I didn't know I was going to have to remember. He was just a man who came to see Dad.'

Apparently, it had never occurred to either Mr or Mrs Dodds that their daughter might have been suspected of her husband's murder, so they showed no signs of relief. Rather, they were bemused. Who would have thought the day before yesterday, they seemed to be saying to themselves, that the whole of life could be overturned like this so quickly and with no warning?

Mrs Dodds appeared to be looking about her for some means of distraction, some way of lightening the atmosphere or removing the seriousness, and she came up with an idea commonplace enough, the universal panacea for the British, but she brought out her offer with an air of triumph. 'Shall we all have a cup of tea?'

'I don't like tea,' said Robert.

And Wexford said, 'Not just now, Mrs Dodds, if you please. It's important I ask Edward a few more questions.' He turned to the boy. 'Your mother was out in the kitchen when the man went into the study to see your father?'

'I suppose so. We left her there. She might have gone into the garden but I don't reckon she did. She was trying to stop her hand bleeding.'

'Where was Sanchia?'

'In the kitchen with Mum. Mum has to help her eat things or she gets them all over the floor.'

'Did this man come in a car?'

Robert starting laughing again. 'He came in a high-speed train. It came up our driveway at a hundred and fifty miles an hour.'

The child's laughter was manic but without mirth or joy, or even amusement. It was the cackle of a parrot or a mynah bird. He opened his mouth, but unsmilingly, and the sound rattled out.

Wexford remembered uneasily how Jane Andrews had said all the children must be damaged by what they had witnessed and heard at home, not the little girl alone. 'Edward?' he queried.

'He must have walked,' the boy said. 'I didn't see a car. Or he could have left it in the road, I didn't see. People don't always bring a car up our drive, they don't know if they'll be able to park it.'

'What did he say to you?'

The boy thought. 'Something like "I've come to see Mr Devenish" or "I've come to see your father", one of those, I can't remember.'

'And you heard nothing from the study after he had gone in there?'

'I told you. I told him to go into the study and then we went, my brother and me. I shut the front door behind us and we went down the road to Mrs Daley's.'

'Daley, waley, scaley,' sang Robert and, suddenly babyish, stuck one finger in his mouth and whined, 'Can we go now? I want to go and play with the aeroplanes, Grandad.'

'You can go,' said Wexford.

When he got back to the station he found Burden waiting for him, sitting in his, Wexford's, office at his, Wexford's, desk drinking tea and eating, very fastidiously and with the help of a paper napkin, a chocolate éclair.

'You won't believe this but that villain Smith, Monty Smith, says someone videoed the whole of that bomb-throwing affair on a Camcorder.'

'The Mitchell woman – where does she live?

Oberon Road? Next door to Smith? Somewhere down there – she's got a Camcorder,' Wexford said.

'She hasn't now. She says she sold it and I can't prove she didn't. Anyway, she says she was in the middle of the crowd outside here and couldn't have filmed it and she's right. Monty Smith says he didn't recognise whoever was filming the whole show. It was no one he knew. Colin Crowne is sticking to his story that he put Flay's petrol bomb in a skip outside 21 Oberon Road – and there was a skip there. The builders had it, the ones that left the pile of bricks about for the Kingsmarkham Six to hurl through Smith's windows. If what Crowne says is true, someone found it there and helped himself.'

'I doubt if Crowne would *give* anything away or, come to that, throw anything away if he could get money for it. Is there any more tea? No? OK, I'll phone down for some.' Wexford sat down. He made his phone call. 'We were wrong about Fay Devenish,' he said. 'This is the one case where the unknown assailant really did come to the door' and he told Burden what had happened. 'It's a funny thing, when Fay told me about the man at the door, about hearing a man's voice, I scarcely gave it credence. It was such a cliché thing to come up with. "No, it wasn't me, it was a mysterious stranger at the door." I *knew* we weren't going to get confirmation, but we did.'

'And you separated those boys from their mother, lest she get at them and tell them to lie for her.'

Wexford grinned. He was feeling inexplicably happy. 'I like your use of the subjunctive, Mike. Must be the effect of Mensa membership. Sure, that was my reason for separating them. I'm very glad I did. Robert confirmed it too. He said the man was carrying a briefcase.'

'Containing the weapon and maybe a raincoat?'

'Presumably. So what I thought would turn out a waste of time, trying to discover who sent those threatening letters and whatever revelation Trevor Ferry has for us, is actually essential stuff. Someone had it in for Devenish and that someone accomplished his revenge or whatever it was.'

'Let's go and see him now. I'll come with you.'

'I don't suppose there's anything in it,' Ferry said.

That phrase, or versions of it, always alerted Wexford. It invariably seemed to be used when the reverse was true and there was plenty 'in it'. He was far less anxious to hear accounts that were vaunted as sensational, hair-raising or calculated, in the storyteller's estimation, to lead to immediate arrests. He said what he always said in these circumstances. 'We'll be the judges of that.'

It was three in the afternoon and they had been admitted to the house by Gillian Ferry. Burden asked her if she had got home early from work and she said her school had broken up two days before. She was a thin, stringy woman with a prematurely lined face and silvering blonde hair, in all respects ordinary but for her large, angry green eyes. Once she had shown them into the living-room, where her husband was again enjoying culinary banalities on television, she left them, shutting the door rather too sharply behind her.

The slam had made Ferry wince. He shook himself as if coming to, returning to the real world from Bolognese kitchens and Tuscan feasts. 'You want to know about the guy Steve Devenish had the tussle with? I'll tell you. It was about two years back. More than that because I was still there and it was around the time Steve Devenish got that big rise. Mind you, I don't reckon anyone would ever have heard of him if they hadn't put that piece about him in the paper with all those photos.'

'The *Kingsmarkham Courier*, you mean?'

'The local rag, yes. They called him a fat cat and had pictures of him and his house, and they even had one of his wife and baby – that was the baby that went missing, right? Well, round about the same time as that there was this chap flying on Seaward to Amsterdam – I think it was Amsterdam – only when he got to Gatwick he was told along with a couple of others that the flight was overbooked. We'd got more passengers than we had seats. It was the sixteen-ten flight, four ten p.m. to the layman.

'Now this doesn't very often happen, not with Seaward, but it does sometimes, especially on the popular flights. The point about Amsterdam – Schiphol, that is – is that you can get a cheap flight from there to the US, I mean cheap*er*. Well, this chap wasn't going to do that, he was going to Amsterdam for a dirty weekend or whatever, or he thought he was, only we were overbooked and something had to give, if you see what I mean.'

Ferry looked expectantly at the two policemen, apparently awaiting approval. Wexford gave it with an encouraging nod.

'So we started making offers to the passengers,' he went on, 'you know the sort of thing: give up your seat on this flight and take the later one – say in three hours' time – and we'll give you a free dinner at the Holiday Inn and a complimentary bottle of wine. Now one passenger accepted so we were left with two. Of course we upped the ante and the other guy, not this chap, he accepted. But we were in trouble because, for some reason – plain inefficiency, I'd guess – we'd issued two tickets for the seat this chap thought was his.

'I was called in – I was the Seaward manager then,

of course – and I talked to this chap, privately like, took him into a room and gave him a drink. Everyone else was on board, waiting for take-off. I knew there'd be trouble, he didn't want the air miles, so off my own bat I offered him a hundred and fifty quid to take the later flight. Well, the upshot was that he accepted, he said he'd take the cash and have the price of his ticket refunded, so I agreed, but he didn't take the flight, he used the cash to hire a chauffeur-driven car to take him to Harwich and go on the ferry over to the Hook of Holland.'

'Why didn't he drive himself?' Burden asked. It was irrelevant but he wanted to know.

'Liked the idea of the luxury. That was what he called it, the luxury. Apparently he'd never in his life been in a car with a driver, not even a bloody minicab, or so he said. Well, he got his car and his driver but he never got to the Hook. The car was in a pile-up on the M25 near the Dartford crossing, and him and the driver were both killed.'

Ferry looked at them with more animation than usual in his face, evidently proud of his dramatic tale.

Wexford said, 'Where does the threat or the menace to Devenish come in?'

'I'm coming to that,' said Ferry with the story-teller's talent for suspense. He looked much brighter, less hangdog, and colour had come into his greyish face. 'This chap had a sister and she was – is, I suppose – married to a very aggressive kind of guy. Lives round here, this guy does.'

Wexford thought he could manage to sort things out fairly satisfactorily, provided Ferry categorised his principal characters as a 'chap' and a 'guy'. 'Go on,' he said.

'Well, this guy knew the story; it seems the chap rang up his sister from Gatwick and told her the tale.

I mean, he was full of it, over the moon, how he'd got this money out of the airline. I mean, I reckon he put it across as if he'd practised some kind of deception.'

Ferry paused as his wife came in with three mugs of tea on a tray. The milk came in a quarter-litre carton and the sugar in a half-empty packet. There were no spoons so it was just as well none of them took sugar. Gillian Ferry left as quickly as she had come in. Handing out the mugs, her husband looked round for something to stand them on, but looked in vain, shrugged and gave up.

'Please go on, Mr Ferry,' said Burden.

'Right. Where was I? Oh, yes. Now you understand there's no question it was anything to do with Seaward, what this chap decided to do with the money. He chose to spend it on a chauffeur-driven car and the car crashed and he was killed. There was no way Seaward was responsible. You might as well say the airline caused the driver's death. But this guy, the brother-in-law, and his wife the sister, they didn't see it like that. For some reason they picked on Steve Devenish and put the blame on him.'

'Because Mr Devenish was, you could say, the boss of Seaward?' Wexford asked.

'Exactly. The way this guy saw it, or the way I suppose he saw it – if you can say an animal like that sees anything – was that Steve Devenish made the company's policy – which was only partly true – and that the company's policy was to overbook flights and – well, "bribe" was the word he used – and put temptation in the way of people like his brother-in-law by giving them large sums of money that went to their heads and they couldn't handle it.'

'Bit over the top, wasn't it?' Burden said.

'Out in the stratosphere,' said Ferry. 'But this guy came to Seaward's office in Kingsmarkham first of all and Steve happened to be there. He made a big scene and threatened to sue. Steve didn't think much of it and he even tried to ignore it when the guy forced his way into his office at Gatwick. That time he said he'd call the police.'

'And did he?'

'Not so far as I know. He didn't have to, Steve threw him out himself. He was a big chap, was Steve, as I dare say you know. Then he got a solicitor's letter from this guy's solicitor, whoever it was, saying this guy's wife had a right to substantial compensation. Rubbish, of course. Seaward's own lawyers soon put him in his place.'

Ferry took a mouthful of tea and set the mug down, making a wet ring on the coffee table. 'Of course,' he said, 'when the death threats started coming Steve should definitely have got on to you but for some reason he didn't. D'you know what I think? I think he didn't want any more hassle.'

'What d'you mean by hassle, Mr Ferry?'

'Well, he'd thrown the guy out of his office, hadn't he? I mean, literally thrown him out. And when a great big bloke like Steve, in what you might call the prime of life, picks up a little guy like this guy and throws him on to his back on to a marble floor, if he doesn't do lasting damage he definitely causes pain. The guy said he'd broken one of his ribs. I don't know, I wasn't there. But it was why Steve didn't want you lot called in.'

It might be the Rachel Holmes story all over again, Wexford thought. You are attacked, physically or verbally, certainly illegally, but in repelling your assailant you injure him and, fearing repercussions, keep silent, or as silent as you can, about the original assault. There ought to be a name for it – how about the Kingsmarkham Defence? He looked up at Ferry and nodded just as Gillian Ferry came back into the room. She kicked open the door because her hands were full with books and papers – schoolchildren's work to mark in the holidays? – but it seemed to Wexford as if she kicked in anger.

'You mentioned death threats,' he said. 'You mean letters?' The tea was very thin, weak and tepid, and he wished there were a potted plant nearby in which secretly to tip it but there wasn't. No green leaves flourished here. 'Did you see any of them?'

Ferry shook his head. 'Steve told me about them. That was just before he told me Seaward were "letting me go". Nice expression that, isn't it? It's what they call a UFO-something.'

'A euphemism,' Gillian Ferry said in a rather sharp, schoolmistressy tone. It told Wexford a lot about her relationship with her husband. She felt she had married intellectually beneath her and it rankled still. Had Ferry attracted her only because once he was well-off and successful? And, finding this not enough, had she been trying to improve him ever since? He said to Ferry, 'Your contention is that the brother-in-law wrote these letters?'

'Who else? Maybe it was his wife who actually wrote them. The guy could barely write, or so I'm told. Steve laughed it off. Well, whether he went on laughing it off I couldn't say. I wasn't there, was I? I'd been *let go*. The guy made phone calls too until Steve had his number changed and went ex-directory.'

It interested Wexford that of all the people he had talked to about Stephen Devenish, Trevor Ferry was the only one to call him by a diminutive of his given name. No one else, apparently, called him Steve. Yet this man, in spite of what he professed, had particular reason for bitterness against Devenish and could never have been intimate with him. Wexford found it hard to believe Ferry bore him no grudge. 'You refer to him as "the guy",' he said. 'What's his name?'

'Oh, didn't I say? His name's Meeks, Carl Meeks.'

This was no special cause for surprise but Wexford was surprised. He remembered Meeks from the various disturbances which had taken place at Muriel Campden, an undersized but fat man with a round face and loose lips, his wife one of those grossly fat women until recently rarely seen in any British communities. Burden had interviwed them in the hunt for Hennessy's killer and Wexford recalled murmuring to him, in a paraphrase, 'It is such fools as you make the world full of ill-favoured children.' But aggressive? Violent?

That this man and this woman might be capable of the literate letter he had found in Stephen Devenish's desk seemed questionable. The language used would scarcely have been available to them.

'When exactly did you leave Seaward, Mr Ferry?'

'I like "leave",' said Ferry with an unamused laugh. 'It's almost as good as "letting go". I *left* in the July, exactly two years ago, struggled to keep up the payments on my house which, incidentally, was in Kingsbrook Valley Drive, Kingsmarkham – a nice part if you know it – failed, sold it for a lot less than I gave for it and bought this dump.'

'So you don't know if the threats went on coming after September two years ago?'

'No, and he can't tell you, can he? Maybe his widow can.'

At least we know he had a letter very recently, Wexford thought. He was rather surprised to hear Burden ask the name of the private preparatory school where Gillian Ferry taught.

'The Francis Roscommon in Sewingbury.'

'Quite a distance,' Burden said. He was remembering the plastic-hooded bicycles in the passage outside. 'You no longer run a car?'

'She gets the bus,' Ferry said shortly.

*

394

Fay took him out into the garden. It was one of the rare mornings of that cool, wet summer when sitting outdoors was just possible. When the sun was out it was almost too hot and when the clouds surged up once more and covered it, too cold. Three wicker chairs were arranged around a wicker table on the broadest area of lawn, under a mulberry tree, so that it looked as if they were expected. But Fay said the neighbours kept coming in. She made them tea and they gave her their condolences, though what sympathy they felt was due to her she couldn't imagine, as most of them had been alerted by the police and the Social Services under Operation Hurt-Watch of her situation with her husband.

The little girl, Sanchia, had a blanket on the grass, on which stood a glass of orange-coloured liquid (or so it appeared from its dregs) that she had managed to knock over, an opened can of Coke, a packet of custard-cream biscuits and another of chocolate-chip cookies, and a welter of toys. It was a happy, comfortable mess and one which, Wexford was sure, Devenish would never have tolerated. Passing through the house with Fay, he had noticed that on only the third day after the man's death it was already less immaculate, less tidy. At ten thirty in the morning two wineglasses with wine dregs in them stood on a table in the living-room, had certainly been drunk from the evening before and left there overnight.

'Jane's gone back to Brighton just for the day,' Fay said to him. 'She was here last night and we drank – oh, nearly a bottle of wine between us. I'm getting sloppy, I haven't cleared up.' It was still necessary for her to make excuses for untidiness. 'I don't know what I'd do without Jane. I had to do without her for so long.'

She looked a lot better. It was strange; to anyone

who hadn't known what went on in that house it would have been monstrous. Her eyes were brighter, her colour better, she even looked younger. Somehow he guessed that the clothes she wore, a short denim skirt, a top that was rather low-cut, had long been banned but never disposed of, had thankfully been put on now the censor and brutal judge was gone.

'My boys are coming home today,' she said. 'I've missed them. It'll be good to have them back.'

'They both go to the same school, I think you said?'

'That's right. In Sewingbury. Edward will be leaving next year to go to Oundle.'

'Don't let them tire you out.'

'I don't think I shall get tired the way I used to. The only thing is I cry all the time. I just start to cry for no reason.'

'I think you've plenty of reason,' he said, then, 'Mrs Devenish, do you remember the threats made against your husband by a man called Carl Meeks? Do you remember how he came to the Kingsmarkham office of Seaward Air, then to Gatwick? And your husband threw him out, allegedly injuring him?'

She said, but without bitterness, 'He was great at injuring people.'

'But you remember these incidents?'

'He never said much to me about them. He didn't talk about his work but he did tell me about this man Meeks. He was proud of hurting him.'

'Do you think Carl Meeks could have sent these threatening letters? They threatened your husband's life, didn't they?'

'He said he'd kill him, yes.' She spoke dreamily, almost as if with a longing for some wished-for event. Then she said, in quite a different tone, 'I loved him so much once. When we were engaged he was so gentle and thoughtful. He hit me while we were on our honeymoon but that was because he was jealous of me talking to a man in the hotel, and he was so sorry afterwards. Only even then, you know, he said I'd made him do it, it was my fault for being – for being flirtatious.'

Her eyes filled with tears. She made a little sound that was between a gulp and a sob, and Sanchia came over to her with the biscuit packet, an offering of comfort. 'Mummy not cry.'

'Mummy won't cry, darling,' Fay said and it was true, she had stopped crying. She put her arms round the little girl and kissed the top of her head. 'I'm so lucky,' she said. 'Look what I've got, all my lovely children, and my health and I'm free, but somehow I keep crying. You see, I always loved Stephen, somewhere the love I had for him was still there. He tried to beat and kick and knock it out of me, and in the end he nearly did, but when I think of the love I once had I cry. And it was true I was the only woman for him, the only one he ever loved, it was *true*. It was just that he had – well, a funny way of showing it . . .'

# Chapter 23

The builders working on the restoration of 16 Oberon Road were sitting on the front step, having their mid-morning coffee break. So far, all they had done was put back the tiles that had come off the roof during the fracas led by the Kingsmarkham Six. The graffiti still remained, 'filth', 'paedo' and 'killer', among the decapitated bodies and the snarling animal faces, all done in red and pink and blue and yellow. The builders would leave repainting the rendering till last. Later in the day, unless it rained, which it looked likely to do, they would set about replacing the glass in the upstairs windows.

They finished their coffee and were just having their second smoke when a van drew up outside from Kingsmarkham Borough Council's Domestic Environment and Landscape Department. The logo on its side was of a female doll holding a spade and a male doll with a bunch of flowers. This reversal of what some would call the accepted order of things had taken place in response to the demands of the militant feminist element on the council. The driver of the van, who had long red hair like a teenage girl, and his mate, with an open mouth and protruding tongue in much the same sort of red tattooed on one wrist, got down from the cab and went round the back to size up the situation.

Daunted by the now waist-high grass, the giant hogweed and man-height thistles, not to mention the iron bedstead, they came back to have a cigarette with the builders. The driver said it was a job for a JCB. All the department's mechanical diggers were in use, so it would be at least three months before one could be spared to start on this garden and in his opinion they would be lucky if they got it done by Christmas. There was the added problem of getting a JCB round the back of number 16.

From her first-floor window in the Muriel Campden tower, Rochelle Keenan was filming the four men on her Camcorder. Kingsmarkham Council had just banned all its employees from smoking in public places and Rochelle intended to produce her film as part of her revenge campaign against the driver of the van. She had had a brief affair with him a couple of years back while her husband was in Stowerton Royal Infirmary (about to be renamed the Princess Diana Memorial Clinic) having a hernia operation, he had been the one to end it and now when she saw him he pretended not to know her. She watched him light another cigarette before sitting down on a camp stool one of the builders had produced from inside the house.

John Keenan didn't know about the affair but he suspected something, largely owing, Rochelle believed, to the youngest Keenan child, Winona, having red hair. He said that as soon as he could raise the £300 it cost, he was going to get one of those home DNA-testing kits and find out for sure. To make certain of getting it right he had already tried taking a swab from the inside of Winona's mouth, only the enterprise came to nothing because the little girl swallowed it. Rochelle didn't know which of them was Winona's dad and she didn't much care. She was far more interested in her video and in getting the redheaded driver the sack or at least a severe reprimand.

A stone's throw away in Ariel Road – 'a stone's throw' at Muriel Campden being more a fact of life than a figure of speech – Maria Michaels had a date with Miroslav Zlatic. He admired powerful women and had somehow managed to make her understand with signs but without words, that he had fallen in love with her when he saw her putt the shot that broke the police station window. Their meeting planned for this morning was to be in the derelict house on the outskirts of Myringham, where Miroslav had taken Lizzie Cromwell and perhaps other young women as well. Leaving the despised Monty Smith in bed, Maria was off to catch the Myringham bus at the York Street stop.

Wexford saw her as his car entered the approach road but he ignored her cheerful wave. Although not one of the Kingsmarkham Six, she was almost certainly responsible for a great deal of the criminal damage caused on the day of Hennessy's death. The difficulty was that, along with other people's involvement, he couldn't prove it. Donaldson drove him the long way round, up Ariel and along Puck, for the purpose of assessing what was going on, if anything. On the street sign the name of this latter road had once more been defaced. 'I don't know why they don't rechristen it,' he said to Karen Malahyde. 'Call it Titania or something.'

'I'm not sure that would be a wise choice, sir.'

'What? No, I suppose not.'

The first few spots splashed against the windscreen, then the rain came in torrents. Donaldson put the wipers on at fast speed but still he felt it wiser to stop until the heavy shower had passed. Someone in number 2 Oberon Road shut an upstairs casement with a slam. Wexford rubbed at the steam on the window but still could see nothing out there, not even the graffiti on number 16, beyond glassy streams and dazzlement.

'This Meeks, sir,' Karen said. 'I suppose he's on the benefit?'

'He's unemployed at any rate.'

'Living on our taxes and from what I hear they're both obese.'

'Being overweight has nothing to do with affluence,' said Wexford. 'It's not so much a matter of you can't be too rich or too thin as you have to be rich to *be* thin.'

'Cheap food makes you fat,' said Donaldson sagely, 'all those pies and chips.' He switched on the ignition and they were off once more, the rain having subsided into a drizzle.

Wexford put on the plastic mac. 'I suppose I shall have to buy a new raincoat,' he said to no one in particular, but Donaldson's shoulders hunched a little.

No one had blamed him for Wexford's loss but he sometimes felt he had been negligent. He was thinking how, if he chanced to see Charlene Hebden while he was up here, he would confront her and get the truth out of her, when he found himself outside 24 Oberon Road and Wexford was telling him to stop and let him and DS Malahyde out.

Karen Malahyde never seemed to notice rain. Her clothes had a rainproof look to them, even skirts and blouses, and on a man her hairstyle would have been called a crew-cut. She stood on the front path, surveying the house, leaving it to Wexford to find shelter under the diminutive porch and ring the bell.

Linda Meeks was immediately recognisable, an often-seen figure in those riotous assemblies. She should have been in the hierarchy, he thought, important enough to enlarge it to the Kingsmarkham Seven, though she had never been one of the ringleaders. A large woman, soft and cushiony, she looked as if her plump, dimpled flesh, mottled pink and white, would hold the impress if a finger were dug into it. It was evident from a flicker of alarm in her pale-blue eyes that she expected these two police officers intended to question her on the subject of DS Hennessy's death. It wouldn't be the first time. Just the same, she had hoped the first time would also have been the last.

Wexford had a feeling he had set her mind at rest when he said he wanted to talk to her and her husband about her brother-in-law who had died in a car crash on his way to Harwich.

'My brother,' said Linda Meeks, 'not my brother-in-law.' She looked very relieved, positively cheerful. 'Come in. You want a cup of tea?'

Wexford said no, thanks, and Karen said no, not now, which for both of them was a way of saying that this matter was too serious for sociable cups of tea. Both expected Meeks to be in front of the television with a can of something and a bag of crisps, which behaviour, as Barry Vine, a golfer, put it, was par for the course at Muriel Campden. Instead, he was out in the garden, in a shed, doing woodwork. He appeared to be making a table, for the legs and base were finished and he was planing what appeared to be the top. When he saw them he laid the plane down carefully on its side and came out, putting up an umbrella.

The garden was exquisitely neat. Vegetables grew in it where others might have flowers. That is, they were not planted in rows as on an allotment, but in clusters as in a herbaceous border: lettuces making a nice contrast with beetroot and runner beans in full scarlet bloom climbing up the fences instead of clematis.

Meeks spotted a tiny plant that shouldn't have been there and in spite of the rain, pulled it out. 'Never pass a weed,' he said philosophically.

He was a little man, shorter than his wife, and with his fatness, as is often the case in middle-aged male beer drinkers, concentrated on his belly. This area of his body was so large and protuberant as to make an onlooker feel uneasy. It looked as if its possessor must be uncomfortable, embarrassed by what was almost a deformity, ashamed of such grotesqueness. But if Meeks felt any of this he gave no sign of it. He walked very upright, carrying all before him, as he led them back to the house where he dropped the weed into a waste bin.

In the living-room it was the boy Scott who had the television on, playing a video game in which the player won points if he could steer a surfer through a stormy sea without bumping into islands, ships and other obstacles. His father was going to leave it – keep him quiet, it's harmless – but Wexford asked him to switch it off and leave them. Scott Meeks, who had never been spoken to like that before, gave Wexford a lowering look, his underlip stuck out, but he did as he was told and departed, slamming the door behind him.

'I'd like to talk to your wife as well, Mr Meeks,' Wexford said, 'but not till after I've had a word with you. Tell me about this trouble with your brother-in-law. For a start, what was his name?'

'Jimmy – well, James, I suppose, James Crabbe.'

If Meeks was surprised to find the police at last taking an interest in his brother-in-law's wrongs, he gave no sign of it. Rather, he seemed pleased to have a chance of talking about what had evidently become an obsession and, before Wexford could ask him anything else, he had launched on a muddled account of the fateful happenings at Gatwick.

'They was all dead against him from start to finish, don't tell me they don't make no difference between passengers and whatever, they was set against letting him on that plane from the start, and it's my belief it was on account of he was wearing shorts, shorts and sandals, and that got up their noses, so they was set on making him a victim, it's my belief they paid those folks to what-do-they-call-it, over-book and then . . .'

'Just a moment, Mr Meeks,' said Karen. 'Would you tell us how you know all this? You weren't there, were you?'

'He gave us a beil,' said Meeks. 'Jimmy did. Him and Linda, they was very close. I mean, they was twins. It hit her very hard, him dying like that, I can tell you. I mean, it upset me, but her, she was devastated, it knocked her for six, they thought she was going to have a mental breakdown. Well, like I was saying, he gave us a phone. He was over the moon, like out on Cloud Nine, bubbling over he was, how he'd got this money out of Seaward and he was going to spend it on a chauffeur-driven car to the ferry.'

'What was he going to Amsterdam for?' Wexford asked. Jimmy Crabbe wasn't gay, he thought, or was he? He wasn't going to buy cheese or porcelain or look at *The Night Watch*. 'Was it just a holiday?'

'It was his girlfriend,' said Meeks. 'She'd got a job as a nanny over there. He was going to have the weekend with her while the folks she worked for was away. But he never made it. The car he hired crashed on the M25 soon after it come out of the Dartford Tunnel. Big truck jack-knifed and went smack into it.'

'But surely that was no one's fault,' said Karen. 'Well, maybe the truck driver's fault or the hire-car driver's fault but not Seaward Air. All they did was give him the money.'

Whose side are you on, Meeks may have been thinking. 'They shouldn't put temptation in a poor man's way,' he said sententiously. 'Folks like Jimmy, they need looking after, they need to be protected.'

'Your brother-in-law wasn't' – Wexford sought about for something reasonably PC and failed lamentably – 'he wasn't mentally afflicted, was he?'

Meeks jumped up. 'What are you insinuating? That Jimmy was backward, is that what you're saying? I never said that, I never meant that. I mean he'd never been nowhere or done nothing, he said as much, he had that car because he'd never been in a chauffeur-driven car. He was thirty-six years old and he'd never even had a girlfriend before this one. Those Seaward folks put temptation in a poor man's way when they should have been putting him on that plane and looking after him, and the air hostesses bringing him beer and a sandwich. D'you know, he'd never been on a plane before? Well, he never went on that one, did he? Thanks to them. Thanks to that bastard Stephen Devenish, he was the one made the rules, he was the one said what they all had to do.'

Linda Meeks put her head round the door. 'I heard you shouting, Carly. You all right?'

'Of course I'm all right. I just got a bit aerated.'

'Leave us for a while longer, Mrs Meeks, will you?'

She retreated without argument and as the door closed Wexford changed tack completely and asked Meeks in an abrupt tone where he had been on the previous Tuesday at eight in the morning.

Meeks looked astonished but he apparently failed to make the connection. 'Out with my dog,' he said. 'I'm always out with my dog at eight in the morning.'

'I don't see any dog.'

'He's in the kitchen with Linda.'

Wexford asked if Meeks had a car and then if anyone saw him while he was out, got a 'no' to the first and a – 'I don't know' to the second, qualified by, 'I go out at half-seven and there's not many about then. Folks round here may have seen me. I go in York Park or out in the fields and there's no one there so early.' Either he was acting or the purpose of these inquiries hit him, rather late in the day. 'He's dead, isn't he? That Stephen Devenish? He was murdered.' More light dawned, an unpleasantly searching light. 'You think I done that? I murdered him?'

'We don't think anything, Mr Meeks,' Karen said. 'We'd just like to eliminate you from our inquiries. You threatened Mr Devenish, didn't you? You made threatening phone calls and wrote threatening letters, and went along to Seaward Air and threatened him.'

Carl Meeks was shaking his head. 'I never wrote no letters.' He seemed to be making up his mind to come out with a confession, he even closed his eyes briefly, screwed up his face, said in a rush, 'I'm not much at writing and reading, never seemed to get the hang of it, I reckon it's not up my street.' He brightened a little. 'The wife can write and read.'

'I think we'll have Mrs Meeks in now,' said Wexford.

'And bring Buster with you,' Carl Meeks called out.

She had changed out of leggings and T-shirt into an all-enveloping check dress like a table-cloth with sleeves. For their benefit? Or because she was going out? But it wasn't her appearance that made the impact. She was pulled into the room, as a bow-fronted carriage might be pulled with a frisky horse in harness, by the biggest dog Wexford had ever seen. It seemed to be a Great Dane, of a slate-blue colour, and it slipped its lead, making straight for Carl, placing its paws on his shoulders and licking his face with a huge, slimy, dark-blue tongue.

'Down, boy, down! Get off me! That's enough now. Get down!'

'I think I've seen enough', said Wexford drily, 'to know you genuinely do possess a dog. Perhaps you'd remove Buster to the kitchen, Mrs Meeks. Thank you.' He waited until she came back, panting from her exertions, and said nothing until she was sitting down, catching her breath. 'You didn't much like Stephen Devenish, did you, Mrs Meeks?'

'I didn't mind him,' she gasped. It took her a few moments to be able to speak. Then she said, 'I didn't know him – well, only by sight. It wasn't just him. It was all of them Seaward people.' Once started, she was voluble. 'That driver was drunk, they found I don't know how many pints of whatever in his blood, and it was those Seaward people told Jimmy to go to them, they said to him, Whatsisname was a good driver, they recommended him, and what did he know? He just did what they said and it killed him, *they* killed him. You said, did I like Stephen Devenish, and I say, what d'you expect when someone throws your husband down the stairs?'

'We heard he'd thrown him out of his office,' Karen said.

'Well, you heard wrong then. He kicked him out of the office and then he picked him up by his coat collar and dragged him to the top of the stairs and threw him down.'

'Is that how it was, Mr Meeks?'

Meeks nodded. He seemed less than pleased, though, that his wife had shown him in such an abject light, as a man who could be thrown hither and thither, wherever his attacker's fancy took him. 'He was a bastard,' he said at last. 'It's a blessing he's dead.'

'But you didn't kill him?'

That made Linda Meeks give a thin shriek. Her

husband said, 'Do me a favour. He was about twice as big as me.'

Compounding her offences, Linda Meeks said, her expression quite serious, 'He wouldn't have let Carl kill him.'

'There's a lot in that,' Wexford said to Burden later. 'We know that whoever stabbed Devenish was shorter than he, so there's your question, why did he let whoever it was kill him?'

'I suppose he was taken by surprise.'

'Well he wouldn't have been taken by surprise by Meeks. If Meeks was the stranger Edward Devenish saw and his mother heard, he was no stranger to Devenish. The moment he was let into that study Devenish would have known who he was and that he meant to do him harm. Are you saying that after Devenish cut his wife's hand he left the knife he used, the certainly blood-stained knife, lying on his desk or a table? And that when Meeks came in he continued to leave it there for Meeks to pick up and use?

'Because the knife must have been there, Mike. God knows where it came from, perhaps he kept a knife in a drawer. Why not? He had a whip. He maybe kept it for the express purpose of chastising his wife, used it that morning and then what? It wasn't in the study, he didn't throw it out of the window – why would he?'

Burden said thoughtfully, 'He could have cut her and then handed her the knife and told her to take it away and wash it.'

'D'you know what that reminds me of? It reminds me of that directive in the Jewish Law. "Thou shalt not seethe a kid in the milk of its mother." It's adding insult to injury.'

'But he was capable of it.'

'I believe he was.' Wexford sat silent for a moment, reflecting with no great pleasure on human iniquity. 'We've had the report on the knives that were in the kitchen. They're expensive knives with horn handles. No traces of human blood on any of them. Her fingerprints on all but two, his on none.'

'Does any of them have a blade that fits those wounds?'

'Two do. But you needn't look like that. These blades are – well, a standard size. Thousands of knives in people's kitchens and on sale in shops are that size and would fit those wounds. The evidence we need is Devenish's blood on a knife and, as I say, there was no blood. Perhaps it was one of those knives but more likely it wasn't and the knife that was used was taken away.'

'By Carl Meeks?'

'Maybe. I don't know. The sequence of events is that Devenish's killer either brought a knife with him and that knife happened to have the same size blade as one of those in the Devenishes' knife block or that he used the knife Devenish had left lying on the desk after he cut Fay. It has to be one or the other. If it is as you say and he gave the knife to Fay to wash, could she wash it so thoroughly as to remove all trace of its previous use? But why would she want to? So the likelihood is that the killer used that knife and took it away with him.'

'Unless there were eight, not seven, knives in the knife block.'

'I don't think there were, because what Fay says is true, and though there are eight slots in the block, if you put eight knives in they jam up against each other. I know, I've tried it.'

'And Meeks?'

'We've a house-to-house going on at Muriel Campden to see if any of the neighbours saw him out with his dog at eight that morning. The Meek-ses's dog is an enormous Great Dane, a bluish-grey thing, name of Buster. It's not the kind of animal you'd miss. Once seen, never forgotten.'

'The way things are going,' said Burden, 'we shall soon know that Muriel Campden lot better than our own families.'

It was a fine evening if rather muggy. The residents of Oberon, Ariel and Puck Roads, and of the tower, sat on their front doorsteps if they had them or in deckchairs on the tower green if they didn't.

'Like a bloody caravan camp,' said Tony Mitchell, who thought it was common, the kind of thing people did who lived in tenements.

They gossiped. They had been talking for weeks about who might or might not have thrown the petrol bomb that killed Ted Hennessy and all of them had different views, depending on the side they took in personal vendettas or the degree of their paranoia. Now they had Carl Meeks to talk about, a subject made even more enthralling by the arrival on the scene of three police officers doing a house-to-house.

Maria Michaels said she was sitting outside to save them the trouble of ringing her bell. She had just seen her old friend Tasneem Fowler go into her own house accompanied by a woman called Tracy Some-thing, and she'd called out to them and said to come over and have a drink when they'd done their business or whatever with Terry and the kids. Maria went into the house and fetched two chairs, which she put on the bit of grass in the front garden, and she was going back for a third when she met Monty Smith coming downstairs, carrying all his belongings in two Tesco carrier bags.

'For two pins,' said Monty, 'I'd smash your face in.'

'You wouldn't do it twice, my darling. I'm not like that poor little cow Tasneem.' Memories of glorious shot-putting days came back to her. 'When I get going you wouldn't know what hit you. Don't shut the door, I'm bringing another chair and a table out.'

Despised, rejected and expelled, Monty Smith went off down Oberon towards the York Street bus-stop. Halfway down he met Detective Constable Archbold who asked if he could have a word. The word was to ask where Monty was at eight on that Tuesday morning and if he had seen Carl Meeks out with his dog. Monty said Archbold must be joking as he never got out of bed before ten, or that had been his habit, but God knew what the future held.

Shirley Mitchell was on the green, picking up litter by hand and dropping the beer cans, crisp packets, cigarette ends, fish-and-chip paper and take-away and hire-car fliers into a shopping trolley she had lined with a plastic bag. Archbold asked her about Carl Meeks and she burst into a long diatribe about dog owners whose pets fouled the pavements. That Buster was one of the worst offenders. She had personally offered to supply Mr and Mrs Meeks with a dustpan, rake and hygienic bags for the disposal of the Great Dane's waste but they had laughed in her face. No, she couldn't say if she had seen Carl Meeks out with the dog on Tuesday morning, but she saw him every morning, or almost every morning, and it was just as well she did, for she was able to run outside and clean up the mess before her unfortunate neighbours trod in it.

One of the few Muriel Campden residents who wasn't sitting outside was Terry Fowler. He and his sons were watching a video he had made of the France–Brazil final in the World Cup. They had seen the match live and since then they had looked at the video twice. This was the third time but Terry, Kim and Lee Fowler never tired of football, especially international matches of this calibre. France had just scored their first goal when a key was heard in the front door lock and Tasneem walked into the room with a strange woman.

She had only got up the courage to come because Tracy egged her on and promised to go with her. On the way they were stopped by Lynn Fancourt and asked about Carl Meeks. Both found this quite exciting but, regretfully, had to say they didn't know because they didn't live here, they were just visiting. The idea of 'just visiting' her own home brought tears into Tasneem's eyes and the marks of the tears were still there when she entered the house and confronted, after many months, her husband and her children.

'What are you doing here?' said Terry, ignoring Tasneem's timid introduction of her friend. 'You reckon you can go away when you want and stay away for a fucking year, do you, and then walk in here as bold as bloody brass like you've just been round the shops?'

Kim and Lee hadn't even looked at her. They were watching France go on to score their second goal.

Tracy Miller glanced about her and said, 'This place is filthy, I bet it wasn't like this when Tas lived here.'

She crossed to the set and turned it off. A great wail went up from the boys. Terry leapt to his feet and there ensued what Tracy's dad used to call a slanging match, beginning with Terry calling her a slag and an interfering bitch, and her calling him an animal.

A string of name-calling ensued, Terry dubbing Tasneem with epithets of such richness and obscurity

412

that Tracy had never heard of half of them before. The boys both burst out crying and Tracy's heart bled for them. She thought Terry was going to hit Tasneem and she was wondering whether to get between them – as if she hadn't had enough of that in her own married life – when Tasneem said, 'OK, I'm going, and that's it, I've had it up to my eyes.'

They got out into the hallway and heard the television go on again. Terry and Lee sat down once more but Kim came running after them, got hold of Tasneem's trousers – she was wearing the salwar kameez – and sobbed, 'Don't go. I don't want you to go.'

Tasneem set up a wail of grief but Tracy said quite firmly, 'You stop crying now, love. You and your brother's going to come and live with your mum and everything'll be *fine*.'

God knew whether it was true. Tracy got Tasneem out of the house and more or less dragged her down to Maria Michael's. Maria was sitting on a chair in the front garden with an elegant little table in front of her, on which were a tray with glasses, a bottle of Scotch, a bottle of gin, two cans of ginger ale and two of orange crush. She said hi to Tracy, that she was pleased to meet her and what was it to be, my darling, whisky or mother's ruin? Tasneem, being a Moslem, asked for orange crush but Maria insisted on something stronger to 'put some lead in her pencil'.

'Come on, that's men,' Tracy said, but Maria said, so what? And hadn't Tracy ever heard of the equality of the sexes?

Both women put their arms round Tasneem and Tracy held the whisky to her lips like a nurse with a feeding cup. Then Maria said she'd something to tell them that would cheer them up, a real bundle of laughs. She'd thrown Monty Smith out, the lazy bugger, and – how about this? – she'd got somebody else. Maria was telling them how Miroslav Zlatic had been a freedom fighter in Sarajevo, had had to flee with a price on his head and how great he was in the sack, when DC Kevin Cox opened the gate, came up the path and asked her about Carl Meeks.

Maria was only too happy to help. She offered Cox a drink but Cox, who had been looking longingly at the gin, was obliged to refuse. Carl Meeks, she said, was a regular out with his dog at eight in the morning. That is to say, she often saw him when she was on her way to work and that dog was more the size of a horse, but not *every* day, my darling, not this morning, for instance. This morning she'd had the day off and she smiled dreamily, remembering.

'What about last Tuesday morning?' said Cox.

'Well, I saw him, but whether it was Monday or Tuesday or Wednesday or what, I couldn't say. As I say, I don't see him every day. Some days he goes down the fields. He goes in the park.'

'I'd like a dog,' said Tasneem. 'When I get my boys back we'll have a dog.'

'Of course you will, my darling, and a cat and a rabbit and a bloody alligator too if you want.'

Cox went off, drew a blank at the remaining houses in Ariel Road where the occupants were out, and called on the Crownes and Sue Ridley, and the people next door and the people next door to them, but three sets of them didn't know Carl Meeks, not even by sight, or they said they didn't, and the Crownes got up too late to see him out with the Great Dane. At the Meekses' house in Oberon Road Lynn Fancourt was questioning Darren Meeks. Darren was still doing his paper round, so Lynn thought he of all people might know where his father was that Tuesday morning, but Darren didn't know, he left for his round three-quarters of an hour before eight. Still, he reckoned his dad must have taken Buster out. The dog made so much racket, whining and howling for his walk, that you took him out just to get a bit of peace.

'So what's new up in millionaires' row?' Maria wanted to know after Tasneem had told her Tracy worked for a lady in Ploughman's Lane.

'That bastard as was murdered,' said Tracy, 'he was another of them, used to beat her up something disgusting. Nobody knew till she kidnapped her own kid to get her out of his clutches and then it all came out. The neighbours was warned to keep an eye on him. Talk about bloody useless when those great places up there are all about ten miles apart.'

'Good riddance to bad rubbish then,' said Maria. 'I suppose she did it.'

'I don't know. It doesn't look like it, not with them asking us all that about whatsisname.'

'Oh, I reckon she did it, my darling. I would have.'

Lord Tremlett's medical report showed that Stephen Devenish had received three stab wounds to his chest and, in his opinion, that these wounds had been inflicted in a frenzy. The one that killed him had pierced the left ventricle of the heart. A woman could have inflicted them, but it was impossible to say whether the perpetrator was a man or a woman. The likelihood was that he or she was shorter than Devenish because the dead man had been so tall.

The murder had been committed between seven forty-five and eight thirty, the original estimate. He was unable to narrow the time down further. The weapon used was a kitchen knife with a blade two inches wide at its widest point and between eight and ten inches long. Devenish, prior to his death, had been a healthy man in his mid-thirties, of an exceptionally powerful physique, a well-made man without bodily flaws or scars. The inquest was opened and adjourned.

Wexford, who had attended the brief proceedings, went to see the widow and told her the funeral could take place whenever she chose.

Jane Andrews was at Woodland Lodge, was apparently staying there, and Fay's two sons were back home. It might have been his imagination but he felt that Sanchia was already a calmer, quieter and perhaps happier child. For the first time he noticed that she was also pretty, looking, perhaps, as her mother had at her age, pink-cheeked with satiny skin and regular features, big, grey-blue eyes and fine, shining hair. That hair was much longer than when the family group photograph was taken and now there would be no confusing her with a boy. It was a feminine, delicate face. She looked up at him and smiled. And he thought how dreadful it was that anyone could die, and moreover die by violence, and leave behind him so much relief and thankfulness.

The whole family – for Jane Andrews fitted in like a family member – were in the big living-room where the french windows were thrown open. The children ran in and out of the garden, bringing grass clippings from the lawn on their shoes and on to the white carpet. There was no one to stop them and no need to stop them now. But when she had shown him in, Jane Andrews suggested to Sanchia that she might like her to push her on her new swing and the child took her hand and pulled her outside, leaving him alone with Fay.

Fay said, in a cold, practical voice, 'Am I allowed to cremate him?'

'Of course. The undertakers you use will see to the formalities. I think it's only that you have to have two doctors sign the certificate instead of one.'

He couldn't read her expression. There's no art, he

thought, to find the mind's construction in the face. Burn him, destroy him, scatter the ashes, be rid of him for ever – was that what she was thinking? Or, more likely, I loved him once, he seemed different once, if only he could have been the way I believed him to be when we were young . . .

'How do the boys seem?' he asked her.

'They're fine.'

'I'd like to talk to them again, especially to Edward, about the man who called here at eight last Tuesday morning.'

Fay nodded, apparently neither shocked nor gratified. 'I'm going to sell this house. I shall put it on the market when all this' – she used an extraordinary phrase in the circumstances – 'has blown over.'

He could find nothing to say.

'He left everything he could to the children, you know. The house is in my name, I don't know why he did that, some tax dodge, I expect. He always said I wasn't fit to manage money. Shall I call Edward in now?'

'I think he's coming of his own accord, Mrs Devenish.'

A little colour came into her face. It was almost a blush. 'Please don't think I'm correcting you, you don't have to remember it now, but I'm going to call myself by my maiden name. I'll be Ms Dodds in future.'

Edward came in from the garden. Wexford could have sworn he had grown in the past few days. He was entering puberty and looked like a teenager.

'Sit down, will you, Edward?'

The boy glanced at his mother and at a nod from her sat down in the least comfortable chair nearby, sat upright and looked straight at Wexford.

'The man you admitted to this house on the morning your father died, you described him as "just a man". Can you be more specific?' Seeing that the boy was unsure of what he meant, he amended that. 'Can you try to describe him to me? Close your eyes and try to get a picture.'

Edward closed his eyes but opened them again almost immediately. Again he looked at his mother, said, 'He was just an ordinary man. About Dad's age, I told you that.' He screwed up his face as if in an effort to remember. 'I think he had jeans on and maybe a jacket. Oh, and he was carrying a case.'

'What kind of a case? A briefcase?'

'A big briefcase,' said Edward.

'Now the doorbell rang while you and Robert were out in the hallway, heading for the front door. The door to your father's study is on the right. Was that door closed?'

'I think so. It might have been just – well, pulled to.'

'I see. Now you answered the door and saw the man with the briefcase there. What did he say? And what did you say?'

'I don't think I said anything. He said, "I'd like to see Mr Devenish."'

'Deep voice, high voice, what kind of voice?'

'Quite deep,' said Edward. 'Just an ordinary man's voice.'

Fay Devenish had attempted to seem uninterested in all this, had turned her eyes towards the garden where Jane Andrews, Robert and Sanchia were slowly strolling towards the house, but now she turned to Edward and watched him inscrutably.

As if on cue, he said, and said with the snobbery of which only the privately educated child of wealthy parents is capable, 'He had the local accent. Like yours only more so.'

Wexford allowed himself to react to this not at all.

Inwardly, he smiled. Impossible even to feel angry with this poor child. 'Was he fat? Thin? Dark? Fair?'

'I don't know. I didn't notice.'

'You'd have noticed if he'd been a big fat man, wouldn't you?'

'He wasn't like that. He was just normal size.'

'Now, did your father come out of the study or did you open the door and show the man in?'

'I opened it. I just said to him "in there", then Robert and I went. We closed the front door after us like we always do. We had to go to Mrs Daley's and we'd have been in trouble if we'd been late.'

'Did you close the study door after the man?'

Suddenly Edward looked bored, as if he had lost interest. 'I don't remember. Can I go now?'

'Yes. But I want to talk to your brother.'

This was a hopeless task. Robert was as childish as Edward was – if not altogether pleasantly – mature.

'He looked like Batman.'

'Can you remember what he said, Robert?'

'He said, "Trick or treat" and I said, "Where's Godzilla?" and he turned into a bear, black fur grew all on him and he roared and showed all his big teeth. I said, "You're not Godzilla, you're the Beast." '

Robert collapsed in helpless laughter. To Wexford's astonishment he rolled on the floor, laughing and shrieking. Jane Andrews came in, prodded Robert with her toe, said in a teacher's tone, 'Get up. Come on, don't be crazy.'

It was effective but only up to a point, for the boy's laughter was succeeded by a storm of tears. Fay put her arms round him and he sobbed against her shoulder. Her eyes met Wexford's above his head but he could see only blankness in them and dismal resignation.

Jane was in jeans and sweatshirt but today her face was made up and she wore earrings, a long silver chain necklace and a big watch with a black-and-silver face. She looked pleased with herself, glad to be busy and useful, the heroine's friend, her mainstay and support. 'I'll be staying here for as long as Fay wants me,' she said, 'as long as I'm needed' and she bent down to pick up Sanchia.

But the little girl, seeing her brother in their mother's arms, exhibited immediate signs of jealousy, pushed Jane away and climbed up beside Robert. The almost-adolescent Edward, not hesitating for long but unable to find a corner in Fay's chair for himself, stood behind it and leant his cheek against her hair.

Wexford and Jane Andrews looked at each other and Jane smiled. 'Love-bombing, as the psychologists put it,' she said.

# Chapter 24

A needle in a haystack is not too different a concept from a knife in a hundred acres of woodland, interspersed with gardens, with shrubberies and hedgerows, and a drainage system branching underneath it. The drains had been investigated for that knife and an unpleasant task been assigned to PC Peach and WPC Brodrick: that of sifting through the rubbish collected that Tuesday morning from Ploughman's Lane by Kingsmarkham's contracted refuse collectors, Agate PLC.

From only one household a knife had been put into the wheelie-bin. But it was just a knife, quite the wrong sort, short and serrated. All the knives taken from Woodland Lodge were returned to Fay Devenish, though before they went back Wexford looked at them closely, probably for the twentieth time, at their long smooth or serrated blades and their horn handles, dark-brown horn or, in two cases, a lighter bleached shade. He looked specially at the two, one with a dark handle, the other with a light, whose blades matched Stephen Devenish's wounds.

'He must have brought the knife with him in that briefcase,' Burden said. 'Brought it with him and took it away. Young Edward says it was a big briefcase. How big, d'you reckon? Big enough to carry something to cover that jacket and those jeans? Say a raincoat?'

'Don't talk to me about raincoats,' said Wexford.

'Dora's taking me to London on Saturday to buy a new one. Another Burberry, she says. God knows what they cost now.' He sighed. 'What you're saying, I presume, is that this guy brought a raincoat with him to cover up the blood-stains on his clothes. Maybe it was mine. It was at Muriel Campden it went missing.'

'Be serious, will you? He would have had to conceal his clothes.'

'Doesn't seem to matter whether he did or not,' Wexford grumbled. 'No one saw him.'

'No, but he couldn't know that, could he?'

Wexford didn't answer. 'No one saw Carl Meeks either. Of course the trouble with checking up on someone who performs some regular task at the same time every day, like dog walking or even just going to work, is that people who see you can't remember *when* they saw you. Everyone says they often do see Meeks and the enormous Buster but not always and they can't remember which days they did see him. Darren Meeks was out delivering his papers, so he doesn't know. Scott was in bed. The primary schools didn't break up for the summer till that afternoon, but young Scott's not a candidate for a perfect attendance prize, always supposing they have them any more. Linda Meeks says he always takes the dog out without fail, no exceptions.'

'Reg,' said Burden, 'do you honestly believe Carl Meeks killed Devenish? It's more than two years since Devenish threw him down those stairs – or whatever he actually did to him. If he was going to get revenge on Devenish, why did he wait so long?'

'And if he did wait so long what triggered off his doing it last Tuesday? I suppose it's possible Meeks encountered Devenish somewhere, even went to one of Seaward's offices, had another go and was again manhandled.'

'No, it isn't,' Burden said triumphantly. 'I've had it checked out. No one among the staff at the Kingsmarkham, Brighton and Gatwick offices of Seaward has had sight or sound of Meeks since the stairs-throwing incident. It's just possible Devenish met him in the street and insulted him or some such thing . . .'

'But we've no reason to think he did.'

'Now I'll tell you something,' said Burden. 'I wonder if you've noticed.'

'Noticed what?'

'Gillian Ferry.'

'What about her?'

'Mrs Ferry is a teacher at the school Edward and Robert Devenish go to. She teaches English at the Francis Roscommon School in Sewingbury.'

Wexford thought about it. 'So she does. Is it significant?'

'I don't know. But it makes, so to speak, a double connection between the Ferrys and the Devenishes. Don't you think it's a bit odd?'

It was a little after ten o'clock when Sylvia put down the phone. She had been talking for twenty minutes to the woman who called but refused to give her name. Thank God no one else had phoned in the meantime. She got up, went to the window and looked down into the gardens. The bright windows of houses in Kingsbrook Avenue punctured the darkness. Lawns looked like strips of grey velvet and cypress trees hooded figures. Sylvia thought there was nothing like hours of solitude working on the helpline for sharpening the imagination. She would so much have liked to tell someone what the anonymous woman had said. Griselda could be told, of course, or Lucy – she wasn't a priest and it wasn't the confessional – but Griselda was on holiday and overworked Lucy was probably asleep.

It was her father Sylvia really wanted to tell but she would only do that with Griselda's or Lucy's permission. Standing there, looking at the backs of houses where the lights were beginning to go out, she thought about her father, and how attentively he would listen and how wisely he would respond. If she didn't feel much better about her husband, Sylvia thought, she did about her father. Another good thing The Hide had done for her.

Reflected in the black glass, the door behind her opened and Tracy Miller came in, wearing a pink tracksuit and with her long hair pinned to the top of her head.

Sylvia turned round and smiled, glad of some company. Tracy often came in for half an hour on her way to bed. Her children would have her up at six in the morning. 'I've had such a – well, frightening phone call, Trace.'

'One of them bastards wanting to chop your tits off?'

Sylvia laughed. She actually laughed, which only proved how hardened you could get or how the passage of time *softened* the worst horrors. 'Not a man. A woman. I want to tell you but I can't. You know the rules. It's absolutely in confidence.'

'I know. It's only on account of they know that, they trust you, that the poor cows give you a phone at all.'

'Did you call a helpline before you came here?'

'Me? I phoned all of ten times before I screwed up my courage and made the break. By that time he'd nailed up the doors on the cupboard so I couldn't get at my clothes and cut up my shoes. I went barefoot for a week. Well, you know what he's like. He scared you when he got over the wall, didn't he?'

Sylvia nodded. 'She asked my advice and I gave it. For what it's worth. I'm not a lawyer. I just remembered something I'd read and I said to be careful. If you've got to lie, lie. Was that wrong, Trace?'

'Don't ask me, love. What do I know? You've got to do what you've got to do, that's what I say.'

The crematorium chapel was no more than five years old, its walls panelled in fine hardwoods, its windows owing a good deal to Chagall's designs for stained glass. The curtains, of dark-green linen, had been embroidered by a local craftswoman with heavenly bodies, galaxies and long-tailed comets, and the pulpit was a cylinder of polished steel with star-shaped cut-outs through which light faintly gleamed. But for all that it was a dismal place, cold, stark and designed to hold more mourners than were likely ever to occupy its inlaid maple pews. Often the number was limited to ten, as was the case today, when his family and a few acquaintances came to cremate Stephen Devenish.

A representative from Seaward Air Wexford thought the man in a raincoat very like his own lost Burberry must be. He sat, looking uncomfortable, with a pale-grey felt hat on his lap. Devenish's PA he recognised, a smartly dressed young woman in a black suit and very high-heeled black patent shoes, sitting two rows behind him. It was extraordinary how ostentatiously the English avoided sitting *next* to anyone they didn't know. Four seats from her was Trevor Ferry.

Anyone may go to a funeral, it isn't obligatory to be asked. But still Wexford was surprised to see him there. Had he come to rejoice and gloat or simply quietly to celebrate? Ferry didn't look in his direction but sat staring at the abstract up on the wall that might have represented an angel or a tree of life, it was impossible to tell.

Fay came in with her father and mother, Jane Andrews walking behind with Edward. That was the extent of the congregation. Devenish had had no parents living but, though he had a sister, she had stayed away. There were no flowers and if any request had been made by Fay that, instead of flowers, donations should be made to a charity, no mention was made of such a suggestion. At one point the Seaward representative got up and seemed to be about to deliver some kind of eulogy of the dead man, but Fay touched his arm, whispered something to him and he sat down again.

No hymns were sung. Handel's *Water Music* was quietly piped, some words from the Alternative Service Book were muttered, and the coffin was slowly drawn away to disappear behind the beige velvet curtains and send Devenish's body to the fire. Without waiting for any valediction, any closing of the ceremony, Fay got up and walked out, the small congregation gradually following her. The officiating cleric looked embarrassed. The music stopped.

Outside, the Seaward man got into the black Mercedes that was waiting for him and was driven away. Wexford found himself walking down the long gravel drive in the company of Trevor Ferry.

'That was a funny old carry-on,' Ferry said conversationally. 'Talk about a good-riddance gathering.'

'Is that what you'd call it?' Wexford said, amused.

'Well, wouldn't you? I suppose you want to know what took me there.'

'If you want to tell me.'

'I don't mind, I'm not proud. The fact is, I'm a poor man – well, you know that. I'm unemployed and likely to remain so, I'm bored. I can't afford cinemas and I certainly can't afford to join clubs. I've got square eyes – that's what they used to call it when I was a kid – from watching TV. So I like to get out sometimes to whatever I can that's free.'

'Like funerals?'

'Why not? You can't get in to weddings. Not if they're any good. Besides, believe it or not after what's happened, I felt sorry for the poor devil. He wasn't so bad. It's an outing, isn't it? Sometimes I go down to the station and watch the INTERCITIES go through.'

Wexford said nothing. It was raining again, a drop fell on his nose and he could see the coin-size spots on the paving.

'Anyway, I got to talk to you. It all makes a change. For instance, another thing I do, I've joined the Kingsmarkham Neighbourhood Clean Streets Campaign.'

They had almost reached the car-park, where Donaldson awaited Wexford. He turned back and cast a look at the sugar-loaf-shaped crematorium, with its steel doors and glass cross on the top. 'The what?'

'Haven't you heard of it? Groups of us are organised to go to specific areas picking up litter. Oh, you don't get paid, it's on a voluntary basis. But you get people to talk to, I've met some very decent people, and they give you mid-morning coffee and biscuits. Tuesday's my day. The only drawback is you have to start so damned early, eight a.m. on the green outside the town hall.'

Wexford was so astonished and at the same time so aghast that anyone would be in such desperate straits of boredom and idleness as to welcome this kind of diversion that it was some moments before he realised what Ferry had said. And when he did, and Ferry was saying he must be off before it started pouring, he had to catch the bus, he said nothing at all beyond goodbye.

That evening Patrick Flay and Monty Smith were caught burgling a house in Orchard Drive. Kaylee was not with them. The neighbours recognised Flay, or they recognised the intruder they saw cutting a pane of glass out of a next-door window, as the man they had once seen involved in a drunken brawl outside the York Arms public house. Whoever he might be, they were sure he had no business gaining entry to their neighbours' home and they dialled nine–nine–nine.

It was eleven forty-five. The police came quietly, entered the house by the same means as Flay and Smith had entered it, and found both men in the master bedroom, putting jewellery and ornaments into a canvas holdall. Monty Smith said he was a law-abiding man who had been led astray by Patrick Flay. Flay's wife had been putting him up since his girlfriend turned him out. Even so, he would never have done it if he hadn't been thrown out of his home and left destitute on the streets. Flay said nothing at all but jumped out of the window.

The result was that he broke one of his legs and, while Smith was driven to the police station, had to be taken away in an ambulance. Next morning, at the Princess Diana Memorial Clinic where he was in traction, he told Burden that apart from the one he had given Colin Crowne, he had sold two of his petrol bombs to John Keenan and two to Peter McGregor.

'Who's Peter McGregor?'

'Chap who lives with Sue Ridley, next door to the Crownes.'

Burden had no comment to make.

'Don't matter telling you lot now,' Flay said,

'seeing as I'll be going down for Christ knows how long. I never said nothing before on account of I was scared they'd get me.'

It all sounded highly unlikely to Burden. 'How about that business with Kaylee and the cat flap?'

'Before I'm sentenced,' said Flay rather grandly, 'I shall be asking for a number of offences to be taken into consideration.'

'I bet you will.'

'I can't talk any more now, I'm in pain. My leg feels like it's on fire. D'you know, you've been in here an hour and you haven't once asked me how I'm feeling?'

Burden met Wexford for lunch in the Europlate. Wexford said three-quarters of an hour was all the time he could spare and he hoped Henri would get a move on. The big Glaswegian appeared as if on cue to tell them that today's specials were *soufflé pomadoro secco* and *osso buco à l'orange*. Wexford said to forget it. He'd have the pike and boiled potatoes and his friend the roast lamb.

'Good choice,' said Burden and refrained from adding that he hadn't been consulted. 'Do you know, Jenny's sister's got an Italian friend who's lived in Tuscany all her life and she'd never heard of dried tomatoes till she had some in a restaurant in Soho.'

Wexford laughed. 'I met Trevor Ferry at the funeral.' He told Burden about their conversation. 'When I got back I phoned the Town Hall – well, not the Town Hall at all, really, these days – the building that used to be the Midland Bank, which now houses Kingsmarkham Neighbourhood Clean Streets Campaign. What do you think they told me?'

'That Ferry turned up at the rendezvous covered in blood,' said Burden sourly.

'Not quite that. They told me that the area covered

on Tuesday mornings was Winchester Drive, Harrow Avenue, Eton Gardens and adjacent roads.'

'So? Winchester Drive's the nearest to Ploughman's Lane and it's still a good half-mile away.'

'Right. I asked for a lot of details about the campaign. Apparently, people may work in groups or individually – that is, one man or woman could work a street on their own. And last Tuesday very few people turned up – the usual fate of this kind of enterprise, I fear.'

Burden considered. 'You're saying Ferry could have been left on his own and while he was alone slipped away up to Woodland Lodge?'

'At any rate I mean to find out. Here comes our delicious Euro-grub.'

A bottle of sparkling water came too. Burden poured them a glass each.

'Karen's gone to Brighton to have another word with Mrs Probyn. Or another ten thousand words. Barry and Lynn are at Muriel Campden, still hoping to find some evidence for Meeks's assertion that he went out with that dog as usual on Tuesday. Or if he didn't, they haven't given up hope of finding someone who saw him out *without* the dog around half-seven.'

Wexford tasted his pike, nodded with grudging approval. 'Not bad. The thing is, Mike, Ferry lied. He lied when he said he was in bed at eight o'clock on Tuesday morning, then, caught off guard, he forgot what lie he'd told last time and told the truth.'

'You mean he was definitely out with the Clean Streets people?'

'The organiser remembered him. So few turned up, you see, that she remembered those who did. One of the others who did, by the way, was Shirley Mitchell.'

'What, the Shirley Mitchell who lives next door but one to the Smith house?'

'The very same.'

'Have you talked to her?'

'Not yet,' Wexford said. 'But if she tells me Ferry disappeared once they got up to Winchester Drive, I'm going to have that house of his turned upside-down.'

Arriving at the police station as requested, dead on time, Shirley Mitchell told him just that. She began with a preamble on the need to be a good citizen and the importance of what she called 'community values'. Litter was the scourge of the age and the principal destroyer of the environment. Wexford listened patiently. Then she said most people who volunteered to take part in the campaign 'fell by the wayside'. Trevor Ferry was one of them. It was her belief he only took it on for the sake of getting a lift up to the top of the hill to enjoy the otherwise unattainable view across the countryside and the Kingsbrook valley.

He was always skiving off. They didn't necessarily work singly, the idea was to work in groups, but when she'd worked in a group with Ferry, as often as not he disappeared. It was her belief he went off for a quiet cigarette, which he couldn't do on the job, Kingsmarkham having a ban on council workers, paid or otherwise, smoking in public places.

'Smokers are some of the worst litter offenders,' she said. 'A lot of people don't know that. They say to themselves, what's one fag end? Well, fag ends mount up. And they're not bio-whatsit, they're not destroyable.'

Wexford saw that he had a fanatic to deal with. 'But does Mr Ferry smoke?'

'Don't ask me,' Shirley Mitchell said sharply. 'I

don't want to know about his filthy habits. You asked me if he was there when I was there and I'm telling you he wasn't. We got up there in the minibus, just the four of us. He got Winchester Drive, I got Harrow Avenue and the other two got the rest of it. Well, I had my tools ready and my bag . . .'

'What tools were those?'

'We have a pole kind of thing with a spike on the end, and you can have a smaller thing like a kind of – well, not a dagger, you wouldn't call it that, more like a metal rod kind of thing with an end that's been sharpened. You can picture it, can't you, sharp so that you can stab something with it and pick it up.'

Silent for a moment, Wexford thought about Devenish and his wounds. Only a knife could have made them, not a spike with a sharpened end. But it was a strange business, far stranger than he had expected. Instead of saying any more, he asked her to excuse him for a moment and went outside. There he picked up the nearest phone and got on to Barry Vine.

'See if the council got all their tools back last Tuesday, Barry, after the morning clean-up session. And if they didn't, what was missing?'

Shirley Mitchell was sitting in his office, staring fixedly at an object which had once, many years previously, been used as an ashtray. When he came back and took his seat opposite her, she pushed the ashtray a little way further away from her as if it still presented a threat.

'So at what time would you say you last saw Mr Ferry that morning? You met at seven thirty, probably got going in the minibus at twenty-five to eight, got to the set-down point at – what? A quarter to?'

'Bit before a quarter to,' she said. 'The set-down point's in Harrow Avenue. That's my patch. The others just went off with their tools. Oh, and Ferry had a bag he was carrying.'

Wexford felt his muscles tense. 'What sort of a bag? A briefcase?'

'I wouldn't call it that. He always brings that bag. Like a canvas thing with sort of leather binding – correction, more like plastic binding. Brings his fags in it, I shouldn't wonder, and maybe a bottle. I've seen him drinking on the job. I've seen him eating sandwiches.'

She could even make this last sound like a crime. He frowned a little. 'So you didn't see him for a while after seven forty-five. When did you see him again?'

'When I got to the end of Harrow Avenue where it joins on to Winchester Drive. I'd got to the end and I was starting down the other side. He waved to me. You want to know what time it was? All of nine, if not a bit past.'

After she had gone Barry Vine told him that one of the campaign's short spiked tools had gone missing on the previous Tuesday morning. The loss hadn't been noticed until after the volunteers had been dropped on the green outside the Town Hall. Wexford sat down and reread the medical report on Stephen Devenish. He had read it at least three times before. It told him once again that Devenish's wounds had been made with a flat-bladed knife with a blade eight to ten inches long. He had taken it for granted the campaign's tool was cylindrical, with a sharpened point like a pencil. He would have to see one.

But first he set about applying for a warrant to search Ferry's house.

'He could have got there in time,' Burden said. 'He could have done it on foot, walked to Ploughman's

Lane, up the path to Woodland Lodge, rung the doorbell, gone in and done the deed by eight.'

'The time's tight, though, isn't it?' It was Wexford's idea but he was dubious just the same. 'It must have been exactly eight when he arrived because Edward and Robert got to Mrs Daley's by five past. I wouldn't call him a very fit man and it's uphill all the way.'

'A gentle slope,' said Burden. 'Even a very unfit man can walk half a mile in fifteen minutes. Once he got there he had all the time in the world. Stephen Devenish may have been killed at any time between seven forty-five and eight thirty. He could have stood there arguing with him for ten minutes before he did the deed.'

'Wouldn't Devenish have thrown him out the way he did Meeks?'

'It's not important,' Burden said airily. 'Besides, the conversation might have been amicable at first. Then they quarrelled. Surely the point is Ferry could easily have done it in the time. He had the means, the opportunity and the motive.'

'Revenge?'

'Look, Reg, we've known all along that whoever did this did it for revenge. That's the only possible motive.'

'I'm off to look at spikes,' said Wexford.

The old Midland Bank building in Brook Road was opposite the Job Centre and the Nationwide Building Society. Brutal refurbishment had removed the pillared portico and the Parthenon frieze, and replaced the front entrance with swing doors in a white metal mesh arrangement rather like a freezer basket. This was the headquarters of Kingsmarkham Domestic Environment and Landscape Department and the man-with-flowers, woman-with-spade logo was over the door.

Entering the foyer, Wexford encountered Rochelle Keenan coming out of the lift. This made very little impact on him beyond reminding him that she was some relation to his informant of the morning, Shirley Mitchell, sister or sister-in-law or something. He went upstairs to the room that housed the Clean Streets Campaign and was shown the tools supplied to the volunteers. Shirley Mitchell had described them accurately and nothing he saw much surprised him.

There was no doubt that either of these spiked implements could have been used to kill a man. The smaller one reminded Wexford of something he had never actually seen but had often read and heard about: the ice-pick, once beloved of the writers of American murder mysteries. But perhaps it didn't in fact look much like this at all.

'The missing one hasn't been returned to you?'

It had not. The woman who had shown him the tools took a philosophical view. So much went missing from the council's property, issued for various reasons to the public – went missing or was destroyed – that really she wasn't surprised more of these hadn't disappeared. Had he heard, for instance, of the fatal damage to Jodi the virtual baby?

'Fatal?' Wexford said. 'It wasn't real.'

'Maybe not.' She sounded huffy. 'But it was very valuable.'

By this time the search of Ferry's house in Oval Road would have begun. He said to Burden, 'There is no way the wounds in Stephen Devenish's chest are going to match up with one of those spikes. They are very precisely described in the medical report. It was a knife, not a spike.'

'What if you find the thing inadequately washed and wrapped up in a towel in Ferry's bedroom?'

'I doubt very much that we will. Even if we do, the

fact remains that a knife of very precise measurements was used and not a spike of any kind.'

'With Devenish cremated ...'

' "Two handfuls of white dust, shut in an urn of brass," only she won't have wasted a good brass urn on him. Makes no difference, anyway. The medical report is a marvel of precision.'

Burden looked dubiously at him. 'Then what are you going to find?'

'Possibly nothing. Possibly something unconnected with Devenish's death. You remember what you pointed out to me and I'd missed? About Gillian Ferry being a teacher at the school the Devenish boys go to?'

'Sure I do. She teaches English at the Francis Roscommon.'

'Sit down a minute, Mike.' Wexford took his seat on one side of the desk, motioned Burden to the other. He pushed away the ashtray Shirley Mitchell had moved towards his side. 'Gillian Ferry is also Robert Devenish's – well, we used to call them form mistresses, I expect there's another term now. I'm no expert in these things but I think Robert is a badly disturbed child, a child who was perhaps more affected by his father's treatment of his mother than either his brother or his sister were. Did he have anyone to confide in? Anyone to tell about the horrors that went on at home?'

'I think I see what you're getting at.'

'Yes, he had his teacher, his class teacher. Suppose he confided in her? She already had cause to hate Devenish, he was responsible for her husband losing his job and, incidentally, for forcing her back to work. Almost any woman – any man, come to that – would be moved by a child telling them his father constantly assaulted his mother. Many would be outraged and angry ...'

'Are you saying Gillian Ferry killed Devenish?'
'No, Mike. I'm saying she wrote the letters.'

# Chapter 25

It was too small a house and too sparsely furnished to give the searchers much difficulty. Less than half an hour after they began they found the spiked tool that was the property of the local authority. Trevor Ferry had made no attempt to hide it but put it into a kitchen drawer along with a hammer and a couple of screwdrivers. Technically, he had stolen it but, more realistically, he had simply taken it home by mistake. In any case, even a cursory examination of the tool made it clear that though it was capable of being used as a lethal weapon, it hadn't been so used.

The bag Ferry had carried with him the Tuesday before and yesterday could never have been described as a briefcase, even by a twelve-year-old. It was a soft, unstructured holdall, shabby and almost dilapidated, made of dark-green canvas with tan-coloured plastic binding. Wexford wasn't going to waste time showing it to Edward Devenish. Would Edward ever have mentioned a briefcase if his younger brother hadn't?

Ferry's indignation at the searching of his house was extreme and he accused Wexford of 'disloyalty' and even of 'betrayal', solely, it seemed, on the grounds that they had left a crematorium together and carried on a reasonably amicable conversation. 'I call it dirty and underhand,' he said. 'Worming details out of me under the guise of friendship.'

Wexford ignored the last bit. It was too ridiculous

to be taken seriously and reminded him of Brian St George. 'You volunteered the information, Mr Ferry,' he said mildly. 'I didn't ask you.'

'I should have known better than to open my mouth in front of you people.'

'Why did you tell me you were still in bed at eight in the morning when in fact you were out with the clean-up campaign?'

'Because that time I had the sense not to open my mouth. I knew what you'd think if I said I'd been in Winchester Drive at a quarter to eight. You already knew there was no love lost between me and Steve Devenish. I may as well say it now.'

'You told me, I quote, "He wasn't so bad." '

The blood came into Ferry's face and swelled the tissues. It even seemed to get into his eyes. 'I hated him,' he said.

'Did your wife also hate him, Mr Ferry?'

Many men would have seen the question as a hint that there might have been sexual relations or a desire for sexual relations between Devenish and Gillian Ferry. In that Ferry did not, that he hesitated and slightly narrowed his eyes, Wexford understood her husband had half guessed she had written the threatening letters.

She had been out while the search was done and knew nothing about it. The anger she suppressed burst out when she saw police in her home and she turned on Ferry, calling him a fool, a spiritless fool with no gumption. 'You're as weak as a baby! You *are* a baby, you've never begun to grow up.'

Wexford had found no evidence of the letters but he hadn't expected to do so. She would hardly have made copies and kept them in a reference file. A Word for Windows program had been used to produce them but the searchers hadn't found a computer. He would have been surprised if they had in this household where money was tight. She would have used one of the computers at the Francis Roscommon School. He showed her the letter, the last line of which threatened to make Devenish's wife a widow and his children orphans, and asked if she was its author.

She held it in her hand and took a long time reading it. He could see in her face that she admired her achievement. When she had finished she was smiling. Defiantly, she admitted authorship. 'Yes. I wrote it. I wrote a lot of letters to that man. More than a hundred. A hundred and sixteen in all, if you want to know.'

She lifted her eyes, opened them very wide so that they looked spherical. In the dark, Wexford was sure, sparks would fly from that white-blonde hair. Her face was contorted as she spoke. 'I wrote them. I enjoyed writing them. I kept them courteous, even quite formal. They all started "Dear Mr Devenish". They were in very good prose, though I doubt if he appreciated that.' Her tone made it clear she believed she had been clever and amusing. 'It was for my own pleasure, my own revenge. It made me feel better about a whole lot of things.'

Her husband stared at her, then put his head in his hands. Gillian Ferry looked at him contemptuously. 'I didn't do it out of love of *you*,' she said, 'so don't think it. I should have left you when you drank yourself out of that job, when you got sozzled every day – God knows why I didn't.'

To Wexford she said more calmly, 'It wasn't for him. At least, it was only a bit for him. Mainly it was because Devenish was such a bastard, punching his wife in the face and cutting her, and letting his kids see, wanting them to see. Robert told me, I teach Robert at school, or I tried to, but you can't teach much to a child who's living a nightmare at home. Kids like that aren't exactly receptive.'

'He told you about his father beating his mother?'

' "Beating" is a word for it, I suppose. It's not the one I'd choose. He told me how the torture started. The poor woman put a horn-handled knife in the dishwasher by mistake once and when it came out the powder or the hot water or whatever had bleached the handle. Devenish cut her for that, he cut her with the same knife.' Her eyes flashed. 'I'd like to meet the guy who killed Devenish, I'd shake him by the hand.'

Wexford cautioned her. She took no notice of his words.

'Will I go to prison?'

'Probably not.'

'Pity. I'd quite like to go to prison. It'd be a change from here and *him*, and that bloody school.'

When he got back to Kingsmarkham Lynn Fancourt was waiting for him with the news that Carl Meeks could be eliminated from the inquiry. Two people had been found who remembered seeing him in the Kingsbrook Meadows with Buster at eight a.m. on the day of the Devenish murder. Her report was on his desk but she'd like just to tell him that the witnesses weren't Carl's neighbours or among the more dubious of Kingsmarkham's citizens. Both were dog owners dog walking, the woman the proprietor of a boutique in York Street, whose premises Patrick Flay had robbed, the man a college lecturer who taught computer studies at Myringham University.

But it was really Buster who was responsible for getting Carl Meeks out of trouble. Once seen, never forgotten, as Burden had said, Buster was a dog to remember. The First Gear owner (with her spaniel) had seen him for the first time that Tuesday, she recalled it because Tuesday was her birthday and she'd wished she could ask her boyfriend for a Great Dane for a birthday present, only she already had the spaniel.

Buster got into a fight with the lecturer's Jack Russell. While gentle enough with human beings, Danes were apparently in the habit of seizing upon smaller dogs, hurling them in the air and shaking them to death. Or so the lecturer said. He had to take Jake to the vet, which was a nuisance because that Tuesday was the day he was due to begin teaching a course at a summer school in Sewingbury.

Carl Meeks was off the hook, as Burden put it.

Wexford said, 'But Ferry isn't, is he? Not really.'

'What d'you mean?'

'Just because he didn't do it with the litter spike doesn't mean he didn't do it at all. And equally, because it was his wife who wrote the letters that doesn't exonerate him. He still has no alibi. He was within walking distance of Devenish's home at the relevant time. He admits he hated the man. And there's another thing – he seems to me not to find life worth living. What has he to look forward to? His retirement pension in twenty years' time. He has no children. His wife dislikes him. His home is a tip. Maybe he did it because, like his wife, he doesn't care what happens to him, anything for a change, even prison.'

'Bit extreme, isn't it? People don't really behave like that.'

' "People don't do such things," as Ibsen says? Maybe. Anyway, we have a far more likely suspect.'

'We do?'

Wexford nodded. Then he said that he'd had it for today and how about a drink in the Olive and Dove? 'I want to tell you a story,' he said.

They walked there, the length of the High Street. It was a mild evening of hazy sunshine, humid and still. A bereavement charity was holding a wine and cheese party in St Peter's Church Hall but by the look of the trickle of visitors it was sparsely attended. Conversely, on its closure at six, crowds poured out of the Heaven Spent mall, laden with carrier bags, flushed from the triumph and deep inner fulfilment shopping brings. Wexford spotted Maria Michaels and Miroslav Zlatic among them. He thought about his lost raincoat and the dismal prospect of buying a new one, then about a previous visit to the Olive and Dove when a newspaper had taken a photograph of him with a beer tankard in his hand and printed it above a ribald legend. He had never forgotten it; he dreaded its happening again. But that had been outdoors, in the hotel garden, and this evening they would be in the quiet and seclusion of the landlord's snug.

'You're very silent,' said Burden.

'I'm thinking. Anyway, I don't think one can be "very" silent. You're either silent or you're not. It's like saying someone is very dead.'

'Like Devenish,' said Burden. 'I don't think I've ever come across a dead man so many people were glad to be dead. Not a dissenting voice.'

'I doubt if his children are glad, Mike. Children have a rare faculty of loving parents who are unworthy of their love. You might say children love their parents as a matter of course. It's sad.'

The garden of the Olive and Dove and its bar were crowded this evening, mostly with people under thirty, many probably under eighteen.

'In the United States they make you produce identification to show your age,' Burden said.

'That's fine if you've got any. If you don't have a passport or a driving licence or a rail pass, what

443

then? Don't tell me they do in America, I know that. The point is they don't here.'

No one was in the snug. It was too small and, with its only window overlooking a yard full of beer-can crates, too dimly lit to attract Kingsmarkham's youth. The three tables had marble tops and the chairs were upholstered in very worn dark-red leather. Another feature of the place, discouraging to many, was a notice on the wall which read: *Don't Even Think of Smoking Here*. You either went to the bar and queued up or rang a brass bell for service. No one came in here otherwise.

They both asked for Adnams. It arrived in glasses which pleased Wexford, though he had once preferred tankards. He hadn't drunk out of a tankard – they called them mugs in here – since that never-to-be-forgotten day. He said an unaccustomed 'Cheers' to Burden and took a long draught of his beer.

'Cheers,' said Burden. 'I've been thinking about that boy Edward, Edward Devenish. He could have killed his father. After he'd seen his mother come into the kitchen with her hand bleeding where Devenish had cut her. He could have gone into the study, picked up the knife and stabbed his father, taken him by surprise. He's a big, strong boy, though not as tall as Devenish, and it's someone shorter than Devenish we're looking for.'

'How about the blood, Mike? Did he cover up his clothes before he went in there? Or wash his clothes before he left for school? And what about Robert? Was he in it too? You're forgetting what I said about children loving their parents.'

'Maybe, but children do kill their parents, it's not unknown, patricide. Yes, by the way, why do we call the act patricide and the perpetrator a parricide?'

Wexford said rather impatiently, 'I don't know' and, uncharacteristically, 'Does it matter?' He didn't wait for an answer. 'In France when they had capital punishment, parricides were sent to the guillotine barefoot and with their faces veiled. I read that somewhere. But Edward and Robert Devenish aren't parricides.' He hesitated. 'I know who did this murder. And it wasn't any of our suspects. I think', he added reflectively and rather sadly, 'I've always known it.'

Burden simply looked at him, saying nothing.

'I said I was going to tell you a story.' Someone carried a crate of empty bottles out into the yard, dropping it with a crash. Wexford winced. 'Silent', still less 'very silent', were no longer descriptions that had much relevance. The countryside was as noisy as the town. He took another drink. Beer was still pretty good. 'Fay Devenish and her son Edward and, more or less, her son Robert, have told us a man, unknown to Edward, came to the front door of Woodland Lodge that Tuesday morning at eight a.m. Give or take a little, I suppose. It may have been two or three minutes to eight, or two or three minutes past. We also know that Stephen Devenish was stabbed to death, receiving three stab wounds to the chest, at some time between seven forty-five and eight thirty.

'The scenario goes like this: at seven thirty-five or seven forty, again give or take a little, Stephen Devenish, seriously displeased with his wife's failure to provide fresh orange juice, gets up from the breakfast table, leaves the room and goes into his study. Perhaps he shuts the door, perhaps he doesn't. Fay, her sons and her daughter Sanchia, remain in the kitchen.

'Within five minutes Devenish calls out to his wife from the study – presumably from the study doorway. He calls out, "Come in here, Fay" or even, knowing him, "Come in here, darling." She knows

445

what is going to happen and the boys probably know but she goes. She hasn't much choice, has she? If she doesn't go he'll fetch her, drag her out of there, an act of violence which Sanchia will witness.

'She goes into the study. Devenish tells her she has to be punished, she's a hopeless housewife and mother, she's mad, she has to learn and a load more of that stuff, no doubt. He tells her to hold out her hand and he cuts her across the palm. Probably she cries out. She may even scream out, loudly enough for the children in the kitchen to hear. Devenish wipes the knife clean on something – maybe his own handkerchief which she will have to wash – and tells her to go. Her hand is bleeding heavily, so she goes across the hallway into the cloakroom where she holds it under the cold tap, then wraps it in the towel that hangs there.'

'OK,' said Burden a little impatiently. 'We know all that. What's new?'

'Wait. The study door is left a little ajar. Fay goes back to the kitchen, her hand wrapped in the towel. Neither boy asks what has happened. They know. Fay tells them to get ready for school, it's their last day of term and they know they have to be at Mrs Daley's by five past eight.

'Within the next five minutes or so the boys go out into the hallway, use the lavatory, wash their hands and prepare to leave the house. The doorbell rings. Edward opens the door and there on the doorstep is a man he has never seen before. This man is about the same age as his father – that is, middle to late thirties – is wearing jeans and a jacket, and carrying a briefcase. He says he has come to see Stephen Devenish.

'Edward calls out something like, "Dad, there's someone to see you" and says to the man, "He's in there," indicating the slightly open study door. Fay, in the kitchen, also hears the man's voice but not Edward's. Possibly this is because a boy of twelve's voice is naturally higher and lighter than a mature man's. Moreover, though Edward can't remember the man's precise words, Fay can. She remembers he said, "I'm here to see Mr Devenish."

'Now, whether Devenish had come to the door by then or was still inside, unseen, we don't know. Edward can't remember and Robert is too young to be a reliable witness. But the man goes into the study, shutting the door behind him. Now, this is quite remarkable. If a stranger calls on you in your house and is shown into the room where you are, he only closes the door if asked to do so by you, doesn't he? Unless he's not a stranger but well known to you and is in fact someone accorded the privileges of a friend, at least of a familiar acquaintance.'

Burden nodded. 'I'd put it more strongly than that,' he said. 'The person coming in would either be a friend of some duration or a person in authority. I mean, I close the door behind me when I come into your office but Lynn wouldn't. On the other hand, Southby would and the Chief Constable would.'

'That's true. However, it's not relevant here. I think there's a third category. And in that category comes someone who is an acquaintance, not a friend. Indeed, it's an acquaintance who *has become an enemy* and, as an enemy, need no longer observe customary social usage or even politeness. He or she wants seclusion and silence, so he closes the door without asking permission of the man inside.

'The door shuts. The boys leave the house, closing the front door behind them. In the kitchen Fay is giving Sanchia her breakfast and trying to staunch the blood still coming from her hand. She has the breakfast dishes to put into the dishwasher and the day's washing to do, not to mention house-cleaning, bed-making, shopping and the day-long care of a three-year-old.

'She doesn't hear Devenish's visitor leave the house and, of course, she doesn't hear Devenish leave. Devenish is dead, his body lying on the study floor, with three stab wounds in his chest, including the fatal one to the heart. Fay thinks he's left for work. She tidies and cleans the kitchen, puts the breakfast things in the dishwasher and starts it, takes Sanchia out of her high-chair and gives her things to play with. At some point in the next hour or so she takes her into the playroom and puts on children's television for her or a video. Then she goes upstairs, makes the beds, gathers up the dirty washing and, along with the towel in which she wrapped her hand, takes it into the utility room and puts it in the washing machine.'

'I suppose all these household management hints are necessary?' Burden grumbled.

'I think they are.' Wexford swallowed the last of his beer, set down the glass, wondering why a glass always leaves a damp ring on a surface even when it's not wet. One of life's little mysteries, only he had the big ones to solve. 'At nine or thereabouts,' he went on, 'Fay checks on Sanchia in the playroom, perhaps puts on a new video. Then she goes into the study to clean it, carrying no doubt a duster and pushing a vacuum cleaner. She finds Devenish dead on the floor and calls us.'

'Yes, but look here,' Burden objected, 'are you saying there were two knives? The one Devenish had used to cut his wife's hand and the one the man at the door brought with him? Because, if you're not, you must be saying the man at the door brought no weapon with him, either because he didn't intend to kill Devenish or because he knew the knife would be there waiting for him, which is absurd.'

'I might be saying that he only thought of killing Devenish when he saw his opportunity in the form of the knife. Perhaps because Devenish said something insupportable to him, he picked up the knife and stabbed him.'

'Well, OK, perhaps. But who was he, this mysterious man no one recognised but who had the authority or the familiarity to close Devenish's study door behind him?'

'First of all,' said Wexford, 'I'd like to talk about the knife − or, rather, the knives. But let's have another drink, shall we? Ring the bell.'

Feeling like someone in a Victorian mystery story, literature his wife sometimes encouraged him to read, Burden picked up the brass bell and gave it three vigorous shakes. There should have been a candle on the table in one of those metal candlesticks with a snail-shaped handle, or at least an oil lamp. The snug looked as if it hadn't seen a coat of paint on its grimy ochre walls and dark-brown woodwork since such a story was first published. The barman came. He was a man who could only have lived at the end of the twentieth century with the ring in his pierced lip, matted dreadlocks and endangered-species tiger-face logo on the back of his hand.

But he had a pleasant manner and an old-fashioned politeness, and he took their order cheerfully, returning in only a few moments with the two glasses and a free packet of cashews, compliments of the management.

'I don't suppose taking these smells of corruption, do you?' Wexford said after the man had gone. 'It won't make us look more favourably on him at the next Brewster Sessions.' He laughed. 'Now, the knives. We both know that the knife block is made to hold eight knives but it contained only seven. However, the remaining slot is too small and short to have contained a knife wide enough or long enough in the blade to have made Devenish's wounds. There was no eighth knife, and when Fay told us there never had been an eighth knife because to insert one made the block too crowded and inhibited the removal of any of the others, she was speaking the truth.'

'We've been through that before.'

'All right. We have. Of those seven knives, all have horn handles, but five of the handles are dark brown and two a much lighter brown, almost a fawn colour. Now this is the effect of putting horn handles into a dishwasher and through a very hot wash. I know. I've tried it and Dora wasn't too pleased with me when she saw what I'd done.'

'Shame,' Burden mocked, 'and when it was all in the cause of justice and truth.'

Ignoring him, Wexford went on, 'Edward Devenish has told me that he knew this happened *to one of the knives* in the block and Gillian Ferry has told me that for this – that is, putting a horn-handled knife through a hot wash – Devenish cut Fay's hand. In fact, it seems that this was the first time he cut Fay and the damage to the knife put the idea into his head.'

'But only one knife, not two?'

'Gillian, quoting Robert, spoke of just one. But there were two. So when was the second knife put through the hot wash? Not, surely, *before* Devenish's death. Fay was often enough punished for nothing, she wasn't going to stick her neck out committing an offence for which she was deliberately cut across the hand the first time.'

'Right. And why was it put through the dishwasher?' Burden answered his own question. 'Presumably, because such a wash, extending over –

what? Forty minutes? – would effectively have removed any blood and any prints that might be on it.'

'Certainly its blade matches Stephen Devenish's wounds,' Wexford said. 'Don't you want to know who the man at the door was?'

'I know you well enough to be quite aware that you'll only tell me when you're ready.'

Wexford grinned. He drank from the new Adnams, nodded. 'Remember, according to Edward, it was a man of about thirty-six or seven, tall but not so tall as his father, wearing jeans and a jacket, and carrying a briefcase. Now there is a woman involved in all this whom, when I first saw her, because of her hair and her lack of make-up and her height, and her thinness and her clothes, I took for a man. Very briefly, a matter of seconds rather than minutes, but I took her for a man.'

'Jane Andrews,' said Burden.

'Without being in the least unattractive or what used to be called "mannish",' Wexford said, 'she can make herself look like a man. She's flat-chested, she's tall, she has the right haircut. These days women's jackets and men's are scarcely different from one another. Jeans are the same for men and women. Let us suppose that Jane Andrews dressed herself in her jeans and jacket, and perhaps added some other masculine touches, men's shoes in a size seven – her size, anyway, I'd guess – a white shirt? A tie? Edward says the man wore a tie. And the briefcase. Most people still associate briefcases with men, though the concept is slowly changing. That would be enough.

'She leaves the house in Brighton at seven or seven-fifteen. Her mother is still in bed asleep and likely to remain so for a couple of hours. There is no one else to see her go or care whether she goes or not. She arrives in Ploughman's Lane, a place she knows very well, though she hasn't been there for years.

'She parks somewhere. Maybe in Ploughman's Close or even down the hill to where it meets Winchester Drive. She walks to Woodland Lodge, carrying her briefcase, in which she has a thin, lightweight raincoat and a weapon, for she intends to kill Stephen Devenish. That is the purpose of her visit.'

'Then what happened . . . ?'

'To the other knife? The one used to cut Fay and which she afterwards put through the hot wash? Wait. Presumably Jane brought a knife with her or even a gun. Why she chose that time of day I don't know. Perhaps she had already tried to set up a meeting alone with him outside the house but he had refused even to speak to her.'

'Her motive, of course, is her affection for and sympathy with Fay Devenish?'

'That and the rage she felt, and has felt for years, against Devenish. Perhaps, too, her empathy with her sister Louise Sharpe . . .'

'It would be a very illogical empathy,' Burden said hotly. 'Devenish may have been a villain and a miscreant but no one could say he was to blame for Louise Sharpe's problems.'

Wexford sighed. 'We're talking about emotion, Mike, not logic.' He paused, looked down at the table, then said, 'Jane Andrews rang the doorbell and the door was opened almost immediately by Edward. She recognised him, of course, but he didn't recognise her. Why would he? He hadn't seen her for years and when he last saw her *she had long hair*. Mrs Probyn told us that her daughter used to have "lovely long hair". No doubt Jane deepened her voice for the few words she had to speak to Edward, not a very difficult undertaking. She already has a deep voice for a woman.

'She goes into the study and for a moment he doesn't know who this stranger is. He says hallo or something and what can he do for her – well, him, as he thinks. She speaks in her normal voice and then he does recognise her ...'

'Why doesn't he throw her out?'

'I don't know, Mike. There are a few loose ends to tie up. The point is that he doesn't. Maybe he welcomes a confrontation. He may suspect she and Fay were still in touch, he may know that they were and he wants to tell her what he'll do if she doesn't stop communicating with his wife. And we know what that might be, don't we? More and severer punishment for Fay. Or he may prefer to deny what Jane says or tell her she's mad, a favourite retort with him. One thing you can be sure of, he doesn't think she's come to kill him.

'What he says drives her over the edge. A knife is lying on the desk. She has a weapon with her but why use that when one is here to hand? She picks it up, catches Devenish unawares and stabs him.

'She wipes the knife – on what? Her own clothes perhaps, which in any case will already be splashed with blood – puts it back on the table, having guessed why it was there and what it was used for *and knowing that in due course Fay will take it away and wash it*. She knows her Fay.

'She puts on the raincoat she has brought with her and leaves the house, picks up the car, drives home, where her mother is still in bed. How's that? It covers everything, I think.'

'Yes, it does. It's the only solution that does.'

Burden lifted his glass. 'Well, congratulations, if that's appropriate.'

Wexford nodded. He didn't drink.

'The only drawback', he said, 'is that it isn't true.'

# Chapter 26

The new raincoat looked uncomfortably new. Yet it wasn't uncomfortable but an excellent fit, the right breadth on the shoulders, the right length. Burden would have enjoyed wearing it. Mystifyingly, Burden loved new clothes, the pleasure of putting them on for the first time, of seeing himself look elegant. Wexford could never understand it. Part of the trouble for him was the newness, the *looking* new. He wasn't a self-conscious man, nor shy, nor desirous of making an impression, but in new clothes he felt everyone was looking at him. With a kind of nostalgia, he thought of his old raincoat, so comfortable, so pleasantly worn, so mildly battered. He even loved the ineradicable small stain, the heart-shaped blotch of something unanalysable that defied the efforts of dry-cleaners.

But once again it was raining. The warm, dryish weather had lasted no more than a day. He would have to wear it, make a start, break it in. The faint sheen on its fabric, the stiffness of its lapels, discomfited him.

On the phone to Burden he said, 'If we have even a week's dry spell after all this rain the water moguls will say we're in drought and put on a hose-pipe ban. You see if I'm not right.'

'What are you really ringing me about, Reg?'

'How well you know me.'

'Perhaps. So what's new?'

Wexford told him, in a sombre voice and with a heavy heart. But Burden knew already. He'd see him later and never mind, what must be, must be. Justice must be done.

The rain was so heavy that Donaldson had to stop the car in Winchester Drive, pull under the trees and wait for it to abate a little. Wexford, in the back, not even bothering to clear a space with his hand in the steamy window, sat thinking whether there was anything he could say, any hint he could give, any adumbration of the terrible risks involved, without jeopardising his career and his very job. Through his head ran such phrases as 'mandatory life sentence' and 'provocation beyond bearing'. The rain crashed on the car roof. Condensation trickled down the glass. 'Give it another go, will you?' he said with unaccustomed roughness. 'We can't sit here all day.'

As he spoke the rain diminished a little. The roar lessened. The wipers could just cope with the flow down the windscreen. Donaldson started the car and drove slowly up the hill, sending fountains of water on to the pavements as the wheels rolled through puddles. In the driveway, an overhanging branch brushed against the car and sent down a cascade of water.

The rendering on the walls of Woodland Lodge was stained dark grey with water. A puddle lay at the foot of the front doorstep and Wexford was faced either with an undignified jump or the prospect of inundated shoes. He jumped. Lynn Fancourt's small leap was more elegant. The bell rang hollowly through the house. He must have rung this bell a dozen times but he had never noted its loudness before, nor the echo that seemed to follow it. At any rate, he reflected while he waited, that cuckoo was gone.

Jane Andrews came to the door with Sanchia close behind her. In a long skirt and silk jumper, she looked very unlike a man today. Her hair seemed longer and a hairdresser had put blonde highlights in it. 'She's expecting you,' she said, then, 'She knows why you've come.'

'Thanks,' he said because he didn't know what else to say.

'I'm going to take the children out. In the car somewhere. I'll think of somewhere we can go in the rain.'

The house looked like a place people lived in, women and children lived in, no longer like a country house interiors museum. Someone's cardigan hung over the banisters. The flowers in the big Chinese vase were dying. In the big living-room where Fay Devenish sat alone books were scattered on the coffee table among two or three days' newspapers. She jumped up when he and Lynn came in.

'Please sit down, Mrs Devenish.'

In a slow, sad voice, not at all hysterical, she said calmly, 'You know, don't you? I knew you would. I just want you to know I wouldn't have let anyone else take the blame for this. I mean, if you'd arrested someone else I'd have stopped it.'

'I'm sure you would.'

'I killed Stephen, of course I did. Didn't you always know?'

He wouldn't admit to her that in his heart he had indeed always known. At any rate, had always feared. It was really that he hadn't wanted to face up to it. Had he, of all people, been wasting police time these past few days?

He said quietly, 'There was no man, no stranger who came to the door. It was just the story that any frightened person would invent, it's the first thing

457

that comes into one's head. It came into your head and into your son Edward's – perhaps *because* you're mother and son – only he went further than you did. He gave the mystery man an appearance: height and clothes and an age. You only gave him a voice.' He cleared his throat. 'Edward loves you, you see. He didn't think twice about lying for you. That morning, when he was at school and the head teacher came and told him, I think he knew then that you'd killed his father. It was so obvious to him. He'd have done it himself – one day.'

Lynn made a small sound behind him, a little indrawing of the breath. Fay had been looking at him impassively but when he spoke of her son her lip trembled. He knew he was talking to postpone the incriminating confession she would soon make.

'No one came to the door,' he said. 'Edward invented that, not knowing that you'd also invented it. He and Robert left for school but by then, for ten minutes before that, your husband was dead. Your husband took the knife from the knife block after breakfast and took it into the study. That's how you knew what he would do when he called you in. You killed him after he cut you with the knife.'

'Yes,' she said.

'Did he cry out? Scream?' She wasn't going to answer him. 'It would have made no difference if he had. If Edward and Robert and Sanchia had all heard him. It would simply have been a change to hear a cry from him instead of from you.'

He saw her wince. A conviction for murder, he thought, carries a mandatory life sentence. Self-defence doesn't always work, often doesn't work. If a woman gives evidence of repeated abuse and it is known that on the final occasion she reacted by killing, a jury is going to want to know what was so special about the last time. Why kill then when in the past she had borne the abuse passively? Pick up a knife and kill an unarmed man? That's murder. It's just as much murder as if a stranger came up to him in the street and stabbed him. And murder carries a mandatory life sentence, there's no choice about it, no second- and third-degree murder such as they have in the United States. Here murder is murder and the punishment is life.

'I am going to take you back with me now, Mrs Devenish, and you will of course want a solicitor to be present.'

'Are you arresting me?'

'Of course.'

'This is what I'm going to say. Stephen always said I was – was mentally unstable and he was right. That morning he cut me and I went mad, I lost control, I don't know what I did or why I did it. I must have just grabbed the knife and stabbed him in a frenzy. I don't remember it, it's all a blur, it was then. They say you see red. I did, I just saw red in front of my eyes. I lost my mind. I didn't even see him when I struck out.' She stared at him as if she saw red now and her whole body shook. 'I went mad,' she said.

He felt an inward sigh relax him. She might be lying, but he didn't care. If she stuck to that story – and her solicitor, her counsel, would love it – she would be saved.

'Jane will look after my children,' she said in the most tranquil tone he had ever heard her use. 'I know I may not see them for a long time. They will be fine with Jane.'

# Chapter 27

In the months that followed the hunt went on for Ted Hennessy's killer but inquiries had reached a stalemate. It was known that the petrol bomb had been thrown by John Keenan or Joe Hebden but neither of them would give evidence against the other and no one admitted possessing or handling one of the bombs.

In the middle of October Brenda Bosworth took her three children out of school for a week and up to Clacton for a holiday in her mother's caravan. As soon as she was out of the way, Miroslav Zlatic and Maria Michaels were married in the new Bridal Bower at the Cheriton Forest Hotel with the maximum of celebration and the minimum of secrecy. Heavily pregnant Lizzie Cromwell, along with her mother, attended the wedding and the buffet lunch afterwards, not at all upset. For, as she told everyone over the Spanish champagne, Miroslav had only got married for the sake of British citizenship and Maria was years and years older than him.

Two weeks later she gave birth to a daughter in the maternity wing of the Princess Diana Memorial Clinic and named her Millennia. During the single day and night Lizzie was in there Colin Crowne, who had been consoling Brenda for Miroslav's defection, moved in with her. Debbie said there was no way she was going to live three doors away from that pair, but instead of 16 Oberon Road (now tenanted by cousins of the Meekses) Kingsmarkham Housing Department, delighted to repossess 45 Puck Road, allotted her and Lizzie and Millennia a two-bedroom flat in Glebe Close.

Further reshuffling took place in the tower when John Keenan finally accumulated enough money to buy DNA testing equipment, used it and proved he was not the biological father of the redheaded Winona. He rented a room in the Mitchells' house – strictly against Kingsmarkham housing rules – while determining his future. Shirley Mitchell, though his wife's sister, was entirely on his side. Her husband was seriously worried about her since she had taken to grabbing and shaking any child she came upon dropping a chocolate bar wrapper or crisp packet in the street. Sooner or later she would hit one of them and get taken to the European Court of Human Rights.

Doing very well at the University of Myringham and showing a particular aptitude for social sciences, Tasneem Fowler had also been rehoused. Kings-markham Housing eventually gave her a 'studio' flat quite near where Debbie and Lizzie Cromwell lived. At their divorce hearing she and Terry were awarded joint custody of Kim and Lee but Terry got care. The two boys, asked with whom they would prefer to live, opted for their father.

Tracy Miller made so much money working from morning till night that she set up her own house-cleaning business with ten employees, called it Tracy's Treasures, and put down a deposit on a house for herself and her daughters in Eton Road.

One morning, leaving a house in Ariel Road which the occupants had been using as the headquarters of a cocaine-dealing syndicate, Wexford saw a man come out of the tower wearing a Burberry. It was a fawn-coloured raincoat with a heart-shaped stain at the hem on the left-hand side. It took him a few seconds to identify the man as Peter McGregor, partner of Sue Ridley, once the Crownes' neighbour in Puck Road. What he had been doing in the tower Wexford didn't know and, seeing the general goings-on, perhaps it was just as well he didn't. McGregor gave him a calm, innocent stare before looking away. Wexford knew he couldn't prove anything. Besides, he had the new one now, no longer new, really, but becoming comfortably battered and even very slightly stained.

He had another call to make, this time in Harrow Avenue. Donaldson drove him there but he was early, so he walked up the hill and saw, with some undefined satisfaction, that the estate agent had put a 'Sold' sign up at the gate of Woodland Lodge. Good. It was hers, in her name. If it had been Stephen Devenish's God knew if she would ever have got the money, seeing that no one may benefit from his or her crime.

Now, nine months after Stephen Devenish's death, she was living in Brighton, she and her children, in a house she had bought next door but one to Jane Andrews. She would still live with and carry through her life the stigma of a conviction for manslaughter. Her plea of diminished responsibility, that she had gone mad and scarcely knew what she was doing, had saved her and she had received no more than probation.

Sentencing her, the judge said, 'We are taught that we should not speak ill of the dead. *De mortuis nil nisi bonum*. Of the dead nothing but good. There must be exceptions to that axiom. Stephen Devenish was a hard worker, a good provider and, I believe, an honest man. He was also, in other respects, a monster. This woman lived a life of unimaginable suffering, abuse and torture at the hands of a miscreant who used her as a punchbag for his sadistic impulses.'

Louise Sharpe had remarried. Her husband was the man who had rescued her when she attempted suicide by walking into the sea. Six months pregnant, she expected the birth of her baby at the end of July.

Revengeful as ever, Rochelle Keenan went to the police with the film she had made of the Kingsmarkham riot, claiming that it showed beyond a doubt that it was her husband John who had thrown the petrol bomb that killed Detective Sergeant Hennessy. Burden, who confronted her, was a little taken aback. He thought he had seen everything, become hardened to everything and that nothing remained to astonish him. But a wife endeavouring to secure for her husband life imprisonment merely because he resented a cuckoo in his nest, that shook him. He put the film on his video transmitter – what else could he do? He was almost glad when the picture that appeared wasn't much of an improvement on a store's closed circuit television, grainy grey images of barely recognisable people. He certainly saw someone throw a bottle with a rag stuffed into its neck – he saw three men throwing bottles and a woman throwing a brick – but whose hand these missiles came from he had no idea at all.

Still, he would keep trying to find Hennessy's killer. He would never give up, he said.

'When you're dead,' said Wexford, 'and they open you up, they'll find *Get Hennessy's Killer* written on your heart.'

'I hope they'll find *He Did* written underneath.'

'We all hope that, Mike,' Wexford said.

These days he often found himself in sombre mood. Sylvia and Neil had at last decided to divorce.

Strangely, they got on better since they had come to this decision than they had for years and sometimes Wexford hoped that this new accord might lead to reunion. They were still living in the same house, if on different floors of it, the old rectory being quite large enough to accommodate this arrangement. The children knew but showed no signs of minding while both parents were under the same roof. It would be a different story, Wexford thought, when Neil moved out.

Or when there was someone else for Neil or for Sylvia? 'An intervener', as Stephen Devenish had called it, in another context. Dora took the attitude that while they were still together, nothing was decided, nothing was definite. But he, when he considered it quietly to himself, asked how he would feel about this pair if they were not his own daughter and son-in-law, the parents of his grandsons. If they were strangers, wouldn't he perhaps think the best course for everyone's ultimate happiness was an absolute separation?

Sylvia was in the house when he got home that evening. He never mentioned the imminent divorce unless she did. She usually did, particularly when she could take advantage of the children's being out with their father to list Neil's manifold faults and sometimes, to do her justice, her own. But this evening she gave him an especially loving kiss when he came in and said she had something to tell him, she had a confession to make.

Wexford's heart sank a little. If her mother had been in the room this couldn't have happened. Neither daughter cared to shock their mother, knowing her tongue could be rough and her opinions strong. But they told their father anything. He was unshockable, or so they believed, and now he was afraid she was going to tell him she had a lover. Or had met someone who would soon be her lover. Or Neil had a girlfriend. Things of that sort – what else could a confession be?

Something quite different.

'Dad,' she said, 'do you remember once saying to me that you couldn't imagine me breaking the law?'

'I think so,' he said guardedly.

'Well, I don't know if I have broken the law but I may have covered up a crime.' She looked at him warily. 'I can't remember if I ever told you how, when I was first working for The Hide helpline, a woman calling herself Anne phoned. Her husband was out in the garden with the baby, she said, and then she saw him coming in and she was afraid of being found talking to me.'

'Maybe you did. Very discreetly, I'm sure.'

'Yes, well, that must have been last April. She was terrified of her husband but like so many of them she wouldn't leave. Her name wasn't Anne at all, of course it wasn't, they do give false names. Well, she phoned again but what she had to say was quite different. He wasn't abusing her any more, all that had stopped, she didn't say why. She said she wanted to ask me about the law relating to – well, to abused women who kill their husbands.'

'Go on.'

'First of all I said I wasn't a lawyer, I couldn't help her. I said The Hide had the services of a solicitor – we have, she does it for free – who would advise her if she'd like to ring this number. And I was going to give her the number when she said she wouldn't do that, she didn't want that, all she wanted was to know what was the best *excuse* a woman could use if she killed her husband. Could she plead self-defence?'

A gentle chill, not unpleasurable, ran through Wexford's body. 'So what's this confession?'

465

Sylvia looked at him speculatively. 'I told her – what I knew. What I'd learnt, that is, when I had my couple of days training for working there. I said that if a woman used a knife or a gun to kill an unarmed man or a sleeping man she couldn't use self-defence. And that was because no matter what he'd threatened to do to her in future or what had happened in the past, the "criterion of immediacy" for manslaughter – I remembered that phrase – wouldn't be there. A jury might be understanding but they couldn't acquit her and she'd get life imprisonment because that's the sentence that's mandatory for murder.'

'And?'

'She said, but what about being provoked to it beyond bearing. I said to forget all that. The only thing was to plead guilty to manslaughter on the grounds of diminished responsibility. In other words, a woman goes mad, picks up the gun or whatever and loses control. You'll always be stamped a criminal, but you probably won't go to prison. That's what I said.

'And then, a few months later, that woman I recognised as abused in the photo came up in court and pleaded guilty to manslaughter on the grounds of diminished responsibility and it all came back to me what I'd said. I knew then, I just *knew* Fay Devenish was Anne and I'd told her how to avoid a life sentence for murder. And my own father was the investigating officer in the case.

'I've wanted to tell you for ages but I've only just plucked up the courage.'

Wexford drew a deep breath. So much depended on when this phone call had been made. Stephen Devenish had died on the morning of 29 July. 'When was this, Sylvia?'

'*When* was it? Let's see. It was ten at night, I do

remember that. The end of July, I think. The children's school had broken up.'

'When did they break up?'

'I don't remember. "Anne" probably phoned on a Wednesday or a Friday because those are the nights I usually work. I mean, there are exceptions but there weren't that week. I've checked. Dad, tell me, have I done something dreadful?'

Seriously perturbed now, Wexford went to find last year's calendar. He always kept calendars for a year or two. If "Anne" had made that phone call before 29 July it meant Fay Devenish's attack on her husband had not been a reaction to his cutting her – perhaps he hadn't cut her, perhaps she had cut herself – but premeditated murder, planned possibly for a long time. Wexford closed his eyes, opened them, found the calendar in his desk pigeon-hole and took it with him, reading it on the way, nearly falling down the bottom four stairs.

'Tell me, Dad,' Sylvia said. 'Don't keep me in suspense.'

'The twenty-ninth, when Stephen Devenish died, was a Tuesday. That was the day school broke up. Your punctilious mother has written it on the calendar. It must have been a Wednesday or a Friday when Fay Devenish phoned you, so it was either Wednesday the thirtieth or Friday, August the first.' He gave her a half-smile. 'You're off the hook.'

'Thank God,' she said, 'but I did tell her how to get herself off the hook.'

'I know. But by then he was already dead. Sylvia . . .' He went over to her and took her hand. 'There's no harm done.'

467

# GOING WRONG

To Fredrik
and Lilian

# CHAPTER
## ONE

---

S he always had lunch with him on Saturdays. This always happened, was an absolute, unless one of them was away. It was as certain as that the sun would rise in the morning, sparks fly upward and water find its own level. He found comfort and reassurance in it when things were bad. Whatever else might happen to bring him doubts and make him afraid, he knew she would have lunch with him on Saturday.

Usually, when he went to meet her at one o'clock on Saturday, he was optimistic. This time he might persuade her to have dinner with him one evening in the week or let him take her to a theatre. She might agree to see him before next Saturday. One day she would, she was bound to, it was only a matter of time. She loved him. There had never been anyone else for either of them.

When he repeated those words to himself as he walked to their meeting, he felt a tremor of apprehension. His heart misgave him. He remembered what he had seen. Then he told himself for the hundredth time that it was all right, he was

1

worrying unnecessarily. He held up his head and braced himself.

He was on his way to a wine bar quite near to where he had first met her. She had chosen it, knowing he would have picked somewhere expensive. If he arrived in a taxi she would remind him of his wealth, so he was on foot, having got out of his cab at the top of Kensington Church Street. He was wealthy by the standards of all but the really rich, and seemed a millionaire in the eyes of most of the people she knew. Lefty, 'green' do-gooders, who thought there was something morally proper about not having a freezer or a microwave, about going on camping holidays and riding a bike. He could have given her anything she wanted. With him she could have a beautiful life.

She would come to their meeting by walking along the Portobello Road. Its picturesqueness appealed to her, the Saturday stalls, the hubbub, the people. That was what he disliked, it reminded him too much of the bad parts of his childhood and youth, of what he had left behind. Instead he took the long austere Kensington Park Road, the wide impersonal avenue which led northwards. The trees were dark green and dusty with high summer. It was hot, the sun white on the pavements, the air above the tarmac distorted into dancing glassy waves by the heat. She disliked his sunglasses, she said they made him look like a mafioso, so he would take them off when he came into the darkness of the restaurant. He was hoping they would meet this side of the restaurant, she coming from the west, from where she lived on the other side of Ladbroke Grove. Then she would see he hadn't come in a cab.

He glanced down the mews on the left. He couldn't help it, though it hurt him rather, bringing a sweet and bitter nostalgia. In one of those pink-painted, window-boxed dolls' houses she had lived with her parents, the one with the balcony like a firegrate and a front door white as whipped cream. It was as if she had chosen this place for their lunch today to torment him. Only she was not the kind who did things like that. The point was she had no idea it would torment him, she no longer

2

understood how he felt, and he had to make her understand. He had to make her feel the way she used to feel about him when she passed the block of council flats where *he* had grown up, a few streets away in Westbourne Park. For a moment he wondered what it would be like to know that she yearned for him as he did for her, that the mere sight of a place where he had lived would bring to her a rush of memories and tenderness and longing for the sweetness of the past. He thought stoutly, I can make her feel like that again.

When he was fourteen and she was eleven they had wandered these streets. His gang. Not innocent children at all, tough kids, white and black, big for their ages most of them, brilliant shoplifters, inveterate smokers of marijuana. Those were the early days of his dealing and very well he had done at it, made a little fortune leading schoolchildren astray. They were rich, some of those schoolkids, with parents living on the 'right side' of Holland Park Avenue. His mother had never known or cared where he was so long as he didn't bother her, and why would he? He was five feet ten and shaving, taking a girl of eighteen about, still going to school most days, but rich enough to forget about all that. Taxis were what he used for transport when he wasn't driving his girlfriend's car.

But she . . . He had loved her from the first, from the moment she came down Talbot Road and stood there on the corner watching them, four of them sitting on the wall having their first joint of the evening. She was small and very young, with a grave face, hungry for experience. The others weren't interested but he went on looking at her and she went on looking at him, it was love at first sight for both of them, and when the joint came round to him he stuck it on a pin and handed it to her and said, 'Here – don't be shy.'

Those were the first words he ever said to her. 'Here – don't be shy.' So gently he said them that Linus had given him his long Muhammad Ali look and spat in the gutter. She took the joint and put it to her lips, made it wet of course, they always did the first time. But she wasn't sick, she didn't do anything stupid, just gave him that heart-breaking smile of hers that ended with a small giggle.

3

Her parents stopped it a month later. They stopped what they called 'playing in the street'. It was dangerous, anything might happen to her. Of course they went on meeting, he and she, after school, on the way to school and the way back. There had never been a time since then when he hadn't known her, gaps of course, three and four months long, when she was at college, but never a real separation. No separation of her from him was possible, he told himself as he came into the wine bar and went down the spiral staircase.

He paused to take off his sunglasses. The place had a thirties theme and the music they were playing was a selection from Astaire and Rogers movies. All around the walls were photographs of old film stars like Clark Gable and Loretta Young and long-forgotten people that meant nothing to him. She was there already, she was sitting at the bar with an orange juice talking to the French boy who was the barman there. He wasn't jealous. He liked looking at her when she was unaware of being watched.

She was a very dark girl in the way Celts can be dark, which is not at all the way of Indians or Middle Eastern people or even the Spanish. Her skin was always brown, summer and winter, but now in a hot summer she was deeply tanned. None of her features was beautiful, except her dark blue eyes, but they added up to beauty, to something entirely pleasing and satisfying. They made you say, this is how a nice, good, intelligent, interesting woman of twenty-six should look. Her face in profile was what he saw now, the small straight nose, the chin that was slightly too big, lips that were a red rose petal and its mirror image, the eyebrows that flew off into her hairline. Her hair was a page's in a Rossetti painting. Her mother had once said that, her *mother*. It was the darkest that brown can be without being black, hanging just below her ears like a metal bell, a fringe cut across her forehead. She was in white, white shorts to the knees, white shirt with big sleeves rolled up, a belt that was red, white and blue joining them up but slack on her tiny waist. Her brown legs were very long, long enough and shapely enough to wear thick white socks and trainers and still look beautiful. Those absurd earrings!

Black vases with double handles, like something out of the mummy's tomb. They moved him, those earrings, to an unbearable tenderness.

The barman must have whispered something to her. She turned round. He would have given anything to see delight dawn on her face, to have seen her face as his would be when he saw hers. If only he could have deluded himself that her expression was not – dismay. Gone at once, wiped away by duty and politeness and the decent goodness that was so much a part of her character, but there first of all. Dismay. Disappointment that he was there already, that he hadn't been late or sent at the eleventh hour a message that he couldn't come. It felt like a long thin pin going into his heart. Then he deluded himself. He was imagining it. She was pleased to see him. Why else make and keep these regular Saturday arrangements? Look at her smile! Her face was suddenly radiant.

'Hallo, Guy,' she said.

When first he saw her, even when she had spoken to him, he found it hard to speak. For a moment. He took her extended hand and kissed first her left cheek, then her right. As he might kiss any woman friend. And he felt her lips move in the accepted way against his left cheek, his right.

'How are you?' He had managed it. The ice that held the back of his tongue frozen was broken.

'I'm fine.'

'Will you have a real drink now?'

She shook her head. Wine she would drink sometimes, spirits never, and she mostly kept to fruit juices and fizzy water. It was a long time since the days when, after school, they had sat on a gravestone in Kensal Green Cemetery drinking the brandy Linus said fell off the back of a lorry. You can drink a lot of brandy when you are eighteen and fifteen. Your heads are strong and your stomachs made of iron.

He asked the barman for another orange juice and a vodka and tonic. Somewhere in the world there must be perfect sun-ripened oranges without seeds, oranges as big as grapefruits and sweet as heather honey. Those were the ones they should have here to squeeze for her into a tall crystal glass, frosted white all over from a freezer, a glass from Waterford, precious, chased with leaves and flowers, which would be smashed when she had drunk the contents. Thinking of it made him smile. She asked him what amused him and began frowning when he explained.

'Guy, I want you to stop thinking about me like that. Stop thinking of me in those terms.'

'What terms are those then?' he said.

'Romantic fantasy. It has nothing to do with the world we actually live in. It's like a fairy story.'

'I don't only think of you like that.' He looked deeply at her, spoke in a slow, measured and reasonable way. 'I believe I think of you in every possible way a man can think of a woman he loves. I think of you as the nicest girl I know and the most beautiful. I think of you as unique, as clever and gifted, and everything a girl should be. I think of you as my wife and the mother of my children, sharing everything I have and growing old with me, and me being as much in love with you in fifty years' time as I am now. That's how I think of you, Leonora, and if you can tell me any other ways a man can think of the brightest star in his heaven, well, I'll do those too. Does that satisfy you?'

'Satisfy me! It isn't a question of satisfying me.'

He knew she had heard that speech of his before, or something very like it. He had composed it long ago, learnt it by heart. It was nonetheless true for that and what else could he say but the truth? 'Please you then. I want to please you. But I don't have to say that again, you know that.'

'I know I'm not going to be your wife, I'm not going to be the mother of your children.' She looked up when the orange juice came, gave the barman the smile that should have been his. 'I've told you enough times, Guy. I've tried to tell you nicely. I've tried to be honest and behave properly about this. Why won't you believe me?'

He didn't answer. He raised his eyes and looked sombrely at her. Perhaps she took this heavy look of his for a reproach, for she spoke impatiently.

'What is it now?'

It was hard for him but he had to ask. If he didn't ask now he would do so later. If not today, he would ask tomorrow on the phone. Better ask now. Better to know. He had to know what he must fight against, if he had an adversary. His throat dried a little. He badly didn't want his voice to be hoarse.

'Who is he?'

His voice *was* hoarse. He sounded as if someone had him by the throat. She was surprised. He had caught her off guard.

'What?'

'I saw you with him. Walking along Ken High Street. It was last Tuesday or Wednesday.' He was pretending, in a breathless voice, a casualness he didn't feel. It was not only the day that he knew, indelibly, but the hour, the precise time to the minute, the precise spot. He could find it if he was to go there now, as if their footprints were engraved in the pavement. He thought he could find it blindfolded or in his sleep. And he could see them, the two of them, images petrified in his memory, their happy faces – no, not that, he was inventing that – outside the Kensington Market.

'A little runt of a fellow,' he said, and now he was savage. 'Ginger hair. Who is he?'

She hadn't wanted him to know. That gave a scrap of comfort. Her cheeks reddened. 'His name's William Newton.'

'And what is he to you?'

'You've no right to ask me these questions, Guy.'

'I have a right. I'm the only person on earth who has a right.'

He thought she might dispute that but she only said sulkily, 'OK, but don't make such a big thing of it. Remember, you did ask, so you have to accept the answer.' Did she know how that made his heart fall through his body? He looked at her, holding his breath. 'I've known him for about two years as a matter of fact. We've been going about together for a year. I like him very much.'

'What does that mean?'

'What I say. I like him a lot.'

'Is that all?'

'Guy, this is very hard for me to talk about when you look at

7

me like that, William is becoming important to me and I am to him. There, now you know.'

'Is he your lover?'

'Does it matter? Yes. Yes, of course he is.'

'I don't believe it!'

She tried to say it lightly. 'Why not? Aren't I attractive enough to have a lover? I'm only twenty-six, I'm not bad-looking.'

'You're beautiful. I don't mean that. I mean him. Look at him. Five feet six, sandy-haired, a face like a zebra without the stripes – and what's a zebra without stripes? What does he do? Has he got any money? No, don't answer that. I could see he hasn't. A poverty-stricken ginger dwarf, I don't believe it. What do you see in him? For Christ's sake, what do you see in him?'

She said equably, looking at the menu, not even looking up, 'Do you really want to know?'

'Certainly I want to know. I'm asking you.'

'Conversation.' She lifted her eyes. He thought she sighed a little. 'If he talked to me all day and I never heard another person talk as long as I lived, I'd never get bored. He's the most interesting man I ever knew. There, Guy, you did ask.'

'And I'm boring?'

'I didn't say that. I said that to me you're not as interesting as William. Not just you, no one is. You asked me why I go about with him and I told you. I fell in love with William for the things he says and – well, for his mind, it's as simple as that.'

'You fell in love?' Oh, the horror of uttering those words! He would have expected to die before he spoke them, or that speaking them would kill him. He felt weak and his hands went out of control. 'You're in love with him?'

She said formally, 'I am.'

'Oh, Leonora, you can say that to *me*?'

'You asked me. What am I supposed to do? Tell lies?'

Oh, yes, tell lies, tell me any lie rather than this awful truth. 'And you go to bed with him for his conversation?'

'You want to make it sound ridiculous, I know that, but, yes, oddly enough, in a way I do.'

8

She ordered melon with prosciutto without the prosciutto, followed by pasta. He had gamba and tournedos Rossini. He made an effort to speak, to say anything, and succeeded only in sounding like some scolding chaperone. 'I wish you'd have a decent meal for once. I wish you'd have something expensive.'

He could tell she was relieved he had changed the subject, or she thought he had. The truth was he couldn't bear to go on talking about it. The words hurt. Her words stayed in his ears, pressing and drumming: I fell in love with him.

'As it is,' she said, 'I don't like you paying. I don't belong in a world where men pay for women's food just as a matter of course.'

'Don't be absurd. It's not a question of sex, it's a question of me earning about fifty times what you do.' He shouldn't have said it, he knew that as soon as he had. It was a fault with him, which he recognised, to be unable to resist expressing pride in his success as a self-made man. The frown was back on her face, drawing together those winged eyebrows. He began to feel angry as well as miserable. That was the trouble. When they were together, on these rare occasions, always in the glare of noon, always in public, he was unable to keep his temper.

'I know you hate what I do for a living,' he said, staring at the two frown lines, the steady blue eyes. 'It's because you don't understand. You don't know the world we live in. You're an intellectual and you think everyone's got your taste and knows what's good and what isn't. It's something you can't understand, that ordinary people just want ordinary pretty things in their homes, things they can look at and – well, identify with if you like, things that aren't pretentious or phoney.'

' "His position towards the religion he was upholding was the same as that of a poultrykeeper towards the carrion he feeds his fowls on: carrion is very disgusting but fowls like it and eat it, therefore it is right to feed fowls on carrion." '

Guy felt himself flush up to his eyes. 'I don't suppose even you made that up.'

'Tolstoy did.'

'I congratulate you on your memory. Did you learn it on

purpose to come out with it today? Or is it one of the things *he* says in his marvellous conversation?'

'It's a piece I like,' she said. 'It's appropriate for lots of the terrible things that people do to other people today. I don't like any of the things you do for a living, Guy, but that's only part of it.'

'Are you going to tell me the rest?'

Her melon came and his prawns. He asked for a bottle of Mâcon-Lugny. He was a long way from an alcoholic but he had begun to drink every day, to drink quite a lot, an apéritif and wine at lunchtime, two or three gins before dinner and a bottle of wine with dinner. If the person he was with wanted to share another bottle or two in the evening, that was all right with him. Even for Leonora he wasn't going to pretend he didn't like a drink or deny himself the cigarette he would have after his steak.

'You have never actually told me, you know. You've said why you fancy the ginger dwarf but never quite why you don't fancy me. Any more, that is. You did once. Fancy me, I mean.'

'I was fifteen, Guy. It was eleven years ago.'

'Nevertheless. I was your first and a woman always loves her first best.'

'Antiquated sexist rubbish, that is. And I must tell you, if you call William a ginger dwarf I shall get up and go.'

'I'm not going to sit here and be insulted,' he jeered in a cockney char voice.

'As you say. I'm glad you said it, saved me the trouble.'

He was silent, too angry to speak. As was often the case at these meetings of theirs he became too angry or too unhappy to eat, in spite of the hunger he had felt a few minutes before. He would drink instead and end up reeling out of the place, red in the face. But he wasn't red yet. He could see himself in the black glass panel opposite, next to the still of Cary Grant in *Notorious*, a very handsome man with strong classical features, a noble forehead, fine dark eyes, a lock of dark hair falling casually over his tanned brow. He put Cary Grant in the shade. Paradoxically his looks made him angrier. It was as if he had everything already, looks, money, success, charm, youth, so what was there left for him to acquire, what was there he could find to sway her when everything was inadequate?

'I don't want a sweet,' she said. 'Just coffee.'

'I'll just have a coffee too. D'you mind if I smoke?'

'You always do smoke,' she said.

'I wouldn't if you minded.'

'Of course I don't mind, Guy. You don't have to ask with me. Don't you think I know you by now?'

'I shall have a brandy.'

'Go ahead. Guy, I wish we didn't quarrel. We're friends, aren't we? I'd like us to be friends always, if that's possible.'

They had been through that before. I fell in love with him. The words buzzed in his ears. He said, 'How's Maeve? How're Maeve and Rachel and Robin and Mummy and Daddy?'

He knew he should have said 'your mother and father' and he wished it didn't give him pleasure to see her small wince when he referred to her parents like that. But he went on, he compounded it, he couldn't help himself, 'And their append-ages,' he said, 'stepmummy and stepdaddy, how are they? Still in love? Still making mature second marriages now they're old enough to know their own bloody minds?'

She got up. He held her wrist. 'Don't go. Please don't go, Leonora. I'm sorry. I'm desperately sorry, please forgive me. I go mad, you know. When you're as unhappy as I am you go mad, you don't care what you say, you'll say anything.'

She prised his fingers off her wrist. She did it very gently. 'Why are you such a fool, Guy Curran?'

'Sit down again. Have your coffee. I love you.'

'I know that,' she said. 'Believe me, I don't doubt that. You'll never hear me say I don't think you love me. I know you do. I wish you didn't. God, I wish you didn't. If you realised what a hassle it is for me, how it blights my life, the way you go on and on, the way you never leave me alone, I wonder if you'd – well, if you'd give up, Guy?'

'I'll never give up.'

'You'll have to one day.'

'I won't. You see, I know it isn't true, all that. You say you fell in love with what's-his-name but it's infatuation, it's a passing phase. I know you really love me. You'd hate me to leave you alone. You love me.'

'I've said I do. In a way. It's just that . . .'

'Have lunch with me next Saturday,' he said.

'I always have lunch with you on Saturdays.'

'And I'll phone you tomorrow.'

'I know,' she said. 'I know you will. I know you'll phone me every day and have lunch with me every Saturday. It's like being sure Christmas will come round.'

'Absolutely,' he said, raising his brandy glass to her, sipping it, then drinking it as he might wine. 'I'm as reliable as Christmas and as – what's the word? – inexorable. And I'll tell you something, you wouldn't come if you didn't really love me. The ginge – this William, you're not in love with him, you're infatuated. It's me you love.'

'I'm fond of you.'

'Why do you keep on seeing me then?'

'Guy, be sensible. I only do it now because – well, I needn't go into that.'

'Yes, you need go into that. Why do you "only do it now because"?'

'All right, you asked for it. Because I know how you feel, or I try to know how you feel. I want to be kind, I don't want to be rotten. I did make promises and whatever to you when we were kids. No person in their right minds would call those promises binding, but just the same. Oh God, Guy, you're on my conscience, don't you see? That's why I have lunch with you on Saturdays. That's why I listen to all this stuff and let you insult my father and mother and my friends and – and William. And there's another reason. It's because I hope – well, I *hoped* – I'd make you see sense, I hoped I'd convince you it was hopeless – sorry about all those hopes – and you'd come to see there wasn't a joint future for you and me. I had this idea I'd convince you we could be friends and that's how it'd have been by this time, you agreeing to be my friend – well, *our* friend, William's and mine. Does that explain it now?'

'Quite a speech,' he said.

'It was as short as I could make it and still say what I meant.'

'Leonora,' he said, 'who's turned you against me?' It was a new idea. It came to him as a revelation might, enlightenment vouchsafed to a faithful believer. Her face, guilty, wary, on guard, showed him he was right. 'I can see it all now. It's one of them, isn't it? One of them's turned you against me. I won't do for them, I don't match up to their idea of what's good for you. That's it, isn't it?'

'I'm grown up, Guy. I make up my own mind.'

'You wouldn't deny you're a close family, would you? You wouldn't deny they've got a lot of influence on you.' She couldn't deny it, she said nothing. 'I bet they're over the moon about this William, I bet he's first favourite with the lot of them.'

She said carefully, 'They like him, yes.' She got up, touched his hand with hers, giving him a look he couldn't understand. 'I'll see you next Saturday.'

'We'll speak first. I'll phone you tomorrow.'

She said in an even, cheerful tone, 'Yes, you will, won't you?'

He walked off one way and she the other. Once she was out of sight he hailed a taxi. He thought of asking the taxi driver to go to the house in Portland Road where her flat was, go there and thrash the whole thing out with her, maybe with William there as well. He was sure William would be there, waiting for her, listening sympathetically while she complained about lunch and him and what a bore it all was, and then giving her the benefit of his brilliant conversation.

But she wouldn't say that. She wouldn't complain about him or say he was a bore. He made a shrewd guess that she wouldn't mention to anyone that she had even seen him. Because the fact was that she really did love him. Would she meet him like that if she didn't? Who would believe all that rubbish about conscience and trying to convince him they could be friends? If a woman spoke to a man on the phone every day and met that man once a week it was because she loved him.

Guy paid off the taxi at the entrance to Scarsdale Mews. He had bought the house ten years before when he was nineteen,

13

an unheard-of thing to do. But he had had the money. It was just before the property boom, which had tripled the price of the house in as many years. The second-best part of London, he called it. He had bought the house because it was a mews cottage like the one her parents, at that time, still lived in. Only his was bigger, in a far more prestigious district. A peer, a famous novelist and a TV chat-show star were among his neighbours. The first time he asked her to marry him was when he was twenty and she was seventeen and he took her home to this house of his and showed her the walled garden with the orange trees in Roman vases, the drawing room that had old Lisbon tiles on the walls and a Gendje carpet. The house had the first jacuzzi ever installed in London. He had an eighteenth-century four-poster bed and a Joshagan rug on the bedroom floor. It was better than anything her parents had. He took her to dinner at the Écu de France where the waiters danced up to you showing you the food on big silver dishes, and then he took her home where he had Piper Heidsieck waiting on ice and wild strawberries.

'The Great Gatsby,' she said.

It was the name of a book. She was always talking about books. The ring he had bought her was a large sapphire, the size of the iris of one of her eyes. On her and for her he had spent the fortune he had amassed in his teens.

'No, I can't, I'm only seventeen,' she said when he asked her to marry him.

'OK, then, later,' he said. 'I'll wait.'

He still had the ring. It was in the safe upstairs, along with a few other, less worthy, commodities. He wouldn't despair of putting it on her finger one day. She must love him. If she didn't love him she would simply refuse to see him ever again. That was what people did, that was what he did with the girls who chased him. He let himself into his house, went straight through to the room she said he mustn't call a lounge, but of course he did, what else, and poured himself a brandy. It reminded him, as beautiful cognac always did, of Linus Pinedo's which they had drunk in Kensal Green. Dazed with love and liquor they had lain in each other's arms in the long grass between the graves while butterflies floated above them on the warm summer air.

'I'll love you all my life,' she said. 'There can't be anyone else for us ever, Guy. Do you feel like that too?'

'You know I do.'

She loved him, she always had. Someone else had turned her against him. One of them. One or more had influenced her against him: William or Maeve or Rachel or Robin or the parents: Anthony her father and Tessa her mother. And they'd married again, the pair of them, which was why neither of them could any longer afford little mews houses in the second- (or in their case third- or fourth-) best part of London. Guy smiled. Now they were Anthony and Susannah, Tessa and Magnus.

They had turned her against him, deliberately. It was part of a deliberate policy to force her into their mould and separate her from undesirable elements. Anthony the architect, her father, and Tessa with the metallic fingernails and lofty know-it-all voice, her mother. Pretty gentle Susannah, the amateur psychotherapist, her stepmother, and Magnus the solicitor, her stepfather, he of the skull face and manner of a hanging judge.

And the others on the fringe: Robin and Rachel and Maeve. They were in a league against him, the eight against Guy Curran.

# CHAPTER
# TWO

When she changed schools it was to Holland Park Comprehensive she went, his school. Her mother didn't like her walking home alone on winter afternoons when it started getting dark at four, so to stop her mother coming for her in the car, Leonora said some 'older friends' would go with her. The older friends were himself and Linus and Danilo, just starting to be known to the local underworld as the Dream Traffic.

Her parents wouldn't just have freaked out if they'd known, they'd probably have emigrated. As time went on, anyway, it was just him walking home. Linus had got himself some O levels and gone to a sixth-form college and Danilo was in trouble breaking into flats. The Dream Traffic had become a one-man show, but going from strength to strength. One autumn afternoon he and she were sitting on a doorstop in Prince's Square, not smoking or anything, just sharing a can of coke and eating potato crisps, when her mother came by in her car. She was driving home up Hereford Road. He expected her to stop but she only waved to Leonora and went on.

'Keep your fingers crossed for me when I get home,' Leonora said.

'Why? What'll happen?'

'I don't know exactly. Maybe a big scene. Maybe I'll get taken to and from school for a few weeks. God, I hope not, that'd be a real drag.'

'You reckon? I bet she does what it says in my gran's woman's magazine.' He spoke in a bright falsetto: ' "Don't forbid your children to see their friends. Much better encourage them to invite their friends home. Then you can get to know them. Remember most people respond well to a happy home atmosphere." '

That made her laugh. He remembered every word of that conversation, every detail of place and time and, of course, of her. She was wearing blue jeans with a white shirt and a dark blue sweatshirt with a teddy bear on the front of it, a nice cuddly-looking blue denim jacket lined with sheepskin, brown leather boots and a long stripy pink and blue and yellow scarf. Her hair was long then; really long, nearly down to her waist. She hadn't got a hat on, it wasn't yet cold enough for that, it was only October. She was thirteen.

That was when she had her ears pierced. He went with her to get it done. The things girls did to themselves which were different from what men did were what he liked, he liked the contrast. Even then he was imagining a future when he would buy her diamond earrings. Her mother had been furious, said it was 'common' having it done so young. Leonora had begun wearing those fantastic earrings she still liked. The pair she had on while they were sitting on the steps were telephones with the receivers hanging on cords.

He remembered everything because that was the first time she told him she loved him. Nobody had ever told him that before, not even the eighteen-year-old (now twenty) whose sofa bed in a tiny bedsitter he sometimes shared and whose car he drove. Why would they? Who would? Not his mother, certainly. Not even his grandmother, who had persuaded his mother to name him Guy because she said Guy Fawkes was the first Catholic to try and bomb the British Government.

17

But when in a squeaky voice he said that about being invited to her home and the happy atmosphere, Leonora started laughing. She laughed and laughed and put her head down on her knees, shook her long dark brown hair and shook the phone earrings, looked up at him and said,

'Oh, Guy, I love you. I do love you,' and put her arms around his neck and hugged him.

She liked him to say funny things or clever things, so he tried saying them as often as he could. It didn't come easily but he tried. He was still trying. And she still laughed, though there was a note in her laughter that troubled him. It was surprise.

The interesting thing was that her mother did exactly as he had predicted and got her to invite him home. That was his first meeting with any of them, any of those people that surrounded her. Robin, her brother, wasn't there. He was away at school, some toffee-nosed public school he went to.

At that time her mother must have been about thirty-eight. She looked exactly like an older, harder version of Leonora: the same olive skin and pageboy face, the dark hair, though hers was done in a sort of knot on the back of her head, the same dark blue eyes, but calculating and watchful. Guy noticed her nails. They were painted silver. They were very long, and curving over at the top like claws but filed to points, and they looked like metal, like pieces of cutlery. Whenever he saw her after that her nails were done a different kind of metal, gold, bronze, brass, or that silver again. Leonora didn't introduce her mother to him. Why should she? Each knew who the other was, it couldn't be anyone else. Just the same, the unanswerable remark was made.

'So this is Guy?'

It was raining. The little mews house was rather dark, with a few lamps lit, making pools of golden light in dim corners. Intense heat came off large gold-painted radiators. There was a polish smell of chemical lemons and lavender. Guy's home was a dump, scarcely furnished. The furniture was tea chests and mattresses on the floor, a huge television set and stereo, Indian bedspreads pinned up to cover the windows. But he knew what was good, what he would have one day. He looked about him at the late-Victorian bits and pieces, the pink chaise longue, the Parker-Knoll armchairs and reproduction Georgian dining table. Leonora's mother said.

'Where do you live, Guy? Not far away, I suppose.'

He told her baldly, in the knowledge of her immediate comprehension. She would know at once that Attlee House was unlikely to be the name of a private mansion block. He could see her brain ticking, the wheels turning and slotting things into place, making contingency plans. Leonora was restive, bored with it all.

'Come on, Guy, we'll go up to my room.'

A hand went out to Leonora's arm and rested there, a long pale brown hand with, it seemed to him, preternaturally long slender fingers, and the nails glittering like implements, like things designed for picking bruised or damaged bits out of food.

'No, Leonora, I don't think so.'

'Why not?'

'We shall be eating the minute Daddy comes in.'

They watched television, side by side on the pink chaise longue. She would have taken his hand, he could sense she wanted to, but he gave a tiny shake of his head, and moved an inch or two from her. Daddy came in. He looked more like a handsome human teddy bear than any man Guy had seen before, fair and blunt-featured and stocky without being fat. He called Leonora's mother Tessa, so Guy did too when he had to call her something. There wasn't anyone he called Mr and Mrs, he never had and didn't mean to start; he'd had endless trouble over it at school. 'Tessa,' he said and she looked at him as if he'd called her a bitch or a whore or something. Those eyebrows that were Leonora's, only the skin round them was old and brown and freckled, went up right into her hair.

'You flatter me, Guy,' she said, very sarcastic. 'I didn't realise we were on such intimate terms so early in our relationship.'

'Oh, shut up, Mummy, please,' Leonora said.

She took no notice. Guy could have sworn the old man – well, he was maybe forty – gave him the ghost of a wink. Tessa said,

'I appreciate you must have a very warm outgoing tempera-
ment, but if you don't mind awfully, I'd prefer it to be Mrs
Chisholm for a while.'

He felt like saying that in that case she could call him Mr
Curran. But of course he didn't. He said nothing, he called her
nothing, he didn't want Leonora kept away from him. They
talked about drugs all through the meal, that is the parents did.
It sounded as though it was all rehearsed. They couldn't know
about him but they had made intelligent guesses. The father
said dealing in drugs was a more despicable crime than murder
or molesting children and the mother said that, much as she
hated the idea of taking life, in her opinion capital punishment
should be introduced for pushers.

He was never asked back, but nor was Leonora forbidden to
see him. No doubt they knew this was something they were
unable to enforce, short of moving away. Sometimes he saw
Tessa doing her shopping, once coming out of the Gate
cinema. She was a very well-dressed woman, he would grant
her that, and her figure was fantastic. She had those very thin
long ankles that make other women's legs look like carthorses'.
But the lines were forming thick and fast on her face; there was
a new deeper one each time he saw her. When he started taking
Leonora about in a more or less official way, her accredited
boyfriend, he was sometimes at the house without invitation.
Then Tessa treated him with the utmost coldness or placed her
little sharp barbs into his most tender places. It was as if she
stuck those silver or copper or pewter daggers on the ends of
her fingers into his eye sockets. He had to shut his eyes and
bear it.

So he wasn't training for anything then? How was his father?
*Where* was his father? Did he think his mother would ever spare
the time to come and see the Chisholms? He did realise, didn't
he, that once Leonora went to university he might not be able
to see her for three years?

But soon after that they split up, she and Anthony Chisholm,
the little mews house was sold and Leonora for a while was
aghast, devastated by a divorce she had never foreseen. Her
father had found another woman, her mother another man.

20

Leonora confided in him that she hated them all, she never wanted to see her parents again, and he rejoiced in secret. Even then, young as he was, he understood the influence they had on her. Now that she wasn't speaking to them, but longing to get away, find a place of her own, shake the dust of their thresholds off her feet, he knew she would come to him. He would have a house to take her to and they would be married. In him she should find mother and father as well as husband and lover.

She came round. The rift lasted no more than a few weeks and suddenly they were all, so quickly, friends again, the two couples hobnobbing, dining out in a foursome. Leonora was again talking about what Mummy said and Daddy did, and now too, incredibly, what Susannah thought and what Magnus advised. She called it civilised behaviour.

Guy accepted it, he had no choice. Besides, he had other things to think about and he told himself that, in spite of everything, he was sure of Leonora. One morning he realised he was a rich man. At eighteen he was much richer than the Chisholms would ever be.

* * * *

He had phoned her every day for years. That kind of statement is never quite true. How could it be? He had *tried* to phone her every day. Most days he reached her. It was a kind of challenge for him or quest, a labour of love.

When she was at university she said she didn't like his daily phone calls, they embarrassed her. He never took that very seriously. In her holidays he phoned her at Tessa's or at Anthony's, wherever she happened to be living. She went on to teacher training college and he tried to phone her every day at the student's hall of residence. Quite often he didn't reach her but he persisted. He phoned her when she went to live with Anthony and Susannah and when she moved into that room with Rachel Lingard and when she got the flat with Rachel and Maeve Kirkland.

Usually someone else answered the phone. He didn't know

21

why that was. When she was at her father's Anthony or Susannah would answer and now at the flat it was likely to be Rachel or Maeve. It was a good many years since she had lived with her mother, and he hadn't heard Tessa's voice since the Portland Road house-warming party. But he recognised it as soon as he heard it. It was Tessa who answered when he phoned Leonora's flat on the day after their lunch in the wine bar.

A languid, 'Hallo?' Tessa was either languid or sharp, these moods alternating.

He said tersely, 'Leonora, please.'

'Who is that?' As if she didn't know.

'It's Guy Curran, Tessa.' He drew a long breath. 'And how are you after all this time?'

It was as if she had two taps inside her head. From one came a drawling sluggish trickle, from the other a swift splashing flow. She turned on the flood tap.

'I'm glad to get a chance to speak to you. Leonora is simply too kind and sweet to say what has to be said. Another girl would have got the police on to you by now. At least. Do you realise it would be quite possible for her to go to a judge in chambers and get an injunction forbidding you to pursue her?'

He didn't say anything. He held the receiver at arm's length, grubbed about for a cigarette. The voice chattered angrily out of the receiver. He held it in the hollow between chin and shoulder, lit his cigarette.

'I know you're still there,' he heard her say. 'I can hear you breathing. You're like one of those heavy breathers and just as sinister. That's the horrible thing, you're sinister, you're a kind of gangster. It's appalling that my daughter should be associated with someone like you – these awful phone calls, day after day, this Saturday lunch thing, like a kind of endurance test. I don't understand it, it's beyond me, unless you've hypnotised her in some way.'

The only course might be to put the phone down and try later. He was thinking that when he heard Leonora say, 'Come on, Mother, give it to me.' She had stopped calling the woman 'Mummy' at any rate. 'I'm sorry about that, Guy,' she said. 'My mother's gone out into the kitchen with Maeve. I don't want you to think I've been complaining about you. It's all in her head really. I'm afraid she's got a very negative attitude towards you, she always has had.'

'So long as you don't take any notice, my sweetheart,' he said.

She didn't tell him not to call her that. 'It's hard not to take any notice of one's own mother, especially if you're as close as we are.'

The chill touched the back of his neck again. So the woman exerted a real influence. Leonora listened to the woman. Why did she want to be close to a person like that? Because she was her mother? He hadn't seen his mother for seven years, let alone been close to her. It was something he couldn't understand, this family unity, but he understood the results of it.

He listened to Leonora's voice, which was as pleasurable as actually taking in the content of what she said. They talked for a while. She was going out for lunch somewhere on the river with her mother, stepfather and brother and, for some reason, Maeve, and meeting up with the ginger dwarf later on. The last week of the primary school she taught at started next day, then the long summer holidays.

'I'll phone you tomorrow,' he said.

Her tone throughout had been very sweet and affectionate. If the evil influence or influences which put her against him were removed the love she had once felt for him would return. He corrected himself. 'Felt for him', not 'once felt for him'. It could never die, only be submerged. Someone had told her, was probably constantly telling her, that the ginger dwarf would be a more secure bet than he, a safe life partner, more suitable. That same person was poisoning her mind against him personally, calling him a crook.

It was interesting to speculate, or would be interesting if it wasn't so vital to his happiness, how things would change if Tessa Chisholm – or whatever she was called now, Mandeville? – were simply removed from the scene. He poured himself a Campari and orange juice with plenty of ice and walked out into the walled garden. A wonderful summer they were having, sunny and warm every day. His orange trees in the blue-and-white Chinese jars had fruit on them, green still, but turning, a lemony bloom on their cheeks.

The garden furniture came from Florence, bronze-coloured wrought iron, and on an island in the little round pond was a bronze dolphin. Clematis climbed the walls, Nelly Moser and Ville de Lyon, pale pink and deep pink, against the dark shiny mantle of ivy. Leonora hadn't been to his house for ages. She had been coming, he now remembered, the previous summer and had phoned to say she couldn't because her mother was ill. Tessa again. He didn't for a moment believe she had really been ill. The woman was a strong as a horse. She ate like a horse too, for all that she was so thin. He imagined her now in the garden of some hotel in Richmond, eating at a table under a striped umbrella, guzzling avocado and roast duck and God knew what, those long gilt-tipped fingers busy with knife and fork.

It was more than possible that she had introduced Leonora to this William Newton. She was the sort of woman who would find a prospective husband for her daughter and bring them together. But he mustn't think like that. He wouldn't even put it into thought-words, the idea of Leonora marrying anyone but him. Tessa would. Tessa would be doing it all the time.

He had long ago lost touch with Linus but Danilo he still knew. Danilo wouldn't hesitate. A couple of grand was all it would take and Tessa Mandeville would be quietly removed from this life without Danilo having sight or sound of it, his hands clean, knowing neither the time nor the place of her death. He, Guy, wasn't serious, of course. But why not be serious? Why make a joke of everything, treading so lightly with dancing steps on the surface of things? Why not confront the situation fair and square, confront the undoubted fact that Tessa Mandeville stood between him and his life's happiness, kept him from his love?

With his glass in his hand, looking at its contents, the most beautiful drink in the world, the ravishing colour of an orange-pink rose, Guy lay back in his bronze chair and remembered. Long ago, nine years ago when he first came here. They had been here in his garden and she had said, looking into his eyes.

'I *am* you, Guy. Just as much as I'm Leonora, I'm Guy.'

She had meant they were so close that she was he and he was she. And then, very soon, all too soon, Tessa Mandeville had come between them. Killing Tessa would be too good for her.

\* \* \* \*

She had married a man called Magnus Mandeville. Absurd name but not one you would forget. He was a solicitor, had in fact been the solicitor she had gone to when she and Anthony Chisholm were seeking a divorce. No wonder she knew so much about going to judges in chambers and applying for injunctions.

The Mandevilles had gone to live in some suburb on the outer extremities of South London, or perhaps Magnus had lived there before. Tessa had never worked, or not since the birth of Robin who was two years older than Leonora, and he remembered Leonora saying she had got married as soon as she left college which had been when she was twenty-one. It was art school she had been at and she was supposed to know all about art. This had been important in his relationship with Leonora or important in *altering* his relationship with Leonora.

When he looked back he could see that there had been a definite precise point when Leonora had changed towards him. Or, rather, when she had ceased to show him a devoted uncritical love. Someone had put her off him, he knew that quite clearly. It had happened when he was twenty-two and she was nineteen. Then it was, when she had come home from college for the long summer vacation, that she had seemed to stop wanting to touch him. In August, which he had looked forward to desperately all summer, she kept finding excuses for not being alone with him, she had begun gently to extricate herself from his embrace.

The strongest possibility was that Tessa had found out he had been Leonora's lover and indicated her violent disapproval. He had never thought of that before. Having that set-to with Tessa on the phone had wonderfully cleared his mind. The more he thought of it the more apparent it became that it was Tessa who had been the prime mover against him.

He phoned Leonora as soon as he thought she would be home from school. This time it was Rachel who answered. Leonora had met Rachel at university and they had been friends ever since. Guy didn't like the sort of girls who were overweight and hyperintellectual, who wore steel-rimmed glasses, took no interest in their appearance and whose greatest ambition was to end up as head of Friends of the Earth.

'Off sick, are you?' he said. 'You'll never make it to the top that way.'

'I have a client here with me,' she said. 'It happened to be more convenient.'

He knew what she meant by a 'client'. 'Some child abuser, I suppose?'

'How did you guess? Leonora isn't back yet. I shan't be here to tell her you rang but she'll know. Surprise day will be when you don't ring.'

Leonora came in before she put the phone down. 'What's she got against me?' he said. 'What have I ever done to her, the bilious bitch.'

'Perhaps you're not very nice to her either, Guy.'

'Have you had a good day?' he said. 'Are you very tired? Will you have dinner with me?'

'Of course I won't. I never have dinner with you. I have lunch with you on Saturdays.'

'Leo,' he said. Sometimes he called her Leo and in the same tone as he sometimes called her 'sweetheart'. 'Leo, your mother doesn't go out to work, does she?'

He understood that she was so surprised at getting an ordinary question from him instead of a plea to love him that she answered without thinking, she answered *gratefully*. 'No, she doesn't, she never has, I thought you knew that. She does voluntary work at some hospital down there. Would it be the Mayday Hospital? Tuesdays and Thursdays, I think. Oh, and sometimes at the CAB on Wednesday mornings.'

'The *what*?'

'Citizen's Advice Bureau. I think she got it through Magnus. And they both work for the Greens.' At least she was realising the question was odd coming from him. 'Why on earth do you want to know?'

'One of the people who work for me mentioned knowing her at art college. She asked if she was working and I said I'd find out.'

This utter fabrication was accepted. Leonora tended to believe what she was told. Habitual truth-tellers do. He was encouraged to press on. 'It's 15, Sanderstead Way they live, isn't it?'

'Seventeen and it's Sanderstead Lane.'

'Where shall we go for lunch on Saturday? Let me take you to Clarke's.'

'I'm just as happy in a wine bar, Guy. Or McDonalds, come to that. I don't really enjoy food when I know that what you spend would buy meals for a whole family in Bangladesh for a month.'

'Would it please you if I sent the cost of lunch at Clarke's to Bangladesh?'

'Yes, very much, but I still wouldn't want to go there.'

'I'll phone you tomorrow,' he said.

When she was fifteen and he was eighteen he made love to her for the first time in Kensal Green Cemetery. If you told people a thing like that – not that he did tell people – they said, How revolting! or How macabre! but it wasn't revolting or macabre. Those who talked like that didn't know the cemetery, which was really like a vast overgrown wild garden that happened to have weathered grey stones among the long grass and wonderful tombs like little houses. There were big dark trees and wild flowers and in the height of summer wreaths dying on new graves. The cemetery was full of butterflies, small blue ones and big brown and orange ones, because there were no poisons or pollution in there to kill them.

Where they were was so quiet and wild and beautiful with long seed-headed grasses swaying and creamy foxgloves growing among the grass, with tall pink flowers he didn't know the name of and moss growing over a sunken slab, moss that had its own tiny yellow flowers growing on it, that it was like a lost paradise. There were bushes with pointed silver leaves and small firs like blue Christmas trees and overhead a great spreading tree covered with green cones. The smell of London didn't come in here. It smelt like when you sniffed the jars of herbs in the health-food shop.

She was wearing a dress, very thin and soft and sort of smoky blue and mauve with a low neck and puff sleeves and no waist. It was one of the few hot days of a cold summer. She was wearing the dress and a pair of knickers and blue espadrilles and nothing else. When she lay on her back her breasts were soft and spread like little silk cushions. He laid her in a nest of grasses and scattered elderflower petals. He lifted the dress and drew it up to her neck. It lay there round her neck as a scarf might. She wasn't afraid, she was very excited, and when he entered her she wasn't hurt. He told her afterwards that was because she loved him and wanted him.

What Tessa said when she saw the creased dress all covered with green stains he never knew. Perhaps Leonora contrived for her mother not to see it. It was when Tessa finally found out that things began to go wrong. If you loved someone like that when you were fifteen, if you loved them so much that though you were a virgin lovemaking didn't hurt you at all and you didn't bleed, that love didn't change. It didn't just go away, it was as much a part of you as your love for your parents or your brother, your love for yourself.

'I *am* you. I am Guy and he's me.'

If Tessa wasn't there that love would return. Unhindered, it would become once more what it had been. If there was no one there to tell evil stories about him, call him low-class and criminal, insult his intelligence, Leonora would be him and her. Still, the idea of harming Tessa seemed grotesque. In all his career he had never really harmed anyone. When Danilo came back after his stay in a borstal institution they had run a very lucrative protection racket up in Kensal and once they'd had to rough up a publican a bit to show him they meant business, but the man only got a few bruises and a black eye. Of course there was the final showdown with Dream Traffic and there was Con Mulvanney's death. But that was no one's fault, certainly not his, it was what might be called an occupational hazard.

He refused to think about Con now. All he ever allowed himself to think of in that connection was that it had marked the end of his dealing. He had had a good run, had made a fortune, escaped from Attlee House and all its associations. His hands were clean and so was his record.

It would do no harm to ask Danilo to have dinner with him and there sound him out on the question of hit men, how to go about it and what it would cost. Not that he cared about the cost.

# CHAPTER
# THREE

When there was a sale of his paintings in a country pub or some other suitable outlet, Guy would sometimes go and see how it went. On these occasions it wasn't his habit to let it be known who he was. He liked to see customers' reactions and was seldom willing to take his agents' word or the sales figures. It was best to see for himself whether the current favourite was 'Man's Best Friend', say, or 'Carry on, Kittens' or 'Lady from Thailand'.

This week one of the sales was at a pub in Coulsden that was nearer to a country club. It was a fine day and the traffic was never terrible in August. Everyone was away. Guy went down in the Jaguar. It was champagne-coloured, though called 'Beige Satin', with cream leather upholstery and an air-conditioning system so good that on really stifling London days he was sometimes tempted to go into the garage and sit in the Jaguar with the engine running to get the benefit of its cool breezes. 'You'll kill yourself if you do that,' Celeste said when he told her and there was some sense in what she said.

The pub was called The Horseless Carriage, which was a

made-up name if ever he heard one. There were more flowers on the front of it in window boxes than at the Chelsea Show. Two large yellow posters outside advertised the sale of 'original oil paintings, £7-£70, all prices, each one unique handwork.' He didn't wince for himself but only when he thought of Tessa Mandeville's reaction. He kept thinking of her. He couldn't get the bloody woman out of his mind.

The sale was in a large room at the back that had double doors opening on to a terrace and a rather shabby garden where the lawn had become a dust bowl and no one had deadheaded the roses. A lot of people were there already, in the saleroom and out on the bald grass. There was one glass of red or white wine for everybody who came. After that you bought your own. Two girls were taking the orders. He didn't know them, had never seen them before, but he could see from the growing lists on their clipboards that the orders were coming in thick and fast.

And why not? They *were* original paintings and each one *was* painted by an artist working individually. The results were a lot more pleasing than ninety-nine per cent of what you saw along the Bayswater Road on Sunday mornings. They were harmless and pretty, their subjects innocent, children and baby animals, young girls, country cottages or views of the sea. He considered some of the pictures he had seen that were supposed to be so good, war and slaughter of men and horses, for instance, that he had once seen on an outing with Leonora to Blenheim Palace, lopsided vases and deformed apples, paintings in that Guggenheim place in Venice of naked women in birds' feathers and furs. He was open-minded enough, God knew, but they had disgusted him. It was madness for Tessa Mandeville to call his paintings 'junk', and what was her other word? 'Obscene'. Those others were truly obscene.

He walked round, studying each one. Even at this late stage he liked to make sure there were minute differences between each copy of the same painting, slight variations in the curls on the weeping boy's head, for example. Tears glistened on the round pink cheeks, but in some versions there were three tears on the left cheek and in others four. 'Lady from Thailand' was again proving the top seller. It was the custom of his agents to attach red stickers to paintings which had been sold – 'as though at a real private view', he had been told was Tessa Mandeville's comment. What was unreal about his sales no one had specified.

All four copies of 'Lady from Thailand' were sold, and they were up in the £70 range. He asked one of the girls if she was taking orders for that particular painting and she said she was, she had already taken twelve, it was the most popular. Guy could understand why. The girl in the painting was very young, fifteen or sixteen, and very innocent-looking. But she was sexy too, with full gleaming lips and big shining doe eyes, and the gold-embroidered bodice she wore parted to show between its braiding and the gold and jewelled necklaces she wore the tops of her smooth young breasts. She seemed to gaze back into the eyes of the viewer with a look that was winsome, yet pleading, shy yet provocative.

Somewhere the original of that girl must exist, for all the paintings were based on photographs. Literally and actually based on photographs which, printed in a pale overexposed version on to plasterboard, were imported by Guy in quantity from Taiwan. They were then painted over according to a prescribed method by his workers at the factory in Isleworth. When Guy, explaining his new business to members of Leonora's family, had said that many of his employees would be art-school graduates, Tessa Mandeville had actually shuddered and said that made things worse.

'They're glad of the work, I can tell you,' he said.

'They'd do better to go on the streets,' said Tessa. 'Better get themselves a beat outside King's Cross Station.'

What did she know about it? She had always had someone to keep her and give her a house to live in and money to save the whales and stop the acid rain and a studio where she could mess about with her paints. She didn't have a clue what it meant to need a job. He would have liked to say that but he couldn't because he had to keep on selling himself to those people, present himself as worthy to pay court to Leonora. The funny thing was – if such things were funny – that he had come along there, to some hotel it was where they were celebrating Leonora's birthday and the end of her teacher training, with the aim of getting himself in good with them all by indicating his abandonment of a life of fringe-crime and explaining his new career as a respectable businessman.

As he looked at the paintings, the Thai girl and the weeping boy, 'The Old Millstream' and the twin Persian kittens, he reflected that that particular evening had marked another watershed in the decline of his relationship with Leonora. It was true that by that time she had ceased altogether to sleep with him but though that had naturally bothered him, it was not his major concern. She had once told him she thought it a bad idea for a girl to be on the pill for more than, say, four years at a stretch. While she was studying for her degree she would be afraid of becoming pregnant. He would, of course, have married her like a shot whenever she wanted it, chance would have been a wonderful thing, but nevertheless he understood she wanted to complete her studies. Then she had been away so much and though he had phoned her every day, they hadn't met for months on end. You expected difficulties, awkwardnesses, coldnesses, in those circumstances.

But she still loved him then. She still loved him publicly and openly. Hadn't she seen to it on that July evening four years ago that he was seated next to her, he on one side and her father on the other? Robin was right down the table, stuck with the horrible Rachel. Later on Leonora had danced with him. She had said to take no notice of what Tessa said. But she, Leonora, had taken notice next day or the next. 'Philistine' was one of Tessa's favourite words but 'Philistine' was the least of what she would have called him. Crook, thug, low-life – he could imagine. Leonora listened to Tessa, was 'close' to Tessa.

Guy helped himself to his permitted glass of wine from the tray. It was Rioja, red and rough. He felt a sudden desire to see Tessa, as one sometimes does wish to see an enemy, to see perhaps without being seen. The wish is to see the enemy in misfortune, in defeat. Had she changed? Was she grey? She was fifty now, a solicitor's wife, living in a suburb, busy it appeared with good works. Living, he realised, in a suburb very close to where he now was.

He walked through to the saloon bar. A girl of about twenty-five sitting on a bar stool alone eyed him. Guy was used to women looking at him and it gave him a certain pleasure even though he seldom responded. He asked for a dry martini and wondered what they would come up with, a glass of warm French vermouth as likely as not. When it came it was passable, at least it had gin in it and a piece of ice. He allowed himself for a moment to imagine that the girl was Leonora and she was with him. In a moment they were going to have lunch and sit long over the table afterwards with their drinks, talking about the past and the future and their love. Then they might drive down to the coast and walk on a beach in the cool evening. They would stay in the best hotel, in the bridal suite. Oddly enough, it was not the idea of making love to her that was paramount. Of course he wanted that, he was full of desire for her, but it was not the most important thing, it was only a part of the whole. What was the most important thing? Being with her, being *her* and she being him. 'I *am* Guy. . .', to hear her say that again!

He had another drink and a dried-up smoked salmon sandwich and then he got back into the Jaguar and drove to Sanderstead Lane. Number 17 was not at all as he had imagined but half of a pair of rambling old houses, three floors high, with imposing windows framed in stone and pillared porches, that had obviously been there for a hundred years or more, long before all the rest were built. The front garden was as long as the back gardens of other houses. White-painted furniture was grouped under a spreading cedar tree.

Guy was long past the stage of hoping to impress Tessa Mandeville with his wealth and success – she never was impressed or she pretended not to be – so he was anxious not to be detected as the driver of the golden Jaguar. But there was no one to detect him, no Tessa obligingly leaning out of a window to show him the grey in her hair and her latest wrinkle, no Magnus Mandeville taking a day off from soliciting to potter about in the garden, hollow-eyed skeleton in a skin that he was.

Like a lawyer in some Dickens serial on TV. That was how Guy had thought of him when they met at that party. He had wondered what there was to attract a woman about a stooping skinny man with a little wisp of grey hair on top of a parchment-covered skull. His money perhaps. Knowing Tessa, that would be it. Magnus had a neck like the gizzard that came in a plastic bag inside a frozen chicken. His voice was high-pitched and chilly and extravagantly, affectedly, dauntingly, Old Etonian. You could imagine him playing the part of the judge with a white wig on, sending some poor devil to be hanged by the neck until he was dead.

Guy drove half the length of Sanderstead Lane and back again. He turned down a side road and saw that a lane between high hedges ran along the backs of the houses. Their gardens had gates into it. He returned to the main road. Number 15, next door to and adjoining Tessa's, looked empty. There were no curtains at the windows and an estate agent's For Sale board was planted in the overgrown front garden.

In the old days, if this had been his area of Kensal and Tessa Mandeville had been running a business and had defaulted on her fees to him for keeping the place intact and not broken apart, he'd have got in there (or someone working for him would have) and either had her roughed up a bit or the fittings made to look less like they'd just come from the Ideal Home Exhibition. Midday would have been the best time, when there weren't many of her neighbours at home, but not on a Tuesday, a Wednesday or a Thursday. Entry by that lane at the back, the chances were the door into it was never locked, even if it could be locked, then try the back door. If it wouldn't open, knock and when she came no games, no posing as a salesman, a market researcher or whatever, but the swift hand closing her mouth, her two hands held hard behind her, quick march her into the middle of the house, silence while what had to be done was done.

Fantasies -- or were they? He began the drive home. Tonight he was giving Danilo dinner. There came quite suddenly into that part of his mind that made pictures, that ran videos, a sight of Magnus Mandeville eyeing him at that birthday party.

Looking at him above the straight tops of his half-glasses as a judge might look at the scum in the dock, puzzled, enquiring, shrewd, astonished, unrelenting. Magnus possibly had influence with Leonora. He was a lawyer, for God's sake. Suppose he had had some inkling of his, Guy's activities, which were then still on the edge or over the edge of what was legal, would he have warned Leonora?

Guy drew into the side of the road and parked the car. These small cameos were expanding into a picture, a panorama or group photograph, of that table on the evening of July 25. He couldn't concentrate on the road. He had to stop. Where had it been, that dinner? Not a very distinguished place, not a great restaurant or famous hotel, not the kind of place he would want to celebrate some important event in *his* daughter's life. But Guy could hardly bear to think of any possible daughter or possible son of his. It was too painful. He had had thoughts of this before and it seemed to tear open a wound somewhere inside him, it made him bleed. If he could know, actually *know*, that sometime he and Leonora would have children together he thought he would die of happiness.

The panorama opened in his mind. At that table there had been eleven people: Leonora herself at the head of it with Anthony Chisholm sitting on her left and he, Guy, on her right. Leonora had been wearing a dark blue dress, plain, of some silken material, austere and rather too old for her. She looked beautiful of course, that went without saying. She was wearing the necklace her father had given her, lapis in a silver setting from Georg Jensen, pretty but not expensive by Guy's standards. Anthony was a good-looking man with a boyish face that would always have something of youth in it. Next to Anthony sat his own mother, an aged crone now dead, Leonora's grandmother.

On his own right sat a cousin of Leonora's called Janice who had later got married and gone to Australia, and next to her Robin Chisholm with Rachel Lingard on his right. Maeve was not in the picture in any sense at that time, Leonora hadn't met her. Old Mrs Chisholm was sitting next to Magnus Mandeville and next to him was Susannah, Anthony's wife. Susannah was a nice-looking woman, very slender with sleek dark hair, no more than thirty-three or -four at the time, who Leonora said hardly ever wore skirts or dresses and was in fact on that evening wearing a black silk trouser suit. Janice's fiancé whose name Guy couldn't remember sat between Susannah and Tessa.

He let his mind's eye rove round that table from guest to guest. The men's suits had been unmemorable, vague greys, but he thought Robin had been wearing a pink tie. Robin favoured his father, was much fairer than Leonora and, having Anthony's boyish look, seemed absurdly younger than his twenty-four years. He was a swap jockey – that is, he had later become one. He swapped sums of money between potential borrowers, thus making dollars quickly available to clients in, say, Germany, and Deutschmarks to clients in Brazil. Guy suspected he was, in a respectable sort of way, just as dishonest and on the make as he himself had once been.

'You'd think he'd like me,' Guy had once said to Leonora. 'I can't understand why he doesn't. We're birds of a feather, aren't we?'

'He's a snob.'

'What does that mean, he doesn't fancy my accent?'

'Let's hope he grows out of it. He's still at the stage of making snide jokes about people who haven't been to public school. I'm sorry, Guy. I love Rob and I always will but he's the only reactionary member of my family. He's a real old-fashioned Tory.'

'I can believe it,' he'd said, though politics didn't interest him. He was an old-fashioned Tory himself if he was anything.

Tessa hated him because he was a so-called Philistine, her husband because he was or might have been a crook – had Robin turned Leonora against him because he came from the wrong background and spoke with the wrong kind of voice? Guy closed his eyes and went on seeing those ten people, nine without Leonora. Tessa in a greenish-gold dress of some pleated silky stuff, a thin gold chain round her neck, her new wedding ring bright and shiny and her nails to match, Susannah in her black trousers and tailored jacket, the open-necked white silk shirt and chunky jet and amber beads, old Mrs Chisholm in brown lace and pearls, Rachel, that ugly four-eyes, in a flowered cotton skirt with a dipping hem and a pink blouse probably from the British Home Stores. The men. Janice, plump as Rachel, round-hipped, wearing fancy-rimmed glasses, pink plastic. Himself and Leonora.

They ate avocados stuffed with prawns. Surprise, surprise. Not to say big deal. The next course was chicken done in an uninteresting way. Guy had read somewhere that chicken, if not the best loved, is the most widely eaten protein food in the world. When they got to the profiteroles Anthony had said to him, across Leonora,

'So what's with you careerwise these days, Guy?'

They knew he was rich. No one else had on a suit from Armani, cuff links that were imperial jade set in 22-carat gold. And he was less than half Anthony Chisholm's age. He answered the question, told them about the paintings, not mentioning his other sidelines of course. They were all soon to go anyway. With the death of Con Mulvanney, imminent, waiting to happen as it were in the unknown, unguessed-at-future, the remnants of Dream Traffic were to be dissolved. The last of that trading Tessa and Anthony had hinted at with such opprobrium, such violence, the first time he met them, was almost over.

Like a vulture Tessa had been at that dinner party, watching the others kill him and then swooping to pick his bones. First that remark about going on the streets and having a beat at King's Cross, then a savage closing in, a lecture to the assembled company about the demise of art and culture in the West (whatever that meant), and Leonora had listened, had later on no doubt been told more, and more . . .

He started the car and drove home.

\* \* \* \*

Leonora had stopped living with her mother in the holidays and moved in with her father and stepmother. That was for the sake of being in Central London. And to be near Rachel

Lingard. If he was honest with himself he had to admit that. Rachel's mother had a flat in Cromer Street and Rachel was living there because her mother was dying of cancer. He had recognised Rachel as a menace from the beginning, the kind of person he didn't want his girlfriend to know. Girls should be frivolous, they should be a bit silly sometimes, mad about shopping, passionate about clothes and perfume, always catching sight of themselves in mirrors, loving to be stared at and whistled at. They should be vain and petulant and with a tendency to be bitchy towards other women. Rachel was a feminist. She never wore make-up. She ate what she liked and grew fat. It was a principle with her to say she preferred the company of women to that of men. Her conversation was clever and to him often incomprehensible. Half the time he literally didn't know what she was on about.

Now he wondered if it was through her that Leonora had met this William Newton. He looked the kind of person she would know. And he too had that quality Leonora seemed to prize so highly, the gift of the gab. He had never seen the point of it, all those discussions, arguments, all that cleverness and wit. Why bother? It might have been necessary once when there was nothing else to do, no magazines, papers, videos, music, television, no places to go to and no electric light. The art of conversation was no more necessary now than the art of writing letters. That was the way he saw it.

The rift really began when Leonora changed her mind about going on holiday with him. He had never known why. He didn't know why she seemed almost *shocked* when he suggested she move in with him. Her attitude was more what her mother's might have been, not that of a girl of twenty-two. After all, they'd been going out together steadily for years. He loved her and she loved him and both knew they would be married one day.

'You're not serious, Guy?'

'Isn't it what people like us do? I've got a house all ready for you. It's in a place you like. I presume you like *me* – well, love me. And I love you.'

'Who are these people like us?'

39

This was one of those 'clever' remarks she was making more and more often. Picking him up on old sayings he used, expressions everyone said but which she called clichés. She had never used to do it. She had caught it off Rachel. And now she was going to share a bedsit with Rachel.

'We thought of Fulham, because of me teaching there, a big room with a kitchen while we look round for a flat.'

Rachel's mother was permanently in hospital now, she would never come out again. Leonora showed Guy the bedsit which was as horrible as Attlee House and much smaller. Fat Rachel, her round eyes magnified by the glasses she wore, saw his expression, whispered something to Leonora and said like someone acting on the stage,

'Prithee, why so pale? Will, when looking well can't move her, looking ill prevail?'

Both girls went into gales of laughter, giggling the way he liked girls to giggle, but not when he was the butt of it. He understood the remark, bit of poetry, quotation, whatever it was, though Rachel might think he didn't. It meant she wouldn't like a miserable hangdog man, so he tried not to look offended but to laugh it off. Rachel's mother died soon after that, which wiped the smile off her face for a while. No doubt she was pleased to have property to sell, though, she was as greedy as the next girl for all her airs. She and Leonora started flat-hunting.

As soon as he heard they were applying for a mortgage – a huge one – he offered to lend Leonora the money. It wouldn't, of course, really be a loan. It would be an outright gift. Secretly, in his heart, he planned this from the beginning, but of course he would let her think it was an interest-free loan.

Why did she have to bring her family and friends into everything? She was nearly twenty-three, for God's sake. Why couldn't she break away from that family? Because they wouldn't let her. They clung to her and to each other like leeches. Her parents, who weren't even married to each other any more, who were married to other people, nevertheless were always meeting, saw nearly as much of each other it seemed to him as when they shared a home.

The night he made his offer she had been staying with Anthony and Susannah in Lamb's Conduit Street. *Staying* with them, if you please, though she had had a home of her own no more than five miles away. Rachel had gone up north to a reunion of people she called 'alumnae' which he thought sounded like bacteria, the kind of thing you picked up from eating supermarket pâté. Of course he hadn't made his offer in anyone else's presence. He and Leonora had been alone, having a quiet drink after the cinema.

'It's very generous of you, Guy,' she had said, and he could tell she was moved. He thought she was going to cry.

'I won't even notice it,' he said, which he shouldn't have said, he knew at once he shouldn't have.

'If only it was possible,' she said, and she took his hand.

They went back to her father's. Anthony and Susannah were both there and her uncle, Anthony's brother Michael, who was something big in television, chairman of a TV company, and her brother Robin, he of the baby face and fair curls. And black heart, thought Guy.

He was embarrassed when she came out with it. He was also proud. After all, he had begun with nothing, less than nothing, and they had all been to universities, come from happy home backgrounds, known people with influence.

'I hope you told Guy anything like that was out of the question,' said Anthony.

You couldn't get more patronising than that. Patronising and what was the word Rachel was always using? Paternalistic.

Anthony looked like a nice teddy bear. His face was boyish, his eyes twinkled. Guy had never seen him look the way he did then. Affronted. Shocked, really. He looked as if Guy had insulted him instead of offering to lend his daughter forty thousand pounds.

The uncle, who was a bigger, older and somehow *furrier* version of Anthony, pursed up his lips and gave a thin little whistle. Robin said,

'How to put a lady in your power in one easy lesson.'

The bastard. Guy had always hated him.

'I just wanted you all to know,' Leonora said, 'because it was

41

so very very kind of Guy.' 'Was'? What did she mean, 'was'? He had been half-sure up till then that she'd take it in spite of them all. But their influence was too strong for her. 'It was a magnificent offer,' she said, 'but of course I couldn't dream of taking it.' And she looked so sad he longed to put his arms round her and kiss her better.

He hadn't given up. He had pressed her to take the money in the weeks that followed. At about the same time she started making excuses for not going out with him, she was going out with him less and less. For years he had spoken to her every day, though it wasn't easy phoning the room in Fulham where the phone was downstairs and shared by about eight people.

A kind of cold panic took hold of him when he felt she was separating herself from him, more even than when she had been away at college. Life wouldn't be possible without her. Sometimes he had moments when there opened before him a cold vision of emptiness, a grey desert from which she had walked away and he was alone.

'What's happened to us?' he said to her one day, when he had steeled himself to it. He was so afraid of her answer. Suppose she said, 'I don't love you any more'?

She didn't. 'Nothing's happened. We're still friends.'

'Leonora, we were more than friends. I love you. You love me. You're my life.'

'I think we should see less of each other. We ought to see more of other people. This sort of monogamous situation we have isn't very healthy when you're young.'

Rachel's expression. He could hear her uttering it.

'I must see you.'

It was a Saturday. They were having lunch together at a French restaurant in Charlotte Street. She hadn't got into that vegetarian nonsense at that time. He could remember what she'd been wearing, a dark blue and dark green striped cotton dress with a tan belt and tan pumps. In those days, three years ago, she still dressed quite nicely.

'I tell you what,' she had said, 'I'll always have lunch with you on Saturdays.'

# CHAPTER
# FOUR

It was a joke. That was how he took it at first. She could hardly have meant that. He could scarcely remember a time when he hadn't been the man she went out with and she the woman he went out with. The girl with the furnished room and the car that he'd known before he met her was a dim memory, a phantom. Leonora couldn't have meant they were only to see each other like people regularly having a business lunch.

Phoning her was very difficult, sometimes he got no answer, often another occupant of the house answered, promising to pass on a message but forgetting. Two days went by without his speaking to her and that declaration of hers, that statement of intent, became less real. He saw that she had been teasing him. How could he have been so silly as to be upset by it?

When he did manage to speak to her he asked her to come to the cinema with him the following night.

'Don't you remember our arrangement?' she said.

He grew cold. 'What arrangement?'

'I said I'd have lunch with you on Saturdays.'

43

'You can't be serious, Leonora.'

She was serious. She'd see him on Saturday. Where would he like to have lunch?

That was long before he began asking himself what the reason for it could be. He hadn't even considered it could have had something to do with his offer of a loan or with his ways of making a living, still less with Con Mulvanney. By then the Con Mulvanney affair was six, seven, months in the past. He told himself that she was upset about the move, the problems she and Rachel had been having in getting contracts signed, exchanged, a completion date decided on. In a month or two, when they had moved into the flat in Portland Road, things would be different. She would come back to him.

Some might say she had never gone away. He began telling himself she hadn't. He saw her regularly, there was no one else for her and no one serious for him, no one that counted. He phoned her every day, much easier now she had a home of her own and her own phone. They had lunch on Saturdays. Every day he heard her voice and once a week he saw her. There were couples he knew who didn't see each other as often as that. If you told anyone you saw your girlfriend once a week and phoned her every day they would say you were going steady. He reassured himself in this fashion, he comforted himself.

But a man can't be expected to live celibate and there were other girls. Naturally, there were. There wouldn't have been if she hadn't withheld herself. Give him the chance and he would be the most constant lover, the faithfullest of husbands. He never told her about the girls, she didn't ask, and he didn't ask her if there were other men. But he had taken it for granted that though he had to have a girlfriend, he was a man, she didn't have to have a boyfriend, she could live without sex.

'A fine example of the double standard,' said Rachel, speaking of another couple they knew.

It wasn't quite like that. He made this compromise because he couldn't face a starker reality. He convinced himself there was no starker reality. This was reality: that she wasn't very highly sexed, for companionship she preferred the company of women. But she loved him – why else would she talk to him every day and have lunch with him every Saturday?

One day, he had thought, things will change. She's enjoying her freedom, she likes supporting herself, doing her job, trying to run a household on a shoestring, putting those absurd principles of hers into practice. But one day the novelty will have worn off. She'll want to get married, *all* women want to get married, and it was him she'd marry. In a way it was as if they were engaged, betrothed since childhood the way some of those Asian people were. These days a girl wanted to prove herself, show she could be as self-reliant as a man. He even said as much one Saturday when, after lunch, he went back to the new flat with Leonora.

The stairs they had to climb were incredible. He wouldn't have believed so many London flats were without lifts. Rachel was there in one of her typical outfits of ancient skirt from a Monsoon sale (probably the first-ever Monsoon sale) and grey Oxfam jumper. He looked at their house plants and their posters, their Reject Shop crockery and the sofa they'd bought off a pavement in the Shepherds Bush Road, and after a while he'd made that remark about women proving themselves.

'You're a Victorian, you know, Guy,' said Rachel. 'The last one. You ought to be in a museum. The Natural History Museum, d'you think, Leonora? Or the V & A?'

'No, you've got me wrong,' he said, trying to keep his temper, catching sight in a fly-spotted mirror of his young handsome face, his thin athletic figure – a Victorian! 'You've misunderstood. I believe women are equal to men. I know women need to have careers and their own money and a job to go back to after they're married. I know what women want.'

They screamed with laughter. They clutched each other. Rachel said something about Freud. He still didn't know what he'd said that was wrong or funny. After a while it didn't bother him much because it was Rachel who'd made the remark, not Leonora. And he laughed at Leonora over Saturday lunch when she reproved him for saying Rachel's trouble was sour grapes.

He was passing through a long phase of *knowing* she'd come

45

round to marrying him one day. The possibility of her meeting someone else never really occurred to him. Or rather, with a chill like the first frost on the air of autumn, the possibility would occur and he would phone her to reassure himself. Not to explain his feelings, for they were only feelings, never as strong as suspicions, but to listen to her voice and attempt to detect in it some change. And on Saturdays he would watch her and listen to the inflexions of her voice, on the watch for some subtle alteration. She was always the same, wasn't she?

She talked as she always did about the old times, about their youth, and then about her family and her girlfriends, what they'd been doing and saying. None of it interested him but he liked to hear her talk. It was funny really what she'd said about this William Newton's conversation when she hadn't really much conversation herself. There was never a word from her about TV or music or the latest West End hit or fashion or sport. He tried to imagine the content of this fabulous conversation she had with Newton, but imagination failed him.

It was now a week since he had seen her with Newton. He was on the other side of Kensington High Street, crowded traffic-laden Kensington High Street, walking in the direction of Church Street, and they had been on the other side, hand in hand. His Leonora and a skinny red-haired fellow, not much taller than she was.

Hand in hand. He had felt a rush of blood to his head, his face grow red as if he was embarrassed, as if he was *ashamed*. Passionately, he hadn't wanted them to see him, and they hadn't. Afterwards, having a drink at home, he had thought of it as one of the worst shocks of his life, comparable to the one he had received on the day when that woman came to his house and told him about Con Mulvanney.

* * * * *

'You aren't looking too good,' said Danilo.

'I'm perfectly OK.'

For a moment Guy felt affronted. In his new Ungaro jacket and thin Perry Ellis sweater he had been pleased with his appearance. It wasn't his habit to spend much time in front of the mirror, a quick glance was enough to convey the desired impression of deep tan, sepia brush of shadow on the hard jawline, white teeth, a lick of black hair. And the hard, muscular, yet thin, body shape. But that glimpse, caught as he left the house ten minutes before, had showed him something else, something tired and worn perhaps, something *haggard*.

'I've been under a bit of pressure,' he said. 'My migraine's been coming back.'

'You want to eat feverfew.'

'What the hell is feverfew?'

'God knows. I read about it in one of Tanya's papers. She's into all this alternative stuff. Seriously though, you don't look too good.'

They were in a restaurant in that expensive region round the back of Sloane Square. Danilo was a short spare leonine-faced man with a big head and yellowish-brown eyes like an animal's, a fierce small carnivore. Though he was no more than five feet four, some inches shorter than William Newton, and had longish springy sandy hair, Guy would never have called him a ginger dwarf. Danilo wore a very casual but very expensive suit of nearly black seersucker with the jacket sleeves rolled up to show the blue silk lining. He had on a blue shirt with fine dark green stripes but no tie. His two rings were of white gold, one set with a round boss of lapis, the other a square block of jade. A few years back, when it was still possible, Danilo had carried on a very profitable business importing imperial jade from China. That was where Guy's cuff links had come from. Danilo was not Spanish or of South American origin and his given name was really Daniel, but there had been no fewer than five Daniels in his class at primary school, so he had rechristened himself. As well as an importer of various illegal substances, Danilo was a one-remove murderer. Or so Guy believed.

The only area in which Danilo wasn't macho was drink. He had a spritzer in a tall glass. Guy drank more than he ate. He tended to do that, though he ate as well, a fine thick strip of Scottish fillet steak, brought to the table whole and charred outside, blue in, divided into two for them with one dextrous stroke of the knife.

Danilo talked about the villa in Granada he had sold and the house he had bought in the Wye Valley, a Welsh castle with thirty acres, which he intended to furnish with the contents of a Swedish baroque manor house. There was an order prohibiting the removal of any of these tables and chairs and pictures from Sweden but Danilo was fixing things to get around that. He wasn't a particularly self-centred man, and if he was callous, he was not hard-hearted to his friends. This invitation had not been extended for him to talk about himself.

'How's Celeste, then? That still on?'

Guy lifted his shoulders. Any mention of Celeste always embarrassed him.

'The works of art – keeping you in the style to which you're accustomed?'

'I haven't got any money worries, Dan,' said Guy. 'That's not a problem. You and I, that'll never be a problem with us, right?' They had once said to each other, years ago, that a man was only half a man if he couldn't make himself rich.

'Then it has to be little Miss Leo.'

Guy wouldn't have allowed anyone else to call Leonora 'little Miss Leo' but he minded Danilo doing it less than he would some other people. Danilo loved her too, in a more brotherly way, of course, and he hadn't seen her for years, but he still retained for her that tender regard which is born out of a nostalgia for old wild times. She had been more skilful at nicking stuff off Boots' counters than any male companion of theirs. Once, in a single swoop, she had pocketed an electric toothbrush, a hair dryer and a set of heated rollers. Thinking of that reminded Guy of another old friend and helped him put off the moment.

'You ever hear from Linus?'

Danilo laughed. 'That one, he came to a bad end. Well, I would reckon, I don't *know*. Someone told me he went to Malaysia and they hung him for having a little bit of weed on him.'

'You believe that?'

'No, I don't believe most of what I'm told. What's with Leonora then? Come on, you're going to tell me, you might as well come out with it? She getting married, is that it?'

It was unpleasantly near the bone. He said stoutly. 'She won't do that. Well, not unless it's to me. I want to ask you, Dan, I mean, if I want to . . .' Guy looked round. There was no one within earshot but he lowered his voice, '. . . get someone out of the way, could you – well, fix things?'

The irises of the yellow eyes didn't change but the pupils did. They seemed to elongate, becoming black stems instead of spots. Danilo touched a red tongue to his thin lower lip.

'The boyfriend?' he said.

Guy was taken aback. 'How d'you know there's a boyfriend?'

'There's always a boyfriend. You want him wasted?'

Again Guy made that impatient gesture with his shoulders. 'I don't think so. I don't know.' He saw that table in the hotel again, planted Maeve there instead of old Mrs Chisholm, put William Newton in the place of Janice and her fiancé. 'There's someone poisoning her mind against me, Dan, but I don't know who. I don't know which one. I thought I did. If I knew, I'd . . . I *just don't know.*'

'It can be done,' Danilo said calmly. 'For a friend I could get a nice neat job for three grand.'

'And ten nice neat jobs for thirty grand? I can't have a massacre, can I? I can't blast the lot of them off the face of the earth. Dan, I know there's just one of them that's turning her against me, one or at the most two, one or two she wants to please and be in good with. They've told her every lie they can fabricate about me.'

'The fiancé it'll be.'

'I don't think so. *I don't know.* Christ, if I only knew. I'm all sorts of a fool, Dan. I've brought you here for bloody nothing. I don't know who to name to you. I've brought you here for nothing.'

'The steak was magic,' said Danilo. 'I'll break my rule and have a small Chivas Regal.'

Guy said, 'Dan, why did you say that? Why did you say that about Newton?'

'What did I say?'

'You called him "the fiancé".'

'You must have said.'

'I didn't. I said she wasn't, she wouldn't. I mean, this Newton, he exists, of course he does, but he's just a chap who takes her about, he's no more to her than Celeste is to me.'

Danilo gave him a hard look, penetrating but not unkind. 'OK, I remember now. Tanya told me. She saw it in some paper. Yesterday or the day before. She said to have a look at this and wasn't it the Leonora Chisholm I know. It said the usual stuff about the engagement being announced and the marriage shortly to take place. Leonora Chisholm and William Newton. That's how I know the guy's name, it must be, you never told me. That's why I thought it was him you wanted disappeared.'

Of course it was not quite like that, it was *not* like that. He had never been anything but honest with Celeste. She knew he was in love with Leonora, or he had told her he was, he had been quite open. It was not his fault if she persisted in taking it in the wrong way.

'I don't mind, sweet Guy, why would I mind? I know I'm not your first, I'd be mad to expect it. You're not mine, are you?'

He wouldn't let that pass. 'I'm in love with Leonora, I love her. I can't imagine life without her. I'd marry her tomorrow if I could.'

She had smiled at him. 'Yeah, sure. You have lunch with her on Saturdays, you're with her an hour and a half. I guess I can stand that. If that's the competition I can take it.'

Her father came from Trinidad where the people have Indian blood. Her mother was Gibraltarian. She had a perfect Caucasian face that happened to be the colour of teak and a body like an Egyptian girl on a vase painting. She was a model. Her hair was a dark russet brown, immensely thick, and grew naturally in deep long waves, like Dorothy Lamour's in some South Seas movie of the thirties.

When Guy took her about men turned to look at her. He could swear that once, walking behind her down the staircase at Blake's, he had heard a man growl at the sight of her. On the other hand, when he was out with Leonora – or *had* been out with her, for now it happened very seldom – no one looked at her. Of course it was true that men on scaffolds and men down road holes whistled at her, she was young and her legs were lovely and she was attractive. But the traffic wouldn't stop for her, no one would stop for her and stare. The odd thing was that this made no difference. The seething, positively palpitating admiration Celeste received and the indifference which greeted Leonora's appearance, had not the least effect on him. He sometimes thought he would be rather relieved if Celeste said goodbye, it had been nice but she'd met someone else.

He reproached himself, it was horrible, it was unfair. But what could he do? He hadn't asked Celeste to chase him, he didn't invite her to be there waiting for him when he got home. He didn't even give her a key. She pinched his spare one and had another cut. She was in love with him as he was in love with Leonora and that, as he put it to himself, screwed him up. But it wasn't as bad for her as it was for him. At least he didn't refuse her, he didn't show her the door, or have the lock changed or tell her to go to hell. He didn't restrict their meetings to lunch on Saturdays. He was nice to her. He slept with her, though he often thought rather sadly that he could if necessary have done without that and he told himself he should have ignored his body, obeyed his mind and heart, and like some knight waiting for his lady, have remained chaste.

She didn't drink coffee. He made tea and put the cup on the bed table beside her, touched her shoulder lightly, and said, 'Cup of tea, love.'

Her eyes half-open, she said what she always said to him when she woke. 'Hi, sweet Guy, love you.'

She took a long time waking, especially if it happened to be a Saturday, if she happened to have come round on a Friday night and be there on Saturday morning. He wondered sometimes, feeling his own wound, if she avoided waking on those mornings because Saturday was his lunch-with-Leonora day, if she needed to postpone consciousness for as long as possible, and awareness of what the day would bring. Perhaps it wasn't like that though, perhaps he was only projecting his own feelings on to her, judging her by himself. There is something very low in trying to gauge the emotions of someone in love with oneself when one is far from being in love with them, and Guy knew it.

He walked up to the macho health club called Gladiators in Gloucester Road that he belonged to. Forty-five minutes with the weights, then the steam room, cold shower, thirty lengths of the pool. He decided to miss breakfast, though he could have had a healthy one at the juice 'n' grains bar. The scales showed him he had put on two pounds. So much for Danilo's comments on the state of his health.

It was still only eleven. If he had thought of it he could have gone to the rifle range in the King's Road and put in an hour's practice but he hadn't thought of it and he only liked using one of his own guns. He was suddenly most unwilling to go back to

# CHAPTER
# FIVE

G uy's bed was a four-poster, japanned, with a canopy in
the Chinese style, made by the firm of William Linnell in
1753. Gilded flying dragons seemed just to have alighted
on the curving scarlet horns of its pagoda-like top. Its curtains
were of yellow silk. There was one very much like it in the
Victoria and Albert Museum. The bedroom walls were covered
with a Shiki silk paper. There was no carpet on the wood-block
floor but Chinese Pillar rugs with dragons and animal masks
and cloud motifs.

At eight-thirty on Saturday morning Guy was in his four-
poster bed with Celeste Seton. She was still asleep but he was
awake, contemplating the making of coffee, eating some small
light thing, as yet undecided on, and then going for an hour or
two to his health club. Guy looked at Celeste's exquisite face on
the pillow, like a precious delicate bronze, and thought how
beautiful she was but avoided otherwise thinking about her.
As soon as he thought about her he was filled with guilt. The
idea that he loved one woman and used another for sexual
purposes was shameful and abhorrent to him.

Scarsdale Mews. Celeste would still be there. Celeste would very likely still be in bed and would put out her arms to him. Most things his situation with Celeste and Leonora brought him he could take, though wincing, but not passing straight from one to the other, even though Celeste knew and Leonora wouldn't care.

Oh, but wouldn't she? It occurred to him that he had never actually, in so many words, told Leonora Celeste was his *lover*, that she frequently slept with him the night before he came for his lunch date, that she *loved* him and often swore she would love him for ever. Perhaps he should try telling her. The idea that Leonora might be jealous made him feel dizzy; he had to sit down on a seat in the park.

Today their lunch date was at Cranks, the original one in Soho. Nothing but love would have induced Guy to go there. Of course he had never been to Cranks but he was aware that it was a vegetarian restaurant and for all he knew alcohol-free. Having decided not to go home first, simply to leave Celeste (not by any means for the first time) to take herself off and perhaps phone him later, he began to walk vaguely in the direction of Hyde Park Corner. He would perhaps pick up a taxi in Park Lane or even walk all the way.

The sky was a soft delicate blue, overspread with a fine network of tiny clouds which did nothing to hinder the passage of the sun's rays. The sun was warm, delightful, but not hot. There was no breeze or sharpness in the air. The lawns to the left of him which bordered the Serpentine were this morning the abode of waterfowl, ducks with russet-coloured heads and black and white ducks with long necks, barnacle geese and pink-footed geese, red-wattled Muscovies and mallards with green satin crowns. A little way ahead of him, at the point where Rotten Row comes very close to the waterside, a girl and a man were feeding the ducks from a bag of bread cubes, or the girl was feeding them while the man stood aside, watching her and polishing a pair of sunglasses with a tissue. Guy slackened his pace. The girl screwed up the paper bag and put it in her pocket, having looked in vain for a litter basket. She and her companion began to walk away. They were on Rotten Row itself, some twenty or thirty yards ahead of him and evidently going in the same direction. Guy had recognised them as Maeve Kirkland and Robin Chisholm.

At first he felt simple astonishment that they knew each other. But nothing of course could be more likely. Robin was Leonora's brother and a 'close' brother, Maeve one of her flatmates for the past three years. They were not holding hands or walking particularly close together, they were not walking as Leonora and the ginger dwarf had been. There was no indication that they were lovers or even close friends.

Guy didn't want to be seen by them. He let them get further and further ahead of him. If one of them turned round he would simply cut across the grass on to the South Carriage Drive. He wondered where they were going and what they were talking about. Both were wearing denim and T-shirts, Maeve's a 'shocking' purplish-pink, Robin's white. In spite of her name, Maeve was not Irish. She was a big statuesque blonde, Valkyrie-like, a good inch taller than Robin, who was himself nearly six feet. Ten years ago women still minded being taller than their men (or the men minded) and if they could have been transported a decade back in time, Maeve would have worn flat shoes and even rounded her shoulders. Now she had on high heels that looked uncomfortable with her short denim skirt, but perhaps were not. In them she towered above Robin.

Maeve was not one of Leonora's childhood or school or college friends. She and Rachel met her when they advertised for a third girl to share the flat, which in the end was far more expensive than had at first appeared. They were aghast at what the monthly repayments on the mortgage turned out to be, but instead of accepting a further offer of help from him, they abandoned the idea of having two bedrooms and a living room, made the flat into what were virtually three bedsits and advertised for a lodger. Maeve was the successful applicant. Mysteriously to Guy, both girls liked Maeve, who became a friend and frequent fellow guest at those dinner parties in the flat, family lunch parties and other outings-in-a-crowd of which Leonora seemed so fond.

Guy found her bossy and noisy and far too tall. As much as Rachel, though in a different way, she took it on herself to dictate to him what his relationship with Leonora ought to be. That amounted, in her eyes, to no relationship at all. She was less subtle about it than Rachel and less obscure. But she was ruder. There was an expression his grandmother had used that he thought would apply to Maeve: fishwife.

Perhaps Robin and Maeve had been going out together for years. Leonora had said nothing but he feared there were many things in her life of which Leonora told him nothing. He watched them ahead of him, walking more slowly now towards Hyde Park Corner, and then suddenly – Robin raised his right arm and put it around Maeve's shoulders. Almost simultaneously, as if she feared someone behind her might see and disapprove, or as if she sensed his presence, Maeve turned her head and looked in his direction.

He knew she would wave. She might not like him, he was sure she didn't like him, but they knew each other, had frequently sat at the same table, constantly spoke on the phone when he rang Leonora and she happened to answer. He began to lift his arm to make the gesture that was obligatory in response to hers. She stared hard and turned away. She didn't wave. Guy felt disproportionately shocked and angry. He felt outraged. Maeve and Robin had their heads close together now, they were talking it seemed in whispers, though why they had need to whisper there in the open with no one within fifty yards of them, was a mystery. They were talking about him. That was very plain. It was only natural to wonder not only what they were saying but what they had *already said* and said to Leonora.

The two heads were so close together that their hair, copious in each case, though Maeve's was longer and fairer, seemed to combine in a bright golden-brown shining sun-suffused mass, like a large silky flower. And now, moved to a need for greater closeness due no doubt to Robin's agreeing with the malicious slanders she was uttering, Maeve passed her arm round his waist. They were entwined, had become Siamese twins joined at the hip. He imagined those slanders, fabrications of what he did for a living, inventions about his private life. Robin, who might well frequent the same nightspots as he did, could easily have seen him with Celeste. They would relay all this to Leonora. And Leonora was far more likely to listen to and be swayed by what her own contemporaries said than by people thirty years her senior.

*He* would be. He imagined the relative effect on him of Danilo's advice or caution and that of Danilo's father, a crafty old man who ran a betting shop. He would take ten times more notice of Danilo. And he would take ten times more notice of the counsel of Celeste than that of, say, his own mother if they ever again encountered each other.

The couple ahead turned off Rotten row on to the path to Serpentine Road and the Achilles statue. Maeve didn't turn her head again. For all he knew, they might be going to meet Leonora for a prelunch drink somewhere, they might be on their way to fill her up with warnings so that by the time he and she met at one, she would be well-armed against him and on her guard. He had surely been wrong to lay all the blame for Leonora's change of heart – or outward change – at Tessa's door. Others were just as much to blame, or more so, Maeve and Robin were even more powerful enemies.

It was still early. Guy retraced his steps a little way, walked through into Knightsbridge by the Albert Gate, and stood looking into Lucienne Phillips' window at the clothes which would have all looked wonderful on Celeste and at one short-skirted dark blue satin dress that might have been designed for Leonora.

\*   \*   \*   \*

'I suppose you had that rubbish put in the paper to please your family,' Guy said.

He and Leonora were in Cranks, which was very crowded. They were not even able to get a table to themselves. As it was, they sat pressed up against the wall while four very young girls dominated the table, giggling loudly, tasting each other's food and talking about office rivalries. Guy had already reproached Leonora for suggesting they come here. It was a very long time since he had been in a self-service restaurant. He had had to queue up for his food which was quiche and salad, the least offensively vegetarian on offer. At any rate he had managed to get a glass – in fact, three glasses – of wine.

They were both speaking in necessarily low voices. Not that their table companions took any notice of them. Leonora was also wearing the summer Saturday uniform of jeans, T-shirt and white trainers. Her jeans were blue denim, her T-shirt blue, white and mauve stripes. She had a mauve headband on between her fringe and the rest of her hair. Guy thought she looked lovely in spite of what she wore but for all that he would have liked to see her in a dress when she came out to lunch with him. The first thing he had looked for he had not found, to his great relief. The absence on her finger of an engagement ring helped give rise to his remark.

She said in a pleasant even tone, 'If it had been entirely up to William and me, no, I don't think we'd have bothered to announce it. I don't think, come to that, we'd have "got engaged". My parents wanted it and so did his. It's a small thing to do to give so much pleasure, don't you think?'

'I see.' He laughed a little. 'I know you always do what your parents want.'

She didn't deny it. 'Why did you call it rubbish, Guy? I told you I was in love with William.'

'I'd call that rubbish too.' He finished the first of his glasses of wine. Leonora was drinking apple juice, looking at him over the top of her glass in what he interpreted as a sulky way. He changed the subject. 'You never told me Maeve was going about with your brother.'

'I suppose I didn't think you'd be interested.'

'Everything even remotely connected with you interests me, Leo, you ought to know that. I saw them in the park. They were walking along ahead of me. Have you been with them before you met me?'

'What, just now, d'you mean? Of course I haven't Guy. Why would I? They don't want to spend their Saturdays with me.'

'Where does he live now?'

'*Now* he lives in Chelsea, he's just moved. I think he'd like

Maeve to move in with him and perhaps she will when I've gone.'

He let that pass. The girls were leaving. The table was littered with their debris but at least, for the time being, it was left to him and Leonora. He leaned a little towards her.

'You haven't really changed in your feelings towards me, have you? You feel the same as you always have, but you think, or you've been persuaded, that being involved with me wouldn't be wise, wouldn't be a good thing for you. That's it, isn't it?'

She spoke carefully, considering. 'I do love you, Guy. I always have and I think I always will. It's got a lot to do with what we were to each other when we were teenagers.'

His heart seemed to take a little happy leap, to dance about inside his chest. He felt the blood mount into his face. He put out his hand to touch hers which lay on the table.

'But Guy, we've nothing in common any more, we don't like the same things. I *hate* what you do for a living. Looking back, I hate what you've done.'

That made him laugh. 'Oh, come on. How about you? I was only thinking the other day how brilliant you were at nicking stuff. D'you remember how we used to get rid of it all down the Portobello?'

Her voice was very low. 'You don't know how ashamed I am of the things I did. They fill me with self-disgust when I think of them. But you still think they were all right, you think anything goes so long as you make money out of it.'

Her hand was flat and limp under his. He withdrew his own and looked at it as if something had stung it and he was watching for the sting to swell. 'I do nothing illegal any longer,' he said. 'Nothing.' Not since the death of Con Mulvanney, he thought, but he didn't say it aloud, she knew nothing of that, and please Christ, she never would.

'It's not just illegal things, it's – well, unethical things. Oh, Guy, you don't know what I'm talking about, do you? That's part of the trouble, we don't speak the same language. Your sole aim in life is to make lots of money and live in luxury and have power and make more and more money. And anyway, you can't wipe out the past just by saying you don't do things any longer. Someone told me you'd actually once run a protection racket. Oh, Guy!'

'Who told you?' he said, very cold.

'Does it matter?'

'Yes. I'd like to know.'

'Well, then, it was Magnus.'

He knew it! Hadn't he guessed as much? 'And?'

'He was acting for a client, finding him a barrister, you know how they do, and this man was some sort of criminal and he mentioned your name in connection with a protection racket up in Kensal.'

'And Magnus told you?'

'He said it couldn't be the same Guy Curran, but Mummy said it was and of course it was, I knew that.'

'You listen to what these people say about me, don't you, Leonora? You listen to all of them?'

She said softly, 'It wouldn't make any difference what anyone said. We're poles apart. We aren't *like* each other.'

He didn't answer that. He said rather slowly and in a deliberate and calculated drawl, 'I've got a beautiful girlfriend. Her name is Celeste. She is twenty-three and a model and she is very lovely. She stayed with me last night. She's probably still at Scarsdale Mews waiting for me to come back.'

For a single horrible instant he thought Leonora was going to smile and tell him how happy she was for him, how delighted. But a shadow had crossed her face. Her expression was fixed, the dark blue eyes steady, the lips compressed. She was jealous! He could see it, he couldn't be mistaken.

'Are you making it up?'

'Sweetheart, if it wasn't you that asked I'd really resent that.' He was aware of echoing what she had said to him when he seemed incredulous about Newton. How close they were really! They read each other's thoughts! 'I'm supposed to be *attractive* to women,' he said, smiling at her. 'Ring her up, go on, ask her. Go and call my house.'

Someone, a woman, had once told him that we always feel jealousy over the loves of our past lovers. Even if we no longer care for them, even if we have a new lover, a true love that will be everlasting, we are still jealous. The pang of rejection is still there, for we are all insecure, all terrified of desertion, all longing to be the first and only, or if not the first, the last. But he forgot that now or didn't think of it. She was jealous, his Leonora was jealous because he had another woman.

'I'm very happy for you, Guy,' she said. 'I hope it goes really well. I'm very pleased.' A thought struck her. 'But, Guy, would she mind about you meeting me like this? She does know? I mean, perhaps we ought to stop if she's likely to mind.'

'Of course she doesn't mind,' he said impatiently, and then, 'If you've finished, shall we go? Shall we go somewhere else, even if it's only sitting on the grass in Soho Square?'

He knew she'd refuse but she didn't. 'All right, just for half an hour.'

He wondered what would happen if he tried to take her hand. Better not risk it. They walked along side by side. The clouds had gone and the sky become a hot, hard blue. He found himself suddenly thinking of a holiday they had planned to take together at this time four years ago. They were going to one of the less-frequented Greek islands and he had seen it, without of course discussing this with her, as the venue for resuming their sexual relationship. The sea was called wine-dark down there and the nights were warm. They were going to stay in a wonderful kind of hotel where all the rooms were little grass-roofed huts and each had its own private path down to the silver beach. She would return to him there, physically return to his arms, and soon after they came back they would be married, the job she was going to take and the bedsit she was going to share with Rachel forgotten.

She had called it off less than two weeks beforehand. It was because he was paying, she said. It was no good, she couldn't pay her share, she couldn't afford to, and she couldn't let him pay for her, so they had to call it off. Even now, remembering it was deeply painful. In his philosophy a woman acknowledged a man's love and her love for him by letting him pay for things. The bargain between them consisted in a kind of loving sale, though it didn't sound pleasant put that way.

He glanced at her Egyptian profile, the firm mouth and chin, the rather severe nose, the dark curtain of hair that hung two inches across her cheek. Her head was bowed as if she was deep in thought.

'You're not going away on holiday this year, are you?' he said, thinking of being deprived of his Saturdays, of maybe missing two or three of his Saturdays.

'Not exactly on holiday,' she said. 'I mean, we'll be going away later.'

His heart leaden, sinking. 'Who's we?'

'I've been putting it off telling you, Guy. But things are different now you've told me about Celeste. I'm getting married on September the sixteenth and we'll be going away after that on our honeymoon.'

# CHAPTER SIX

It was five weeks away.

The wedding would be at Kensington Register Office, the usual routine ceremony with Maeve and Robin as witnesses. They weren't religious. On the evening of the wedding day Leonora's father and his wife were giving a party for them. Anthony and Susannah Chisholm lived in London, not in the Notting Hill mews but in a flat on two floors of an early nineteenth-century house in Lamb's Conduit Street that had belonged to Susannah and her first husband. William Newton's father and mother lived in Hong Kong and wouldn't come for the wedding because they would be in England for Christmas, but his sister and brother-in-law would be there.

She told him all about it.

'It's not him, though, is it? You wouldn't have me if he was dead, for instance, would you? It's something else.'

'He won't *be* dead, Guy. Why should he? He's a healthy man of thirty.'

'If I thought it was him I'd like to kill him. I'd like to fight him, challenge him to a duel and kill him.'

'Don't be ridiculous.'

'Can he handle a gun? No, don't tell me. I don't want to know about him. He's just an excuse, anyway. Any man but me. I'd like to know why, Leonora. I'd like to know what happened to turn you against me.'

This conversation took place not in Soho Square but on the following Saturday in a restaurant which, for once, she had allowed him to choose. It was in that part of Notting Hill called Hillgate Village, on the southern side of the Bayswater Road. Leonora was wearing a dress. It was a hot day and the dress was short and made of some clinging diaphanous fabric, white with misty pink and mauve flowers and a plain mauve belt or sash. She had white tights on and flat pink shoes. On the coat rack at the entrance to the restaurant she had hung up her hat of fine white straw with lilac ribbons. After lunch she was going to the wedding of a friend of William Newton's, mention of which had given rise to talk of her own.

Guy wished she would always dress like that. He ached with desire for her. He heard his own voice cross-examining her and he hated himself for the bullying tone, the reiterated questions, but he had to know. She gave him an injured, sullen look. She wouldn't have a dessert, cheese or coffee, in case she was late. Pressed, she said nothing had happened to turn her against him. No, it wasn't his offering to buy her a flat that had done it, nothing had 'done it', it had been a gradual process that began in her late teens. She had grown out of him and wished he would grow out of her.

'You were jealous when I told you about Celeste,' he said. 'I could see it in your eyes. That means you really love me still.'

'That's nonsense, Guy.'

'If you marry him while you love me you'll be committing a crime against yourself and me.'

She laughed at him. He thought her very cruel but understood it was a defence. If she hadn't laughed she would have burst out crying. It was a hard unwomanly sound, that laughter, more pain in it than amusement.

She went away to William Newton's relative's wedding after that and left him sitting at the table drinking brandy.

Maeve and Robin, Anthony and Susannah, Tessa and Magnus, Rachel Lingard, one of them or one set of them had done this. But done what? Convinced her that he was entirely unsuitable so that, bowing to their coercion, she had thrown herself into the arms of the first man who came along. They had probably brought the man along themselves, found him and vetted him and introduced him to Leonora.

He phoned her as usual on Sunday, on Monday and Tuesday. He refused to admit the possibility that she would actually get married on September 16, but if anything so impossible and *wicked* did happen, just if, he intended to go on phoning her every day. Sometimes he imagined still doing it when they were old and she was a grey grandmother and he an aged millionaire, single but with many beautiful unloved mistresses. But it wouldn't happen because one day, if not this year or next year, the year after or the year after that, she would marry *him*. Out of his path he would clear those who stood between them. Rachel answered the phone on Sunday, Maeve on Monday and Tuesday.

Rachel said, 'I'll fetch her,' followed by a heavy theatrical sigh and a remark which made him grind his teeth: 'She guessed who it would be. She had the sort of premonition psychic people have just before a road accident.'

Maeve said when he asked to speak to Leonora, 'Must you?'

He was furious. 'What the fuck d'you mean, "must I"? What affair is it of yours?'

'Don't speak to me like that, please. You won't get to talk to Leonora by using obscene language.'

'Oh, won't I? I'll keep ringing this fucking number till I do. And by the way, thanks very much for ignoring me in the park last week. Charming manners you and your boyfriend have.'

'I never saw you in the park, last week or any other time.'

She went away and Leonora came on the line. Next day Rachel answered the phone again and said there was such a thing as having Telecom change the number, did he know that? He didn't reply.

'Alexander Graham Bell's got a lot to answer for,' said Rachel.

She really hated him, there was venom in her voice. It was extraordinary the way these women, Tessa, Rachel, Maeve, thought they were *being loyal to Leonora* by putting her against him, when in fact the best possible thing they could do for Leonora was encourage her to marry him and thus ensure for herself, apart from the love and romance aspect, a future free from financial worry and a life of happiness and luxury.

Guy never stayed at home in the evenings. What would he do there? He hadn't made a fortune in order to sit in his house eating takeaways and watching videos. Susannah Chisholm, who had always been nicer to him than any of the rest of that lot, had once told a story of someone she had met in New York who said that since he came to live in Manhattan he had never once eaten his dinner at home. The other people there had laughed and wondered at this and been amazed but Guy, though he didn't say so, had wondered what all the fuss was about as he, since he came to Scarsdale Mews, had never eaten dinner at home either. Going out in the evening meant drinking out, eating out and then going on to a club for more drinking out.

He seldom went to a theatre but occasionally to the cinema, to please Celeste. Having flatly refused to consider *Women on the Verge of a Nervous Breakdown* at the Lumière, he had consented to go to *Paris by Night* at the Curzon West End.

They had been to the six fifty-five showing because both preferred to eat afterwards and it was only nine o'clock when they came out. Guy had booked a table at a restaurant he particularly liked in Stratton Street, where Leonora would never have allowed him to take her for lunch. It was a warm airless evening after another hot day. Celeste was wearing a dress of white cotton broderie anglaise, short and tight but not obviously so because she was so slender. She had white sandals with straps of alternating white and gilded leather, white and green bracelets on both arms, and each separate tiny plait of her hair, at least fifty of these, ended in a gold pointed tip. Guy wore a linen suit in a very light greyish-beige with a bitter chocolate-coloured open-necked shirt, a belt of plaited grey leather and white trainers with a grey leather trim. He had thought, some hours before, that they made a handsome couple but this was simply an opinion, it gave him no particular pleasure.

As they were coming out of the cinema he saw Leonora and William Newton leaving ahead of them. Although he had spoken to Leonora that afternoon, he still felt at the sight of her those extraordinary and characteristic sensations, which were even stronger when on very rare occasions he came upon her by chance. His heart seemed to stand still, then to beat not faster but somehow more *loudly*. Those people who surrounded him and her, a considerable crowd of people, mostly young or youngish, who until he saw her had seemed attractive and colourful, some of them very well worth looking at, now faded to faceless shadows, the dead perhaps, or extras in an old monochrome film. Only he and she existed in the world.

This sensation lasted a few moments. By the time the crowd had faces again he and Celeste, she and Newton, were all out on the pavement. Leonora turned her head and looked straight at him. She was pleased to see him, he could tell she was. She was smiling her lovely, carefully governed smile and, taking hold of Newton's sleeve, drawing him over in their direction.

'Guy,' she said, 'you didn't say you were going to the cinema.'

'Nor did you. This is Celeste. Celeste, Leonora.' He wasn't going to utter Newton's name.

'This is William.'

Loving her so much, he could admit to himself that she looked awful. A couple of hippies left over from the sixties they might have been, Newton in a pair of khaki cotton loons from Dirty Dick's and a T-shirt that must have been a pale blue before it was put through the cold wash with a lot of navy and red garments about a hundred times. Her dress was one of Laura Ashley's less successful lines, bought no doubt in a sale three or four years ago, a now faded or washed-out navy and white viscose print with elasticated waist and too-long short sleeves, a hem that came halfway down her awful scuffed red leather boots. Guy was pleased. A woman who would dress like that to go out with a man couldn't care much about him.

He told them about the restaurant in Stratton Street and suggested they join him and Celeste. Newton said he didn't think so, thanks. Guy's eyebrows went up. Well, had they eaten or hadn't they? They had to eat.

Guy thought a ghost of a smile crossed Newton's face at that remark, he couldn't think why. Newton was a bit taller than he remembered, by no means a particularly short man, though the horsy face and ginger hair were just as he recalled them. *And* he was wearing glasses. Guy thought that any young person with a scrap of self-esteem who had trouble with his eyes would have gone into contact lenses.

'We eat at home, Guy,' Leonora said. 'We had something earlier.'

'That must be hours ago.'

'We'll come with you and have something cheap,' she said.'We'll have pasta, just one course.'

She wanted to be with him! Now they'd met she couldn't bear to go straight home! She could see him in contrast to Newton. She could see him *with Celeste*. He felt a great warmth and affection for Celeste quite suddenly and he took her hand. The gesture was not lost on Leonora who looked at their joined hands but did not take Newton's. When they got to the restaurant the two women went straight to the ladies' cloakroom. He was left alone with Newton and girded himself for a fight or a silence.

But Newton, who Leonora had said at lunch on Saturday was something at the BBC, a producer of documentaries on social questions or something equally boring, began to talk about the film they had just seen. He asked if Guy had liked it and why. Guy hadn't much liked it but he found it hard to say why not, so he changed the subject by asking Newton if he liked Paris, if he had been there recently and would he have liked to be there for the two hundred years' anniversary of the Revolution. He lit a cigarette because that helped him concentrate.

Newton didn't wave the smoke away or anything like that, but he moved his chair a little. To Guy's surprise he had a drink, gin and tonic, the same as Guy himself, instead of alcohol-free beer which might have been expected. He'd been to Paris in the spring, he said, to see the Gauguin exhibition, which he began to describe and praise. Guy wondered if this was designed to get at him, a snide attack on his hand-done original oil painting enterprise. Newton seemed to see that he was bored, stopped talking about Gauguin and said Paris would be too crowded and anyway he usually went to Scotland for a couple of weeks in August, though he wouldn't be doing that this year.

Guy knew why he wouldn't be doing it this year. Why he *thought* he wouldn't be. Where had the women got to? They had been away ten minutes. Perhaps they were scratching each other's eyes out somewhere over him. Scotland in August meant only one thing, as far as he knew. He had to find something to talk to the man about.

'Shoot, do you?'

'Only in self-defence,' said Newton, 'and no grouse has attacked me yet.'

Whoever said that sarcasm was the lowest form of wit was right, thought Guy. 'It's surprisingly easier to become a good shot than you might think. There's something very satisfying when you bring down your first bird.'

'If that's the way you look at things, yes, I expect it is. Considering the stalwart band of thickies who do it excellently, it must be. I shouldn't care to shoot birds or animals. The fact that they've been bred for the purpose of being shot rather makes things worse.'

'What would you like to shoot then? People?' Guy laughed rather loudly at his own joke.

'I've managed to live for thirty years in reasonable contentment without shooting anything, Guy, and I expect I can go on in the same way for another thirty. A death-dealing banging about doesn't appeal to me.'

'A man should be able to handle a gun,' Guy said. 'I belong to a rifle club. Of course, we shoot at targets.'

Newton slightly inclined his head, the way a bored person does who doesn't really want to be rude but doesn't care much either. Guy said, 'The girls have been a long time.' Another nod from Newton. Guy didn't know what made him think of it but having thought of it, he felt an inexplicable surge of excitement. 'Ever done any fencing?' he said.

Now Newton turned to look him fully in the face. He looked right into Guy's eyes. The smile was there again, very slight, somehow in the eyes and inside his head rather than in any movement of the lips. Guy saw that his eyes, which he would have remembered as greyish or fawnish out of Newton's presence, were in fact a deep blue-grey, of that shade which is less like an animal's than any other.

He took a long time replying. Then he said, 'At school.'

'At *school?*'

'And a bit later on. You belong to a fencing club, do you?'

'Me? No, why should I?'

Guy knew Newton must be getting at him, something he wasn't going to put up with, and he was about to repeat his question when Leonora and Celeste came back. They both looked pleased with themselves, Guy thought. Leonora asked what they had been talking about and Newton said, grinning, that it had been about martial arts.

They gave their orders, Leonora and Newton sticking to their decision to eat pasta, though Guy did his best to make Leonora change her mind. He didn't care what Newton ate. That wasn't quite true as he would really have liked to see him eat something poisonous, something laced with cyanide perhaps or infected with one of those fashionable germs, listeria or salmonella, and roll about the floor in front of the women, groaning and frothing at the mouth. He hated Newton and his grin and his cool clever eyes. He was talking more about fencing now, or rather about early prize fighting, in the sixteenth and seventeenth centuries, when before the days of bare-knuckle fighting men attacked each other on public stages with blunted blades and often with 'sharps'. Guy thought it an unsuitable subject at the table and with women present.

This then was an example of Newton's vaunted 'conversation'. Apparently he possessed a pair of sabres which, crossed, ornamented a wall in his flat in Camden Town. He was thinking of selling them, Leonora didn't want them in their new home. Guy would have liked to know where they had in mind but wasn't going to ask. Celeste asked.

'I'm selling my flat. Leonora's selling her share of their place to her friend who owns half of it already.'

'Rachel's grandmother died and left her some money, so she'll buy my half,' Leonora said. 'We're not in a hurry, anyway. I shall live at William's place in the meantime.'

Why did no one ever tell him these things? Why was he kept in the dark? It was a wonder that Rachel bothered to work at all, the way her rich relatives kept dying and leaving her slabs of wealth. His steak arrived, an enormous bloody wedge of it, which he fancied Newton was looking at in a mocking way, though when he raised his eyes he saw that the other man had his back to him and was saying something to Celeste. Guy was drinking rather a lot. No one wanted any more out of the second bottle of wine, so he finished it and began drinking shorts, dry martinis without ice though it was so warm.

Before the bill came Newton leant towards him and said they would split it.

'Absolutely not,' Guy said. 'I invited you.'

'Please, Guy,' Leonora said, 'we'd much rather.'

'I wouldn't dream of it, I wouldn't entertain it for a moment.'

'Well, thanks for entertaining us then,' Newton said and he immediately got up and went off to the men's.

Had that been a dig at him for using a phrase which a clever bastard like Newton might think was incorrect or out of date or silly or whatever people like him did think? He was instantly sure that Newton was double-crossing him and meant to sneak up to the waiter and pay his share before the bill came to Guy. That this had not happened, that the bill when it came was for the four of them, surprised him very much. What was the man up to? What was his game?

A taxi now had to be secured. Leonora looked tired, she looked as if she hadn't enjoyed the evening, had found it for some reason a strain and was worn out. She had seen Newton and him together of course for the first time. Was she, after what she had seen, having – glorious idea! – second thoughts about Newton? Had he compared them, as he must, Newton would have come out wanting.

'If you're going north,' he said to Newton, 'why don't you take the first taxi? Leonora can come with us and we'll drop her on our way.'

'I can't do that, Guy, I'm staying at William's till Friday. And we won't take a taxi, we'll go by tube.'

'Green Park to Warren Street and then up the Northern Line,' said Newton, smug and cool. 'Nothing easier. Good night. Good night, Celeste, it's been nice meeting you.'

In the taxi Guy said, 'I should have asked her for his phone number. If she's at his place I won't be able to talk to her tomorrow.'

'Try the phone book,' said Celeste.

'Yes, he'll be in the book. What did she say to you all that long time you were in the ladies'?'

'This and that. She talked about us and about William.'

'He's a bit of a shit,' he said.

'I liked him, I thought he was very nice.'

'But you can't imagine a woman falling in love with him, can you? The idea's grotesque.'

'I'll tell you what she said if you like. She said she was really happy to see you so happy with me. She said I was beautiful and you were lucky to have me and she was sure you knew your luck and she hoped we'd be very very happy. D'you want to know what else she said?'

'Not really,' said Guy. 'It doesn't sound very inspired. I don't suppose you want to come back with me, do you? Not if you have to get up early for that L'Oréal job. I'll tell the driver to go along the Old Brompton Road, shall I? Celeste, you're not crying, are you? For God's sake, what is there to cry about?'

Guy fell asleep very quickly and dreamt he was fighting William Newton with swords. They were in Kensington Gardens, on the lawn by the Albert Memorial below the Flower Walk. It was very early in the morning, dawn, the sun not yet risen, and there was no one about but themselves and their seconds. His second was Linus Pinedo and Newton's was a man whose face Guy couldn't see because it was covered by a fencer's mask. Guy had done a certain amount of fencing some four or five years before, had taken lessons and belonged to a club, but had given it up in favour of squash which was so fast and better exercise. But in the dream he was very good, he was like some thirties film star in *The Prisoner of Zenda*.

His aim was only to wound Newton, though perhaps severely, but the man was clearly terrified and scarcely able to put up a defence. Guy, intending a thrust to his left arm – Newton, at any rate in the dream, was left-handed – jumped forward, executing the move called the 'balestra' and followed it by a 'fleche' at great speed which passed in a single swift lunge through Newton's heart.

Newton made no sound but sank onto his knees, his foil dropped, his hands clasped together on the forte of Guy's sword. He fell over onto his side onto the green, now blood-splashed grass. The death rattle issued from his pale lips and he gave up the ghost in the masked man's arms. Guy withdrew his sword, which came out clean and shining.

Linus looked into Guy's eyes and said, 'That'll give you breathing space, man. That'll give you time.'

Guy felt happy, he felt an enormous relief. Newton was dead, so Leonora couldn't marry him. Now he could discover *at his leisure* the slanderer who had poisoned her mind against him. He bent over the dead man, feeling grateful to him, almost caring for him. The masked man, in a single swift gesture, took off his mask and revealed to Guy, who was now trembling and horrified, his identity. It was Con Mulvanney.

\* \* \* \*

In the morning, still quite shaken from the dream, Guy looked up Newton's number in the phone book, found his address in Georgiana Street, which he then looked up in the *ABC London Street Atlas*. Linus's opinion in the dream, that getting Newton out of the way would give him time, now returned to him. Newton might not, as a man, be a serious threat, but he was *there* and Leonora would marry him on September 16, no doubt soon regretting the step she had taken, though by then it would be too late. One thing to be glad about was that divorce was relatively easy.

Why had Con Mulvanney come to him in the dream? If Guy had inherited little from that hopeless feckless mother of his, and derived less, he had at any rate brought with him through the years and changes, some of her superstitions. To this day he would not walk under ladders. His broken-down pushchair had been made to take avoiding detours, often with very real danger from passing cars to the dirty-faced infant occupant. He touched wood in times of anxiety, and threw salt over his left shoulder when some was spilt. Omens he trusted, while saying he didn't believe in them. Premonitions he recognised in sudden vague apprehensions. The totally unexpected appearance of Con Mulvanney in his dream, something that had never happened before, he had never before dreamed of Mulvanney, was a clear omen. What else could it be?

He began to wonder if it was possible anyone had told Leonora about Con Mulvanney. On the face of it, it seemed unlikely. Very few people knew. Of course hundreds, thousands, knew who he was and what had happened to him, though no doubt most of them had now forgotten, but surely only he himself and that woman knew his own connection with Mulvanney's death.

The police knew. Correction – the police had been *told*. It wasn't the same thing. They had found nothing, they had probably in the end not believed her or knew it would be hopeless to prove it.

The woman had a name he would never forget, no one could forget, she was called Poppy Vasari. She had threatened to tell everyone she knew. But what would be the point in naming him to people as the supplier of LSD to Mulvanney when his name would mean nothing? To the police now, that was another story.

But suppose she had carried out her threat and talked of it to friends and acquaintances, given some sort of description of him? 'A handsome, dark man, very young.' He had been only twenty-five at the time. Or 'very well-off, the way these people are, living in one of those pretty houses in a mews in South

Ken.' Those details would be enough to arouse the suspicions of anyone who knew him only slightly. Robin Chisholm, say, or Rachel Lingard. Suppose they then asked his name? Poppy Vasari would tell them, of course she would. She had nothing to lose.

And they would have told Leonora.

No surer way could have been found to put her off him. Four years ago. That was about the time she began radically to change towards him, to change her mind about that holiday, to turn down his invitations, to *wean* herself gradually away from him, to refuse his offer of money to buy that flat. And once she was in the flat, to cease altogether to go out with him in the evenings, to cease kissing him (except in the way she kissed Maeve, on both cheeks), sending others to answer the phone when he rang, gradually achieving the present situation of daily phone calls and lunch on Saturdays.

At ten he dialled Newton's number. Leonora answered. There was a pause, a silence, when she heard who it was, then she spoke cheerfully as if she was really pleased, asking him how he was, saying how much they had enjoyed the previous evening and meeting Celeste.

'Where would you like to have lunch on Saturday?' he said.

'Anywhere you like, Guy. Clarke's if that's what you'd like. After all, we've only got four more.'

# CHAPTER
# SEVEN

Some of the people who worked there called it a factory,
Guy had been told, but to him it was always the studio. It
was at Northolt, in Yeading Lane. Guy usually drove out
there every couple of weeks to see how things progressed. His
other enterprises, the travel agency and the club in Noel Street,
got on perfectly well without his presence, and if he went to the
club sometimes that was because he enjoyed it.

Tessa, the fine arts graduate, had called the studio a
sweatshop, though of course she had never seen it. This was in
any case a manifest lie as the people Guy called his workforce
painted in clean, light, airy surroundings, with plenty of space,
did not work particularly long hours and were reasonably well
paid. He could have paid them more because the paintings
were selling better than he had ever imagined they would, but
as it was they earned more than they would have by teaching,
more for instance than Leonora did. Instead he was seriously
thinking of starting a second studio to cope with the demand.

No one seemed to mind him looking over their shoulders
while they worked. No doubt that was because, as he frankly

told them, he knew nothing about art but admired what they did. He paused and watched a very talented young Indian girl who had been at St Martin's School of Art painting in the tears on the cheeks of the weeping boy. It was wonderful to see the skill with which she did this. How wet the tears looked! Like real drops of water, as if someone had lightly splashed the painted face. And surely she had managed to make the child look sweeter than usual and sadder. Guy could almost identify with him, recalling distant days of deprivation in Attlee House.

What Tessa, and to a lesser extent Leonora, meant by saying that what was done here was morally and – there was some other word, yes, 'aesthetically' – wrong, remained a perpetual mystery to him. It was true that his artists had a basic pattern or guide to follow, that there were affinities here, though remote ones, with painting by numbers. But was that very different, *any* different, from what went on in the studios of those Old Masters? Guy remembered his feeling of triumph when, on holiday in Florence, he had found out from a guide how people such as Michelangelo had workshops like his with young painters in them learning their craft, copying the master's pictures, filling in backgrounds, working regular hours and working to order. Leonora had laughed when he told her this and said it wasn't the same thing, though she had not explained how it differed.

And it wasn't as if these people's original work was any good. The girl he watched putting the finishing touches to 'King and Queen of the Beasts' had actually once shown him one of her own paintings. He had said, 'Very nice,' but it was terrible, just lines of sludge with something that might have been eyes peering out. In the house in Scarsdale Mews he had a Kandinsky which was the nearest thing to it he had ever seen, but at least the Kandinsky was in bright colours and very big and complex which accounted, no doubt, for the very high price he had had to pay for it.

He had coffee with his artists and one of them asked him if he had any paintings from the studio on the walls of his house. He said he had, though this wasn't true and made him wonder obscurely why he hadn't. There was another sale that day in

South London, in Clapham this time, and he had thoughts of dropping in and buying a painting like an ordinary member of the public.

Guy drove south and crossed the river by Kew Bridge. This was a mistake as he didn't know this part of London at all well and got lost. By now he had given up all ideas of buying a painting, he could much more easily have one sent to his home, and was even wondering if he would get to Clapham Common before the sale was over. Somehow he had managed to get himself and the Jaguar south of Wimbledon Park and he must make his way northwards.

If asked, he would have said he had never been in this neighbourhood before. The commons of South London were confusing, there were so many of them, but this certainly wasn't Clapham Common, perhaps Tooting or Tooting Bec. A sign here pointed to Clapham, Battersea, Central London, and he found himself in a big thoroughfare that seemed vaguely familiar. It was Balham, that was where it was, this was Bedford Hill and in that pub, that great Victorian mansion of a pub, where he had on that fateful night been accosted by Con Mulvanney.

'Have you got any shit?'

The question, ugly, ridiculous, meaningless but having a special meaning to those in the know, remained in his memory, the words reverberating there like so many plucked strings, while much of the rest of what had happened that evening had faded. He hadn't replied of course, he had pretended ignorance, disgust even, had turned his back, but the man had been insistent, had returned to the attack, now rephrasing his question, now simply saying,

'Have you got *anything*?'

Guy drove on up to Clapham Common, where the sale was being held at Broxash Hotel. One last space remained in the hotel car park. He walked about looking at the paintings with a glass of Rioja in his hand. He had sometimes asked himself what he should have done to escape Con Mulvanney on that night, to give him the slip, but he hadn't then known that giving him the slip was important. He had understood only that Mulvanney did not know his name, and that seemed to him all that mattered. Come to that, although he thought of him *in the context of that time* as Con Mulvanney, he had not then known his name either, had not known it until the man was dead or even, in a curious way, until some time after that.

The woman who was presiding over the sale, an untidy dark woman in a black dress, reminded him faintly of Poppy Vasari. She wasn't really like Poppy Vasari, who had been thinner and wilder looking and dirtier. Guy was no longer used to dirty people, to men and women who seldom washed their clothes and hardly ever bathed, and they disgusted him. Perhaps it was something to do with there having been rather a lot of such people around in his childhood. The woman selling his pictures and taking orders was probably quite clean, the ingrained dirt in her fingers the result of gardening, the dandruff on her black shawl collar due to mischance. He noted that, unlike in Coulsden, the painting of the noble lion standing on the rocks with his crouching mate beside him was the best seller here, and then he left.

This must have been the way the taxi took him home that night from the pub in Bedford Hill, over Battersea Bridge, up Gunter Grove, Finborough Road, or perhaps up Beaufort Street and into the Boltons. Could you go that way? Would the traffic system permit it? It had been late and very dark. Too dark to see or at any rate to notice the little dark red 2CV following the cab.

\* \* \* \*

Guy never went to pubs. He only went to this one because it was a party and anyway he didn't know it was a pub till he got there. Robert Joseph, the man he was going into partnership with in the travel agency, was celebrating his fortieth birthday. He described the pub to Guy as a hotel.

Sensibly, he had come late. The pub had an extension till half-past midnight and Guy didn't get there till nearly eleven. A female impersonator, very old and hideous, in black sequins and yellow feathers, was capering about on a stage and singing a song of such incredible obscenity that Guy could hardly believe he was hearing those words in that sequence. A youngish man standing at the bar ventured a mild protest and was immediately, almost before finishing his sentence, frog-marched by two heavies to one of the doors and put outside. The doors were closed and locked. Guy decided to drink a lot in order to make things bearable.

Bob Joseph, by this time, was drunk but not too drunk to notice Guy was there, to throw an arm round his shoulder and call him his best pal. A group arrived on the stage and began singing old Beatles songs. Guy had another vodka martini and another. It was then that Con Mulvanney, whose name he didn't know, came up to him and asked his question.

'Have you got any shit?'

He meant hashish. Guy had never dealt in hashish. He had at one time been involved in an enterprise supplying Thai sticks, but later was interested only in cocaine and the best marijuana, usually Santa Marta Gold. In any case, not since he was a young boy had he actually purveyed the stuff himself, handled it. He was altogether loftier than that. At the time Con Mulvanney came up to him with his question it was almost exclusively cocaine in which he was dealing, though giving some thought to the possibility of this new thing called crack, which was smoked.

This time, in reply to the question, 'Have you got anything?' he said, 'I don't know what you mean. Go away, please.'

'I know you have. I was told about you and that you'd be in here tonight. You were described to me.'

That made Guy feel very odd and very vulnerable. Afterwards he wondered why he hadn't asked who had said he would be in there, who had described him. But he didn't ask. He said,

'You're mistaking me for someone else.'

The man who was Con Mulvanney didn't persist. At least, not then. He was a thin, slight man, neither short nor tall, with narrow shoulders and a slight stoop, who looked unwell, who looked a generally rather unhealthy person. His face was long and pale, and the lips and chin were like a woman's, as if they could never grow hair. The hair of his head was longish, wispy, no colour or the colour of dust. His eyes were a light greyish-brown and they shifted away from Guy's when he tried to meet them.

Guy walked away from him and started a conversation with Bob Joseph and then, after Joseph had moved away into another group, with some neighbours of his, a man and a woman who lived near him in Chingford or Chigwell or wherever. The encounter with Con Mulvanney, whose name he didn't then know, sent him in quest of another drink. When he had had two more vodka martinis he thought he had had enough, of drink and these people and the awful place, and anyway it was gone midnight. He didn't call a taxi but walked out into the street and one came obediently along. As it moved off a dark red 2CV moved off behind it.

Guy didn't see the 2CV again all the way. He didn't look out of the back of the taxi. When they got to Scarsdale Mews and he was paying the cab driver, he saw a small car moving away from the end of the street. That is, he thought afterwards that he remembered seeing a small car at that point. He remembered that on the following evening when, just as he was leaving to go out to dinner somewhere, Con Mulvanney appeared on the doorstep.

The doorbell rang and Guy thought it was the taxi he had ordered. At the sight of him, Con Mulvanney said facetiously,

'Mr X, I presume?'

'Yes, you do presume,' Guy said. 'I've nothing for you. Would you go, please?'

'Look, can I explain what it is I want?'

'You have. Now go.'

'I haven't actually,' said Con Mulvanney, and then he said, 'You can call me Mr Y.'

'Don't be ridiculous,' Guy said. 'Please go away. I've nothing for you. I am just going out.' The doorstep and the hall floor were on the same level, without further steps, and Con Mulvanney or 'Mr Y', the absurd name but the only one Guy knew to call him by then, had got himself onto the doormat and one foot on the hall carpet. 'I didn't invite you in. I don't want you in my house. If you force me to, I'll put you out.'

'I want a hallucinogen,' Mr Y said, lowering his voice. 'Whatever sort there's available. I know nothing of these things. You must know. I'll pay the market price. Don't they call it the street value? I'll pay that.'

Guy said, 'I haven't got anything like that.'

He was beginning to think Mr Y was a policeman. The man didn't look like any policeman Guy had ever seen, but of course they wouldn't use a man who looked like a policeman, they would use someone who looked like Mr Y. The front door was still open and now Guy's taxi arrived. The driver got out and Guy called to him to wait a minute. He shut the front door. He said to Mr Y that he would meet him later, he would meet him at ten – but where? Nowhere was safe. There were just some places safer than others. Mr Y said that when he hadn't got his car he used the Northern Line and how about Embankment Station? Guy said the middle of Hungerford Bridge at ten o'clock.

He didn't go. Of course he didn't. He had no intention of going. But he thought about it all through dinner and afterwards. He saw himself standing in the middle of Hungerford Bridge, that cold exposed dark footbridge, where someone had told him murders took place, meeting Mr Y, and then as he returned to the Embankment end, two men stepping up to him out of the shadows. Returning home an hour or so after the time he had set for the meeting, he wouldn't have been surprised to find Mr Y waiting for him but there was no one. It was not until the following day that Mr Y came back, this time in the dark red 2CV.

Guy pretended not to see him. He put the Jaguar in the garage, entered the house from the inside. The doorbell rang. Guy let it ring. He had a small quantity of marijuana in the house, some capsules of Durophet and a little LSD. He could open the door to Mr Y, *give* him the grass, close the door on him and forget him. That might be the best way. The doorbell rang again, insistently, in a prolonged way. Guy went upstairs and looked out of his bedroom windows. There were no cars in the street at this end except the 2CV, no one who could conceivably be watching the house unless they were planted in the houses opposite which Guy realised was extremely unlikely. He opened the safe in which Leonora's sapphire engagement ring was in its box alongside the various drugs. He took the marijuana out, locked the safe and went down to the front door as the bell began ringing again.

Mr Y said, 'I don't want what you've got there. It's a hallucinogen I want.'

'You what?'

'Mescalin maybe or psylocybin. That magic mushroom stuff. I didn't really want cannabis resin. It was just that someone told me if I asked for it and called it shit you'd know I was serious.'

A policeman who could be that naïve, in that way, could sound like that, would have to be a genius. To the Drugs Squad he would be worth his weight in gold – worth more than his weight in the best Colombian gold. He had to be genuine. Guy said, 'All right. You'd better come in. I don't want to know your name.'

'I don't want to know yours.'

Why had he done that? Why had he invited Mr Y in? Because, if Mr Y didn't know his name, he plainly knew him as a dealer, knew where he lived, could revenge himself for rejection by giving this information to the Drugs Squad. Of course, by that time, Guy would see to it that the house in Scarsdale Mews was totally clean, but that was not the point. He didn't want the police there. If the police came once he knew he would have to give up dealing, he would have seen the writing on the wall.

Up until now he had been spotless, a citizen of the same irreproachable respectability as any of his neighbours, and he must keep clean. A single blot and it would all be over.

He reminded himself of something which he kept ever before him, which always hovered a little below the thin top skin of his consciousness: the maximum penalty under the Misuse of Drugs Act for possession of Class A drugs with intent to supply is fourteen years' imprisonment.

Mr Y came into the house but showed no desire to go further than the hall. He sat down in one of the Georges Jacob side chairs. He said, 'You didn't come last night. I waited a long time. I went in the end because I was afraid of missing my last train.'

'What exactly is it you want?'

Guy had not, until this point, thought of Mr Y as mad. Odd, naïve, eccentric, peculiar, up to something perhaps, but not mad. What the man said next radically altered this opinion.

'I must tell you that I am a reincarnation of St Francis of Assisi.'

Guy just stared. He said nothing.

'You know who I mean? You've heard of St Francis?'

Guy made an impatient gesture. He said, 'I asked you what you wanted.'

'The proof is in my hands.' Mr Y held out his hands, palms uppermost. They were not very clean. 'You can see the stigmata very well today.'

'The what?'

'St Francis – and therefore I – was the first man to exhibit on his own body the wounds inflicted on Christ at his crucifixion. There is no real dispute about this. The claims of St Paul the Apostle and St Angelo del Paz can in no way be allowed. In the case of St Francis and therefore myself all the marks are present, the nails on hands and feet, the spear wound in the side and the marks of the crown of thorns.'

His tone had become pedantic, professorial and rather shrill. Guy could see no marks on his hands except those of ingrained dirt and when Mr Y lifted his hands and smoothed back his wispy dust-coloured fringe, saw nothing on his forehead either.

'All right, but what has all that to do with me?'

Mr Y began to talk in a very rambling way about all nature being the mirror of God and about the new Franciscan rule of life which he would formulate. It had something to do with the only hope for mankind being in a return to communion with God through a new reverence for nature.

'But I can't do this unless I can get into my own inner space.'

That was something Guy understood. Years ago, when he was a young teenager, he had heard someone who had used a psychedelic drug say he had 'got lost in my own inner space', a phrase which at the time he had found disquieting.

'I haven't got any mescalin,' he said. 'I've no peyote or anything like that.'

But up in the safe he had some lysergic acid diethylamide, LSD-25, which he would quite like to be rid of, out of his house and his life. It was in tablet form.

\* \* \* \*

In those days he had been seeing a lot of Leonora. She was coming to the end of her teacher training course at a college in South London. She had no other boyfriend, he was sure of that, but they did not make love, they had not made love for years. He told her that he wanted her, that he longed for them to be lovers again. She didn't exactly say they would be but she didn't say no. Once even, he thought he remembered she had smiled and said 'one day'. That of course meant 'one night'. Their earliest experiences notwithstanding, those cemetery idylls, she wouldn't go to bed in the afternoons, or at any time but night-time, come to that. It was her excuse. She was at college, her room was not private, there would be difficulties, staying overnight at his house wasn't possible.

That was the time when she was saying she had no real home any more. Though a bedroom was religiously kept as hers at Tessa's house in Sanderstead Lane and another at Anthony's flat in Lamb's Conduit Street, it was not 'the same'. In any case she couldn't possibly take him there. Not for the night. It would be awkward, it would be embarrassing. But they went out together. They went to the cinema, they went out for meals, for walks, they spoke often on the phone. Though there was no lovemaking, he was her boyfriend and she was his girlfriend. They had arranged to go on holiday together and then, he told himself, the long period of chastity imposed by Leonora would be ended.

While she had been at university there had been long separations. Sometimes he hadn't seen her for a whole term. She hadn't asked him what he did for a living but he knew that the time would come when she would and he must be prepared. It was in a large part due to the presence of Leonora in his life that he had acquired a share in the club, then become sole owner, embarked on the travel agency business, started the paintings enterprise. He couldn't have told her he lived by dealing. He had to tell her lies and make them into truths. Eventually, when they were lovers again, when marriage was coming, the dealing would have to be given up altogether.

Four years ago, all of it had been almost exactly four years ago. Mr Y who was Con Mulvanney, had sat in his hall on the Georges Jacob chair, on one of the last days of July, perhaps the very last day, after that party anyway, talking about St Francis of Assisi and how to get into one's inner space. And he, Guy, to shut him up and get rid of him, had given him the acid he had in the safe. *Given* him, not sold him, though he couldn't remember now why he had shown this unusual generosity. Panic probably, an overwhelming wish to get Mr Y out of his house.

Guy himself had never used LSD. He had never used anything but marijuana very occasionally and cocaine twice. Because he was afraid of snakes, the commonest of phobias, he had never dared experiment with LSD in case he had a 'bad trip' and 'saw' snakes. Besides, acid which was so popular during the late 1960s and early 1970s, the hippy phenomenon, had gone out of fashion in his own teenage years and was only recently coming back. But he knew enough about it to give Mr Y a routine warning.

'Have you ever used it?'

Mr Y said no. 'I know the risk is you can get confronted with too much reality too quickly.'

'Never mind that. Just have someone there when you do it. Don't be left alone. You want to come back from that inner space, not get left in there.'

No money passed. Guy told himself that this was good, though he really knew it made no difference. When Mr Y departed in the dark red 2CV he experienced an enormous relief, a great sense of lightness. He went back upstairs to put the marijuana back in the safe with the amphetamines and then to lock the safe. For some reason, simple caution perhaps or one of those superstitious feelings, one of those premonitions, he didn't do this. It went against the grain, he might regret it, but just the same he took the drugs into the guest bathroom and flushed them down the lavatory. In the light of what happened, it was just as well.

Two nights later he was taking Leonora out. She was living with her father and stepmother in Bloomsbury.

Anthony Chisholm was nicer to him than any of the other people who were close to Leonora. Anthony and Susannah. She was nice to him as well. Of course she was only eight years older than he was, there was no feeling that here was another parent. Like an old-fashioned suitor, Guy called for Leonora in Lamb's Conduit Street and took her home.

He got there early. He always got there early when he went to fetch Leonora. She was in the bath. Anthony, who was an architect, a partner in a City firm called Purdey Chisholm Hall, was not yet home from work. Susannah did PR for a cosmetics company and some toymakers and handled her accounts from home. She gave him a drink, said they had people coming and she was cooking something tricky – would he excuse her? The evening paper which Leonora had brought in with her was lying on the arm of the settee.

Guy drank his drink and read the front page. There was a bizarre story about a man in South London being stung to death by bees.

The man's name was Cornelius 'Con' Mulvanney, which meant nothing to Guy, who read the story and then another about a tennis player's divorce and had started on one about a fire in Fulham when Anthony came in.

# CHAPTER
# EIGHT

W hen Guy phoned Leonora's flat on the day after their
lunch at Clarke's, Rachel Lingard took the call.
    'I'm afraid Leonora isn't here.'
'Where is she then?'
'I'm not my sister's keeper.'
'What?'
'We may not know what God said to Cain after he made the
statement I paraphrased but I emphatically dissociate myself
from that kind of involvement.'
    She talked like that. She often did. He had long ago ceased to
ask her what she was on about.
    'She's round at the ginger dwarf's, I suppose. OK, you
needn't answer that. I've got his number.'
    There was no reply from Georgiana Street. He tried again an
hour later and an hour after that and then every half-hour. He
took Celeste out to dinner and then to a drinking club in Green
Street called Greens. From there at eleven he again dialled
William Newton's number and again there was no answer. It
wasn't very late for him but he knew it was late for most

people. They were either not in or Newton had a plug-in-phone which made a ringing tone to the caller even if unplugged. Newton had unplugged his phone to make it impossible for Leonora to speak to him. Most likely, almost certainly, Leonora did not know this.

Next day he tried her at home. There was no reply. The phone was not answered throughout the evening and the phone in Georgiana Street was not answered. Just before ten he asked directory enquiries for the number of an M. Mandeville in Sanderstead Lane, South Croydon, obtained it and phoned Tessa.

When she heard who it was she said first of all that she had no idea where Leonora was. Leonora – she called her 'my daughter' – was twenty-six and 'her own woman'. Then she said,

'You know it's only right to tell you I think you must be a very seriously disturbed person. You ought to be having therapy. Though it may be too late for anything like that to do any good. Permanent damage was done long long ago.'

'What's that supposed to mean?'

'I used to think of you as a criminal but it's more pity I feel now. I pity you, I really do. All that filth you took into your system over the years is bearing fruit now. You're reaping the whirlwind.'

Guy put the phone down, badly shaken. It was the first confirmation he had ever received that she, or anyone connected with Leonora, knew what he had once done for a living. Was there anything the Mandevilles didn't know about him? Leonora herself had said Magnus knew about his protection network in Kensal. Tessa, however, had got it wrong. He had never been an addict. Had Leonora told her he was? The notion of Leonora talking derogatorily to her mother about him was deeply painful.

But there was another way she might know, or think she knew. Tessa lived in South London. So did Poppy Vasari, so *had* Con Mulvanney. Of course there must be about five million people living in the vast metropolitan area south of the river, but Poppy Vasari was a sort of social worker. And so in another way was Tessa Mandeville. Hadn't Leonora told him about her mother's doing voluntary work in a hospital and having some sort of job at the Citizen's Advice Bureau? What more likely than that she and Poppy had encountered each other?

Suppose Tessa and Poppy had met regularly, at the CAB or chauffeuring geriatrics about. Guy was vague in his ideas about this but it could be something like that. Poppy, talking about the death of Con Mulvanney, might so easily have described him, Guy, to Tessa and told Tessa in her indignation what he had done. She knew his name, she had found that out. She could have told Tessa his name.

There had been no mention of Poppy in that original story, the account of Con Mulvanney's death he had read while in Anthony Chisholm's flat. But Poppy was not Con's lover, didn't live with him, perhaps wasn't even all that close a friend. Some of those do-gooders could get very steamed up about what they called 'social injustice' or 'outrageous' breaches of something or other. As for him, he had read it and been interested, mildly appalled at Con Mulvanney's fate, an awful fate however you looked at it. This Mulvanney, whoever he was, seemed to have taken the roof or lid off a beehive and been stung all over his head and face and neck by bees. Could you *die* of that? Apparently. There would be an inquest. Con Mulvanney was described as being thirty-six and unemployed, living in the 'garden flat' or ground floor of a house in Upper Tooting.

Anthony Chisholm arrived home. Since his second marriage he had more than ever that look of a handsome teddy bear, his smile more boyish, his eyes less tired. No wonder. Any man would feel himself in a seventh heaven of bliss to have escaped the clutches of that bitch Tessa. It was a mystery to Guy how he had stuck her so long. At that time, that summer four years past, Anthony was being very nice to Guy, very pleasant.

'Have you got a drink, Guy? Oh, good, Susannah's been looking after you. Where's that girl of mine? No, don't tell me, I can guess. I thought two bathrooms were more than anyone could want in a mere duplex, that's what the Americans call them, you know, duplexes, but I now see three are needed.'

Guy asked if he minded him smoking. He wouldn't have asked Tessa, just got one out and lighted it.

'D'you know, I think I'll have one too. Officially, let's say *matrimonially*, I've given it up, but having one of yours doesn't count.'

What could be more comfortable? More matey? The easygoing, cultivated, urbane and affectionate parent with his prospective son-in-law. His wealthy jetsetting, successful prospective son-in-law. Guy was sure Anthony saw him in that light. He did *then*. Anthony wasn't any more worldly or greedy than the rest of them but he was a sensible realist, he had an eye to the main chance. Whatever Leonora herself might have thought of this attitude, she with her feminist ideas, Anthony saw a rich successful husband as a snip for his daughter. Guy had had a Porsche at that time. Anthony would have seen the Porsche outside (on a double yellow line before the days of clamping – who cared about the fine?), would have heard from Leonora about Guy's house, knew from that none-too-happy birthday party of Guy's business interests. He might in his heart have preferred some intellectual for Leonora but intellectuals often aren't rich and a bird in the hand is worth two in the bush.

So Guy reasoned in those days and was pleasant to Anthony, accepted another drink, gave him another cigarette, said what an awful case that was in the evening paper. Who would have thought a man could die from bee stings?

Guy, who remembered everything that had happened during those days, recalled that on the following morning he went to his rifle club for the first time. He was taking lessons, it was his first lesson. The instructor said he had a good eye and his control was good. After that he took a taxi into the West End to pick up his air tickets for the holiday on Samos. The travel agency he and Bob Joseph were setting up was still at the planning stage. Guy had booked the hotel's 'honeymoon hut' which was actually on the private beach. They were flying first class and he was wondering if he could possibly trick Leonora into believing that this luxurious mode of travel was in fact economy class. She insisted on paying for herself from the proceeds of some holiday job she had taken. Perhaps he could make her think the airline had 'upped' their seats because there were vacancies in first class.

He foresaw trouble with Leonora over payment. She would realise that the hotel was astronomically beyond her means. They might even have the price of the 'honeymoon hut' up on a notice somewhere, inside the clothes cupboard or behind a door. By that time, however, it would be too late for her to do anything about it, she would have to put a good face on it and let him pay as he wanted and indeed longed to do.

Guy had a lunch date with Bob Joseph and a lawyer who was fixing up the lease of their new premises in Milner Street in the most advantageous possible way. He intended to go to Gladiators for a workout later so he thought he was justified in drinking rather a lot. When he got home it was nearly four.

There was a woman in a car outside, having an argument with a traffic warden. Scarsdale Mews had resident's parking throughout most of its length and five meters at the Marloes Road end. Guy pointed out to her that someone had just pulled away from one of the meters. If he had known this was Poppy Vasari and what she had come about he wouldn't have given her any help, he'd have liked to see her car towed away. She didn't say who she was or that she wanted him. He let himself into the house.

Two or three minutes later the doorbell rang. There she was. She said her name and that she was a friend of Con Mulvanney's. Guy, who had forgotten the name of the man in the bee sting story though not the story itself, said he had never heard of Con Mulvanney.

'Oh, yes, you have, Mr X,' she said.

'Am I supposed to know what you're talking about?' He did though, or he had an inkling.

'You gave him a hallucinogenic drug,' she said.

She said it out loud, in her normal voice or louder. Guy thought he was going to faint, fall on the floor. He said, 'For God's sake,' and then, because anything was better than having her go on like that out here, 'You'd better come in.'

She was a big, gipsyish woman, wearing large gold hoop

earrings and gold chains and strings of coloured beads round
her neck. She had a lopsided, raddled, much-lined but vivid
face, a hooky nose, black burning eyes. She was dark and her
long wild hair was black. Her clothes were draperies perhaps
worn to conceal bulk or just for their loose floppy comfort, a red
tunic, a black layered skirt, a long loose grey cotton jacket, a red
and blue shawl. Bare legs, bare feet, sandals.

He must have taken all that in later, he certainly wasn't
capable of it at the time. In those first moments she was
Nemesis, come to make him mad and then destroy him. Her
wild look, her clothes, were even appropriate. But he smelt her
smell as she pushed past him. Instead of perfume and toilet
water and bath oil and body shampoo which the women he
knew smelt of, there emanated from her a powerful reek of
sweat. She smelt like a cheap hamburger restaurant. Ever
since, he had associated the smell of cooking hamburger with
her.

'You'll have read about it,' she said when they were in his
drawing room. 'You'll know all about it or what the papers
know.'

'I didn't know it was him,' Guy said.

She looked at him. She laughed. It was the most unpleasant
laugh he had ever heard. 'So this has been a shock?'

'You could put it that way, yes.'

'Good. I like to think your punishment is beginning.'

She wasn't the least bit afraid of him. She was a woman, a
good fifteen years older than he was and out of condition, she
was in a strange house with someone she no doubt thought of
as a criminal, at his mercy, but she wasn't afraid. She held her
head high and looked fiercely into his eyes. And she was right
not to be afraid. The strength had gone out of him. The drink
had too. None of its magic remained to give him false nerve.

'He begged me to give him something. He pestered me, he
gave me no peace.' Guy knew he was being indiscreet, worse
than that, but there were no witnesses. 'I didn't take any
money,' he said, as if this were a defence. 'I warned him to take
it under supervision.'

'He did. My supervision.'

'Yours?'

'I was there. I'd been working in a drugs rehabilitation centre, I ought to have known better.'

'Yes, you ought.' Guy clutched at this straw. 'Fine bloody supervisor you were.'

'Shut up,' she said. 'Shut up. Don't you dare speak to me like that. D'you want to know what happened? I'm going to tell you anyway. It'll all come out at the inquest. D'you want to know?'

'Of course I want to know.'

'Well, then. He didn't know your name, only where you live. I know it, I asked the people next door before you came back. He told me he was going to take the tablets you gave him in order to get into his inner consciousness. Some tripe like that. I told him not to. I said he didn't know enough about it, didn't know how long you'd had it for instance or where it came from. I said its use had to be properly controlled. He talked a lot more rubbish. If I wouldn't be with him he'd take it on his own, he said. He was as daft as a brush anyway, all that reincarnation tripe. I used to be a nurse on a psychiatric ward and I can tell you that's one of the first signs of a psychosis, people claiming they're reincarnated.

'He was the last person who should have been allowed near a substance like that. But you can't tell people what to do, not without putting them under restraint. That bloody acid filth – God, and I thought that was the end of it when it went out in the seventies. OK, well, the upshot was he took it and he – I was going to say he had a bad trip, but he didn't, he had a *good* trip. He kept saying he could see lovely things, lovely colours. There's a garden where he lives – lived. The flowers in it weren't marvellous, well, they wouldn't be, but he started describing the flowers, daisies they were, that you get in lawns, he said they were sunflowers, as big as dinner plates and with the scent of roses. The sparrows were kingfishers and parakeets and God knows what. He started talking to butter-flies. They were cabbage white ones but he said their wings were blue and purple and scarlet.'

'What about the bees?' said Guy, dry-mouthed.

She looked grim. She stretched her mouth into a nasty smile.

'The bees, yes. The bees were in a hive in the garden at the end of his garden. Some of the neighbours had complained to the council – I work for the council – but there were just as many liked the bees on account of they were good for flowers and fertilised their fruit trees. This'll be the end of them now, that's for sure.' Her eyes came back to meet his, 'He climbed over the fence.'

'But *why*?'

'To talk to the bloody bees. He was St Francis – remember? Brother Bee and Sister Butterfly. There was a lot of that and then he got over the fence. It wasn't very high and there was a wooden box he stood on, on his side. I couldn't stop him – how could I? He did what he wanted, people do. The couple who lived in the house, the beekeepers, they were out at work. Everyone was at work or somewhere.

'He went up to the beehive, talking to the bees. He liked bees, though I don't think he talked to them when he was – well, normal. It's a wooden hive with a top that comes off. He leant very close and said to me it would be all right, the bees would recognise him, they would know their friend. I got hold of him and he pushed me away. He said I'd upset the bees and maybe I would have, maybe I *did*. Anyway, he took the top off the hive.

'The bees came out. I mean, hundreds, it seemed like hundreds. A great swarm of them, all angry. I knew they were stinging him because he was shouting and slapping at them. He ran and fell and the bees came after him. Bees aren't like wasps, they do come after you. They sting you and they leave the sting inside you and half of themselves with it. That's why they die. Christ, it's amazing, people actually believe in a God that'd make a creature whose way of defending itself is its own death.'

The tears were running down her face. She made no attempt to wipe them away. Guy felt he was gaping at her and he turned aside.

'They stung me,' she said. 'They got in my hair. They stung my hands and my neck. They leave the stings in and half of their bodies with them. I was full of stings and bits of bee.'

'You didn't die, though.' he said stupidly.

'I'm not allergic.'

'He was *allergic*? You'd have thought that'd have stopped him. Why did he go near the bees if he was allergic.'

'He didn't know he was,' she said. 'He can't have known. You don't if you've only been stung once before. The first time nothing much happens, it's a question of getting sensitised. It causes a strong adverse reaction to later contacts with the substance, whatever it is. Bee stings or shellfish or poison ivy, it's all the same.'

'And that's what he had?'

'I didn't know,' she said. 'I tried to drag him back. Those bloody bees . . . I started screaming, you can scream a hell of a lot in London before people take notice. A man did come. I said to get help, a doctor, ambulance, the police, anything. The bees were there, everywhere and angry, it was hell.'

'The police,' he said. 'Did the police come?'

She jeered at him, 'Is that what worries you? Is that all that worries you? No, they didn't. They're never there when you want them. Another thing, it's bloody hard to convince people in a situation like that, they don't believe you, they don't believe you, they don't believe someone's going to die of bee stings. I could *tell* he had an allergic reation, they would have been able to tell in a hospital if we could have got him there in time. He was dead before that, he was dead in less than an hour. He choked to death. He swelled up and choked to death.'

Guy said nothing. He just sat there and he looked away. He looked out of the windows on to his own pretty town garden with its round pond and the island in the middle, no bronze dolphin then, no Florentine furniture, the orange trees tiny in their Chinese vases, up against the wall blue and dark green junipers he had later had cut down to make way for the clematis. It was raining a little, the raindrops puncturing the surface of the pond. A single pink water lily had been in bloom. He remembered everything.

'He wasn't able to speak,' she said, in a cool neutral sort of voice.

Did that mean he had told no one about the LSD?

'I know what you're thinking. He didn't tell anyone.'

'He'd told you.'

She laughed. 'Oh, yes. That filth you gave him may show at postmortem, I ought to know that but I don't. Anyway, it doesn't matter.' She looked slowly round the room. He knew, as if she had said it aloud, what was going through her mind. He's got all this, ill-gotten gains, but not for long, oh, no, not for long, all to be swept away, all lost. Fourteen years, thought Guy. 'I told the police,' she said. 'I told them everything I knew. I imagine they'll be coming here. They said I shouldn't try to see you, but I had to. I had to *confront* you. I'll go now.'

'How was I supposed to know he was allergic to bees?' Guy said.

He would have liked to kill her but of course he didn't touch her. She was crying when she left. Crying seemed to make her body smell worse. He wasn't too keen on his neighbours seeing a weeping woman in flapping robes and with dirty bare feet leaving his house, but there was nothing he could do about it.

Less than an hour later the Drugs Squad arrived.

# CHAPTER NINE

What makes you love someone? Why can't you choose, when you can choose almost everything else in life? If you're rich, that is. You can choose what to do for a living, where to live, what kind of a house and a car and clothes and entertainment to have. Why isn't the person you love a matter of choice too?'

Guy often asked that about himself and Leonora. Why was he in love with Leonora when he didn't want to be, when it was so inconvenient, when it was so destructive and time-wasting? She looked beautiful to him but he knew she wasn't all that good-looking, she didn't dress well, she didn't like any of the things he liked and he disliked most of the things she liked. They hadn't anything in common. She wasn't interested in eating and drinking and expensive clothes, staying up all night, exotic places, fast cars, sunny beaches and going to the races. Sport meant nothing to her. She had never been skiing or on a yacht. Diamonds might be a girl's best friend but not her sort of girl, and she campaigned against the fur trade.

She liked books and serious films, preferably made in Japan or

Chile and with subtitles. She liked camping or hostel holidays with a backpack, health foods, fruit juice, Badoit and Ramlosa, cycling, fringe theatre, classical music and 'green' documentaries on BBC 2. He would make himself get to like all that if they were together again but at the moment he hated it. He hated her clothes and the fact that she hardly ever wore make-up, wore it even less often since she had taken up with the ginger dwarf, never put varnish on her nails. Hairy legs would be the next thing, he sometimes thought.

But when he saw her coming towards him, coming into their Saturday restaurant, his heart moved. His heart turned a little sideways and beat hard as in shock. Every time that happened. Something inside his head, the skull itself perhaps, expanded with a kind of warmth, with a faint pain. But his body grew cold, if he did not exactly shiver, he felt the cold stroke him, running down his arms and sides, touching his heart. Every time.

And why? It was something about her, that was all he could say. Perhaps that was what it always was with love. Something about someone. A glance, a smile, a way of opening the eyes wide, a gurgle in the laugh, a movement of the shoulders, some little thing. That of course didn't explain why the little thing could do so much. With him and Leonora it was her smile, the way she smiled, a curious tightness of her lips that never stretched quite as far as you imagined they could, a kind of control in her smile. The teeth of course were perfect, small, white and even. The only smile like hers he had ever seen had been Vivien Leigh's in *Gone with the Wind*.

Did her smile mean so much to him, madden him and pain and delight him, cause him to long for something he couldn't define, not because it was controlled but because he knew it could break the bounds of control and be full and complete, but never would be for him?

Three days had passed without his speaking to her. On the fourth day, in Georgiana Street, she had answered the phone. They had been out a lot, she said, they hadn't been at home much. William had been working. William had been working on a film about men who had to care for their disabled wives at home. What a thrilling subject! The viewing figures would really be something else! As if he cared where bloody William had been. He would have liked to kill William several times over.

Where shall we have lunch, he said, and she said what about going back to that place in Kensington Park Road. So there he was, the first to arrive this time, sitting at the bar being served a vodka martini by the French boy who was the barman there. He had taken off his sunglasses, not wanting to be accused of looking like a mafioso.

Passing the mews where once she had lived had made him think of love and of her smile. It was August 19, exactly four weeks to go to her wedding day – well, to the date she called her wedding day. He wasn't giving in as meekly as that. He wasn't giving in at all. He had made himself not look at the spiral staircase, and he was just thinking he would have to look, he would have to turn round, when she touched him on the shoulder.

'Guy, you're dreaming.'

The shiver went through him and his heart moved. He looked at her. She smiled at him and he told her what he had been thinking about her smile.

'It's why I love you. It's sort of the essence of why.'

'Suppose I had plastic surgery and the shape of my mouth was altered, would you stop loving me?'

'I don't know. Maybe. I always have this feeling that you don't smile properly for me, you don't smile as much as you could. You *govern* your smile when you smile at me.'

'Don't be ridiculous, Guy,' she said.

'What does Newton think about you having lunch with me on Saturdays? Does he hate it?'

'He understands,' she said.

They sat at their table. Leonora had an orange juice and he had a Campari soda. She ordered grapefruit and avocado cocktail and stuffed courgettes and he ordered escargots and then calves liver in a raspberry coulis. He thought about Newton's 'understanding'. Big of him to 'understand', the patronising bastard.

'Someone started turning you against me when you were nineteen,' he said.

'Oh, nonsense. What nonsense.'

'Didn't you like my house?'

'I loved it, it's a beautiful house.'

'It's better than your parents' house was, isn't it?'

'Much better, but I don't see where all this is leading.'

'I want you to tell me something. I want you to tell me if there was anyone else between me and Newton.' A little humility would be in order, he thought. 'I suppose I've no right to ask, but I hope you'll tell me.'

'There was no one very serious,' she said.

'He didn't care for that, it caught him by the throat. 'But there were other men between me and Newton?'

'Of course there were.'

'Who were they?'

Her eyes sparkled. He couldn't tell if she was pleased or angry. She said crisply, 'All right, if you insist, there was Robin's friend that he was in partnership with, and two men at university and, yes, now I come to think of it, there was someone I met at Robin's twenty-fifth birthday party. Is that what you want to know?'

'Did you sleep with them?'

'That's nothing to do with you, Guy, it's not your business. You said you'd no right to ask and you haven't.'

'You did then.' Having a heart attack must be like this, it would be the same kind of pain, clutching at his chest, bringing a kind of paralysis. 'I just wonder what your father would say,' he burst out.

'You *what*?'

'I said I wondered what your father would say to that. He'd be horrified. Any man would be about his daughter. Your father would very much have liked you to marry me. He would have liked me to be the one and only, I know he would, he'd die if he thought you'd been promiscuous.'

'I wasn't promiscuous. Don't be silly.'

'One man after another, what else is it? Why, anyway? What was wrong with me? Were they better looking, richer? What had they got that I haven't got? I was the one your father would have liked to give his daughter to.'

She started laughing. Then she shook her head.

'What's so funny?'

'You are. You're so old-fashioned. You think of yourself as a sort of trendy Yuppie – well, you've yupped – young and trendy but in fact you're really old-fashioned, and a sexist too. "I just wonder what your father would say." Really, Guy, you sound like someone of sixty. My father himself wouldn't say a thing like that. And men don't give their daughters in marriage any more, hadn't you noticed?'

'Don't deny your father has a lot of influence over you, Leonora.'

'That has nothing to do with it. I'm not denying it. I'm only saying we've come a long way since men chose husbands for their daughters.'

Hating the look on her face, her smile, he said morosely, 'He changed towards me, your father.'

From that night forward, he thought. That evening when he came to take Leonora out and read the story about Con Mulvanney in the paper, that was the last time Anthony Chisholm pressed him to have another drink, smoked his cigarettes, treated him like an old friend. It was a few weeks before he saw him again and the change was marked. At the time he had thought Anthony preoccupied with business cares, worried about something, and after that evening months went by before they saw each other again. When they did he, Guy, was making his offer to 'lend' Leonora the money for that flat and Anthony, who had somehow been brought in on it, was stern and dismissive. The loan was not to be considered, he understood Leonora had already refused, just as long as Guy understood his offer was appreciated but must be utterly out of the question.

Guy ordered himself another Campari. He lit a cigarette while they waited for the food to come. 'You never told me how you met Newton,' he said.

'Why would I? You never asked.'

'Well, how did you? Where did you?'

She gave him an odd sideways look, as well she might, considering what was coming. 'In Lamb's Conduit Street.'

'At your father's? Come on, say what you mean, Leonora.'

'And you can come on, Guy. Who else do I know in Lamb's Conduit Street? As a matter of fact, my father introduced us.'

'What? He what? You see! I am right. I'm not all those things you said, old-fashioned and sexist and whatever. *Your father introduced you to the man he wants you to marry.*'

'*I* want to marry him, Guy. I am going to marry him. Anyway, it wasn't like that.'

'What was it like then?'

'William was making this programme about architecture. It was sparked off by something Prince Charles said. He came to see Dad for a preliminary interview at home and I happened to be there.'

'When was this?'

'Don't interrogate me, please, Guy. It was about two years ago. Well, it was July.'

'You weren't living with them then. You'd been in your flat for over a year by then.'

'I didn't say I was living with them. I said I met William at their place. It was Dad's birthday. I called in with Dad's birthday present and William was there.'

'That doesn't explain how you started going out with him. Or did your father arrange it? Maybe he told Newton you'd got an undesirable boyfriend and he'd welcome someone more suitable. Maybe he gave him your phone number.'

'I gave him my phone number,' she said. 'He asked me for it.'

How was it possible to be so angry with someone and still love them? How could you dislike almost everything about the way a person dressed and behaved and still love them? Love them better than anyone else in the world. Better than yourself.

'If you're so – I think the word's progressive. If you're so progressive, why do you think of marrying him? Why don't you go and live with him?'

'I am living with him now – more or less.'

Their food came. Leonora asked for some water, he for a

bottle of red Graves. 'Why marriage?' he said when the waitress had gone.

'To make a public commitment is the usual reason, isn't it? Yes, I suppose that's what we want to do. Commit ourselves to each other for life.'

'For *life*. You're counting on this lasting for *life*?'

'Why not? People used to take it as a matter of course that marriage would last for life. I hope ours will. I don't know, I can't tell, how can anyone tell? All we can do is try.'

She had taken a roll from the basket but wasn't eating it. Her left hand lay on the table. He took hold of the wrist, held it loosely like someone feeling for a pulse, then tightened his grip.

'Do something for me.'

He thought she sighed. 'What would that be, Guy?'

'Don't get married. Wait. Wait a year. You're young, he's young – what's a year? Live with him. I don't mind that – well, I do but I can bear it. Live with him and see.'

She looked at him, shaking her head very slightly from side to side. 'Let me go. You're hurting me.' She pulled her hand away.

'Do that for me. It's a small thing.'

'A small thing! To postpone my marriage because a friend, an ex-boyfriend, tells me to!'

'I'm more than that to you, Leo. I am the love of your life and you know it. If you refuse me I'll stop you. I won't let you get married. I have a right to forbid your marriage and I will.'

'Guy,' she said, 'sometimes you say things to me which make me very seriously question your sanity. *I mean that*. And it's getting worse. I honestly think you need to do something about it.'

'You've been listening to your mother.'

'Why not? Yes, maybe I have. I do listen to my mother sometimes. I think she's got a lot of sense. But I haven't been listening to her on the question of your sanity, I've never discussed it with her. I think you're losing your mind, Guy, and all because you've got this crazy idea in your head that you and I would be happy together. We wouldn't. You'll do much better with Celeste, if only you'd look at it rationally. Actually, it'll be better when I'm married and out of your way, when you can't see me. You'll get over it then.'

They were neither of them able to eat their lunch. He drank the wine, though, he could always drink. She drank her water and made the bread roll into a heap of crumbs. She said that these days meeting him only made her miserable and him too, but she promised to have lunch with him again on the following Saturday.

She had given him a lot to think about. When had he made the offer to pay for her flat? It must have been in the December and January three and a half years ago. Between then and the previous August someone had told Anthony Chisholm about the Con Mulvanney affair. Perhaps Leonora had told him. But who had told her? Who was it had said,

'Do you know the sort of person you've been going about with?'

But it had happened long before he offered the 'loan', it was just that he hadn't seen Anthony for six months. No doubt Anthony had deliberately avoided him. He must have known a few days after Poppy Vasari put the police on to him. Poppy had immediately started telling people, as she had threatened to do, and one of the people she had told was – why hadn't he thought of that at once? – Rachel Lingard.

The chances of Poppy coming across Tessa were not very great. Tessa was only a voluntary worker in a hospital and the CAB. But Rachel was a social worker for some London borough, he couldn't remember which one, if he had ever known. If she worked for the Social Services in some South London borough while Poppy worked with addicts, what more likely than that they knew each other? They might even be friends.

'His name's Guy Curran, he's got a luxury mews house in just about the best part of Kensington.'

'Guy Curran?'

'Don't say you know him!'

'Oh, I know him. My best friend's thinking of marrying him.'

She *had* been thinking of marrying him once. The first time he took her to see his house, on the way there in his car – he'd had a Mercedes in those days – 'It'll be your house too,' he'd said, and she had given him that smile, only he remembered it as freer and more open then, less contained. 'When we get married,' she'd said.

She *had* said that? He hadn't imagined it? Of course he hadn't. He wasn't losing his mind. She had loved him entirely but the separations imposed by university and training college had driven them apart. It was natural, it would have happened to anyone. The point was that she was coming closer to him again, she had agreed to go on holiday with him, they were going out together two or three times a week. And then Con Mulvanney died.

It seemed no more than ten minutes after Poppy Vasari had gone that the Drugs Squad arrived. They searched the house and found nothing. There was nothing to find. Thank God he had put that grass and those amphetamines down the john three days before. They had been known to take the drains apart. Not that they did that in Scarsdale Mews. He could tell they were impressed by the house, they couldn't help being, and it had to affect them, the elegance of it, the quietness, the beautiful things.

They questioned him at home and at the police station. The interrogation went on for hours. He denied everything. The club was doing well at that time, the travel agency was well past the planning stage, the original oil paintings business had started bringing in the money. They could see where the money came from.

His two new rifles came to light, each in its case. He had his gun licence, as a member of an accredited rifle club. He said he had never heard of Cornelius Mulvanney, the man had never come to his house. One thing he would like to tell them, he said, was that while he was at a party in a pub in Balham at the weekend, someone had come up to him and asked if he had any cannabis resin. In those words? Well, no, not in those words, he didn't want to repeat the words, but if they insisted, what he had asked had been, 'Have you got any shit?' How did he know what that meant? He had been curious, he had asked a man in the pub who had told him.

Describe the man. Which man? The one who asked him for the cannabis resin. Guy had said he couldn't, he couldn't remember. Eventually he came up with a vague outline of a thin man, pale with longish fairish hair. The name of the pub? The time? Whose party was it? What time did he leave? On and on it went. At midnight they let him go home. He never heard from them again.

Poppy Vasari, however, returned a few days later. She said she wouldn't come in, thanks. (He hadn't asked her.) She'd stay on the doorstep because he might do her a mischief if she was alone with him in there. That made him laugh. As if he would even touch someone so repulsive! The smell was still there, ingrained in her clothes probably. He stood holding the door and laughing at her, it was all so ridiculous.

'You murdered Con,' she said, 'so why not me? It wouldn't make any difference to you. You're evil.'

He was forcing himself to keep on laughing, it didn't come naturally. If he shut the door she would only keep banging on it until he opened it again.

'You're safe from the law,' she said, 'but you're not safe from your peers.'

'What d'you mean, peers,' he said, getting a sort of picture of the House of Lords.

'I'm telling everyone I know about you, everyone. And I'm telling everyone Con knew. I'm telling them the truth, that Con may have died from bee stings but he only got stung because of the drug you gave him. You murdered him by giving him a lethal drug and that's what I'm determined everyone's going to know. I've started at home. Now I'm going to start here. I'm going to find your friends and tell them. I'm going to knock on every door in this street and tell people what you did.'

The trouble with doing that sort of thing, at least in Britain, is that the recipients of statements of this kind, delivered like that, think the messenger is mad. He or she is a 'poor soul' who ought to be put away, ought never to have been let out, needs looking after, is best ignored, forgotten, and as for the information thus relayed, no one gives it credence. No doubt the neighbours in Scarsdale Mews did think Poppy Vasari mad if she carried out her threat – Guy didn't look to see – and perhaps she was temporarily a little mad. I mean (thought Guy), imagine it, the TV chat-show chap coming to his door and getting an earful of,

'I think you ought to know that the man who lives at number seven killed my friend with drugs.'

It didn't even worry him much. If she thought these people were his friends she was making a big mistake. He had never been matey with the neighbours. An invitation from one set of them to drop in for a Christmas drink he had refused. In the ensuing days he was a bit wary with them but everyone went on just as they had been before, either saying 'Good morning' or 'Hi' or not saying anything. As he thought, they hadn't listened. But that was a far cry from Poppy Vasari telling someone she knew personally, someone she worked with, especially when she had calmed down a bit. It was a far cry from her telling someone *who knew him, who recognised his name*.

Rachel Lingard.

It was within a fortnight of the Con Mulvanney inquest that he and Leonora were going away on holiday together. Nothing of importance came out at the inquest. His name, thank God, wasn't mentioned. Poppy Vasari got a reprimand from the coroner for sitting by and doing nothing while Con Mulvanney took a prohibited substance, a dangerous hallucinogen. She was specially to blame in the light of her training and the job she had been doing, from which, the coroner was pleased to inform the court, she had resigned. The verdict was accidental death. But Rachel must have been busy because in the middle of the following week when he and Leonora met in Cambridge Circus – he was taking her to the theatre to *Les Misérables* – she told him she wasn't coming to Greece.

She wasn't abashed about it, she wasn't awkward. There was no question of saying to him that she hated telling him, that she felt awful. She came straight out with it.

'I can't come, I'm sorry.'

He was appalled, he protested. Was it the cost that was

worrying her? Was it because he would have to pay for both of them?

The shock of it made him careless and he uttered the phrase she hated and he had promised himself not to use. 'I won't even notice an amount like that.'

It always made her wince. 'It's that, and other things. I can't. Don't ask me to explain, it would be painful to explain. Let's just forget it – can we?'

Once he had thought it was the money and perhaps – unpleasant notion – she might feel she'd *have* to sleep with him if he'd paid, so it was better not to go. Now he knew differently. Rachel had told her about Con Mulvanney.

She lived with Rachel, Rachel was always there, poisoning her mind, influencing her against him. He would like to kill Rachel.

# CHAPTER
# TEN

The barbecue at Danilo's was operated by cooks in striped aprons and high white hats and the food served by waitresses dressed like eighteenth-century dairymaids. The barmen and barmaids were dressed like Hawaiian dancers. Fortunately, it was a warm evening. The garden of Danilo's neo-Georgian house in Weybridge was enormous, planted here and there with imported, nearly mature palm trees, which were doing all right this summer but might be less happy by next spring. His latest novelty was the fountain, installed in an ornamental pool on the lawn below the terrace. The fountain was floodlit this evening, pink rosetrees in pink pots stood round the marble coping and pink dye had been put into the water. Danilo explained to people admiring the effect that the natural-looking rocks were real rose quartz.

About a hundred people had come. Guy knew some of them slightly. Bob Joseph was there with his girlfriend and Bob's ex-wife was there with her new husband, Danilo's wicked old father with his third wife, and Danilo's brother who had taken over the turf accountant's business and now had a chain of betting shops. There were a lot of friends of Tanya's in the rag trade and a lot of girls who looked like models but probably weren't. Danilo and Tanya, though always talking about getting married 'one day' had not yet done so, in spite of having four children.

These four, intolerably spoilt in Guy's opinion, instead of being in bed or supervised in some distant suitable place by their two nannies, ran about among the guests screaming, throwing food about and splashing anyone who came within the line of fire with pink water from the fountain. They were dressed up to the nines, the two boys in striped trousers and monkey jackets with bow ties, the girls in white organza with layers of petticoats, as if their parents were Italian peasants made good instead of Cockney parvenus. The elder boy, Charles, but always known as Carlo, had got himself a Bellini, which because this was Tanya's party, had brandy in it as well as champagne and peach juice, and surrounded by shrieking girls in hip-high miniskirts, was swigging it down and smacking his lips.

Fairy lights were strung among the palm trees along with ultraviolet mosquito repellent rings. A tape was playing music of the down-below-the-Rio-Grande type, thus fostering the illusion Danilo and Tanya liked to create that they really were of Latin origin. The garden smelt of burning oil and charred steak in spite of the patchouli-scented candles. Guy understood that he could never have brought Leonora here. She would call it vulgar, or worse, would laugh. Her idea of a party was fifteen people in a flat in Camden Town, drinking white wine and Perrier and talking about the environment. But giving up Danilo and Tanya for Leonora would be an endurable sacrifice.

The night sky was purple, starless, with a lemon-coloured sickle moon which must be real but looked as if Danilo had hung it up there when he dyed the fountain. A slight breeze moved the palm fronds. Guy had drunk one Bellini for form's sake, then moved on to vodka. He could see Celeste enjoying herself dancing with Danilo's next-door neighbour, a millionaire and former member of a highly successful sixties rock group. She had a bright red ankle-length skirt on and a black and gold tank top that left bare two inches of golden midriff. Her hair in those scores of gilt-tipped plaits was like the crest of some glorious tropical bird. The smallest of Danilo's children, a little girl in a bouncing white tutu, came running up to her and Celeste drew her into the dance, the three of them holding hands. Celeste loved children, he had seen signs before.

He was walking towards the bar for a vodka refill when a more than usually loud splash and shriek from the direction of the fountain made him look to his left. There, among a knot of guests brushing waterdrops off their clothes – Carlo had been active at the fountain edge – was Robin Chisholm.

Guy fetched his drink, moved to a shadowy point of vantage where only scented candlelight penetrated. Robin was talking to Tanya, a man Guy didn't know and two string-thin bizarrely dressed women with hair like huge cumuli of candyfloss, lemon and strawberry respectively. Tanya's hair was not dissimilar, except that candyfloss does not come in ink flavour. Tanya was wearing a kind of camisole in gold lamé with black and gold striped pleated trousers and high-heeled green shoes that she had probably put on by mistake and then forgotten to change. There was no sign of Maeve.

Robin looked as if he had stepped straight out of a musical set in Edwardian times. All that was lacking was the straw boater. He had taken to wearing his fair wavy hair parted in the middle. It looked very strange. His face was as youthful as ever, not simply youthful as a man of twenty-seven's is, but like a boy's ten years younger. His cheeks were rosy, his lips red as a girl's. He had white flannels on and a striped blazer, seemed prosperous and immensely pleased with himself.

Guy said to Danilo, 'I didn't know you knew him.'

'I used to know him just like you did. Not so well, maybe, till lately. He swapped some pesetas for me. I sold my villa and it was a question of getting the funds out. I should have asked little Miss Leo, eh? Is that what's going through your mind? Little Miss Leo and the fiancé?'

'Not at all,' Guy said stiffly. 'How did you run across him again?'

'I wonder why you ask. Still, my life is an open book between friends. It was a chance meeting. Tanya's sister had a flat in the same block as him by Clapham Common. That's her talking to him, the strawberry-blonde one.'

'In *Clapham*? He lives in Chelsea.'

'This was three or four years ago.' said Danilo. 'Why are you so interested all of a sudden? Oh, I begin to see. You aren't putting a contract out on him, I hope. He's valuable to me. Where shall I find another swap jockey with a baby face and no scruples? Look at him, he looks about twelve.'

Guy· fetched himself another drink. What he would have liked to do was walk up to Robin Chisholm and throw the drink in his face, see what happened. He had never thrown a drink in anyone's face but the idea of doing this was suddenly very attractive. It was as if this was something he had to do before he died. The evening was no longer very warm. For the first time in his life Guy thought, nights are never warm in this country – well, maybe one a year might be warm. Then he walked up to Robin who was still with Danilo's strawberry-blonde sister-in-law and, by now, an elderly man someone had said was a dress designer.

'Hallo, how are *you*?' He said it in that transatlantic manner which places all the stress on the 'you' and runs the words together in a meaningless way. It was deliberate, unaccompanied by a smile.

Robin chose to answer this rhetorical question literally, which made the strawberry blonde laugh. 'Oh, I'm marvellous, never been better.' He gave Guy a purposely vacuous grin, looking like one of the 'big boys' in *Just William*.

'Maeve not here?'

This occasioned an offensive pantomime search. Robin looked to either side of him, stretching out his neck and peering round the back of the dress designer. His eyebrows rose, he immediately became short-sighted, baffled, looked at the ground, pursed his lips in a silent whistle. 'She doesn't seem to be,' he said at last. 'No, I'd say not.' He had assumed, for the evening only perhaps, for Guy only perhaps, a hearty ingenuous manner. 'I say, is that awfully pretty girl with you?'

It was a mistake to ask which one but Guy asked it.

'The coloured one with the Rastafarian hair.'

Guy threw his drink in Robin's face.

Danilo's sister-in-law screamed. The dress designer shouted, 'For heavens' sake!' Robin shook himself, spat, tossed back his hair and leapt for Guy with arms extended like a cat fighting. The whole party was silenced, was staring, movement suspended, adrenalin rising. Guy's fist shot out and caught Robin not where it was meant to on his jaw, but against his right collarbone. Almost immediately Robin's flailing hands made contact with Guy's face, the longish nails extended, tiger-like. Guy struck again as people began to intervene. Someone seized him from behind as someone else grabbed Robin by the shoulders, but not before he had slammed his fist into Robin's left eye.

They were both gasping, snorting really.

'Stop it, cut it out,' someone was saying.

'Are you crazy?'

'This is *my* party.'

'What in God's name is going on here?'

'I couldn't believe my eyes.'

'Yes, he threw his drink at him, right in his face.'

'He's a shit,' Guy said. 'He's the biggest shit in London.'

'And you're a criminal psychopath and murderer,' said Robin, holding one hand over his eye. 'Why don't you fuck off back to the slum you came from?'

\* \* \* \*

Celeste drove them home. Guy sat beside her, nursing his bleeding face. He had been scratched on his right cheek, the right side of his upper lip, the left side of his chin and on his neck.

'I shall probably get blood poisoning. God knows what filthy bacteria a shit like that carries, listeria, hepatitis B, it could be anything.'

'Silly Guy,' said Celeste. 'You're so silly. You can go to the doctor tomorrow. He'll never believe it was a fellow did it – you can say I did it, right?'

He didn't love her but he loved the way she talked, that accent. Rastafarian, that shit would call it. Tomorrow was 'tomorr-*oh*' and doctor 'd'ctah'.

'Celeste, I want to tell you something.'

It was dark inside the Jaguar. Darkness helped. He lit a cigarette. He would rather have died than tell Leonora about Con Mulvanney but he was going to tell Celeste and tell her without many qualms, with hardly any inhibition. Was that because he didn't really care what she thought of him, whereas what Leonora thought of him was all-important? Was it because if she said as a result of what he told her that she no longer wanted to know him, he would be indifferent? Or something else altogether – that Celeste knew him for what he was and loved the man she knew, the real man, he had no need to pretend with her. Leonora on the other hand, for all their long and close association, didn't really know him and he didn't want her to know him, he wanted her to keep her illusions about him.

'Go ahead, then,' said Celeste.

He told her, he didn't conceal anything. It all came out, his doubt, his trepidation, his cowardice, his later awareness that someone had passed it on to Leonora. Rachel Lingard, he had thought it must be, but at the party he understood it wasn't. It was Robin Chisholm. At the time Robin had been living in Clapham, only half a mile away from Poppy Vasari.

'And that's why you threw your drink at him?'

The real reason had been because of Robin's racist remark directed at Celeste, but he wasn't going to say this. It might hurt her, besides showing him in a ridiculous, chivalrous light. 'More or less, yes.'

'Guy, sweetheart, you are a bit crazy, do you know that? You are a bit obsessed with this thing about Leonora. Do you even know if someone told her? Have you asked her? No, because that would tell her the truth if she doesn't know it already. Don't you see this is all in your head, and your head is very strange these days, Guy, let me tell you.'

'She changed towards me. Within two weeks of what

happened to Con Mulvanney, she changed. She wouldn't go on holiday with me.'

'She didn't want you to pay. She wouldn't go because of the strings attached, right? That was the only way she changed. OK, so I'm not like that. A man want to pay for me, he can, he's welcome, I'm happy. If he want me to do things he want and I don't want and he come on strong, then I throw him out the window. I have not been going to t'ai chi classes for five years for nothing, I can tell you.'

Guy laughed in spite of himself. He glanced out of the car window but he knew where they were without looking. This was Balham Hill and over there to the left was Clapham Common. Con Mulvanney country. He had a sensation of it as crossed with a million invisible wires, a network of transmission, each carrying whispers of his crimes and his culpability. Robin Chisholm's voice spoke to him again: Psychopathic criminal and murderer. How could Leonora's brother have known that those were the words to use unless he had been told the facts?

Celeste was driving them across the river by Battersea Bridge. 'Sweet Guy,' she said, 'I don't want to hurt you.' He smiled to himself. That made two of them, each not wanting to hurt the other. 'But, Guy, isn't it most likely she changed because she was realising you'd nothing to share any more? You're not the same kind of people. Even I can tell and I've only seen her once. OK, so I'm biased, I'm jealous, it's true, I am. But that doesn't mean it's not the truth. She woke up, she got to understand.'

'At that precise moment? That would make it the biggest coincidence of all time.'

'Well, maybe it would, if you were lovers right up till then, if you were living together or sort of living together like us I mean, if you'd promised things and were going to make it permanent. Then it would be really strange. If it was *me* it would be really strange. But was it like that, Guy?'

He said nothing. He shrugged. It was she who didn't understand. The streets were dark but shiny with yellow light, the brassy light from lamps, a cold summer night, the cold small hours of a summer morning. The scratches on his face felt sore. He told her to leave the car in the street, not to put it away. A cat crouching on the opposite wall gave him a long inscrutable look from its light-filled almost pupil-less yellow eyes. Perhaps it was a connoisseur of scratches. If people asked he would tell them he had been clawed by his neighbour's cat.

This was a night when he would have preferred not to have Celeste with him. It would be unthinkable to send her home. Poor thing, he thought, poor fellow sufferer. And then anger filled him, anger against Rachel Lingard and those Chisholms, all the Chisholms. His fists clenched. Celeste went ahead of him upstairs, but not jauntily, not with any air of part possession of the house, more as if she expected him to call her back, even send her away.

She sat on the Linnell bed, picking the gold tips off her plaits. 'Guy, she said, 'sweet Guy, was it just marijuana you dealt in, and maybe a bit of acid?'

How he would have seized this lifeline if Leonora had asked him! There was no point in prevaricating with Celeste. He didn't have to impress her. It wouldn't be true to say he didn't care what she thought of him, rather that he believed in her unqualified forgiveness. 'The hard stuff too,' he said. 'Everything.'

'Opium?'

'Heroin, yes. Heroin's opium, isn't it?'

How absurd that, after all these years and the fortune he had made, he still didn't quite know. Perhaps he hadn't wanted to know. She nodded, watching him.

'People don't come to any harm from the stuff itself,' he said. 'It's the related things, dirty needles, infection, unrestricted use. And it's no worse than being addicted to drink, only alcohol's socially acceptable. And as for dealers, you might as well condemn a wine merchant.'

'I've a friend whose grandfather was Kurdish,' she said. 'He was an *aga*.' She must have seen his incredulous smile starting. 'No, that's not only a Swedish stove, it's a kind of feudal lord in parts of Turkey. They all grow poppies there, they make base morphine. It's what you do in that place, that part of Asia. It's funny what you say about the man and the bees because that's what they once did, kept bees, but now the smugglers pack the hives full of the drug.

'Her mother's family is very big. They have four laboratories processing morphine in the villages near Van. Her grandfather sent the young men away to learn the chemistry and two of her uncles got caught in Iran and executed. Thousands of smugglers and chemists get executed in Iran all the time.'

'Why do they do it then?' he said hollowly.

'Poverty.'

The word fell with a hollow sound. Poverty was a condition he had once known well, but the word itself was seldom heard in this house.

'You could say it's not all bad then, not if it creates employment.'

She went on as if he hadn't spoken. 'They don't use it themselves. No way. And there's no other work, not even in the fields. They don't have a choice about what they do. You can earn £6,000 taking a kilo of heroin to Istanbul and much more per kilo if you're a chemist.'

He had never heard her talk like this before, that serious tone, that articulate almost authoritative manner replacing her usual lazy simple speech. It was more the way Leonora and her friends might talk.

'I expect it's much the same in South America,' she said. 'You may not die through using it, though you do, thousands do, but you sure do die getting it to the users.' She said in a voice he'd never heard from her before, hard and clear and aimed straight at his guilt, his soft sensitivities: 'Shame on you, Guy, shame on you.'

He wasn't angry, he felt rather sick, It came to him that he had drunk a great deal, but the effects were only now becoming apparent. Not able to see very clearly, suffering a slight duplication of vision, he looked at the cuts on his face in the bathroom mirror, the deep scratch across his upper lip that would probably scar, the scoring on his throat. What kind of a man would scratch another man? Now that Guy thought of it, he remembered Robin had always worn his nails rather long, another unpleasant habit.

Celeste had got into bed and was lying with her arms over her head and her face in the pillow. He lay beside her, reached for the switch and turned out the light. The sudden darkness moved his memory. The last time they had had lunch together, he and Leonora, last Saturday, she had confessed to him she had been out with a friend of Robin's. Someone Robin had been in partnership with was one of the men between him, Guy, and William Newton. And there had been another man she had met at a party given by Robin. It wouldn't be going too far to say Robin had hated him so much that he had thrown one man after another in his sister's way. He had practically pimped for her. Guy heard himself make a sound, a kind of groan.

Celeste heard him too. She put her arms round him and held him close.

# CHAPTER
# ELEVEN

---

Something Guy hadn't thought of on that night was that Leonora might be angry with him because he had given her brother a black eye. That he had done so he was certain. Robin Chisholm would have more explaining away to do than he had. Guy's doctor had looked at the scratches and not believed the story of the cat. He had scarcely believed the true story of a fight with another man but he gave Guy an anti-tetanus injection.

Leonora was in Georgiana Street. He reached her there in the afternoon. Yes, she knew all about the fight, Robin had told Maeve on the phone that morning and Maeve had told her and then Robin himself had told her. Guy wasn't surprised. It just confirmed what he already knew of the closeness of that family and the influence each one of them exerted over the others. Robin was telling everybody how Guy had sprung upon him 'like a madman' for no apparent reason, only he privately knew that the reason was his absurd obsession with Robin's sister.

'Not at all,' Guy said coldly. 'He insulted Celeste.'

*That* interested her. 'Did he? What did he say?'

Guy told her, not minding in the least that she knew he could be heroic and chivalrous. 'Are you angry with me?'

'Not more than usual. I expect it was six of one and half a dozen of the other.'

'Has Robin told you awful things about me?'

There was a hesitation. 'When? D'you mean recently?'

He could hardly have asked for clearer confirmation. 'Never mind,' he said. 'Where shall we have lunch on Saturday?'

Suppose she wouldn't because he had given her brother a black eye? The silence lasted about fifteen seconds but it was an hour to him. 'You choose,' she said. 'I'm always choosing, it's time you did, especially as there won't be many more.'

He winced at that. 'We've got three more from now,' he said. Hundreds more, he told himself stoutly, that wedding's a dream, it'll never happen. He said, making his voice light and teasing.

'Come off it, sweetheart, you know you're not really getting married.'

There was more silence. This time it really did last for nearly a minute. A click on the line made him think for an awful instant that she had rung off.

'Leo, are you still there?'

'I'm wondering,' she said in a remote voice, 'what to say. I don't know what to say to you when you talk like that. I suppose that if you want to live in a world of illusion I just have to let you.'

He let it pass, he even laughed, a knowing sophisticated laugh. 'Where shall we have lunch?'

'Come and have it with me in Portland Road.'

'We wouldn't be alone.'

'We aren't exactly alone in restaurants. Rachel's hardly ever there on Saturdays and Maeve will go out with Robin. They always do.'

'I'd love to,' he said.

* * * *

After the Drugs Squad had searched his house he had given up dealing. Well, he had phased it out. And it hadn't been altogether easy. He had been in actual danger. One of his suppliers had threatened him, if not with death, with some kind of attack, with spoiling his 'handsome face'. It was rubbish saying only women cared about their looks, he no more wanted to be scarred than a girl would. He had gone about in fear for a few weeks, had carried a gun. Nothing had in fact happened and within six months he had given up all dealing. He never heard from the police again or from Poppy Vasari. No direct evidence came from Poppy or anyone else that she had carried out her threat and whispered everywhere his part in Con Mulvanney's death.

But in the ensuing months the Chisholms changed towards him. Leonora changed. He didn't care about the others, but Leonora was his life. First, she wouldn't go to Samos with him, then the other refusals began. Less and less would she go out with him in the evenings. Anthony became cold and distant. Now, when he looked back, he could remember Anthony's almost violent repudiation of the money he wanted to 'lend' Leonora for that flat.

'You must see it's out of the question.'

'It would be a loan,' he had said. 'She has to get a loan from somewhere. Why not me?'

'Are you seriously asking that?'

'Yes, of course I am. Why shouldn't I offer her an interest-free loan?'

'Because you're a man and she's a woman,' Anthony had said roughly. 'Good God, man, you're not a relation, you're not her brother or her cousin even. What kind of an obligation would that put her under?'

And Robin, at that time, in those months? The trouble was that Guy couldn't remember Robin at all that autumn and winter, apart from that remark about getting a lady in your power in one easy lesson. But he could imagine all too well the conversations between him and Poppy Vasari, the woman who was his neighbour in the block of flats by Clapham Common.

'Your sister's thinking of *marrying* him?'

Robin cocking his head on one side, his fair curls bobbing,

his face winsome as a ten-year-old's. 'That wouldn't be a good idea?'

'You won't ask that question when I've told you how he makes his living. I'd like to start by telling you what he did to my friend.'

But if he gave Danilo £3,000 to dispose of Robin Chisholm – and he could imagine doing that, he could imagine not being too worried if the 'disposal' was that far removed – it wouldn't undo the past. It wouldn't, at any rate, undo what Robin had told Leonora in that fateful August four years ago. Perhaps not, but it would prevent Robin poisoning her mind against him now, and he had no doubt that was going on at present, all the time. How many more vile slanders had been repeated, for instance, during that phone conversation about Robin's black eye? And there was another aspect. If all else failed, there was no way Leonora was going to go through with her wedding on September 16 if her brother was killed two weeks before that date.

He was unpleasantly aware that he was no longer talking to Leonora every day. It was no longer possible to get hold of her every day. Living as she did for three or four days a week in Georgiana Street, she never answered the phone during the day. When he asked her why not she said it hadn't rung or she was out. He could hear Robin saying,

'Don't answer it, there's your remedy. Nothing will happen to you if you don't answer the phone, you know. There are no *penalties* attaching. There's no inquisitor going to get hold of you and have you up before the bench and make you say why you didn't answer the phone. Let me give you three little words on magnets to stick on the fridge: LET IT RING.'

She could so easily. No one important would phone Newton in the day. They knew he was at work. Few people knew she was there. If it rang it would be him, and however much she might want to speak to him, she could be made to believe it was wiser not to. Her family had her under their thumbs, under their five thumbs, six if you counted Rachel Lingard, and you almost had to, she and Leonora were so close, like sisters.

It was Friday when he phoned Danilo.

'No need to apologise,' said Danilo. 'These things happen in love and war.'

Guy hadn't been going to apologise. He knew very well that the fight had considerably enlivened a flagging party and given the guests a subject of conversation that would last for months.

'Tanya was upset, but she'll forgive you.' Danilo laughed so loudly that the phone made a noise which hurt Guy's ear. 'So what's with you then?'

'Dan,' Guy said, 'it's him, he's the one.'

He felt reluctant to speak an actual name. It had physical symptoms, a constriction of the throat, a whisper of nausea. Danilo was silent but his breathing was just audible, the faint small gasps a man makes before he sneezes. The sneeze didn't come but a snigger instead, very soft and breathy.

'How about my financial transactions?'

'There are other swap jockeys.'

Danilo seemed not to be listening. He said, 'It was a good party, wasn't it? We were lucky with the weather.'

'Fuck the weather. Do you want the money now?'

'Of course I do. I trust you, but there are limits.'

* * * *

He had only twice been to Portland Road. The first time was soon after they moved in when he was invited and Rachel called him Victorian. The next occasion was a house-warming party Leonora and Rachel and Maeve had given. They had been in the flat two or three months. By then he had lost his special place in Leonora's life. No one, least of all she herself, would have described him as her boyfriend. Nobody would have spoken of him to the Chisholms as the man 'your sister' or 'your daughter' was going to marry. She still sometimes went out with him. She had told him they ought to meet less often, they ought to 'see'.

A year and more was to pass before the coming of William Newton. Perhaps that was why, although he hated him, he didn't blame Newton for her defection. She had already, long since, allowed her family to persuade her he and she were unsuited. There was no man at the party for her but himself, though Maeve had someone, Robin Chisholm's predecessor, and even Rachel had an owlish fellow in glasses. He tried to remember if Robin, on that occasion, had been particularly antagonistic or if Rachel had, but he could only recall the malicious false sweetness of Tessa who, encountering him for the first time since those loan and mortgage discussions, commented that she was surprised he wasn't married yet.

'I was sure you'd arrive with some glamorous creature in tow. I said so to Magnus, didn't I, Magnus? Guy Curran will turn up with some beauty from a TV commercial, I said.'

\* \* \* \*

The street was unchanged, the Prince of Wales still looking like a nice pub to take your girl for a pre-dinner drink. He could live here – give him half a chance! He hated the fantasies that came to him unbidden but he was often unable to control them. Now he imagined in spite of himself buying one of these houses, the whole house of course, because a miracle had happened, because Leonora said she had really loved him all along. She liked the area, she would want to stay. Dinner at Leith's, he thought, drinks first in the Prince of Wales, just he and she, dining out in the first week after they came back from their honeymoon. He'd have taken her to India: Kashmir, Jaipur, Agra and a week in the Maldives. Hand in hand, by moonlight, they would approach in awe the gleaming palace that was the Taj Mahal, turn to each other and kiss in the shadow of its shimmering walls.

The top bell had all three names on a card above it. Her voice came out of the entryphone, polite, hostessy, expressing pleasure that he was so early. The stair carpet was already worn, the walls already marked. It was a long way up too, forty-two stairs. He counted. And when he considered what he could give her. . . ! She need never climb stairs again so long as she lived.

She was wearing a tracksuit. Gear for a day at home, no doubt. It was dark blue and had probably looked all right until the first time it was washed. Since then it had been washed about five hundred times. He reminded himself that she didn't dress up for Newton. It was a good sign, those dark blue pants and top, bare feet and Dr Scholl sandals. She could be relaxed with him, she didn't have to bother.

'Fantastic earrings,' he said.

She smiled, and about as widely as she ever did for him. The earrings were cheap Indian things, he could tell that at once, but pretty: white enamel daisies with yellow centres. They nestled against the peach-pink lobes, the golden-brown neck, like real flowers tucked through her ears.

He didn't know what he had expected of the flat, perhaps that they might have done great things with it. But what could be done with three bedsits, a kitchen and a tiny bathroom? Posters and house plants, things from the Reject Shop and things from the Indian shop. Fasitidiously, he noted that it wasn't even very clean, not the way his house was with Fatima coming in four days a week. He stood in the kitchen while she opened packets from Marks and Spencers and cut up a loaf from her favourite Cranks. After a while he lit a cigarette.

'Do you mind, Guy? This flat is a smokeless zone.'

'I don't believe it,' he said.

'None of us smokes and we don't like the smell, so we decided it was only sensible to have a total ban.'

'Can I have a drink?'

'Oh, God, I'm sorry. I forgot. You should have asked before. There's sherry up on the shelf there and white wine in the fridge. It's in one of those box things, you turn the tap on.'

They inhabited different worlds. It wasn't that she preferred her world, he thought, no one could. The point was that it was all she could afford and she was proud. The 'box thing' had a printed pattern of vine leaves and grapes all over it. He turned the plastic tap and the pale yellow wine dribbled out. He hated sherry, so there wasn't much choice.

'If you have to have a cigarette you can always go out on the balcony while I'm seeing to this.'

It opened out of her bedroom. The bed was made but in the sort of way people do make beds who only use a duvet and two pillows. He couldn't help asking himself how many times William Newton had shared it with her, perhaps even the previous night. The room had an air of having been hastily tidied. A drawer in a chest was stuffed too full to shut properly. One leg of a pair of green tights hung out. There were books on the floor on one side of the bed, one of them lying open and face downwards. The glass doors to the balcony were open. He went out, leaned on the iron rail and lit a fresh cigarette.

The roofs and spires of Notting Hill lay below him, the looped crescents and the great bow of Ladbroke Grove. Dusty trees made nests of dark green among the custard-coloured Victorian terraces, the new red blocks, the dove grey of stucco and the dark grey of stone. Yes, it would be right for them to live somewhere near here, in the place where they had been born, where they had first met, where their lives had been interlinked.

He felt a yearning nostalgia for it, as if he couldn't bear to be away another instant. To return to South Kensington would be like going into exile. Why hadn't he come to live on her doorstep, sold his house and bought another here, so that he would see her every day and she him?

He would find a pretty house. There were plenty on the market, estate agents' windows were full of them. With prices falling, a million would buy a little dream at the 'best end' of the Grove. Lansdowne Crescent perhaps or some other street among those concentric circles of faintly shabby elegance. He imagined her furnishing it. He would come home for lunch and find her sitting on the floor among carpet samples and books of fabric and books of wallpaper, some poovey interior designer nodding and smiling, suggesting this and that while she concentrated, her face wearing that grave frown . . .

'Lunch is ready, Guy,' she said behind him.

He surfaced. It was like emerging from a warm scented bath in which one has fallen half-asleep. Awakening from these dreams brought him a sharp unhappiness but still he couldn't stop them or even control them. He followed her through the room, carrying his empty glass and his pinched-out cigarette end.

She had laid the tiny table in the kitchen. He sat squashed up against the side of the fridge. The wine box was on the table next to a carton of orange juice and between two plates, pastrami and salad for him, cheese and salad for her. He longed for a cigarette, and in spite of being here alone with her, having achieved if temporarily what was the summation of all his wishes, he felt his temper rising. It was her pride he was fighting, he thought, the arrogance that made her stoutly endure this poky, dirty kitchen, eschew decent food, deny herself good clothes.

'Do you remember saying you'd share my house with me when we got married?' he said.

'No, I don't remember.'

'It was a long time ago. Nine years. It was when you first came to the house.'

'Yes, I remember, but I don't think I said that.'

'All right. Do you remember saying "I *am* Guy and you are Leonora"?'

'Oh, Guy, probably. I was a child. I did *Wuthering Heights* for O levels.'

'What's that got to do with it?'

She was eating bread and cheese, putting up a pretence of enjoying it more than all the delicate food he offered her. 'It's a book,' she said kindly. 'The girl in it talks like that – well, she says "I am Heathcliff".'

He shook his head impatiently. 'I don't understand why people want to be always saying things out of books. Surely life's more important.'

'Sometimes things in books apply to life.'

He didn't understand and her laughter irritated him, making him angrier. He said in an abrupt change of subject, 'Do you think what your brother does for a living is exactly what you'd call pure and ethical?'

'*What?*'

'Swapping sums of money. He must be contravening currency regulations all the time.'

She got up to take away their plates, took Greek yogurt and a dish of stewed dried fruit out of the fridge. 'I'm not responsible for what Robin does for a living or what anyone else does, come to that. It's nothing to do with me. I'm only responsible for what I do – oh, and maybe what William does.'

Greatly daring, 'Does that apply to me too?' he said.

'I'm not responsible for you, Guy, or what you do. I've told you before, I know how you make a living and I don't care for it, but it's not my business. Except, well . . .' He saw her face change. She laid down her spoon. 'I suppose I really ought not to let you buy meals for me if I don't approve of the source of your income.'

'Oh, for Christ's sake!' He pushed the yogurt away from him. 'I can't eat this muck, Leonora. It's like being at the fucking Festival of Mind, Body and Spirit. I can't eat fermented sheep's milk.' He took out a cigarette without thinking, saw her eyes on it, crushed it in his palm, his anger boiling. 'Who does bloody Robin think he is telling tales of me? It's not as if his own hands are clean. He's lucky not to be in jail.'

She said, 'Guy, I really don't know what you're on about and I don't think you do.' She was filling the kettle, bent on making filthy instant coffee, he thought. 'Do you know anything about nervous breakdowns?' she said.

'What?'

'Nervous – mental – breakdowns. People do have them, you know. It's when everything gets too much for them and they lose their hold on reality and can't cope – all that sort of thing. Only, Guy, I think you're having one. Well, I think you're going to have one if you aren't careful.'

That made the second woman this week to tell him he was going mad. He hoped the look he was levelling at her, patient, controlled, bored, though with seething undercurrents, would silence her, maybe make her say she was sorry.

With near disbelief he heard her say, 'Guy, William's got a friend he was at university with who does Jungian therapy, he's very good.' Mercifully, she was interrupted before she had said more than, 'If you'd just think of seeing . . .'

The kitchen door opened and a tall, thin, almost unrecognisable blonde girl came in. Her face was white, her eyes glazed. Pausing in the doorway, holding the handle, swaying a

129

little, she stared past them. Guy thought she was drunk and
silently cursed this unexpected interruption.

Leonora jumped up in consternation.

'Maeve, what is it?'

'Robin . . . It's Robin, he's been in an accident.'

# CHAPTER
# TWELVE

---

Robin Chisholm wasn't dead or even badly injured. Guy felt angry with Maeve for causing Leonora unnecessary anxiety. The woman made a drama out of everything. No doubt going in the ambulance to hospital with him and seeing him taken off for a brain scan had made her hysterical. But as far as Guy could tell, Robin had simply got a mild concussion and a few cuts and bruises. To add to that black eye, he thought.

She had told her tale after Leonora had ministered to her with an aspirin and a glass of the stuff he wouldn't dignify with the name of wine that came out of that cardboard box.

'We were coming out of the park, you know that bit where the roads sort of meet and come out into the Bayswater Road and there are lights and everything, where the Royal Lancaster is. I don't know what you call it.'

'The Victoria Gate,' said Guy.

She took no notice of him. She hadn't since she came in. He might as well not have been there, except that it wasn't natural when talking, to avoid ever looking to the right side of the

131

room. She kept her head turned away the way she might if there was vomit on the floor.

'Well, we were coming from the Kensington Gardens side, we were going to go in the Swan for a drink. You know it's always dicey crossing the road there because the traffic tears round the – is it called the Ring? So we were very very careful but naturally looking to the right, if you see what I mean, we didn't think the left mattered on account of the light being red and nothing being there anyway. And then it happened. This car came tearing out of whatever that road's called by the side of Hyde Park Gardens . . .'

'Brook Street,' said Guy, expecting no acknowledgement and getting none.

'Robin had gone over ahead of me. My shoelace was undone. I was bending down doing up my shoelace, only he didn't realise and he'd gone on over. This car came tearing out of nowhere – well, out of – ' She looked at him at last, ' – Brook Street, I suppose, right through the red light, the lights might not have been there for all the notice he took. Thank God Robin's pretty quick on his feet and I saw and I yelled. I screamed out, "Robin! Look out!" The car hit him, but only a glancing blow. It didn't hit his head, he hit his head on the lamppost.

'There are never any police about when you want them, are there? A great crowd gathered though, you can always depend on that. I wasn't in shock then, the shock didn't hit me for about an hour – well, it doesn't, does it? Most of the people came there just to gawp and get the maximum thrill – you know the type – but there was one man with a bit of sense who phoned for an ambulance. The ambulance man asked me if I got the number of the car but of course I hadn't, you have other things to think about at a time like that.'

Guy felt a certain relief, though Danilo's hitman would certainly have used fake registration plates. A failure but a brave attempt. Better luck next time. Maeve at any rate had no suspicion, as far as he could tell, that the incident in the park had been any more than the result of a piece of reckless driving. What Guy would have liked to say was that it served Robin right for having the bad manners to go across a fairly dangerous street on his own, leaving his girlfriend on the pavement tying up her shoelace, but he thought better of it. Leonora seemed both upset and relieved, Maeve much restored by having told her tale and got it off her chest.

'Is there anything to eat?' she said. 'We never got around to lunch as you can imagine.'

If Leonora had chosen that moment to go to the bathroom or something he could have said what he wanted to, something on the lines of, 'Oh, really, how amazing, I'd have expected them to be serving caviar and blinis in the ambulance', or 'You mean you never went to the dear old Swan after all?' But Leonora stayed, dispensing extravagant sympathy and a pastrami sandwich.

Fortified, Maeve gave a deep sigh, helped herself to more from the vine-patterned box. Her face had grown pinker, she was really a very pretty girl, if you could use that word about someone so statuesque, with such flashing blue eyes and so much lion's mane hair. Guy was just thinking that her legs were the same sort of length as another girl's height, when she turned to him and said with the utmost venom.

'It's all thanks to you. If you hadn't *bludgeoned* him he'd have had a better idea of what he was doing. He was half-blinded, do you know that? He's been having the most crushing headaches. If anything shows up on the brain scan it's just as likely to be through you.'

Guy's reply was to extend his neck and turn his face from side to side so that she could see the deep scratch marks, which, though healing, looked rather worse than they had immediately after Robin had inflicted them.

She said with a light scathing laugh, 'Oh, I've no doubt he had to defend himself.'

'Yes, like a fucking tomcat,' said Guy, he couldn't help himself. 'They do tend to get run over in the Bayswater Road.'

Both girls were on him for that. How could he? How could he talk like that? When poor Robin was lying in a hospital bed, when he might have some serious injury. Hadn't he any ordinary human feelings?

'Haven't you any affect?' said Maeve incomprehensibly.

He apologised to Leonora who said that that was all right but perhaps he had better go now. She would have to phone her parents. Perhaps she would go to the hospital to see Robin, she and her mother would go together. It pleased Guy that there had been no mention of the ginger dwarf in all this. He, it appeared, was quickly forgotten. If only Maeve had taken herself off after the announcement had been made, he was sure Leonora would have come running into his arms for comfort. When the story was being told, at one point, she had actually rested her hand on his shoulder, as on the natural place to steady herself. He must, ideally, try to be with her when the news ultimately came of Robin's death, as in a day or two it must.

Next day, as usual, he phoned her. She was at home. That in itself was good, was reassuring. You would expect her to run to the man she talked of marrying but she hadn't done that, she had stayed at home. He had no qualms about ingratiating himself with her.

'How is Robin?'

'Do you care?'

'Leo, of course I care. Just because we had a bit of a disagreement when we were both pissed – I mean, for God's sake. Men do fight, it's the way they are, you have to accept that.' Did they? Not in her world perhaps. 'It doesn't mean I'd bear a grudge, no way.'

'I suppose I don't really understand. It's not just me as a woman. William wouldn't either.' His heart dropped. His heart was a small cold stone dropping through him. 'Robin's OK,' she said. 'They're keeping him in till tomorrow. It isn't just the accident. They're harking back a bit to that trouble he had four years ago – you know, when he was in hospital all those weeks?'

It had been around the time she had changed her mind about going to Samos with him. Weeks had gone by and she had been cold to him and he angry with her. But he seemed to remember some trouble of Robin Chisholm's – headaches, dizziness,

suspected epilepsy. Of course, it ultimately turned out there
was nothing wrong with him.

'It so happens it was exactly four years ago,' Leonora said.
'Well, he must have gone into hospital the first week of August
and he stayed there till nearly the end of September. I don't see
how that could affect him now, do you, Guy?'

Guy said, no, he didn't think so and especially (trying to
keep the sarcasm out of his voice) since all the tests that first
time had been negative. Was Maeve feeling better?

'She's in a really bad nervous state, Guy.' He loved the way
she kept calling him by his Christian name in that confiding
way. 'It must have been an awful shock. I think she's very
much in love with Robin.'

Too bad, thought Guy. She'll just have to bear it when her
love comes to nothing. I'm very much in love and who gives a
shit about me? Something was bothering him, something
about Robin Chisholm, though he couldn't think what it was.
Often these days he experienced this fuzziness, a cutting off
almost. To call it confusion was too strong, it wasn't as bad as
that.

'Will you have dinner with me tonight?' he said.

'No, Guy, dear, I never do. You know that.'

'No one need know, Leo. I'll be very discreet about it. They
needn't know.'

'Who's they?'

He expressed it carefully. 'Your family. The people who're
close to you.'

She was silent. When she spoke she sounded distressed.
How is it that you can love someone and yet be *glad* when
they're distressed? 'Oh, Guy, how I wish . . . It's no use.
Phone me tomorrow,' she said.

His heart, which seemed to have shrivelled to the size of a
pea, was suddenly huge, was swollen and soft and palpitating.
*She had sounded as if she was going to cry.* And over him. *She had
been moved to tears by him.*

'Darling Leonora, have dinner with me tomorrow, any day,
you name the day. Or I'll come over. Shall I come now?'

135

'No, Guy, of course not.'

'Then let's meet tomorrow.'

'We'll have lunch on Saturday,' she said. 'Goodbye.' The phone went down before he could protest.

When he dialled her number next morning he still hadn't been able to identify what was haunting him, what unease lay just below the surface of his consciousness. He had had a curious dream. He was an observer, watching but invisible, at a meeting of the residents' association of a block of flats in Battersea Park. This mansion block was in fact where no buildings could be, in the centre of the Pleasure Gardens, overlooking the pier. The residents included Rachel Lingard, Robin Chisholm and Poppy Vasari. They were discussing applications from people who wanted to come and live in the flats. One was from himself. Rachel read his letter and read out his name.

'Guy Patrick Curran, 8 Scarsdale Mews, W8.'

Dreams were strange because that wasn't quite his address. His address was 7 Scarsdale Mews. Robin Chisholm said nothing. He spat. He spat the way he had after Guy had hit him at Danilo's party. Poppy Vasari, who was even dirtier and more unkempt than in reality, said,

'We don't want him. He's a murderer. He murdered my lover with a substance classified Class A under the Misuse of Drugs Act, 1971.'

After that Guy wanted to leave. Even though they couldn't see him he wanted to escape. Knowing he was dreaming, that this was dream substance and dream time, he began willing himself to wake up. Before he did a man he didn't know and had never seen before got to his feet and began to sing a song about opium. He sang that opium poppies first grew on the spot where Buddha's eyelids fell when he cut them off to stop himself falling asleep. Guy woke up shouting and groaning.

He tried to phone Leonora at ten in the morning. There was no answer. He made a second attempt at just before eleven and got Rachel Lingard.

'You get a lot of holidays in the Social Services.'

She had an accent like the head of a women's college at

Oxford making a television appearance. 'I'm not on holiday. I'm at home in bed with a bug. You got me up.'

Guy restrained an impulse to say that was the only thing she was ever likely to be in bed with. It wouldn't be true anyway. Even the plainest, most repulsive girls got men these days. He didn't know why but it was so. Rachel had never been without a man all the time he had known her, she always had some bearded or spotty-faced intellectual in tow.

'Where's Leonora?'

'I don't know. I was told to say if you rang that Robin is better and coming out today.'

'Well, fuck him. When you were "told" that where were you "told" she'd be?'

'Please don't take that hectoring tone with me. And you can leave out the "fuck", it's offensive. I get quite enough of that from the low-life I encounter at work. Perhaps you'd like to get this clear: I don't know where Leonora is because, knowing you'd ask, I was careful not to ask her. I'm not lying to you, I don't tell lies. Do I make myself plain?'

'You don't need to, my love,' said Guy, knowing he would regret it. 'Nature did that for you.' He slammed down the phone.

He dialled William Newton's number. The line was engaged. That would be Rachel ringing Leonora to repeat to her what he had said. Anger began to rise inside him in that uncontrollable way it had. It was happening all the time these days. It would start in the way nausea started, a stifling feeling that worked its way up to his throat where it settled and needed not to be vomited but screamed out. Only he had never yet screamed it out. He walked across the room to the double doors. It was sunny again, it was like being in Spain or Italy. The flowers on the water lilies in the pool were all open to the sun. He turned back, picked up the Chinese vase that stood on the red lacquer cabinet just inside the doors and smashed it down on to the stone flags.

The shattering of the vase had an effect on him, if not quite the one he had aimed at. Certainly his anger was temporarily appeased, it had done that. It awed him too and brought him a kind of fear of himself. Why had he done it and without thought? He had simply done it, on an impulse.

It was August Bank Holiday Monday so not one of Fatima's days. He kicked the fragments, pushed them into a heap with his toe. The vase was *famille noire*, cherry blossom and linnets on a black glaze worth about fifteen hundred pounds. Thinking of that made him shudder. He lifted the phone, dialled William Newton's number and got no reply. If he stayed here any longer he might break the place up, that was the way he felt, so he took a taxi to the rifle club and practised target shooting. Gladiators after that, the weights and some acrobatics on the parallel bars. He weighed himself and found he had lost those two pounds plus three more. In the steam room a gay Norwegian eyed him lustfully. What wouldn't he give for Leonora to look at him like that?

He tried her again in the afternoon. There was still no answer. Suppose he couldn't get through to her all week? They hadn't yet named a restaurant for their Saturday lunch date. Suppose he couldn't get in touch with her, what would happen to their Saturday lunch? Most likely she had gone to Robin's. She and Maeve would have gone to Robin's to be there when he came back from the hospital. Guy started looking up Robin's number in the phone book.

It wasn't there. No Robin Chisholm was listed anywhere in Battersea. Then he realised that of course Robin didn't live in Battersea any more, he lived in Chelsea. He realised a few more things with startling suddenness. Why was he so confused these days? Why had he been telling himself for days now that Poppy Vasari had lived in the same block of flats as Robin when it was not she but *Danilo's sister-in-law* who had lived there? And wasn't there something else he hadn't thought of which was now staring him in the face?

Robin *couldn't* have been told about Con Mulvanney by Poppy or anyone else in August four years ago because he was in hospital undergoing those brain tests. He couldn't have been told and he couldn't have passed that information on to Leonora. He wasn't there. Leonora must have known about Con Mulvanney two weeks before they were due to go to

Samos because that was when she changed towards him, but it wasn't Robin who had told her. Robin was shut up in Barts or St Thomas's or somewhere, interested no doubt in nothing but the fate of his own head.

Guy had a quick image of a white-coated surgeon bending over Robin's bed and applying a scalpel to his throat instead of a stethoscope, or of an armoured truck ramming the taxi which was taking him home to Chelsea, of two hooded men with sub-machine-guns jumping out of the back of it. He reminded himself he wasn't living in a TV thriller and went back to the phone book. Chelsea. There it was: St Leonard's Terrace, a very nice address. He must be doing well. Guy dialled the number. He wouldn't have been surprised not to get a reply, but Maeve answered.

'Yes? Who is it?'

What a way to answer the phone! For the first time he noticed her rather 'common' voice, more akin to his own than to Robin's patrician accent.

'It's Guy, Maeve. I just wanted to ask how Robin is.'

She was stunned into silence, as well she might be. Then she said in a tone in which suspicion seemed to war with a willingness to live and let live, 'He's really quite OK.' Evidently thinking furiously, she paused. 'Thanks, Guy I mean, well thanks.'

'I'm glad to hear he's doing all right.'

For a moment he thought she was going to ask if he was kidding. She didn't. 'They're very pleased with him. There won't be any, you know, ill effects or whatever from the concussion.'

'You tell him to take care.'

This was the true purpose of his call. 'I shouldn't let him go out again today. Keep him quiet.' He nearly said, don't answer the door. She would think him crazy. 'Say hallo to him for me, will you?'

'Sure, I will, yes, Guy, thanks.'

He hesitated. 'Is Leonora there?'

'No, she's not.' The former tone, surprised, gratified,

touched, had changed to Maeve's aggressive voice. 'Why ever would she be? Of course she's not. Is that the real reason you rang?'

He said goodbye. He tried to phone Danilo. This was never easy as it was always possible for Danilo to be in any of about ten different places, clubs, two Soho offices, his old dad's place, one of the establishments of his brother the turf accountant, or at a race meeting. Five attempts having failed, he got Tanya at her Richmond boutique. Danilo was in Brussels, she didn't say why, he would be back tomorrow very late in the evening.

Guy was by now almost certain it was Rachel Lingard and not Robin who had told Leonora about Con Mulvanney. That is, he was certain it wasn't Robin and not quite sure about Rachel – nearly sure but not absolutely. Removing Rachel from Leonora's immediate circle would in any case be a good thing. He wished he could, with a word or by the pressure of a switch, divert Danilo's hit squad from Robin to Rachel. He really didn't wish for Robin's death any longer, it would be inconvenient, it would be *unnecessary*.

He poured himself a drink, the first of the day, a very strong Campari-orange, three-quarters Campari and about a spoonful of orange juice. As he was dialling Newton's number the doorbell rang.

Guy's doorbell hardly ever rang unless someone was expected. Celeste had a modelling job out at Totteridge, it couldn't be her. Anyway, she had a key. Listening to the phone ringing on and on, in an empty place unanswered, he thought: it's Leonora. He put the phone down. Of course it was Leonora – what could be more likely? On the phone the day before he had felt her changing, returning to him, her better instincts taking over, all that perverse stubbornness of the past years faded, gone.

'Oh, Guy, how I wish . . .' she had said. Wished what? That she could bring herself to swallow her pride, of course, to come back to him and be as they once were.

The bell rang again. He set his drink down. A second thought made him thrust it behind a vase. He must not die of happiness when she came into his arms . . . It was all he could do not to run to the door. He strode there, threw it open, already smiling a delighted welcome.

On the doorstep stood Tessa Mandeville.

# CHAPTER
# THIRTEEN

His disappointment was so terrible, worse he thought than on that day four years before when Leonora had said she wasn't coming to Samos with him, that he couldn't have spoken to her. He was quite dumb, staring like a fool, yet seeing her only through a haze. Unable even to answer her, he stood there while she pushed past him into the hall.

At any other time, he would have been gleefully proud of showing off his house to one of the members of Leonora's family. None of them had ever been there. Well aware of the suburban Victoriana in which Tessa herself lived, he would have taken great pleasure in watching her note the evidences of his wealth, the carpets, the antiques, the Kandinsky. She, of all people, would very likely know it *was* a Kandinsky. But as it was, he cared not at all. He followed her silently into the drawing room.

She was dressed as usual very smartly. She had a tobacco-brown linen dress which, though waistless and quite straight, could only have been worn by a very thin woman. To the hot weather she made few concessions, wore shoes the colour of polished acorns and tights patterned with sprays of leaves. More lines had appeared on her face since last he saw her. She had a young woman's shape and legs and hair and a wizened face with lines as deep as scars. Her fingernails were painted the colour of a copper kettle in an antique shop.

'It's quite brave of me to come here alone, isn't it?' she said.

He found his voice. It came out like a sigh. 'Brave?'

'Though I'm warning you at least half a dozen people know where I am. In case you want to try anything, you won't get away with it.'

'Don't be ridiculous,' he said.

'You persecute my daughter, you beat up my son, you attempt to run my son over in a car . . .'

He was indignant at the unfairness of that. 'I was having lunch with Leonora when that accident happened, I was in her flat.' Then he realised there was in fact nothing unjust in her accusation. 'Tessa, I went to Leonora's in a taxi. Anyway, I wasn't anywhere near Lancaster Gate. You can't believe I'd . . .'

'Can't I? It's funny you knew all about it. Maeve said you corrected her, you told her exactly where it had happened. You kept on saying things like "Brook Street" and "Victoria Gate" as if you'd been there. I think you're mad. All you want is to wipe out the people who're close to my daughter, kill them or disable them. I should never have let her have anything to do with you, I blame myself for that. I should have put my foot down all those years ago. You'll do some harm to William next. I know what you're up to, I know everything, I saw you parked outside my house that time in that flashy car of yours.'

There was an uncanny accuracy in what she said. She was quite close to the truth. He moved away from her, opened the French windows. He no more fancied being closeted in here with her than she did with him. The heat came in, the scent of his climbing rose. He saw the pile of broken china still on the paving stones and she saw it too.

'Been smashing the place up, have you?'

'What did you come here for, Tessa?'

He hadn't asked her to sit down but she did. Probably his calmness, his air of indifference, had reassured her he meant to do her no harm. She stared at him without speaking. He picked up his drink and, aware of the absurdity of it, asked her if she would like one.

'Of course I don't want a drink!' She almost spat the words.

'What do you want then?'

'To tell you this. First of all my husband will get a court order to stop you molesting Leonora if you don't leave her alone from this moment. Is that clear? Secondly, Leonora is getting married on September the sixteenth. At twelve noon at Kensington Register Office. I'm here to give you a very serious warning, very serious indeed, not to start anything on that occasion. Right?'

'What would I start?' he said, very nearly amused by her. She was a figure of fun, glaring at him like that, long bony fingers with those copper-kettle nails clasping exposed polished knees. The intensity of her frown contorted her face grotesquely.

'Anything, I don't know, a – a ruckus! You're quite capable of turning up there and shouting things – well, forbidding the banns or something.'

'They don't have banns,' he said, though uncertain what banns were.

'You're capable of attacking William, grabbing my daughter – oh, anything! Shouting that you've got some insane prior claim on her.'

'So I have.'

'So you have not, Guy Curran! How dare you speak like that! She loves William and he loves her and they're going to be tremendously happy. I will not have a clod like you, a common piece of rubbish from a council house, from the worst part of London, interfering with my daughter!'

Anger began to well up inside him. Her snobbery had cut into him where her threats never could. He would have liked to tell her this was his house and to get out of it, not to speak like that to him in his house, but he thought of Leonora, of all this getting back to Leonora. It was bad enough, the way he had insulted Rachel, or she would think so. He must stay calm. With extreme controlled calmness he said,

'She isn't going to marry him. She'll never marry him.'

Tessa Mandeville went quite white. 'You filthy drug trafficker,' she said. 'Oh, yes, you can look like that. I tell you, I know everything about you. A very good friend of Leonora's told me all about your drug peddling, ruining young people's lives, giving their parents a hell on earth.'

'What friend?' he asked.

'Oh, yes, I'm likely to tell you, aren't I? So that you can go and beat them up, I suppose. A good friend, that's all I'm saying. Someone who's been a better friend to Leonora than you ever could be.'

He said, 'I don't want to put you out of here, Tessa. You're Leonora's mother and I can't forget that. I'm going upstairs and while I'm away perhaps you'll go.'

It was to be alone really, not just to get away from her. So he had been right about Rachel. It was Rachel who had done and who was doing all the damage, Rachel who was probably with Leonora even at this moment, feeding her poison. Leonora had been more gentle with him, more loving, that day than at any time he could remember since she moved into the flat. True, it had been on the phone. But Saturday it hadn't been on the phone. 'Oh, Guy, how I wish . . .' What had she been going to say? How I wish we could be as we once were? How I wish I'd never met William?

Now, though, she would be back home with Rachel, sickbed-bound Rachel. He could imagine her sitting on the side of Rachel's bed and Rachel repeating what he had said to her, adding 'What can you expect from low-life like that?'

Downstairs he heard Tessa's footsteps. They stopped. She had paused. Of course. She had stopped in front of the Kandinsky, was taking it in, valuing it. The footsteps started again, the front door closed hard if not quite with a bang. He went into his bedroom and watched from the window. She was going in the Marloes Road direction, looking for a taxi. He hoped she wouldn't get one, she probably wouldn't, not at this hour.

So it was Rachel. The connection must have been the one he first thought of, through the social work she and Poppy Vasari had in common. He went downstairs and was starting to dial one of the numbers he had for Danilo when he remembered what Tanya had told him, that Danilo was in Brussels. It slightly troubled him that he was as yet unable to call off the dogs that menaced Robin Chisholm but there seemed nothing to be done about this.

Something was puzzling him and continued to do so on and off throughout the night. Dining with Celeste at the Pomme d'Amour, meeting Bob Joseph afterwards for a drink at the club in Noel Street, his mind kept reverting to Tessa Mandeville and the things she had said. What had she really come for?

That was all rubbish about getting a court order preventing him from 'molesting' Leonora. How could you molest someone when she wanted your company? It was Leonora herself who, three and a half years before, had made that arrangement to lunch with him on Saturdays. When Rachel and the rest of them no doubt had persuaded her to stop going out with him in any real sense, to stop being his girlfriend, she had proposed the regular Saturday meetings. Leonora wanted those lunch dates as much as he did, that was certain. She wanted him to phone her. Hadn't she said when he left her on Saturday, 'phone me tomorrow'?

So Tessa hadn't really meant that at all. That was just a cover for something else. What she had come for was ostensibly to stop him making some sort of scene at Leonora's wedding but really to *tell him where Leonora's wedding would be*, a venue he knew quite well already. He was suspicious of them all and now he was even more suspicious of Tessa. What was she up to? Why come all that way, visit him at home as she had never done before, just to tell him that?

Then he understood. He nearly laughed out loud, there in front of Celeste. The woman told him Kensington Register Office because it wasn't going to be there at all. It was going to be at the Camden Register Office, which was at King's Cross, and in Newton's borough. You could get married in your own borough or that of the person you were marrying, it was a matter of choice. She had told him Kensington in case he decided to go along. The woman was so transparent it was really quite funny.

Not that it mattered. Leonora wouldn't get married. She wouldn't *want* to get married. He heard her voice again and the tone seemed infinitely soft and yearning as she expressed her wish for what might have been. 'Guy dear', she had called him when she had explained she couldn't dine with him. They probably threatened her with all kinds of things when she told them she was thinking of going back to him. Rachel, for instance, who was buying Leonora's share of the flat from her – Rachel had very likely told her the deal would be off if she persisted in having any further to do with him. Anthony Chisholm was capable of cutting her out of his will or at least of stopping any money he might be making over to her.

'Guy, sweet,' said Celeste. 'A penny for your thoughts.'

He told her about Tessa's visit. Her face clouded over. She said nothing. 'I've got a headache,' he said. 'I usually have these days. D'you think it's being angry most of the time?'

She went home with him. 'You have to accept it,' she said gently. 'Sooner or later you have to accept she's going to marry William.'

'You'd like that, wouldn't you?'

She knelt on the paving, picking up the pieces of broken vase. He wished he hadn't said what he had said but she didn't reply. Danilo would be back tomorrow night, he'd keep on trying to phone him from ten onwards. Probably, to compensate for all the trouble he was causing, he'd have to give Danilo another fifteen hundred, but who cared? Celeste said,

'Buy her a really nice wedding present, why don't you?'

She was never bitchy but this time. . . ? Surely she didn't mean it seriously? He poured himself a last drink, vodka on the rocks, realising that he had been drinking non-stop since the Campari orange he had had when Tessa came at five.

In the morning, while Celeste was still asleep, he phoned the flat in Portland Road. Maeve answered. She was about to leave for work. He didn't ask for Leonora, not immediately.

'How's Robin?' He really wanted to know. Worrying about

Danilo's hit man getting at Robin had kept him awake most of the night.

'He's fine,' she said. But did she know? Had he just been fine when she left him the night before?

'You've spoken to him this morning?'

'Just now, Guy.' Oh, the relief! It wasn't that he cared about Robin Chisholm's fate but he realised, after that black eye and what Tessa had said, that Leonora might so easily blame him for any harm that came to her brother. 'He rang me. He'd had such a super sleep, he was feeling really refreshed, you know, he sounded on top of the world. Isn't that great?'

Guy said it was and could he speak to Leonora?

'She isn't here, Guy. She's at William's.'

He phoned the Georgiana Street number. It was early, of course, it wasn't yet nine, but he was still surprised to hear Newton's voice – no more than that, astounded, thrown. He nearly put the receiver down. Instead he said, 'It's Guy Curran.'

'Oh, hallo.' It wasn't said in a friendly way. But Guy would have despised the man even more than he already did if he had spoken in a hearty or ingratiating manner.

'How're *you?*' he said in his best transatlantic style, but coldly.

'I'm extremely well and I hope you are. Now, what can I do for you?'

'I'd like to speak to Leonora.'

Most people, before imparting unwelcome information, say that they are afraid. 'I'm afraid I've something rather unpleasant to tell you . . .' Newton didn't do that and Guy noticed.

'She's not here.'

'Now, come on,' said Guy, the ready anger rising. 'I've just been told less than five minutes ago that she's with you.'

The man sounded bored, still within the limits of patience. 'Less than five minutes ago she was. Two minutes ago she went out. Would you like me to tell you where?'

'Of course I would. Where is she?'

'At her father's. Susannah's mother has died and Leonora

has gone with her to see to things, register the death and see undertakers. I've now told you all I know, so if you'll excuse me I'll ring off as I'm already late. Goodbye.'

He had no idea where Susannah's mother had lived, had barely known Susannah had a mother. Hopeless to try and find them, hopeless to pursue that inviting image of himself sitting in a waiting room with Leonora, talking to her softly, then taking the two of them out to a wonderful lunch somewhere. A comfort for Susannah, whom he had never disliked, taking her mind off her mother whom she had probably been fond of. He would have to catch Leonora later in Lamb's Conduit Street.

He took a cup of tea up to Celeste.

'Thank you, sweet Guy,' she said.

She opened her eyes and then she put out her arms to him. It was weeks since he had made love to her. Sexual desire seemed to have been drained out of him by all that had happened, by fear and anger. But he bent down and let her hug him. She was warm and sweet and she felt silky to touch. He lay down beside her and held her, not realising how very hard he must have clutched her until she struggled and freed her nose and mouth from the pressure of his face, until she gasped, 'No, Guy, you're hurting!'

While she was in the bath he called Anthony Chisholm's number. The line was engaged. Five minutes later it was still engaged. He got the operator to check it, was told the number was indeed engaged speaking, and decided to give up until the afternoon. Fatima arrived as he was leaving the house. She made a noise like a distressed henbird with a lost chick when she saw the black and pink shards, 'Aiee!' Guy got his car out. He was going to Northolt to the studio, then to make a check on a picture sale at a motorway hotel at the start of the M1. Backing the car across the cobbled mews, driving slowly down towards the Earl's Court Road, he wondered if perhaps he had outgrown his house. In his position he was past the little mews house stage. After all, he would be thirty in January. A house in Lansdowne Crescent or maybe even something in the neighbourhood of Campden Hill, Duchess of Bedford Walk . . .

Would Leonora mind being that side, the *good* side, of Holland Park Avenue?

'Carry On, Kittens' did better in Barnet than even 'Lady from Thailand'. The woman who was running the sale and with whom he had a nasty lunch in the motel dining room (oval plates piled with gristle-bound blackened steak, tinned peas, tomato halves, chips, mushrooms as slimy as slugs, and broccoli spears like toy farmyard trees) told him she could sell twice, three times, as many. Guy undertook to provide that number. On the motel phone he tried to call Lamb's Conduit Street and failed but succeeded in getting Tanya at her boutique. Danilo was expected home in the late evening, certainly by eleven.

Guy had a ferociously unpleasant image of Robin Chisholm pressing the button on his entryphone, opening the door in his towelling robe to the man who had come to mend something or read some meter. The silenced gun or cosh, or if Danilo's 'help' was being really vicious these days, the thin swift stiletto.

He drove to the travel agent's. Business was booming there too. In the office at the back he phoned the flat in St Leonard's Terrace. There wasn't going to be an answer, the bell rang and rang, ten times, fifteen. He put the receiver back and redialled. This time Robin's voice answered after four rings. Probably he'd misdialled that first time. It was a great relief to hear Robin saying, 'Hallo, hallo?' with increasing irritability.

They buoyed him up wonderfully, the considerable and varied successes of the day. Things hadn't gone so well for a long time. Going home, even going to the West End, it would have been usual to take a route north of Regent's Park, but he found himself approaching the Euston Road. Across Tavistock Place, into Guilford Street, and Lamb's Conduit was just down there . . . He wasn't supposed to see her except on Saturdays, except for Saturday lunch, but – well, come *on*. She wanted to see him. Hadn't she said how much she wished they could be together again?

It was hot, the still yellow heat of London in sunshine. Any place he had been to with her and been happy brought him pain. It was as if he had two levels of feeling about her, the upper in which he was optimistic, cheerful, confident and the lower where fear was and doubt. The places they had been together evoked images in that lower world. He remembered rejections, he remembered with something that was more like panic than pain, that it was now six years since they had made love.

The houses in this part of London are old, early rather than late nineteenth century. Their brickwork is a dark greyish brown, their doorways and windows long and narrow, their roofs invisible. Very little green was to be seen except distant treetops showing like vegetation in a walled garden. Susannah had window boxes which contained, instead of the usual geraniums, small-leaved ivies and plants with yellow-grey fluffy foliage. Guy rang the bell, preparing himself as he always had to, for his first sight of Leonora.

The door was answered by a woman he recognised but couldn't immediately place. She seemed to be having the same difficulties identifying him.

'Guy Curran,' he said.

'Oh, *yes*. I'm Janice. We met at Nora's birthday party.'

He hated the diminutive that was allowed to her family but not to him. The woman who had used it he now remembered as the cousin who had been going to Australia to get married. She was rather plump with a pale moon face, prominent eyes and a great deal of long mousy hair worn in a French plait. Guy particularly disapproved of Indian cotton dresses (cheap, badly cut and shapeless) and she of course had one on, tan-coloured with black hieroglyphs and white bits. Her hips were round and the effect in his opinion was of someone going to a fancy-dress party as a granary loaf.

'I thought you were an undertaker actually,' she now said. 'Susannah's expecting an undertaker. You know her mother died?'

'Yes. Someone told me. Can I come in?'

Janice admitted him grudgingly. He felt she was looking him up and down as if he was committing some awful social *faux pas*. 'She's just lost her *mother*. I mean, mostly people write or phone.'

'It's Leonora I've come to see,' he said impatiently.

But at that moment Susannah herself put her head over the banisters. The living room was on the upper floor of the flat, the bedrooms on the lower. Susannah didn't react towards him as did all the other women close to Leonora – including this indignant Australian – in an aggressive or judgmental way. She called out to him and said how nice of him it was to have come. Obviously she hadn't heard his remark to Janice. When he got to the top of the stairs she came up to him and putting her arms round him, kissed him in an almost motherly way, though she wasn't anywhere near old enough to be his mother.

It was quite a shock to be kissed *nicely* by a woman, though of course Celeste did it all the time. But this was different. Susannah very evidently took the purpose of his visit to be one of condolence. Well, that was all right with him. He felt warm towards her and approving. Susannah might be sad and in mourning but it didn't show. She was carefully and quite heavily made-up, which Guy thought proper for women, her thick wiry dark hair was teased into a fashionable sea-urchin shape, she wore black silk trousers with a chocolate and black striped top and a lot of rather elegant silver jewelry of the chain-mail kind, including a wide glittering belt. What a pity Leonora couldn't or wouldn't learn from her example!

As he followed her into the living room where he hadn't been for nearly four years he thought of the time when Leonora had lived here after leaving teacher training college, and of calling to take her out and being given drinks by Anthony Chisholm. Well, it wasn't so long ago . . . The first thing he saw, even before he saw Leonora, was a white card on the mantelpiece with a silver edge. A wedding invitation, it had to be, but he couldn't read the print at this distance.

Leonora got up when he came in. His heart had already done its turning-over stuff, sending a beat up into his head. She looked horrible but what did he care?

She kissed him. There was no hugging and not much warmth but then she hadn't just lost her mother. (More's the pity, thought Guy.) Janice, behind him, was going into some long tale about recognising him and not recognising him, then thinking he was an undertaker or a florist. Leonora wore black-and-white plastic earrings. Not a scrap of make-up of course and her hair looked greasy. She had green tracksuit pants on and a black sweatshirt, rusting with age and bad washing. Since knowing Newton, Guy thought, whatever dress sense she had once possessed had gone to pot. The fool probably told her he loved her for herself, not her appearance.

At any rate she didn't ask him what he was doing there. He remembered in time to say something appropriate about Susannah's mother.

'It was really thoughtful of you to come, Guy,' Leonora said, beaming. He thought her smile was surely fuller and freer than he had seen it for months. 'We've had such a day. Some of those people are so insensitive. D'you know what the registrar said to poor Susannah? It was a woman, apparently they mostly are. Men won't take the jobs, they're too badly paid, it's the old story. She said, "Is it the first death you've ever registered?" and when Susannah said it was she said, "I don't suppose it'll be the last. Good morning." Can you imagine?'

Janice had departed to make a cup of tea, having had some whispered communication with Susannah. Leonora began explaining how her cousin was staying with Anthony and Susannah, her cousin's husband would be coming over next week, and it was very sad for poor Janice who had been particularly fond of Susannah's mother and arrived too late to see her alive. No other family Guy had ever come across had been so closely interlocked as these Chisholms. Even those on the outer fringes of the root system, people not even related, were mad about each other. Leonora was giving the impression this Janice had come twelve thousand miles to be at the deathbed of an old woman, the mother of her aunt by marriage, that she had probably only met once or twice in her whole life. How right he was not to underestimate the influences that worked on Leonora!

From where he sat he kept trying to see the mantelpiece and the card on it but Susannah insisted on remaining standing, and in front of the carefully preserved Georgian fireplace, leaning on the mantelshelf. He didn't like to dodge his head about too obviously. Susannah had begun talking about the funeral.

'We find ourselves in a dilemma, Guy. We really don't know what to do. Shall we ask his advice, Leonora? Perhaps a fresh mind, do you think?'

Leonora gave him another lovely smile. 'We'll see what he says.'

'Now my poor dear mother didn't leave any instructions about – well, I mustn't mind saying it bluntly – about whether she wanted to be buried or cremated. Of course most people are cremated these days, but cremation seems so . . . I nearly said "so final" as if death itself wasn't final but perhaps you know what I mean.'

'Oh, I know what you mean,' said Guy, craning his neck.

'And then it's a question of where? All the nice London cemeteries are full and it means going right out into the sticks. My mother lived in Earlsfield but the churchyard there of course is out of the question and has been for about a century I should think.'

Janice came in with the tea which she placed on a table in such a way as to oblige Guy to turn his chair round with its back to the fireplace. It was near enough to real drinking time for him not to want tea but he drank it, refusing a slice of the peaches-and-cream *torte* which fat little Janice should have known better than to tuck into. A plan was forming in his mind of managing to drive Leonora home – well, of getting her in his car, starting to drive her home and then persuading her not to go back but to have dinner with him.

Janice was telling an elaborate story – in the worst of taste, Guy thought – about the adventures of someone she knew scattering a loved one's ashes from the Cobb in Lyme Regis. Susannah said that was a coincidence because she and Anthony were going for a short holiday in Lyme in a couple of weeks' time. The doorbell called Janice away from further anecdotes. Though repeatedly told by the others to sit down and do nothing, she seemed to have appointed herself a temporary au pair. To Guy's great pleasure he and Leonora found themselves for a moment or two alone. The undertaker had arrived and Susannah was summoned downstairs.

'I do hope she's made up her mind,' said Leonora. 'She'll have to tell him one way or another.'

'Have dinner with me, Leo.'

'Oh, I can't Guy. I'm awfully sorry but I can't.' Not 'I never do' or 'I have lunch with you on Saturdays', not that any more. 'I'm staying here and William's coming over. We're all going out for dinner so that poor Susannah doesn't have to cook.'

There went his plan to drive her home . . . But, 'I'm really sorry,' she said. 'It would have been nice. Maeve told me you rang up this morning to ask after Robin. That was kind of you, I do appreciate it.'

He dared to reach across the sofa and take her hand. He *knew* she would snatch her hand away but she didn't. She even let the fingers nestle softly in his and she turned on him a look of such sweetness, such compassion, that if Janice hadn't come back at that moment he would have lost control of himself, he would have had to jump up and seize her in his arms. He did jump up, but only to go. There was little pleasure in being here with that fat gimlet-eyed one staring censoriously at him.

'Lunch on Saturday?' he said.

'Yes, Guy dear, of course. Where shall we go?'

'The Savoy,' he said. 'We'll go to the River Room at the Savoy.'

She didn't protest. She was changing towards him, she was changing *back*. He kissed her goodbye, stood up, turned to face the fireplace and saw that the wedding card had gone. It had been there when he came in half an hour before and now it was gone.

Someone had quietly moved it so that he shouldn't see.

# CHAPTER
# FOURTEEN

He had known Leonora for quite a long time before he met her brother. One winter's day, just before or just after Christmas, he went with Leonora into the living room of her parents' house where a boy was standing by the window with a paper in his hand that he was reading. He must have heard them come in but he didn't look round immediately, he read to the end of the page. There was something headmasterly in this behaviour or even policeman-like, something deliberate and scornful, though the boy himself looked almost babyish. He was tall enough, a lot taller than his sister, but his face when he finally turned his head was that of a five-year-old, plump, innocent, with toddler's skin and a rosebud mouth. The voice that issued from those baby lips was therefore all the more amazing. Instead of shrill and lisping, it was deep and rich, it was *fruity*, with an accent that can only be acquired (Guy learned later from Leonora) by attendance at one of those schools within the Headmasters' Conference.

'Is this your beau, Nora?'

Guy had heard the word before, but only on television. He

would – then and now – have given a lot to have a voice like that. Leonora introduced him.

'Robin, this is Guy. Guy, this is my brother.'

Already, at the age of fifteen, Robin Chisholm was practising that teasing mockery that was such a feature of his unpleasant character. It wasn't clever or amusing, it was just rude.

'Guy,' he said. He said it slowly and with a certain puzzlement. He said it again, thoughtfully, as if it were the name of someone he had known long ago but couldn't quite place. 'Guy. Yes – don't you find it difficult being called that? I mean, if Nora hadn't said, I'd have put you down as a Kevin, say, or a Barry. Yes, Barry would suit you.'

He looked like an innocent child, smiling, wide-eyed, his cheeks plump and rosy, defying the object of his insults to take offence. For they were insults, Guy was in no doubt about that. Leonora's brother was implying that his name was far too upper-class for its possessor.

She defended him. 'Oh, shut up. You're in no position to mock people's names. Robin may be all right now while you look like an infant but it'll be no joke when you're old.'

Even then, in a very unnatural way, Robin Chisholm was proud of looking younger than he was. Most people are at thirty but not at *fifteen*, for God's sake. Guy, seeing him occasionally, not often but too often for his own comfort, thought he purposely cultivated the baby-face look. He wouldn't have been surprised to see Robin with his thumb in his mouth. Well, he would have been surprised, he'd have run screaming from the room.

The Chisholms had sent their daughter to a state school and a prestigious university. Their son had attended a public school with high fees but dropped out of the polytechnic he just squeezed into and went instead 'into the City'. He was twenty-three when he started having those blackouts. They thought it was a tumour on the brain, then epilepsy. There turned out to be nothing wrong with him. Guy privately thought Robin had carefully planned and staged it all to extricate himself from the firm he was working for, an investment company that was plunged into a financial scandal of mammoth proportions a week or two after he entered hospital.

He was the sort of person the world would be better without. Someone else could see to his destruction though, not Guy. It wasn't he who had told Leonora about Con Mulvanney. Further to that, Guy, who having failed to get hold of Danilo that evening, had been considering the matter for half the night, decided that her brother, of all those who surrounded her, probably influenced her the least. Of course she loved him, that went without saying – she said it often enough for all that, said it of far too many people, Guy thought – but Robin irritated her, she didn't altogether approve of him.

All this made him dream of Robin. Robin was dead, pushed down all those flights of stairs in Portland Road, his bleeding body discovered by Maeve. This wasn't at all a fantastic or irrational dream and it therefore alarmed Guy all the more. He couldn't phone St Leonard's Terrace before eight-thirty or Danilo before nine at the earliest. Making coffee for himself, he kept touching wood as he moved about the kitchen. It was an old habit of superstition he had believed long shed.

If you touched wood the action fended off disaster. It kept away – what? Evil spirits? His grandmother, from whom he had learned wood-touching, not helping others to salt, not passing a knife to a friend, avoiding the divisions between paving stones, hadn't specified the precise function of these acts. They just kept you safe. Funny, he should think of her now when he hadn't for years. Luckily, the kitchen, lavishly re-fitted in limed oak, was a paradise for wood-touchers.

A sleepy Danilo answered the Weybridge phone at ten-past nine. Guy was nearly out of his mind because there had been no answer from St Leonard's Terrace in spite of his trying ten times between eight-thirty and now. He was sure Robin must be dead, and with his death Leonora lost for ever, but he called Danilo's hit man off just the same. Danilo took his change of heart with a show of ill temper but agreed to meet him for a drink at a club called The Black Spot at six. Certain now that he was too late, that Robin's corpse was even at this moment being identified by Maeve in some mortuary, Guy nevertheless had another try at the Chelsea number.

Rather a strange thing happened. The phone was picked up but before anyone spoke into the mouthpiece Guy heard Robin's voice bellowing from a distance,

'Answer the bloody thing, can you? I'm in the bath.'

Then accents like his grandmother's, it must be the Irish cleaning woman, said, 'Hallo, who's speaking? Mr Chisholm's busy.'

Guy gasped with relief. He was on the point of saying, 'Tell him to go back to bed and stay there,' but thought better of it.

\* \* \* \*

The Black Spot was all bar and floor. There were no tables, nowhere to sit except on a stool up at the long black and silver counter. It was very dark, American-style. The first person Guy saw was Carlo sitting on a stool next to his father and drinking something dark and frothy from a brandy glass. It was probably Coke but the glass it was in made it look sophisticated, even sinister. Guy was rather surprised. Then he reflected that he would very much have liked to go into bars like this one when he was ten, only he had never got the chance.

Carlo was wearing junior designer jeans and a black sweatshirt with *Breadhead's Kid* printed on it in luminescent pink. He said 'Hi' to Guy and continued eating prawn fries out of an ashtray. Danilo was in caramel-coloured herringbone silk tweed, a suit with an enormous, wide-shouldered jacket, and under it an open-necked crimson shirt.

'You're not looking too good,' said Danilo.

Guy shrugged impatiently. That was what Danilo always said every time they met. 'It's the light in here, if you can call it light.' He asked the barman for a large vodka martini. 'We can't talk,' he said to Danilo, cocking a thumb in Carlo's direction.

'I can't help it, mate. What was I to do? One of the nannies has got flu, the other's walked out. Tanya's sister'll have the other kids, she won't have him. Last time he was there he put her *Apocalypse Now* video in the microwave. He said he wanted to see what would happen.

'Mervyn,' he said to the barman, 'Take him round the back and let him watch *Mork and Mindy*. Five minutes, that's all I ask.'

'It's not on, Dad. There's only *Buck Rogers in the Twenty-fifth Century*.'

'Go round the back and watch that then.' Danilo had to have another glass of the red wine he favoured. 'Don't ever do that to me again,' he said dramatically to Guy. 'Don't ever.'

'Don't ever do what?'

'Bell me with that changed-me-mind crap.' He lowered his voice deeply. 'You could have made a murderer out of poor old Chuck, d'you realise that?'

Poor old Chuck, whoever he might be, was certainly a murderer already, several times over. Besides, what was the difference, it was either one victim or the other? Guy knew arguing with Danilo was quite useless. He said he was sorry, he realised he'd been a bit thoughtless.

'Immature,' said Danilo. 'That's what you've been. Call a spade a spade. Now you listen to me, Guy. We've nearly had a very nasty accident in this particular area. I want you to think carefully. Do you or do you not want me to pursue this matter? The original party you wanted wasted I quite understand is out of the firing line, and for personal reasons I'm not sorry, but from what you said on the blower this morning I got a sort of hint you'd someone else in mind. No, don't answer now. Name no names. I want you to think very carefully, like I said.'

'I have thought.' They were alone in the bar but for a man and a girl kissing up at the far end. Guy thought, that's just what the fuzz would do, it's an old one that, a WPC and a DS in a clinch but all ears really. Just the same he said, very softly, 'Rachel Lingard,' and he gave the address in Portland Road. Because Chuck might only need to recognise her and not know her name, he took one of his cards out of his pocket and wrote on it: *Short, round-faced, fat, glasses, dark hair scraped back, about 27,* a cruel but accurate description of Rachel so that there could be no confusion with Maeve or – for God's sake! – Leonora.

\* \* \* \*

In the light of this, it struck him as odd there was no reply at all from their flat when he phoned at nine, at midday, at four and at ten. In the meantime he also phoned Georgiana Street. No one answered there until ten-thirty at night when Newton finally replied to his fourth call.

'Leonora's in bed. She was tired and she went to bed early.'

'She'll talk to me.'

'She won't. I've told you, she's in bed.'

'Surely you've got a bedside extension.'

Newton said obscurely, 'I'm a poor man, Your Majesty,' and put the phone down.

It was much the same the next day. Guy had to see his accountant, so phoned the flat in Portland Road from the restaurant where he was giving the man lunch. He tried Georgiana Street, then St Leonard's Terrace. Maeve answered.

'I'm living here. I was going to move in with Robin after Leonora's wedding anyway, so we thought I might as well now.'

'Do you happen to know where Leonora is?'

'I should think you say that in your sleep, don't you? It'll be on your tombstone. Guy Curran, 1960 to whatever, RIP, "Where's Leonora?" No, I don't know where she is. You're a bloody menace, d'you know that?'

He had to go back to the accountant. Coffee had been brought in the meantime. Guy had a large brandy with his. A taxi took him back to Scarsdale Mews and his own telephone. The room and the green garden seen through the French windows seemed to turn red, dyed by his anger. To keep his anger down he had to hear her voice; it was like a tranquillising drug. He needed his fix of her voice.

She wasn't at Portland Road, she wasn't at Georgiana Street. Where does she go, he thought, where does she hide? Probably Rachel hides her, takes her to work with her, anything to keep her from me. Later on he phoned Lamb's Conduit Street. Janice picked up the receiver.

She'd only been out there four or five years but she already had an Australian accent. For some reason the sound of his voice made her giggle. It was as if she and Susannah had just been talking about him – no, more as if she was recalling some trick played on him.

'I'm sorry,' she said. 'I was laughing about something when you phoned and I couldn't stop. I'll fetch Susannah.'

A nice woman, Susannah. You often couldn't understand why people married other people, mostly you couldn't, but in this case he could easily see what there was about Susannah that had appealed to Anthony Chisholm.

'Hallo, Guy,' she said with real warmth, putting a thrilling emphasis on his name as if she were really pleased to hear from him, as if he were someone she loved and hadn't heard from for months. 'It was so nice to see you the other day. It must be ages since we last met.'

He had meant to be cool and light, to make small talk. But her words moved him. He was near the edge today anyway, he was nearly out of control. 'Too long,' he said, and, 'You were always good to me, Susannah. You alone of all of them. Even Leonora's father turned against me.'

'Now, Guy I'm sure that's not true. Anthony and I have always liked you. The thing is . . . Excuse me just a moment.' He heard her lay the phone down and go to close the door. This was so that giggling little Janice didn't hear. 'Guy, Leonora's a grown-up woman, she has her own life. I understand how bitter it must be for you to see her prefer William, but if she does what can anyone do about it? As a matter of fact I'd like you to know I think your – well, your constancy to Leonora is a very beautiful thing. You've been like one of those knights of old who were devoted for years to their ladies. You really have. But, Guy, my dear, it has to be over now – you see that, don't you?'

'It will never be over,' he said, speaking low.

'What did you say?'

'It will never be over, Susannah. You see, I believe, I *know*, she'll return to me. I know we'll be together for the rest of our lives and we'll look back on this as a temporary madness.'

'If you like to look at things like that, I can't stop you. I'd just like to save you from prolonging your unhappiness, that's all.'

Why not come right out with it? 'There was an invitation to the wedding on your mantelpiece yesterday. It was there when I came but before I left someone had taken it away.'

She answered immediately with no hesitation. 'Oh, no, Guy. You must be mistaken. Anyway, we wouldn't have an invitation, would we? We're *giving* the wedding.'

That was unanswerable. Was it possible he'd imagined it? He thought, Susannah wouldn't lie to me, not Susannah. He asked her if she knew where Leonora was. No, but she expected to see her tomorrow. Leonora was coming to her mother's funeral.

Probably the lot of them would go, Guy thought after he had rung off. Tessa and Magnus Mandeville, Robin and Maeve, William Newton and even some of the Newton relations. They were all drawn into the great Chisholm spider's web. A little fantasy showed Guy a glimpse of a future in which, now Leonora and he were married, the Chisholms drew in *his* family, or what there was of it, what could be found. They were capable of going hunting for his mother, for his grandmother, if the old girl was still alive. He imagined them all at some vast dinner table, celebrating something. Robin's wedding? *His* wedding to Leonora? Why not?

He made several more attempts at Georgiana Street and Portland Road. No reply at either. Newton was preventing her from answering the phone or Rachel Lingard was. The latter was actually more likely, for Leonora would have had to go home to find suitable clothes to wear at the funeral. Still, tomorrow should not only see the end of Susannah's mother but also of Rachel.

No doubt Chuck or Chuck's man had so far had no opportunity of doing the trick. Guy would know if he had. It wasn't that he expected Danilo to phone and tell him the deed was done. Leonora would. Leonora would turn to him in trouble. It brought him a small qualm to think how unhappy she would be. She was really fond of that ugly, fat, ego-tripping Rachel with her superior manner and her ruthless manipulating of other people's lives. Learning that Rachel had died in a car accident (or been lethally mugged or fallen off a river bridge) would upset her so much that she certainly wouldn't go ahead with that absurd wedding. She would turn to him for comfort.

In the morning he phoned the flat in Portland Road as early as he reasonably could, just after eight. He was in his bedroom and he touched wood, this time the Linnell bedhead. Someone took off the receiver but didn't speak. He knew who it was.

'I know that's you, Rachel,' he said. 'It's pointless pretending with me.' He wanted to say what the kids where he came from said when they begged from a woman and got nothing: 'Die, bitch, die,' but she really *would* die and someone might overhear. 'I'd like to speak to Leonora, please.'

She put the phone down.

He dialled the number again and let it ring. When it was clear she wasn't going to answer and was stopping Leonora from answering, he laid the receiver down so that the ringing would go on and on to torment her. Perhaps he should go to Susannah's mother's funeral but he didn't know where it was. It was now three days since he had spoken to Leonora. Had it ever been so long, apart from at holiday time or when she was at college? Even when she had the bedsit and the phone was downstairs, it had never been as long as three days. He panicked when he thought that way, so he made an effort to rid his mind of it. The receiver restored to its rest, he went off in the Jaguar to a paintings sale at Wallington in Surrey.

Driving back, he came to the gates of Croydon Crematorium. This would be the place, he thought, and he parked the car halfway up the pavement and waited. It came to him how wonderful it would be just to see her. If he did he would leave the car and go in, follow the mourners, sit discreetly at the back of the crematorium chapel. He imagined her the way he would dress her to go, for example, to her own mother's funeral, an event devoutly to be wished for in four or five years, say, after their own wedding. A simple black dress by Jean Muir with a single flounce six inches from the hem, a wide-brimmed black hat, black suede pumps and gleaming black tights with seams. He liked the idea of her in a veil, her face mysteriously hidden, disclosed only to him.

They would walk in side by side, he supporting her, she clinging to his arm. He imagined her in the front pew kneeling to pray a little before the service started. The long thin coffin containing Tessa's long thin body appeared, borne by half a dozen bearers, Magnus, Anthony, Michael Chisholm, Robin – but he would be there too surely among them? Trying to solve the dilemma of how to be at Leonora's side and at the same time an undisputed member of the inner family, Guy looked up to see a slow sad procession of cars moving out from the gates.

He jumped out of the Jaguar. The first car was full of very old people, white heads like dandelion clocks. He peered, he scanned them. The second car was full of very old people. Two slightly younger grey-headed people sat in the third car. Someone said behind him,

'Excuse me, you can't park there.'

It was a traffic warden. He drove home. Fatima was still there, polishing. Guy went upstairs and tried to phone Leonora on his bedside extension. It reminded him of what Newton had said, mocking him, calling him 'Your Majesty'. No one answered, either in Portland Road or Georgiana Street.

She wouldn't forget about lunch with him, would she? They had made no arrangements as to time. But perhaps there was no need for that, they always met at one. The Savoy, he thought, at one. The front door closed as Fatima let herself out. He went down and made himself a large drink, vodka and ice and a few drops of Angostura. That wedding invitation kept returning to his mind. It occurred to him for the first time that if they were sending out invitations to this ridiculous wedding, it was odd that they hadn't sent one to him. Odd, that is, in their assessment of things. Not in his. In his it would be grotesque inviting him to Leonora's marriage to someone else. But they wouldn't see it like that. They would see him as an old friend with the same sort of right to be invited as that bitch Rachel –

more right because he'd known Leonora longer. So why hadn't they invited him?

Because they weren't sending out invitations? Because that silver-edged card had never been there. He'd imagined it. He had got into a state and imagined it. The garden was green again, the waters of the pool lay still and gleaming, bearing dense sheaves of lilies, leaves that were green above, crimson-lined, their flowers a veined streaky rose or ivory. He noticed that the roses were over and he walked about removing the dead heads. It was quite quiet out there, tucked away in the mews, the traffic a distant throb. There was peace here and an air of healing. You would never lose your mind, have strange inexplicable things happen inside your head and to your imagination, if you sat calmly here.

After about an hour the phone rang. Intuition told him it would be Leonora, he knew it would be Leonora. It was years since she had phoned him but he knew it was she. He went indoors so fast that he knocked over the red lacquer table inside the door on which the Chinese vase had once stood. His heart thumping, he picked up the phone. It was Celeste. Had he forgotten he was taking her to her friend's party? There was going to be dancing on a terrace above the river at Richmond. Only he'd said he'd phone her and he hadn't.

Guy had forgotten. He knew he ought to go, it was the sort of thing he enjoyed, he'd accepted the friend's invitation and promised Celeste but just the same he said he didn't feel like it. He'd got a bug, he thought, some virus, or a migraine coming. She took it resignedly, she didn't try to persuade him. After she had rung off, with the phone still in his hand, sick with disappointment, he thought he might as well take the opportunity and phone Georgiana Street.

No reply. He made himself another drink and dialled Portland Road. He touched the red lacquered wood – was it wood? No reply. Rachel might be already dead. Chuck would probably do it down in Brixton where Rachel worked. A lot of people said it wasn't safe for a woman, particularly a white woman, to walk about alone in the back streets of Brixton. Guy had never quite believed that but he thought he might start believing it now.

A scenario took shape in his head. The police would want someone to identify Rachel's body. They'd call on Leonora or Maeve – Leonora most likely because she still lived in the same house as Rachel while Maeve did so no longer. Of course she'd ask William Newton to go with her, she'd be beside herself with grief and terror, but Newton wouldn't go because he was squeamish, he was the kind of person who couldn't face the idea of seeing a dead body, particularly a body in the state Rachel's would be in. So in despair she'd turn to the one she could depend on, her own true love, and together they'd go to Brixton. He'd drive her in the Jaguar. Once there, he'd take matters into his own hands. 'I know the deceased quite as well as my fiancée does, Sergeant. Leave this matter of identification to me.' She'd cling to him afterwards in the car. 'It was always you really, Guy. I must have been mad . . .'

After two more stiff vodkas he was perfectly sober but his speech was a bit slurred. He practised talking to himself in the mirror and confessed honestly that he didn't really want Leonora to hear him speak like that. When he got back from the restaurant would do for a last try.

He walked. He needed the air. It was very unusual for him to eat alone or in a place where he hadn't previously booked a table. A little way along the Old Brompton Road was an Italian restaurant where he had once had a good pasta with Celeste's predecessor, a half-Chinese girl who was a stewardess on a Boeing 747. Four days since he had spoken to Leonora . . . It was better, safer, to concentrate on Rachel who might so easily be lying dead somewhere by now, almost certainly was. It was nearly eight o'clock, more than forty-eight hours since he'd tipped the wink to Danilo.

The restaurant was somewhere in this row of shops. A man, a beggar, down-and-out, whatever you liked to call it, was lying full-length along one of the doorsteps, the threshold of a health-food store, long closed. He was black, a youngish man, tall apparently and thin to the point of emaciation, dressed in blackish rags. A cap lay on the pavement beside him and the single five-pence piece in it was the only indication that this was not simply headgear cast temporarily to the ground.

He lay on his back with his hands folded behind his head, staring upwards. His lips were parted, the teeth very white with a gleam of gold among them. He didn't look at Guy and Guy gave him only a rapid glance but he was sure it was Linus. A Linus terribly changed, brought low, with a growth of beard on his once glowing cheeks and an ugly jagged scar across his once shapely cheekbone, but the same man. Guy walked on, quite sober now but trembling. His hands shook, he felt as if his legs could scarcely carry him, but for all that he kept walking. He forgot about finding the Italian restaurant and walked unsteadily down the Boltons, along the Fulham Road. All that mattered was to put as great a distance as possible between him and the poor derelict on that doorstep who might have been, who *was*, Linus.

Yet once he was in the restaurant he found in Cale Street, had gone to the bar and ordered a large vodka martini before asking for a table, he wondered almost with a groan why he had run away. Why hadn't he stopped and asked how he could help his friend?

That, of course, was to simplify things. But he might have made a start by asking the man if he really was Linus. The precise identity of a black person is no more readily discernible to a white than a white is to a black. There will not be that instant indisputable recognition. In Guy's mind a slight doubt lingered. When he last saw Linus he was a lithe, fit, beautiful, prosperous, young gangster. He was always well and gaudily dressed. He had a gold tooth, Guy remembered, rather unusual in the young but not so unusual in someone of Caribbean origin.

Guy sat down at his table, ordered some sort of chicken dish and another vodka martini while he waited for the food. The beggar on the step had a gold tooth. Going back in his mind to half an hour before, he saw again the parted lips, full and gleaming, with a bluish tinge, and among the white molars a glint of gold. It was Linus. What had happened to him that he had come to this?

Fifteen years ago . . . The teenage street gangs knew nothing of racism. It was something to be proud of now, something to be pleased about, but in those days none of them thought about it from that aspect, only marvelled when the police and social workers talked about race troubles among the young in Notting Hill. Guy could almost have said – almost but not quite, if he was honest – that he didn't notice another person's colour. He was aware that in some people's eyes to be Irish, as he was, was a liability. Linus had been a young devil. Once, on the Central Line tube between getting in at Notting Hill and getting out at Queensway, he had taken five hundred pounds off three American tourists without their knowing a thing about it.

The food came but he could only pick at it. He drank a carafe of the house wine. Why had he stayed to eat anything? He should have returned immediately to the place in the Old Brompton Road where he had seen Linus lying. He had run away. Getting up now, paying the bill, he told himself he must go back. He must go back and find the young black man on the step and confirm that he was Linus.

He walked down the street looking for a taxi, looking for that glowing golden cube moving towards one that is the most welcome of all streetlights. Approaching him along the King's Road, arm in arm like an old married couple, were Robin Chisholm and Maeve Kirkland.

Of course it was less surprising that they should be here than that he was. They lived only a street away. The King's Road was their High Street. Guy expected them either to pretend not to see him as on that day in the park or to start a row in the street. He braced himself and stared as they approached. They were going in for that twin-dressing again, perhaps it was a feature of their relationship. Identical pink shirts this time. It was the jeans which differed, hers the brushed sooty kind, his stonewashed blue denim. Robin showed no signs of having narrowly escaped a serious accident and his eye was no longer discoloured. Guy had to stop himself putting his hand up to his cheek where the faint mark of a fingernail still was.

They were both grinning widely. 'Bygones be bygones, old man?' said Robin.

Guy had never heard anyone under sixty call another 'old man' before. 'How are you?' he said, and then, for politeness, 'Good to see you up and about again.'

'Oh, I'm fighting fit.' It seemed an unfortunate choice of words. Knowing Robin, Guy had no doubt it was a matter of choice. 'What brings you,' said Robin in his fruity tones, 'to this neck of the woods?' Without waiting for an answer, he asked Guy round to St Leonard's Terrace for a drink.

All this warmth staggered Guy. What was Robin up to? 'Sorry, I'd like to but I'm in a bit of a hurry.'

'You haven't asked where Leonora is,' Maeve said rather spitefully.

It was true. He realised he hadn't thought of Leonora for the past hour. It must be a record. 'No,' he said. 'No. She's at Portland Road, I suppose. I'm having lunch with her tomorrow.'

'She's moved out to William's on account of Rachel not being there. There's no point in her staying in the flat alone.'

He felt a thrill of excitement. 'What do you mean, Rachel not being there?'

'She's gone away on holiday, hasn't she?'

'On holiday?' he said.

'This morning. She went to Spain with Dominic. Why are you looking like that, Guy? It's Rachel I'm talking about, not Leonora.'

A taxi came. He hailed it, told the driver to drop him in Bolton Gardens, said goodbye to them and got in. As it drove off he could see Maeve's face through the rear window, her mouth a little open, her head shaking. So Rachel had escaped him, or rather, had escaped Chuck. Rachel had gone off on holiday with one of those egghead men of hers. The important thing, of course, was not that she should be dead but that she shouldn't be *there*. Well, she wouldn't be there.

The evening had grown windy and no longer warm. Autumn was coming. The concrete of a doorstep was cold and hard, piercing through thin soot-coloured clothes like pain. He got out of the taxi in Bolton Gardens and walked the few yards back into the Old Brompton Road.

There was no one in the doorway. Linus, if it was Linus, had gone. The only evidence of his past occupancy was a cigarette end, a tiny stub, much smaller than that left behind by most tobacco smokers. Guy picked it up and smelt the sweetish, slightly dizzying scent of marijuana.

# CHAPTER
# FIFTEEN

She was late. He sat at their large round corner table in the gracious room, determined not to look at his watch again. His drink had been ordered and he resolved not to look at his watch until it came. The cigarette he had not been able to resist lighting was attracting censorious glances from a woman in a pink hat. Guy forced himself to look out of the window.

The brandy he had ordered arrived. It was the strongest thing he could think of, short of something totally way-out like absinthe or zubrovka. Even the Savoy probably didn't have those. He looked at his watch. It was twelve minutes past one. He hadn't spoken to her on the phone for days. This date at the Savoy had never been confirmed. He thought, she's not coming. They've beaten me, they've moved her away to Newton's place, they're never going to let her speak to me again. I'll wait till twenty past. If she hasn't come by twenty past – what will I do then? What shall I do?

Go to Georgiana Street, he thought. Find her. He hadn't spoken to her since he saw her in Lamb's Conduit Street on Tuesday. It was four days. He ought to have persisted, he ought to have found her before this. She might be anywhere, she might have gone with Rachel to Spain. He caught the waiter's eye and asked for another brandy. Of course she wasn't coming, he knew she wouldn't come now. He looked at his watch. It was twenty-two minutes past.

The second brandy was nearly gone by the time the waiter showed her to the table. Guy jumped up. He forgot the agonies of his long wait. She looked *beautiful*. For him and for this special place she had for once dressed up.

But perhaps not for once. Perhaps for ever. It was part of the changing process, the change back to him. He forgot the unanswered phone, the silent days. She wore a linen suit. The short skirt was of a rich dark but not navy blue, the long, high-buttoned, tight-waisted flared jacket, dark blue and dark pink in wide vertical stripes. The sleeves were turned back to show the pink and blue spotted lining. She had mauvish tights and blue suede shoes and her earrings were dark red glass roses.

Her hair shone. It looked as if it had just been cut, and well cut for a change. There was a glow on her face so that for a moment he thought she was made-up. She kissed him, one cheek, then the other, nothing unusual in that.

'I'm sorry I'm so late, Guy. There was trouble on the tube.'

Who cared about the tube? Her eccentric modes of travel made him laugh, 'Darling Leonora,' he said. 'You look so beautiful. I want you to look like that always.'

'It was my mother. She said, you can't go to the Savoy in jeans. I'd just bought this suit so I thought, well, why not?'

'Your mother wanted you to dress up for lunch with me?'

She smiled, the tight smile with the corners of her mouth restrained. 'My mother would want me to dress up for lunch with anyone.'

That was best ignored. 'Have something nice to drink for a change,' he said. 'Don't spoil things with orange juice.'

'All right. I'll have a sherry. No, not a dry one, a lovely dark brown sticky Bristol Cream.'

'So you've moved into Georgiana Street,' he said.

She began explaining why. He told her about meeting Maeve and Robin. The apparent truce or *détente* between him and

173

Robin seemed to bring her great pleasure. She reached across and squeezed Guy's hand. No, she wouldn't eat meat even to please him, she said. She'd have fish. Lobster? Guy suggested. That made her shudder but she would have sole, Creole prawns first and then sole and fried potatoes – why not? – and vegetables instead of a salad. A proper meal, Guy said, he was delighted. Although he had never contemplated doing so, he told her about Linus. She did remember Linus?

'Of course I do. He didn't like me. I'll never forget it, the first time we met, it was out in the street, Talbot Road or somewhere, and you were nice to me, you passed me a joint – though, God knows, Guy, you shouldn't have – and Linus, he spat into the drain.'

She remembered all that. She remembered how he had been that first time. His heart was full. 'There was the end of a joint left behind on the step,' he said.

'He never liked me,' she said again. 'There was no reason. He was just one of those gay men who didn't like women.'

'Linus wasn't gay.' He was astounded sometimes by the things she thought of, the *layers* of her, the things that went on in her pretty head. 'What makes you say that? He had that girlfriend Sophette, she was old enough to be his mother but she was his girlfriend.'

'Exactly,' said Leonora with a little laugh. 'Are you sure it was him on the doorstep?'

'Almost positive.'

'You'd better be entirely positive before you start doing something.'

She ate her prawns with gusto, she ate all her fish and most of the potatoes. She wouldn't have a second sherry but she shared the Frascati with him. He had to order a second bottle.

'Guy,' she said, very serious, 'it's very good of you, very kind, to want to help Linus if that's really him and he's down and out, but I think you've got to remember something. Linus was a pusher, he was a dealer in dangerous drugs. That's how he made his living. He's probably come to this state through his own addiction. Had you thought of that?'

He had to stop himself gaping at her. Didn't she know?

Didn't she know that what went for Linus also went for him?

'It would be a bit strong,' she said, 'to say he only got what he deserved but you could say he brought it on himself.'

'So he's to be left in the gutter? Who gives you these ideas? Newton?'

'You're identifying yourself with Linus, that's why you feel so deeply about him. You see yourself in him, brought low by some means or other. Oh, not poverty or crime now, I don't mean that, but something else. You were in the same line of life, you see, you're the same age with much the same background, the same way of making a living once.'

'You've caught that way of talking from Rachel.'

She didn't answer.

'What do you know of my way of making a living, Leonora?' he said heavily.

She said innocently, 'You sold marijuana, didn't you? I always knew that.'

The moment passed, the terror. She drank a second glass of wine, would have no more, but was excitedly prepared to have a wonderful sweet, a kind of sculpture in chocolate with leaf-thin whorls and petals, white, milk and dark. The decision about the sweet, its arrival, shifted them from the subject. He began to think about the two weeks ahead, the wedding that everyone *said* would take place on September 16, a fortnight from today. Of course it wouldn't, but . . .

'I couldn't get you on the phone at all last week,' he said.

'No, I know. I *am* sorry, Guy. But I'll be in Georgiana Street all the time now.' She smiled at him, her head a little on one side. 'I do have to go out sometimes, you know.'

'You've left the flat in Portland Road for good?'

'It looks like it. With Maeve gone and Rachel away, there didn't seem much point in going back there. As a matter of fact we're lending it to Janice and Gerry while they're in this country. It's nicer for them to have a place of their own than stay with Daddy and Susannah. Then when Rachel comes back we'll exchange contracts and it'll be all hers.'

When they had finished they walked down on to the Embankment. He took her hand and she let him hold it. The words were in his head and he wanted to bring them out but he was afraid. They were there, in his mouth now, waiting to be uttered. She talked about the river, the craft on it. There had been an accident to a pleasure boat the week before, the worst river disaster for more than a hundred years, fifty people drowned. She was talking about what it would be like trapped below deck, shuddering. He said because he had to, because the words crowded into his mouth were choking him, they exploded from him:

'Con Mulvanney – the name – what does it mean to you?'

Innocent eyes, an uncomprehending gentle gaze. 'Nothing. I don't know. What is it, Guy?'

'A man who took LSD and died of bee stings.'

'Ah.' He saw light dawn and his heart dipped. 'Yes, I heard about that. A long time ago. I never knew if it was true.'

'It was true.'

'What am I supposed to say? Do you want to tell me about it?'

'He begged me for the stuff. I didn't want to give it to him. But I was devastated afterwards. Leo darling, I was so ashamed. And I didn't want you ever to know, I knew what it would do to you and me. How you'd feel about me.'

'I knew there must be a reason why you did it,' she said. 'It didn't make any difference.'

'It didn't make any difference?'

'To the way I felt about you,' she said.

He took her in his arms. She was leaning against a round smooth stone pillar and he put his arms round her and kissed her. There had been no kisses of that kind between them for years, five years, six. It was a long and sweet, open-lipped kiss with tongues meeting, of the kind that precedes love-making, not a kiss for a river-breezy corner with people passing and a ship on the water sounding a long blast on its siren.

'I love you Leonora,' he said 'I've always loved you. I shall love you till I die. Come back to me now.'

She said with infinite sadness, 'It's too late, Guy.'

'Why is it too late? It's never too late. I love you and you love me, and you know you'll never go through with that crazy marriage, that ridiculous marriage. Don't you see it would be a crime against you and me to marry that man? I know you won't, though. I know you love me. You've shown me. I know you love me now.'

'Let's walk, Guy,' she said.

They walked along the path in the Victoria Embankment Gardens. It was cool and windy and there were little grey waves on the river.

'Promise me,' she said, 'not to press me about this. It's hard enough for me without that. Things are hard enough.'

'My darling, I won't do anything you don't want me to do. I'll do anything you ask. You've made me so happy.'

'You do nag rather, you know, Guy. You do go on and on. But you won't any more, will you? You won't pin me down?'

'Now I know you love me I'm so happy I won't say another word.'

'Come and have supper with us on Wednesday,' she said. 'Would you do that? Phone me tomorrow and Monday and Tuesday and come and have supper with us on Wednesday at about seven-thirty.'

What's supper? he might have said if it had been anyone else. Dinner is what you eat in the evening. Tea, of course, was what he had eaten in the old days with his mother, if there had been anything to eat. 'Who's "us"?' he said.

'William will be there, of course. Guy, it's William's flat. Be reasonable. Be *nice*.'

'I'll be nice. I'll come. I'll get to see you twice in one week. Where shall we have lunch next Saturday?'

She laughed. 'We can talk about that on Wednesday.'

After she had parted from him he didn't take a taxi. He walked. She had kissed him again when they said good bye, a warm sweet, loving kiss. And now he was alone again. She had told him she loved him, that nothing made any difference to that, she had renewed her love for him. Of course she had also said it was too late to come back to him but she didn't mean that. Probably she thought he wouldn't really want her after her inconstancy, but she was wrong there, she was quite wrong.

It occurred to him as he walked along the Embankment that when people in their circumstances come together again after a split, when they start again, it would be usual for them to go home together. The natural thing would have been for Leonora to go home with him now. But he understood why she couldn't do that. Hadn't she said things were hard for her? 'Things are hard enough without that,' she had said. Nothing could have declared more plainly the pressure she was under from her family to stay with William Newton. They had found him for her, brought them together, and now they were all united in binding her to him.

All they wanted, and this was very clear, was to get September 16 over and that wedding with it. They were like some royal family in history or a fairy story who locked the princess up in a tower until she consented to marry the – ginger dwarf. He smiled to himself when he thought of it like that. But he was soon angry again, angry for *her*, whom they had made unhappy, his sweet and beautiful love who found 'things hard enough' because she was being forced into marriage with a man she didn't love.

It began to rain and he hailed a taxi. Once back in Scarsdale Mews he thought he would check up at once in his engagement book to see what he was doing on Wednesday that he would have to cancel. Nothing – on Wednesday. For a moment he could hardly believe what he read, then believed it only too well. He *remembered* it.

On Monday, her birthday, he was supposed to be driving Celeste to Stratford-on-Avon, taking her to the Shakespeare Memorial Theatre and afterwards staying the night at the Lygon Arms in Broadway. *Supposed* to be? He had the tickets, had made the booking. She had taken his letting her down last Friday very well. He couldn't do that to her again. As he reassessed the next few days he started planning his phone calls to Leonora. On Monday he ought to be able to reach Leonora before he left and on Tuesday he could phone her from the hotel . . .

\* \* \* \*

Celeste spent Sunday night with him. She arrived in the late afternoon just as he rang off from talking to Leonora.

It was necessarily a bland and on the whole meaningless telephone conversation they had due to Tessa and Magnus being there. Leonora was back in Portland Road for the day, packing up some of her personal possessions, she said, for her mother and stepfather to take home with them in their car and store in their garage. This made Guy reflect to his satisfaction that if she really intended marrying Newton she would have her things taken round to *his* flat.

'Darling,' he said, 'I would have brought it all here. Why didn't you ask me?'

He understood she had to speak in a very neutral way, make small talk really, with Tessa there. With Tessa, doubtless, breathing down her neck, noting every word to rebuke her with it later. He could *see* Tessa, that stick-insect woman, darting about the flat, picking up this and that, choosing to take things off a shelf just behind Leonora while she was on the phone. He could see her stringy brown hands, a skeleton's bone hands with a bit of dried leather covering them and the nails painted like silver knife blades, her small head with the dark hair scraped back on a neck like a tortoise's questing out of its shell.

'I have to go away on business, Leo,' he said. 'Just tomorrow and Tuesday.' It was untrue but now was no time for admitting he was taking another woman away for the night. Telling a lie about it would only be bad, Guy thought obscurely, if he had *wanted* to go off with Celeste. 'But I'll still phone you, I'll make sure I get to a phone.'

It wasn't until very early next morning that, waking up in the Chinese bed beside Celeste, he began to recall what Leonora had said to him about Con Mulvanney. Her kiss, her declaration of her continuing love for him, her disclosures, so revealing, about the pressures she was under – all this had driven those simple remarks of hers from his mind. He hadn't even remembered them when he talked to her on the phone yesterday afternoon. But they were back with him now, in the dark mad small hours. He could see the luminous hands of his small carriage clock showing four-thirty.

'I heard about that,' she had said. 'A long time ago. I never knew if it was true.'

*She had heard about that.* He had never really doubted, he had never needed proof, but now his belief was confirmed. Why hadn't he asked her who told her? Because he was so overwhelmed with joy by what she had said next that none of it made any difference. Anyway, he knew. Rachel had told her, Rachel who had gone away on holiday to Spain with a man called Dominic. And what a difference that had made! Rachel was scarcely removed from the sphere of influence she had set up, for Leonora to be back in his arms.

He was painfully aware just the same of her not being in his arms at that moment. Only a fool wouldn't have asked why she couldn't just walk out on Newton, get in a taxi and come here to him. But he knew why she wouldn't. Her family's pressures and threats were still too much for her, she had to be liberated from that and liberated by him. If there was any possibility of her arrival, Celeste wouldn't be here now, her sable-dark hair spread over the pillow, her brown shoulders emerging from the white ruffled tulle of her nightgown. There had been no occasion for the removal of that pretty garment last night or on any night for a while now. The odd thought came to him that she would never take it off for him again.

When he thought sleep gone until the next night, in some Cotswold bed, sleep came to him and held him until past eight. Celeste was up before him, making the phoning of Leonora difficult in theory, impossible in practice. They were away by ten. At the place where they had lunch he couldn't tell Celeste he had to make a phone call on business. She knew too much, she wouldn't believe him. It was her birthday, she was enjoying herself. He had just bought her a magnificent lunch, promised her a present, anything she wanted from the nicest dress shop in Stratford. She looked wonderful with her beautiful hair plaited and coiled on top of her head, in a cream silk trouser suit and caramel shirt. Men turned their heads, looked at her, then at him. He couldn't go and make a phone call to Leonora now and tell Celeste a lie about it – still less, tell her the truth about it.

It was *Romeo and Juliet* they saw. Guy had seldom, if ever before, seen a Shakespeare play on the stage. Maybe on the TV by accident but not on the real stage.

'You thought it would be boring, didn't you?' said Celeste, as they got into the Jaguar. 'But I could see you loved it. You're like a kid that's only done Shakespeare at school and can't believe it's the same thing when he sees it done for real.'

'I don't remember Shakespeare at school,' said Guy.

'Sweet Guy, they did it on the days you were shuckin' 'n' jivin' round Notting Dale.'

'Maybe,' he said. 'Do you know what that play reminded me of?'

She didn't answer. He could feel her silence, warm and distressed. Then she said, 'Yes,' with great finality.

It was their own story, his and Leonora's, the star-crossed lovers, the repressive autocratic family. He hadn't killed anyone, of course, but in their eyes he had: Con Mulvanney. Con Mulvanney was his – what was he called? – Tybalt. The play stayed with him as he drove south, reproducing glowing pictures in his mind. That bit in the orchard and on the balcony, he could so easily replace Romeo with himself and Juliet with Leonora. He wished he could remember some of the lines, he wished he could talk about it with Celeste. Something about the way she was sitting, her shoulders stiff, her profile bronze hard and staring ahead of her in the dark, told him he couldn't.

By the time they were in their hotel bedroom it was midnight. The day had gone by and he hadn't phoned Leonora. He had longed and longed to phone, even during the intervals of the play he had thought about phoning her, about escaping from Celeste and finding a phone, but it had been impossible. It wasn't the first time a day had passed without their speaking on the phone. Far from it. In the previous week, though he had seen her at Susannah's, he had spoken to her only once. But it was the first time they hadn't spoken because *he* had failed to call.

Celeste didn't maintain her silence. She was speaking again, talking about the room, the view they would have in the morning. But the confidence that had existed between them, the wonderful way that, though he didn't love her, he had been able to say anything and everything to her, they had been able to share each other's minds, that had gone.

It was lost, he had killed it, it would never come again.

What did it matter? He thought as he lay in the twin bed a yard away from Celeste's that he would be bound anyway to lose her once he and Leonora were together again.

# CHAPTER
# SIXTEEN

'**Y**ou didn't phone me yesterday.'

'Darling, I'm so sorry. Were you worried? I haven't upset you, have I?' Guy was so happy that she minded his not phoning her that he couldn't keep the note of excited joy out of his voice. 'I couldn't get to a phone. It just wasn't possible. Will you forgive me?'

'Oh, it doesn't *matter*, it's not that. I only meant it was odd, it was so unlike you.'

She must have waited in for his call. His heart sang. His head felt tumultuous as if someone inside it was doing an energetic dance. 'You stayed in, waiting for the phone to ring? Oh, Leo.'

'I happened to stay in. I'd nothing to go out for.'

Ah, yes. A likely story. He almost laughed aloud. 'Leo, will you tell me something. It's about what we talked about on Saturday. I don't know why I didn't ask you then. You said you knew all about – well, Con Mulvanney. Do you remember?'

'Who?'

'The man who died of bee stings. You said you knew all

about him, you'd heard about that and it was a long time ago. It was exactly four years ago, as a matter of fact.'

'Yes,' she said, 'it would be about that. I was still living with Daddy and Susannah. It was before I moved into that room in Fulham with Rachel.'

'Leo, who told you about it? It was Rachel who told you, wasn't it?'

'Rachel?'

It was so clear in his mind, he began to tell her the story as he understood it. 'Con Mulvanney lived in South London, in Balham, and so did this woman who was with him when he died. She was some sort of social worker and Rachel's a social worker in South London, so you can see how she came to tell her. She said she'd tell everyone . . .'

'Guy,' she interrupted him, 'what are you talking about? Do you know what you're talking about? Because I don't. It was Susannah who told me, *Susannah*.'

The name exploded in his ears. *Susannah*, whom he had thought of as his friend, the woman who of all Leonora's family and friends had been kindest to him – it was she who had betrayed him and alienated his love. He should have thought of it before. Why had he been such a fool?

'Of course.' He heard himself stammering. 'Susannah's mother lived in Earlsfield, which is east Wandsworth, which is next to Balham, she was in hospital there.'

'Guy, I honestly don't know what you mean. i. wasn't like that, Susannah's mother never came into it. I suppose I'd better tell you, though I promised myself I never would.'

'Tell me what?' He touched the wooden frame of the French windows and held on.

'A woman wrote to Susannah – well, she wrote to Susannah and my father, I mean to Mr and Mrs Anthony Chisholm. I was there when the letter came. I suppose she thought they were my parents, I mean that Susannah was my mother. She wrote warning them off you, for my sake, I mean. Look, Guy, what is this? What does it matter? I've told you it didn't make any difference. I have to go, we've been talking for half an hour.'

'Please don't go, Leo, please don't ring off. This is terribly important to me, I have to know. Who wrote to your parents?'

'To Daddy and Susannah,' she said. He could hear a growing impatience in her voice. 'Well, I'll tell you quickly and then I must go. I've told you it made no difference to the way I felt about you and you must believe that. This woman's name was Vasari, I've always remembered because it's the same as the man who wrote about the lives of the artists.' He didn't know what she meant, he was lost. 'Vasari,' she said. 'Polly or something. She wrote to them to tell them they shouldn't let me marry you. My God, I was twenty-two years old. They were to stop me marrying you because you were a social menace and you'd given drugs to her boyfriend. It was something like that. Susannah opened the letter because it was addressed to both of them and Daddy had gone to work.'

'And she told you just like that?'

'I was there when she opened the letter. Of course she showed it to me. Look, phone me later if you want to but I do have to go now, this minute.'

He said he would phone her at seven. She said goodbye quickly and put the phone down. He sighed. Clarifying the mysteries of the past and the present only led to further complications. Of course it was easy to see how Poppy Vasari had found out about his association with Leonora and found out too who Leonora was. In those days they were often together, he was always calling at Lamb's Conduit Street. She would have followed him, read the name by the bell push on the door. How that vindictive woman must have enjoyed writing the letter that would ruin his life!

And Susannah, that treacherous woman, that snake in the grass . . . Surely a nice person with any idea of loyalty would have thrown that letter away in disgust after reading the first line. The sort of woman he had thought Susannah was wouldn't have believed a word of it, the last thing she would have done was show it, and show it immediately, to the girl it was intended to caution. The hypocrisy of it made him indignant. It wouldn't have been so bad coming from Tessa who had never pretended to like him, who had never concealed her hatred. He remembered Susannah's kindly proffered advice, her Judas kisses.

He phoned Leonora again at seven. It was Newton he expected to hear and he braced himself for the man's exasperated, surperior-sounding voice – after all he was going to have to spend tomorrow evening with him – but Leonora answered the phone.

'Can he hear what you're saying?' he asked her.

'If you mean William, he's not here. He's been in Manchester all day and he's not back.'

'Will he be back by tomorrow evening?'

'Yes, of course. He'll be back tonight, any minute now I should think.'

'Leonora, tell me about the letter Poppy Vasari wrote to Susannah.'

'Oh dear, I wish you'd forget it. I wish I'd never told you. You're making far too much of it. Poppy – is that her name? – Vasari wrote to Daddy and Susannah and told them you made your living by selling dangerous drugs. I think she called them Class A drugs. She said you'd given a hallucinogenic tablet, those were the words she used, to this Mulvanney man and he'd gone crazy and stuck his head in a beehive. Well, that part had been in the papers. There was a photocopy in with the letter of an account of the inquest from a newspaper. Susannah showed it to me – well, I was sort of reading it over her shoulder. She said she didn't think she'd even tell Daddy. She was quite upset.'

'What did you say to her?'

'As a matter of fact, I said I thought it was probably libel putting things like that in a letter.'

'Did she tell your father?'

'I don't know. I didn't ask and he never said. She told Magnus.'

'*She did what?*'

'Guy, please don't get in a state. She told Magnus because he's a solicitor. She rang him up at his office and asked him what one ought to do about letters like that. She meant should she tell the police, I think.'

'Oh, Christ,' said Guy. 'Christ.'

'Anyway, you needn't worry because he said the best thing to do with it was burn it. I suppose he thought it was a poison-pen letter, though it was in fact signed.'

'No doubt old skull-face told your mother.'

'Possibly. Well, yes, I expect he did. My mother and I never discussed it. I wish you wouldn't call Magnus that. Susannah and I talked about it quite a bit. She's very understanding, you know. I told her we all smoked grass in those days and she said she had too, and I said I expect you *had* dealt in drugs when you were younger. It was the background you came from and the people you associated with – you didn't mind my saying that, did you, Guy?'

'I don't mind anything you say,' he said.

'All Susannah said was that it might have mattered if I was seriously thinking of marrying you but I wasn't.'

'She said that?'

'There isn't any point in going over and over it. *It made no difference to the way I felt.* Guy, you *know* how I feel, I've told you often enough. Listen, I can hear William coming in. We'll see you tomorrow night, right?'

'I'll phone you first thing in the morning.'

'No, don't do that. I shan't be here. I'll see you about seven-thirty tomorrow.'

He was going out to dinner with Bob Joseph and a man who was chairman of a Spanish hotel chain. They were meeting at a restaurant in Chelsea, not far from the one where he had dined on the evening he had seen the street person who might have been Linus. Guy walked down to the Old Brompton Road. What had Leonora meant, she wouldn't be there 'first thing in the morning'? She was there now. Where could she possibly be going? Then he realised. Tomorrow would be September 6 and very likely the first day of her school term. The children would be returning to school tomorrow. She would be going to work.

But, wait a minute. That was a bit odd, going back to school as a teacher when you intended to get married less than two weeks later and take a fortnight off. Teachers never did that. Teachers were expected to get married and go on honeymoons in the long school holidays. But of course, it meant only one thing, she wasn't getting married, she had never really intended to get married. It was all a fantasy. Was it perhaps designed to make him jealous? If so, it had certainly succeeded. He smiled to himself. Women, he thought, were like that.

He turned out of the Earl's Court Road and began looking for Linus. In a doorway, though not the doorway of the health-food shop, a man lay asleep, curled up in the foetal position, his face and head covered by a newspaper. Guy thought it was the same but he couldn't be sure. Nor could he bring himself to wake the man. The realisation he had come to about Leonora and her fake or dream wedding made him feel so happy and buoyant that his interest in Linus was temporarily weakened. There was nothing anyway that he could do about it. To lift up the newspaper and look at the sleeping man's face seemed to him an outrageous act, a piece of insensitive impertinence. This evidently was Linus's beat. He would find him again.

A taxi came and he got into it. He thought of Susannah with hatred, picturing her in that flat in her smart black trousers and top. She was leaning over the banisters and smiling. He followed this welcoming presence into the living room. The white card with the silver border was on the mantelpiece. It was probably an invitation to someone else's wedding. Yes, that would be it. It was an invitation to another couple's wedding, the ceremony had already taken place, and because the card was now therefore useless, Janice had picked it up and thrown it out as she went to make tea. This explanation satisfied him completely.

\* \* \* \*

Flowers, chocolates, wine – or a real present? He had never seen her eat chocolates. She was a health foodie. Flowers had to be put in water which would mean her going away and leaving him with Newton. A real present could only be jewellery for her, earrings for instance, and he sensed this would somehow be out of place, over the top, ostentatious. After all, unimportant as William Newton might be, a mere stooge or puppet set up by Anthony and Susannah, it was his home, he still no doubt thought of Leonora as engaged to him, even as due to marry him on Saturday week. Guy didn't think he could give Leonora a pair of earrings worth, say, three hundred pounds, in Newton's presence.

He settled for champagne. A single bottle of Piper Heidsieck. Should he wear a suit? He couldn't imagine Newton even possessing a suit. Maybe designer jeans and a sweater would be best. It wasn't going to be warm. Guy realised he was as nervous and uneasy about the evening ahead as if he had never dined out in his life. Would there be other people there? If only he could phone her. There was an idea in his mind of finally winning her away from Newton on this evening, carrying her off under his nose, a happy victim of kidnap, bringing her home here for ever.

A night's sleep had cooled his anger. He no longer felt he hated Susannah. He blamed her, he never wanted to see her again, if he had met her in the street he would have passed her by with head averted, but his hatred had gone. After all, she had failed. In spite of her vindictive motives, she hadn't succeeded in turning Leonora against him. Leonora herself said it had made no difference. Susannah had interfered inexcusably in his life but her interference no longer mattered, had never mattered, it was simply of no account.

Yet his discovery altered the situation. Rachel, designated Chuck's victim, was very obviously not guilty. Rachel had never spoken to or even heard of Poppy Vasari, Rachel had never been told about his activities as a dealer, so Rachel did not merit death. But Guy, not usually cowardly, baulked at saying so to Danilo. Having changed his mind about Robin Chisholm and been roughly handled by Danilo on account of it, he hesitated to ring Danilo up and say he had been wrong about Rachel too.

It wasn't as if he could even say, forget Rachel Lingard, Susannah Chisholm is the one. Susannah *wasn't* the one, he didn't want Susannah killed, he just never wanted to speak to her again. Dressing for the dinner party ahead, deciding finally – the sun having come out – on a pair of white linen trousers and black silk shirt with a white-and-cream-patterned V-necked silk pullover, Guy came to the conclusion that there was no need, at least at present, to tell Danilo anything. Rachel, after all, was out of the country, safe in some Spanish resort. Chuck probably knew this, or knew she had gone away, and would do nothing until she returned on September 15.

Just before he left, he poured himself a stiff brandy, then another. He needed it and there might not be much on offer in Georgiana Street. The taxi waited while he went into the wine shop and bought the champagne. He was going to be early. He got the driver to set him down in Mornington Crescent and began to walk the rest of the way, cradling the heavy bottle that was wrapped up in mauve tissue paper. It was still only twenty past seven when he got there. The houses here had scrubby front gardens, tiny plots of brown grass and dusty bushes. Steps went up to the front door and there was a deep basement. In the front garden of the house where Newton lived was planted a pole with an estate agent's board attached to it on which was printed: *One-bedroom luxury flat* and *Sold, subject to contract*.

There were five flats, one on each floor. Guy, before he even rang Newton's bell, had a very good idea what the 'luxury' as described by the estate agent would amount to. A bathroom that actually had tiles on the walls and some sort of central heating. He didn't much like to think of Leonora living in this place, a backstreet that looked as if it would be unsafe at night, a grey-brick house whose paintwork needed renewing.

Newton's voice, coming out of the grid, instead of asking who it was, said, 'Come up,' and the lock on the door buzzed.

A steep staircase and two long flights to climb. Another one of those dreary walk-ups. Newton was on the landing, outside an open front door, waiting for him. He said, 'Hi,' and held out his hand. After a moment's hesitation, Guy shook hands with him. He was glad he hadn't put a suit on. Newton wore jeans and a grey jumper with a hole in one of the elbows. His longish ginger hair stuck up like a punk's, only it grew that way, the effect hadn't been achieved with styling gel.

Leonora was in the living room, looking awkward, Guy thought, or embarrassed perhaps. As well she might in this barn of a room with a surprisingly low ceiling and two small sash windows giving on to the grey façade opposite. He had got over all his heart-turnings on the way upstairs and advanced towards her with no less diffidence than if she had been Celeste. She kissed him, a light peck. Of course she would, with Newton watching. He handed the champagne to Newton who said,

'How grand. What are we celebrating?'

That made Guy smile. The little red-haired man was really very unsophisticated. Guy felt powerful, in control. He said kindly, 'Quite a lot of people drink champagne as an apéritif these days, you know. There doesn't have to be anything to celebrate.'

'Oh, I see. Then it would be appropriate to drink it now?'

'Don't be absurd, William,' said Leonora, looking uncomfortable, though Guy couldn't see what was absurd about what he said.

He was taking a good look round the room. The furniture was the kind of thing rejected by comfortably-off middle-aged achievers and passed on to poor young relatives. He assessed the carpet as coming from one of those sales held after a store fire. You could even see the burnt patch in one corner. Up on the wall, above a Victorian fireplace of cast iron and floral tiles, a fireplace that was there not because Newton had found it in an antique shop but because it had been put in with the rest of the dilapidated fittings in 1895, hung the swords.

They were crossed at the point Guy remembered was called the forte. One was bare, the other in a rather worn and shabby embroidered scabbard. They recalled to Guy that dream he had had in which he was fighting Con Mulvanney with swords in Kensington Gardens and had stabbed him through the heart. He remembered Newton had said he wanted to sell the swords. He had also, on that occasion after the cinema, said something about selling his flat.

'Is it this flat that's been sold?' he had begun to ask when Leonora came back with three glasses (one champagne flute, one hock glass and something that looked as if designed to hold half a grapefruit) on a tray. Guy nearly offered to open the champagne, but stopped himself because he wanted to see Newton make a mess of it and in Leonora's presence.

She was looking worried and far from her best. Gone was the elegant fashionable young woman in the dark blue and pink linen suit, the pretty tights and shoes. Being with Newton simply didn't suit her. That was an inescapable conclusion, anyone would see it. Those white pants would only look good if freshly laundered each time they were worn and as for that faded sweatshirt . . . Her hair was hauled on to the back of her head with one of those awful crocodile clips. The red glass roses hanging from her ears looked ridiculous with the rest of the get-up.

Newton opened the champagne without mishap. It must have been one of the easy bottles, Guy thought, you sometimes got them. They began to talk about the sale of Newton's flat and Guy asked him where he was going to live. He asked where *he* was going to live but Newton said,

'I expect we shall buy a house.'

Guy ignored that 'we'. 'You don't want to leave it too long. Remember property's the best investment. Even in a recession in the property market it's a great mistake to sell your home and invest the proceeds in something else.'

'I'll remember that, Guy,' said Newton.

Guy was quite well informed about the property market and he talked some more about it. He said something about his own plans for moving, perhaps of buying a house at the 'best end' of Ladbroke Grove. What did Leonora think of Stanley Crescent, the abode, he had heard, of TV personalities and one world-famous singer, a million-pound Italianate villa in fashionable Stanley Crescent? William said he hardly supposed what Leonora thought would make any difference to whether Guy bought or not. He said it coldly and Guy wondered if the two of them had been quarrelling before he arrived. Leonora went off to do the final dinner preparations and Guy changed the subject. He intended to be tactful, to behave well while he could.

'Very autumnal this evening,' he said, looking towards the window.

'The nights will soon be drawing in,' said Newton.

Guy looked narrowly at him to see if he was taking the piss, but it was all right. Newton's expression was both serious and pleasant. He began to talk about the summer that was past, the sunniest of the century.

It wasn't much of a meal. If people couldn't or wouldn't cook properly, Guy thought, it was better to buy smoked salmon and a cold roast chicken for guests than attempt strange meat loaves. He was even more dubious when Leonora told him there was no meat in the loaf, it was all soya and herbs. The only good thing was the wine, a surprisingly good claret, of which Newton actually produced two bottles. Guy complimented him on the wine. Drink, as it always did, made him feel a lot better. Just the same, he knew it would be impossible for him to pass a passive evening here and to go home alone. The brandy, the wine, had wonderfully clarified his mind. He saw that this was the crunch, the time had come. But it wasn't this decision of his which was responsible for the change in atmosphere, the rapidly ensuing trouble. It was the question he asked Leonora, in all innocence, about her first day back at school.

* * * *

'It's a shame you've had to cook. We could have gone out to eat.'

This remark was partly prompted by the dessert she served, a home-made sorbet, the colour and texture of three-day-old snow but with large ice crystals in it like splinters of glass. The sorbet was as tasteless as snow too, though Guy guessed it was supposed to be lemon.

'Why is it a shame, Guy? Because the food's so awful? I'm sorry, I know I'm not much of a cook. But William's worse except with curry. His curry's marvellous, only we didn't know if you liked it.'

The idea of a man possibly being expected to cook for guests rather shocked him. But he didn't say so. He hastened to assure his Leonora – that she should apologise to him! – that he only meant she must have had a hard day at school, today being the first day of the new term.

She reddened. It was years since he had seen her blush like that. Newton didn't seem to notice. He was busy with the mousetrap cheese which was all that was on offer. But he looked up and said, with his mouth full,

'She hasn't been in today. She's given up – remember?'

Remember? What did the man mean? 'Leo, have you left your job? You didn't tell me.'

'I resigned,' she said, 'as soon as I knew . . . I mean, I resigned in June.'

'What were you going to say?' he said. 'As soon as you knew what?'

Newton picked up the wine bottle. He looked at Leonora who shook her head, filled Guy's glass and then his own. He took a long slow drink, said,

'As soon as she knew I was going to work for BBC North-west.'

Guy looked at her. 'I don't understand.'

'There's no particular reason why you should need to.'

Newton could be quite simple and innocent-sounding and, suddenly, he could become crisp. The crispness was starting to gel into ice. 'I have a new job. In Manchester. BBC Northwest studios are in Manchester. Therefore, in the nature of things, since I'm not a happy commuter, I shall live there. Are you answered?'

'*You*, yes,' Guy said. 'I don't see why Leonora has to give up her job because you're going to live in Manchester.'

'Don't you? You're rather slow sometimes. I've noticed it before. Let me explain in simple language. Leonora has given up her job in West London because she intends to get another one in Manchester. She is going to live in Manchester with me. From the end of this month. Leonora is going to live with me because she *will be married to me*.'

'Why didn't you tell me about this, Leonora?'

'Because she's afraid of your reaction. She's afraid of what you'll do. And who can blame her? Now let's talk about something else. Let's change the subject. We can revert to any of those things you're so fascinated by, house-buying or the autumnal weather, any bloody thing, only for God's sake let's not get our tempers running any higher.'

He was hardly going the right way about reducing Guy's temper. Guy jumped up. Before he could speak Leonora said,

'Please stop quarrelling, the pair of you. Please stop now. I should have told you, Guy, but William's right, you're so *violent*.'

'Would you expect me to take it lying down? That he's preparing to take you away? To take you up to the north of England?'

'Why not? She'll be my wife. I'll be her husband. If she'd got a job in Manchester I'd have followed her. The idea of being married surely is that you share each other's lives.'

'I want to hear what Leonora has to say, not you. Let her speak for herself. She's quite capable of that, I assure you. Now you tell me, Leonora, you weren't going to leave me, were you? You weren't seriously contemplating going to Manchester?'

'What do you mean, "leave me"?' said Newton, very cold now. 'You can't leave someone you're not with. Leonora left you seven years ago.'

'It's a lie!' Guy shouted. 'She loves me, she's told me so a hundred times. She isn't going to marry you. What makes you think she is? Her family found you for her and pushed her on to you but they can't control her mind, they can't touch her heart. She's mine and she always will be.'

'Guy . . .' Leonora came round the table to him. Newton still sat there staring, calm, as cold as ice. 'Guy,' Leonora said, 'you must stop this, you must.'

'Get him to stop lying to me and then I'll stop all right.'

'He isn't lying. I'm going to marry him and I'm going to Manchester with him.'

'I don't believe it. I *won't* believe it. I'll see you dead before I let you go away with him.'

'Do you wonder I didn't tell you about it when you go on like this? The reason I didn't tell you was to avoid you going on like this.'

Guy looked at her, feeling a tide of misery gathering and

mounting inside him. He had never felt more like weeping in her arms. He wanted to take her in his arms and beg her not to go. 'You won't go, will you, Leo?'

She made no answer but her face was twisted as if she was in pain.

'That's why you're selling your flat,' he said. 'That's why he's selling his.'

'Please don't Guy, don't go on. Please stop shouting.'

It was slowly becoming clear to him. 'That's why he's getting rid of –' he flung out an arm '– all this shit. All this rubbish,' he said, 'these swords. He said he wanted to sell his swords.'

Guy was trembling. He took two steps to the fireplace and pulled down the swords from the wall. Newton sat there, looking incredulous. Guy threw the naked sword down on the table and tugged the other from its scabbard. Leonora seized his arm. He flung off her hand and leapt back, brandishing the shining sabre.

'I'll fight you for her! We'll fight a duel.' He was trembling no longer. Adrenalin poured through him, quenching misery. 'I'll fight you to the death!'

# CHAPTER
# SEVENTEEN

William Newton picked up the sabre from the table and stood looking at it as if it were some strange implement he had heard of but never seen before. He laid it down again, said to Guy.

'Why don't you put that down and go home.'

'He's afraid to fight me, Leonora,' Guy said.

'It might be unwise.' A little smile, probably nervous, had appeared on Newton's horsy face. 'They're old fighting sabres, they're not ornamental.'

'You coward,' said Guy. 'Where's your honour? Admit it, you're chicken. This is the man your parents chose to be your husband, Leonora. Pathetic, isn't he?' He raised the sabre. It was years since Guy had taken his fencing lessons but he was strong and fit. He held the sword at an angle, the point level with Newton's eyes.

Leonora said in a breathless voice, 'I'm going to phone the police.'

'Why?' said Guy. 'Nothing's going to happen to me.'

'I'm going to phone them unless you put that sword down *now*.'

'No, you're not my dear.'

The phone on a small side table had a long trailing lead. It wasn't the kind you can plug in. Guy brought the sabre down with a long slicing movement across the lead six inches from where it emerged from the wall. The phone bounced off the table but the lead remained intact. Guy made a grab at it, pulled the lead and wrenched it out of the wall socket.

'For God's sake. Are you mad?'

'Don't say that to me, Leo. You shouldn't have talked about phoning the police. Stand back, please. Go in the other room, if you want.' He added contemptuously, 'If there is another room.' He turned back to Newton, who had said nothing, who had responded to none of Guy's insults, but merely stood there, the smile still twitching his lips. 'Ginger dwarf, miserable runt. Fucking prig.'

Casually, Newton picked up the sword. Its blade was dull but it looked sharp. For all their shabby appearance on the wall, the swords had been kept in good condition. The two men faced each other, each holding his weapon, but not crossing them, not performing any preliminary ritual. They looked at each other and Leonora watched them, one hand up to her open mouth.

Guy was the first to make a move. He swung the sword in two sideways sweeps, to the left and to the right, then made a swift fierce stab at Newton but the other man skipped quickly round the table, avoiding the lunge. Guy stabbed again, over the table top, knocking over the wine bottle. Newton ducked, then sprang up at the end of the table where he had been sitting. His sword and Guy's clashed with a high ringing sound. Guy thrust again and the swords crossed and recrossed. Playing for a moment or two, like a tennis player in a knock-up before a match, Newton suddenly made a sweeping movement which turned Guy's weapon aside.

'Pimp,' shouted Guy, 'ginger dwarf, yes-man, wimp, egghead.'

Newton started laughing. 'I have to tell you,' he said, 'that

I've done quite a bit of this, so if you want to stop now that'll be OK.'

'He's trying to say he's good,' Leonora shouted. 'He fenced for his university.'

'So did I,' said Guy, 'the university of life! Now wipe that grin off your face,' he yelled at Newton and lunged at him.

Leonora put her head in her hands. The swords were simply clashing now, Guy smashing his this way and that, in wild movements without any finesse or control. He sprang back and drove his weapon at Newton in a scooping movement like an underarm serve. Newton didn't skip aside his time but deflected the blade with a single sweep. Guy could feel Leonora behind him. One of her hands clutched at his shoulder. He shook it off. He backed, defending himself. She cried out,

'Please, Guy, please stop. I'll get the neighbours, I swear I will. I'll go down to the street and phone the police. You must stop.'

'For Christ's sake, keep out of this!' He had never spoken to her like that before. She gave a sob. 'I love you,' he shouted. 'I'll always love you. I'll win you!'

Newton stood there, legs apart. He wasn't smiling any more. He threw back his ginger hair. For a moment they faced each other, perfectly still. Guy had the feeling Newton would like to stop, would welcome a truce. That made him spring forward and whirl his sword in a movement which, if successful and the blade sharp, would have severed Newton's head. Leonora screamed. But the stroke wasn't successful. Newton parried it. He did so easily, and in a way that maddened Guy, it was so smoothly done and with a grace that made the ringing clang of the blades the more shocking.

Newton made a quick riposte, a feint really. He was teasing Guy. He danced with his sabre, making swift covering moves as Guy's sword lunged wildly. Leonora was struggling to raise one of the window sashes. Guy forgot everything he had learned about fencing. He was just a man with a stabbing cutting weapon. He was doing what an unskilled man with a sword will do, pushing it back and forth to the right and left, and yelling curses with each attack. He could hear himself roaring.

She couldn't shift the window but collapsed against it for a moment, her head on her hands. Guy beat at the air, at Newton's blade when his came into contact with it, once striking the shade of the central light and setting it swinging wildly. Leonora's coming away from the window, standing there and watching them as if hypnotised, gave him a fresh impetus. But the silent Newton was no longer menaced by anything Guy did. He was in absolute control of the bout. Sometimes his weapon grazed Guy's, sometimes beat lightly on it. Guy's rage, at boiling point, rose another inch and spilled over. He leapt outside the range of Newton's sabre and made a wild attempt to run him through from the side.

The blade missed Newton, not because he parried it with his own but because he contracted his muscles in the nick of time. The sabre point went through his sweater at the waist and ripped the wool from hem to neckline.

Newton growled like a bear. His sweater flapped open like an unfastened straitjacket. He pulled his arms out, stood there in a grubby white T-shirt, his breath rasping angrily. Guy was laughing in triumph. He pulled off his own jumper and threw it across the room. From his success he had gained skill, or at least energy. He began to make slashes, stabbing, crowing and making Wild West yells. Leonora was watching wide-eyed, like a first-time spectator at a bullfight, horrified, yet compelled.

Guy began directing his blade in a low line, pointing at Newton's genitals. He twirled the point. He laughed. Shouting insults, he danced up and down, the sword jumping and bobbing in a half-circle at thigh level. It was designed to lull Leonora's lover into a state of unpreparedness and if the surprise thrust he now made had hit its target, Newton would have got to his feet a eunuch. But this was the last blow Guy was to attempt. It was all over with a frightening suddenness. Newton parried the lunge with a neat turn of his wrist in a lateral defensive movement, riposted at once and caught Guy on the left arm. The point of the sabre cut him in a straight line from wrist to elbow.

Guy's sword fell from his hand. With blood fountaining from his wound, he toppled over, seizing what first came to hand to break his fall. It was the edge of the tablecloth and with it came plates and glasses, wine bottle, knives and forks. He collapsed on to the floor covered in a litter of sticky china and glass. He could hear Leonora screaming, a manic animal sound. She dropped the window sash and ran to him. Guy shut his eyes, opened them and sat up. His arm was streaming with blood.

'Oh God,' Leonora sobbed. 'Oh God, oh God.'

'It's all right,' he whispered. 'I'll be all right.'

He held the wound but his hand wasn't large enough to cover it. Leonora started ripping up the tablecloth, tearing it into strips. The first bandage she put on was immediately soaked in blood. She was sobbing and gasping.

'Don't worry, darling,' Guy said, 'it's only a flesh wound.'

This, for some reason, evoked a crow of laughter from Newton, who with ridiculous coolness was wiping the sabre blade and replacing it, unwashed, in its scabbard. He hung both swords back on the wall.

'Still want to buy them?' he said.

'Oh, William, don't. Haven't you done enough?'

'I'm sorry,' Newton said. 'I shouldn't have fought him.'

'No, you shouldn't. It was awful. Look what you've done. Phone for an ambulance, now, please.'

'I can't phone for anything, can I? Not now he's buggered up the phone.'

Leonora unwrapped the tablecloth bandage and started applying a fresh one. Guy was still sitting on the floor. He got to his feet. His left arm felt rather numb, without pain. There had been no pain, only the initial sting, like an insect biting, when Newton's sword point ripped the skin. Newton sighed and said, 'I'll drive you to hospital. I'm sorry about this, Guy. It's a mess. All we can do now is go and find some casualty department.'

'Thanks, but I'd rather die than have you drive me anywhere.'

'OK, be like that, but you'll have to have something done about your arm.'

'I'll drive him' said Leonora. 'I'll drive you, Guy.'

Everything that had happened was worth it to hear her say that. She had another go with a fresh strip of tablecloth, binding more tightly this time. One of her scarves made a sling for his arm. 'Put your sweater round you.' She picked it up off the floor. 'Do you want a coat? I expect I could find you a jacket.'

'Not one of his,' said Guy.

Newton grinned. 'He'd rather die of cold.'

That made Guy start for him, fists up, in spite of his bleeding arm. Leonora grabbed him, pulled him round, and then the wound did start to hurt, a deep throb beginning. Guy groaned. Leonora's face was wet with tears. She wiped it on another bit of tablecloth. Newton touched her arm and she looked at him, but Guy couldn't read that look. He would have liked to hold on to her going down the stairs but pride forbade it.

At the bottom a front door opened and a man, a sleek yuppie with a small moustache, put his head out.

'Everything all right?'

'Only a duel,' said Leonora, with an hysterical edge to her voice.

The man didn't seem to take this in. 'I thought I heard something. My wife said it was builders.'

They found a casualty department open in a big hospital halfway up a hill. Guy didn't know the name of it. He didn't really know north London. It seemed to him he must have lost pints of blood. His shirt was soaked with blood. It had cost him nearly two hundred pounds, a deceptively simple and casual garment. The blood would never come out. Some of it had got on to Leonora's tracksuit top and there were smears on her white trousers. The pair of them looked as if they had come off a battlefield.

He was happy. Of course he realised that it was awful, what he had done. He would be scarred for life. But she loved him. He had won her. Hadn't she reproached the wretched Newton? Hadn't she rushed to him and sacrificed a perfectly good tablecloth to bind up his wound?

'I'll pay for the phone to be reconnected,' he whispered.

She started laughing. It was humourless hysteria. Sobs punctuated it.

'Come on,' he said. 'Everything'll be OK. You'll see. I'll buy him a new sweater.'

After that his name was called. A weary houseman cleaned the wound and of course wanted to know what had caused it. An accident with a carving knife, Guy said, an explanation which wasn't believed but the doctor said no more for the time being. He gave Guy an anti-tetanus injection, put half a dozen stitches in the wound. It was really no more than a deep scratch.

'Do you know what that looks like to me? Just as a matter of interest? As if someone quite skilled with the sabres wanted to, if you'll forgive the pun, make his point. Show he meant business but that was enough for now, right?'

'I don't know what you mean,' said Guy.

'I do a bit with the sabres myself or I used to in the days when life was normal and I had, you know, what's it called, leisure. Run along now. You can come back next Wednesday and have the stitches out.'

In the car Guy said, 'Are you angry with me?'

'I don't know. I think I'm just tired, fed up, sick of the whole thing.'

'My darling, I understand. I know how you feel.'

'No, you don't, Guy. That's the trouble. You don't know how I feel, you never have and you never will. Now I'm going to drive you home. Will you be all right on your own?'

'I hoped you'd stay with me.'

'I can't do that. What good would that do? Shall I phone Celeste?'

He shook his head. They were waiting at traffic lights and he reached out to take her hand. 'Stay with me.'

'Guy, I'll come in with you and see that you're OK and make you a hot drink. I'll phone you in the morning.'

He understood she couldn't leave Newton just like that. Newton, who was a madman, a psychopath, was capable of coming round to look for her, armed probably. Besides, she probably wanted to be alone with Newton and tell him in no uncertain terms what she thought of his violent behaviour.

He said it again and this time she didn't argue. 'Have lunch with me on Saturday.'

'I always have lunch with you on Saturdays.'

That she came in with him as she had promised nevertheless surprised him. 'Your lovely house,' she said. 'It's the nicest house I know.'

'Is it? It'll be yours one day.'

He waited for the denial but it didn't come. 'I can't remember where the kitchen is.'

'You don't need the kitchen. I don't want a drink, not that sort anyway. You shall sit down, my darling, and I'll make you a drink. Something strong, you need it after all that hassle.'

'I'm driving,' she said. 'Remember?'

'Oh, come on. No one's going to breathalyse you.'

She took the glass from him, poured soda water into it. He was impeded by his disabled left arm. Something from the past evening came back to him. Perhaps it was the sight of the television set in the corner that he hardly ever switched on. He poured his brandy, a generous measure.

'Haven't you got an uncle in television? Something with the BBC? Haven't I met him?'

She nodded. 'My father's brother, my uncle Michael. He's the chairman of TVEA. Why?'

'I suppose it was through him Newton got this job?'

'Of course it wasn't, Guy. It had nothing to do with it. William's going to work for BBC Northwest. He *told* you.'

'It all comes to the same thing, though, doesn't it? Back-scratching. What's the word? Begins with an n.'

'Nepotism. Only it isn't. Guy, are you all right to be left? I ought to go.'

'Where shall we have lunch on Saturday?'

'Anywhere you like.'

'D'you know, I thought for a while in the car that you might say you wouldn't have lunch with me, you might be too cross.'

She smiled, got up. 'Well, now you know. I'm not. Too cross, I mean.'

'Clarke's again?' he said.

'Could it be – well, more central? Didn't we once go to a nice fish place in the Haymarket?'

'The Café Fish in Panton Street.'

'That's right. One o'clock? Guy. . . ?' She took his hand. They walked out into the hall together. He stood inside the front door looking at her, his left arm still supported in her red and black silk scarf. 'Guy – I don't know how to say this.' She was trembling. The light in the hall was dim but he could see she had gone pale. Her eyes glittered. 'I want to – could we spend the day together on Saturday? I mean, could we have lunch and be together for the rest of the day? Maybe go to the theatre or the cinema, have dinner – oh, I don't know. I'd just like to – but your poor arm! Perhaps you won't feel like . . .'

'Oh, darling!' He put his good arm round her. She nestled against him. 'I wouldn't have minded if he'd cut off my arm if this is the result. Don't you know by now you don't have to ask if we can spend the day together? Don't you know it's what I long for?'

'That's all right, then.' She put up her face.

He kissed her as he hadn't kissed her for years, not even that time by the Embankment Gardens. Her warm responsive lips opened under his. He felt her breasts press against him. His heart knocked and made his hurt arm throb. The strangest thing of all was that he was the first to draw back, to pull away. He had to because of the pain where her body crushed against his wound. She wasn't smiling but gazing at him with a curious, half-hypnotised concentration.

'I must go,' she said at last.

'You said you'd phone me in the morning.'

'Of course I will.'

He stood watching the car turn on the cobbles. The night was chilly, very clear. For once, as very seldom happened, stars could be seen up there in the radiant purple, swimming points of light. She waved from the open car window, rolled it up, disappeared rather quickly. It was almost midnight. He went indoors and drank some more brandy until he began to feel light-headed and his arm no longer hurt.

# CHAPTER
# EIGHTEEN

He overslept. He had been dreaming he was going to be married. It was Leonora he was going to be married to and in church, or he thought it was, he couldn't be entirely sure. He arrived at St Mary Abbots in a taxi and hurried into the church alone. He was late and the guests, hundreds of them, were already there. Breathless, he arrived at the chancel steps, only to realise he had forgotten the ring. He stood, wondering what to do, while behind him a swell of giggling arose from the congregation. It gathered force and became a long sustained roar of laughter. Guy looked down and saw he was dressed in the costume of a fencer, the tight jacket, gloves, breeches and white stockings. For the first time he was aware he had a mask on his face.

The phone ringing pulled him out of this dream before worse humiliation could happen. He reached for the phone and, turning over, felt pain from his sore arm. Memory of the previous evening returned as he lifted the receiver, and with it came a surge of panic. What had he done? He said a cautious, 'Hallo?'

'How are you this morning, Guy?'

He could hardly believe it was Leonora's voice he was hearing. How long was it since last she had phoned him? Years. But, of course, things had changed. He remembered more about the night before. Almost incredulously, he began remembering what she had said.

'Guy? Are you all right?'

'I'm fine, darling. I'm perfectly OK.'

'Did you get some sleep?'

'Like a log. I died. As a matter of fact, the phone ringing woke me.'

'Oh, I'm sorry. I did wait till nine. I was anxious about you.'

He closed his eyes at the bliss of it. He said softly, 'It's wonderful to hear your voice.'

'Do you think you should go and see your own doctor today?'

'Why? Everything's been done that can be. It's only a bit sore.' Downstairs he heard Fatima let herself in and the front door close. 'It really *is* nine. Listen, Leo, did I dream it or did you say you'd spend all Saturday with me?'

'You didn't dream it.'

'Thank God. I've had such strange dreams I don't know what's real and what isn't. If I get tickets for a show what would you like to see?' He remembered too late that she didn't like that word 'show' but preferred 'play' and he waited for her to correct him. She only said,

'I don't mind. You choose.'

'I know you don't like musicals. I won't get a musical. Leo?'

'Yes, Guy?'

'Afterwards, in the evening, will you come back here with me?'

He knew she would say no. She always did. Her hesitation meant nothing, only that she was looking for the kindest way to say no. One day she would say yes but he wasn't absurdly optimistic, he knew it would be a long time. He waited stoically. The pause was a long one. He heard her sigh.

'Yes, I will,' she said. 'Of course I will. Anything you say.'

'Leo, did you really say that? Did you really say you'll come back with me? You'll stay with me?'

'I did say that.'

'Leo, I'm so happy. I'm so happy, darling. I know I've said it before. I can't help it. I'm so happy. Leo, you're not crying?'

'Guy,' she said, 'forgive me.'

That made him laugh. 'There's nothing to forgive. Say you love me. Say I'm the only one for you.'

'You're the only one for me. I love you. One o'clock on Saturday, then?'

'One o'clock on Saturday, darling. Goodbye till then. Take care, save yourself for me.'

It had happened. She had come back to him. Not a promise of next year, not years ahead, but now, the day after tomorrow. He could confess to himself now that he had doubted, he had sometimes lost hope, but the constancy, the struggle, had not been in vain. He had won her. He had fought for her and he had won. The battle scar on his arm he looked at with pride. If he had lost his arm it would have been worth it.

*  *  *  *

When he had had a bath, for showers must be avoided for the time being with that arm, he wondered if it would be wise to keep the sling on. No blood had come through the dressing. His arm was sore but no more than that. Slyly, he saw through his own doubts about the sling. What he really meant was that he wanted to go on wearing Leonora's scarf. Wasn't that what knights of old did – well, they did in movies – wore their ladies' favours? Susannah had called him Leonora's knight, had said his constancy was beautiful.

The scarf Leonora had given him was a silky woven red and black thing. He dressed carefully in blue jeans, a pink shirt, a sweater he hardly ever wore but was coincidentally very much like the scarf, a ribbed pattern in vertical stripes of dark grey and Venetian red. Guy found himself looking into the mirror for longer than he usually did. He was so much better looking than William Newton, so superior a physical specimen, that it was almost a joke.

What he would have liked to do was spend the morning at the rifle club but that would only make his arm worse. He started phoning theatre box offices. Andrew Lloyd Webber's *Aspects of Love* was what he would have preferred. The price of tickets in the black market would be astronomical but that never bothered him. Leonora didn't like musicals, so that was out. Celeste had told him what *M. Butterfly* was about and he thought he might have enjoyed seeing it with her, but it wasn't the kind of thing you could take the woman you were going to marry to see. In the end he settled for Ayckbourn's *Henceforward* and booked two seats on his American Express Gold Card in the third row of the stalls.

Next day Celeste phoned to remind him they were dining with Danilo and Tanya and some American friends of theirs who were in London. Guy considered refusing on the grounds of his injured arm but thought better of it. It would pass the time until tomorrow. The dinner party was at the Connaught. The obvious thing would have been to call for Celeste in a taxi. He decided instead on the Jaguar. The idea appealed to him of driving it one-armed. He was going to tell everyone the truth, that he had got his wound in a duel.

'You're kidding,' Danilo said.

The Americans looked to Guy like a couple of gangsters. They were both short, dark, Italianate, showily dressed. One of them had a scar on his cheek the circular shape of the broken-off base of a wine bottle. Tanya was up to her old trick of forgetting to change her shoes and was wearing white sandals with her smart black minidress and black tights. She gave one of the Americans a wink.

'Someone got fresh with Celeste, did they?'

'It had nothing to do with Celeste,' Guy saw her wince, though he had already explained everything to her in the Jaguar on their way there. 'A private matter.'

'Be honest,' said Danilo the abstemious. 'You did it yourself when you were pissed.'

It wasn't a very successful party. Tanya talked about her children. The Americans responded as if children were a rare species of mammal and one in which they were uninterested.

This didn't deter Tanya who told anecdotes about Carlo putting red dye into the swimming pool and telling her the gardener had cut his throat before falling in. Guy drank a lot. He moved on to brandy. He had promised Celeste they would leave by ten-thirty at the latest. She had to be at a photo call in Kensington Gardens before eight in the morning. When it got to ten forty-five she said she had to go.

'Just half an hour and I'll be with you.'

'No, Guy. It's all right, I'll get a taxi.'

'I'm not letting you do that.' He struggled to his feet and suppressed a cry at the pain in his arm. 'I'll drive you like I said.'

'You're not fit to drive and I really have to go. I've already asked them to get me a taxi.'

He was aware of only one thing. This way he wouldn't have to have her back to spend the night with him. Her hand rested lightly on his shoulder. 'I'll see you tomorrow night,' she said.

They must have made some arrangement. He would phone tomorrow morning and stop her, he couldn't come out with it in front of everyone. Feeling guilty, feeling obscurely ashamed, he touched the lightly resting hand. She said goodbye and was gone.

'Nice little looker,' said one of the Americans unbelievably.

Guy thought how extremely embarrassing it would be to take Leonora home with him and find Celeste there. Or for poor Celeste to arrive while he and Leonora were there together. He must give some serious thought to explaining to Celeste the turn events had taken.

'We'll drive you home,' said Tanya. 'I mean, we'll drive your car. We came in a cab, so we can take you home and get a taxi to take us on.'

Danilo didn't say anything. His frog face was set in grim lines. Guy couldn't remember where he had parked the car and they trudged through the dark, empty Mayfair streets, looking for it.

'I'm going to love you if they've clamped it,' said Tanya.

They hadn't. Guy got in the back. The fresh autumnal air had brought him round. It was nearly midnight, nearly the day that would mark the beginning of his life with Leonora. What would Danilo and Tanya have to say to that?

He could have driven himself. He felt perfectly all right apart from his aching arm. They were driving along Knightsbridge when he remembered about Rachel Lingard. Tanya knew all about Danilo's activities – or as far as he knew she did.

'Can you put a stop on Chuck, Dan?'

'Can I *what*?'

'Just call it off, will you?'

Danilo was silent. Guy could tell he was upset. He went the wrong way and got them into the Fulham Road. With a little shrug Tanya said, 'Don't mind me. I've had to learn when to shut my ears.'

'Turn right when you can,' Guy said. 'Look, I'm sorry. I don't want the three grand back.'

'I should fucking think not,' said Danilo.

'But you can do it?'

'Ah, shit, Guy, I can live without this.'

'But you can manage it?'

'Frankly, I don't know. I don't know who Chuck's put on the job and Chuck's been in Ireland. Maybe he's still in Ireland. I don't even know if Chuck's boy's doing it or Chuck's boy's boy.'

Danilo turned left along the Old Brompton Road. Guy said, 'You've got a whole week. Well, a week tomorrow. She's away for another week.' He was suddenly aware of where they were and what they might see.

Danilo said in a bad-tempered way, 'Yeah, yeah, OK. It'll take time but maybe not that long. Only don't reckon on doing that kind of business with me again, right? Christ, what is it now?'

Guy was tapping on his shoulder. 'Please stop, will you? Just for a minute. Just park over there. It won't take long, I promise.'

'What is all this, Guy?' Tanya was losing patience with him now. 'I have to be in the shop tomorrow morning.'

'Please pull in over there, Danilo.'

They had to walk back. The tall thin man lay stretched out on

211

the doorstep of the health-food shop. He was dressed in the same soot-coloured rags but this time he lay on his back with the cap, which had been a receptacle for alms, covering his face. Guy said, 'It's Linus.'

'You're joking.'

'No, I'm sure it is. This is the third time I've seen him. I know it's Linus. It's been worrying me, on my conscience, you know. Dan, we can't just leave him here. We'll have to do something for him.'

Danilo went across the pavement, took hold of the cap and lifted it from the man's face. It woke him. He sat up and began screaming at them, his face contorted, his bright white perfect teeth bared. A stream of meaningless obscenity poured from him.

'Ah, for Christ's sake,' said Danilo. He stuck up two fingers at the screaming man.

Guy could see now that it wasn't Linus. It was no more like Linus than he was like Danilo. 'At least give him something.'

'Give him something yourself,' said Danilo and he walked back to the car, followed by Tanya.

Guy felt deeply disturbed. What was going on in his mind that he had confused this derelict with his old friend? He gave the man a tenner which had the effect of shutting him up but not of eliciting thanks. He took the note, thrust it into his trouser pocket and rolled back on to the doorstep, once more covering his face.

'Linus is dead,' Danilo said when he was putting the Jaguar away in Guy's garage. 'They strung him up in Kuala Lumpur. Have you ever thought of joining the AA?'

'I've been a member for years.'

'Danny didn't mean the Automobile Association,' said Tanya, by this time laughing helplessly. They went off together to find a taxi.

* * * *

He would drink less when he was with Leonora all the time. If she wanted him to give up smoking he would have a go at that too. In a month's time he would be thirty and it wouldn't be very many more years before he'd be unable to hold the drink like he could now. When he was happy all the time, leading a contented life, he wouldn't need the drink to cushion him against blows, he wouldn't need his consciousness changed from misery to limbo.

He felt none the worse for the excesses of the night before and his arm was much better. The sling wouldn't be needed any more but he wanted to wear it because it was hers. Sentimentally, he thought of wearing her scarf today for the last time and then, when she was back here with him, returning it to her ceremoniously. She would smile her Vivien Leigh smile for him and at last it would be full and unrestrained.

What to wear this morning was something of a problem. Although he knew she had never been that keen on Newton, he had been procured for her and she persuaded to take him, there was something about the man that appealed to her apart from his conversation. And Newton always dressed in clothes that were a combination of the Housing Trust charity shop and Dirty Dick's. It had to be faced that nice clothes didn't interest her, either for herself or her man. Perhaps he should start learning to care less about them himself. With that end in view he chose the jeans he had worn the day before, a plain blue shirt in sea island cotton and a blue-and-grey striped seersucker jacket. It still looked over the top or would to her. Changing the jacket for yesterday's sweater was a real sacrifice for him, but he made it. Carefully, he reknotted the ends of the scarf and arranged it around his neck to support his arm.

He was on the point of leaving when he remembered the ring. He still had the engagement ring he had bought for Leonora all those years ago. It was in the safe. He hadn't used the safe, hadn't opened it, for four years, there had been no need to do so. The last time had been after Con Mulvanney's visit. He went back upstairs, opened the safe and took out the ring. It was in a small blue leather box and the ring itself, a large square-cut sapphire with 'shoulders' of diamonds, sat in a bed of midnight-blue velvet. Guy put ring and box into his pocket.

It was twelve when he left the house, much too soon for an

appointment in the West End at one. But he had nothing to do. He had already made a careful tour of the house, checking that everything was as it should be to receive her. He had refilled the ice trays in the fridges in the kitchen and the drawing-room bar, arranged on the coffee table the *Guardian*, *The London Review of Books* and *Cosmopolitan* which, wonder of wonders, the newsagent had remembered to deliver, and put into the bathroom which would be *her* bathroom, the various Paloma Picasso toiletries he had yesterday sent Fatima out to buy. There was nothing left to do and sitting about reading the paper was intolerable. He had made several attempts to phone Celeste and stop her from coming before he remembered she was out being photographed somewhere. At twelve he left to walk part of the way, stopped to look in an estate agent's window and on an impulse went inside.

On their books they had a beautiful house in Lansdowne Crescent, Notting Hill. The price, they said, ran into seven figures. When they saw he didn't flinch they told him precisely what the price was. Photographs of interiors were produced, a grand staircase, swan-neck-shaped, a magnificent drawing room forty feet long, octagonal bathrooms in each of the turrets. Guy made an appointment to view for Monday afternoon. By now it was twenty minutes to one, nice time to get there punctually in a cab.

The traffic was less dense than usual and the taxi put him down outside the Café Fish. It was two minutes to one. She might be there already, it had been known, and those familiar sensations repeated themselves, the little jump his heart gave, his insides tightening, pressure in his head. He paused on the pavement for a moment, gathered himself, went into the restaurant.

It was crowded but she wasn't there yet. The girl who came to show him to his table told him that. Smoking or non-smoking? One day he would choose non-smoking to please Leonora but that time hadn't come yet. He lit a cigarette the moment he was sitting down.

Obviously it was a mistake to come here. The food was good and there was a big choice but unfortunately a hundred other people knew it too. Of necessity the tables were close together. They wouldn't be able to talk intimately. Guy flicked his fingers at a waiter and when the man came over ordered a large gin and tonic. Brandy would have suited him better but he also realised brandy might not be a good idea at this stage.

With careful thought, he had chosen his theatre tickets for the matinee. The performance began at five-thirty which meant they could have dinner soon after eight. There was plenty of time for everything – it would all be leisurely and beautiful. If there was any time left this afternoon between leaving here and the theatre, she would surely let him take her shopping. The engagement ring he already had, but perhaps a bracelet? Cartier? Asprey? Or perhaps some earrings. He imagined diamonds close up against her glowing face. When they were no more than children and she had first had her ears pierced, he had dreamed of the day when he could buy her diamond earrings.

The gin came, it was very welcome, he was thirsty for it. The first sip of the day was always wonderful. It spread peace through his body on long divergent feelers. He sat back in his seat, looking at the pattern in the weave of her scarf, then at the menu which was written on the card as well as up in chalk on blackboards. What would she have? She was eating more fish lately, he had been glad to see. She didn't get enough protein. He adjusted the sling on his arm and in doing so caught sight of his watch. It was nearly a quarter past one.

That was what came of trusting to the Northern Line instead of taking cabs. It was going to be the Savoy experience all over again, but in less luxurious surroundings. He finished his gin and ordered another. She had been over twenty minutes late, he remembered, for their lunch at the Savoy. It would be just like her to walk here from wherever the nearest Northern Line station was, Leicester Square probably.

The people at the next table, four of them, were laughing immoderately. It wasn't coarse laughter or particularly raucous, but it irritated him. His second gin went down very fast. If only you could ask for the bottle in these places and just help yourself like you could at home. He didn't quite like to ask

215

for the bottle. Danilo and Tanya's remarks of the previous evening about Alcoholics Anonymous repeated themselves unpleasantly. The time was twenty-five past one. A waiter came up and asked him if he would like to order. Guy said, 'No,' rather abruptly. More gales of laughter shook the table next door. They were drinking champagne, evidently celebrating some anniversary. He had begun to feel hungry in the taxi going round Hyde Park Corner but his hunger had left him. In spite of the gin his mouth was dry. He asked for a large glass of white wine.

At twenty to two he began to feel sick. She was forty minutes late. He couldn't remember her ever having been more than twenty-two minutes late. She wasn't coming. He couldn't delude himself any longer that she was coming. Either something terrible had happened and she had met with an accident or she had been prevented from coming. Some member of that awful family of hers had found out what she planned to do, to spend the day, then the rest of her life with him, and had stepped in to stop it. For another ten minutes he sat on, staring at the street door. Then he got up.

He told the imperturbable sullen-faced waiter he didn't want anything to eat after all, a remark to which the response was a Gallic shrug. He paid for his two gins and his wine. Luckily and for once he had a pocketful of small change. In the first empty phone box that he found he dialled the Georgiana Street number. It was years since Guy had used a phone box, they had changed in the interim and he had to read the instructions carefully before getting it to work. The ringing began but there was no answer. He dialled again to make sure. Still no answer. He closed his eyes and imagined opening them to see her walking down the street towards the restaurant, running rather because she was in a panic at being late.

Of course she wasn't there. He scooped out the money that had come back and dialled Lamb's Conduit Street. All these numbers were stamped on his memory. He knew them better than his own phone number, bank account number. The bell rang and rang but no one was answering there either. There was no reply when he dialled the St Leonard's Terrace number and none from Portland Road, though that was a long shot, unless one of them had somehow contrived to imprison Leonora in her former home. The last place he tried was the Mandevilles' house in Sanderstead Lane and he tried in vain.

They couldn't *all* be out. It was plain what was happening. They had ganged up to stand solid against him. They were all refusing to answer their phones. She had told them what had happened on Thursday night, told them in all innocence, still believing she could make her own choice as to her future life. Somewhere she had been made a prisoner. No doubt it was principally her father who had done that, her father who, once his wife had poisoned Leonora's mind against her lover, had produced a husband for her, a tame lackey, an ugly egghead, and then to make absolutely sure, with his brother's help, found him a job up north where his wife would accompany him.

Only it wasn't going to happen that way, Guy thought. Where would they keep her? Portland Road or Georgiana Street? He went back to Scarsdale Mews in a cab. Although he had drunk quite a lot and eaten nothing, he felt clear-headed and very calm.

At home he tried phoning again. Methodically he tried each number: Lamb's Conduit Street, Sanderstead Lane, St Leonard's Terrace, Georgiana Street, Portland Road. Again there was no answer from any of them. He imagined all the phones unplugged or those people, Anthony and Susannah, Tessa and Magnus, Robin and Maeve, Newton himself, sitting there listening implacably to the continuous ringing. The time was two forty-five.

He tried all the numbers again, to unnerve them, to make them jumpy. Then he went upstairs and took his .22 rifle from its case.

# CHAPTER
# NINETEEN

On the way to Portland Road he tried to find an explanation. At last he thought he could understand. It was the duel he had fought with Newton which was responsible for all this. The last straw, her family would call it. He couldn't imagine Leonora telling them about it but Newton would have. While Leonora was out taking him to the hospital Newton would have been on the phone to her father and then her mother with an account of what had happened. He could hear Tessa's voice:

'He's mad, of course. He's a violent dangerous madman. He'll stop at nothing to get Leonora. The only thing is to keep her away from him until the sixteenth and then you can take her up north and he'll never see her again.'

And Anthony Chisholm:

'He attacked you with a sword? That's a bit much, isn't it? No, I quite agree, it won't do for Leonora to see him again.'

And Magnus Mandeville:

'Leonora should have gone for the police. Of course you couldn't have left her alone with him, I quite see that. But you should have made *her* go. That was assault, you know, it might even be called attempted murder.'

And Susannah:

'Poor Guy, he's so emotional, so *violent*. But there's such a lot of good in him too. He's really bad for Leonora, the last person for her. If there's no other way – well, it's very regrettable, but she'll have to be kept away from him by force.'

He double-parked the car, hoping that as it was Saturday afternoon it would be all right. The rifle was in the boot in a black leather golf bag. He was already coming to see it as an awkward sort of weapon to carry on a mission of this kind. Leaving it where it was, he went up the steps and rang the bell which was still marked: Lingard, Kirkland, Chisholm. No one answered. He wasn't surprised.

His arm felt fine if he didn't move it much, and with automatic transmission there was no need to. He rested it lightly on the wheel. The traffic had thickened up since the morning and it took a long time getting to Camden Town. This time he took the rifle in the golf bag with him. After he had rung the bell and was standing there waiting, he had the sensation of someone looking down on him from above. It was very strong, this sense of being watched. He stepped back, went down a stair or two and looked up. No one was there and all the windows were closed, though it was a mild afternoon.

Lamb's Conduit Street next. That wasn't so far away. A parking space was empty directly outside the house. Susannah's window boxes had just been watered. Water was dripping from them onto the flagstones below. That told him they must be in, someone must be. No one answered the entry-phone. He pressed the bell again and heard footsteps on the stairs. A woman Guy had never seen before opened the door. He didn't know her but even before she spoke he sensed that she had been expecting him.

'Laura Stow,' she said. 'I'm Susannah's sister.'

He could see the likeness. She was a bit older, dressed in jeans and a shirt, a towel twisted turbanwise round her head. She had been washing her hair. He hadn't known Susannah had a sister but he wasn't surprised. Did they have any *friends*, these people? Did they know anyone who wasn't family? Everyone you met at their houses, everyone you were introduced to, was a relation.

He said bluntly, 'Guy Curran.'

She nodded, looked at the golf bag in his hand. Anyone with a grain of intelligence could see it was a rifle in there or a shotgun.

'I'm looking for Leonora,' and then, 'You do know who I mean?'

'Yes, of course I do. She isn't here. No one's here but me. I'm looking after the house while they're away.'

'Away?' he said.

'On holiday. They've gone away on holiday today.' She was patient with him but her eyes went to the golf bag again. 'I'm sorry but I'm afraid I can't help you.'

It was rehearsed. Someone had prepared her for his visit, taught her to say all this. 'Are you sure she's not here? Are you quite sure she's not upstairs somewhere?'

For a moment he thought he had frightened her. She had retreated a little. He made his voice gentler, he tried to smile. 'Do you think I could come in and – well, look? I'm an old friend of the family.'

'Look for *Leonora*? I've told you she's not here. Of course I can't let you in.'

'I'm going to marry Leonora,' he said patiently.

She stared, a nervous smile now trembling on her mouth.

He shouted in the direction of the stairs, 'Leonora! Leo! Are you there? Leonora!'

She made an incoherent sound and shut the door in his face. Without being able to see, he sensed she was leaning back against the door, gasping.

He hadn't really believed Leonora was in there. She would have come down long before. Even he couldn't believe she was actually imprisoned, tied up, locked in a room. They wouldn't do that – or would they? He imagined this Laura Stow getting on the phone at once to Anthony and Susannah in their holiday hotel. She would probably phone them all to report his visit.

Perhaps she'd make her first call to Robin and Maeve at whose flat it now seemed Leonora was most likely to be.

He drove home, left the car in the mews and went upstairs to replace the rifle in its case. It was an unwise choice, that cumbersome weapon. The time was five-thirty.

His hunger had come back. There was never much food in the house, no more usually than the basic materials for breakfast: bread, various cereals, eggs, Dutch cheese, marmalade, orange juice. Having poured himself a vodka and filled the glass with orange juice, he wondered if he knew how to cook an egg but decided against it. He had some bread and Gouda, finished his drink and dialled the St Leonard's Terrace number.

They still weren't answering. They were still letting the phone ring. Guy cut himself more bread, poured more vodka. He dialled in vain Sanderstead Lane, Georgiana Street, and – out of devilment, as he told himself – Lamb's Conduit Street. Laura Stow answered. She sounded nervous. He laughed in a sinister way and she slammed the phone down. By now he was feeling enormously better. To say he felt fighting fit, in spite of his arm, wouldn't be an exaggeration. A challenge had been made to him. It was as if they had thrown down a glove in front of him and dared him to fight them all.

He was suddenly involved in a savage fairy story or cloak-and-dagger adventure. The beautiful princess had been imprisoned in a tower by her cruel father and stepmother. Marry the ginger dwarf or stay there for ever! But her rescuer was coming, in his armour and with his weapons, if not on a white horse, in a golden car.

He went back upstairs and took out of the wardrobe the new handsome jacket in battleship-grey calfskin he had bought from Beltrami in Florence last May. He changed his shoes for grey leather half-boots. Reluctantly he took off the sling, but he hardly needed it any more. There was no reason why he shouldn't wear the scarf wound round his neck.

In the third bedroom, one of the two at the back which looked on to the back of houses in Abingdon Villas, he went to the bureau which stood against the rear wall between the windows. From the top drawer he took the heavy Colt .45 which had been in his possession since he was seventeen but which he had never used.

* * * *

Danilo had got that gun for him. It was while he was protecting the shopkeepers of Kensal. He had let it be known discreetly that he would like to possess a real gun instead of the convincing-looking replica he carried about with him. Danilo brought it into the pub in Artesian Road one night, showed it to him in the men's and by the time Danilo had pulled the flush, Guy had paid cash for it and the ammunition that came with it. Leonora had seen it and called it a ghastly weapon. He saw what she meant.

He hadn't a holster for it. That had seemed unnecessary. He put in on the passenger seat of the Jaguar with his leather jacket on top of it.

The evening was growing cold. It was already dusk. For the first time in months he was using the car heater. He lit a cigarette. It took no more than ten minutes to reach St Leonard's Terrace. Guy couldn't remember if he had actually ever been in this street before but now he was here he was impressed. Robin was evidently doing better for himself than the rest of the family with their shabby duplexes in Bloomsbury and their suburban villas. The flat was in an elegant but substantial house, its architecture classical, with a noble dark blue front door set under a portico whose domed roof was supported by Corinthian columns. Guy wouldn't have minded living there himself.

The framed card above the bell was printed: Ms M. Kirkland, R. H. Chisholm. Very formal. The flat he thought must be theirs had a huge bow window. He had put on his jacket and stuck the gun in the right-hand pocket which luckily was large. No one replied on the entryphone when he rang the bell. Guy tried again and then once more. He was coming down the shallow steps when he saw Robin and Maeve approaching from the end of the street.

They were arm in arm, closer than that, somehow intertwined, her head turning onto his shoulder, and they were in high spirits, laughing, squeezing each other. But more remarkable to Guy was the way they were dressed. Gone were the jeans and twin sweatshirts, gone the socks and trainers. Maeve was in a pale pink silk suit, very low cut, the neckline plunging in a deep V, the puffed sleeves ballooning from padded shoulders, the skirt very full and very short. It revealed her long legs in white lace tights from halfway up the thighs. Her shoes were pink and high-heeled and in her left hand she carried a white cartwheel hat, covered in pink roses.

Robin wore a pale beige suit, probably wild silk. His tie had obviously just been removed. The tail of it, bronze-and-cream-patterned silk, protruded from his jacket pocket. When they saw Guy they stopped, looked at each other and burst out laughing. More rehearsing had been going on, he thought. They began to walk towards him, smiling broadly.

Guy said, 'Where is she?'

This had the effect of almost doubling Maeve up. She crowed with laughter, she clutched at Robin gasping. They were both very much the worse for drink. Robin giggled foolishly.

'Tell me where she is, please.'

Guy could feel the gun in his pocket, heavy, cold, weighing down his jacket on the right side. He rested his hand on it through the leather.

'I know you've hidden her. You've no business to do that. This is a free country. You can't keep people prisoner against their will.'

They made their way up the steps to the front door. Robin had his key out. They were still laughing. Maeve actually had tears on her face. Guy could see Robin smiling at her indulgently, amused in spite of himself by her amusement, trying in vain to achieve a straight face. He let out a final apparently irrepressible burst of shrill laughter, the neigh of a skittish horse, got his key into the lock, said to Maeve,

'Go in, go in, for God's sake. You're making me worse. Every time I look at you it starts me off.'

Guy was very cold. The adventure story he had been living

223

in for the past half-hour began to dissolve, to melt and flow away. They were real people in a real street and this was reality. He would have liked to take out the gun and shoot them both, there on the steps. He would have loved to do that. If he did, he thought, he would never see Leonora again. That stopped him.

'Where is she?' he said again.

Robin, who had stopped laughing now Maeve was inside the house, said like a little boy, 'You'll have to ask Mummy.'

'I'll *what*?'

Growing up suddenly, Robin drawled, 'That's what we agreed on. If you turned up, I mean. We decided my mother was the one to tell you. Right?'

He went into the house and shut the door.

* * * *

By the time Guy crossed the river it was dark. He chain-smoked as he drove. A drink was what he would have loved but the drink must wait. He had his leather jacket on with the Colt .45 in the pocket and Leonora's scarf wound round his neck. It smelt very slightly of her scent.

At the northern end of Sanderstead Lane he stopped, parked the car and loaded his gun. The streetlamps were alight, smoky yellow globes, some half-buried in the thick dark foliage of the trees with which this long street was lined. The surface of the roadway gleamed. No cars were parked along it. All the houses had garages. No one was about, no dog walkers, no girls walking quickly and fearfully on their way to an evening date. A car passed, then another. The place was silent, still, and colder than inner London.

He drove on to the Mandevilles' house. There it lay at the back of its long front garden and it was ablaze with light. There were lights on in the bedrooms as well as downstairs, but Guy had no sense that the house was full of people, that for instance a party might be in progress. The house looked all the more incongruous because the one next to it, the unoccupied one joined on to it, was in total darkness. Not another car was in sight. No shadow moved against the light behind the drawn but transparent curtains. Yet he had the feeling that he was expected, they were waiting for him.

No doubt Robin had phoned his mother and she was prepared. She and Magnus were prepared. Perhaps she had also roped in a bodyguard. He felt the gun in his pocket, patted it like a patrolman in a film. The iron gate clanging shut made a loud clear ringing sound in the quiet. He began to walk up the path. The lighted house seemed to be looking at him.

He wasn't to have the chance of getting all the way there, of ringing the bell or using that lion's-head knocker. When he was halfway there, when he had just passed the point of no return, Tessa Mandeville opened the front door. She stood looking at him, silent, unsmiling, apparently unafraid.

'Where is she?'

Maeve had said that would be on his tombstone. Maybe. Perhaps it would be the last thing he ever said, his dying words. He didn't care. It was all he wanted to say. He repeated it.

'Where is she?'

'You can come in,' Tessa said. Her tone was remote. She seldom used his Christian name, she hardly ever had. 'Come in, please. We may as well get it over.'

Magnus was behind her. Tessa was as elaborately dressed as Maeve had been, in a copper-coloured close-fitting dress with a scroll pattern at neck and hem in bronze and gold beads. Her wrinkled neck with the prominent tendons was hidden under ropes of amber beads. But Magnus was in a pair of old serge trousers and a grey jersey as if stripped for action. For all that he had the transparent fragile look of a grasshopper.

They went into an airless overfurnished living room. It was intensely hot. Two huge vases held bouquets of flowers which were wilting in the heat.

'You'd better sit down.'

'I prefer to stand,' Guy said.

'Just as you like. You asked me where Leonora is.' Tessa looked at her watch in an overacted, ponderous way. She raised her eyes to his. 'As of this moment I imagine they're twenty thousand feet over northern France. Leonora got married at one o'clock today.'

# CHAPTER
# TWENTY

The flowers in the two vases seemed to be wilting visibly. They were pale, exotic, full-petalled. Guy could see they were wedding flowers, formerly bouquets or table decorations. His head swam. Although he had said he wouldn't sit down, he did so. The scent from the flowers was sweet and stale, there was something obscene about it. It was like perfume on an unwashed body.

Tessa said, 'That's my daughter's scarf you're wearing!'

'She gave it to me.'

He was aware that his voice sounded weak, barely under control. He cleared his throat and said it again. 'She gave it to me.'

'I suppose you've come here for an explanation.'

Tessa had seated herself opposite him on a sofa whose chintz cover was patterned with flowers curiously like those in the vases, pale pinkish, whitish, pallid lilac and peach-coloured blown roses. She was a little, sharply cut figure, sitting upright with her hands clasped about her knees. Because of the bright brown of her dress and the gloss on the material, her dark hair shiny and her skin walnut colour, she looked as if cast in metal or carved from wood. Her eyes were very bright, sparkling with satisfaction, with triumph. Guy had taken too hard a knock, been too bludgeoned by it, to stand up to her and fight. His energy had gone and he could feel pressure inside his head. A chill, in spite of the heat of the room, drew his skin into gooseflesh. Hovering nervously, with a kind of ghoulishness, Magnus must have seen this, for he said hastily,

'Would you like a drink?'

Guy shook his head. Later on he wondered if this was the first time in his life he had refused an offered drink. He summoned from somewhere a voice that approximated to his normal voice.

'Is that where you all were? At her wedding?'

'That's right,' said Tessa. 'You've got it right first time. She was married at one, then we had lunch.' She was unable to keep herself from smiling, though he could see she tried. Her lips twitched and she sat up very straight. 'We've been partying ever since. It was a lovely wedding, everyone said so. We saw them off on their way to Heathrow and Robin tied a shoe to the back of the taxi! He's so naughty, there's no stopping him. I'm sure you'll want to know where Leonora and William have gone. Greek islands – Samos, actually.'

He didn't believe her. It was to Samos that Leonora had been going with him. Tessa's eyes flickered when she told the lie. He understood she wouldn't dare tell him where they had really gone. He said desperately, though he hated showing them how terribly he had been hurt, how wounded almost to death.

'She said she was getting married on the sixteenth. She told me over and over it was the sixteenth, *you* said it was.'

Even as he spoke he understood about that wedding invitation on the mantelpiece in Lamb's Conduit Street. It *had* been to Leonora's wedding, Janice and her husband were no doubt the invitees. The true date of the wedding would have been on it, the ninth, one week earlier than they had deceived him into believing. They had rushed to remove it. If he had seen it the whole plan would have been spoiled.

'Why did she tell me the sixteenth?'

Tessa was smiling now, an arch smile with her eyebrows up. He had never seen her look like that before.

'Why did she say she'd meet me for lunch as usual today?'

The rest of the promises she had made he couldn't bear to utter. Tessa's face had relaxed a little. He sensed, with a kind of shame, that his feeble voice had touched her, that she, savagely triumphant though she was, had begun to *pity* him.

'You have to try putting yourself in our position. Try to think of others for once. My daughter was very seriously worried that if you knew the date of her wedding you'd go to it and make trouble. I mean, she *knows* you. We all know you. We know what you're capable of. Look what happened last week when you got drunk and started fighting William. With *swords*. I mean, it's unbelievable. Fighting someone with swords in this day and age. You're capable of going to a wedding and breaking the place up. You might have forced your way in and shouted to the registrar to stop it – anything. You might have done anything. My daughter has been *afraid* of you for literally years. She's been living in a nightmare of terror about what you'd do next.'

By a subtle rearrangement of hope and inhibition, Leonora had become 'my daughter'. Guy sensed Tessa would never again refer to her by her name when speaking to him.

Magnus said in his mild dry way. 'That is why, if my advice had been taken, we would have sought legal means to prevent you from annoying my stepdaughter. No doubt, it would have been an unpleasant step to take initially but in the long term it would have saved a great deal of trouble and distress.'

Guy lifted his eyes, which felt heavy as if full of unsheddable tears. His eyes felt swollen. He looked at Magnus. Through the fine soft leather pocket of his jacket he could feel the uncompromising shape of the gun. But it was distanced from him, it was as if he lacked the strength not only to use it but even to lift it out of its hiding place. The numbness that comes with shock wasn't unknown to him, but it was a long time since he had felt it. 'Forgive me,' she had said on the phone yesterday morning. He understood now why she had said it. 'Forgive me.' Her voice had been thick and unsteady as his eyes were now, full of tears. 'Forgive me for the lies they've made me tell you, for deceiving you, for this ultimate terrible lie that I will meet you tomorrow and be with you for ever.'

Tessa had been speaking. Words, sentences, whole paragraphs, had flowed out of her unheard by him. He picked up a word or two here and there: 'cream silk', 'yellow roses', 'white gold'. He turned to her. Again the feeling he had was unfamiliar, a sense of agony that people are capable of such refined and calculated cruelty.

'I don't want to hear about that,' he said, and his voice was stronger. In a curious way it was a new voice, hard, clipped, stiff with contempt. I have died, he thought, and been born again differently with a new voice, a new set of values. 'I don't want to hear about that.' Anger was beginning to return and that was the same, the same old anger. 'Don't give me that rubbish, what she wore, the fucking flowers, don't give me that shit.'

'And don't you speak to my wife like that!'

'Are you going to stop me?' He felt the gun again. Magnus made a pettish sound, a 'pshah!' sound, and Guy knew he was afraid. He could have laughed if laughter had been something he was capable of. But his head felt heavy, his eyelids were heavy. 'Whose idea was this?' he said.

'I beg your pardon?' Tessa sounded very sarcastic, all superiority and Lady Muck, the short-lived pity vanished.

'I asked you whose idea it was, to con me into thinking Leonora was getting married a week later than she was. It wasn't her idea, was it? She didn't think that up.'

'What does it matter whose idea it was? I can't remember whose idea it was. It wasn't mine. I wish it had been, I wish I'd thought of something so – well, so simple and so effective. Let me tell you, my daughter may not have thought of it herself but she was extremely happy to go along with it. She jumped at the chance.'

'She was corrupted,' he said. 'All of you, you corrupted her.'

'If getting someone away from a person who's frightening them to death is corrupting them, then long live corruption.'

'Leonora wasn't frightened of me. She loved me. She asked

me to forgive her.' Guy turned to Magnus and said, 'I will have that drink, after all.'

Tessa burst into laughter. 'You're incorrigible, aren't you? You've got the devil's own nerve.' She mocked his tone, 'I will have that drink, after all.' You're not a friend of ours, you know. You're not a friend of this family. You forced your way into it God knows how many years ago and we've been trying to get rid of you ever since. You never seemed to understand, *you've no place among us, you're not our kind of person.* To be perfectly frank, no matter how much money you've made, you don't belong in our class. Basically, you're still an Irish yob, a street toughie. It'd be an insult to the working class to say you're working class, you're not, you're an erk from a slum and you always were.'

There was a tap on his shoulder and he looked up to see Magnus's death's head above him, a glass of something held out in the papery slightly tremulous hand. He hadn't been asked what he wanted. Something Magnus thought suitable (or something he'd got most of or didn't himself like) had been brought. Medicine. A remedy for shock. In fact, it was whisky, slightly diluted with water. The taste of it brought Guy the faint nausea whisky always did, then the beginnings of a surge of energy.

'The absurd thing,' Tessa was saying, 'is that you ever supposed my daughter might marry you, might be *allowed* to marry you.'

'She's of age, Tessa,' said Magnus, legal as ever. 'No doubt she could make her own choice about that. She *had* made her own choice, in point of fact.'

'No, she hadn't,' Guy said. 'Not in point of anything. Others made it for her, and that's the real point. Your wife was right when she said that about not being allowed. You lot, you Chisholms and whatever else you are, you didn't allow her to do what she wanted.'

'What utter nonsense! I honestly wish I'd made a tape recording of the things my daughter said. I honestly do. The number of times I asked her why she bothered with you and she said seeing you was the only possible way. She played

231

along for the sake of peace, for the sake of being free to do what she liked for the rest of the week, that's what she did.'

'If only she'd seen the perfectly reasonable step of applying for an injunction as feasible. . . .'

'Well, she didn't, Magnus. She didn't want to, I quote, "hurt his feelings". She was always far too soft-hearted for her own comfort. Unlike our guest here, she put others first. She would have done anything to avoid hurting him. But it doesn't matter now, it's over. She's married. And when she and William come back from – er, Samos, they're going to Samos, they're going straight up north. They won't be coming back to London. And if you imagine I'm telling you my daughter's new address you must be even more mad, disturbed, whatever they call it, than I thought.'

Guy felt for his cigarettes. They were in the pocket that the gun wasn't in. He put one in his mouth and lit it, watching her. She reacted predictably.

'I don't allow smoking in this house.'

'Too bad,' he said. 'If you want me to put it out you'll have to do it by force. D'you want to have a go? You or him?'

'It's outrageous,' she said.

'You shouldn't make rules like that if you can't enforce them.'

'Magnus,' she said, 'make him put that cigarette out.'

Magnus's reply was to produce an ashtray which he set at Guy's elbow. Guy said, 'Your ex-husband got Newton that job through his brother. Leonora as good as told me that. He introduced Newton to her and then he pulled all the strings he could to get him a job in the north.'

Tessa began a pantomime coughing. She covered her mouth, shivered a little. 'That may be. I know nothing about that. I haven't seen Michael Chisholm for years.' She put out a hand to he. husband. 'I think I'll have a drink too, darling. I notice you didn't ask me. Gin and ginger ale and why don't you have one too? Since,' she added, 'we're apparently saddled with a protracted discussion about his – well, what would you call it? Paranoia?'

'Frankly, Curran,' said Magnus, 'don't you think it's time

you left? My wife's told you a great deal more than you could reasonably have expected in the circumstances.'

'I'm not going yet. I want to know whose idea it was to set me up.'

Tessa said in a bored voice, 'I'm not sure if I follow you. How were you "Set up"?'

'Deceived, then. I was led to believe the wedding was next Saturday.' Guy hesitated, re-phrased it. 'No, I was led to believe there would be no wedding.' I love you, I'll come to you, anything you say. He remembered her kiss on the night when his arm was wounded and he touched his arm, touched the silky stuff of the scarf. If I sob when I start speaking, he thought, I will kill them both. 'Who,' he said, and his voice was steady, 'put her up to that? Who made her tell me the wedding was on the sixteenth and then make me think the wedding was off? Who was it?'

'I told you, I don't know.' Tessa took the glass her husband held out to her. She held it up as if for a toast, was going to say something, but thought better of it and drank. 'It doesn't matter who it was, we all approved.'

'She shouldn't have told him untruths,' Magnus said unexpectedly. 'I mean, if he's right about her saying she told him she wasn't marrying William, she really shouldn't have done that.'

'*What?* Whose side are you on, pray? Let me tell you, she was entirely justified in telling him anything. Anything. And if you say another word about an injunction I shall scream.'

Magnus took no notice. The creases on his face ironed themselves out a little, like screwed-up paper smoothed by painstaking fingers. He was smiling. He said, 'I recall perfectly whose idea it was. I was quite taken aback. It seemed so – well, audacious.'

His wife made an impatient gesture with her hand. 'It's quite unimportant who thought of it. The thing is that it worked and all that miserable business in the past *is* the past.' She began staring hard at Guy, looking into his eyes, into both his eyes. He could tell she wasn't in the least afraid of him, and he wondered at that. She was observing him quite coolly, even clinically, like a state torturer gauging the reactions of a victim.

For a moment he thought she would ask him briskly if he had anything to say before she started with the thumbscrew, but she didn't. 'That's it then,' she said, 'all out in the open. And now I think you should go.'

'Oh, I'm going. I don't want to stay here. Why would I?' Guy stubbed out his cigarette but left it smoking a little. He looked at Magnus. 'OK, whose idea was it?'

'Idea? You mean, who thought of that business of the wedding date? There ought to be a name for the relationship. I ought to be able to say something like my 'stepwife' but that wouldn't quite do, would it? I'm simply obliged to call her by her name, that is Mrs Chisholm, Susannah Chisholm.'

The man enjoyed saying all that, Guy thought disgustedly. He enjoyed spitting out all that pedantic rubbish. Then he realised what the man had said. 'Susannah thought of it?'

'We were at some family gathering. Very civilised. It couldn't have happened when I was young, ex-husbands and ex-wives all matey together. But it's very pleasant, I'm not complaining. Mrs Chisholm – that is, Susannah – came out with it. It certainly appealed to my wife, didn't it, darling?'

'Yes, it did. Of course it did. I was thrilled.' Tessa, who had said she couldn't remember, now seemed to have acquired total recall. 'I was tremendously grateful to Susannah. I was only too happy to help work out the details. I played my part in it, don't you remember? I'm sure you remember my coming to that house of yours and making a point of telling you the wedding was on the sixteenth. If I'd had my way you'd have been sent an *official invitation for the sixteenth*.'

Her husband nodded. He nodded and nodded like one of those wobble-headed dogs drivers have in the rear windows of cars. 'Leonora didn't care for it, though. Wouldn't do it at first. She said it was wrong, but I said to her, there's nothing illegal in telling a white lie.'

'I don't remember that, Magnus. I think you dreamed that up.' She coughed again, reached over and with a shudder ground out Guy's cigarette end. 'It was wonderful for Leonora, it took away all her worries.'

'Needs must when the devil drives,' said Magnus, his eyes

gleaming, leaving little doubt as to whom he meant by the
devil.

Guy got up, patting his pocket where the gun was. Tessa's
eyes followed his hand. The telephone was beside her on a low
table, within easy reach. He had no sword to cut the wires.
With his wounded arm, he lacked the strength to pull them out
of the wall. He wouldn't have wanted to anyway, but he put
his hand into his pocket and felt the smooth cold metal.

'Where have they gone?'

'Where have who gone?' Tessa had got up too.

'Anthony and Susannah. They've gone away on holiday.' Or
was that a lie too, put about by the sister? 'I was told they were
away.'

'Only for a few days. I wouldn't dream of telling you where. It's
been quite bad enough our having to put up with this interrogation, but I took that on myself. I volunteered. I said to send you
here and I'd be the one to face you. That was to save the others. I
felt it was the least I could do, so you can be sure I'm not going to
drop poor Anthony and Susannah into it at this stage. Anyway,
they can't tell you any more than I've told you.'

He felt the gun and thought again of killing them. If he did
that he would spoil his chances of finding Anthony and
Susannah. He took his hand out of his pocket. Breaking the
place up, even kicking the vases of flowers over, would spoil
his chances with Anthony and Susannah. Magnus Mandeville
was the kind of man who wouldn't hesitate before getting on to
the police. He was probably on to the police about something
or other every couple of days. Guy looked from one to the other
of them and then he looked away, sickened.

He thought, she is married. While I waited for her in that
restaurant, at the very moment set for our meeting, she was
getting married. I tried to make those phone calls, I went from
house to house, I saw myself as her rescuer. All the time I was
doing that she was at a party, her own wedding party. She was
drinking champagne and laughing and being congratulated.
The flowers in this room had been in that room, she had
probably smelt them, touched them, perhaps even carried
some of them as a bouquet.

He walked out of the room and across the hall, opened the front door, slammed it and walked down the long path to the gate.

They were watching him, he knew that, but he didn't look back. They had won, all of them. Tessa and Magnus, Rachel, Maeve and Robin, Anthony's brother and Susannah's sister, Anthony and Susannah. They had done what they had set out to do four years before. It had taken four years to accomplish it but they had done it and the instigators, the leaders of the plot, were Anthony and Susannah.

He sat in the Jaguar. He switched on the engine and saw the digits on the clock light up: eight fifty-two. All these things had happened, his life changed, himself changed, and it was still only ten to nine. It wasn't believable, so he looked at his watch. Ten to nine. He drove a little way and parked the car again. He parked simply because there was a space at the kerb and no yellow line. The cigarette he lit was so comforting it nearly made him cry. How could he have considered giving up smoking? He would never give it up.

When his head cleared and he could think again he would remember where Anthony and Susannah had gone. Susannah had *told* him where they were going. She had told him that day when he called in at Lamb's Conduit Street. He had forgotten but it would come back. On the other hand, he could phone the sister. What was her name? Laura Stow. He could phone Laura Stow. It was only ten to nine – well, five past now. He could be home by a quarter to ten. That wasn't too late to phone someone. He wouldn't be himself on the phone, he would think of some tale – an urgent message for Anthony, a package to be delivered express. . .

All of them were guilty, Magnus and Tessa, Rachel, Robin and Maeve, Laura Stow and Michael Chisholm, but most of all, Anthony and Susannah. It had started with Susannah's opening that letter from Poppy Vasari. That was the beginning of their vendetta against him. Then Anthony had set to work, forbidding her to go on holiday with him, preventing her from borrowing the money for the flat in Portland Road from him. Negative moves, all of them, but the next one was positive. The next one was finding a husband for her, introducing her to William Newton. It was as bad as Indians arranging marriages, he thought.

The husband secured, all that remained was to get a job for him in the north of England, far away from the man she really loved. And the final step was Susannah's plan to get her married in secret, a week in advance of what he had been led to expect. Anthony and Susannah had master-minded the whole thing, made plans, carried out the operation, brought it to a triumphantly successful conclusion. The others were no more than their servants, willing and obedient, awaiting instructions. And Newton was their pawn, an innocent nonentity. How much had they paid him to fall in with their plans?

Guy started driving home. On Battersea Bridge he stopped, left the car and looked down at the brown gleaming dirty water of the river. He took the blue leather box with the sapphire engagement ring in it out of his pocket and after a very small hesitation threw it into the water. His thoughts reverted immediately to Anthony and Susannah Chisholm. The world was not big enough to hold within it himself – and them. He wouldn't rest while Anthony and Susannah were still alive.

# CHAPTER
# TWENTY-ONE

It was normal for the lights to be on. There was a timer arrangement which switched them on as dusk fell. He left the car in the mews, let himself into the house and went straight to the phone in the living room. The directory in his brain which held a list of Chisholm numbers came up immediately with the one for Lamb's Conduit Street.

A man answered. Laura Stow probably had a husband. Guy said he was Wing Express Carriers of South Audley Street with an urgent packet for Mr Chisholm and where could he reach him? If Laura Stow herself had answered he would have disguised his voice but with the husband it wasn't necessary. The man wasn't suspicious. He gave Guy the name of a hotel in Lyme Regis.

Guy fetched himself a drink, a very large brandy, a triple. On the table, where he had left them, lay *The London Review of Books* and *The Guardian*. He thought he had left *Cosmopolitan* magazine there too but he couldn't have because it wasn't there now. Other things came to mind, the Paloma Picasso perfume and bath essence he had put in the bathroom, the house he had arranged to view on Monday. Rage that was as much misery as anger took hold of him and he seized the two papers, pulling them to pieces, tearing the sheets. He cursed as he did it, holding his head up, shouting at the ceiling – or God. He could hear his own voice raving as if it were someone else's. He kicked the table, drummed with his fists on the wall.

'Guy,' someone said, 'Guy, what is it?'

He turned round. Celeste was standing in the doorway.

'Sweet Guy, what's happened?'

Oh, God. Oh, Christ. He had forgotten their date, or rather forgotten that he hadn't succeeded in cancelling it. They had arranged for her to come here and she had come. How long ago? It was almost ten. 'Celeste.' He simply spoke her name, his voice all ragged and rough from the shouting. 'Celeste.'

'I thought something had happened to you. I thought, Guy's had an accident.'

As if it were not himself but another man seeing her, as if he saw through that other man's eyes, he thought how wonderful she looked. Her long dark chestnut hair hung loose but still in the ripples made by plaiting. An inch-wide gold band held it off her face. She wore a black silk sweater and a black skirt densely embroidered in turquoise and blue and pink and red. Everything was perfect, from the tiny gold studs, snail shells, in her ears, to the bracelets of gold wire, to her flat gold-embroidered blue-and-green silk pumps. He closed his eyes and saw Leonora in navy-and-white washed-out cotton and dirty trainers. The pain of it made him wince.

'Are you hurt?' she said. 'Is it your arm?'

'Celeste, I'm sorry I wasn't here. I forgot you were coming. I'm sorry.' If he used those words and asked her to forgive him ('forgive me') he would start crying. 'Awful things,' he said carefully, trying to be careful, 'have been happening.'

'What things, Guy?'

He lit a cigarette and gave her one. He tasted the brandy. It was good but it made him shudder. 'I've got to go out again. I only came home to make that phone call. But I've got to go out soon. I'll drive through the night.'

'Can I come with you?'

'No. I have to go alone. You stay here and sleep. OK?'

'I'd like to come with you. I could drive you.' She didn't say he soon wouldn't be fit to drive but that was what she meant. Still looking at him, she knelt down and began picking up the pieces of torn newspaper.

'Oh, leave that.' He put his hand up to his head. 'Celeste, she didn't come today. She's married. She got married while I was waiting for her in the restaurant.'

'What?'

He said it all again. It was easier the second time. She sat beside him and he told her all about the Chisholm conspiracy. Celeste listened in silence. When he had finished she was still silent, then she said,

'That was a terrible thing to do.'

He nodded. He had always liked the way she spoke, with that faint touch of accent that is Caribbean, the stress on the last syllable of words. 'Terri-bull' was what she said. He looked at her affectionately. It came to him that she understood, she had always understood.

'They ganged up against me,' he said. 'They set out to turn her against me and they succeeded.'

'I meant what she did was terrible. What *she* did. It was wicked, Guy. A good person wouldn't do that.'

He jumped up and stood a few paces from her. The warm feelings he had had a few minutes before were gone. She continued to look at him.

'She's twenty-six years old,' she said. 'She does her own thing. She does what she wants. You have to face that she wanted it. No one could make her, she's not a child or an animal, she's intelligent, she's got a lot more brain than me and I'm younger, but I'd never do what people told me, never, never. And she didn't. She did what she wanted. She enjoyed it, I really think she enjoyed it. You said she stood there and watched you fight William. She liked you fighting over her and making a goddess of her and not asking for anything in return.'

His body trembled. He would have liked to kill her. His right arm itched to rise and his hand to strike her a swinging blow. Something stopped him, an old gallant shibboleth that you don't strike a woman. You may kill her but you won't hit her. He held his hand in the other hand and the scarf touched it, the silky scarf that was Leonora's. All that he would ever have of her, he thought.

'You're jealous,' he said. 'You always have been.'

She shook her head. He didn't know if she meant yes by it, or no. 'Leonora's in love with William, Guy. Her father didn't find her a husband, she found him. She loves him.'

'How would you know?'

'She told me. That day in the restaurant. She said, "I'd like to think of Guy loving someone the way I love William and them loving him back."'

'It's funny you never mentioned that before.'

'I tried to tell you. You wouldn't listen.'

He went to pour himself another drink. The night had become very quiet, though it was Saturday and early yet. He heard her say,

'Where are you going?'

'A long way. To Dorset.' The brandy nauseated him. It had never had that effect before. 'I want to see Anthony and Susannah.'

There must have been something in his eyes to tell her. 'I've hidden the ammunition for your gun. When you didn't come I had a sense, a premonition.' By gun, she meant his .22. She didn't know about the Colt. 'I'll never tell you where it is. You'd have to kill me first.'

'You can stop interfering in my affairs, Celeste. You're not my wife. You're not even my girlfriend. You're just *a* girlfriend. Isn't it time you got that straight?'

He wanted to hurt her. Sometimes, in the past, he had seen her wince and he wanted to see it again. But her face was calm. She was still. 'Have you ever thought,' she said, 'that if you hadn't been chasing that dream, you had what was best for you right here at home? You and I, we've got everything in common, Guy. We like all the same things. We want to do the same things. We've got the same tastes. You don't love me but you would one day if you gave it half a chance. I love you. I don't have to tell you. We've been good lovers, haven't we?

We've been good to each other there, haven't we? There's never been a better lover for me – has there for you? Has there? Be honest, Guy. Have you had a better, more loving lover than me?'

'I told you,' he said, 'from the first I was in love with Leonora.'

'I know what you said. What you say and what really is, they're not the same. D'you know your life's one hundred per cent illusion?'

'You're talking about things you don't understand. Leonora is the great love of my life. She *is* my life.' He remembered that utterance Leonora had denied, had attributed to a character in some book. 'I *am* Leonora,' he said. 'We were one person.' The brandy was making him wild and slurring his speech. 'I'm dead without her. Life's meaningless without her.'

For a moment he thought Celeste was going to laugh at him. She didn't. She said softly, 'How many times did you actually make love to her?'

It struck him as a monstrous impertinence. 'That has nothing to do with it,' he said stiffly.

'From that first time you told me about, on a grave or whatever, all those years ago – how many times, Guy?'

It was like one of those anti-Catholic jokes, priests in the confessional and the little Irish girl kneeling. 'How many times, my child?' Celeste was looking at him very seriously, though. She wasn't joking. He thought back to those early years but he could only remember Kensal Green, the long summer grass and the butterflies.

'Does it matter?'

'I should think it matters to you.'

'Five or six times,' he muttered.

'Oh, Guy,' she said. 'Oh, my sweet Guy.'

He shrugged his shoulders, looked away. Suddenly he was aware of tiredness, heavy and dark, covering him like a blanket. He reached for the brandy and drank what was left. The cigarette he lit tasted ashen from the first draw.

'She liked it,' Celeste said. 'You were right when you said she wanted to meet you on Saturdays and have you phone every day. She liked having you on a string. What did it cost her? Nothing. It was flattering, having you hanging after her, you so handsome and rich and nice, Guy, and her not wanting anything from it but people knowing you were in love with her. She could get herself another boyfriend and fix up to marry him but you'd still be there, phoning her every day and taking her out to lunch on Saturdays, and her not having to pay a thing, not even sleeping with you.'

'It wasn't like that,' he said, but it had been. 'Get me another drink, would you?'

'Aren't you going to drive through the night?'

'Get me another drink, please.'

He would go to Dorset first thing in the morning. That would be best. When Celeste was asleep. He always woke early. Fresh, revived, he would make a start at eight and be there by midday. It occurred to him that he had had nothing to eat all day except that bread and cheese in the afternoon, but he didn't want anything. For the first time in years he hadn't gone out to a restaurant or someone else's house to eat dinner.

In the Chinese bed he lay for a little while apart from Celeste. He was thinking about his plans for tomorrow. It would be better to have a night's rest first. When he got to Lyme he would walk straight into the hotel and ask for them. The clerk in reception would tell him they had gone out and he would go in search of them, along the cliffs maybe – were there cliffs at Lyme? There must be. He would see them in the distance, walking along the beach at the water's edge. The Colt was still in the pocket of his leather jacket. Let it stay there. In the morning he would put on his jacket and go. How would they feel, what would they do, when they saw him in the distance, walking along the sands to meet them?

The wide empty beach, the vast sea, no one else there. Nowhere to run to but they would run . . . An image came to him of Leonora's smile, coquettish, controlled, secret, Vivien Leigh's smile in *Gone with the Wind*. It was her wedding night. Not that this meant much, she had been living with the man on and off for weeks. How cruel she had been to him! He had never supposed he could think of Leonora as cruel but he did now and with self-pity and wonder.

Celeste's slender hands touched his face and she brought her lips to his, very soft and warm. She could speak through a kiss, he had never known anyone else who could do that.

'Sweet Guy, I love you. I want you to make love to me.'

He did. He thought that in order to do so he would have to conjure up Leonora, never difficult for him, but this time she refused to appear or Celeste's presence was too strong to admit ghostly intruders. It was as if Celeste was determined to dispel by her love everyone but herself and him. This was Celeste in his arms and no one else, her eyes open and shining, her voice silenced. He could feel emanating from her a curious concentrated power, and the word 'witchcraft' came into his mind. Inside her body, her self, was a healing white magic.

\* \* \* \*

It was a kind of boast of his that he could never sleep late. He had hardly expected to sleep at all, only to rest. But when he woke up the hands of his carriage clock told him it was after nine and Celeste still lay wrapped in sleep, as deeply burrowed into sleep as if it were still the small hours.

This way it was better, he could make his escape without her knowing, go without her. He showered. It struck him as absurd that a man should bother to wash his body all over, soap himself and stand under these power-driven cascades of hot water, before going off on a killing mission. Why bother with anything? Why stand here making tea, waiting for the kettle to boil? Why consider, wrapped in his towelling robe, what clothes to put on? There should be nothing between his determined aim and its accomplishment. He should already have been on his way.

A light mist lay over the little garden. The sun's rays had already begun to pierce it. All summer long the lilies had bloomed on his pond, they were still in bloom now in the autumn. He had a ridiculous absurd desire, immediately suppressed, to go out there and stroke the bronze dolphin's head. But he opened the French windows and felt the mild breath of the morning.

His head ached, but normally. Most mornings his head ached. It didn't amount to the monumental, hammer-ringing, bone-splitting wrenching apart of brain fibres he called a hangover. Housework wasn't something he ever did, not even washing a cup, but he knelt down now and began picking up the torn pieces of paper from the floor and carrying them to the kitchen. The kettle boiled, its light went out. He made tea, a tea bag in each mug, then decided against waking Celeste.

Silently, so as not to disturb her, he put his clothes on, jeans, a black T-shirt, the most sombre pullover he had, a plain navy thing with a polo neck. It came to him that he dressed like that because this most resembled the garb of an executioner. He put Leonora's scarf round his neck, took it off again and pushed it into a drawer. In the mirror he saw himself as Anthony and Susannah would see him, approaching them along the beach. He imagined the jacket, the heavy pocket, and he mimed reaching into it for his gun. And then he said to himself, you're playing games, stop playing games, you know you're not going to Lyme, you're not going anywhere and you're not going to kill anybody.

Last night he had been. Hot with angry pain, he had cared for nothing but his revenge, nothing else mattered. There was no future. A night's sleep had changed that, Celeste had changed it. He would have gone, he thought, if she hadn't been there. He would have gone last night. And Anthony and Susannah would be dead by now and he arrested or else dead by his own hand.

I don't want to die, he thought. I don't want to be imprisoned. I want to be free. He *was* free. By what Leonora had done she had freed him. There would be no more enslavement to the phone, no more Saturday lunches that brought as much suffering as pleasure. The idea was so novel that he sat down to think about it, sat down outside in the pale sunshine on one of the white chairs.

He wouldn't stop loving her, he couldn't. He would always love her. In a cool, sane, very grown-up way he knew he would be in love with her all his life. That was the way it was. It sounded melodramatic but it was true that he'd met his fate that day in the street when he was there with Danilo and Linus and she had come along, a little girl, and stood there watching them.

But she was gone now, she was lost to him. He had thrown the ring he bought her into the Thames. She had married someone else and if they ever met again it would be in the company of others and with all of them there: Tessa and Magnus, Anthony and Susannah, Robin and Maeve, Rachel Lingard and Uncle Michael, maybe Janice and her husband. And he would be there with Celeste.

Why not Celeste? She had saved him last night. She always saved him. It was true what she had said about the way they were together. They were good together, they had everything in common, they could *talk* to each other, they could be silent together, there was between them no shame or pretence. She loved him the way no one had ever, all his life long, loved him, and he was fond of her. Even he, tough as he was, streetwise baby grown up, one-time dealer in Class A drugs, gangster, entrepreneur and sharp businessman, even he needed to be loved.

Why don't we try, he thought. Why don't I try to make a go of it? What can we lose? He felt an extraordinary hollow lightness at the thought of no more phone calls, no more fantasies, no more sick longings. If he had exacted his revenge he would have lost everything.

'Oh, Leonora,' he said aloud as he went back into the house. It had been such a long haul, so long for someone of his years, only twenty-nine years old but for fifteen of them in thrall to love. 'Oh, Leonora.'

Passing into the hall, he had a look at the Kandinsky. He had never liked it. No matter what people like Tessa Mandeville said, it was hideous. Having it there was all pretence. He would sell it. He took the Colt out of his jacket pocket, sat down on one of the Georges Jacob chairs and emptied it of its ammunition.

From upstairs Celeste was calling to him.

'I'll bring you your tea,' he said.

If it were Leonora lying up there, in his bed, his wonderful Chinese William Linnell bed, waking to put up her arms to him . . . The time for these fantasies was past. He carried the mug of tea upstairs. She said.

'Sweet Guy, thank you. Did you sleep well? Do you feel better? Ah, yes, I can see you feel good this morning.'

He sat on the bed beside her. He held her hand as he might hold the hand of a sick person in a hospital bed. Celeste wasn't ill, she was young and healthy, glowing with health and vitality. Her dark hair shone like a tiger's-eye jewel. He thought he would buy her a necklace of tiger's-eye. I will try to love her, he thought, oh, I will try. If willing it will do it, I will do it.

The doorbell rang.

He couldn't help remembering how once, when that had happened, he had been sure it was Leonora. It couldn't be Leonora now. It couldn't be any of her family either. He let go of Celeste's hand, said to Celeste,

'We'll do something nice later. We'll drive out to the country. We'll have a nice day.'

The doorbell rang again when he was halfway downstairs. Someone was very insistent. He opened the door and saw two men standing there, the older one, a white man in a suit, looking like an accountant. The black man, who was about his own age, wore jeans like his own and a polo-necked sweater also like his own. He looked like an executioner and there was also something familiar in his face. The man in the suit said,

'Mr Curran? Mr Guy Curran?'

Guy nodded.

'I'm a policeman, we're policemen. I expect you'd like to see our warrant cards, save you asking. I'm Detective Inspector Shaw of the Serious Crimes Squad and this is Sergeant Pinedo. May we come in, please?'

It was Linus. He must know Guy, recognise him as his old street companion, but he gave no sign of it, and Guy said nothing, only looked at him. So that was what had happened to Linus, he wasn't a down-and-out or a drug bandit executed for smuggling, but a policeman. The dark face, fuller now, less handsome, seemed rigid, fanatical. They said a knife edge separated the policeman from the criminal, while the affinity between them was strong. Linus had chosen to hunt rather than be hunted.

Guy backed a little to let the two men in and the light from the open door fell on his Colt which still lay on the little table. Shaw said,

'Do you have a firearms certificate for this weapon, Mr Curran?'

'Yes, of course.' But he hadn't and they would ask to see it. 'For a rifle, yes,' he said. 'For a .22.'

'This isn't a rifle,' said Shaw.

He didn't touch the gun. He walked down the hall and into the living room, Linus following him. Linus still walked with that pimp roll, hips stiff, thighs together, shoulders on the move. The thin man in the grey suit sat down on the sofa in Guy's living room, having looked neither to the right nor the left, having ignored the Kandinsky.

'What is it you want?'

'We're making enquiries into the death of Mrs Llewellyn-Gerrard.'

'I don't know any Mrs Llewellyn-Gerrard.'

Guy felt enormous relief. This must be some neighbour. They were enquiring at every house in the mews. It was one of those cases of a woman found stabbed in a bedroom or dead of an overdose. It happened all the time. Shaw was looking narrowly at him.

'Mrs Janice Llewellyn-Gerrard,' said Linus, 'of Portland Road, West Eleven.'

'Janice,' Guy said, all wonder. 'Yes. Yes, I suppose I do know her. If it's who I think it is. But Portland Road? I know some other people in Portland Road.'

He sounded confused and breathless, he could hear it in his voice. Shaw was looking at him. Linus was looking at him. 'She's dead?' he said, trying to make things better. 'What did she die of?'

'She was murdered.' Linus's gold tooth gleamed.

He was all innocence. He didn't understand, he said. 'How was she murdered?'

'It went wrong,' Shaw said. 'The man was seen. He's in custody.' Guy thought he sounded proud of himself. 'He's been in custody since an hour after it happened at eight last evening.'

'You mean she was mugged?'

'No, I don't mean that. He rang the doorbell but the entryphone didn't work, something like that, so she went down. He shot her at point-blank range, through the chest and the head. She died immediately, she can hardly have known what happened to her. But her husband had come down behind her and saw it all. He was able to make an identification.'

'We'd like you to come with us, Mr Curran,' said Linus. He had lost the accent, Celeste's Caribbean. He talked like any policeman on his way to the top. The first black commissioner, thought Guy. 'Down to the station. We'll do better down there.'

'Me?' said Guy. 'Why me? You've got someone for this, you said so. You said you'd got him in custody.'

'Charlie Ruck, yes. Would you like to see this card we found on Charlie Ruck? It's got your name and address on it.'

Guy read the card, though he didn't need to. He had recognised it. He had given it to Danilo in the Black Spot when arranging for the 'wasting' of Rachel Lingard: *Short, round-faced, fat, glasses, dark hair scraped back, about 27.*

'I can explain this,' he began, and then he understood that he couldn't.

He had forgotten, but now he remembered, that one of them had mentioned how Janice and her husband would be staying in Portland Road. Perhaps it was Leonora who had mentioned it. Always he could remember when Leonora told him something, but he couldn't now and knowing this, he felt a bitter pang.

The two policemen were watching him.

'Come along then, Curran,' Shaw said. The 'Mr' had been dropped. That was the beginning.

He called out bravely to Celeste, 'See you later.'

'I doubt it,' said Linus.

They went out into the mews. One of Guy's neighbours gave them an indifferent glance. Guy got into their car and they took him away.